HOLD BACK THE SUN

U.S. Asiatic Fleet Battles Japan

A Novel

Warren Bell

For Glenn

Warren Bell

5/17/2014

HOLD BACK THE SUN

ISBN-13: 978-1492307006
ISBN-10: 149237009

This is a work of historical fiction. All characters, organizations, and events portrayed in this novel are either products of the author's imagination or are used fictionally.

The book cover was designed and produced by Karen Bell Williams. Mr. Bill McCallum of the Defense Logistics Agency painted the portrait of the U.S.S. *Marblehead* for the author as an end-of-tour gift.

The map of the 1930's Pan American Pacific Clipper Route is from the collection of the San Francisco Airport Museum and is used with permission.

The map of the Malay Barrier was drawn by the author.

The map of Java is from *They Fought With What They Had* by Walter D. Edmonds. The rights to this work are held by the U.S. Air Force Historical Research Agency and are in the public domain.

Dedication

This book is for my daughter

KAREN BELL WILLIAMS

without whose selfless assistance it would

never have been published.

Acknowledgements

Hold Back The Sun could not have been completed without the assistance of a number of people. My wife and partner of over five decades, Annette, read, critiqued, and edited the entire manuscript. She is also the best copy editor I have ever met. Very little gets past her eagle eye. Our daughter, Karen Bell Williams was involved in many ways. Karen designed and produced the cover and formatted and integrated all the graphic images. She also managed the launching of the book. My son, Stephen, my son-in-law, David Williams, and my grandson, David Arvelo, all read and critiqued passages of the book. Many thanks to all for their valuable assistance.

Internet websites provided vital information. I must especially mention *U.S.S. Marblehead & Dr. Wassell* (http://www.ussmarblehead.com) and its link to *The Marby*.

I also thank the city government of Perth, Western Australia, for providing information on U.S. Navy activities in the city in early 1942.

Major Characters in Order of Their Appearance

MAJOR KATSURA OKUMA -- a resourceful and ruthless Japanese paratroop commander.

LIEUTENANT FRANK RHEA -- a daring floatplane pilot on the cruiser, USS *Marblehead.*

COLONEL JAN DIJKER – Dutch commander of Java's richest oil region.

CAPTAIN GARRIT LATERVEER -- RAF fighter ace commanding a Dutch squadron in Java.

CINTA VAN WELY -- Frank's former lover, a beautiful young Dutch physician.

LIEUTENANT JACK SEWELL -- gunnery officer of the destroyer, *USS Rust.*

NICOLAAS VAN WELY -- Cinta's father, a brilliant Dutch oil executive for Royal Dutch/Shell.

TONIA IVANOVNA -- an exiled White Russian countess, Nicolaas's mistress

COMMANDER WILLIAM "BILL" GOGGINS –Executive Officer of U.S.S. *Marblehead.*

WARRANT OFFICER "TONTO" COACOOCHE -- Frank's Seminole air observer

CHIEF GUNNERS MATE PATRICK MULDUNE– Leading Chief of *Rust*'s Gunnery Department

PAMELA MALLORY -- a bewitching English refugee from British Borneo.

CATHERINE VAN ZWEDEN -- Garrit's fiancée, a Dutch Army nurse.

LIEUTENANT COMMANDER CORYDON WASSELL – a Navy doctor caring for wounded U.S. naval personnel in Java.

CHAPTER 1

(One)
Salon Kitty
11 Giesebrechtstrasse
Berlin, Germany
21 July 1941

S *hosa* (Major) Katsura Okuma, Imperial Japanese Army (IJA), stifled a yawn without visibly changing expression, then sipped politely from his glass of champagne. He wished to heaven that one of his military friends would come and rescue him from the minor *Gestapo* functionary who had cornered him at the buffet table. After all, this was his going-away party. He was supposed to have fun, not be bored to death by this buffoon's empty-headed blather about the *Führer's* military genius.

Okuma was big for a Japanese, about 182 centimeters (six feet) when barefoot. His gleaming brown cavalry boots made him even taller. Okuma's olive M.98 service dress uniform was impeccably tailored about his muscular frame. He had hardly an ounce of fat on his body. Raven hair was cropped close to his bullet-shaped head, and a pencil mustache graced his upper lip. A German decoration hung between the points of his Prussian collar.

He let his dark eyes drift around the enormous, high-ceilinged room, the former parlor of a Jewish millionaire industrialist. Dazzling crystal chandeliers sparkled in the subdued electric light. The floors were polished marble; the tall walls, covered with red and gold wallpaper; the windows, masked with red velvet draperies. A twenty-foot mahogany table groaned with *hors d'oeuvres*, all delicacies from the recent Nazi conquests: Polish hams and sausages; Norwegian smoked salmon and sardines; a variety of Dutch and Greek cheeses; Danish pastries; even Russian caviar. The hard bread was French, as was the champagne, which everyone was drinking. Still pretending to pay attention to his companion,

Okuma spread sturgeon eggs on a piece of bread and began to munch on it.

On the eve of completing a two-year posting as Assistant Military Attaché at Japan's Berlin embassy, Okuma was currently the toast of the city. He was an asset to any hostess, a strikingly visible symbol of Hitler's new alliance with the greatest power in East Asia. Most German women considered him cultured and witty, while others knew him as a skilled and considerate lover. But their husbands recognized him for what he really was--an utterly dedicated military professional. He had come to Germany to study modern warfare. He was leaving as an expert on airborne operations.

"Ah, here you are, Katsura," came a familiar, welcomed voice. "You'll excuse the *Major*, I'm sure," the young *Luftwaffe* lieutenant colonel said to the man with Okuma. The colonel wore the uniform and polished jump boots of the *Fallschirmjäger* (Hunters From the Sky), the German Air Force' paratrooper wing. An Iron Cross, First Class, hung at his throat. "I simply must introduce him to our Madame Kitty."

"Thank you for getting me away from that moron, Ernst," Okuma said when they were out of earshot of the table. Ernst Echart was his best friend in Germany. They had been close since they were classmates at the Spandau paratrooper's school.

"Indulging politicians is the price we must pay or military glory," Ernst replied with a shrug. "*Mei fa tzu.*"

Okuma smiled at the familiar phrase, which he had taught to his German friends. It was the Chinese equivalent of *C'est le vive*. "I must confess that I'm anxious to meet our hostess. I understand that her girls are the best in Berlin."

"Not just Berlin," Ernst said with a laugh. "In all Germany."

The party was being given for Okuma by Ernst and his first cousin, Hermann, who was a *Schutzstaffel* (major) on *Reichführer* Heinrich Himmler's staff. The two Echarts were prototypical Nazi Aryans: blond-haired, blue-eyed giants with athletic builds. Hermann had cultivated contact with Okuma in the days immediately following the signing of the Tripartite Pact, which established the Berlin-Rome-Tokyo Axis. Okuma realized that his initial objective was purely political, but that had not inhibited the development of a genuine friendship. While Ernst was a true comrade-in-arms, Hermann's access to the inner sanctums of German power was a valuable source of intelligence for Okuma's superiors in the Second Bureau of the Imperial General Staff--Army Intelligence--and the *Kempei Tai*, the IJA military police and espionage service. Okuma enjoyed Hermann's more worldly contacts. The mansion in which this farewell was being staged was an exclusive *Gestapo* bordello.

"There's Madame Kitty now." Ernst indicated a voluptuous, dark-haired woman who was circulating among the guests. She had a younger woman in tow, a strawberry blond with a "peaches and cream" complexion. Both wore strapless evening gowns. Ernst waved them over.

"Madame Kitty, this is our guest of honor, *Major* Okuma," Ernst said in introduction.

"I'm charmed, Madame," Okuma added suavely.

"I'm very pleased to meet you, *Herr Major*." The madam's voice was low and husky. "Let me present Mademoiselle Genevieve, our new dancer from Paris. She'll be performing for us later this evening."

The French girl immediately intrigued Okuma. Although barely five feet tall, her emerald gown revealed a striking figure, and her face held a delicate beauty. Her bare shoulders were the color of polished alabaster. "That will surely be the highlight of the party," he said as he gallantly kissed Genevieve's hand. She was wearing a delicate French perfume.

"You have a long journey ahead of you, *Herr Major*," Madame Kitty commented. "How will you get home, now that the route through Russia is closed?"

"Katsura's flying back," Ernst put in.

"Truly? I didn't realize that's possible."

"Pan American still operates a Clipper service from Lisbon to New York," Okuma explained. "They have another flight that runs from San Francisco to Manila, then on to Hong Kong. Once there, I can connect with *Dai Nippon*."

"What a fascinating time you're going to have," said Kitty, her eyes wide with wonder. "I wish I could come with you."

"I'd welcome your company, but you'd have to buy your own ticket. I doubt that my government would be willing to pay the fare."

"I suspect that *Kuma* will be doing more than just sightseeing," quipped Hermann, who had walked over to join them. He wore the black uniform of the *Waffen SS*.

"*Kuma?*" said Genevieve quizzically.

"My Japanese nickname--meaning 'Bear,'" said Okuma. "It's a play on my size and my name."

"The Pacific Clippers land at the American military bases in Hawaii and the islands to the west," Ernst put in.

"Midway, Wake Island, and Guam are key links in the Americans' line-of-communications to their Philippine colony," said Okuma. "I could hardly fail to observe the details of their defenses."

"I couldn't help noticing your medal, *Herr Major*," Genevieve said to Okuma in a seductive French accent. "Isn't that the *Ritter Kreuz* (the Knight's Cross of the Iron Cross)? I wasn't aware that it was awarded to foreign attaches."

"*Kuma's* no ordinary military diplomat," Ernst said with enthusiasm. "See that parachutist's emblem?" He tapped the silver *Waffenfarbe* badge on Okuma's left breast, a diving eagle encircled by an oval wreath. "This man jumped into Crete with us. Without him, we might have lost the battle. We call him 'The Bear of Maleme.'"

"The *Führer* himself hung the *Ritter Kreuz* around his neck," said Hermann.

"But how can that be?" said the French girl in surprise. "Surely you're a neutral in the war with the English."

"Ernst and Hermann arranged for me to go along as a war correspondent for a Tokyo newspaper," Okuma said modestly. The decoration was something of an embarrassment to him. The Japanese Army would never have given him a medal for what he'd done. Such conduct was routinely expected of true *Samurai* warriors. "I fought the Anzacs because there was no other way to stay alive."

"And you actually talked with the *Führer?*" Madame Kitty's eyes took on a messianic sparkle, and her face flushed with excitement. "I'd do anything for such an honor! What did he say to you?"

"He's an admirer of *Bushido*, our warrior ethic," Okuma replied. "He'd like to bind your German forces to its doctrines. I gave him a translation of *Senjinkun*, our Field Service Code."

"To a *Samurai* like *Kuma*, war can have only two possible outcomes," Hermann interjected. "Victory or death."

"It's more than just that," Okuma continued. "Our armed services live by a set of precepts we call 'The Grand Way of Heaven and Earth,' which our Emperor Meiji proclaimed when we became a modern nation. Every command from a superior is taken as a direct order from our divine Emperor. Loyalty and faithfulness to the death, what you would consider uncommon valor, are considered our simple duty."

"Does the *Führer* actually believe that European troops would live by such rules?" asked Genevieve, raising an eyebrow in doubt.

"Perhaps not the *Wehrmacht*," Hermann replied, "but the caliber of our *Waffen SS* recruits is so high that we can become a caste of German *Samurai*."

"You'll need them before you're finished with the Russians," Okuma observed.

"Surely, you're jesting," said a surprised Ernst. "Our *panzers* are ripping the Reds to shreds. They're surrendering in droves. We'll have them beaten before the first snowfall."

"You Europeans don't appreciate the geography of Russia," Okuma responded. "I came to Germany by rail from Vladivostok, crossing those interminable steppes. You could lose the whole of Western Europe out there and never miss it."

"But the Red Army's coming apart at the seams," Hermann insisted. "Their government will have to capitulate when we've taken Moscow."

"Napoleon took Moscow, but the Czar didn't surrender," Okuma replied. "Russians have always traded space for time, wearing invaders down by drawing them deeper and deeper into their vast territory. Beware of overconfidence when you do battle with them."

"This is all quite fascinating," said Genevieve, flashing Okuma a peek down her bodice as she deposited her champagne on a table, "but I'm afraid that I must change for my number. I do so want to hear more about your exploits in Crete, *Herr Major*. Perhaps you'll tell me about them later."

"Nothing would give me more pleasure," he lied. He could think of innumerable things that he could do with the Frenchwoman that he would enjoy more than telling war stories. Once he got his hands on her, he knew she would be unable to deny him anything. During the past two years, he had seduced dozens of European women, making love to them in ways they had never dreamed possible. For Okuma was a master of the ancient Taoist Arts of the Bedchamber. His most prized possession was an original copy of *I-shim-po*, the Tenth Century classic on erotica, which he knew completely by heart.

I'll have to figure out how to make the tale about Crete short, he thought as she took her leave of the group and went out of the room. Unconsciously, he started stroking a freshly healed scar along his right cheekbone.

Three bullets slammed into the rocks above Okuma's head in rapid succession, forcing him to press his body even harder against the rocky soil of Crete. *Goddamn those Tommies*! he cursed silently. *How can they shoot so straight*? He had done two years of combat with Japan's Kwantung Army in China, but never had he encountered infantrymen who could deliver such a volume of massed, accurately aimed rifle fire as the British and Anzac troops on the hill above.

Opening his eyes for the first time in several minutes, he surveyed his immediate surroundings. The remnants of Ernst Echart's company of paratroopers were scattered in disarray in front of the south slope of a round-topped hill that dominated the Greek airfield at Maleme. The parched plain between them and the sea was a charnel house of shattered German bodies, the result of a hellish, low-level drop through intense British small arms and antiaircraft fire. The enemy must have realized that the airfield was a logical target for airborne attack, for they had been prepared. Like Okuma, the lucky *Fallschirmjäger* who had reached the ground unharmed were cowering behind whatever cover they could find. With blood still leaking from leg and shoulder wounds taken during his first moments on the ground, Ernst was hunkered down with his runner behind a low stone wall about twenty meters uphill from Okuma, trying desperately to get a wireless set to work so that he could call down air support. The British and commonwealth troops remained in firm control of the airfield. The German air-landing formations waiting in their transports in mainland Greece might as well have been on the moon.

Another volley of rifle fire peppered Okuma's boulder, spraying his head with fragments of rock. His padded, rimless parachutist's helmet deflected most of the shards, but one plowed along his right cheekbone, laying open the flesh like a saber cut. Unreasoned anger and shame boiled up within him. What was he doing hugging the ground like a coward? He was a *Samurai*. He had to fight back!

Springing to his feet, he sprinted toward Ernst's position, crouching low and zigzagging to throw off the aim of the enemy soldiers above. The *zing* of rifle slugs whipping close around him filled his ears. A Vickers machine gun opened up, its bullets kicking up puffs of dust as they chased him across the bone-dry field. Drawing on a final burst of adrenaline, he dived through the air to land in the shelter of the stone wall beside Ernst. The Vickers gun lashed the front face of the wall, showering them with dust and more fragments of rock.

"You're either the bravest man I ever met or the most foolish," said Ernst as Okuma lay gasping for breath.

Okuma ignored the comment. "Did you have any luck with the wireless?" he asked when he was able to speak.

"None at all." Ernst threw the radio to the ground in disgust. "It must have taken a round when we first landed. We've no way to communicate with our air support."

Okuma dug a cigarette out of one of the pockets of his camouflaged smock and lit it, then shaded his eyes and looked up into the pale, blinding sky. High overhead, a number of ugly bent-wing *Stuka* dive-bombers were orbiting aimlessly, their pilots apparently unsure as to where the enemy positions lay. He pushed himself up on his elbows and scanned the plain between the wall and the sea, memorizing the positions of the pinned-down German troops for future reference. A cluster of corpses about forty meters from the wall drew his attention. The shattered remains of three *Fallschirmjäger* were draped over what looked to be a heavy weapons container.

"Let me have your glasses," he said to Ernst.

Without a word, the major lifted his Zeiss binoculars from his neck and handed them to Okuma. As the attaché focused the eyepieces, he saw that the object beneath the dead Germans was what he had hoped, a half-assembled infantry cannon.

A few feet beyond Ernst was a section of wall that had partially collapsed. Okuma crawled carefully to the spot and searched until he found a gap between the stones that was large enough to peer through with the glasses. Squatting on his haunches to remain hidden, he studied the enemy position on the hilltop for several minutes. The Tommies were dug in deeply just behind the military crest, their trench line reinforced with a number of machine gun nests. He estimated the range to be five hundred meters. Closing his eyes for a moment, he did spherical trigonometry calculations in his head, then crawled back to Ernst.

"I'm going to need some help." He explained what he had in mind.

"Take Lance Corporal Steiner." The *Luftwaffe* officer nodded at his runner. The man was slightly built, but wiry and tough.

Slithering on their bellies like snakes, it took Okuma and the German almost half an hour to reach the small cannon. The dead gunners had gotten well along with assembling the weapon before falling to enemy fire. The barrel and trail were already fitted together, and one of its spoked bicycle wheels was in place. The other lay alongside the drop container, which held a ten-round pack of ammunition.

Speaking in colloquial German, Okuma told Steiner what he wanted him to do. The lance corporal worked his body under the barrel of the piece until it rested on the center of his back. On Okuma's order, he heaved himself upward, using the full strength of his arms and legs to lift the weapon. Okuma slipped the second wheel onto the axle and dropped the retaining pin into its socket. Then they began the long crawl back to the wall, pushing the gun ahead of them and dragging the ammunition behind. Realizing what was happening when they were about halfway home, the soldiers on the hill began shooting at them. Miraculously, they reached shelter unharmed. After resting for a few minutes, they moved the gun to the collapsed section of wall.

Okuma snapped an order to Steiner and rotated the operating lever of the breach. The gun broke open like a double-bore shotgun, the barrel swinging up to clear the fixed breechblock. After the German slammed in a 75-millimeter shell, Okuma swung the lever to cam the barrel back down against the block. He laid the piece himself, carefully lining it up toward the end of the enemy trench line and spinning the elevation wheel until the muzzle was pointing almost straight up. Then, leaving Steiner with the firing lanyard, he went back to his gap between the stones. When he got his glasses lined up, he gave the signal to fire.

The sharp crack of the gun nearly burst Okuma's eardrums. Mentally cursing himself for not having the sense to plug his ears, he observed the fall of shot. The projectile landed about fifteen meters in front of the trenches. He barked the correction instructions to Steiner. Two minutes later, the little cannon spoke for the second time. Okuma let out a whoop of elation when the shell fell right into the end of the trench, blowing several bodies straight up into the air. He crawled back to traverse the piece for the next shot, which took out another section of enemy defenses.

Five thousand feet above the battlefield, the *Stuka* squadron commander witnessed the bursting shells on the hilltop and decided to investigate. Alerting his wingman, he went screaming down to level off a scant four hundred feet above the beach before speeding inland. His sharp eyes picked out the scattered bodies and huddled survivors. Then the infantry gun behind the stone wall spewed out another plume of dirty smoke. Moments later, its shell exploded in a machine gun nest on the crest of the ridge. The fortifications were patently British, a precisely laid out trench system with heavy weapons bunkers. The squadron commander strafed them with his wing machine guns, and his rear gunner took out several men who raised their heads as the *Stuka* soared skyward.

"It's going to work," Okuma crowed to Ernst as the dive-bomber rejoined its formation. He loaded the last shell into the infantry gun and carefully laid the barrel on the machine gun nest at the north end of the hilltop position. He paused then, waiting for the airmen to act.

The first *Stuka* nosed over and dived straight for the Tommies, the air-powered siren beneath its belly wailing like a banshee. Okuma jerked the firing lanyard, dropping the 75-millimeter shell directly onto the machine gun bunker. Zeroing in on that marker, the dive-bomber zoomed toward the ground until it seemed sure to crash. At the last possible moment, the pilot pulled her up sharply, releasing a cluster of anti-personnel bombs to fall squarely on the sharp-shooting Tommies. As the plane zipped by close overhead, Okuma saw that a leering shark's mouth was painted on its nose.

Again and again, the dive-bombers pounded the hill until it was shrouded in a cloud of dust and smoke. The enemy's rifle fire slackened, then ceased altogether. From all over the coastal plain, paratroopers rose up from their hiding places and raced toward Okuma's wall. The number that had survived unscathed amazed him. Overpowering battle lust suddenly swept over him. Nothing mattered except the compelling necessity to shed enemy blood.

Scooping up an MP-40 submachine gun from a dead *Fallschirmjäger*, Okuma vaulted onto the wall and shouted in German for the gathering soldiers to follow him. Then he went racing up the hill toward the British position. The *Fallschirmjäger* screamed at the top of their lungs as they swarmed up the slope behind him, firing their automatic weapons from the hip.

A low parapet of sandbags loomed up in front of Okuma. Without pause, he sprang up onto its lip and dropped down to the firing step below. The trench was empty except for bomb-smashed corpses. Dashing recklessly ahead, he turned a corner and found himself face to face with a section of towering New Zealanders. The submachine gun came alive in his hands, chattering and bucking as its bullets swept the trench like a deadly broom, knocking bodies helter-skelter. Then he realized with a start that the weapon had stopped firing. It was empty, and he did not have a spare magazine!

With a roar that was scarcely human, one last Kiwi came charging up the trench, the monstrously long sword-bayonet on the end of his Enfield leveled at Okuma's gut. Reacting without thought, Okuma flung the empty MP-40 at the bull-like soldier. It struck him dead in the face, breaking his nose and bowling him over backwards. Grabbing the muzzle of the Enfield as he fell, Okuma tore the rifle from the New Zealander's grasp and swung it high in an arc, crushing the man's skull with a single stroke. The force of the blow snapped the weapon's stock at the pistol grip.

The trench was rapidly filling with Germans bent on revenge. Okuma unsnapped the sword-bayonet and flung the useless rifle barrel aside. Never aware that he was now speaking Japanese, he waved the long blade above his head and shouted for them to follow him as he charged off in search of the remaining defenders. An irresistible tidal wave of death, the *Fallschirmjäger* swept quickly through the New Zealanders' positions. It was all over in twenty minutes. Those Kiwis who survived the slaughter huddled submissively in front of their command post to witness their colonel's surrender. None would ever forget the ferocity of the blood-smeared Asian officer with the dripping bayonet to whom he capitulated.

In less than an hour, the first Junkers 52 transport plane put down on Maleme aerodrome and disgorged a platoon of air-landing troops. Soon, a steady stream of aircraft was coming in, pouring reinforcements into the airhead. Over a week of hard fighting lay between the Germans and total victory, but from the moment Maleme fell, the issue was never really in doubt.

The ringing tones of a spoon rapping on a glass snapped Okuma back to the present.

"May I have your attention, please," Hermann said when the guests had quieted. "I hope that everyone's having a good time."

A collective murmur of approval interrupted him briefly. He held up his hand to signal for silence.

"Madame Kitty always entertains us royally. But we're here tonight to honor a departing friend of the *Reich*--Major Katsura Okuma, the assistant military attaché for our ally, the Japanese Empire."

A round of enthusiastic applause caused Hermann to pause once more. When it finally subsided, he continued. "I'm sure you all know that Major Okuma's not your run-of-the-mill attaché, content to attend social functions and charm our Berlin ladies. He's a graduate of our elite *Luftwaffe* paratrooper school, and his exploits while observing our invasion of Greece and Crete are already legend. The *Führer* expressed the admiration and gratitude of our nation to the Major during a decoration ceremony earlier today. However, the many friends he's made here wish to present him with a small token of our affection. But before we do that, I believe that Madame Kitty has some special entertainment planned."

"Some very special entertainment," the madam purred. "It's a floor show, so I must ask you to please clear the center of the room."

As the guests moved back toward the walls, the small orchestra, which had been playing muted classical tunes, switched to a burst of wild Oriental music dominated by Berber hand drums and a shrill *mizmaar*, the oboe-like instrument of snake charmers. The short introduction climaxed with a tambourine and drum fanfare. When it ended abruptly, gasps of surprise and pleasure broke the sudden silence as Mademoiselle Genevieve sprang into the parlor through the open door.

She was attired as a Turkish odalisque, the blue fabric of her brief garments contrasting starkly with the creamy white of her skin. A *yashmak* of white voile veiled her face. As the music resumed, she began to strut seductively around the room, adding the constant jangle of *kasiks,* tiny cymbals worn like rings on her fingers, to the torrid, exotic melody. Light shimmered from her costume as she moved: gold gleaming from the band of coins which held her hair in place and anchored her *yashmak,* from serpentine armbands and bangle bracelets and anklets, from the double waist chain which secured a star sapphire in her navel; jewels flashing from the gold lame halter which scarcely confined her full breasts; innumerable beads glistening from the medallions and dangling strings which adorned the low-slung, satin cincture supporting her diaphanous skirt. When she reached Okuma, she paused in front of him and put her palms together, bowing low in the Japanese fashion. Then she launched into a dance that was at once both artful and unimaginably wanton.

Okuma immediately realized that this was no burlesque parody, but authentic *du danse ventre*--North African belly dancing.

After several minutes of spectacular spinning and shaking, Genevieve sidestepped over to Okuma, moving in so close that they were almost touching. The musky aroma of a different perfume inflamed his senses. Her hands dropped to her temples and the *yashmak* fell free, baring her face to him. Then, rising onto her tip-toes, she wrapped the length of silk around his neck and pulled his face down until their lips met in a steaming kiss. He was sure from that moment that she was dancing solely for him, that all the others did not matter to her at all. A warm flush of self-esteem swept over him, followed closely by a wave of overpowering lust. More than anything else in the world, he wanted to possess this woman.

She kept her belly oscillating while she slowly sank to her knees at his feet. Her whole upper body was horizontal now, bent backwards just a few inches off the floor. Her arms imitated a swimmer's backstroke while her hips lasciviously rose and fell.

Then she arched her neck again until the back of her head touched the floor just as the music soared to a frenzied climax, ending with a crash of cymbals. For several moments, she remained as rigid as a statue. Then the mesmerized audience burst into applause.

"This, my lucky friend, is our parting gift to you," Ernst announced to an exhilarated Okuma. "Mademoiselle Genevieve is yours for the night."

(Two)
Central Security Office
Prinz Albrechtstrasse
Berlin, Germany
21 July 1941

Oberfeldwebel (Master Sergeant) Wolfram Röhm lit a cigarette and let his eyes wander proudly around his personal realm. The basement room contained five tables, each equipped with an electronic console and two recording turntables. Expert *SS* signals technicians manned the stations, each intent on monitoring his assigned circuits. Two were making recordings on wax discs. To Röhm, that was a clear indication that most of the patrons of Salon Kitty were still at the party in the drawing-room. When the action really got going, his men would be hard pressed to keep track of what was happening in all the bedrooms. Every room in the bordello was wired with super-sensitive microphones, all connected by amplified cable circuits to this listening post in *Gestapo* headquarters. During the one and a half years that it had been in operation, the brothel had provided *Reichsführer* Himmler tons of detailed reports on the attitudes of high German officials and foreign diplomats, poured out in fits of post-coitus euphoria to skilled *Waffin SS* courtesans. Unaware that their bedrooms were bugged to a recording studio, the women also prepared written reports on each assignation for their superiors.

One of the console operators raised his hand to attract Röhm's attention. I think you'll want to hear this, *Herr Oberfeldwebel,*" the man said when Röhm reached his position. Stripping off his earphones, he passed them to the master sergeant.

After several minutes, Röhm handed the earphones back. "Put it on the speaker," he ordered the operator.

For the next few hours, the studio staff listened in fascination to the sounds emanating from Room 7--the rhythmic squeaking of the bed, animalistic male grunts, feminine moans and sighs, and shrieks of ecstasy.

"My God, the man must be an absolute satyr," Röhm finally opined. When the action finally quieted, he made sure that the recording discs were properly labeled and packed for shipment to *Brigadefürher* Walter Schellenberg, the head of "Operation Salon Kitty." He had no doubt that Himmler himself would be listening to them before a day had passed.

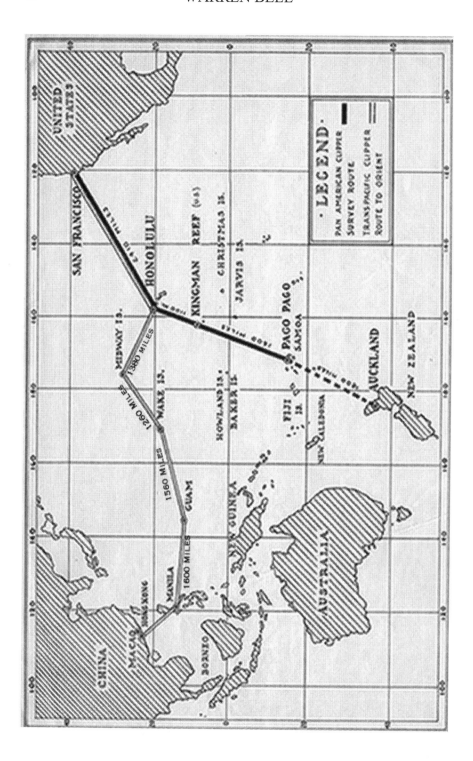

CHAPTER 2

(One)
Skies Above the Northern California Coastline
7 August 1941

L ieutenant Frank Rhea sat quietly in the starboard gun blister
of the PBY-5A, enjoying the view of the Monterey Bay
coastline three thousand feet below. Cruising at 120 knots,
the Navy patrol plane seemed to be moving in slow motion. The
thunderous roar of twin 1200-horsepower radial engines mounted on
its high parasol wing made conversation with the crew of the plane
almost impossible, but Frank was content. The rugged shore of his
native state had a natural beauty that always moved him, and this
would be his last chance to drink it in for months, perhaps even
years. He was on his way to San Francisco to take the Pan
American Clipper to Hawaii, the first leg on the long flight to
Manila, in the Philippine Islands. To avoid the usual month-long
ocean voyage on a Navy transport, he had purchased the airline
ticket with his own money.

A radioman tapped Frank's arm to get his attention. "Beggin'
your pardon, sir," the man yelled to be heard above the engine noise.
"The Skipper says our ETA's in about twenty minutes. If you're
gonna stay back here, you'd better strap yourself in."

"That's a Roger," Frank replied to indicate his understanding,
then settled into the gunner's seat and fastened the lap belt.

The *Catalina* dipped its right wingtip and turned inland above
the foothills of the Santa Cruz Mountains, breaking out over San
Francisco Bay just south of San Mateo. Compared to the boiling
surf of the Pacific beaches, the protected waters of the Bay looked
placid. A few minutes later, the pilot swung north again to parallel
the Eastern Shore. Frank watched the shadow of the plane dance
across the barren stretches of the Oakland mud flats. Up ahead, he
caught sight of the Alameda Naval Air Station on a long island that

pointed like a finger toward San Francisco across the Bay. New construction was evident everywhere. Hangars, parking aprons, and runways now covered acres, which had been empty marsh during his last visit to the area.

When Frank was released from active duty in 1938, the U.S. Navy owned fewer than a thousand airplanes. The Two-Ocean Navy Bill of 1940 authorized over fifteen thousand aircraft for the Sea Service. It took time to build aviation facilities and tool up the factories, but even longer to train new pilots. As the production lines began to flow, The Navy recalled Frank and hundreds of other Naval Reserve aviators to active duty. A bachelor with no entanglements, he accepted the recall without protest and applied for retraining in fighters. The Bureau of Navigation had other ideas. The detailers noted that he was still qualified as a cruiser floatplane pilot and posted him to U.S.S. *Marblehead,* an Asiatic Fleet cruiser home-ported in Manila.

Frank was disappointed but far from shattered. A cruiser pilot could become a more complete naval officer than his carrier-based counterparts. As assistant division officer of the "V" (Aviation) Division of *Marblehead's* Gunnery Department, he would again become a qualified Officer of the Deck, as adept at running the ship from the bridge as any of his surface warfare contemporaries. If war broke out, the "V" Division would play a crucial role in any combat action. Their *Seagull* floatplanes were the cruiser's "eyes in the sky," vital for locating the enemy and spotting fall of shot for her guns. Some senior officers felt that it took more courage to fly *Seagulls* than the new *Wildcat* fighters. In a pinch, a fighter pilot always had high speed and maneuverability as assets. Floatplane pilots relied on their wits and raw flying skill, enlisting the sun and any cloud cover available as their allies.

With a clamorous squealing of hydraulics, the *Catalina's* wingtip floats unfolded in preparation for a water landing. The pilot eased the big bird down until her keel began to kiss the calm surface of the bay. Spray cascaded against the Plexiglas of Frank's gun blister as the plane settled deeper into the water, and then the frantic clamor of the engines modulated to a deep-throated growl as the pilot taxied toward the air station. More mechanical groaning followed by a resounding *thump* announced the extension of the landing wheels from their wells in the sides of the fuselage to lock in a down position. Then the *Catalina* climbed a seaplane ramp to the broad parking apron that ran along the waterfront. Five minutes later, it came to a halt in front of the air station operations building. The engine noise died, and the propellers coasted to a stop. The sudden silence was startling.

The plane captain, a lean little chief aviation machinist's mate who looked like a leprechaun, dropped down from the flight engineer's station in the wing pylon and came back to the waist gunner's compartment. "Need any help, Lieutenant?" he asked Frank.

"No, thanks, Chief," Frank responded in a deep, resonant voice. "I'll just find a head and change clothes." He'd worn a flight suit on the run north from San Diego. To leave the base, he must put on his dress uniform.

"You can use the head up front, but there's a lot more room in the one in the ops building."

"That's good advice. I'll take it."

Frank splashed hot water on his cheeks to wash away the last of the shaving lather and then inspected the results in the mirror above the washbasin. Pale blue eyes set in a deeply tanned face stared back at him. It was a good, strong-featured face, handsome in a rugged sort of way. His thick shock of brown hair was unruly, so he wet his comb and slicked it down. After packing away his shaving gear, he began to dress.

Frank felt a twinge of pride as he fastened the gold buttons of his double-breasted blue blouse. The twin rings of gold lace that marked the rank of full lieutenant encircled the sleeves, and the gold wings of a Naval Aviator glowed softly above the colorful splash of ribbons on his left breast. The uniform was over six years old, but it still fit perfectly. He'd been a track star during his years at the University of California, Los Angeles, and exercise remained a part of his daily routine. Standing an even six feet in his stockings, he weighed one hundred and eighty pounds, mostly muscle.

Frank finished repacking his flight bag, then set his white cap on his head at a jaunty angle and went out into the lobby of the operations building. The freckled-faced petty officer manning the information desk dropped the magazine he had been reading and sprang to his feet.

"I was just about to call you, Mister Rhea," the man said in a pronounced Georgia drawl. "Your car from the motor pool just pulled up. Do you want me to get your bag?"

"I can handle it. Thanks for your help."

"Anytime, Lieutenant. Good luck out there in WESTPAC."

"I have a feeling I'm going to need it."

The driver of the gray Navy sedan at the foot of the steps popped Frank a snappy salute as he held open the door. "Bosun's Mate Brown, at your service, sir," the petty officer bellowed.

"Afternoon, Brown," Frank responded as he returned the salute and climbed into the rear seat. "How long's the run to Pan Am?"

"About an hour, sir. Got to pick up another officer at the Oakland train station. He's catching the Clipper, too."

Frank chatted with Brown while they exited the burgeoning air station and merged with the Oakland traffic. Brown had been an Atlantic Squadron sailor until recently, so they shared their experiences in the ports of Europe and the Caribbean. When they reached the train station, Frank stayed with the car while the driver went inside to look for his other rider.

(Two)
Treasure Island
San Francisco Bay
7 August 1941

Master of Ocean Flying Boats Marty Ryan puffed confidently on his pipe as he marched up the pier toward Treasure Island. The strong breeze sweeping in off San Francisco Bay whipped away the smoke and tore at his salt-and-pepper hair. It was a perfect "Chamber of Commerce" day: clear, blue skies, temperature in the seventies, a good sailing wind.

The stocky mid-westerner was among the most senior pilots in the vast Pan American empire. A true aviation pioneer, he had flown a Martin 130 flying boat on the first passenger run from San Francisco to Manila back in 1936. Only nine hardy travelers had ventured that inaugural 8210-mile flight. Today, he would be carrying thirty-four passengers on the sleepover leg to Honolulu and sixty-eight on the daylight continuation to the Philippines. His aircraft, a Boeing 314 named *Manila Clipper*, was docked at the

"Port of the Trade Winds," the protected basin formed by Yerba Buena and Treasure Islands and their connecting causeway. The wonder of modern commercial aviation, the mammoth four-engine flying boat had performance and payload characteristics undreamed of a scant five years before.

For the past two days, 185 mechanics and inspectors had toiled around the clock, going through the 1,500 checklist items required to ready the big bird for her trans-Pacific flight. On the previous afternoon, Marty had reviewed and approved the preparations, then taken *Manila Clipper* up for a test flight before accepting her for the mission. Since then, the officers of his crew had toiled over the elaborate flight plan that the long, over-water flight demanded. At last satisfied that matters were now well in hand, Marty was on his way to the Pan Am offices to look over the passenger list. Expected to play congenial host for the airline on the five-day flight, he made it a point to memorize the names and key facts about important customers before they arrived. When he reached the shore, he knocked the fire from his pipe and vaulted up the steps at the end of the terminal building.

The Treasure Island facility was the most elaborate in the Pan American system. Originally built for the Golden Gate International Exposition, the three-story, 400-foot semicircle of concrete held restaurants, a weather station and a control tower in addition to offices and the passenger terminal. Marty's leather heels echoed loudly off plaster walls as he went through a short corridor and entered the curved central concourse of the building, where the ceiling soared over fifty feet above the polished terrazzo floor. Sunlight streamed into the huge room through tall windows behind the front mezzanine observation gallery. The Pan Am offices filled a ring along the back wall of the concourse. Marty made straight for the check-in counter.

"Anything special today?" he asked the curly-haired booking clerk.

"About the normal mix, Captain" the young man replied in a squeaky voice. "Mostly businessmen. We have four military officers: two Dutchmen, two American Navy. I put them together in Compartment Three with a Dutchwoman doctor."

"Hope the lady isn't a pacifist." Marty's eyes narrowed as he scanned the manifest. The clerk obviously was not up on the air war in Europe. He made a mental note to give the second Dutchman a special welcome. "Anyone checked in yet?"

"Just one, a Colonel Dijker of the Dutch Army. That's him over on the couch--the guy with the newspaper."

The passenger got up when Marty walked over to introduce himself. Jan Dijker would have been an imposing figure anywhere. At three inches over six feet, he towered above Marty. His thick, bushy hair was snow-white, but his plain-featured face suggested a man in his mid-forties. They chatted politely, but their conversation lacked warmth. In precise, Oxford English, Dijker thanked Marty for his attention and expressed satisfaction with the arrangements. After chatting for a few minutes about the route and the schedule, Marty excused himself and went out to complete the pre-flight check on *Manila Clipper*.

"He's a cold bird," Marty muttered to himself as the doors closed behind him.

Had he known how Dijker spent the last year, Marty might have been kinder in his judgment of the man. Until five weeks previously, the Dutchman was Britain's most successful spy in occupied Holland.

Hearing English spoken with a Dutch accent, Jan Dijker looked up from his newspaper. He immediately recognized the blond, square-faced young man at the counter, although they had never actually met. Captain Garrit Laterveer of the *Militaire Luchvaart-Koninklijk Nederlands-Indisch Leder* (Netherlands Indies Army Air Corps) was well known in London military circles, his name whispered with reverence in occupied Holland. He was a triple ace, the highest scoring ML-KNIL pilot serving with the British RAF. Puzzled to find him here in San Francisco, Jan walked over to his countryman and introduced himself.

"Are you going on leave?" Dijker asked after they shook hands.

"I'm being transferred home to teach advanced fighter tactics at our flying school at Andir." Bitterness laced the younger man's low-pitched voice. "I doubt that I'll do much good unless someone gets us some decent aircraft."

"I don't understand," Jan commented as they walked to the couches in the waiting area. "I thought that our purchasing commission was ordering modern American equipment for our forces. I've seen the small arms and light armor, and they're all first rate."

"The airplanes are obsolete junk!" Garrit snorted in disgust. "Have you ever seen a Brewster *Buffalo*?"

"Can't say that I have."

"The damned thing's aptly named. It wallows about the sky. I could whip a whole squadron of them with a single *Spitfire*. If we go to war against the Japanese in those things, they'll cut us to ribbons"

"Perhaps it's well that the High Command picked a man of your credentials to train our pilots."

Garrit laughed cynically. "I beg your pardon," he finally apologized, "but that's almost a joke. They pulled me out of combat because they think I've gone stale. They couldn't afford the bad propaganda if some German shot me down."

"Have you gone stale?"

"No, but the brass has good reason to think I have. Let me put you in the picture, and you can judge for yourself."

In April of 1941, after downing his fifteenth kill to become a triple ace, Garrit was promoted to captain and ordered to London to be decorated by Queen Wilhelmina. He met Juliana Kortie at the Ministry of War. Like many wartime romances, theirs blossomed with volcanic intensity. Within a fortnight, they were sleeping together and planning marriage after the war. Then, in late May, the news that Juliana had been killed in a bombing raid shattered Garrit. Unhinged by grief, he refused to stand down from flying. It proved a fatal mistake. After losing his wingman on one mission, he was himself shot down in the Channel. Rescued by an RAF flying boat, he found his fate sealed when he got out of the hospital. Until he got over the girl, he would employ his great store of experience by training the fighter pilots so desperately needed in Java.

"I understand how you feel," Jan said sympathetically. "I lost my entire family--my parents and my wife and children--when the Nazis bombed Rotterdam last year. I'll hate Germans until the day I die. It took a direct order from the Minister of War to make me leave for the Indies. He convinced me that the revenues they produce are vital to continuing the war against Hitler. We simply can't afford to lose them to the Japanese. Besides, I'm too hot to go back into Holland for the foreseeable future."

"Are you that Colonel Dijker?" asked Garrit, his voice filled with new respect. "My god, I didn't connect the name. Juliana told me about your narrow escape from the *Gestapo*."

"We were betrayed," Dijker replied without rancor. "I strangled the assassin they sent for me with my bare hands. I still have the Mauser pistol he meant to kill me with, a silenced *Gestapo* special."

Other passengers began to arrive as the two Dutchmen continued their conversation. Garrit let his eyes wander among the newcomers as he described the climate of Java to Dijker. A pair of vivacious young women caught his attention. He had a strange feeling that he should know them. They were obviously sisters, and each was strikingly beautiful in her own way. The younger woman, who was dressed in a carefully tailored suit of gray gabardine, held a black medical bag.

"Is something wrong?" asked Dijker.

Garrit realized with a start that he had stopped talking. "Oh, no, sir. It's that woman doctor. For some reason, I feel that we've met before."

"Her name's Van Wely--Cinta van Wely. We were introduced last night at the hotel. The other woman's her sister, Alette. The man's Alette's husband, Tommy Hawkins."

"Of course," Garrit exclaimed, snapping his fingers. "They're *Indische Jongens*--Dutch born in the East Indies--from Batavia. Their father's a big wheel with BPM."

"I beg your pardon. What's a BPM?"

"*Bataafsche Petroleum Maatschappij*, the Royal Dutch Shell subsidiary in the Indies." Garrit eyed Alette closely, remembering her rumored promiscuity before her marriage to the American. She was a pretty piece, all right, but then, so was her sister. He considered going over to greet them, but decided against it for the moment. They seemed to be involved in some sort of an argument, and he did not wish to become involved.

Cinta van Wely pretended interest in the conversation with Alette and her husband, but she actually was bored almost to tears. They'd been bickering constantly since the three of them left Houston, Texas, in Tommy's private DC-2 on the previous morning. Sometimes she wondered how Alette put up with her husband. Coupled with his big mouth, his Texas-sized ego was often just too much to stomach. Cinta had to concede that Tommy was a good father to her two nephews, and the fact that he insisted on doing productive work even though his father was one of the richest men in Texas was to his credit. But she suspected that he had physical attributes that were also scaled to Texas proportions, which she knew would count heavily with her sister. Alette was a very sensual woman, and Ada, the Indonesian *baboe* who virtually raised the sisters after their mother's death, taught them to express and gratify desire rather than suppress it.

"It still beats hell out of me why Little Sister's got to go all the way out to Borneo to practice medicine," Tommy was complaining. "There's plenty of sick people back in Texas. If she wants to treat burns, men are getting hurt every day in our oil fields."

"We've been over this a hundred times," Alette replied with exasperation. "Besides, if she's there, she can make Papa come back with her if the Japs start a war with us."

"That'll be the day," Tommy snorted. "Your old man's the best engineer Royal Dutch Shell has in the Far East. They'll never let him go, and he wouldn't walk away from a fight even if they would."

"At least, she could try." Eight years of living in Houston had tempered Alette's voice with a grating Texas twang, surprising for a woman who had grown up in Batavia, Java

Sometimes, Cinta found it hard to believe that sisters who looked so much alike could be so different. Each was a perfect size eight with a shape to turn men's heads at any gathering. The fine-boned features of their faces were almost identical, and their eyes were the same sapphire hue. But while Alette was a glowingly healthy blond, Cinta's shoulder length tresses were raven black, the legacy of a Spanish grandee in their ancestry. She looked younger than her twenty-six years, her fair complexion unblemished by time or the terrible stresses of her life as a physician.

Psychologically, the sisters might have been from different planets. Cinta became an introvert, an intelligent, dedicated professional who drew her fulfillment from always doing her very best. Alette lived for the moment. Spontaneity was her strong suit. With an intensely social personality, she was happiest when entertaining. Before Tommy came out to Java on a survey for his father's oil company, Alette took a number of lovers, glorying in the practice of their *baboe's* vast repertoire of Asian wiles.

A chorus of masculine guffaws drew Cinta's attention to the street entrance to the concourse. Then her hand shot to her mouth, and her heart came up into her throat.

(Three)
Oakland Train Station
7 August 1941

Petty Officer Brown came out of the train station trailing a sandy-haired lieutenant in rumpled blues. The driver stored a large leather suitcase in the boot of the car.

"Welcome aboard," Frank greeted the wiry stranger. He introduced himself.

"Jack Sewell," the man responded. He had a strong New England accent.

"Did you come far?" Frank inquired as Brown nosed out into the street.

"From Norfolk, Virginia. I just finished the Gunnery Officers course." Jack took out a gold cigarette case and offered a smoke to Frank.

"Naval Academy?" asked Frank when he noticed a heavy class ring on Jack's hand.

"Harvard Business School. I got my commission through ROTC. What about you?"

"I took ROTC at UCLA. They just called me back to active duty."

"What did you do as a civilian?"

"I'm aeronautical engineer for Hughes Aircraft."

"Wasn't that a war-essential job?"

"If we're going to have a war, I'd just as soon fight. I want to fly high-performance aircraft."

"You a fighter pilot?"

"Not yet, but I'm working on it." Frank explained his dilemma with the detailers. "I'm headed to Manila to join *Marblehead*, the old 'Gallopin' Ghost of the China Coast.' What's your assignment?"

"The *Jonathan B. Rust*, a recommissioned 'four-piper' destroyer. She got 'Shanghaied' into the Asiatic Fleet last month."

"Those little 'cans' bounce around too much for me. Have you done duty in them before?"

"Four years in the North Atlantic. I've been going to sea in little ships since I was old enough to walk. My dad owns a fleet of fishing boats out of Gloucester, Mass. I was running the financial end of the business when I got my recall notice. It's kind of good to get away for a while. The folks keep pressuring me to settle down and get married. Don't have anything against matrimony, but I haven't found a woman I want to spend the rest of my life with."

The Navy sedan broke free of the city and began the ascent to the trestles of the San Francisco-Oakland Bay Bridge. Brown turned off at Yerba Buena and took the ramp down to the low-lying Treasure Island, stopping in front of the crescent-shaped Pan Am terminal building.

The two lieutenants placed their bags in the care of a porter and thanked the bosun before he drove away.

"Will you look at that view!" Jack exclaimed in wonder. "I should've come out earlier and spent some time here."

The panorama before them was spectacular. To the left were the triple towers of the suspension bridge to the mainland; directly across the crystal waters of the bay was the San Francisco skyline; to the right, in the distance, the graceful lines of the Golden Gate Bridge were shrouded in sea mist. The lowering walls of Alcatraz Prison in the middle of the bay completed the picture.

Jack began to tell a ribald tale about a Mediterranean cruise he had been on back in 1936. As they came laughing into the passenger concourse, Frank suddenly stopped and whipped off his teardrop sunglasses.

"Good God, Frank," said Jack. "You look like you've just seen a ghost."

"Not a ghost, pal," Frank replied slowly. "It's the only woman I ever asked to marry me."

"What's wrong, Cinta?" Alette said with alarm. "Are you ill?"

"No. I'm all right. It's just that Frank Rhea's here."

"Really?" Curiosity laced Alette's voice. "Show him to me."

"Who the hell's Frank Rhea," Tommy interjected, annoyed at being cut out of the conversation.

"You know, Darling, the California boy who proposed to Cinta before she came to Texas. Now, Cinta, which one is he?"

"The Navy pilot. The one who's coming this way."

Frank was walking briskly toward them, leaving his companion standing with a puzzled look on his face.

"Is it really you, Cinta?" asked Frank, taking off his hat.

"It's good to see you again, Frank," she said warmly, offering her hand. "You're looking well. Life at sea must agree with you."

"I've been a civilian for three years. They just called me back. You're as beautiful as ever. I guess I'm supposed to call you 'Doctor' now." He nodded at the medical bag in her hand.

"I just finished my residency. I'm going out to Borneo to live with my father. But I'm being rude. Let me introduce my sister and her husband."

They shook hands all around and made small talk. Jack Sewell came over and joined the group. Finally, as the flight time approached, the two lieutenants excused themselves to finish checking in.

"I'll see you on the plane, Cinta," Frank said in parting. "We've got lots of catching up to do."

As he walked away, Alette eyed Frank with approval. "I always thought you were a little crazy, Cinta, but now I'm certain. I can't believe that you let him get away just so that you could stay in school. You must have been out of your mind."

"He seemed like a nice enough fellow," Tommy commented, "but, Honey, you've got to remember that Little Sister had to make some sacrifices if she wanted to take on a man's job."

"There you go again," Alette retorted. "Who says that medicine's only for men? She stood first in her class at med school, didn't she?"

"And a damned good thing it was. After all the strings I pulled to get her into Texas Med, I'd have been the laughingstock of the Alumni Association if she'd quit to get married."

The couple continued their banter in the good-natured manner of people who have lived together for years. Cinta scarcely heard them. Inside, her feelings were in turmoil. The chance meeting with Frank had awakened emotions she'd thought long dead. It had taken all her willpower to calmly converse while her heartbeat was racing, her body tingling all over at his nearness. Eight years before, Frank had forced her to choose between their love and medicine. Poor Frank never had a chance. She had been wed to her obsession to become a doctor since she was ten years old.

Entering *Manila Clipper* through the main access hatch from the port hydro-stabilizer, Frank was struck by an aura of spaciousness. He and Jack were assigned to the compartment just aft of the lavishly furnished passenger lounge. When one of the stewards showed them to their seats, he was pleasantly surprised to find Cinta already situated on the other side of the aisle, deep in conversation with the two Dutchmen he had noticed in the concourse. She glanced up and smiled sweetly at him.

Unbuttoning his blouse, Frank took the outboard seat by the porthole, while Jack sat down opposite him. They tossed their hats onto one of the empty chairs. When the last passengers finished filing through to the compartments farther aft, Frank stepped out into the aisle and introduced himself to the Dutchmen. As they cordially shook hands, he struggled to remember where he had heard Garrit Laterveer's name before. Marty Ryan's arrival saved him the embarrassment.

Ryan welcomed the group aboard, explaining his role as their Captain and host. Then he turned to Garrit. "I wanted to tell you, Captain Laterveer, what an honor it is to have a famous ace on board. You're invited to come up to the flight deck after we're airborne. We're very proud of *Manila Clipper*."

"Thank you, Captain," Garrit responded. "Perhaps I could bring Lieutenant Rhea along. I see that he's also a flier."

"Of course. You may all come up two or three at a time if you wish. If you'll excuse me now, I must see to the preparations to get underway."

Frank sat spellbound at the window as the pilot taxied *Manila Clipper* out onto the bay, turning her nose into the prevailing wind. The roar of her four 1600-horsepower Wright Cyclone engines rose to a fever pitch, and the plane began to rise out of the water. For the longest time, she seemed suspended between sea and sky. Then her keel broke free, and she was airborne. Alcatraz flashed by to starboard, and the long fingers of the San Francisco docks loomed ahead. The Clipper climbed steadily as she crossed the city.

"Take a good look, buddy," Frank remarked to Jack. "It'll be a long time before we set eyes on the USA again."

They could see the Golden Gate Bridge for several minutes as the pilot continued his climb to the cruising altitude of 11,000 feet. Soon, there was nothing left beneath but the white-capped tops of the dark blue waves.

Listening to Cinta and Dijker conversing in Dutch, Frank felt a stab of irritation. He realized that he was jealous of the colonel sharing her company and thoughts while he was excluded. Cinta van Wely was the one great love of his life, but his selfish pride had spoiled their chances of happiness. When they first broke up, he thought he would eventually get over her, but he never really did. In the years that followed, passionate women from the ports of the Americas, the Caribbean and Western Europe shared his bed but never his heart. He became the consummate lover who never fell in love. Frank's felt elated when he recognized Cinta in the terminal. Was he being given a second chance? If he showed patience and understanding of her need for professional fulfillment, could he possibly still win her love? One thing was certain: if he didn't make the attempt, he would regret it for the rest of his life.

"Are you a fighter pilot?" asked Garrit Laterveer's voice startled Frank from his musings.

"No such luck. I've been trying to get into fighters, but the Navy hasn't cooperated. I fly SOC's off cruisers."

"I'm sorry. I don't understand your acronyms."

"I should have realized. That's our unique Navy way to designate airplanes. We confuse our Air Corps guys, too. The first two letters stand for, 'scout, observation.' The 'C' means that Curtiss Aircraft was the manufacturer. We tag a number on the end to specify the model. An SOC-3 is the third plane of that type we've bought from Curtiss."

"I believe that I like the British system of simply naming the aircraft better."

The two aviators were soon engrossed in a deeply technical conversation. The Dutchman was a natural teacher, his thoughts well organized and their verbalization articulate. He was demonstrating the "four-fingers" fighter formation that the RAF copied from the German *scharms* when Marty Ryan appeared in the doorway. He suggested that Cinta accompany Garrit to the control deck, to which she readily agreed.

"That's a lot of woman," Jack remarked after Cinta had gone. "How'd you let her get away from you?"

"I couldn't compete with her career," Frank replied glumly.

Cinta and Garrit returned in about twenty minutes. Ryan invited Frank and Jack to visit the flight deck next. They passed a few passengers in the lounge, where chess sets, picture puzzles and cards were available for those who wished to pass the time with games. Some were simply sipping cocktails and conversing. The two lieutenants followed Ryan into the nose, where a stair led to the upper deck.

"I'll be damned," Jack swore as they reached the top step. "This place is bigger than the bridge of a destroyer."

"I've been on cruisers without this much chart house room," Frank agreed.

After Ryan introduced them to the rest of the crew, the First Officer, Harry Beall, let Frank sit in the copilot's seat while he explained the elaborate controls. Up ahead, Frank saw a wall of clouds stretching along the horizon. The solid undercast stretched out a thousand feet below the Clipper's cruising altitude, and within a few minutes, *Manila Clipper* soared in brilliant sunlight above what looked to be an immense, level snowfield. Homing on a radio beacon sent out from Hawaii, Harry Beall was unperturbed.

After Frank left the cockpit, Marty Ryan showed him the aircraft log and the elaborate system of "howgozit" curves with which the crew charted the flights progress. By tracking fuel consumption against hours of flight and miles to destination, changed conditions such as wind velocity could be identified and compensated for. Miles versus fuel consumption on three engines were also tracked to assure the ability to return to base or continue to the destination if the "point of no return" had already been passed.

The passenger lounge was bustling when the officers came back down the stairs. A steward brought them cocktails, and Jack stayed on, attracted by a lovely Eurasian girl who seemed to be unattached. Frank took his Johnny Walker Scotch back to their compartment and resumed his discussion with Garrit about flying fighters. The time passed rapidly. The sun was far down against the cloudbank when Jack returned to flop down in his seat.

"Any luck?" Frank asked jokingly.

"Absolute zilch." Disgust was evident in the New Englander's voice. "She belongs to that fat old Englishman from Hong Kong."

"The fortunes of war," Garrit chimed in with a laugh.

A little later, a steward came through to explain that dinner would be served in six relays because of the limited lounge capacity. Dijker, Jack and Garrit all asked to eat early. When Cinta decided to wait until later, Frank jumped at the chance to be alone with her.

"Some privacy, at last," he commented when the others had gone. He moved across the aisle to sit facing her.

She smiled wistfully at him. "The years have been good to you, Frank. You don't seem to have changed very much."

"Maybe not on the outside, but I've grown up a lot. I've quit expecting everything in life to go my way. But you've certainly changed. You're lovelier now-- more serene."

"I see you're still the glib charmer." She raised an eyebrow. "You've never married?"

"Couldn't find anyone who could measure up to you."

"Oh, Frank, you must have had other women."

"Nothing serious. Just passing fancies. What about you, Cinta? Are you involved with anyone right now?"

"I'm married to medicine. You, of all people, should know that. I've had men in my life, but I'm just not ready for any long-term relationships."

"Still the same single-minded pursuit of medical science?"

"Exactly. I nearly drove Alette crazy. She's been trying to play matchmaker for me for years. I've had to fend off droves of rich Texans since I left UCLA."

"I was in Fort Worth on business when I read in the paper that you graduated from UT Med School. You can't imagine how proud I was that you were at the top of your class."

"Why, thank you, Frank." She flashed a broad smile "Coming from you, that's especially pleasing."

Frank leaned forward, his face suddenly dead serious. "I could see later how selfish I was when I insisted that you leave school for me. At the time, I only knew how much I loved and needed you."

"It all worked out for the best," Cinta said with a sigh.

"Maybe so. How long will you stay in Borneo?"

"A year or two. What happens with the Japanese will have a lot to do with it. I want Papa to leave if war becomes a certainty."

"Our fleet makes port calls in your islands. I'd like to visit you there if the opportunity arises."

"I'd like for you to meet Papa. The two of you are a lot alike. But you mustn't get romantic again."

"That's a promise I can't make. I never really stopped loving you."

"You're dreaming, Frank. We're two entirely different people now. A third of our lives have passed since we broke up. You may discover that you don't even like what I've become."

"You're wrong there, Doctor. I like you even better."

"Tell me about yourself. It's pretty obvious what I've been doing for the past few years. I know nothing of your life since college."

"There's really not much to tell." But under the gentle prodding of her questions, he began to relate what life had been like for a fledgling Naval aviator in the mid-thirties. He found her laughing at his old sea stories and keenly interested in his descriptions of the ports he had visited in Europe. When the others returned, the steward shepherded the couple into the lounge for dinner, putting them at a table for two. They continued their reminiscences over braised roast beef served on fine china.

"Enough about me," Frank finally said as the mess attendant poured coffee. "Your life hasn't been all school and books. Tell me about those wealthy oil men your sister's been trying to marry you off to."

"Oh, Frank," she laughed. "It's all so dreadfully boring."

"It won't be to me."

As Cinta told of her life in Texas, Frank realized what complete dedication it had taken for her to reach the goal she had set for herself so many years before. While the medical profession put up no official bars to women, her path had not been easy. Only when she spoke of Alette's endless rounds of parties did levity enter her story. Her descriptions of some of her suitors were downright hilarious.

After they finished eating, Cinta excused herself and went to check on her sleeping arrangements. Gripped by nostalgia, Frank returned to his seat and sat staring out the window, oblivious to the conversation around him. The moon had risen, casting bright, silver light on the flat plain of the cloudbank below. He closed his eyes and dozed until the steward woke him to make up his berth.

By 11:00 P.M., all the passengers except Cinta were lost in slumber. She lay tossing in her bunk, memories of her college days with Frank flooding her consciousness. She wondered what her life would have been like if she had given in and married him when he graduated. They'd been so young then, so full of life, so much in love. But the answers were all too obvious. She would be a housewife with small children, alone in San Diego grieving for her man gone off to war. Her self-assurance returned. She had chosen the only course in life that could have given her the professional achievement her soul demanded. Perhaps sometime in the future, she could have the other, more traditional rewards of a woman as well. She turned over and closed her eyes. Very soon, only the crew on *Manila Clipper's* flight deck remained awake.

CHAPTER 3

(One)
Above the Hawaiian Islands
8 August 1941

Frank watched through the window as the volcanic landmarks of Hawaii crept up over the horizon. At first, he saw but a blue smudge. Then towering cliffs with clouds piled high above them became visible, and he recognized the distinctive outline of Diamond Head. The Clipper flew on past Honolulu with its snowy beaches and quaint, New Englandish hotels. Ahead, he made out the extensive runway system of Hickam Field, the Army Air Corps's big airbase. The large, landlocked harbor for which the flight was bound loomed in the distance.

Slowed by a head wind from the north, *Manila Clipper* dropped smoothly toward the waters of the entrance channel. Harry Beall eased her down until her hull was skimming along the surface of the Pearl Harbor. She settled into the water to become a monstrously large boat. Approaching the mooring float of the Pearl City terminal, Beall cut the engines, letting the flying boat coast in. Within minutes, the big bird was snugly tied up alongside the float, and a gangplank had been lowered onto one of her "water wings"-- the big hydrostabilizers at her waterline. On the shore, an Aloha band struck up an island tune, and hula dancers began to gracefully sway to the beat of the music.

"Will you be coming into Honolulu?" Cinta asked Frank as they walked up the boardwalk to the terminal building. A sign over the door read, "San Francisco 2404 Miles, Midway 1304 Miles."

"I'm not sure. I'm going over to Ford Island to see an old friend."

"I've reserved one of the best rooms in the Royal Hawaiian for tonight," Jack remarked. "You're welcome to stay with me."

"I may take you up on that. Let's see how things work out."

A Pan Am motor launch dropped Frank at the officers' boat landing at Ford Island, where the petty officer in charge called for a car. As he rode past the flight line of the naval air station, Frank was impressed with the variety of aircraft parked there. Floatplanes from cruisers and battlewagons rested on wheeled cradles. He recognized both the Curtiss *Seagulls*, which he would fly off *Marblehead*, and the later monoplane *Kingfishers*. A large number of PBY flying boats filled one parking apron, while another held carrier planes, including dive bombers, torpedo planes and the new *Wildcat* fighters. A few of the older Brewster *Buffalo* fighters--now hopelessly obsolescent—stood nearby.

After the bright sunlight off the water, the inside of the air operations building seemed still and gloomy. Frank ambled down the hall until he found the door with "Assistant Operations Officer" painted on the glass panel. He opened it without knocking. Across the room, a heavy-shouldered lieutenant with curly brown hair looked up from the report he was reading. Lieutenant Steve Henley's deeply tanned, cherubic face creased into a toothy smile.

"Frank, you old son-of-a-bitch," Henley said, springing from his chair. "Come on in." He met Frank halfway across the room and pumped his arm.

"Make yourself comfortable." Henley indicated a rattan chair beside his desk. "Want some coffee?"

"Never pass up a good cup of Java. You look fit."

"Never better. I work out and swim every day." Henley called a yeoman to bring the coffee. "When did you get in?"

"About an hour ago. Flew in on the Pan Am Clipper."

"Hey, that's high-class living. I didn't know the Navy was that hard up to get pilots out here."

"They're not. I bought my own ticket."

The yeoman brought in two mugs of coffee. Frank wrapped his fingers around the plain ceramic cylinder and sipped the steaming liquid.

"How long will you be in town?" Henley continued.

"Overnight. We shove off for Manila before daylight."

"Oh, hell, that's too bad. I've got to go to a party at my skipper's quarters tonight. I'd like to have you out to dinner. You've never met Helen, have you?"

"No. You got hitched after I went back to San Diego."

"She's an angel." Henley shoved a framed picture at Frank. It showed a shapely blond in a one-piece bathing suit.

"Very nice," Frank commented. "You're lucky."

"You still a bachelor?"

"Yep. It's just as well. I've got orders as second aviator on *Marblehead.*"

"I should be giving you something stronger than coffee. That's a suicide assignment when the balloon goes up. Those old SOC's will be sitting ducks."

"Thanks a lot, buddy," said Frank, smiling wryly. "How're things here at Pearl?"

"The place is lousy with battleship supremacy people," Henley replied, suddenly agitated. "Admiral Halsey's the only flag officer around who really knows the score. The others can't accept that carriers are all that count anymore. They're obsessed with their precious battle line. But what's worse, they bring the whole shebang into this rat hole every weekend and tie up for liberty. Here, let me show you something."

Henley led the way out into the hall. A few minutes later, Frank followed him up into the Ford Island control tower. It had windows on all sides, giving a panoramic view of the island and the surrounding harbor. After ordering the petty officer in charge to "carry on," Steve swept his hand along the east window.

"Just look at this place," he said. "Before the airplane, it was a perfect set-up. Plenty of sheltered water. You could put the whole fleet in here. Now it's a damned death trap in any kind of an air attack. Let's just say the big boys are all tied up along Battleship Row." He indicated the moorings along the eastern part of the island. "There'd be a dozen or more cruisers at the Navy Yard and around the harbor. The `pig boats' would be over at the Sub Base." He pointed to a big indentation north of the Yard, a harbor within a harbor. "There'd be `tin cans' moored all over the lochs. Now suppose, just suppose, that the Japs hit us with a surprise attack like they laid on the Russians back in 1905, but this time with aircraft. Can you imagine what this place would be like? Ships milling around all over the harbor and trying to get out down that funnel of a channel?"

"You paint a depressing picture," Frank commented. "But it can't really be that bad. Someone must be responsible for air defense."

"Don't bet on it. The Air Corps has that ball, and they're booting it. They don't have any kind of a warning system. No radar. No nothing."

"You make me glad I'm going out to Manila." said Frank as they descended the stairs.

"Just farther out on the limb, old pal. When the Japs saw it off, we'll both take a tumble. Matter of fact, I may be joining you out there before long. A call came around for volunteers to fly PBY's in Patrol Wing Ten. Helen doesn't know it yet, but I put my name on the list. Want to have a look around the base?"

"Sure, why not?"

Henley gave Frank a jeep tour of the island for the next hour and a half, finishing in front of the officers' club. "You look like a man who could use a drink," he said as he punched Frank's chest with a finger. "The bar just opened."

They ate peanuts and drank bourbon on the rocks in the darkened bar for the next hour, retelling old sea stories, then continued their conversation over lunch.

"I've got to get back to the salt mines," Henley said after polishing off a thick hamburger. "Otherwise, there's a certain commander who'll be ready to skin me alive. Where will you be staying tonight?"

"I'd thought about the BOQ here, but one of the guys on the plane offered to let me share his room at the Royal Hawaiian."

"Take him up on it. Hell, you'll have lots more fun in town. Look, if you want to stick around until quitting time, I'll drive you down."

"That's okay. I can get a taxi at the Fleet Landing."

"It'll cost you an arm and a leg."

"You forget that I've been a rich civilian engineer. I can afford it."

"You'll have some coming down to do, considering what lieutenants make these days."

After the heat of the tropical afternoon, the elevator in the Royal Hawaiian Hotel seemed downright frigid. Frank shivered as the chill penetrated his sweat-soaked white uniform, reflecting that it must be unhealthy to keep buildings so cold in so hot a climate. He got out at the third floor and began searching for Jack's room. Pausing before a door, he checked the number he had written on a piece of paper before rapping hard on the knocker. Waiting several minutes without a response, he knocked again.

"Yeah. Who is it?" Jack's voice was muffled.

"Frank Rhea. I've come to accept your invitation."

"Wait a minute."

There was a rustling of bedclothes, and Frank would have sworn that he heard a woman laugh. Several minutes elapsed before the latch on the door clicked and it swung open.

"Wasn't expecting you this early," said a tousle-headed Jack. He was dressed in a satin bathrobe. "Come on in."

The room was large and well decorated in Spanish motif. It held two double beds, one made up and the other recently used. Broad windows on the opposite wall overlooked Waikiki Beach.

Jack lit a cigarette and blew out the smoke. The smell of rich tobacco blended with the unmistakable aroma of human lovemaking. Frank parked his flight bag on the made up bed and dug out his own Camels.

"Looks like I interrupted something," he laughed as he lit up.

"You just shortened the afterglow," Jack replied, a devilish grin splitting his face. "I knew I was taking a chance, but it seemed worth it."

At that moment, an attractive brunette emerged from the bathroom, buttoning a clinging silk frock. "Oh, don't mind me, Honey," she said in the accent of the Pacific Northwest. "I was just about to go."

"I wouldn't mind you at all," Frank shot back with a laugh.

"Then perhaps I should stay." His comment had obviously piqued her interest.

"Thanks, but no, thanks. I'm in pursuit of another lady."

"If you strike out, our Jack knows where to find me." The woman smiled coyly.

"Will this cover it, sweetheart?" asked Jack, handing her a twenty-dollar bill.

"Sure. Anytime you want a repeat, I'm available." She straightened her hair before the mirror and let herself out the door.

"Where'd you pick her up?" asked Frank.

"Olivia? At the hotel bar. Stopped by for a cool drink after a swim on the beach. When I saw her, I decided I'd better get my licks in while I had the chance."

"Was it worth it?"

"Every penny."

Frank considered hitting the beach but decided against it. There would be plenty of beaches on the islands on the journey ahead. What he really wanted was a shower and a nap before dinner. He hoped to be up very late that night.

"Have you thought about dinner?" asked Jack.

"Not yet."

"There's a great restaurant right here in the hotel. Serves the best steaks in the island, I'm told."

"I thought you were a seafood man."

"Just because my family sells fish doesn't mean I like them."

"I'm going to clean up and rack out for awhile. Gotta be fresh for tonight."

"Sounds great to me. I could use a little shut-eye myself."

Just past seven-thirty that evening, the two lieutenants entered the hotel bar. Jack wore a white linen suit, the tropical uniform of a wealthy white man, while Frank sported blue seersucker. As they sat down at a table, Frank spotted Olivia laughing and talking with a man at the bar. The strains of a polished dance band drifted through the door to the verandah restaurant as a couple came in from outside. Jack ordered *mai tais* for them both, and as they sipped the tropical drinks, Frank told him about the conversation that morning with Steve Henley.

"He sounds like a real pessimist to me," Jack commented.

"That's what worries me. He's usually a `gung ho' character. I'll admit that he's one of those aviators who thinks battleships are dinosaurs, but even that doesn't explain his attitude. He's convinced that Hawaii's wide open to air attack."

"That's hard to swallow. The Naval War College has been studying that contingency for years. They must have considered every possibility a hundred times."

"I hope you're right. What bothers Steve the most is that the Air Corps is in charge of air defense. Those guys haven't been to the Naval War College. How about some chow?"

"I'm starved. Let's see if this place lives up to its reputation."

Jack slipped the headwaiter a ten-dollar bill, and they were rewarded with a table next to the dance floor. The band was very good, although Frank did not care that much for steel guitars. They played a blend of island tunes and those popular on the mainland.

As Jack predicted, the steaks were excellent. Frank attacked his inch-and-a-half slab of rare sirloin with a will. Intent on enjoying the meal, he didn't notice the party being ushered to the table directly behind him.

"Don't look now," Jack said softly, "but your old flame just sat down at the next table."

Frank swallowed his bite of meat half-chewed, washing it down with the good French cabernet Jack had ordered. Then he turned his head slowly so that he could see. Facing the dance floor, Cinta was talking avidly with the Dutch colonel and Garrit Laterveer. She was wearing a filmy blue cocktail dress with spaghetti straps at the shoulders. Her white skin seemed out of place among the beach tans of the other patrons. To Frank, she looked like an angel.

The floorshow began. A young Hawaiian with a mellow, tenor voice sang a number of traditional island songs. Then a dozen grass-skirted dancers took to the floor, their hips gently swaying in the stately hula of Hawaii. Frank kept a sharp eye on the performers as he finished his steak. Most were of mixed Asian and Polynesian blood, which produced delicate beauty and willowy figures. He pushed back his chair and shifted in his seat to get a better view of their graceful movements.

"Enjoying the island scenery, Frank?" Cinta said close to his ear, startling him. He turned to find that she had moved to a chair just behind him.

"Naturally. It's beautiful, don't you think?" he replied, tongue in cheek.

"It depends on your point of view."

Frank exchanged greetings with Garrit and Dijker, both of whom immediately went back to watching the show. It was approaching its climax, with the star dancer performing the frenzied, uninhibited *Te ote'a mau purotu* of Tahiti. The eye could hardly follow the wild gyrations of her hips. Then she was suddenly finished, and the steel guitars played an *aloha* melody while the dancers trooped toward the stage entrance.

"Looks like a good exercise to keep the waist slimmed down," Frank remarked.

"I should think so," Cinta agreed. "I see that you've already eaten."

"Jack wanted to get an early start. He feels that this is his last crack at civilization for a while."

"We ordered just before the show. I'm starved after an afternoon of hard shopping."

The band settled into dance music, and couples began to drift onto the floor.

"Care to dance while you're waiting?" asked Frank.

"I'd enjoy that," she answered with a smile. "It's been a long time."

Frank led her onto the floor and swept her smoothly into his arms. She moved with practiced poise, effortlessly following his lead. They seemed to float across the polished hardwood. Casual observers might have mistaken them for a professional team.

"You haven't forgotten," he whispered into her ear.

"Dancing is like swimming. Once you learn, you never forget."

He slipped his left arm more tightly around her waist and drew her to him until her body was molded against his. She looked up suddenly with a mischievous grin.

"You're in for a bad case of epididymal hypertension," she chided.

He momentarily frowned, then grinned as he remembered the meaning of the medical term for aching testicles. "Hope springs eternal."

"It does spring up. Stop torturing yourself."

"I still love you, Cinta."

"How many times do I have to tell you that I'm not the same girl that you knew in California? I meant what I said yesterday, Frank. I don't have room in my life for romance."

"Do you recall how we used to walk barefoot on the beach in the moonlight?" he asked, changing the subject.

"How could I forget? Those are precious memories."

"We're only a few yards from the finest beach in the world, and there's a full moon tonight."

"Are you suggesting that we go for a moonlit stroll?"

"Why not? For old times' sake. Don't you trust me?"

"Should I?"

"Of course. I'm an officer and a gentleman."

"I haven't eaten yet."

"Meet me afterwards. I'm sure that the good colonel won't be offended."

They danced on in silence for a few minutes.

"Well?" he finally asked.

"Shall we say ten o'clock, in the lobby?"

The tune ended, and Frank took Cinta back to her table. The waiters had already begun clearing the one at which Jack sat alone.

"Want to check out the bar again?" Jack inquired as Frank took his chair. "I think the headwaiter wants to put someone else here."

"We might as well, but don't try to get me loaded. I have a date later tonight."

A stiff ocean breeze sang a song in the tops of the towering palms that fringed the beach, but it was barely audible above the roar of the surf. The full moon cast a ghostly light on sand and wave. Frank and Cinta walked hand in hand toward the Royal Hawaiian. She carried her shoes and stockings in her free hand and dug her toes into the cool, wet sand with every step. Frank had his coat slung over his shoulder. They walked in silence for a good bit of the time, each lost in private thoughts. Occasionally, one or the other would make a remark or voice some reminiscence. The faint strains of the band wafted out to them from the hotel. Frank stopped beside a gigantic tree.

"Bring back old memories?" he asked.

"Too poignantly," she replied wistfully. "It was on a night like this that I succumbed to your charms."

"I still feel the same way, Cinta. You're the only woman I've ever really wanted. Even in this mixed-up world we have today, I'd gladly share whatever comes with you."

"Don't spoil it, Frank. I've told you how I feel. You'll only hurt yourself if you keep on like this." She turned and walked out to where the waves were lapping at the beach and stood staring out to sea. Frank followed. Putting his hands on her shoulders, he turned her to face him.

"I hear what you're saying," he said with feeling, "but I can't bring myself to believe you. I won't accept that what we shared is completely dead."

"Believe it, Frank," she sighed, almost pleading. "It has to be dead. I've struggled for ten years to get to this point. I can't throw it all away."

"That's not what I'm suggesting."

"It might as well be. Look, I'm going out to Borneo so that I can practice medicine on the oil field workers and perfect my ideas on new burn treatments. If war comes, I intend to get my father out of there and get back to the States while there's still time. Let it drop, Frank. There's no point in pursuing it any further."

"I don't give up any easier than you do," he replied stubbornly. "One of these days, you're going to realize that we were meant to be together."

"This isn't getting us anywhere. I think we'd better go in. The flight leaves at an ungodly hour in the morning."

"One kiss, Cinta? For old times' sake?"

"Oh, all right. One, but that's it."

Frank pulled her gently towards him and bent his face to hers. He kissed her tenderly, but with all the emotion that was boiling up within him. Her mouth melted into his, their lips moving together in familiar harmony. Then she stiffened suddenly and pushed herself away.

"Good night, Frank," she said in a voice not a little shaky. "I don't think we should be alone like this again." Spinning on her toes, she ran across the sand to the beach entrance to the Royal Hawaiian.

At five-thirty on Friday morning, the Pan Am bus from Honolulu pulled to a stop before the Pearl City air terminal. The jolt of the brakes startled Frank from sleep. He stretched his kinked muscles as the lights came on in the vehicle.

"Watch it, pal," said a sleepy-eyed Jack Sewell, who was seated beside Frank. The New Englander had come in after three that morning. Frank wondered why he had bothered to rent the hotel room.

Having been promised their previous seats by Captain Ryan, the two lieutenants waited until the aisle was clear before debussing.

Although the number of passengers had doubled, the efficient terminal crew processed them in a remarkably short time. The sky beyond Honolulu was just beginning to turn pink as the attendants led them down the boardwalk and across the float to board the brightly lighted Clipper. A cool breeze from the north just ruffled the surface of the harbor.

Cinta, Garrit and Dijker were already seated when the two naval officers arrived. A pair of machinery salesmen on their way to Hong Kong now filled the spaces that had been vacant on the flight from San Francisco. Greetings were exchanged cordially, then Frank and Jack settled into their seats. Jack fastened his lap belt, slumped into the cushions and promptly fell asleep. Frank peered out the window toward Ford Island. Each rotation of the airfield beacon on the control tower swept across the water. Signal lamps blinked between the shadowy Navy ships. Beyond, the city was still asleep.

Several minutes passed without action after the last passengers went aft. The stewards impatiently flitted up and down the passageway.

"Is something wrong?" Frank asked one of the stewards.

"No, sir," the man replied. "Nothing with the plane, anyway. We're waiting for a couple of diplomatic passengers--gentlemen from the Japanese Consulate."

There was a clatter of footsteps from forward, and two Asians in dark business suits came in from the lounge. The first was very thin, almost emaciated, and had a furtive look about him. The other, who followed at a casual pace, was big for a Japanese but moved like a cat. His well-cut suit could not conceal the powerful muscles underneath, and his black hair was cropped close to his scalp. He carried himself with great dignity.

"I say," Garrit remarked after the Japanese had disappeared from view, "did the steward say those chaps were diplomats?"

"That's right," Frank responded. "They have the big VIP suite back in the tail."

"That last one isn't fooling anybody. He's Jap Army through and through."

Almost immediately, the big radial engines roared to life. Moorings were cast off, and *Manila Clipper* began edging away from the float. Then she taxied slowly out into the harbor, heading for a stretch of open water with enough room for her long takeoff run. Frank checked his watch as the pilot turned the Clipper's nose into the wind and poured on power. The flight was ten minutes behind schedule.

The first rays of sunlight were lapping over the mountains beyond Honolulu and spreading over the city. The plane gathered speed rapidly, and Frank felt her lifting onto the step of her keel. At last, she tore free of the water and was airborne, circling to gain altitude before heading west.

Frank looked down at Pearl Harbor through the window, and the vision of horror that Steve Henley had articulated with such eloquence suddenly flashed through his mind. He tried to block it out, but it lingered to haunt him for more than an hour as he watched the lesser islands of the Hawaiian chain move by below.

Katsura Okuma settled comfortably into the thick cushion of his chair as the coastline of Oahu faded into the horizon. He vividly remembered seeing Mount Fuji vanish in similar fashion three years before when the *Dai Nippon* airliner bore him away toward the Soviet Union. Only six days now, and he would be home again. Emotional patriotism welled up within him. He knew that he was returning to aid his homeland in fulfilling its glorious destiny.

The rustle of a newspaper drew his attention back to the luxurious private compartment he shared with Yonai Shimada, a long-serving member of Japan's professional foreign service. Until being called home three weeks before, Shimada was the fourth senior official at the Japanese Embassy in Washington. They were chance companions. After a week of close contact, they barely remained on speaking terms. Okuma despised the soft-bodied, balding Shimada, considering him muddle-headed and out of touch with reality. The diplomat had some crazy idea he was being returned to Asia to reopen oil negotiations with the Dutch. Having once served in Batavia, Java, Shimada considered himself the perfect choice to convince the *Oranda-jin* (Dutch) that they should ignore Roosevelt's pressures to halt sales to the island empire. To Okuma, such talk was nothing but blather. Anyone as devoted to peace as Shimada could prove a hindrance to the government in the days ahead. Okuma suspected that Shimada was recalled so that the *Tokko Keitsatsu*, the Special Security Police, could keep him under surveillance. Roughly equivalent to the German *Gestapo*, the *Tokko*

Keitsatsu could teach Himmler's bullyboys a thing or two. Shimada's greatest fault was that he lacked the rudder of a clear political philosophy. Katsura Okuma suffered no such weakness.

Okuma firmly believed in *koko*--the "Imperial Way"--a complex melding of religion, political philosophy, and mysticism. The son of a retired IJA colonel, he had had drummed into his head since infancy that the Japanese Emperor and his people were superior humans, the descendants of the Sun God. He believed that Japan was destined to free Asia from the domination of the white colonialists and unify all Asians under the benevolent rule of the Emperor. Japan should logically be the center of this universe. The lesser countries must provide the resources to create a self-supporting empire capable of total war with any potential enemy--either the Soviet Union or the Western Powers. Of necessity, the IJA would play a central role in achieving this New Order in Asia. Military attaches in Turkey had brought back word of how a determined cabal of young officers had seized the reins of power and propelled that country forward in a very short period. It was the duty of every citizen to support the will of the Emperor as enunciated by the Army. Weak-willed civilian politicians must be swept aside, by force if not by persuasion.

The steward brought in a tray of tea and set it down on a table. The two Japanese shed their double-breasted coats, and the man stowed the garments in a closet before serving the steaming beverage. Okuma took vicarious pleasure in being waited on by a white man. After three centuries of white supremacy in Asia, he felt a reversal of roles to be long overdue. Taking out his cufflinks, he rolled his sleeves back to the elbows and picked up his day-old San Francisco newspaper to reread the accounts of German progress in Russia. The headlines trumpeted the fall of Smolensk. The *panzers* were only two hundred miles from Moscow.

The Western press was sure that the Soviets would be defeated before winter, but Okuma retained his doubts. He knew the strengths of Germany's well-oiled military machine, but several weeks of touring the Nazi empire with the visiting Lieutenant General Tomoyuki "Tiger" Yamashita during the previous year, including a flight over London at 40,000 feet in a Junker 86P during a bombing raid, had revealed some of its flaws as well. And, as he had tried to tell his friends at Madame Kitty's, with Russia there was always geography to be dealt with.

Okuma knew that controversy had raged for months within Japan on whether the inevitable war for territorial expansion and natural resources should be directed northward against the Soviets or southward against the Western empires. He passionately believed that the move must be against the effete colonial powers. The French and Dutch were now isolated, their homelands overrun by the Germans. The British were stretched to the breaking point by the attacks of the *Luftwaffe* and Hitler's U-boats. The recently announced embargo on oil shipments to Japan by the Western powers made early action to secure new supplies an absolute necessity. Now was the time for Japan to act, before the shortsighted Americans woke up and began to prepare for war. The only point on which he and Shimada agreed was that the Americans would not fight unless they were themselves directly attacked.

Finishing with the war news, Okuma put the paper aside and let his mind wander for a few minutes. Recalling his conversation with Madame Kitty, he wished that he could have brought Genevieve on the trip with him. That night with her in Berlin had been one of the most pleasurable he had ever enjoyed. A smirk touched his lips as he reflected on how the eyes of the *gaijin*--the Japanese derogatory term for Westerners--would have popped to see the gorgeous blond on his arm. In Japan, his opportunities to socialize with white women would be severely limited. Before embarking on the crusade his country was about to launch, he wished he could take a Caucasian to bed one final time. His prospects were not promising. There were only one or two women on the plane who were worth the effort, and they seemed to be closely attended by their own men. One woman in particular had caught his eye, a ravishing brunette in Compartment Three. Closing his eyes and leaning back in his seat, he fantasized about how he would go about seducing her. After a few minutes, he dozed off, faintly smiling as he slept.

CHAPTER 4

(ONE)
Midway Island
9 August 1941

Humid heat hit Frank's face like a wet towel as he stepped out onto the Clipper's hydrostabilizer. He squinted his eyes agains the brilliant sunlight and its reflection off white coral sand beaches. *Manila Clipper* lay moored to a large float anchored out in the cobalt-blue lagoon. A power launch pulled away with passengers from the forward compartments. Ashore, wood paneled station wagons waited to ferry the travelers to the Pan Am Hotel. A few minutes later, the boat returned to take another load to the pier on the beach.

The first object that his eyes focused on was the sign over the gangway, which identified the landfall as Midway Island and gave the distances to Honolulu and Wake Island, the next stop on the flight.

A colonnaded porch ran along the center section of the hotel, a low white building with a carefully groomed lawn. Raised letters spelled out "Gooneyville Lodge" across the top of the porch. Chinese porters speaking excellent English were ready to usher the passengers into the lobby of the solidly built, well-ventilated haven. The room was furnished in Phillipine rattan. The manager, a dapper little man with slicked-down black hair and a mustache, welcomed them to the island and announced the agenda for the rest of the day. Those who wished could swim, sunbathe, or dive with "underwater goggles" at the beach. Dinner would be served at seven, with the first round of the flight-long bridge tournament to follow. Frank was disappointed that he did not play the game, for Cinta asked him to be her partner before settling for Colonel Dijker.

As the passengers began filing toward their rooms, a Navy

lieutenant in sweat-soaked khakis came in through the main entrance. He took off a pith sun helmet and squinted at the crowd, then walked across to catch Frank and Jack just as they were entering the hallway.

"Would you gentlemen be Lieutenants Rhea and Sewell?" asked the newcomer, who wore the crossed-dividers insignia of the Civil Engineer Corps on his left collar.

Frank identified himself and introduced Jack.

"I'm Bill Lafond, the ROICC over at the naval base," said the engineer. Lafond was wiry and of medium height. His black hair was buzzed in a Marine haircut, and he had a "farmer tan."—his arms and lower face bronzed by the sun while areas shaded by his helmet remained white.

"The what?" asked Jack.

"The Resident Officer in Charge of Construction. I run the contract for building the base."

Lafond wanted them to hand-carry some classified construction reports to his counterpart on Wake Island, where an almost identical facility was being built. When Frank agreed, the ROICC invited them to tour his projects. They spent the afternoon watching tough construction men of the Contractors Pacific Naval Bases--CNAB—a consortium putting up hangars and piers and laying runways. The almost-finished air station would be able to handle heavy bombers and long-range patrol planes. Surface ships and submarines headed west could refuel at the new piers. By the time a Navy launch brought them back across the lagoon to the hotel, Frank and Jack had developed a healthy respect for the professional competence of Lafond and his civilian aides.

Clean-scrubbed and comfortable in mufti, the two naval officers came into to the cool, spacious hotel dining room at six forty-five. It was furnished with small round tables, which could accommodate no more than four diners; Cinta, Garrit and Dijker were already seated together. Cinta waved a greeting to Frank as the headwaiter led him and Jack to a place near the screened windows that opened toward the lagoon.

Considering the isolation of Midway, the meal was splendidly done. After a salad of fruit, nuts and lettuce, the waiters served tasty beef stroganoff over egg noodles. The portions were so generous that Frank had to pass up the cheesecake dessert.

Someone began beating on a glass, and Frank looked up. The hotel manager, who reminded Frank of New York Governor Thomas Dewey, was standing near the center of the room.

"May I have your attention, please," the manager began. "Our bridge tournament will be starting at eight thirty. We have an unusually large number of people wanting to take part, so we will have to play here in the dining room. We'd appreciate it if you'd retire to the lounge when you've finished eating."

Coming out into the lobby twenty minutes later, Frank noticed Cinta seated alone in one of the wicker easy chairs, seemingly lost in contemplation. He walked over to join her.

"You'll be playing with Colonel Dijker?" he asked.

Startled from her daydream, she took a few moments to gather her wits. "Yes. We've drawn north-south seating. I hope I'm not too rusty. I haven't played much since before med school."

He began telling her about his visit to the naval base. All too soon, people started drifting back into the dining room.

"Wish me luck," she said as she got up to join the other participants. "I'll need it."

"The very best, always."

The remnants of supper had been cleared away and the tablecloths changed. Eight tables were set up for play, each provided with a tray containing four, pre-dealt hands and a place card designating the table number.

"May I have your attention again," said the manager. "We have a total of thirty-two contestants, hence eight tables." He explained that the rules of duplicate bridge would be employed, with scoring on the match point system. Five complete rounds would be played, three during the overnight stops and two during the intervening flights. Total points would be compiled after the final round on Guam, and the couple with the highest point score would be declared the winners.

Several players queried the manager on one point or another. When the questions had all been settled, the participants took their places, and the tournament began.

Frank circled the contest area, watching the card play. The heavyweight contestants quickly became evident. The two Japanese diplomats drubbed their first opponents before the other tables were half finished. Frank was even more astonished by the performance of Cinta and Colonel Dijker. The colonel showed a total command of the game and was a ruthless competitor. Frank would have understood had he known that Dijker had been trained for weeks by the finest memory experts at Oxford as part of his spy schooling. Bridge was one of the classroom exercises, and the teachers kept Jan at it until he could always remember every card that fell in every trick.

Frank watched three tricks, reflecting that it was a pity that, since both were on north-south seating, the two most skillful teams would never face each other. His smoking made him thirsty, so he headed to the lounge for a drink. Jack was ensconced at a corner table with the Eurasian girl, whose patron was playing in the tournament. They were talking softly with their heads close together. Spotting Garrit Laterveer at the bar, Frank went over to join him. They struck up a conversation about American isolationism that lasted until the card game broke up for the night. The Eurasian girl slipped away from Jack as the chairs scraped against the floor in the dining room. All passengers were soon on their way to bed. Breakfast would be at five the following morning, with takeoff for Wake Island at six.

(Two)
Skies Above the Marianas Islands
11 August 1941

Frank sat pensively by his window, watching the coastline of Guam creep up over the horizon. The island looked like an enormous, green footprint with the toes pointed southward. As the Clipper crossed over its southern tip, he could make out hundreds of coconut palms planted in even rows on the copra plantations.

For passengers not involved in the continuous rounds of bridge, the two-day flight from Midway to Guam seemed interminable. Irritated that the tournament was denying him contact with Cinta, Frank soon tired of watching her and the colonel subdue one set of opponents after another. Except for occasional technical conversations with Garrit Laterveer, it was a time of unmitigated boredom. The night on Wake Island had proved a pleasant diversion. After delivering Lafond's report, Frank dined with Lieutenant Pete Carbone, the ROICC, at the construction camp. They spent the evening discussing the significance of the string of outposts that the Navy was building across the Pacific. In addition to their importance to the Navy, the new runways at Midway, Wake and Guam were vital links in the Army Air Corps' route to reinforce the Philippines.

Jack was sprawled comfortably in his seat, reading a book with the title, *Our Navy*, ingrained in gold leaf in the blue leather cover.

"Learning anything?" Frank asked without enthusiasm.

"Just brushing up on the duties of my new job." Jack went back to studying a quote from Navy Regulations on the responsibilities of the Gunnery Officer:

> *"The gunnery officer of a ship is the officer detailed by the Chief of the Bureau of Navigation to have supervision and responsibility for the entire ordnance equipment, and is the head of the gunnery department.*
>
> *The gunnery officer shall, if practicable, be the line officer next in rank to the executive officer.*
>
> *"The gunnery officer shall assist the executive officer in carrying out the provisions of article 933(4), especially in connection with fire control and the drill, exercise and efficiency of the armament as a whole; and to this end he shall have, subject to the executive officer, the necessary authority over all officers connected with the armament. He shall make such inspections and perform such duties at drills and exercises as the commanding officer shall direct.*
>
> *"The gunnery officer shall be held responsible for the efficiency of the armament and all appurtenances connected therewith, and for all ordnance workshops, and for all ordnance storerooms not turned over to the supply officer of the ship..."*

The bridge players came back to their seats just before *Manila Clipper* began her descent toward Guam.

"You and Colonel Dijker seem to be doing quite well," Garrit commented to Cinta.

"Yes, I really think we have a chance to win. Not that I'm such a great bridge player, but Colonel Dijker's quite fantastic. I've never played with anyone that good before."

"You're up against some stiff competition, though," Jack put in. "The two Jap diplomats are cleaning up, too. The muscular one's their bridge-master. He'll have some ideas of his own about that trophy."

Katsura Okuma did indeed covet the bridge trophy, and he was scheming on how to win it at that moment. He calculated that the only real competition would come from the Dutch colonel and Doctor van Wely. The strength of that team was the colonel, of course. The woman could be discounted as a threat. Mere women did not have the powers of concentration required to really master games like bridge and chess. It was a pity that there would be no opportunity to play the Dutch head to head. Okuma was certain that he and Shimada would dispatch them in short order. Whatever else Okuma might think of his companion, he had to admit that the man was a first-rate bridge player.

The steward came to clear away the leavings of lunch, which had been served to the diplomats in their cabin. Okuma let a malicious smile curl his lips. He was still enjoying this preview of the new order in Asia, under which yellow men would be the masters and whites the servants. That thought brought his mind back to the Van Wely woman, whom he had observed closely during the flight although never being able to actually converse with her. What a waste that she was devoting her life to medicine! He had possessed enough Caucasian women to allow him to mentally undress her with precision. A body like that should be used to bring pleasure to men, not be shut away in a hospital or physician's office. He knew exactly what he would do with her if given the chance. Berlin and Paris had been great places for picking up new ideas along those lines.

Manila Clipper softly kissed the surface of Guam's Apra Harbor, then settled into the calm waters in the lee of Orote Peninsula. Harry Beall taxied her quickly up the long dredged channel through the island's treacherous coral reef, finally reaching the protected basin at Sumay, on the headland's north shore. The hotel at the old Marine Corps Air Station there occupied several buildings and was more comfortably appointed than those on the tiny atolls to the east. Guam was a large and well-populated island, so a substantial staff of friendly Chamorro locals was on hand to speed the weary guests to their rooms. After the walk up from the harbor in the sticky heat, all that Frank could think about was a cold shower. As soon as the porter who had brought their bags left with Jack's fat tip, Frank stripped off his sweat-stained suit.

"Flip you for the first shower," Jack offered.

"This is a case of rank having its privileges," Frank retorted. "I'm senior to you by at least a dozen numbers."

"Snob," Jack said with disgust. "Buy your own wine tonight."

Practically the whole passenger list turned out for the final round of the bridge tournament. The spacious hotel lounge and screened *lanai* were laid out with sufficient rattan tables and chairs. The stewards placed comfortable wicker seats around the perimeter of the playing area for those who wished to observe the contest. White-coated waiters circulated among the spectators serving cocktails. A cool, gentle breeze blew in from the Philippine Sea. The rooms reverberated with the echoes of loud conversation until the game master rang his bell for the match to commence, and the assembly fell silent.

Frank watched Cinta and Dijker complete their first game. The colonel played with zestful abandon, Cinta with cool competency. They were finished well ahead of the rest of the competitors, having won by a handsome margin. They chatted with their opponents until time to shift to another table. After three rounds, the Japanese team ended up at the table nearest Frank. Both of the Asians played with intense concentration. They, too, won big and with dispatch. When the contestants next got up to rotate, Frank searched for Jack among the spectators but could not find him. The Eurasian girl whom the New Englander had been cultivating was also missing.

It was close to ten-thirty when the last hand was completed and the players turned in their scorecards. The tournament judges, Marty Ryan and the hotel manager, began tallying up the scores. They seemed to be in confusion for some time, and it was obvious that they were rechecking their figures. Frank sensed someone beside him and turned to see that Jack had rejoined him.

"What's happening?" asked Jack. He wore the expression of the cat that swallowed the proverbial canary. Frank noticed the

Eurasian girl slipping through the crowd to rejoin her patron.

"They haven't announced the score yet," Frank replied. "There seems to be some problem."

Just then, Marty Ryan rose to his feet, and the buzz of conversation faded. "Ladies and gentlemen," he began, "we have a most unusual circumstance. For the first time in the memory of our officials, we have a tie for first place."

An excited murmur ran through the audience.

"We have no problem with the east-west winner," Marty continued. "Leading that group with an overall score of 9,280 points is the team of Messrs. Courtright and Harvey."

Amid a polite round of applause, the two British businessmen from Hong Kong came forward to receive the small trophy offered by Captain Ryan. Then he motioned for them to stand to one side.

"And now," Marty went on, "we come to our dilemma. We have two north-south teams with identical scores of 18,260 points." A soft whistle of breath came from the audience. "They are the team of Messrs. Okuma and Shimada..." Scattered clapping interrupted Marty as the two Japanese rose to their feet. He quieted the noise with a wave of his hand. "...and that of Doctor Cinta van Wely and Colonel Dijker."

Another burst of applause broke out as the Netherlanders stood up. Both winning couples came forward to the judges' table. They shook hands and waited until the room quieted.

"Obviously," said Marty, "these teams also tied for first place in the overall tournament. Unfortunately, we have only one set of trophies."

"I believe that I have the solution to your problem, Captain," said Dijker, "if the Japanese gentlemen are agreeable."

"What's your idea?"

"One rubber of regular bridge, winner take all."

"Agreed," snapped Katsura Okuma without the slightest hesitation.

"Very well," Marty concurred. "We'll recess for fifteen minutes and then begin the playoff."

The hotel staff readied a single table in the center of the room, arranging a ring of chairs around it for the onlookers. The two teams took their places at the appointed time and held a brief discussion to agree upon the rules to be followed. The hotel manager brought a new deck of cards, shuffled them thoroughly, and spread them face down on the table. The players drew for the first deal, Okuma winning with an ace of spades. He shuffled the cards quickly and dealt the hand. The Japanese got the contract with a four-hearts bid. After a tensely played game, with Dijker battling all the way, Okuma made his bid on the last trick.

The deal passed to Dijker, who bid and made a five-diamonds contract. Both teams were now vulnerable, but the Japanese were leading on points. Shimada shuffled and dealt the third hand. Bidding was desultory. The diplomat bid and later made three spades, pulling him and Okuma within ten points of clinching the second game and the rubber.

Okuma cursed inwardly as he spread the cards Cinta van Wely had dealt him. It was his worst hand of the night. The only face cards it contained were the ace and king of diamonds.

The Dutchwoman passed, and Okuma was forced to do the same. Dijker bid two no trump. Okuma's eyes narrowed perceptibly. The Dutchman had twenty-two to twenty-four points in his hand, almost enough to win the game without help from the woman. Shimada passed, and Okuma began to seethe inside. The *gaijin* might already have the game and the trophy in the bag.

Cinta bid three hearts, and Okuma was forced to pass again. Dijker responded with four hearts. Gritting his teeth, Okuma considered the situation. The Hollanders had a game bid, and he was holding but two cards in the prospective trump suit. If he did nothing, they would clearly win everything. He looked up at Shimada, who was staring straight into his eyes. Okuma dropped one eyelid slightly. Better to be set by several tricks than to concede both game and tournament.

"Five diamonds," Shimada bid defensively.

"Five hearts," bid Cinta, giving Okuma slight optimism.

"Six hearts," said Dijker after Okuma's pass.

The major could barely contain his elation. The Dutchman had overbid to a small slam when he did not need the points for either game or rubber! Eyeing his own ace and king of diamonds, Okuma was now certain that he could take the two quick tricks necessary to set the whites. Even better, if the trump suit remained the same, the woman rather than the devilishly clever colonel would have to play the hand, with Okuma having first lead. Beating a woman should prove child's play.

"Double," bid Okuma at his turn, confidence oozing from every pore.

"Redouble," Dijker answered coolly.

Shimada and Cinta passed in turn. Okuma pulled the king of diamonds from his hand and played it. Dijker began to lay his cards face up on the table. First came the diamond suit, a queen, jack and nine. Okuma let his breath out slowly. There would be seven diamonds spread between Shimada and the woman. He tasted victory already. The impressive array of face cards that Dijker laid out would prove futile. The woman's failure was assured.

Cinta sloughed the nine of diamonds from the dummy, Shimada dropped on the four, and Cinta played the deuce from her hand. Okuma raked in the trick and neatly stacked the cards. Then, flushed with triumph, he played his ace for the setting trick. Cinta played the jack from the dummy, Shimada the five from his hand. Okuma was already lifting his hand to claim the trick when Cinta dropped the deuce of hearts on the pile, trumping his ace. For a moment, he was totally stunned, incredulous that luck had given the woman a singleton in his strong suit. Then violent rage boiled up within him. Only one trained in such matters would have recognized Okuma's emotions from his outward appearance. His facial expression remained unchanged, but the muscles at the back of his head tightened, pulling his small ears back against his skull.

With deliberate speed, Cinta played out her hand. She dropped one high trump card after another until none remained to her opponents. Then she moved to the board, established herself there and played Dijker's aces, kings and queens. After corralling the last of these, she looked up at the two Japanese.

"I believe, gentlemen," she said tensely, "that the remaining tricks are mine. I have only trumps left, you see."

The taste of ashes in his mouth, Okuma threw down his cards, capitulating. As the spectators burst into applause, his mind seethed with humiliation. He felt himself mocked by the smug satisfaction displayed by the whites that one of their own had defeated him. He paid no attention to the announcement of the final score. With slam bonus, doubled and redoubled, the two Hollanders had far exceeded the points scored by the Japanese. Controlling himself with great effort, Okuma rose, politely bowed to each of his opponents and shook their hands. He looked on dispassionately as Captain Ryan presented the trophies to them. Then, as soon as propriety allowed, he excused himself and Shimada and headed for their room. Once inside, his control broke, and he kicked a chair halfway across the suite.

"Calm yourself, Katsura," Shimada chided. "It was only a game."

"*Baka* (idiot)!" Okuma screamed back. "*Kao-ni doro-o nutta* (they flung mud in my face)! Have you been among the *gaijin* so long that you didn't feel them gloating at our loss? It was a disgrace to be defeated in a game of strategy and skill, and doubly so to lose to a woman!"

"I don't think..."

"Oh, shut up! You're incapable of thinking like a true *Nihonjin* anymore. Our time will come, and it's not far off now. The two who humbled us are on their way to the Dutch East Indies. When we go to war, that's where we'll strike first, to get their oil. I'll have my revenge within the year. Before I'm finished with her, the Van Wely woman will curse her god for allowing her to be born!"

Frank finally made his way through the crowd to Cinta's side. "Congratulations, sweetheart. You were superb," he said as he took her hand.

"Thank you, but no endearments, please," she replied coyly. "Tomorrow, we'll be going our separate ways."

"One final moonlight walk?" he suggested hopefully. "Sumay's a friendly little town, and the ocean breeze is very pleasant."

"I really doubt if I should. I might not be able to resist your charms again."

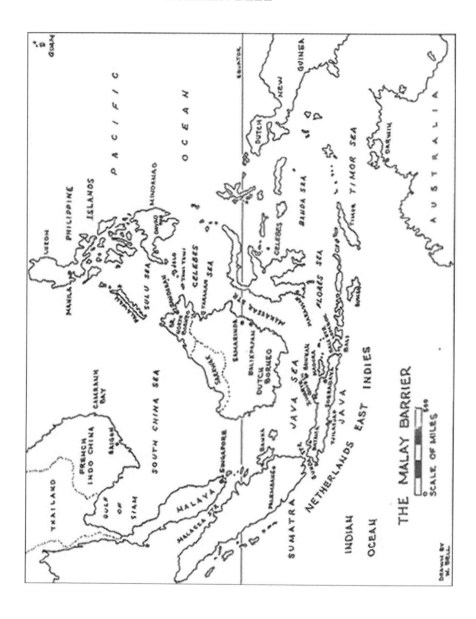

CHAPTER 5

(One)
Skies Above the Philippine Islands
12 August 1941

Frank Rhea watched with Marty Ryan from *Manila Clipper's* flight deck as the plane approached the city for which she was named. The long leg from Guam had taken almost all day, and the sun was well down on the horizon. Most other passengers were napping, but Frank had jumped at the chance to sit in the cockpit during the spectacular flight across Luzon, with its numerous bays, lakes and rice fields terraced up steep-sided mountains. Now they were nearing their final landing.

As *Manila Clipper* crossed the city and then circled to lose altitude, Marty pointed out the landmarks. Frank was struck by the mostly modern appearance of Manila. Tall, white buildings of obvious American design dotted the skyline, especially near the great bay. Thousands of automobiles crawled about like colorful ants on broad thoroughfares that criss-crossed the newer parts of the city. Marty indicated the mansions of the rich along shady Dewey Boulevard on the oceanfront. Splitting the city was the wide Pasig River, bright yellow with mud except where floating green islands of vegetation dotted its surface. Marginal wharves stretched along its banks, berths for freighters, inter-island steamers and native sailing ships. On the southern bank, near the bay, was the old Spanish Walled City with its lowering Fort Santiago, whose massive walls had stood for over three centuries.

The modern port lay along the bay to the south of the Pasig. Seven up-to-date, covered piers jutted into the water. There were acres of high-grade warehousing there, along with gleaming, white office buildings. Beyond the port stood a number of luxury hotels, the most prominent being the famous Manila Hotel, which fronted on an indentation in the coast. The piers were full, and a number of ships anchored in the roadstead, waiting for docking space. Surprisingly, he saw no Navy ships except for a few small auxiliaries.

A few miles to the southwest, a long peninsula became visible. As *Manila Clipper* drew near, Frank made out the drydocks, shops and wharves of the Cavite Navy Yard and the seaplane base at Sangley Point. The little city of Cavite was just south of the Navy Yard.

"Better go back to your seat now, Lieutenant," Marty finally said. "We'll be landing in a few minutes."

Frank was the first passenger to clear customs. As he walked out into the waiting room of the terminal, he scanned the area, looking for anything Navy. He saw no one in uniform, but one couple caught his eye. The tall, large-framed man wore the well-tailored white suit of a successful businessman, but the skin of his hands and still-handsome face was burned to a mahogany hue by long exposure to the tropical sun. His blond hair was bleached platinum. It was hard to gauge his age, but Frank guessed him to be about fifty. There was something vaguely familiar about him, but Frank could not put his finger on it. The woman at his side was just as striking in her own way. Of medium height, she had a splendid figure, which was accentuated by the cut of her silk dress. Now in her mid-to-late thirties, she must have been a rare beauty in her youth, for the face framed by her dark brown hair could still stop a man dead in his tracks. She had the poise and bearing which Frank had seen in European noblewomen.

"Nobody waiting for us?" said Jack at Frank's elbow.

"Apparently not. Let's check at the desk."

The Pan Am clerk offered to call the motor pool at Sixteenth Naval District headquarters, and Frank accepted.

"It'll take them about half an hour to get here," said the clerk. "Might as well make yourselves comfortable."

Cinta saw her father the moment she left the customs stand. He looked exactly as she remembered him, solid as a rock, indestructible. She had to fight hard to keep from running into his arms as she had as a child. He had seen her and was coming to meet her, smiling broadly. Her control broke, and she moved forward as fast as her high-heeled pumps would allow. Tears of joy welled up in her eyes, blurring her vision. Then a massive pair of hard-muscled arms encircled her, lifting her clear of the floor, crushing her to his chest.

"Oh, Papa, Papa," she murmured, kissing his weathered face. "It's so good to see you again."

The big man laughed joyfully. Then he set her back down on her feet and held her at arm's length to look at her.

"My God, Cinta, how you've changed," he exclaimed. "You were still a little girl when I let Alette take you off to California. Now you're a beautiful woman, and a doctor as well. I'm so proud of you that I could burst." He enfolded her again with his arms and hugged her tenderly. She saw that his piercing, blue eyes were also damp with tears.

"I'm forgetting my manners," Nicolaas said suddenly. "A friend came with me to meet you." He took Cinta's hand and led her to the lovely, dark-haired woman who had been standing with him earlier. "Countess Tonia Ivanovna, may I present my younger daughter, Doctor," he emphasized the title, "Cinta van Wely."

"I'm so pleased to meet you, Doctor," said the woman in a pleasant voice, her Russian heritage evident in her accent. "I feel that I know you already. Nicolaas and I are old friends, you see."

"I'm happy to meet you, Countess," Cinta replied, realizing that she and the Russian woman were sizing each other up like a pair of felines. "Thank you for coming with Papa."

"I've heard him speak of you for years," the Countess continued. "I had to come and see if he were exaggerating."

"You must admit now that I spoke the truth," said Nicolaas.

"I conceded the point. She is, as you said, a beauty who is also blessed with brains."

"You embarrass me with such talk," said Cinta, blushing. "Will we be staying long in Manila, Papa?"

"Overnight at the Manila Hotel. I have *Belle of Borneo* at Nichols Field."

"*Belle of Borneo*?" Cinta queried.

"My airplane. Well, the company's anyway. She's a new Lockheed *Lodestar*, a beautiful, responsive bird. We'll fly home in the morning. I've made appointments for you in Batavia to resolve your licensing."

"A *Lodestar's* fairly large, isn't it?"

"Ours is rigged to carry fourteen passengers, and we have extra fuel tanks for more range. Why do you ask?"

"There are two Dutch officers headed for Batavia on the Clipper. They were planning to take the next flight to Singapore and go on to Java from there. Perhaps we could give them a lift."

"And save the Queen the cost of commercial passage. I'd be happy to do it."

"Here they come now," said Cinta. She waved for Garrit and Jan to join them, then introduced the officers to her father and Tonia.

"It's good to meet you again, *Tuan Besar* (Big Boss)," Garrit said as he shook Nicolaas's hand.

"You're from the islands?" asked Nicolaas. Then his eyes narrowed. "Good Lord, you're Anton Laterveer's boy, the Battle of Britain ace."

"Yes, sir. Have you seen my father lately?"

"Last week. He's hale and hearty, as ever. Your mother's in good health also. They'll be delighted to have you home."

Across the room, Cinta noticed a pair of Navy enlisted men come in and take Frank's and Jack's bags. They were clearly about to leave. Cinta waved to Frank and motioned for him to come over. He said a few words to Jack, who went on out, then came towards the Netherlanders.

"Papa, here's someone I'd like you to meet," said Cinta. "This is Frank Rhea. I wrote you about him several times." She went on to introduce Nicolaas and the countess to Frank.

"Tonia and I debated earlier as to which one of the officers you were," said Nicolaas. When he saw the look of surprise on Frank's face, he explained. "Alette, my other daughter, called by radio telephone the day the flight left San Francisco. She told us about you."

"Which one did you pick?" asked Cinta.

"The right one, of course," purred the countess.

"I'm having a small dinner party at the Manila Hotel tonight to celebrate Cinta's return," Nicolaas said to Frank. "I'd be pleased if you'd join us."

"I'd like nothing better," said Frank, "but I'm afraid the Navy may have other plans. My ship's off on maneuvers somewhere, and I have to catch up with her."

"What a pity," said the countess. According to Alette, the young man was worth getting to know, and she tended to agree. Tonia had a wealth of experience at judging men.

"I understand the demands of duty," said Nicolaas. "Perhaps another time. If your ship comes to Balikpapan, you'll always be welcome in my home."

"Thank you, sir. I may take you up on that. It was good to meet you." Frank said his farewells to the others, then turned to Cinta. "I guess this is *au revoir*."

"I hope it's not goodbye," she replied, taking his hand. They walked a few steps from the group.

"I'll write. I got your address from Pan Am."

"You're resourceful, as ever. Remember what I told you in Honolulu, though. I really meant it."

"You won't be rid of me that easily."

"Take care of yourself." Cinta suddenly stood on her tiptoes and kissed his cheek. He felt the pressure of her lips against his face as he walked out to the waiting car.

"These two gentlemen have agreed to fly south with us tomorrow," Nicolaas informed Cinta when she rejoined the party, "and they've accepted my invitation to dinner."

"Will we take a cab to Manila?" she asked.

"No. I've driven the Cavite road before. It's twenty miles of potholes. I have the company launch outside. We'll be across the bay in a fraction of the time a motor car would take."

Cinta followed her father across the vast pavilion dining room of the Manila Hotel. She'd never seen a restaurant so large. Located on the Bay side of the hotel, it was open to the fresh breeze blowing in off the water. Birds flitted about the rafters, sometimes daring to dive and snatch crumbs purposely thrown on the floor by diners. Slippery with wax, the polished hardwood surface caused the birds to skid about like children on a frozen pond. Cinta had trouble keeping her own balance on the gleaming floorboards. The white-clad headwaiter led Van Wely's party to a large table near the western dance floor. A respectably good band was playing a Tommy Dorsey tune as waiters held chairs for Cinta and the countess. They were hardly seated when a portly British gentleman of about fifty was escorted to the table. Nicolaas introduced him as Reginald Forester, director of Royal Dutch /Shell interests in Manila.

"Have you a wife, Mister Forester?" asked the countess as he kissed her hand in the continental manner.

"Alas, no, my dear lady," Forester replied. "I'm a confirmed bachelor." He had salt-and-pepper hair and a white mustache. His dress was the ubiquitous white suit.

"That's a shame," she said with genuine concern. "Every man should have the support of a good woman."

"Here's the report I promised you," Forester said to Nicolaas, handing him a heavy envelope. "It came out by special pouch from London."

"I shall read it with great interest," the oilman replied.

"I've never seen such a place," said Cinta as they resumed their seats.

"It covers an acre," Forester explained. "As you see, it also has two bandstands. A few months ago, it would have been filled with Americans. Since their Army and Navy sent all the dependents home, it's not so gay anymore."

A waiter arrived to take orders for cocktails.

"You're all my guests tonight," Nicolaas announced. "Order whatever pleases you. This is a very special night for me. My heart bursts with joy to have my daughter with me again."

As the drinks were being served, the countess commented on the beauty of the sunset across the sparkling waters of the bay.

"Manila is famous for its sunsets," said Forester. "Every one is different, but they are all equally beautiful."

The menu might have come from a posh restaurant in America. Most of the party ordered steaks, one of the house specialties. Nicolaas bought champagne for the table.

"They did get you in the new wing of the hotel?" Forester asked Nicolaas.

"Yes," the Dutchman replied. "The arrangements are excellent."

"It's almost too cold," said Cinta. "The air conditioning is very efficient. I'll need a blanket to sleep."

"Better than a mosquito net like mine in the older building," said Garrit. "The windows there have no screens. The window lights are quite unique, made of thin sea shells."

"*Mijnheer* van Wely," Dijker spoke up, "you've looked very familiar to me ever since we met. I suddenly realized where I've seen your face before. It was in *Life* magazine, I believe. You were with Doctor van Mook at the economic negotiations with the Japanese last year."

"That's right. We managed to string them along for some months before they caught on that we weren't going to give in."

"They wanted oil?" asked Garrit.

"Of course," said Nicolaas. "They insisted we sell them all their current needs and let them develop new areas in Borneo. They've been getting most of their supply from the United States, and Roosevelt's been threatening to cut them off ever since they attacked China back in thirty-seven."

"And you gave them nothing?" said Dijker.

"That's correct. The Americans convinced the Queen's government that all the Western powers should act in concert to put pressure on Japan to quit China."

"Bloody foolishness," Forester interjected. "We're strapped with a war for survival itself in Europe, and here the Yanks are trying to make us pick a fight with the Nips out here. And over what? Old Chiang's as much a fascist dictator as Hitler or Mussolini. Why should we stick our heads in the fire to pull his chestnuts out?"

"The Americans have romanticized notions about China, brought back by their missionaries," Nicolaas continued. "At least, that's what my daughter in Texas tells me."

"Pearl Buck's book, *The Good Earth*, had a lot to do with it," said Cinta. "The smartest thing old Chiang ever did was to marry a Christian wife," Nicolaas reflected.

"He's better than most who have ruled China," said Tonia with authority, "but his government is corrupt beyond believing. I have first-hand knowledge on that subject."

"I can't understand why Roosevelt's so bent on provoking the Japanese," said Forester. "Last year he cut off scrap iron and steel; now, he's frozen Japanese assets in America, which shuts off their oil."

"I don't think the President wants war with Japan," Dijker offered. "Our embassy people in Washington don't think so. It's their Secretary of State who's so damned inflexible."

"Cordell Hull?" asked Cinta.

"An old-fashioned Baptist moralist with the world view of a Tennessee mountaineer," Dijker continued. "He just doesn't comprehend the differences which cultural background makes in the way men think."

"Their ambassador in Tokyo, Joseph Grew, knows the score," said Nicolaas. "Our people there speak very highly of him. But Hull doesn't pay attention to his warnings. Hull's set on forcing Japan to withdraw from China."

"The Nips could no more pull out of China now than the Americans could cede California back to Mexico," Forester snorted with finality.

"You're saying that there's bound to be a war?" asked Cinta.

"The seeds have already been sown," said Nicolaas sadly. "When we joined the British and Americans in embargoing oil to Japan last month, we might as well have declared war. A modern industrial nation cannot exist without a secure source of oil. The Japanese have only four thousand wells in their Niigata district fields. Their total yield is just under two million barrels a year, only seven percent of their total consumption. To deny them imports when we don't have the military strength to protect ourselves was the height of folly."

"You're against the embargo?" asked Garrit.

"For now, I am. Roosevelt's promises of military support are all very well, but our sources question his ability to deliver when the chips are down. What do you think, Captain Laterveer?"

"I've visited the American factories and training establishments. They're expanding their air forces at a remarkable rate. In another year, they'll be a first class air power."

"There's the rub," said Forester. "We won't have a year's grace. The Nips have only so much oil stashed in their reserves. If they aren't allowed to buy more before they're down to the danger point, they'll come and take it from us by force."

"They couldn't just attack the Netherlands' possessions," Cinta commented. "They'd surely have to take on the British and Americans as well."

"If the Nips were really smart, they'd be selective," said Dijker. "With all the dissension the America First crowd is stirring up, I doubt Congress would act unless Japan directly attacked American territory."

"So, there we have it," said Nicolaas. "One things certain, though. If the Japs come to Borneo, they'll find nothing of use there. We'll blow up and burn everything and then stage a *puputan* that will go down in history."

"*Puputan* is Malay for a fight to the finish," Garrit explained to Dijker.

"Like the Texas Americans at the Alamo," Cinta put in.

"Must you men always talk politics?" asked the countess. "I thought this was going to be a party for Cinta."

"You're right, my dear, as always," Nicolaas conceded. "Politics can wait until another time." He motioned for the waiter to refill the champagne glasses. "I have a toast," he went on, rising to his feet. "To my daughter, the physician. May she always enjoy success and happiness.

"Hear, hear," the men echoed before emptying their glasses.

The conversation turned to domestic life in the Dutch East Indies. Cinta had not really had much time to talk with her father before dinner. She wanted to know about the house at Balikpapan and the servants, especially her old *baboe*, Ada.

"Ada's indestructible," Nicolaas commented. "She keeps pestering me to tell her about the men in your life. Too bad Lieutenant Rhea couldn't join us."

"It's probably just as well," she sighed wistfully. "He has his job to do, and I have mine. It's better that we go our separate ways."

Countess Ivanovna eyed Cinta reflectively, trying to fathom this single-minded daughter whom Nicolaas had sired.

The group lingered on in the pavilion for another hour, enjoying conversation over good brandy and dancing now and then to the orchestra music. Cinta took the floor with each of the men but found herself more comfortable with Garrit. Finally, the party began to break up. Forester excused himself to return to his office. Dijker and Garrit went to their rooms to sleep. Nicolaas paid the bill, leaving an enormous tip, and then took the women back to the new wing of the hotel. After the comfortable tropical evening, the air conditioning seemed almost frigid. The Van Wely's said goodnight to the countess at her door, which was next to Nicolaas's. Cinta went on to her father's suite for more talk before bed.

Nicolaas's had the most posh accommodations in the hotel. His sitting room was furnished in Chinese motif, with intricately patterned Tsientsen carpets, red and gold silk wall coverings, rosewood tables and chairs, a Coramandel screen, and elegant vase lamps. Thankful for her shawl in the chill air, Cinta settled into an overstuffed sofa while her father poured Napoleon brandy into two snifter glasses.

Countess Tonia Ivanovna sat down in a large rattan chair, put a cigarette into an ivory holder and lit it. Feeling relaxed and freshened after a warm bath, she was eager to lie naked in Nicolaas's arms. She guessed rightly that his daughter would be with him for some time yet. Later, when Cinta retired to her room, Tonia would go to him.

From all outward appearances, this exquisitely groomed, shapely noblewoman seemed pampered by life. Yet only a woman of the toughest fiber could have survived her past, much less amassed the riches she now possessed. She had endured rape and imprisonment during the Bolshevik revolution, then the loss of her first true love in the civil war that followed. Her father, whom she virtually worshipped, was killed while fighting as a mercenary for the infamous Chinese warlord, Chang Tsung-chang. She had been enslaved for three years in the *tuchun*'s harem, becoming his favorite among forty-two concubines. When Chiang Kai-shek's armies swept Tsung-chang's empire away, she stole a fortune in jewels from his strongbox and fled to Shanghai. Within a few years, she was the proprietress of six fashionable brothels, each with a stable of the most attractive White Russian girls in the French Concession. By the mid-thirties, she was expanding into real estate, running her operations from a fancy office in the commercial district of the International Settlement. But in 1937, the Japanese brought war to Shanghai, and business began to plummet.

Realizing that it was but a matter of time before the entire Far East became entangled in warfare, Tonia began to make plans to leave Shanghai. She sold property at a loss and put her capital into portable assets, mostly jewels bought at a fraction of their value from the Jewish refugees who flocked to Shanghai after the war in

Europe began. Her greatest quandary resulted from her refusal to leave her girls to the tender mercies of the Japanese. With her connections, she could have easily arranged immigration for herself. A mass migration of White Russian courtesans was quite another matter.

In the summer of 1940, she found her solution but lost her heart in the bargain. She met Nicolaas van Wely at the Sky Terrace of the Park Hotel. He was in Shanghai to coordinate deliveries of Borneo oil to the Japanese, a task he despised. His sheer animal magnetism reminded her of her long-dead father. They ended the night in bed together and remained lovers while he was in the city. When she told him of her dilemma, he offered to arrange to move her "family" to the Dutch East Indies. She learned of his influence with his government when the immigration papers were approved in record time. He flew her in his private plane to Borneo, where she bought an excellent hotel for her demimondes in the oil port of Balikpapan. After a year of healthy profits, she opened another establishment in the boomtown of Zwarte Gouden on Java's north coast, commuting regularly on the flights of *Koninklijke Nederlandsch-Indische Luchtvaart Maatchappij* (KNILM) to check on operations. Nicolaas resented the time she spent away from Balikpapan, where he had become General Manager of the vast BPM complex, but he understood that business was business.

Tonia jumped at this opportunity to accompany her lover to meet his daughter. She had always wanted to see Manila, but even more, she welcomed the chance to size up the young woman before they returned to Borneo. She wondered how Cinta would react to the relationship she and Nicolaas shared. Cinta was hard to gauge, for she clearly kept her feelings on a tight rein. The handsome American lieutenant was quite the opposite. His deep attachment to Cinta was readily evident. The coolness that she displayed toward him did not bode well.

The countess checked her wristwatch. The girl should be gone to her own room by now. Approaching the door that joined her room with Nicolaas's, Tonia put her ear to the wood. Hearing nothing, she slipped her key into the lock, unlatched it and cracked the door to peek inside. Swathed in a Javanese sarong and smoking a long cigar, Nicolaas was sitting in an easy chair opposite the door, engrossed in the report Forester had brought to him.

"That must be a fascinating document," Tonia said petulantly. "I was beginning to think you'd lost interest in me."

"Never, my love!" Nicolaas declared vehemently, rising and coming to meet her. Still holding the report, he wrapped his arms around her and kissed her fiercely.

"May I ask what it is, or is it some sort of secret?" she said when they came up for breath.

"It's no secret," he laughed. "Actually, it's a bit of history. Back in 1916, a British colonel named Norton-Griffiths wrecked the Rumanian oil works just before the Germans captured them. This is a detailed report on the methods he used."

"Do you think it will come to that here?" She was suddenly sobered.

"I hope not, but one must always be prepared. But enough of that. We have more important things to do at the moment."

Their lips barely touched before he was busy untying the fastenings of her robe. Her own fingers tore at the knot of his sarong until it came loose and fell to the floor.

(Two)
Manila Hotel
13 August 1941

The alarm clock in Cinta's head woke her promptly at six a.m. After ten years of rising at that hour, her inner timing mechanism never failed her. Even the time zone changes made no difference. In the chill of the air-conditioned room, she was tempted to lounge for a while in the warmth of the bed. Nicolaas had suggested a midmorning departure for Borneo, however, and she preferred not to be rushed. They were to have breakfast in her father's suite at 7:30. She wanted to finish repacking beforehand. Reluctantly, she threw back the covers and got up.

It took her far less time to get ready than she had expected. Only thirty minutes elapsed while she showered, dressed and combed her hair. After placing the last of her things back into her trunk, she was surprised to find that it was only 6:45. She decided to go to Nicolaas's suite for more conversation before breakfast.

The corridor was deserted at this early hour. Walking briskly to her father's door, she rapped on it. There was no answer, so she knocked on the polished wood again, this time with more force. Then she tried the knob and found it unlocked.

"Papa?" she called tentatively as she cracked the door. Again, there was no response. *He must still be sleeping.* she thought as she slipped into the room and closed the door. As she started across the sitting room, she heard her father sigh heavily from the adjoining bedroom. The thick carpet muffled her steps as she walked toward the open door of the boudoir. About to call again, her eyes caught movement in the large dresser mirror inside the room. What she saw in the glass froze her limbs in midmotion. She stood rooted in her tracks, unable to move. Her heart raced and moved up into her throat, constricting her breath.

Nicolaas was not alone. Tonia Ivanovna was there with him, and they were making love. Cinta felt a red flush sweep up from her neck to her hair roots. She wanted to run, but her feet would not obey her brain. Mesmerized, her eyes remained locked on the mirror while her mind boiled with conflicting emotions: shock at seeing her father *en deshabille* with a woman; guilt and shame at spying on their intimacy; titillation at the joyous abandon of their lovemaking.

The scene in the bed rushed on to its inevitable climax. Embarrassed by her inadvertent voyeurism, Cinta felt a blind compulsion to escape. As she turned to flee, her arm caught a vase lamp and sent it spinning to the floor, its ceramic base exploding.

"What the...who's there?" Nicolaas's gruff voice broke the silence.

"Papa?" Cinta called, dropping to her knees to gather the pieces of the lamp. "Are you up yet?"

"Wait there, Cinta," he replied. "I'll be out shortly. I'm not decent at the moment."

A peal of feminine laughter followed this last pronouncement. Moments later, knotting a satin bathrobe, Nicolaas came out of the bedroom.

"I didn't expect you so early," said the big Dutchman.

"Obviously," Cinta responded, her emotions still in turmoil. Their eyes met briefly. Nicolaas suddenly raised an eyebrow, and at that instant, she realized that he knew that she had seen him with the Russian.

"It's polite to knock before entering someone's room." The

anger in his voice was barely masked. "I thought we taught you better manners."

"I did knock, Papa. You seem to have been too preoccupied to hear."

"I suppose you're right," he said with a sigh. "I apologize for not being more discreet. I've gotten used to not worrying about such things in the years since you left. A man gets lonely, you see, after all his children have gone."

"Oh, Papa, I'm not a prude," she said, rushing to his side. "And I'm not the innocent little girl you sent off to school ten years ago. You learn a lot about real life fast in the medical profession. I wouldn't expect a healthy man like you to live like a monk. It's just that you took me by surprise."

"It's probably best to be honest about these things, anyway." He wrapped his big arms around Cinta and hugged her.

"Is the countess your mistress?"

"You might say so, but not in the sense that she's a kept woman. I've been helping her relocate her business operations from Shanghai to our islands. We care deeply for one another. I assure you that you'll not be embarrassed by our relationship." He turned to the bedroom. "Come on out, Tonia."

The White Russian glided through the door and went straight to Nicolaas. She had covered herself with a floor-length robe of blue silk, but the thin material showed every curve of her splendid body. A half-filled glass of champagne was cradled in her left hand.

"Alas, my love, she knows the worst," said Nicolaas with mock severity.

"But what does she think of it?" Tonia was totally serious.

"It's between you and Papa," Cinta replied. "It's really none of my business."

"But it is, my dear," Tonia insisted. "Your life will be affected by our affair."

"I'd not stand in the way of Papa's happiness, and I won't be jealous of you. I'm glad you've brought love to his life."

"You're very wise for one so young," said Tonia. "I hope we can become friends."

"I can't see any reason why we shouldn't." Cinta took Tonia's hand and squeezed it.

"Within the bounds of propriety," Nicolaas interjected, "considering the differences in your professions."

"Look who's speaking of propriety," said Tonia playfully and tugged at Nicolaas's ear. The three of them burst out laughing.

(Three)
Nichols Field
Manila, the Phillippine Islands
13 August 1941

The Army Air Corps sentry at the gate to Nichols Field waved the Royal Dutch/Shell vehicles through without stopping them. The driver of Nicolaas's car knew exactly where he was going. Skirting the main base and shops, he headed straight to a small parking apron near the control tower, pulling up beside a sleek, twin-tailed transport which was painted in the RDS livery.

"Isn't she beautiful?" Nicolaas said to Cinta as they got out of the car. He was comfortably dressed in a khaki bush jacket and slacks.

"I can see why you love her," she replied. She had long appreciated her father's attachment to fine machinery.

The drivers began passing luggage from the trunks of the cars to the waiting ground crewmen. Just as Dijker and Garrit got out of their Lincoln, a flight of streamlined fighter planes streaked by close overhead.

"American P-40's," Nicolaas commented. "What do you think of them, Captain Laterveer?"

"The RAF calls them *Tomahawks*." Garrit responded. "We sent those the Yanks sold to Britain out to Egypt to fight the Eyeties. They wouldn't last a minute in the air with a Messerschmitt or Focke-Wulf."

"Who's this optimistic character?" asked a burly man of about thirty-five who had just stepped out of the *Lodestar*. He was as tan as Nicollas and had brown hair and eyes. He was wearing a military flight suit.

"This is Larry Nobis, our official company pilot," Nicolaas said in general introduction to the group. They shook hands with the pilot, patently an American by his accent, and told him their names.

"Flight plan's all filed, skipper," Nobis said to Nicolaas.

"Everything's all set to go."

"Good," the Dutchman replied. "I'll take her up."

"You grab all the fun for yourself," Nobis said with disgust. "All aboard, folks. It's a long haul to Borneo."

After the Boeing Clipper, the inside of the *Lodestar* seemed cramped to Cinta. The seats were large and comfortably padded, but there were only six rows, with one seat on each side of the center aisle. A fully equipped flight galley took up a good bit of space. Nicolaas settled the women into the row just behind the cockpit, and the two officers took the next one. A white-coated flight steward took their uniform jackets and hung them away while Nicolaas went forward to complete his cockpit check. Then the engines roared to life, drowning conversation.

Nicolaas taxied the machine out near the end of the runway, where they had to wait on the taxiway while the *Tomahawks* landed. Then he swung the *Lodestar* out onto the pavement and gunned the engines. It gathered speed rapidly and smoothly, lifting into the air after using a mere third of the field. The landing gear retracted with a groan of hydraulics and a loud thump. Nicolaas turned the plane to the south immediately, gaining altitude and speed for the long run to Borneo.

(Four)
Skies Above the Central Borneo Coast
Netherlands East Indies
13 August 1941

Drifting back to consciousness after a late afternoon nap, Cinta became aware that the sky around the plane was darkening. Up ahead, she saw jagged flashes of lightening. The *Lodestar* veered a little to the west, and she realized that her father was searching for a path between the towering thunderheads. Then the nose of the aircraft lifted ever so slightly, and it began a steady climb. Soon, they were out in brilliant sunlight again, while an endless snowfield of clouds stretched out beneath them. Larry Nobis came back into the passenger cabin.

"We're damn near home, folks," said the gregarious American. "To get to Balikpapan, we'll have to go down through the rainstorm. There's nothing to worry about. The skipper's done it hundreds of times. He has a good radio fix on our position."

"We have full confidence in the *Tuan Besar*," said Garrit. "I watched him work while I was in the cockpit earlier. I've never seen a better pilot."

"I've flown through lots of stuff worse than this around England," Dijker commented.

The *Lodestar* began to drop slowly toward the top of the cloud layer. Then the vapor closed around the plane, blocking everything from view with its filmy whiteness. The cabin grew darker as they dropped farther from the open sunlight. Air currents buffeted the plane, rocking it from side to side, and large drops of rain began to pound incessantly against the thin aluminum skin. Glancing at the countess, Cinta saw that she was staring straight ahead, her jaw set firmly. Tonia was clearly frightened half out of her wits but struggling valiantly to control herself. Turning back to the window, Cinta watched blue sparks dancing about on the wings. She peered downward through the gloom, trying to catch sight of something to draw her attention away from her own uneasiness.

The metallic groan of the landing gear going down startled Cinta from her trance. A moment later, the *Lodestar* broke out underneath the cloud cover. Less than a thousand feet below, she caught sight of the surface of the sea, all whipped into frothy whitecaps by the storm winds. The plane was flying in a straight line now, dropping steadily, lining up to land. Through the haze of rain, Cinta briefly glimpsed a snow-white beach, then there was the dark green of land beneath them. A few moments later, the *Loadstar* touched down onto a large paved airfield. Nicolaas used the entire runway in slowing the plane to a near halt. Then he turned and taxied her through the rain and mud to the terminal building. Only when he finally cut the engines did Tonia relax.

"I'm afraid that our weather's less than hospitable," said Nicolaas when he came back out of the cockpit. "A pair of motorcars will be here in a few minutes. We'll have to get a little wet getting into them. You'll all be my guests at my home tonight."

The rain continued unabated for the duration of the half hour drive from the airfield. The first time that anything could be seen through the side windows was when the car braked to a stop beneath the covered entrance of a large house.

"Here we are, Cinta," said Nicolaas. "These are the humble

quarters which the company provides us to live in.”

“Don’t be sarcastic,” the countess chided. “The Controlleur would covet such a place.”

A uniformed butler held open the massive front door to the house. The chauffeur sprinted around and opened the car door nearest the entrance. Nicolaas got out quickly and helped the women from the vehicle. They sprinted into the house.

Pausing in the entryway, Cinta glanced about the room. The house had been built by BPM in the early twenties and represented the best in Dutch colonial architecture of the period. The ceilings soared twenty feet above the tile floors in the core of the building. Walls louvered near the floor and open at the top created a continual updraft of cool air. The location atop the hill, with no barriers to break the ocean breezes, guaranteed pleasant temperatures even without air conditioning. Colorful birds flitted and chirped about the rafters. Since mosquitoes were their natural prey, few of the pests reached the living space below. From the size of the mansion, Cinta sensed that it must have a score or more of rooms.

A dozen male and female servants stood in a line, waiting to greet the returning lord of the manor. At the far end, one of the women leaned forward, peering toward her. A flash of recognition shot through Cinta’s brain.

“Ada?” Cinta called aloud. “Ada, is that you?” Then she was running across the tiles toward the middle-aged woman, her still-dripping arms open wide. The two women met in a rush, embracing.

“*Ibu kecil say* (my Little Mother),” Cinta laughed through her tears. “It’s so good to see you again.”

“And for me to hold you, child,” said the Javanese woman in shrill tones Cinta recalled from her childhood. “But you’re soaking wet. We must get you out of those damp clothes and into a warm *mandi* at once.”

“You’ll never give up mothering me, will you?” said Cinta happily.

“Not as long as you require my guidance,” Ada responded. “You may have become a *dajoeng* (witch doctor) in America, but you still have much to learn about life.”

“Ada’s right about getting out of those wet things,” said Nicolaas, who had come up behind them. “She’ll show you to your room. One of the other women will bring your luggage."

"All right, Papa. What time is dinner?"

Nicolaas consulted his watch. "Shall we say at eight?"

"That's fine with me. That will give Ada and me a chance to get reacquainted."

The room to which Ada led Cinta was spacious and airy, furnished with a huge four-poster bed with a canopy of mosquito netting, a full-sized table for tea, and several comfortable chairs. French doors opened onto a shaded verandah. Ada went into the adjacent bathroom and began filling a tub while Cinta took off her wet clothing.

"I shall attend you," the older woman proclaimed as they walked across thick Indian carpets, "as I did when you were my terrible little girl."

"No one has scrubbed my back since you did it last, Little Mother," Cinta said as she dropped her sticky blouse onto the bedroom floor tiles.

"Truly? I would have thought some man would have done that by now."

"Why, Ada!" Cinta said coyly, "what a shocking suggestion."

"Your wiser sister would not think so."

Cinta got up from removing her shoes and mud-splattered hose and went over to a large dressing table to pin her hair up on top of her head. Then she slipped out of her silk panties and padded into the bathroom, feeling not the least immodest to be nude before Ada. The *baboe* had changed her diapers as a baby and bathed her almost every day of her life before she went away to school.

While most bathrooms in the NEI held simple "dipper baths", this one was elaborate and elegantly appointed, reflecting both Nicolaas's technical skills and the good tastes of some woman-- probably Tonia Ivanovna. Hot water from a solar heater on the roof fed the oversized Victorian bathtub, a separate shower stall and a washbasin. The flush toilet was contained in its own small alcove. Several oil paintings of seaside landscapes hung on cream-colored walls, contrasting pleasantly with the red tile floors. The ubiquitous electric ceiling fan stirred filmy sheers over a high window framed by red draperies. The fragrance of dried flowers wafted from turned ebony bowls on a rosewood vanity table with a bank of mirrors and low bench.

Ada looked up from the tub when Cinta entered the bathroom, reflectively surveying the young woman. Her eyes took in Cinta's long, finely tapered legs, gently swelling hips and flat belly. Rounded, uptilting breasts and a swan-like neck drew her nod of approval. "You may have the mind of a *dajoeng*, little one," she said impishly, "but that body was made for love."

"I wish you wouldn't call me a *dajoeng*, Ada," said Cinta, testing the water with her toe. "I'm not really a witch doctor, you know. In the West, medicine is considered a science."

"*Dajoeng*, physician, what does it matter," Ada responded, helping Cinta into the tub. "You all heal the sick. What worries me is that all those years in schoolrooms may have dulled your vital forces. You're twenty-six years old and have no husband."

"There's plenty of time for that," Cinta laughed, sliding down in the warm water.

"Time slips through your fingers like this water," Ada retorted. "Before you know it, you'll be old and dried up like me. You need a man, now."

"You sound just like Alette," Cinta chided. "She's been trying to marry me off for years. I'll tell you what I told her. Such things must wait until my medical practice is established."

"*Aieeee!*" Ada moaned. "Such foolish talk. The gods didn't give you that beautiful body to waste in a hospital." She dipped a bowl into the water and poured the warm liquid over Cinta's shoulders. Then she soaped the younger woman's back before massaging the muscles where her neck met her body.

"*Uhmmmm*," Cinta purred. "No one can relax me like you do, Little Mother."

"If you're not ready for a husband," Ada persisted in her train of advice, "then you must at least find yourself a lover. No woman can retain her vitality unless she couples regularly with a man."

"I'm not going to tell you anything more about that part of my life," Cinta responded, "and I stick by what I said earlier. There's no room in my life for a man right now."

"Then you'll have to change your plans. Now that you're back with me, I'll get you straightened out on what's really important."

"That will be quite enough on that subject," Cinta said with exasperation. Ada held a large towel for Cinta as she got out of the tub, then helped dry her off. "Such fruits should not be hidden away," she said as she rubbed the terry cloth over Cinta's ample bosom. The gentle massage caused her nipples to stand up pertly. "The people of these islands have known that truth since a time before time. Binding them up is unhealthy."

"You would have had Alette and me running around half naked all the time if Papa had allowed it," Cinta laughed.

"You once didn't mind baring your *dada* when no men were around," Ada reminded her.

"How else could we have stood the heat?"

"Do you recall how to put on a sarong?"

"One hardly forgets."

"Then wear this until dinner time," said Ada, handing a length of blue silk to Cinta. "It will be much more comfortable than that heavy robe."

Cinta took the garment and expertly folded the silk about her hips, tucking it securely in place. It was a *kain*, the classic ankle-length Malay sarong. On the taller Dutchwoman, it fell only to mid-calf. Her firm breasts barely rippled as she walked back into the bedroom, but the unfamiliar kiss of air caused her nipples to tingle and harden.

"I'll help you unpack," said Ada, "but you really must tell me about your lovers."

Nicolaas rapped on Cinta's door at just after seven.

"Just a moment, Papa," she said, searching about for something to cover her upper body. Ada produced a *kabaja,* the loose blouse of the island women, and Cinta slipped into it. "You can come in, now."

Her father opened the door and ambled into the room. He was wearing a sarong of brilliant red batik print and puffing on a curved pipe. The heavy growth of blond hair on his chest starkly contrasted with his bronzed skin.

"I see that Ada has you back in island dress already," he observed.

"It's more comfortable in the heat."

"I like it for lounging about the house. One of these days, the company will give me air-conditioned quarters, and I'll freeze to death. I've just been on the telephone with Batavia. You have an appointment with the Minister of Health at ten a.m. the day after tomorrow."

"Was that really necessary, Papa? I've forwarded Photostats of my American credentials. Surely some lesser bureaucrat could have completed the arrangements."

"I suppose I'm just used to dealing with people at the top. Anyway, he'll have your licensing documents ready to present to you, as well as your appointment to the hospital here."

"When do we leave for Batavia?"

"At ten in the morning. The flight's all arranged. We have reservations at the *Hotel des Indies* for tomorrow night."

"I always loved that hotel, especially the miniature deer in their park. I assume we'll dress for dinner?"

"Of course. With guests in the house, it's an obligation. I'm sure you have something suitable."

"Several. Alette took me shopping in New York last spring."

"If you let Alette pick out your clothes, they'll be scandalous by our island standards."

"You're probably right," Cinta agreed. "She always preferred bare backs and shoulders."

CHAPTER 6

(One)
Skies Above the Sulu Sea
Philippine Islands
13 August 1941

Dimly, through a fog of sleep, Frank Rhea realized that the roar of the PBY's engines had taken on a new, more deep-throated pitch. The plane was beginning to slow down. A hand touched his shoulder and shook it.

"Hey, Frank." He recognized the voice of Lieutenant Tom Chase, whom he'd met when the PBY was loading. "We'll be landing in a minute. If you want to get a look at the fleet, you'll have to hurry."

Frank swung his legs over the edge of the bunk and sat up. Rubbing his eyes as he checked his wristwatch, he saw that it was just before noon. The pilot up front had managed the seven hundred mile flight from Sangley Point in less than five hours. Chase and Jack Sewell were back in the starboard waist gun position, staring down at the sea. Pulling on his "choker neck" white blouse, he went to join them.

On the horizon, the jungle-covered mountains of Borneo were blue beneath a smoky haze. Nearer at hand was a long, narrow island that must be Tawi-Tawi. Frank could just make out the shapes of the ships anchored in the big bay on its southern coast. As the PBY drew nearer, he could identify their types.

"Well, gents," Tom Chase remarked, "there it is, damned near the whole Asiatic Fleet. That's my ship, *Black Hawk*, over there." He indicated a big tender with several old "four-piper" destroyers of World War One vintage moored alongside.

"Admiral Hart claims that all our 'cans' are old enough to vote," Chase continued. "We have one hell of a time keeping them all on line. The half-baked carrier's *Langley*. She's a seaplane tender now--serves as flagship for PatWing (Patrol Wing) Ten."

Frank leaned out of the gun hatch to get a better view. *Langley* was a touchstone of naval aviation history, the American Navy's first real aircraft carrier. Now she looked like a half-dressed old lady. Shorn of the forward part of her flight deck to make room for heavy seaplane cranes, she would never again launch and recover aircraft while underway. Beyond *Langley*, he caught sight of the familiar silhouette of an *Omaha* class cruiser. From a distance, *Marblehead* could easily have been mistaken for one of the flush-deck destroyers, to which she bore a strong resemblance. Four smokestacks towered high above her decks behind her tall, ungainly superstructure, and she had the delicate pointed fantail of the "cans." Only her heavy armament set her apart. She had twin, six-inch turrets fore and aft, and six similar guns were casemated into her superstructure, four forward and two in the back corners of her after deckhouse. It was an archaic arrangement in keeping with the overall appearance of the ship. Only the two *Seagull* floatplanes perched amidship on catapult frames appeared modern.

Frank knew *Marblehead's* vital statistics by heart, for he had served more that a year aboard *Omaha* in the Atlantic. She was just under twenty years old, having been completed in 1923. Over five hundred and fifty feet long and with fifty-five feet of beam, she displaced some seven thousand tons. Her secondary armament included seven dual-purpose three-inch fifties and eight 50 caliber machine guns. Three-inch armor belts girded her sides and one and a half inches her decks. One of her most important assets was her speed. Flat out, she could do thirty-five knots. *Marblehead* carried a crew of over four hundred and fifty, including thirty officers. Of these, three were pilots for her *Seagulls*.

"Which one of the 'cans' is *Rust*?" Frank asked Jack.

"Can't tell from up here," Jack replied. "They've all got awnings rigged. Without them, she'd be easy to spot. She has a different weapons layout. Her three-inch antiaircraft gun is on the forecastle instead of the fantail."

"There's our real firepower," Chase remarked, pointing out a modern heavy cruiser, *U.S.S. Houston*, flagship of the Asiatic Fleet. Her nine eight-inch guns were the heaviest in the force.

"What about those 'pig boats?'" said Jack, nodding to a cluster of big fleet-type submarines moored alongside the tender, *Canopus*. "Considering what the Nazis are doing in the Atlantic, I'd put my money on them."

"I have a hunch that Admiral Hart might agree with you," Chase responded. "He's an old submariner, you know--set up the first submarine desk in the Secretariat. Rumor has it that he riled the President when he did it. Mr. Roosevelt was Assistant SECNAV back then. They say that's why Hart's out here now instead of being Chief of Naval Operations."

"What's the admiral like?" asked Frank.

"A tough, no-nonsense old bird," Chase replied. "Thoroughly professional and a fighter to boot. There was a lot of teeth gnashing when he sent the dependents home last year, but he's used the time since to good measure. This conglomeration of old ships is as ready to fight as they'll ever be. He's hard as nails, though. Used to be Superintendent at the Academy. Likes spit and polish too much for my taste."

"Sounds like the kind of guy you wouldn't mind fighting for," Jack commented.

Apter 7"Where to, gentlemen?" the snappy-looking coxswain growled as Frank, Jack and Tom Chase boarded the boat which *Langley* sent to take them to their ships. They gave him their destinations, and he chose *Marblehead* as the first point of call. As the launch chugged across the smooth, sparkling waters of Chingao Bay, Frank was struck by the wildness of the scenery. Beyond its border of snowy beach fringed with coconut palms, Tawi-Tawi seemed to be covered with dense jungle. The rank odor of rotted vegetation floated out from the shore.

"Good luck, Frank," said Jack as the boat hovered at the foot of *Marblehead's* accommodation ladder.

"You, too," Frank replied, pumping the New Englander's hand. "Don't fall off that little 'can.'"

"I'll try not to."

"We'll take good care of him," Chase put in. "*Rust* is one of *Black Hawk*'s brood."

"Need help with your baggage, sir?" the coxswain asked.

"No, thanks. I can manage," said Frank. He lifted the heavy flight bag in his left hand and hefted it. Then he double-timed up the ladder with the easy strides of an athlete. Reaching the top, he turned toward the stern where the Stars and Stripes hung limply on the fantail flagstaff and saluted. Then he faced the canopied quarterdeck and saluted the lieutenant, junior grade, who was standing by the podium there. The officer wore Yangtze "River Rat" Whites, a uniform of which Frank had heard but not seen before-- short-sleeved white shirt with metal rank devices, short white pants, white shoes with white anklets. All of the officer's bare skin was tanned nut brown. A .45 automatic hung from his pistol belt.

"Lieutenant Rhea reporting for duty," Frank spat out in crisp syllables. "Request permission to come aboard, sir."

"Permission granted," said the jaygee, returning the salute. "Welcome aboard, Mister Rhea. We've been expecting you. I'm Bracken, the signals officer. If you'll give me a copy of your orders, I'll log you aboard."

Frank was expecting this formality and had a copy ready. Bracken looked them over and made his log entry, then picked up a nearby battle phone.

"O.O.D. calling Mister Blessman," Bracken said into the mouthpiece. He waited several seconds for a response. "Your new pilot just got here, Ed. Want me to bring him down?" He listened for a moment, and then put down the instrument. "A messenger from 'V' Division is on the way to get you, Mister Rhea."

"I could have found my own way. I served on *Omaha*."

Standing in the shade of the canopy, Frank took in the sights and sounds around him while he waited. Up forward, part of the deck gang was scrubbing down the teak planking. On the bridge, a clattering signal lamp flashed a message to the flagship. Just aft, three Marines were reassembling a Browning .50 caliber antiaircraft machine gun. He suddenly felt at home, like a traveler returning from a long journey.

"Here comes Mister Blessman," said Bracken.

Startled from his reverie, Frank turned to see a lanky, sandy haired lieutenant in khakis coming out of a nearby companionway.

"Hi, Frank, welcome aboard," said the newcomer, offering his hand. "I'm Eddie Blessman, senior "Airdale" on the ship."

"Glad to be aboard," Frank answered as they shook hands.

"Did they feed you on the flight down?"

"No, but I stoked in a good breakfast before we left Sangley Point."

"We finished lunch a little while ago. I'll see if Fook Liang will rustle you up a sandwich. But first, we'd better check in with the Exec."

Blessman led the way forward to a watertight door at the base of the ship's tall bridge structure. A strong aroma of cooked onions and beef greeted them as they stepped through it into the wardroom, the inner sanctum of "officers' country." *Marblehead*'s wardroom was large, extending all the way across the ship. Half a dozen Chinese mess attendants were just clearing the leavings of the noon meal from the dining tables. Frank felt a twinge of nostalgia. He might well have been back aboard *Omaha*. Blessman continued on into the passageway that led to the officers' staterooms.

"You're bunking next to me," the senior aviator said, opening the door to one of the cabins. "Park your gear here and smarten up a bit. Then we'll go see 'Sergeant York.'"

"Who's he?" asked Frank as he put his flight bag on the narrow bunk and surveyed the compartment. It was spartan, a simple steel box containing the bunk, a metal washbasin and a desk and chair.

"The Exec. When he reported aboard a few months ago, somebody decided he looked like Gary Cooper, so they hung the moniker on him. He's tough as armor plate, but fair. Has to be. Good-guy captains always have son-of-a-bitch execs. Captain Robby's the best there is. He's the finest naval officer I've ever met."

"What about the Gun Boss?" asked Frank as he took a brush from his bag and smoothed his unruly hair. The "V", or Aviation, Division on a cruiser was part of the Gunnery Department.

"Commander Van Bergen's right up there with the skipper. He's a natural leader and knows the gunnery business inside out."

"Sounds like I've landed on a happy ship."

"The old 'Gallopin' Ghost of the China Coast' is that, all right," Blessman said with a laugh. "She's damn well run, too. When the balloon goes up out here, we'll be ready."

Commander Bill Goggins was standing over his desk reading Frank's service record when the new pilot entered his office. Frank immediately noted the resemblance to Gary Cooper's portrayal of the World War One hero in the exec's lanky body. Goggins was dressed in "River Rat" Whites with silver oak leaves gleaming on his collar points. When Goggins looked up, Frank saw that he had a round face and hooded eyes beneath a shock of black hair.

"Come in, Mister Rhea," Goggins said in a firm, commanding voice. "Glad to have you aboard." He shook Frank's hand.

"I'm glad to be here, Commander," Frank responded.

"Sit down." Goggins indicated a chair beside his desk. His eyes flashed over Frank from head to foot in a lightening inspection. "I see that you're a reserve officer. What kind of civilian work were you doing?"

"I'm an aeronautical engineer, sir. Worked for Hughes Aircraft, in San Diego."

"That's defense work. I'm surprised that you weren't exempted from the call up."

"I wanted to come back on active duty. If there's going to be a war, I'd just as soon fight."

"That's the spirit. I see here that you were a qualified OOD underway on *Omaha*."

"That's right, sir."

"Good. We'll put you on the watch bill under instruction right away. You shouldn't have any trouble requalifying quickly. We can always use another good deck officer. You'll be assigned to 'V' Division, of course, as assistant division officer. I expect you know what that entails?"

"Yes, sir."

"You're already qualified in SOC's, so you'll be assigned flying duties at once. You can have the next flight we send up. You have a good record and should fit in nicely here.

"This is the best goddamned ship in the Asiatic Fleet, and we intend to keep it that way. That means that every officer and man on board has to do his job and do it well. Measure up to that standard, and you'll be a success. Any questions?"

"No, sir," said Frank with enthusiasm.

"Good. Report to Commander Van Bergen, the Gun Boss."

"Thank you, Commander." Frank got up to leave. Goggins was buried in his paperwork before Frank was out of the compartment.

Commander Nick Van Bergen took a smoking briar from his mouth and flashed a toothy smile as Eddie Blessman introduced Frank to him. "Glad to have you aboard," the big man boomed. "Are you settled in yet?"

The force of the Gunnery Officer's personality impressed Frank at once. The man had magnetism, infectious enthusiasm that sparked a similar reaction in those around him. He had brown hair and an athletic build. He wore "River Rat" Whites.

"Yes, sir," Frank responded. "Eddie has everything all set up."

"We'll introduce you to the rest of the wardroom at supper tonight. You'll be Eddie's assistant division officer. I expect the Exec outlined the standards of the ship."

"That's right, Commander."

"The Gunnery Department has to be in top form all the time. This isn't the most modern ship in the fleet, but we'll give a good account of ourselves if ever called on to fight. Are you married, Frank?"

"No, sir. I'm a bachelor."

"So am I. I'm married to the Navy. We may be the lucky ones, with war coming on. We can concentrate all our energies on our duties."

After leaving the Gunnery Officer, Blessman took Frank on a tour of the "V" Division spaces, which were far from plush. The capacity to operate aircraft had been grafted onto *Marblehead* several years after her launching. She had no hangar space for working on the *Seagulls*. The catapults were the only place the aircraft could be stored, so all maintenance had to be performed in the open unless the offending part could be removed and taken below.

In mid-afternoon, Frank was going over the roster of personnel with Blessman in the "V" Division offices when a stocky, swarthy-skinned man in grease-stained coveralls pushed through the door. His jet-black hair and distinctive features identified the newcomer as a Native American.

"Number Two *Seagull's* ready to Fly, Mister Blessman," the man said in a deep, gravelly voice. "Had to practically rebuild the carburetor, but it'll be good for another five hundred hours."

"Good work, Tonto," said Blessman. "The skipper'll be pleased as hell to have both birds tomorrow."

"This the new 'Lone Ranger?'" asked the Indian.

"Frank," said Eddie, "meet Warrant Aviation Machinist Jim Bob Coacooche, alias, 'Tonto'. He's the best damned mechanic in the

Asiatic Fleet. He's also your observer and radio operator."

Frank introduced himself and shook Tonto's hand. "Now, what's this 'Lone Ranger' stuff?"

"Pretty simple, Mister Rhea," said the Indian, chuckling softly. "Ever since I was in boot camp, nobody's been able to pronounce my name right. My company chief hung the nickname, 'Tonto', on me there, and it's stuck ever since. When I came to *Marblehead* four years ago, the Captain started calling whatever pilot I flew with, 'Lone Ranger.'"

"It's a tradition now, Frank," said Blessman.

"I can think of worse things to be called."

"Glad you see it that way, *Kemo Sabay*," Tonto continued, "cause you're stuck with it whether you like it or not. Did somebody say that you're a Reservist?"

"That's right. I was just recalled."

"He did four years in cruisers in the Atlantic," Blessman commented, "including a year on *Omaha*."

"An old hand, then," said Tonto with satisfaction. "I'm sure it'll be a pleasure flyin' with you, Mister Rhea."

"Lone Ranger," Frank corrected him.

"Yeah, *Kemo Sabay*. *Adios* for now. Number One bird needs some adjustin' to her elevator cables."

At supper that night, Frank met the other members of the wardroom. Since the Commanding Officer preferred to dine alone in his stateroom, the Exec presided over the meal with the rigid formality customary aboard major warships. Frank tried to take in all the names. They rattled around in his brain, some registered at once, others quickly lost. He did't worry about it. They would all be sorted out in a couple of days.

"Could I see you for a moment, Mister Rhea," the Exec interrupted Frank's conversation with Lieutenant Commander Wildebush, the medical officer.

"Certainly, sir." Frank excused himself from Wildebush.

"The Captain will see you at 1930 for your office call," Goggins informed him.

Frank knocked on the Captain's door at precisely seven thirty. A Chinese steward opened the door immediately. Frank handed him a calling card and announced that he had come to call on the Captain.

The man disappeared for a moment, then returned and swung the door wide open. As Frank stepped into the ship's citadel of power, he was struck by how modest the surroundings were. Few keepsakes adorned the space.

"Welcome to our ship, Mister Rhea," the Captain said in soft but confident tones. The slight man with sharp features pumped Frank's hand.

"I'm proud to be here, Captain. She's a grand ship."

"We tend to think so. Would you care for some coffee?"

"I never pass up the opportunity, sir."

The steward filled two cups from a pitcher as the conversation continued. Frank sipped the steaming liquid, finding it strong and flavorful.

"I noticed from your record that you were working for Hughes Aircraft when you were recalled," the Captain continued. "Do you by chance know Howard Hughes?"

"I've met him a couple of times, but I couldn't really say that I know him. He paid more attention to his movie studio in the last year than he did to his aircraft plant."

"I've heard that. My wife was in show business before our marriage. Perhaps you've heard of Inez Buck?"

"Why, yes, sir. I didn't realize that she's your wife."

"You had the makings of a celebrity, as I recall. I remember your days on the UCLA track team. I was surprised when you passed up the Berlin Olympics."

"I was more interested in learning to fly, Captain."

The conversation went on in a similar vein for half an hour. Only when it was nearly over did two facts occur to Frank. On the one hand, the Captain had been drawing him out, encouraging him to express his thoughts openly. On the other, he had displayed an encyclopedic knowledge of Frank's life before joining *Marblehead*. Frank began to understand why Arthur Granville Robinson--Captain Robby to the crew of his ship--was held in respect and awe by the men who served under him. As he excused himself and rose to leave, the Captain's firm grip once more fastened about his hand.

"You have good men in 'V' Division, Mister Rhea," said Robinson. "Take care of them and they'll take care of you." There was a twinkle in the piercing eyes and an expression of pride on the Captain's face.

"I'll do that, Captain," said Frank, meaning every word.

Jack Sewell's reception on the U.S.S. *Jonathan B. Rust* was similar to Frank's on the cruiser, but far less formal. The launch dropped Tom Chase at *Black Hawk* before proceeding to the destroyer. Jack went up the accommodation ladder two steps at a time, stopped to salute the fantail flagstaff, and reported himself to the lanky jaygee manning the quarterdeck.

"We're pleased to have you aboard, Lieutenant," said the OOD in a slow, mid-south drawl. "I'm Henry Logan. Right now, I'm acting Gunnery Officer, and I reckon I'll stay on as your assistant. Most folks call me Hank."

"Glad to meet you, Hank," said Jack. He did a quick lookover of the jaygee. The starch in Logan's khakis was already wilting in the heat, but he was clean and had good military bearing.

"I'll have you fixed up in a jiffy. The Exec's in the wardroom. Harvey here will show you the way." Logan issued instructions to one of the quarterdeck messengers, who responded with a southern accent, then led Jack to officers' country. It was damnably hot on the deck, even under the canvas awnings. Jack found it much cooler in the small wardroom. As he entered, a slender, red-haired lieutenant with a freckled face glanced up from some papers he was working on.

"You must be Jack Sewell," said the lieutenant, giving the newcomer a quick once-over. His accent was almost identical to Logan's. As he rose from the table, Jack saw that he was wearing khakis also.

"That's right, sir," Jack responded, assuming that this was the ship's executive officer.

"I'm Jerry Busch, and I'm damned glad that you're here. We've been short-handed ever since your predecessor left last month. Got all your stuff with you?"

"Yes, sir."

"Good. We'll bunk you with Hank Logan. Ford here will show you to your cabin." He indicated the black mess steward who was cleaning the tables. "Dump your gear and come right back. Then we'll go see the Captain."

"Tell me something, Ford," said Jack as he dropped his flight bag on the narrow bunk of his tiny stateroom. "Why do all the people I've talked to on this ship sound exactly alike?"

"Cause we're all from the same place, Lieutenant," the black man laughed. "Just about everybody in the crew's from a Naval Reserve unit from Memphis, Tennessee."

"Well, I'll be damned," Jack responded. He should have known. Naval Reservists manned almost all the destroyers the Navy had recommissioned in the past couple of years.

"Captain's in his cabin," Jerry Busch remarked as Jack reentered the wardroom. "Let's go see him."

The Captain's cabin was about as big as the one Jack and Hank Logan would be sharing. The man at the tiny desk was of medium height and build. His black hair was slicked straight back. He had bushy eyebrows, black eyes, and his face was handsome in a rugged sort of way. The gold oak leaves of a lieutenant commander were pinned on the collars of his khaki shirt.

"Captain Hoskins, this is Jack Sewell, our new Gunnery Officer," said Busch as they entered.

"Glad to have you aboard," said Hoskins in a surprisingly tenor voice. "You got here fast."

"Bought myself a ticket on the Pan Am Clipper," said Jack.

"Good for you. We'll put you straight to work. You understand the duties of a Gunnery Officer?"

"Yes, sir. I was on a destroyer when I was on active duty before, and I've just come from the Gunnery Officers School in Norfolk."

"You'll take over the Gunnery Department right away. Hank Logan has been acting. He'll remain as your assistant and Antiaircraft Battery Officer. You'll also have Ensign Elroy Brown as Torpedo Officer. They're both solid kids. All they need is a steadying hand."

"That's good to hear, sir."

"Are you married, Jack?" Hoskins continued.

"No, sir."

"That's just as well. It looks like we'll be out here on the Asiatic Station until further notice."

"I was surprised when they told me that you'd been transferred out here from Pearl," said Jack. "I was in school when it happened."

"We were Shanghaied," snorted Jerry Busch. "We were supposed to be training at Pearl Harbor for another six months. We happened to be in Manila with a convoy we'd just brought in when a freighter collided with old *Toland*. It bashed her up so bad that they had to send her all the way back to Mare Island for repairs. Admiral Hart needed a replacement fast, so we were elected."

"He wasn't all that thrilled at getting a ship full of Reservists," Hoskins put in. "I was the only Regular Navy officer aboard when we got here. I'm Academy, Class of '27. You're Harvard, I believe."

"That's right, Captain. R.O.T.C."

"We'll fill you in on the situation with the rest of the ship later. Get Hank Logan relieved of the watch, Jerry, so that he can start the turnover to Jack right now."

"You get anything to eat on the way down from Sangley Point?" asked the Exec as they left the Captain's cabin.

"Not to speak of."

"One of the mess boys can whip you up some eggs, if you'd like."

"Sounds great," said Jack, fully conscious for the first time of the protestations of his empty stomach.

"Change into khakis and go on down to the wardroom. I'll send Hank as soon as I get the supernumerary to take over the watch."

Jack was polishing off a plate of scrambled eggs when the lanky Logan appeared at the wardroom door.

"What do you want to see first, Lieutenant?" drawled Logan, "the people, the paperwork or the hardware?"

"Let's go look at the weapons first," said Jack. "We can talk over the people while we do that and meet them afterwards. The papers can come last. Might as well start at the forecastle and work aft."

"Shall I have the crews stand by their weapons, sir?"

"No. Not in this heat. We'll have the department officers and chiefs in for a meeting later. I can meet the rest at Quarters tomorrow morning."

Logan led the way along the deck toward the bow. They passed the radio shack beneath the wheelhouse and went through the watertight door in the front of the bridge structure that led to the foredeck. A canvas awning shaded the forecastle all the way to the bow, affording some relief from the scorching sun. Stripped to the waist, a crew of sweating enlisted men was busy cleaning the deck gun nearest the bow under the unyielding gaze of a tall, husky chief petty officer.

"Attention on deck," the big chief bellowed as the officers approached.

"Carry on," snapped Jack quickly.

The chief relaxed and hitched up his dungaree pants. "Afternoon, Lieutenants," he said smartly.

"Mister Sewell," said Logan, "this is Chief Gunners Mate Muldune, the Leading Chief of the Gunnery Department."

"Glad to make your acquaintance, sir," said Muldune. The face beneath the white chief's cap was burned brown by years of exposure to the tropical sun, highlighting the deep blue of his eyes. His blond hair was bleached almost white.

"The pleasure's mutual, Chief," said Jack, extending his hand. The massive paw that came up to meet it was twice its size. The big forearm exposed by the rolled-up sleeve bulged with muscle, and there was an anchor tattooed on it. Muldune's grip was like a vise.

"Number One Gun's about ready," said Muldune, motioning toward the now gleaming piece. Jack recognized the Mark 9/5 four-inch gun. These old-fashioned broadside weapons of World War One design were known as four-inch fifties, denoting a bore of four inches and a barrel length fifty times the bore. They could throw a 33-pound shell almost 16,000 yards. This one was in a Mark 12 "P" mounting, with a thin splinter shield to protect the gunners. Jack walked over and inspected the weapon closely. The breechblock and bore were spotlessly clean.

"Good work," Jack commented.

"Thank you, sir," said the beaming gun captain.

"They gotta be that way if you want them to shoot straight," said Muldune with authority.

Back near the bridge was another gun, a little Mark 14 three-inch twenty-three. Disparagingly called a "pea-shooter" because it could only reach about 17,000 feet, the gun was the backbone of the ship's antiaircraft battery, augmented only by a pair of amidships .50-caliber Brownings and a handful of old Lewis guns. Logan led the way over to look at the sky gun.

"This baby's like a signature on our silhouette," said the jaygee. "All the other 'cans' in DesRon (Destroyer Squadron) 29 have their three-inchers on the fantail. But then, they've all been in service since the last war and got different conversions. Old "Rustbucket" spent eighteen years on Red Lead Row in San Diego."

"Rustbucket?" asked Jack.

"That's what we call the old girl. It fit when we first took her over. Captain Hoskins soon had us whipped into shape, though."

"Would you like for me to come along, Lieutenant?" asked Muldune as the two officers started through the watertight door on the starboard side of the bridge.

"That's a good idea," Jack responded.

Rust carried a powerful surface armament. There were three other four-inch fifties, one on either side of the amidships deckhouse and one on the after deckhouse. Almost a third of the ship's length was devoted to her twelve 21-inch torpedo tubes, which were mounted in two triple banks on either side. Trailed by Hank Logan and Chief Muldune, Jack inspected every weapon minutely, opening breeches, peering down barrels, and checking the mechanisms that swung the torpedo tubes outboard.

"I'm impressed, Chief," Jack said to Muldune. "Keep everything like this and we'll get on famously."

"Piece of cake, Lieutenant," said a grinning Muldune.

"That's all the weapons, sir," said Hank. "Want to go up to Central Fire Control?"

"The tour wouldn't be complete without it."

While modern destroyers had an enclosed director with rangefinders and radar and servomechanisms to automatically point their guns, old *Clemson* class vessels like *Rust* had only a Dotter rudimentary gunfire director on an open platform above the piloting and navigation bridge. Operated by one man, the device had a split-telescope range finder. The operator rotated the director to point at the target and adjusted the split telescope to get the range. A Ford Range Keeper Mark II down on the bridge transferred the range and bearing numbers to dials on the weapons. Sound-powered battle phones connected the platform to the gun captains. The Gunnery Officer's battle station was up here in the open, where he had a clear view in all directions. The space was cramped. A searchlight stood at the front of the platform and the sides held sockets for machine guns. An almost vertical ladder led up to the crow's nest on the foremast. From this lofty perch, every inch of *Rust*'s three hundred foot hull was visible. To Jack, her lines were distinctly feminine.

He found himself loving her already.

"Well, that's it except for the sound shack," said Logan.

"Might as well make it a clean sweep," Jack commented. "Let's go."

Later that afternoon, Jack sat in the Gunnery Department office discussing the roster of personnel with Chief Muldune.

"These Reservists are a good bunch of kids, sir," Muldune remarked. "Different from us old Asiatic Fleet salts, but hard workers."

"Why did you transfer to *Rust*, Chief?"

"Hell, Lieutenant, I just like it out here. I'm an old China Station hand from way back. Admiral Hart wanted to stick some veterans from *Toland* in to stiffen the Reservists, and I jumped at the chance. Most of the boys who came over have 'bamboo families' in Manila and didn't want to leave them high and dry."

"Pardon my ignorance, but what's a 'bamboo family'?"

"You know. They been livin' with native women ashore on more or less a permanent basis. Kinda like common law marriages back home. Some got kids and everything."

"I see," said Jack, uncertain about his feelings on such arrangements.

They spent hours pouring over the department books and the records of the men. By suppertime, Jack began to feel that he had a grasp of the situation. As he and Hank headed for the wardroom, he decided that he was ready to take over the department.

Though *Rust* carried only eight officers, the wardroom seemed overcrowded when they were all inside. Jack had a way with names, so he soon had them all matched to the faces. The comradeship of the group was readily evident from the conversation. Rustbucket was clearly a happy ship, and Jack felt immediately at home in the closely-knit society. He was filled with respect for Hoskins and the way he had welded this mixture of Reservists and very junior regular officers into a smoothly functioning organization. Small ships were the place to be if you were going to be in the Navy.

Dawn the following day found the ships of the Asiatic Fleet steaming northward through the Sulu Sea. *Houston,* with her escort of destroyers, was in the van. *Marblehead* followed in line astern, flanked by her own bevy of 'cans.' The ships knifed smoothly through a moderate sea, great 'bones' of water thrown up by their bows. Schools of flying fish seemed a part of the formation, the rays of the sun flashing off their colorful scales.

Frank Rhea sat in the cockpit of the *Seagull* on *Marblehead*'s starboard catapult, finishing the final checklist before engine startup. Satisfied with the results, he turned to Tonto, who was standing on the lower starboard wing ready with the starter handle. The combined speed of the ship and the stiff breeze into which she was running was sending a good forty knots of wind across her decks. It shrieked about the open cockpit, making verbal communication impossible, so Frank raised his right hand and made a spiraling motion. The Indian nodded his understanding, then bent his back to spin the heavy crank. Frank switched on the ignition as the two-bladed aluminum propeller started to spin slowly, then pick up speed. After coughing asthmatically a couple of times, the 550-horsepower Wright engine caught and began to roar in a businesslike manner. Tonto stepped lightly back across the wing and climbed into the observer's cockpit.

"Ready back there?" Frank said into his intercom mike a few moments later.

"All set, *Kimo Sabay*," came the response.

Frank looked across to the port catapult where Eddie Blessman and Tex Jennings, his observer, were preparing to launch. Down between the catapults, Bishop, the jaygee whom Frank had displaced as second aviator, was acting as launch officer. Frank revved up his engine until the *Seagull* was vibrating all over, then gave Bishop the ready signal with his hand. The launch officer acknowledged the signal, warned the crew to stand clear and jerked the firing lanyard. Propelled by an exploding charge, the piston in the catapult tube shot forward at blinding speed, dragging the attached aircraft cradle with it. The skin on Frank's face sagged backwards, and a giant hand seemed to bear down upon his chest and stomach as the *Seagull* accelerated from a standstill to over a hundred miles an hour in the span of a few seconds. Flung clear of the ship, the plane skimmed just above the wave tops as it gathered speed. Frank eased back on the control column and clawed for altitude, then glanced back at *Marblehead* just in time to see Eddie Blessman's perfect launch off the port catapult.

The old exhilaration of flight took hold of Frank's emotions as the *Seagull* soared higher and higher above the formation of ships. From three thousand feet up, the obsolescent features of most of the vessels were blurred. They seemed a powerful armada, ready to sally forth and defeat any potential enemy.

Down below, the catapults on *Houston* threw another pair of *Seagulls* into the air. Each of the four airborne planes was assigned to fly a preplanned search pattern. In war, part of the cruiser pilot's job was to find the enemy. Frank flew steadily to the northeast, his eyes constantly scanning the deep blue surface of the Sulu Sea. For a long time, both sea and sky remained empty, but when he was almost an hour out from *Marblehead*, a dark smudge appeared on the horizon. After a few minutes, a dim silhouette became visible. He turned the plane a little to the left to give Tonto a clear view with his binoculars.

"Can you make it out?" Frank asked over the intercom.

"It's a fair-sized tanker," reported Tonto. "Can't see her flag yet."

"Send a message to *Marblehead*," ordered Frank, then rattled off the facts to be reported. Tonto tapped out the signal on his Morse key.

Frank flew on toward the tanker. As they drew closer, he saw that the ship was big, around fifteen thousand tons, and looked almost brand new.

"I see her colors now," said Tonto. "She's a Jap. Must have been one of the last to leave Java before the Dutch joined the oil embargo."

Frank circled the vessel once, and then resumed his search pattern while Tonto sent a supplementary report to their ship. After the tanker faded into the distance behind them, they made no further sightings on either the dogleg or the long flight back to the fleet.

The American cruisers were now separated, steaming in small task forces about five miles apart. Frank picked out *Marblehead*'s archaic shape easily and headed for her. A signal lamp began to wink from the cruiser's bridge, ordering him to prepare to land. In the rear cockpit, a hand-held lamp rattled as Tonto acknowledged the signal. Having read the code himself, Frank nosed the *Seagull* over and began to lose altitude, circling to come in astern of the ship, which was now headed into the wind.

Marblehead executed a sharp turn to starboard. Steaming across the wind, her five hundred-foot hull became a moving breakwater, calming the sea on her lee side. Frank plopped the *Seagull* down carefully into the protected patch of water and taxied rapidly up alongside the ship. Her amidships boat boom swung outboard to stream the recovery net--called a "sled"--just under the surface. He made straight for it. With the engine at high revs, the floatplane stayed nose-up with the prow of her main pontoon just clear of the water. Now came the tricky part of the recovery. Frank had executed it many times aboard *Omaha* but only twice during his years with the Reserves. He eased the front tip of the pontoon forward until he was certain that it was above the "sled," then abruptly cut power to the engine. The nose of the *Seagull* dropped, snagging the pontoon hook in the netting. The plane was securely caught now, being towed alongside the ship. Overhead, the big aircraft boom swung outward, and a hook started to creep down toward the floatplane. A few minutes later, half a dozen "V" Division men were snugging the bird down on the catapult cradle.

Frank peeled off his dog-eared, khaki aviator's helmet and ran his fingers through his sweat-soaked hair. Standing on the lower wing, Tonto offered him a hand out of the cockpit.

"Want to change pilots?" asked Frank, laughing.

"Not on your life," Tonto responded. "You're okay, Lone Ranger. I'll stick with you."

Jack Sewell watched the tricky aircraft recovery from the dizzying perch of *Rust's* fire control platform. Simulating action with battle drills, Tom Hoskins had kept the ship at General Quarters all day. In retrospect, Jack realized that he had enjoyed the experience. True, it was damnably hot up here in the open with the old fashioned "soup plate" tin hat strapped on his head, but he had an excellent view of all the fleet maneuvers, and he was quickly getting to know his battle team. Chief Muldune's knowledge and capabilities were especially impressive. He would be a solid rock under the stresses of combat. Later in the day, battle drills permitting, Jack would stand his first bridge watch under instruction. He looked forward to the experience. Running a ship as OOD had been one of his favorite tasks during his previous active duty.

Up ahead, the towering thunderheads of the tropics loomed in a solid front. Unperturbed, the fleet plowed on toward the squall line.

"Looks like we're gonna get wet, Lieutenant," boomed Muldune, grinning.

Just then, the public address system let out an ear-piercing squeal, followed by the monotone voice of the quartermaster of the watch, "Now hear this. Secure from General Quarters. Set Condition Zed throughout the ship."

The fire control party stripped off their helmets, life jackets and communications equipment, carefully stowing them away in watertight lockers. Then they scurried down the ladder to shelter beneath the bridge wings just as the torrent of the squall line struck the ship.

WARREN BELL

CHAPTER 7

(One)
Imperial Japanese Army Headquarters
Ichigaya Heights
Tokyo, Japan
4 September 1941

"Major Okuma reporting as ordered, sir." Okuma saluted smartly as he snapped to attention in front of the general's plain teak desk.

"Be seated, Major," replied Lieutenant General Ko Tsukada. Returning the salute, he bent back over some papers. "I'll be with you in a moment."

Okuma settled into a straight wooden chair and sat rigidly upright. He had no idea why he had been preemptively summoned to the office of the Army Vice Chief of Staff, but he felt no discomfort. His experiences in Berlin had made him at home in the presence of generals. Still, Tsukada was known to be as fiery as he was brilliant, so there was a hint of danger in the air. He glanced about the room, which was hardly larger than his own small office. Like the War Minister, General Hideki Tojo, Tsukada was an ascetic patriot, shunning personal aggrandizement.

"I've read your reports on German airborne operations," the general finally said. "I found them very professional and enlightening."

"Thank you, General." Okuma was not surprised by Tsukada's comment. Since joining the Army General Staff upon his return from Germany, he had become widely recognized as Japan's premier authority on *rakkasan-butai* (airborne units).

"I'm sure that you're aware of the high-level debate that's been going on over where we should conduct operations to seize natural resources. I'm authorized to tell you that a decision has been reached to prepare for a rapid move to the south."

Excitement quickened Okuma's pulse, and he leaned forward.

This was the very course that he believed would lead to a glorious destiny for his homeland, one that he and like-minded younger officers had begun to think would never come. It was well known among the *chuken shoko*--the staff majors and lieutenant colonels who did most of the work at the War Ministry --that the Chief of Staff, General Sugiyama, had strongly resisted the idea of attacking the Western Allies.

"If his Majesty decides on war, it's imperative that we seize all the Western colonial possessions before they have time to react," Tsukada continued. "This is the outline of the preliminary plan." He handed a thin folder to Okuma. "Analyze it from the viewpoint of where best to use such airborne forces as can be readied within the specified time limits. I'll expect your appreciation within three days."

"Yes, sir," said Okuma with enthusiasm.

"A word of caution. We suspect that some civilians from the Foreign Ministry who crave peace above honor may have leaked some of our intentions to *gaijin* diplomats. You are to breathe nothing of this to anyone not directly involved in the planning, no matter how high the position. Is that clearly understood?"

"Of course, General."

"Then, go to it. Set up an appointment through my aide when you're ready to report."

The Japan to which Okuma had returned earlier that month was a nation grappling with the necessity to make historic decisions under severe time constraints. Most civilian statesmen wished to avoid war with either Russia or the Western powers at any cost, a view shared by the Navy high command and many senior military officers who were mindful of the vast disparity in natural resources and industrial capacity that Japan would face in such a conflict. But Hitler's easy conquest of Western Europe in the late spring of 1940 had whetted the appetites of the younger Japanese militarists. The rich colonial empires of Southeast Asia appeared to be ripe fruit ready for plucking. All the physical resources necessary to assure Japan's industrial independence and a successful conclusion of the long war in China--rubber, tin, tungsten, manganese, coal, quinine, abundant rice, and, above all, the oil of the Dutch East Indies-- beckoned to the would-be conquerors. "Don't miss the bus" became the rallying cry of the idealistic super patriots of the *chuken shoko*.

Prince Konoye's new government was swept up in the enthusiasm for expansion. Adopting the aim of establishing *Tao Shinchitsujo* (a "New Order in Greater East Asia") the government pressured the faltering French into closing the rail link from Hanoi into south China, Chaing Kai-shek's last reliable supply route. Stung by the American response of embargoing sales of scrap iron and steel to Japan, Konoye enhanced his freedom for action by signing the Tripartite Pact with Germany and Italy and a new non-aggression pact with Stalin. Emulating Hitler's posturing in the years before Munich, Japanese diplomats tried to browbeat the government of the Netherlands East Indies into granting immediate concessions of oil and raw materials. The Army and Navy began planning for a war to overrun the colonial empires. But in the spring of 1941, their German allies upset all the careful Japanese calculations.

When Hitler's armies slashed into the Soviet Union, he at once called on the Japanese to invade Siberia. As one swift German victory followed another, many officials in the government recommended a delay in the southern operations to allow helping their allies carve up the Soviet empire. They argued that after eliminating the threat of world communism, the plums of Southeast Asia could still be plucked at Japan's leisure. All through the summer, the debate raged back and forth at the Liaison Conferences, at which the politician and military leaders hammered out national policy. Initially confirming the Navy's position of *hokushu nanshin* ("defend in the north, advance to the south"), in late July the government bullied the French into allowing the peaceful occupation of all Indochina by Japanese forces. The unexpected American reaction stunned the nation. Roosevelt froze all Japanese assets in the United States and suspended all trade between the countries. Britain and the other Western Allies followed suit almost at once. The island empire was suddenly isolated from all sources of vital materials, especially oil. Her internal industry of 4,000 wells produced less than two million barrels a year, a tiny fraction of military requirements. At the current pace of operations in China, existing fuel stocks would be consumed in less than two years. If a naval war erupted, they would be gone in a matter of months.

A sense of anger and desperation pervaded the General Staff when Okuma arrived in Tokyo. Imbued with the belief that the moral superiority of Japan's *kokutai* (national essence) would overcome any material inadequacies, the younger Army officers suffered no doubts about what Japan should do: attack the Westerners and seize the resources they needed! Attack now, while stocks of strategic materials were sufficient to allow victory! Their more prudent seniors and the civilian politicians were frantically seeking to negotiate some sort of tolerable settlement with Washington. While they debated, fuel stocks continued to dwindle. The firebrands among the *chuken shoko*, Okuma included, had begun to despair that a decision for war would ever be reached. Now, at last, the Supreme Command was authorized to prepare to move south when the negotiations with America inevitably failed.

Back in his own Spartan office, Okuma eagerly poured over the draft plan that Tsukada had given him. Its scope was breathtaking. While the Navy fended off the American fleet to the west, three amphibious thrusts would tear the colonial empires of Southeast Asia to shreds. The 25th Army under Lieutenant General Tomoyuka "Tiger" Yamashita, his friend from Germany, would conquer Malaya and Singapore; Lieutenant General Masaharu Homma's 14th Army, the American Philippines. The Dutch East Indies with their vast stores of oil and rubber would fall to Lieutenant General Hitoshi Imamura's 16th Army. As soon as Malaya was well in hand, Lieutenant General Shojiro Iida's 15th Army would spring out of Thailand to seize Burma and threaten India. The bulk of the Navy would be employed to screen these far-flung operations, providing air cover from shore bases and light carriers. The entire operation would be commanded by a new Southern Army group in Saigon under General Count Hisaichi Terauchi.

Okuma immediately realized that he was confronted with a daunting assignment. The planned operations presented innumerable opportunities for the productive employment of airborne troops, far more than could be executed by the few units he could hope to activate in time. Like an economist, his primary task would be to select those targets that promised the most significant return for the use of his scarce resources. To him, that suggested the capture of the economic assets for which Japan was about to go to war, especially mines, oil fields, refineries and rubber facilities. His first step must be to get as much information as time allowed from his friends in the Second Bureau of the General Staff -- Army Intelligence.

He turned to Major Tsunehiro Shirai, a classmate from the Central Military Academy at Ichigaya, who ran espionage operations in Organization F, the Special Services Agency. Shirai agreed to provide the data he required but insisted that he review the files without removing them from the SSA offices.

Although he had some idea of the scope of Japan's secret intelligence networks from his days at the embassy, Okuma was astounded by the depth and breadth of information contained in the files. Fishing fleets had charted every possible landing site. For years, Japanese agents had been infiltrating the colonial empires through lawful immigration. Japanese nationals managed tin mines and rubber plantations; Japanese engineers worked in oil fields and refineries; the photography business was dominated by Japanese expatriates, allowing copying of all snapshots with any military significance. Even the ubiquitous brothels and silk shops provided useful information casually dropped by their customers.

One of the last files he reviewed was an extremely detailed dossier dealing with Dutch Borneo. A Japanese firm had obtained a timber concession there a few years before, and he was intrigued to discover that they had not only pinpointed Dutch defenses but had also cleared air landing grounds near the strategic city of Balikpapan. As he scanned through a series of photographs of the vast oil works near the timber concession, one face jumped out and galvanized his attention. Was it the man who had met the infernal woman doctor at the Manila airport? A quick perusal of the caption confirmed his assessment. The Dutchman was Nicolaas van Wely, General Manager of the Royal Dutch/Shell interests in Balikpapan. Thumbing on through the most recent pictures, he discovered a shot of the oilman and the hated woman together at a social event. The accompanying note identified her as his daughter.

A malicious smile crooked Okuma's lips as he circled the name of Balikpapan on his inventory of potential targets and drew an arrow to move it to the top of his list. He kept out the Borneo file when he replaced the others in their cabinets, then went back to his classmate's office.

"Could I ask a personal favor, Tsunehiro?" he began.

"If it's within reason."

"These photographs from Borneo are very detailed."

"They should be. Our agent's the official photographer for the Dutch oil company."

"I'm interested in learning more about this woman."

"Still the ladykiller, *Kuma*?" Shirai inquired as gazed at the image of Cinta van Wely. "I hear you cut quite a swath in German society."

"I have other plans for this one." Okuma briefly outlined the incident on Guam.

"I understand how you feel," Shirai commented. "I'll get you all the information on her I can. I only hope you have the opportunity to make her pay for the affront."

"Oh, I shall, my friend. There's no question about that in my mind."

Okuma worked far into the night. It soon became apparent that the limiting factor for airborne operations in the immediate future would be the paucity of suitable aircraft. The new Nakajima L2D2's--the license-built Douglas DC-3's--were only now beginning to come off the production line. His initial inclination was to impress the older DC-2's of *Dai Nippon*, but Colonel Takushiro Hattori, the Chief of the Operations Section of the General Staff, vetoed the idea. Civilian air service must continue undisturbed in order to lull the Western Allies into a sense of complacency. The *rakkasan-butai* program would have to make do with aircraft already in the Army's inventory. This essentially limited Okuma to the Mitsubishi Ki-57, a twin-engined transport that superficially resembled the DC-2 but carried a smaller payload of eleven passengers or 3,000 pounds of cargo. The numbers were not promising, allowing for only a single airborne brigade. He proposed that a regiment of heavy bombers be made an integral part of the unit. The aging Mitsubishi Ki-21's could be used to ferry troops as well as for strike missions. A few Kawasaki K-46's, license-built versions of the Lockheed *Lodestar*, would be available as cargo carriers. What rankled him most about the aircraft limitations was the knowledge that he would have to compete with the Navy for production allocation. Never content to let the Army have a mission unchallenged, the sea service was forming its own paratroop detachment, the Yokosuka Special Naval Landing Force.

Given the strict limitations on time and resources, he reluctantly gave up his hope of including Balikpapan in his list of initial targets. The oil installations there and at Tarakan were among the richest in the Indies, but they were right on the seashore and vulnerable to amphibious attack. Seizure of economic assets that might be destroyed by the enemy before conventional forces could reach them had to be his primary focus. The mammoth Uyodiraff and Sungeigelong refineries at Palembang, Sumatra, were much more vital targets for the new brigade. Similar but smaller oil works at Tjepu and Zwarte Gouden in Java took second priority.

By 1700 hours on the second day, Okuma's clerk had completed typing the smooth draft of his report. Reading it over one final time, he concluded that it contained everything that General Tsukada could expect and more. He had included appendices on the proposed organization, equipage and training of the proposed airborne units as well as recommendations on doctrine and tactics. Finally satisfied, he stamped the document with his *hanko*--the personal seals used in Japan in lieu of signatures--and locked it in the Operations Section safe for the night.

"*Kuma*, you great hulking bastard, wait a moment," someone shouted as Okuma went down the front steps of the old two-storied wooden structure on Ichigaya Heights that housed the Army General Staff and the War Ministry.

Turning, he recognized Major Etsuko Miyagi, a friend from his days with the Kwantung Army in Manchuria, coming out of the War Ministry entrance. A thin, sallow chain smoker, Miyagi wore thick glasses and affected a Hitler-style mustache.

"It's good to see you again, Etsuko," Okuma said as they exuberantly shook hands. "Are you here with the Staff?"

"At the War Ministry. Do you have plans for dinner?"

"I was going to eat in the officers' mess."

"Forget that nonsense. Come with me to a *machiai* (tea house), and we'll discuss these interesting times while we dally with the *geisha*."

"You're on, old friend. Do you have any suggestions?"

"Of course. I'm in charge of the bureau responsible for troop welfare. We recruit and organize the Army's *Ianfu Gundan* (Comfort Women's Corps). Let's take a taxi."

On the way to the restaurant, Miyagi regaled Okuma with tales about the advantages of his present assignment. Furnishing mobile brothels for its soldiers was a fairly new practice for the Japanese Army, prompted in part by the worldwide criticism of the barbarity displayed by Japanese troops during the Rape of Nanking in 1937. But there was another, more pressing reason as far as Imperial Headquarters was concerned. Letting the soldiers go berserk had resulted in a widespread breakdown in small unit discipline. Insolence towards junior officers and other conduct bordering on mutiny had become commonplace, drastically undermining military effectiveness. The government had decided that perhaps the most practical measure that could be taken to keep the lusts of the troops within manageable limits was to provide them with their own "comfort women," as the enterprising General Okamura had done in Shanghai back in 1932. The subsequent campaign that led to the capture of Hankow had proved the value of the concept, and brothels had accompanied the Imperial Army in all subsequent operations.

Being responsible for the efficiency of the Army's brothel service gave Miyagi many high-level contacts in *Karyukai*--the almost separate society peopled with *geisha* and courtesans. In stark contrast to Western notions, this "world of flowers and willows" was accorded a reputable status within Japanese culture.

"How do you convince young women to join your service?" Okuma inquired. "Considering the hardships in a field *Ianjo* (comfort station), you must have quite a selling job to do."

"It's done mostly through private contractors, who actually run the brothels. Here in Japan, they basically appeal to the women's patriotism. We usually get as many recruits as we need for the officers' *Ianjo* because the patrons typically tip the *Ianfu* well. The brothels for the troops do sometimes present a problem. We get a lot of our girls from Korea. The life of the peasants there is so hard that anything to escape their daily drudgery seems attractive to them. Of course, we sometimes have to send press gangs out to the villages to conscript women to fill our quotas. That's standard operating procedure in the conquered areas in China."

An idea suddenly took root in Okuma's mind, provoking a fiendish smile. For weeks, he had filled his fantasies with the torment he would inflict on Cinta van Wely when she fell into his hands. Perhaps here was a way to make a living hell of whatever life remained to her after he took his personal revenge. "Your units accompany the fighting troops?"

"Right up to the battle lines. A little *tsutsumutse* (pussy) before a fight is great for the morale of our troops."

Okuma chuckled at Miyagi's use of the direct term for sexual intercourse. Japanese usually spoke of physical love in Taoist euphemisms. "I assume you're involved in the current contingency planning?"

"Naturally. If we have to execute them, my bureau will be hard pressed to fill our quotas. We'll need a whole legion of new *Ianfu*."

"The Germans conscript *feld-hures* (field whores) from their concentration camps, and I understand that the Red Army fills its brothels with the wives and daughters of political prisoners. You should be allowed to draft the women of our conquered enemies, especially those of the Western Imperialists."

"That's a policy question that hasn't been settled yet. I'm certainly in favor of it. Think of the loss of face the haughty *gaijin* would suffer when we told all East Asia that their women were servicing our troops."

"Not to mention the humiliation of the arrogant bitches themselves. The myth of White Supremacy would be shattered forever. I have a specific situation along that line I'd like to discuss with you."

Miyagi listened intently as Okuma outlined his idea. "What poetic justice!" he exclaimed when the paratrooper finished his discourse. "It would be perfect *tenchu* (the punishment of heaven) for the *gaijin* witch. Give me the particulars, and I'll do everything I can to make it happen."

CHAPTER 8

(One)
Aboard USS *Rust*
Manila Bay
28 November 1941

Jack Sewell took off his "soup-plate" helmet for a moment and mopped the sweat from his forehead with a wrinkled handkerchief. For four grueling hours he had manned his battle station at Central Fire Control while *Rust* steamed "figure-eights" outside the minefields protecting Manila Bay. Patrolling in the tropical darkness against intrusion by hostile submarines, the ship had been virtually blind for most of the time due to a failure in her underwater detection gear. If a Japanese "pig boat" were out there, her captain could slip a fish into *Rust* with no more warning than a glimpse of a torpedo wake.

War jitters were rampant throughout the Far East. The months since Jack reported to *Rust* had brought steadily mounting tensions as Japan's piecemeal war with China threatened to spill over to the American and European possessions on the rim of Asia. With their assets in Western nations frozen and faced with a total embargo on scrap iron and oil, the Japanese retaliated by completing their progressive occupation of French Indochina and tightening their grip about the European concessions in Shanghai. Although a diplomatic break appeared inevitable, special envoys of the Japanese emperor were even now in Washington, ostensibly trying to heal the fast developing rift with their formerly close friends.

The Asiatic Fleet had been on a war footing for months. Since sending all dependents home in the autumn of 1940, Admiral Tommy Hart had driven his command hard to prepare for combat. The exercise at Tawi-Tawi was but one of a series of maneuvers to familiarize his commanders with their potential theater of war.

Battle drills were the order of every day. Hart believed firmly that the best way to deter the Japanese was to stand up to them diplomatically and demonstrate an instant willingness to fight if provoked. But the progress of events left him more and more pessimistic about the prospects of continued peace. In mid-November, he called all American merchant ships in Asiatic waters into Manila Bay to shelter behind the minefields and the guns of the Fortress of Corregidor.

"Here comes *Pope* out to relieve us, Lieutenant," Chief Muldune's gruff voice snapped Jack back to full alertness. Muldune's battle station was to operate the gun director.

Jack raised his binoculars and peered toward the dark shadow of Luzon. The first pink streaks of dawn silhouetted the shape of another "four-piper" destroyer steaming out through the swept channel in the minefield. A Morse light began to blink from the newcomer. Moments later, one of the lamps on *Rust's* signal bridge rattled out a reply.

"Now hear this!" squawk boxes blared all over *Rust*. "Secure from General Quarters. Set Condition 'Yoke' throughout the ship."

Jack heaved a sigh of relief and took off his tin hat. "I'm going down to the 'sound shack,'" he said to Muldune. "Tell the OOD he can reach me there."

"Aye, aye, sir," Muldune responded, then issued instructions to the telephone "talker."

Jack was well pleased with the big chief, who ran a taut, first-rate Gunnery Department. He never hesitated to leave routine matters to Muldune while attending himself to special problems. Dropping quickly down the steep ladder beside the foremast, he stepped into the open combing of a deck hatch. His destination lay far down in the bowels of the ship, where the sonar equipment for locating submarines was located. Since she had just been refitted, *Rust's* sound gear was more modern than that carried by the older Asiatic Fleet veterans. Arriving at last at the "sound shack," he undogged the watertight door and went inside. A skinny sailor, who was stripped down to his dungaree pants and sweating profusely in the heat, was working through the open back of an electronics cabinet.

"Find the trouble yet, Matthews?" Jack asked the young man.

A freckled face topped with orange hair popped up over the cabinet. "We got ourselves a regular gremlin in here, Mister Sewell," the sailor replied. "I'll catch the bastard before we get back to Cavite, though. Got a 'bamboo babe' waitin' on the beach for me."

"Keep at it, then." Jack had every confidence that Matthews would make good on his promise. His rustic manner was deceiving. Despite his youth, he was the best soundman on the ship. "Better be careful when you hit that liberty. Don't come back with a case of the clap."

"Don't fret yourself about that, Lieutenant. I don't mess around with any cheap whores. This one's special."

"If you say so. Let me know when the sonar's back on the line." Jack started out the watertight door.

Bong! Something solid striking the hull sent vibrations rippling through the ship.

Bong! It struck again, then grated back along the port side of the hull with a rasping screech.

"Goddamn, Mister Sewell," exclaimed a wide-eyed Matthews. "That nearly scared the shit out of me. Did we hit a reef?"

"Not likely. These waters are too well charted."

"Then, what the hell..."

Rust began to shake forcefully, as if in the grasp of some giant sea monster. Jack clawed at the door combing to keep from falling as she heeled over in a tight turn to port, then went dead in the water. The nerve-jangling clatter of the General Alarm went off, and he headed for his battle station.

Lieutenant Commander Hoskins was standing at the back of the bridge with his glasses glued to his eyes when Jack came up the ladder.

"What's happening, Skipper?" he asked.

"Something fouled the port screw. May have wiped the shaft bearings and the turbine. Wait. There it is! Have a look." Hoskins handed his binoculars to Jack and pointed about two hundred yards astern of the ship.

Jack adjusted the eyepieces to focus the glasses. He picked out the barnacle-encrusted, four-foot sphere at once. "A mine," he said flatly.

"That's what I thought," the Captain agreed. "We're lucky as hell it didn't go off. It must have been sucked into the screws and got jammed against the hull."

"Do you think it's a Jap mine or one of ours, sir?"

"Definitely ours. Jap mines work. Admiral Hart sent Washington a scorcher last month about our high rate of defective mines."

"Should we put a boat in the water and try to salvage it?"

"Hell, no! The damned thing might be armed now. Sink it with gunfire. I want to get a diver over the side at first light to see how much damage we took."

"Aye, aye, Skipper." Jack sprinted back along the flush deck and climbed to the top of the after deckhouse, where the crew was standing by Gun Number Four. He pointed out the mine to the gun captain and ordered him to fire at will. The slender, four-inch fifty recoiled sharply seconds later, emitting an ear-splitting crack. A mushroom of water erupted twenty feet beyond the mine. The second shot was dead on target, sending an ugly ball of smoke boiling skyward as the projectile and mine went off together.

Just after first light, Jack was on the pointed fantail with Hoskins when Lieutenant (jg) Jim Thomas, the Engineering Officer, completed his underwater damage survey. The jaygee panted as he climbed the accommodation ladder in a heavy pressure suit.

"Port screw's a goddamned mess, Captain," Thomas reported. "Two of the blades are crushed, and there's a cable tangled on the shaft. Near as I can figure it, the mine was loose and trailing its cable when it bounced along the side. The wire caught in the screw and wound around the shaft, pulling the mine down. It must have slammed into the screw before the cable snapped."

"What about the shaft and strut?" Hoskins asked. "Are they bent or out of line?"

"Not as far as I can tell. Looks like she'll be good as new if Cavite can replace the screw."

"What about the turbine and shaft bearings?"

"Chief Rothchild saved our ass. He shut down the port engine when the vibration started."

"I'll commend him in my report. Any problems running back to Cavite on the starboard engine?"

"No sweat, Skipper."

By noon, *Rust* was moored safely at the Cavite Navy Yard's Guadeloupe Pier. A party of engineers came aboard as soon as she docked to confirm the damage. They were closeted with Hoskins, Jerry Busch and Jim Thomas for over an hour. Then "Officers Call" blared over the squawk boxes.

Tom Hoskins stood quietly at the front of the wardroom as his officers assembled. In the days after reporting to the ship, Jack had discovered that the Captain was the epitome of the professional Navy man. A superb seaman and engineer, he led by exceptional personal example, never asking of his men what he was not prepared to do double himself.

"Gentlemen," Hoskins addressed his seven subordinates in his usual businesslike manner, "it looks like we'll be here for four or five days. The drydock, *Dewey*, is booked solid with higher priority work. They're going to dock us on the old marine railway the day after tomorrow. It'll take about two days out of the water to fix the screw.

"I want every minute of this time in the yard used to get your departments ready for combat. There will be no liberty. Before you get worked up about the effect on morale, let me tell you why. Admiral Hart just sent a war warning to all ships in the fleet."

A murmur swept through the room, and the officers leaned forward on the edges of their seats, their attention galvanized by the Captain's announcement.

"We're to execute the dispersal plan at once. Most of the fleet will head for Dutch ports in the Indies. We won't get our sailing orders until our repairs are finished. 'Cans' are in short supply with *Peary* and *Pillsbury* out of service." The two destroyers had been damaged in a collision a few days earlier. "Questions?"

The discussion that followed was crisp and to the point. The officers were grim-faced when they filed out afterwards. Jack stayed behind for a few private words with the Captain and Exec.

"Skipper," Jack began in a conspiratorial tone, "I assume that a few 'midnight requisitions' won't be frowned upon if the good of the ship is involved."

"What did you have in mind?" asked Busch.

"Anything we can shoot at airplanes with. I've been studying ways to beef up our antiaircraft battery. We need to add at least a couple of .50-caliber machine guns."

"See what you can come up with," said Hoskins, "but don't steal anything unless I okay it first."

"Chief Muldune has his spies out already."

Jack was on watch later that evening when *Houston* backed away from the nearby wharf where she had been undergoing installation of radar and an upgrade of her light antiaircraft battery. The heavy cruiser was a magnificent sight with her eight-inch guns and her wind-whipped flags and her *Seagull* floatplanes perched on her catapults. The heaviest American warship west of Pearl Harbor, she was to become the nucleus of a task force that Admiral Hart was forming in southern Philippine waters.

Tom Hoskins had explained the necessity for the dispersal of the fleet to his wardroom following a classified briefing for commanding officers at Hart's headquarters. Until the previous week, the admiral had intended to keep his ships in Philippine waters, contesting any attempt to invade the islands. The Navy Department had vetoed his plans. On paper, their logic was irrefutable. Intelligence reports indicated that the Imperial Japanese Navy had ten battleships, ten aircraft carriers, thirty-six cruisers, over a hundred destroyers and several hundred aircraft available for operations in Southeast Asia. The Asiatic Fleet was puny by comparison: *Houston*; the light cruisers, *Marblehead* and *Boise*; the thirteen old "four-pipers" of Destroyer Squadron 29; six minesweepers; some old China gunboats; and the twenty-eight PBY *Catalinas* of Patrol Wing Ten. Joint plans worked out earlier in the year between the American, British, Dutch and Australian governments called for the surface units of the Asiatic Fleet to retire to ports in the Netherlands East Indies. The British were deploying the battleship, *Prince of Wales*, the battle cruiser, *Repulse*, and an armored aircraft carrier to Singapore. By combining the Anglo-American forces with the cruisers and destroyers of the Dutch, Australian and New Zealand navies and providing air cover from the numerous British and Dutch airfields, a fleet of sufficient strength to hold the Japanese at the Malay Barrier was envisioned. From a Navy point of view, it was all very logical. General MacArthur and his Army people were bound to feel that the fleet was running out on them.

Admiral Hart did have one ace up his sleeve--his twenty-three modern, fleet-type submarines supported by six aged S-boats. An old submariner himself, he was going to keep his headquarters in Manila and take the war to the enemy with undersea craft for as long as the Army held Luzon. Torpedoes and submarine spare parts were dispersed around the city to preclude losing them all in an air attack. The tenders, *Holland*, *Otus*, and *Canopus*, would remain in Manila Bay to support their broods. PatWing 10 and its tender, *Langley*, would also stay on to provide reconnaissance.

"Are you sure that this thing is going to work?" Jim Thomas said to a sun-bronzed lieutenant in sweat-soaked khaki coveralls. They were standing with Jack between the tracks of an ancient marine railway, staring down its steep incline to where two yard tugs were nudging *Rust* toward the shore. Submerged except for the tops of its bow blocks, a massive carriage bearing timber bracing to fit the hull of a destroyer lay waiting on the lower, underwater section of the railway.

"Don't worry," replied Richard Anderson, one of Cavite's engineering officers. "I've had half a dozen 'cans' up here already,"

"But you'll have forty feet of her keel out of the water before her stern comes down on the blocks," Thomas persisted. "That'll put tremendous bending stresses in her hull, maybe even break her back."

"She can take it," Anderson insisted. "These old girls are a lot stronger than they look."

Anderson's Filipino crew was skilled and well-drilled. They took a bow line from *Rust*, wrapped it around a power winch and towed the ship's bows into the blocks of the semisubmerged carriage. Then Anderson engaged the forty-year-old electric motor driving the hauling winch, drawing the heavy towing cable taut as a bowstring. Amidst a din of creaking and rattling metal, the wheels of the carriage began to inch up the rails, lifting *Rust's* stem out of the water. Out on the bay, the yard tugs kept the destroyer lined up on the railway. Finally, with her plates groaning in protest at the strains induced by the flexing of her hull, *Rust's* stern settled onto the cradle and broke free of the water, revealing the crippled shaft and screw. Jim Thomas's initial evaluation of the damage was right on target. Steel cable was tangled around the shaft outboard of its supporting strut, and two of the four blades of the nine-foot propeller were grotesquely bent down against the hub. It would clearly have to be replaced.

As soon as the destroyer was securely blocked into place on the upper end of the rail bed, the shipfitters went to work preparing to pull the damaged screw. Jack and his soundmen made a thorough inspection of the retractable sound dome in the bottom of the hull.

"She's in good shape, Mister Sewell," said Matthews confidently. "Don't even need adjustin'." Like the rest of the crew, Matthews had taken the lack of liberty in stride when the reason was explained to him.

"You're absolutely certain?' said Jack.

"You can stake your life on it, Lieutenant."

"All of us will if we run into 'pig boats.'"

"Beggin' your pardon, Mister Sewell," Chief Muldune's voice boomed from behind Jack. "Could I have a word with you, sir?"

"Sure, Chief. Just a minute." After giving instructions to Matthews, Jack walked out of the shadow of the vessel to where Muldune was standing. The sun's heat hit him like a physical blow.

"I hit the jackpot, Lieutenant," said a grinning Muldune.

"Let's have it."

"Been talkin' to an old buddy of mine in the Yard Ordnance Department. When *Houston* pulled out, they left behind a whole quad mount of 1.1-inchers they didn't have time to install. Somebody's already copped a couple of the guns, but he thinks that a word from the Skipper to Commander Bowers will get us the other two."

"What good would they do us without proper gun mounts?"

"Got that figured out. I know a chief who runs a machine shop at the yard. He's got some old Spanish mounts he found in a warehouse. Says he could spring-balance the 1.1's to where they would handle like machine guns."

"Sounds too good to be true. We could mount them on either side of the funnels at the rear of the galley deckhouse."

"That's just what I thought too, sir. We'll have to jury-rig a water pump and hose for each gun. They got water jackets to cool their barrels just like the .50-calibers."

"What about more machine guns?"

"Talked to a gunny sergeant at the ammo dump. He says that they got more fifties than they can man. Says to talk to a Gyrene lieutenant named Keene."

"Let's go see the Skipper now."

Before the day was out, Muldune was supervising a party of mixed ratings--machinist's mates, shipfitters and gunner's mates—working to install supports for new gun tubs at the back of the midships gun platform. First welding pipe columns to the deck, the fitters topped them with a steel framework. "Diamond back" steel plate was stacked nearby, ready to be used as decking for the extensions. Other parties were laboring to install similar structures between the after banks of torpedo tubes to house additional machine guns. In theory, permission from the Bureau of Ships in Washington was required for such modifications, but Tom Hoskins had no intention of needlessly hazarding his ship to enemy bombers while waiting for some bureaucrat to make a decision.

"Everything squared away with the 1.1's, Lieutenant?" Muldune asked Jack as he came up the steep ladder from the rail bed.

"I'm afraid not. The Skipper and I spent an hour with the Inspector of Ordnance, but he wouldn't budge. He said that he couldn't release the guns without authority from fleet headquarters. He did set up an appointment for me to see Captain Collins over there at ten hundred tomorrow. I have to make some sketches to show him. Come by the department office when you knock off here. I'll need some help with the gun mounts."

"Let me brighten your day. My Gyrene buddy went ahead and talked to his lieutenant. They're gonna give us four fifties, complete with mounts. Travers is over at the ammo dump now pickin' them up."

"Well done, Chief! Keep it up."

(Two)
Asiatic Fleet Headquarters
Manila
2 December 1941

A sudden chill set Jack's teeth to chattering as the doors of the air-conditioned elevator closed behind him. His high-collared white uniform had been crisp with starch when he left Cavite, but the ride across the bay aboard the ferryboat, *Dap-Dap*, had wilted it with perspiration. Now the damp cotton cloth was clammy against his skin.

One of the most modern buildings along the Manila waterfront, the Marsman Building made an ideal location for Asiatic Fleet headquarters. Most of the major shipping companies had their offices there, and the staff could use flags and signal lamps to communicate directly with the ships in the harbor from their third-floor windows.

Captain John Collins looked up, half scowling, as Jack was ushered into his office by a yeoman. A thickset man in his early fifties, he had the face of a bulldog, and his salt-and-pepper hair was cropped closed to his sun-blackened scalp. "You may sit down, Lieutenant," he said in a voice that was almost a growl. "What's this that Tom Bowers tells me about you wanting to steal *Houston*'s pom-poms?"

"I'm Gunnery Officer on *Jonathan B. Rust*, Captain..."

"I know who you are, Mister Sewell. Get on with it."

"You must know that the antiaircraft batteries on our old 'cans' are pretty pathetic, sir. We figure that the chances of *Houston* coming back to get the rest of her 1.1-inchers are almost nil. My Gunnery Chief has come up with a way to improvise single mounts for a couple of those pom-poms on *Rust*. It would give us at least some sort of chance against a dive bomber."

"None of you people over at Cavite has any business speculating on what we'll do with *Houston*," said Collins gruffly. "But since you're here, I might as well look at what you have in mind."

"Thank you, Captain." Spreading his sketches on Collins's desk, Jack outlined Chief Muldune's scheme for marrying the automatic antiaircraft guns with the old Spanish gun mounts. The captain asked all sorts of technical questions about gunsights, train and elevation controls and the system for circulating cooling water to the barrels. Having prepared himself well, Jack was able to field all the queries to Collins's satisfaction.   "Ingenious," Collins finally commented. "You say a chief gunner's mate figured all this out?"

"That's right, sir. Chief Muldune's my leading chief."

"I like his initiative. Where do you propose to mount the guns?"

Jack produced a diagram of the planned positions on either side of the smokestacks.

"Uhmmm....," the captain sighed as he contemplated the drawing. Then he pushed a button on his desk intercom. A few minutes later, a commander in immaculate whites came into the room. Jack had met the newcomer before. He was Harry Slocum, the Asiatic Fleet Operations Officer.

"This young pirate wants me to give him the pom-poms *Houston* left behind," Collins said to Slocum. "He's half convinced me to let him mount them aboard *Rust*. Do you think the cruisers will come back?"

"I figure the odds are at least fifty-fifty that we'll be at war within a month," Slocum replied, stroking his chin thoughtfully. "If that happens, we won't see the cruisers again until the Battle Fleet gets here from Pearl Harbor."

"Very succinctly put. Thanks, Harry. That'll be all." After Slocum had left, Collins rang up his yeoman. "Get Commander Bowers at Cavite on the line." Collins turned back to Jack. "I'm going to give you those guns, Mister Sewell. If those Jap Bastards do attack us, I'll expect you to shoot down at least a dozen of their planes in the first week. Now get the hell back to Cavite and prepare to fight."

"Aye, aye, Captain," Jack replied, grinning broadly. "And thank you."

Jack arrived at the shipyard a little after noon. As he climbed the tall ladder to *Rust*'s weather deck, it struck him as odd that there were no civilian yard workers around the marine railway. The ruined screw had been removed and carted away, leaving the nub of the propeller shaft looking obscenely bare. When he got to the quarterdeck, Jack asked the OOD what was happening.

"Some goof-up back in the States," Ensign Brown replied. The chubby, baby-faced officer was one of Jack's subordinates, in charge of the torpedo battery. "Cavite only had one destroyer screw. The manufacturer bored the hole for the shaft too small. They had to take it back to the shop to redrill it. Looks like we'll be stuck up here for a couple of days."

"Damn," Jack swore, looking over the immobile ship. If war did break out without warning, *Rust* would be a sitting duck for any Japanese planes that got through to Manila. He resolved to get the new sky guns mounted in record time.

After changing into khakis in his cabin, Jack made for the gun platforms to inspect the progress of Muldune's working parties. He was pleased to find all the structures finished except for painting. Muldune himself was not around. Gunner's Mate First Class Travers, one of Jack's gun captains, told him that the chief was at the shops checking on the improvised gun mounts. He also passed the word that the last of the .50-caliber machine guns from the ammo dump had been delivered during the morning.

"Go ahead and set them up," Jack ordered. "We can paint all this stuff later. Right now, the sooner we're ready to shoot, the better I'll like it."

During the two additional days that *Rust* remained in drydock, the harbor continued to fill with merchant ships until over forty were swinging on their hooks in the broad bay. A surprising number of Navy ships were still in port. The fleet tankers, *Trinity* and *Pecos*, had yet to join the general exodus of surface ships. The "four-pipers," *John D. Ford* and *Pope*, remained behind to help convoy the auxiliaries out when the time came. There was a veritable flock of minesweepers, but these were part of the Inshore Patrol, the unit designated to protect the Army's seaward flanks. Work continued around the clock at the shipyard. *Peary* and *Pillsbury* required extensive repairs for damage suffered in their recent collision. Two big fleet-class submarines were under overhaul, and numerous smaller ships were in some stage of maintenance or refit.

Rumors were rife around Cavite. Jack discovered that the most accurate information came through the CPO grapevine. On the morning of December 4th, the day that *Rust's* new screw was due to be fitted, Chief Muldune came to see Jack right after morning quarters.

"Looks like the shit's about to hit the fan, Lieutenant," Muldune began. "I was over to the Chiefs' Club at Sangley Point last night. Ran into an 'Airdale' chief I used to know in San Diego. Old Buz says that PatWing Ten is flyin' patrols every day now, all the way to Indochina in the west and Formosa up north."

"Maybe they're running drills to sharpen their crews."

"Practice, hell, Mister Sewell!" Muldune snorted. "Them boys have been flyin' neutrality patrols for over two years. Practice is the last thing they need. There's somethin' else that's even scarier."

"What's that, Chief?"

"There's a big harbor over in Indochina called Camrahn Bay. Day before yesterday, there was a whole bunch of Jap transport ships and destroyers there, with more on the way in."

"They could be beefing up their Indochina garrison. They're trying to cut the Burma Road to China."

"Buz says the intelligence boys don't think so. The troops ain't goin' ashore. They could be headin' for Thailand or Malaya, or they could come this way."

"They'd never make it across the South China Sea. Our subs and the Air Corps' B-17's would cut them to pieces."

"Maybe so, Lieutenant, but I ain't seen one of them Flying Fortresses sink no ship yet. Something's sure up with the Japs. Their recon planes are comin' over every day to check out the Philippine coast. They stop just out over international waters. PatWing Ten is keepin' watch on them. Both sides are mannin' their guns. Sooner or later, somebody's trigger finger is gonna get itchy.

"Anyway, what I really wanted to see you about is this ban on liberty. A couple of the guys who came over with me from *Toland* have got 'bamboo families' over in Manila. Those guys need to get home and make arrangements for their people. We could be pullin' out of here any day, and who knows when we'll get back?"

"Who are you talking about, Chief?" asked Jack, searching his conscience. He really didn't approve of sailors having common-law marriages with the locals.

"Jennings and McAndrews, sir."

Jack pondered for a moment. They were two of his best petty officers. "You're not afraid they'll go AWOL?"

"Not them boys. Hell, Lieutenant, me and old Jennings was together on *Toland* for over ten years."

"I'll speak to the Exec," said Jack, his mind made up. "When can you spare them?"

"Most anytime, sir. The new fifties is all in place, and we'll get the 1.1-inchers this morning."

The yard workers showed up at ten that morning with the new screw. Lieutenant Anderson came himself to see to the fitting of the propeller onto *Rust's* naked shaft. The Filipino riggers handled the several tons of bronze expertly, using a truck-mounted crane to lift it off the lowboy trailer, then swinging it smoothly into place with the crane boom and tag lines. A big forklift with a pusher pad mounted on the front shoved the screw onto the shaft.

Just as the crane was finishing its work with the propeller, another heavy truck rumbled up alongside the tracks of the marine railway. Muldune met the driver, for he was delivering the remounted 1.1-inch antiaircraft guns. Leaning over the railing of the midships deckhouse, Jack saw that the weapons looked just like the sketches he had shown Captain Collins. Overgrown machine guns, they were fed from the top by box magazines. Sporting a new coat of haze gray paint, the old Spanish gun mounts on which the 1.1-inchers were slung looked appropriate. Muldune personally supervised the rigging and lifting of the guns to the new platforms flanking the funnels.

"Ain't they purty, Lieutenant?" the chief commented after the 1.1's were bolted into place.

"Gorgeous," Jack responded, admiring the professional job that the Cavite shops had done on the sky guns. Once strapped to the curved shoulder stocks, a gunner could spin and elevate the spring-balanced pieces with ease.

"I'll feel better when we get some ammo for these babies aboard," Muldune continued.

"Commander Bowers promised us 4,000 rounds."

"That won't go far when we start pumping it up at the Japs. By the way, Jennings and McAndrews can take off to catch the late ferry to Manila. We're going back into the water tomorrow morning, then moving to Sangley Point to take on fuel. They can meet us there at 1600."

"Thank you, Mister Sewell. I appreciate you goin' to bat for them. They'll be back on time."

Jack was the Officer of the Deck the following morning when the yardworkers completed their preparations to put *Rust* back in the water. Jim Thomas had fired his boilers earlier, and steam was already up. Tom Hoskins came to the bridge and took the con just before the undocking began. On Dick Anderson's signal, the ancient railway carriage slowly inched down the rails, creaking and banging as it went. From the bridge, the ship appeared to be racing backwards. In fact, the movement was deliberate and under full control. *Rust*'s screws and rudder slipped smoothly beneath the surface of the harbor, then buoyancy lifted the stern, stretching the thin bottom plates as her hull flexed like a bridge beam. Two yard tugs put their padded bows against her sides to hold her steady as the carriage angled on down beneath the water, freeing her stem at last.

"Signal the tugs to stand clear," Hoskins ordered. "Both back, slow. Rudder amidships."

The engine-order telegraph jangled loudly as the quartermaster moved its pointer to the directed position. *Rust* vibrated gently as her turbines and shafts came to life. The screws bit into the water and began to draw the ship away from the land. Ashore, she had seemed an inert hulk of metal. Back in the water, she was a living soul again.

"Well, Jerry," Hoskins said to the Exec, "are we ready to fight?"

"We may be just a bunch of Reservists, Captain," Busch replied, "but if there's a 'can' in DesRon 29 in better shape for battle, I'll eat the proverbial hat."

"We'll soon find out," said Hoskins, no element of doubt in his voice.

Later that afternoon, while *Rust* filled her bunkers at the Sangley Point fuel pier, Jack watched with interest as Gunner's Mate Second Class Jennings explained the workings of the starboard 1.1-incher to his five-man crew. One would never have guessed from his demeanor that the man had just said goodbye to a family he might never see again.

Chief Muldune touched Jack's arm and pointed toward the air station boat landing. "Ain't that Admiral Hart's barge pullin' in, sir?"

Jack raised the powerful binoculars that hung from his neck and focused on the boat. The four-star flag of a full admiral was fluttering from its staff. "You're right, Chief. Wonder why he's over here?"

As if in answer to Jack's question, the drone of a large airplane swept up the bay from the south. A PBY bearing RAF markings passed over the pier, then circled and made a perfect landing on the water. Taxiing straight to one of the wide seaplane ramps, the Catalina put out its wheels and rolled up the incline to the adjacent parking apron. As Jack watched with fascination, a diminutive figure in a white uniform deplaned through the passenger hatch. Through his glasses, he could see that the man wore the sway-backed shoulder boards of a Royal Navy admiral.

"Well, I'll be damned," Jack muttered.

"Who is it, Lieutenant?" Muldune inquired.

"There's only one British admiral that small. It's 'Tom Thumb' Phillips, the naval commander from Singapore."

"You mean the guy that just came out in *Prince of Wales* and *Repulse*? What's he doin' in Manila?"

"Your guess is as good as mine, but it looks like trouble to me."

"That's a sure bet. They're not likely to cut us in on their business, anyway."

Neither the men on *Rust* nor those on the other ships in port would learn the details of the conference which took place that night and the following day at Sangley Point. Admiral Hart hosted the meeting, supported by Rear Admiral William Purnell, his chief of staff, and Rear Admiral Francis Rockwell, Commandant of the 16th Naval District. Rear Admiral William Glassford, just in from Shanghai with the last of the Yangtze River Patrol gunboats, joined the group on the morning of the sixth. They held a wide-ranging discussion of the military situation in Asia and began cooperative action to prepare for the worst. Phillips astounded Hart with the assertion that Washington had promised him the immediate support of two Asiatic Fleet destroyer divisions. Only four destroyers had come out from England with his battle force, far too few to screen the capital ships.

Lieutenant General MacArthur came in for a few hours to expound at length on the massive reinforcements in aircraft he had been promised by the following April, an armada of over two hundred and fifty bombers and two hundred P-40's. Admiral Hart responded that the real question at the moment was the present defensibility of the islands. The picture was far from rosy. The Far East Air Force had just twenty-five B-17's and about a hundred P-40's to defend the entire Philippine chain. MacArthur's ground forces were totally inadequate, only 22,000 trained troops of the crack Philippine Division and 100,000 raw recruits. Nevertheless, the general remained confident that he could meet the invader at the beaches and throw him back into the sea.

Throughout December 6th, a pall of uncertainty hung over the discussions. The American reconnaissance planes had been unable to penetrate heavy weather blanketing Indochina for the last two days. Briefing the flag officers, Captain Frank Wagner of PatWing 10 confirmed that the location of the huge Japanese convoy which had been in Camrahn Bay earlier that week was now unknown. The force could already be poised to strike at several points in Southeast Asia, but none of the potential victims could be sure until either the weather broke or the impending blow struck home.

CHAPTER 9

(One)
Aboard USS *Marblehead*
Tarakan Roadstead
Borneo, Netherlands East Indies
5 December 1941

"Now hear this! Now hear this!" the public address system blared irreverently in *Marblehead*'s wardroom. Frank Rhea, Eddie Blessman and Tonto looked up from their game of gin rummy. "Lieutenant Rhea, report to the bridge immediately."

"Damn," Frank swore, throwing down a sure-win hand. "Wonder what it'll be this time."

"Probably an antisubmarine patrol," said Blessman. "What are you griping about? At least you'll have the chance to get out of this heat."

"Yeah, *Kimo Sabe*," Tonto put in. "I'm all for that. You can volunteer us for a mission if they don't have one laid on."

"Those old *Seagulls* won't climb high enough to get up where it's really cool," Frank responded as he picked up his flying helmet and Mae West life preserver. His khakis were stained with sweat where they had been pressed between chair and skin.

The heat was the most frequent topic of conversation aboard *Marblehead*. Tarakan was less than three degrees off the equator, and the temperature inside the cruiser's hull was hovering around 105 degrees Fahrenheit. The humidity was almost one hundred percent.

Frank headed up a series of companionways to the bridge at the top of the ship's armored conning tower. Commander Goggins was not waiting patiently. His hooded eyes flared as Frank reported. A former instructor at the Naval Academy, Goggins believed it his mission to turn every junior officer under his command into a potential admiral. He placed punctuality next to godliness.

"You took your time," Goggins snapped.

"Sorry, Commander. I got here as fast as I could."

The Exec was sweating profusely despite his "River Rat" Whites. "I have something different for you today. *Whipple's* blown a bearing in her main gyroscope, and none of the ships here have a spare. The closest one's in *Black Hawk*, down in Balikpapan. The Captain decided to send a plane for it, and you're elected. Take Tonto along and check the coast for Jap subs on the way. The Dutch Navy's reported unidentified submarines in Makassar Strait."

"That's a long haul, Commander," Jack commented. "Do I come back this evening?"

"Remain overnight on *Black Hawk* and return tomorrow. In a way, I envy you the chance to get away from this hell hole for awhile." Goggins eyed the muddy waters of the harbor and the jungle shores hemming it in.

Marblehead was swinging on her hook in the roadstead off Tarakan Island. Fabled for crude oil so pure that it could be burned in boilers without first being refined, Tarakan conjured up visions of a tropical paradise. In fact, the heart-shaped island was a land of jungle-shrouded mud. The trees had been leveled by the Dutchmen to clear space for hundreds of oil wells and scores of storage tanks. Tarakan Town, where most of the Europeans resided, was a mile and a half inland, hidden behind the forest. Only the port of Linghas was visible from the roadstead. Industrially functional, its most impressive features were the massive oil tanks. From the muddy shoreline, a fuel-loading pier stretched far out across the shallows to the deep water of the harbor. The berths were all occupied by hungry tankers of *Bataafache Petroleum Maatschappij*. The business of oil took precedence over the looming threat of war. Besides *Marblehead*, the destroyers, *Whipple*, *Alden*, *John D. Ford*, *Edwards* and *Edsall* were also anchored out in the stream.

Finding Tonto waiting by the port catapult, Frank filled him in on the flight plan.

"How far is it to Balikpapan," the Seminole asked.

"Four hundred miles. We'll have to cross the equator to get there."

"You a 'shellback,' *Kimo Sabe*?"

"You won't get the pleasure of initiating me. I crossed the line twice in the Atlantic. Better pack a musette bag for tonight. Meet me here in fifteen minutes."

Frank made a quick pass by his stateroom, throwing a change of khakis, some skivvies and his shaving gear into an overnight bag. When he returned to the deck, Tonto was already standing over the forward cockpit of their *Seagull*, guiding the plane boom hook into the lifting slings on the upper wing. With no wind across the decks, a catapult launch would be dicey. They would have to take off from the water.

"She's ready to go, Boss," said Tonto as Frank climbed up beside him. "I've checked her out real good since we've been in port. She'll be smooth as glass."

"Great," Frank responded. "Let's get this show on the road." He dropped into his cockpit, and Tonto took the observer's seat in the back. The big aircraft boom plucked the little biplane off the catapult and set it gently down in the water. Tonto unhooked the slings, stowed them in a hatch in the top wing, then resumed his seat.

"Ready back there?" asked Frank over the intercom.

"Ready, *Kimo Sabe*."

Frank engaged the starter, and the two-bladed propeller began to spin as the engine caught. The Wright radial was as smooth as a kitten's purr. Tonto's reputation as the best aircraft mechanic in the Asiatic Fleet was well deserved.

Only a slight breeze was blowing in from the Sesajap River to the north. Giving the Dutch minefields a wide berth, Frank taxied almost to the south shore before swinging back into the wind and pouring on power. The floatplane gathered speed rapidly as it skimmed across the harbor. Then came the characteristic bump as the main float broke free of the water, and the aerodynamic lift of the wings rocketed the *Seagull* skyward. Frank dipped the right wing tips, putting her into a tight turn to the south while continuing to climb. As they flew across Tarakan, the tidy streets of the Dutch city contrasted starkly with the surrounding jungle.

With the cockpit canopy open, the heavy, moist air buffeted Frank's face, a not unpleasant sensation as long as his goggles protected his eyes. The higher the *Seagull* climbed, the cooler grew the air. Five thousand feet up, the sticky discomfort of the equatorial climate had all but vanished. Enjoying himself immensely, Frank reflected that only men who have flown could comprehend the calming peacefulness of the sky.

"Hey, Lone Ranger," Tonto's voice in his headphones broke Frank's reverie. "You awake up there?"
"This thing doesn't fly itself."
"They really expect us to find any Jap subs down here?"
"Could be. With their warships and convoys all over the South China Sea, they might have something over here too."
"Okay. I'll keep a sharp lookout."
The view along the Borneo coast was monotonous. For long stretches, there were no beaches, only a clean line where the lush growth of the mangrove swamps met the brilliant blue of the sea. Farther out, the white froth of churning water marked the coral reefs that made the eastern shore of the big island a mariner's nightmare. Occasionally, they flew over tiny offshore islands scattered like emerald studs on the azure surface of the ocean. Sixty miles south of Tarakan, the *Seagull* cruised high above their first checkpoint, the tiny village of Tandjung Batu.

An hour into the flight, a barrier of land running far out to the east crept up over the horizon. Frank recognized the mountainous finger of Cape Mangkalihat, which funneled the waters of the Celebes Sea into Makassar Strait to the south. The cape was shaped like the pendulous breast of an aged woman, complete with a withered nipple.

Despite the coolness of the outside air, the sun beat down unmercifully into the cockpit. Frank mused that he would be sunburned by now if his skin were not already nut-brown from swimming almost nude in the sea for several months. Admiral Hart had kept the fleet deployed on maneuvers almost constantly since he reported to *Marblehead,* and the fliers from the cruisers often swam and picnicked on the beaches of the remote anchorages they frequented. He was getting very thirsty now, so he slid the canopy shut and fumbled with his thermos bottle. The coffee tasted good, and he could feel the stimulus of the caffeine seeping out through his limbs. But by the time he finished the cup, the greenhouse effect had pushed the temperature inside the closed cockpit up several degrees. He was glad to cap the thermos, pull down his goggles, and slide the canopy open again.

"Hey, Boss," Tonto called over the intercom, "if this chart's right, I figure we just crossed the equator."

"You're right, *amigo*. We're in the Southern Hemisphere now."

Checkpoints were few and far between as they cruised on down the coast. Civilization in Borneo went inland only as far as the Dutch found it profitable. In the vast interior of the island, the jungle Dyaks lived more or less as they had for centuries. The two aviators kept up a steady banter over the intercom to fight off boredom.

Out over Makassar Strait, the weather began building up, a common afternoon occurrence in the tropics. The sun evaporated tons of water from the surface of the sea and sent it boiling up into the heavens with rising hot air to form thunderheads.

"We're gonna have to race that storm," Tonto observed. "How long 'til Balikpapan?"

"Another thirty minutes. That was the Mahakan River we just passed. There's a town about forty miles upriver called Samarinda. The Dutch are supposed to have an airfield nearby."

Frank's estimated time of arrival proved accurate. About fifteen minutes after Tonto's query, the coast began to fall away to the west. Frank turned the *Seagull* and followed the coastline. There were real beaches here where the shore ran east and west--brilliant white ribbons of coral sand. Switching on his transmitter, he tried to raise flight control at Sepingyang Airfield to get landing instructions. The replies came back in Dutch. Finally, an Oxford English voice told him to put down in the bay north of the city, giving a stern warning about mines around the harbor entrance.

Frank could see Balikpapan Bay now, a long, thin finger of water pointing inland to the north. From the air, it resembled a Scandinavian fiord. At least three large rivers fed the bay. Broad, palm fringed beaches bordered the sea here, and the orderly streets and hipped-roofed white houses of the Dutch suburb of Klandasan contrasted with the jumble of the native quarter to the south. Steep, tree clad ridges separated the residential areas from the industrial port inside the bay. There was a slight wind blowing up the fiord, so he decided to land from north to south.

The layout of the great oil center beneath them unfolded as the *Seagull* rapidly lost altitude. It sprawled along the eastern shore of the lower bay for over a mile. The huge refinery was pumping tons of steam into the sky. Six tanker piers jutted into the stream from a shoreline and slopes covered for hundreds of yards inland with countless ugly oil tanks. Frank recognized the familiar shape of the destroyer tender, *Black Hawk*, moored to the most northern of the three general cargo wharves. Nested two abreast, four slender `cans' of Destroyer Division 57 occupied the other berths at the pier.

Frank dropped low over the wooded hills to the east of the town, which were sprinkled with large estate houses. Concentrating on his turn, he failed to see the largest of these as the *Seagull* skimmed a scant three hundred feet overhead.

"Damn, *Kimo Sabe*," said Tonto, "did you get a look at the layout we just passed?"

"That's a negative. What did I miss?"

"Must be the palace of the king of Balikpapan. Looked like a big plantation house back home in Florida. You also missed a couple of pretty girls in the driveway."

"Maybe I should go back."

"You'll fly right into that storm if you do. Let's get this bird down into the water."

Frank made a perfect landing in the long bay, then taxied straight to *Black Hawk*. One of her boats led them to the Dutch seaplane base, where they moored the *Seagull* to a buoy. Just as the fliers boarded the tender's boat, the bottom dropped out of the sky, drenching everyone aboard in a tropical downpour. By the time they reached *Black Hawk's* accommodation ladder, Frank was soaked to the skin. Since he was senior officer in the boat, he left first, sprinting up the ladder. He saluted the ensign that hung limply on the fantail staff.

"Request permission to come aboard, sir" he mumbled at the OOD, then stepped onto the sheltered quarterdeck before the jaygee had a chance to respond. Tonto arrived seconds behind him.

"Welcome to *Black Hawk*, Mister Rhea," said the OOD. "I'm Bob Lee. The Exec wants you to come down to his office right away. The messenger will show you where to go."

"Hang onto my dry clothes," Frank said to Tonto. "Meet you in the wardroom as soon as I can."

The messenger led Frank through a maze of ladders and passageways to an office with the title, "Executive Officer," engraved on its brass plate. Frank rapped on the steel door.

"Come in," came a familiar voice from within.

As Frank entered the compartment, he recognized Tom Chase, the officer with whom he'd shared the Catalina ride to Tawi-Tawi. Chase was wearing shiny new lieutenant commander's oak leaves on his collar.

"My God, Frank, you look like a drowned rat," said Chase, getting up from his chair and extending his hand.

"Feel like one, too. Good to see you again, sir."

"It's still Tom to you. How about some coffee?"

"I could use it. You sure you don't mind me dripping water all over your deck?"

"We'll get you some dry duds in a minute," Chase said as he poured coffee into two mugs and handed one to Frank. "As a matter of fact, that's why you're here right now. I've got to get you sized up in dress whites. All the officers are going to a party ashore tonight, and the Skipper wants you and Tonto to join in the fun. What's your uniform size?"

"Forty-two coat, thirty-four trousers."

"You're in luck. We're two peas from the same pod. I'll loan you my spare whites, and I still have my old lieutenant shoulder boards. You'll have to spring for a pair of shoes from the ship's store."

"That's no strain. Who's throwing this shindig?"

"The local Controlleur—that's what they call their mayor. All the officers in the division are going. Should be quite an affair. The bigwigs of the town will all be there."

"Sounds like fun." Frank could barely contain his glee. If she were still in Balikpapan, Cinta was almost certain to be at the party. "What about the gyro part I came to get?"

"It's all crated and ready to go. You can be off in the morning as soon as you want."

Outfitted in borrowed "choker-neck" whites, Frank and Tonto left their cabin a little before six that evening and joined *Black Hawk's* officers in the wardroom. Commander Harris, the Captain, said a few words about decorum and diplomacy to be observed with the locals. Then the group filed toward the gangway. Officers were already swarming onto the big pier from the nearby destroyers. The afternoon thunderstorm was long gone. Tropical stars sparkled brightly in the evening sky, but the air was moist and permeated with the rank smell of crude oil. Dutch military busses waited at the head of the pier, and it took but a few moments for the Americans to file aboard. Then, with engines growling and gearshifts squealing, the caravan set out for the Dutch club.

While the officers of DesDiv 57 were preparing to rub elbows with Balikpapan society, the conference in Manila was drawing to a close. Lieutenant General MacArthur left after confirming joint Army-Navy reconnaissance plans. Hart and Phillips came to a general agreement on future cooperation between the Asiatic Fleet and the Royal Navy.

One of Phillips's aides entered the room and handed him a dispatch. The admiral's face clouded as he scanned the words.

"Read it aloud," he ordered the aide.

"It's a signal from the high command at Singapore," the lieutenant began. "The missing Japanese convoy has been sighted by the RAF at latitude eight degrees north, longitude one oh four degrees east. Course is two sixty-five degrees."

"That's headed straight for Malaya," said the suave Admiral Glassford.

"Or the neck of Thailand," said Phillips. "I should be at sea. I must signal my ships at once and then get back to Singapore."

"All my facilities are at your disposal," said Hart. "One more thing--about those destroyers you asked for. I'm sending a message to my closest destroyer division ordering them and a tender to proceed to Batavia. They can be in Singapore in two days if you need them."

Sounds of festivity were already spilling out of the high arched windows of the Dutch club when the busses bearing the Americans arrived. As he stepped down onto the gravel driveway, Frank saw that the place looked very like the Army-Navy Club in Manila. The spacious white stucco building was surrounded by wide verandahs and had rounded corners in the Art Decco fashion. The officers started sorting themselves out by rank to go through the receiving line. Frank was behind Tom Chase, and they joked about the time they had spent together in Manila as they shuffled through a paneled foyer to the entrance to a substantial ballroom. Polished teak floors reflected the light from electric chandeliers. The tall exterior walls were mostly windows, except for a long stretch of French doors on the side facing the seaward verandah.

Near the front wall, the reception line was strung out beneath large portraits of Queen Wilhelmina and Winston Churchill. On a raised platform, a small orchestra played crisp marches to speed the line along. As his eyes scanned the dignitaries, a stab of intense pleasure shot through Frank. With the bearing and poise of a royal princess, Cinta van Wely was smiling brightly as she greeted the guests. To Frank, she was a vision of loveliness.

"What's with you, Frank?" asked Chase. "You look like the cat that swallowed the canary."

"I just spotted someone I was afraid to hope would be here," Frank answered cheerfully. "I thought she'd be safe in Java or Australia by now."

CHAPTER 10

(One)
BPM Hospital
Klandasan, Borneo
Netherlands East Indies
5 December 1941

Cinta van Wely stripped off her rubber gloves and began to wash the perspiration from her hands and arms in the scrub sink. Still dressed in her operating cap and gown, her face showed the strain and fatigue of concentrated effort, but there was satisfaction there also. Catherine van Zweden, the competent young nurse who assisted Cinta in the operating room, was at the adjacent lavatory. They had just spent three hours working on a Canadian driller with third-degree burns over thirty percent of his body, a casualty of an oil field fire. When they finished washing, the two women put their soiled operating garments in a hamper and went to their lockers in the adjoining dressing room.

"If I may say so, Doctor," said Catherine in a soft alto voice as she donned her starched white uniform, "that was the most wonderful piece of medical magic I've ever witnessed."

"It's not magic, Catherine, just the cutting edge of medical technology. The approach was pioneered in Texas over four years ago."

"All the other doctors I've worked with would have removed the skin from the entire burned area."

"And probably sent him into fatal shock. The fundamental doctrine of Dutch medicine has always been, 'not cutting, healing.' Thank God that we continue to learn."

Cinta put on a white blouse and skirt, then sat down at a vanity to repair her hairdo before reaching for her compact. She applied makeup sparingly--a touch of powder to dull the sheen of her skin, a tiny bit of rouge for her cheeks and a subdued shade of lipstick. Then she returned to her locker for her white medical smock. Catherine was pinning up her long platinum blond hair, and her pale blue eyes held a lively twinkle.

"Would you like some coffee?" asked Cinta as she hung her stethoscope around her neck. "We've both earned a break."

"Yes, thank you, Doctor. I could use a pick-me-up."

Cinta's office was efficiently organized. She had a large polished teak desk and a bookcase for her medical library, cushioned rattan chairs for visitors, and a laboratory bench. A large ceiling fan whirled languidly overhead, keeping the room comfortably cool by pulling in air through floor level screened louvers.

Cinta asked Catherine to sit down, then lit a Bunsen burner and placed it under a decanter of water. Taking a bottle of coffee concentrate and two mugs from a cabinet, she measured a small amount of liquid into each mug and poured in the now-boiling water. After giving Catherine her drink, she sprawled back in one of the comfortable armchairs.

"Ummm," sighed Catherine as she sipped the steaming liquid. "Our Indies coffee has to be the best in the world."

"I quite agree," Cinta responded. "I must admit that I had an ulterior motive for asking you here. We should get to know one another better since we'll be working together a lot. Tell me about yourself."

"You flatter me, Doctor," Catherine said, clearly embarrassed. "There's really not much to tell." She was the daughter of a government clerk and the eldest of a family of three daughters and two sons. They grew up in Malang, Java, but her father recently transferred to Zwarte Goud for a promotion. The family budget was always tight, and she became a nurse only by winning a scholarship to the school in Soerabaja. She still sent money home.

"I sometimes wish that our family were larger," said Cinta wistfully. "There's just my sister, Alette, and me. Mama died when we were little girls, and Papa never remarried. I suppose he's married to BPM."

"Everybody knows your father. He's the oil rajah, the *Tuan Besar*."

"I am very proud of him." *As well I should be,* Cinta thought. Nicolaas van Wely had come out from Holland less than thirty years before almost penniless, but his brilliance as an engineer and astute management ability had been recognized early on by the directors of the oil empire. His rise to his current position of General Manager of all BPM operations at the mammoth Balikpapan oil field and refining complex had been meteoric. It was already rumored that he was being groomed for the job of Director General of the company when the current incumbent, Wilhelm Oosten, retired.

"Are you going to the party for the American Navy people tonight?" Cinta picked up the conversation.

"I don't think so. I wouldn't know anybody, and I really haven't anything to wear."

"You mustn't feel that way. The Americans are here to protect us, and they must be terribly lonely. Their commander sent their dependents home months ago."

"I realize that, Doctor. I'd like to go, but I wasn't joking about my skimpy wardrobe."

"Stand up and let me look at you." Cinta got up herself, measuring Catherine with her eyes. "We're about the same size. I have the perfect dress for you. It's white chiffon. All you'll need are your hose and some white pumps."

"But I wouldn't think of imposing..."

"Nonsense. Better yet, why don't you go to the party with Papa and me and then spend the night at our home? I'll charge you just one favor in return."

"It sounds delightful," said a bubbly Catherine. "What's the favor you want?"

"It's quite proper for you to call me 'Doctor' while we're on duty, but you must call me Cinta the rest of the time."

"I'll try, but it won't come easy. You don't realize what an inspiration you are to the nurses. You're the only woman doctor any of us have ever met."

"That's a lot to live up to." Cinta was somewhat taken aback. She checked her watch. "It's time for my rounds. I'll pick you up here after work."

"Are you sure that I'm not imposing?" Catherine asked when she met Cinta at the end of their shift. She was carrying a small suitcase.

"Of course not. I've warned Papa and the servants. To tell the truth, I've been dying for someone nearer my own age to talk to. I've nothing in common with most of the women I've met here."

They chatted pleasantly as they exited the solid white masonry building and walked out to the parking lot. Cinta guided her companion to a bright red LaSalle convertible Coupe.

"Papa has a weakness for fast machines," said Cinta. "He even flies his own plane."

"It's beautiful." Catherine exclaimed, fingering the leather upholstery.

A muted rumble of thunder rolled in from the east. Cinta raised her eyes and saw that tall thunderheads were building up over Makassar Strait. "We'd better hurry, or we'll get a bath from Mother Nature."

They hopped quickly into the low-slung car, and Cinta fired its powerful engine. A stiff ocean breeze whipped Catherine's hair about her eyes as Cinta turned out onto the black ribbon of asphalt that ran along the oceanfront. Within moments, the young nurse was in terror for her life. Clearly, Nicolaas van Wely was not the only one in his family who loved fast machines. His daughter drove like a maniac, pushing the Alfa up to dangerous speeds on the long straightaway. The palm trees along the road whipped by in a blur. Leafy tamarinde trees shaded the streets when they reached the Dutch residential area of Gundung Dubbs. Catherine did not relax until Cinta braked sharply and turned into a tree-lined lane that wound up the steep slopes of Parramatta Ridge. She stopped in the circular driveway of a rambling mansion surrounded by flaming hibiscus.

"What a marvelous view!" exclaimed Catherine as they got out of the car. From the front lawn, the land dropped away sharply, exposing a wide panorama of the city and the harbor.

"We'd better put up the top, or the car will get soaked," Cinta observed.

They were just finishing when an American Navy floatplane buzzed by close overhead. It skimmed down onto the water of the harbor just before the pregnant storm clouds spilled the first heavy raindrops onto the two women as they sprinted for the house. A liveried servant opened the massive door as they approached, giving them a stately bow as they dashed into the vestibule.

"Nurse van Zweden, this is our *mandur* (butler), Yuni," said Cinta formally. The man was tall for a Javanese, well over five feet. He was perhaps fifty years old. After bowing politely, he glided away to other duties. When he was out of earshot, Cinta added, "We don't address any of our male servants as *'jongos'* (boy). Papa thinks it demeaning. Your bedroom's this way."

With difficulty, Catherine kept from gawking at the opulence of the mansion. She had never before been in such luxurious surroundings.

A wizened old servant woman was waiting at the door to Cinta's bedroom.

"This is Ada, my *baboe*," Cinta said in introduction. "She practically raised me."

"And badly botched the job," Ada quipped as she bowed to Catherine. The nurse was surprised at her audacity.

"I like a snack in my room after my bath, especially when dinner will be late," Cinta continued. "Will you join me?"

"Gladly. I'm starved. I'm used to an early supper at the nurses' refectory."

"Good. Don't worry about dressing until afterwards. There aren't any men in the house except Yuni, and Ada would skin him alive if he came near our quarters. You have your choice of baths. There's a shower and European tub in my bathroom, or you could have a *gagoeng mandi* (dipper bath) in your bedroom. Ada could bring in a tub."

"I'll have the *mandi*. I haven't had one since I came up from Java."

Cinta undressed leisurely in her private bathroom. Encasing her hair in a rubber cap, she got into the shower and turned on the water. She stayed there for a long time, letting the firm liquid jets massage away the stresses of the day. Finally closing the valves with reluctance, she began to dry off with a thick towel.

"Cinta?" came Catherine's voice from the bedroom.

"I'm here. I'll be out in a minute." Cinta placed the towel on the rack and lifted a red batik sarong from the hook beside the shower. Expertly wrapping the garment about her hips, she secured it with a tuck beneath her navel.

Dressed in a seersucker bathrobe, Catherine was vigorously toweling her freshly washed, short blond hair when Cinta came back into the bedroom. "I don't know about that *baboe* of yours," she said through the terry cloth covering her face. "She offered to shave me after the bath, and I don't think she meant my legs. I did them myself yesterday..." she broke off in astonishment when she uncovered her eyes. Then she blushed bright scarlet.

"Do I embarrass you?" asked the bare-breasted Cinta. "If so, I'll put on a halter."

"Oh, no. Please don't," said the flustered Catherine. "It just startled me. Do you dress like that often?"

"When there aren't any men in the house. It's the most comfortable garment in the world. I put on a *kabaja* when Papa's around. Would you like to try a sarong?"

"Yes, why not?" Catherine was finding this lesson in how the rich lived very entertaining. But when Cinta got another sarong from her dresser and handed it to her, she modestly turned her back before shedding her robe. Cinta demonstrated how to wrap and secure the garment.

"I feel deliciously wicked," Catherine laughed. The unaccustomed kiss of air against her breasts caused her nipples to tighten and stand up.

"You should be proud of your body," said Cinta admiringly. Catherine had a magnificent figure, with flaring hips and high, firm breasts that hardly rippled when she walked. "Medical training opens one's eyes to what a marvelous creation the human body really is. God could not have meant such perfection to shame us."

"I never thought of it that way. I believe you're right."

"Let's get you outfitted for tonight." Cinta walked to the louvered doors of her closet. "This is what I had in mind for you." She lifted a long gown of white chiffon from the rack and handed it to Catherine.

"It's divine!" Catherine squealed with delight, clutching the dress to her as she ran to a full length, free standing mirror. She held it out and examined it closely. "What kind of a brassiere do you wear with this?" she asked, puzzled.

"You don't. It has built-in cups."

"Oh, I see. May I try it on?"

"Certainly."

Catherine stepped behind a Coromandel screen to change. She came out smiling broadly. The gown fit as if it had been tailored for her. She turned this way and that before the mirror, obviously pleased with what she saw. "Oh, Cinta, how can I ever thank you?" she said happily.

"By enjoying yourself tonight. Better take it off for now. Ada will be here in a few minutes with cakes and coffee."

"Ummm," said Catherine, biting into a muffin. "These are delicious. Did Ada make them?" They were seated at a gate-legged table on which rested a steaming silver pot of coffee and a tray of small cakes.

"Yes. She's a wizard in the kitchen. She can cook anything, European or Oriental."

"I think she meant to shave me all over after my bath."

"She did," Cinta laughed. "Ada's of the old school, South Asian variety. She was taught to view hair on a woman's body as distasteful. She's been after me about it for years. She also taught my sister and me the Javanese *Tantra*."

Catherine almost choked on her cake. "That's their lewd sex religion, isn't it?"

"More like a philosophy on sex than a religion. They do revere their *Serit Centani* somewhat like a communist might view the works of Marx. Anyway, it wasn't for me. Alette was Ada's *Kama* disciple." She remembered how fascinated she had been the first time she watched Alette stand nude before her mirror to stroke her body and chant a mantra.

"You mean she's not a Christian?" said Catherine, obviously horrified.

"I don't mean that at all. She's a Southern Baptist. Alette's the most sensuous person I know, but she's not promiscuous. She's very devoted to her family. You'll never find a more contented husband than Tommy Hawkins."

"She sounds like an interesting person. I'd like to meet her. Does she live in Java?"

"Her home's in Houston, Texas. Tommy's father's one of America's richest oil men."

"Oh, yes. I remember when they got married. It was front page news in Zwarte Gouden."

Nicolaas van Wely came storming into the house at just after half past seven. He'd been out at a new oil well all afternoon, and his bush jacket and slacks were soaked with sweat and stained with crude. Miraculously, he was knocking on Cinta's door fifteen minutes later, freshly showered, shaved and dressed in white dinner jacket and black tie.

"Are you decent, daughter?" his big voice boomed.

"Yes, Papa. Come in."

Cinta got up from her dressing table where she was finishing her makeup to kiss his cheek.

To Nicolaas, she looked utterly stunning. Her hair was a glistening frame for her lovely face. The emerald green rayon gown fitted her splendid body like a glove. He would have been happier if the halter bodice had less *décolletage*. It plunged deeply into the cleft between her full breasts and completely bared her back.

"You'll be the most beautiful woman there," he said proudly.

"You won't say that once you've met our guest," she replied with a smile.

When Catherine entered the room a moment later, Nicolaas had to agree that a beauty contest between them would have ended in a tie. Cinta introduced him to the young nurse.

"I'm honored to meet you, *Tuan Besar*," said Catherine, sweeping low in a curtsy.

"Nonsense, young lady. The pleasure is all mine. I'll be the envy of every man at the reception, escorting two beauties. You must tell me about yourself on the way. If we don't get moving, we'll be more than fashionably late."

Yuni drove them to the party in Nicolaas's company car, a white Cadillac. The three of them fit comfortably in the rear seat, and Nicolaas insisted on sitting in the middle. Catherine found him utterly charming and surprisingly witty. He had vitality and exuded masculinity. She soon thought of him as a jungle cat, sleek, handsome and powerful. How could he have remained a widower for over twenty years? He could surely have his pick of any woman in the Indies.

When they arrived at the club, Nicolaas took Cinta on his left arm and Catherine on his right before entering the rapidly filling ballroom. Everyone who counted in Balikpapan society appeared to be there, the men in white dinner jackets or dress uniforms, the women in evening gowns. All were conversing avidly and drinking cocktails. A hoard of white-uniformed servants circulated about the room, offering fresh drinks and collecting empty glasses.

Nicolaas got each of the young women a rum punch, then led them across the room to where the dignitaries were gathering to form a reception line beneath life-sized portraits of Queen Wilhelmina and Winston Churchill.

"Ah, good evening, Nicolaas," said the towering Controlleur Woltz. He was known as a great eater, and his bulk confirmed it. He was wearing his dark blue uniform with a gold lace embroidered Prussian collar. An ivory-hilted sword hung at his side. "You're just in time. The busses with the Americans should arrive shortly. And I'm delighted to see you, Cinta. Who's this young lady you've brought along?"

"My nursing assistant from the hospital. May I present Nurse Catherine van Zweden."

"I'm most pleased to meet you, Nurse. This is my wife..."

The introductions were made with great formality. If anything, *Mevrouw* Woltz was fatter than her husband, and she lacked his heavy bone structure to carry weight gracefully. Haughty and disdainful, she looked down on anyone not of pure white ancestry. Cinta disliked her intensely.

The Controlleur asked Nicolaas to join him in the reception line and insisted that both young women do likewise. Cinta stood next to Colonel Rotteveel, the local military commander. He had a reputation as a tough bush campaigner, but she knew him as a cultured gentleman who cared deeply for the welfare of his men. They were chatting amicably when the major domo announced that the Americans were arriving.

Aware that the U.S. Navy was strong on protocol, Cinta was not surprised that they trooped through the receiving line in strict order of seniority. First came the ramrod-straight Commander Harris, then Commander E.M. Crouch, the "Commodore" of DesDiv 57. The Captains of the destroyers were next in line. She was shaking hands with a lieutenant commander named Chase when a familiar voice galvanized her attention.

"Doctor van Wely and I are acquainted," the man was telling Rotteveel. "We went to college together."

Cinta turned to find herself face to face with Frank Rhea. "Frank, what a marvelous surprise!" she exclaimed in surprise, smiling broadly. "I had no idea you'd be here tonight."

"I didn't know myself until two hours ago." He was beaming with pleasure. "I flew down from Tarakan to get a part for one of our `cans.' We've got to talk later."

"Of course. I'll ask Papa to get you put at our table."

"I'll count on it."

Then he was gone, leaving her with her heart up in her throat and her pulse pounding in her ears. She took a deep breath and went on shaking hands and making small talk with the junior officers, but she scarcely noticed their presence.

When the reception line broke up, Cinta found Frank with a swarthy-skinned warrant officer talking to Jan Kuyper, the young Assistant Controlleur, and his placid, fair-haired wife.

"Come join us, Cinta," said the dapper Kuyper. "These two gentlemen were just telling us about their quaint nicknames."

"Nothin' quaint about it," said the Native American. "Ever since I was a Seaman Deuce, nobody could pronounce my real name. 'Tonto' was the moniker they hung on me in boot camp, and it stuck. Since I took up flyin', my pilot's always been called..."

"The Lone Ranger?" Cinta interjected.

"Yup, Ma'am," Frank affected a mock western drawl, "you hit the nail on the head."

Cinta burst out laughing. "That's precious," she finally said when she'd caught her breath. "It fits you, Frank, the crusader riding out to fight the forces of evil."

Frank just grinned back at her.

"I wouldn't go that far," said Tonto, "but he's a damned good pilot."

"Well, Mister Coacooche," Cinta continued after formal introductions, "I won't get your name wrong. Since I was born and raised out here in the Indies, I'm used to even more complicated ones."

"I'd just as soon you called me Tonto, Doc. That's what I'm used to."

"All right, if you prefer."

A trumpet sounded a little fanfare, and conversation in the ballroom died down. The major domo solemnly announced that dinner was about to be served. Controlleur Woltz led the procession into a sumptuous banquet room, and Commander Crouch followed with the stocky *Mevrouw* Woltz on his arm. Still squiring Catherine, Nicolaas was among the first to go in.

Unerringly, Cinta guided Frank through the confusion to her father's table, one of dozens of rattan pieces with matching chairs. It was near the Controlleur's, where most of the senior people were congregating. Each table was set with rice China, sparkling crystal glasses, and full silver service. A perfect host, Nicolaas made sure that everyone was introduced. He placed Frank between himself and Cinta.

"Lieutenant Rhea knew my daughter in California," Nicolaas remarked to the others.

"We were good friends at UCLA," Frank said respectfully.

"I'm pleased that you've come. Cinta doesn't get the chance to see many young people here in Balikpapan. Have you had our *rijsttafel* before?"

"No, sir. I'm not sure what it is."

"You're in for a treat."

"It means 'rice table,'" Cinta explained. "As a doctor, I must warn you not to eat too fast. There'll be about twenty courses."

"Sounds like my kind of meal," said Tonto, who was seated across the table.

After the minister of the local Dutch Reformed Church said grace, dinner began. An army of white-liveried waiters descended on the tables, each bearing bowls of rice or toppings and frosty bottles of good Dutch beer. Frank quickly lost count of the dishes he consumed. The waiters served stewed vegetables, beef, several chicken dishes, and skewered pork cubes with peanut sauce. Sweet courses followed, with delicate fruits and spices. He improvidently tried a bite of rice soaked with scorching *sambal* sauce and had to drain his glass of beer to quench the fire.

Nicolaas laughed heartily at his distress. "You'd make a good colonial, Lieutenant," said the Dutchman. "Anyone who can eat like that is a brother to us."

"I'd soon grow out of my uniform." Tom Chase's trousers were already uncomfortably tight about Frank's waist.

"Don't try to change him, Papa," Cinta chided. "I rather like him the way he is."

"I understand that you're an engineer," said Nicolaas, changing the subject.

"That's right, sir. An aeronautical engineer."

"How do you happen to be in the Navy? I'd think that you'd be more valuable to America designing new airplanes."

"That's what I was doing when I got my mobilization orders, but I didn't want to sit out a war at a drafting table. I'd rather be in the thick of it."

"I'm afraid you'll get your chance all too soon." Nicolaas went on to ask several questions about Frank's plans for after the war: where he would live, what sort of work he wanted to do, what his ultimate goals in life were.

"Quit pumping Frank like a potential suitor," Cinta finally scolded. "He's just a friend."

Wrapped in a heady sense of contentment, Frank heard her words but refused to accept them. He had pushed Cinta to the back of his mind since the previous summer by concentrating on his work. Now, the certainty that she was the only woman he would ever love had returned.

After the sumptuous meal was washed down with countless bottles of beer, the major domo announced dancing in the ballroom. Frank started the first waltz with Cinta, but a lieutenant commander cut in after a few steps. It was over an hour before he was able to recapture her from a countless stream of partners.

"I'm about to strangle in this borrowed uniform," he commented after they had danced for a while. "Could we go somewhere and get some fresh air?"

"All right. There's another verandah on the other side. Follow me."

Cinta led Frank through the fringes of the crowd to a line of open French doors. A moment later, they were out under the stars on a wide porch, where ocean breezes cooled the air. A waning moon provided just enough light to see by. He lit a cigarette.

"You look fit," she said, leaning against a masonry column. "You're darker than I've ever seen you."

"I've been swimming off half the beaches in the Philippines. What about you? Is being a doctor everything you'd hoped?"

"Even more. I saved a man's life this morning. There's nothing in the world to compare with that." Her eyes misted at the thought.

"I'm glad you got what you wanted. By the way, do you know that you're beautiful in the moonlight?"

"I'll bet that you say that to all the girls," she quipped, trying to keep the conversation lighthearted.

"I've done a lot of thinking since last summer. I know now how important your work is to you. You could have both medicine and me, if you wanted."

"I believe you're proposing to me again," she said tenderly, touching his cheek with her hand, "but I still must refuse. I told you on the Clipper that I'm married to medicine. I'm afraid I can only handle one marriage at a time."

"At least think about it, Cinta. Remember that I'm one love you can always count on."

"You've got to put such thoughts from your mind!" She was almost pleading now, her voice quivering. "You're wasting precious time you could be spending with someone who could really make you happy."

"You're the only one who'll ever matter to me," he said, shaking his head. Then he tossed his cigarette away and caught her by the shoulders, abruptly pulling her into his arms. She stiffened in surprise and started to resist, but he smothered her protests with his lips, kissing her hungrily. Then some dam deep within her shattered, and she returned his kiss with equal ferver.

Just then, a trumpet sounded, "attention."

"Could I have your attention, please," Commander Crouch's voice boomed through the open doors. "I've just been handed a message ordering our ships to sea immediately." He gave a short speech thanking the Dutch for their hospitality and expressing regret at having to abandon the party. Controlleur Woltz responded with a short farewell. Then the Americans began shaking hands and filing toward the door.

"Must you go, too?" asked Cinta, a touch of despair in her voice. She was still trembling from the passion of their embrace.

"I'll need to get my cargo and gear off *Black Hawk*," Frank said with reluctance. "I'll have to fly back to *Marblehead* at first light. This could mean war at any moment. What are your contingency plans?"

"Papa intends to fly me to Australia. He has a personal plane, a

Lockheed *Lodestar*."

"Get out as fast as you can. We're not strong enough to hold the Jap fleet short of here."

"Oh, Frank, take care of yourself," she blurted out as tears sprang up in her eyes. She threw her arms about him and kissed him fiercely again.

"You can bet on it," he replied after catching his breath. "I have to go now, or I'll miss the bus. Say goodbye to your father for me."

"He seemed like an intelligent young man," Nicolaas remarked as the Cadillac sped back to their home.

"Frank?" Cinta responded. "Yes, he's smart, and he has a lot of common sense also."

"I think he's a marvelously interesting man," said Catherine.

"A very solid young man," Nicolaas agreed.

"Will you two stop matchmaking," Cinta said in exasperation. "I've no intentions of getting involved with a man just yet."

"I seem to remember the two of you vanishing for some time during the evening," Nicolaas commented.

"We were just talking over old times."

"Is that how Lieutenant Rhea got lipstick all over his face?" Catherine said with a laugh.

Cinta invited Catherine to her room for cocoa before bed. As they sat sipping the hot drink, the roar of Nicolaas's Alfa Romeo came through the open window.

"Is your father going out at this hour?" asked a surprised Catherine.

"He has a lady friend." A wistful smile crooked Cinta's lips.

"You mean a mistress?" Shock was evident in Catherine's voice.

"It would be more accurate to say that they're lovers. It doesn't bother me. I like her, and she's very good for him. Men just can't live without women, Catherine. It's a simple biological fact."

CHAPTER 11

(One)
Streets of Tokyo
6 December 1941

Katsura Okuma seethed with frustration and rage as he sat in a taxi driving from the Tokyo railroad station to Imperial Army Headquarters. It was bad enough that, after all the weeks of personal effort he had put into the project, Colonel Seiichi Kume received command of the First Parachute Brigade. Activated at Nittabaru Airfield on Kyushu on December 1st, the unit included the 2nd Parachute Regiment and the 98th Air Regiment of heavy bombers. Okuma had been assigned as operations officer for the brigade. He planned a number of immediate improvements in doctrine for the unit, but there was little time to put them into effect. The ink was hardly dry on the brigade's commissioning orders when Tokyo directed Kume to deploy his unit to Pnompenh, Cambodia, to await further orders. Okuma's staff toiled long hours preparing for the move. Then, just as the brigade was loading up to deploy, he received message orders to return to Army Headquarters. He was being robbed of his chance to fight in the vanguard of conquest!

"You look troubled, *Kuma*," said Colonel Takushiro Hattori when Okuma reported in at the Army General Staff.

"I don't relish cooling my heels here in Tokyo with the fighting about to begin," Okuma told the Chief of the Operations Section.

"So that's it. I should have guessed. Don't worry on that score, my ferocious young bear. You'll get your chance for combat, and soon. Why are you so sure that war is about to break out?"

"If not, why is everything going south?"

"You're right, of course. I can tell you in confidence that the Council of State gave the diplomats until midnight on November 30th to reach a negotiated agreement with Washington. The deadline has now passed, so war will begin automatically."

Despite his frustration at being recalled to the capital, elation flooded through Okuma. The debate at the Liaison Councils had dragged on for months, at last resulting in the fall of the Konoye government. None of the available civilian candidates for Prime Minister was acceptable to the military, which could exercise veto power by refusing to name War and Navy Ministers. The Emperor finally asked General Hideki Tojo to form a government. He continued the interminable negotiations with Washington while secretly preparing for war.

"Why was I brought back to the General Staff," Okuma asked.

"You can blame our old boss, General Tsukada. He's down in Saigon now as General Terauchi's chief of staff. They've decided that one parachute brigade won't be enough for the coming operations. The Count's demanding another independent parachute regiment for the invasion of Java."

"Where will we get the transports?" asked Okuma, suddenly excited. He could sense what was coming.

"From *Dai Nippon*. The die's cast, now. As soon as war begins, we'll commandeer what we need."

"I want all their DC-2's. They carry twice as many men as a Ki-57."

"You'll get enough for your regiment. You're to return at once to Nittabaru and form a new regiment of parachutists. We called you here to allow direct input of your material and manpower requirements to the General Staff. Time is of the essence. Count Terauchi wants you available for Java operations by March first."

"It shall be done!" Okuma declared without hesitation.

"There's an additional benefit. A parachute regiment rates a *chusa* (lieutenant colonel) in command, so we're promoting you today."

"I appreciate the Army's confidence." Okuma's chest was bursting with pride.

"Considering the shortness of time, we're granting you wide discretion in the equipage and training of your command. The staff will get you whatever you need."

"I know what I want already."

Okuma's tables of organization and allowances raised a few

eyebrows on the staff, but Colonel Takushiro's orders had been explicit that his requests were to be granted without question. A pattern quickly developed as the *chuken shoko* compared notes. The 6th Independent Parachute Regiment--actually a reinforced battalion--would have more firepower than any comparable unit in the Japanese Army.

Okuma adopted the *Luftwaffe* organization for his command. The parachute infantry would be deployed in three companies, using eleven-man machine gun sections as the basic building block. Their weapons were the most modern in the Japanese arsenal. Each section would be armed with a Type 99 7.7-millimeter machine gun (the Japanese version of the British Bren), five Type 100 submachine guns and five rifles. Remembering how the New Zealanders' Enfields outranged the Germans at Malame, Okuma selected the Type 99 *Teraju* rifle, which fired the same new rimless 7.7-millimeter *Shiki* cartridge as the machine gun. In keeping with the Imperial Army's predilection for cold steel, the *paras* would carry the standard 40-centimeter bayonet for close combat, and officers would bear *wakizashi*--the Samurai short sword. Three sections would make up a platoon; four platoons, a company. Each company commander would have a section of three Type 89 50-millimeter grenade throwers at his disposal. To counter enemy armor, a section of three Type 97 20-millimeter anti-tank rifles would also be attached to each company. Rather than the usual machine gun company of tripod-mounted Nambus, Okuma armed his heavy weapons company with twelve additional Type 99's and six of the compact Type 99 81-millimeter mortars. Although it weighed less than half as much as the comparable German model, the Type 99 had a greater range. Mindful of how crucial his own actions had been to the German seizure of Malame, he included a battery of three Type 92 70-millimeter battalion guns, placing them directly under the his headquarters. An airborne engineer company completed the regimental staffing.

One factor that Colonel Takushiro did question was the decision to dispense with reserve parachutes. Okuma's answer was simple. His unit would be trained to jump from an altitude of 200 meters to assure a swift descent on their targets. There would not be enough time to use a reserve parachute if the primary one failed. In their stead, Okuma designed a quick-opening chest pack to contain torn-down weapons and ammunition.

Once all his requests were in the pipeline, Okuma finally took time to visit Major Tsuneshiro Shirai in Intelligence.

"Ah, *Kuma*, I've been meaning to get in touch with you," Shirai said in greeting. "My agent from Balikpapan just came in on our last timber ship out of Borneo. He brought an interesting report on your Doctor van Wely."

Okuma took the file from his friend and sat down to peruse it. The report was very detailed, giving precise accounts of the young doctor's routine. Scanning it quickly, he moved on to a sheaf of photographs. There were about a dozen of them, most depicting the Dutchwoman at social events or at the hospital where she worked. The last three were taken around her home, obviously with an excellent telephoto lens. When he reached the final shot, Okuma popped his eyes in surprise.

She was standing just inside a floor-length window, her arms raised in the obvious act of opening the curtains to the light of early morning. Her hair was loose, falling in dark cascades about her shoulders. But what filled Okuma's mind with glee and his groin with hot blood was her scant attire. She wore a native sarong about her hips, but she was bare above it

"I thought you'd like that one," Shirai commented. "That's why I saved it for last."

"Where the hell did your man take this from?"

"A tree some distance from her father's house. He chanced it the day before he pulled out. Your doctor seems to have strange fashion tastes for a white woman. Did you ever see such teats?"

"In Germany, many times. Perhaps some day I'll carve my *hanko* into that soft white flesh. Or better yet, burn it there with a hot iron the way the *Gestapo* brands their Jewess *feld-hures* from the camps."

"It would be a pity to mar their perfect symmetry. I'd give a month's pay to bang her until she begged for mercy."

"I'll do my best to arrange it for you." Okuma related his conversation with Etsuko Miyagi.

"You really are a vengeful bastard, *Kuma*," Shirai commented. "A comfort woman in one of those field stations has to service troops right up at the battle front."

Shirai picked up the topless photograph of Cinta van Wely and stared at it for several moments. "If it were up to me, I wouldn't waste this one on sergeants and other ranks. I'd put her out on consignment in an officers' *Ianjo* and get rich off her fees."

"That's certainly an alternative worth considering," Okuma responded, stroking the scar on his cheek. "Can I keep the file?"

"It's yours. I made duplicate copies of the photos for my own pleasure. Say, what are you doing tonight?"

"I've nothing planned yet. I'll probably shove off for Kyushu tomorrow."

"We ought to celebrate your promotion. I think a night in the *Yoshiwara* would be appropriate. It may be your last chance for some time."

"An excellent idea!" Okuma responded. "After looking at these pictures, I could use an *ichiya-zuma* (wife-for-the-night)." "Let's see if Etsuko will go with us. With his connections, we're sure to find the best *joros* in Tokyo."

(Two)
Yoshiwara District
Tokyo
6 December 1941

Okuma turned up his overcoat collar and hunched his shoulders against the raw December wind as he waited for Shirai to pay the taxi driver who had brought them to the entrance to the *Yoshiwara,* Tokyo's world-famous pleasure market.

"Hurry up, Tsunehiri," snapped Etsuko Miyagi. "This cold will shrivel my Jade Stalk."

"That would be disastrous," Shirai shot back, "since it's so tiny to begin with."

"You two quit bickering," Okuma chided. "This is my last night in Tokyo, and I don't want to waste any time."

The three friends had already spent two hours at a *machiai* restaurant, drinking *sake* and feasting on raw fish and *tori no mizutaki* (spicy chicken and vegetables) while *geishas* entertained them with music and polite conversation. Okuma was ready for some physical action.

Entering the Omon Gate, they stalked quickly down a long lighted hall where clusters of patrons were examining photographs of the girls available in the various *joro-ya*, picking out their partners for the evening. Miyagi had already arranged for their entertainment by phone. He led the way out into the chill air of the *Nakanoche*, the street that passed between the many houses of pleasure. The flickering light of paper lanterns lit the ornate entrances, and the sounds of music and high-pitched voices beckoned from within. The wind whistled in the branches of the ancient willow just inside the gate--the *Mikaeri Yanagi*. Once accepted into service within the *Yoshiwara*, no woman was allowed to pass out beyond this "Look-back Tree." The *Hikite-Chaya*--the Guide House from which this "willow world" was governed--towered above the many trees of the quarter. With no desire to tarry in the winter air, the three officers made straight for the house Miyagi had selected.

"*Irrasshai, Chusa*," said the pre-teen girl who took Okuma's coat. "You are welcome, Lieutenant Colonel."

He knew that she and those greeting his two friends were *kamuros*, young virgins being trained to become courtesans.

"*Irrasshai, shinshi*," exclaimed an older woman, advancing to meet the officers. She was the *obasan*, the madam who managed the house for the owner.

"Good evening, Auntie," Miyagi said cheerfully. "I've brought some friends for a night of merriment."

"We are honored to serve such distinguished soldiers. As you requested, the house is yours alone for the evening. I assume you want to change?"

"But, of course."

The *kamuros* helped the officers out of their boots and uniforms and brought silk kimonos for them to wear. Toasty warm from the glowing coals of a large *hibachi*, the room's floor had straw *tatami* mats and black satin *zabuton* cushions. A lone *geisha* plucked a jolly tune on her banjo-like *samisen* as the men settled down to accept cups of warm *sake* and dishes of *tempura* and smoked eels from a pair of *shinzo*--slightly older apprentice courtesans. There was a stirring behind the paper *shoji* partitions at the end of the room, followed by soft peals of feminine laughter. Then the *shoji* parted, and six women came out into the light.

Okuma recognized at once that these were *oirans*, proficient courtesans at the peak of their beauty and skills. Attired in gorgeous silk kimonos, they had their hair coifed in the traditional *maga* style. All skin that showed above their garments was powdered ivory white. Their lips were painted a brilliant vermilion; their cheeks, rouged; their eyes, outlined in red and then black.

The *obasan* introduced the girls to the officers. Their names were charming pseudonyms. One was called *Osugo* (Pretty Cloud); another, *Shiragiku* (White Chrysanthemum). Okuma was at once attracted to a young beauty named *Kaoru* (Sweet Aroma). No more than eighteen, she had the dignified air of a great lady.

"Will you dance for me, *Kaoru?*" Okuma asked after the introductions.

"If you wish, your excellency," the girl replied politely with downcast eyes.

"Let's see them all dance," Miyagi put in. "It will help us decide among these gorgeous flowers."

As the officers sprawled back against their cushions on the *tatami* floormats, the *oiran* formed a circle near the musician. The *samisen* struck up a lively melody, and they began to move together in steps as fluid as a flowing ballet. Heads rocked to the music as they chanted endearments at their patrons; arms moved up and down to flutter the shining silk of their sleeves, forming patterns reminiscent of the erotic *shunga* prints that decorated the walls. They became a whirling pinwheel, the brilliant colors of their costumes blurring together in the lamplight. One after another, they left the spinning circle to dance solos, exquisite appeals to join in physical ecstasy. They began to sing about the joys of love.

Okuma leaned forward expectantly, for he knew what was coming. Shirai laughed and shouted encouragement to the women.

"*Chonkina, chonkina, chonkina, hai!*" As the women stopped chanting, they froze in place, like European children playing "eenie-meenie-minie-mo." *Kaoru*, who was an instant later than her sisters, paid the penalty by forfeiting her *obi* sash. After a *kamuro* took the garment away, the women resumed their spinning dance.

The game went on for another half-hour, with garment after garment disappearing until at last all the dancers were completely nude, flaunting their bodies at the electrified *chuken shoko.* Then the music suddenly ended, and the women darted away behind the *shoji.* When they returned a scant five minutes later, they were arrayed again in all their finery.

"Do you gentlemen wish to choose now?" asked the *obasan*.

"I know I'm ready," replied Okuma. He took the tiny hand of *Kaoru,* who smiled demurely while keeping her eyes on the floor.

"I see the Germans have taught you to hurry, *Kumo*," laughed Miyagi. "Were the ladies of Berlin so eager to get you to bed?"

"Always!" Okuma replied with a laugh.

Kaoru went ahead of him down the narrow passageway to her room.

CHAPTER 12

(One)
Aboard USS *Rust*
Manila Bay
8 December 1941

Jack Sewell took a steaming mug of coffee from the duty steward and wrapped his fingers around the ceramic cylinder. In the chill, early morning air, the warmth felt good. He checked the luminous dial of his wristwatch and saw that it was 0230.

Through the wheelhouse windows, he could see the sprawling skyline of Manila. Even at this hour, a few lights were showing, although President Quezon had ordered a blackout. Sounds of festivity still drifted across the water from the Manila Hotel, where the Air Corps officers were winding down a birthday party for General Brereton, the Philippines air commander. With *Rust* tied up to a mooring buoy in the harbor, duty as Officer-of-the-Deck was not really that demanding. Except for the minimum required departmental watches, the sleek warship was as asleep as the city across the calm waters of the bay. Jack enjoyed these moments of relative quiet, but he suspected that they must soon end forever. Walking out onto the port bridge wing, he looked back along the length of the ship. The decks were completely deserted, giving her a ghostly air.

A communications circuit buzzed inside the wheelhouse, and the duty quartermaster picked up the sound-powered phone.

"It's the radio shack, Mister Sewell," the petty officer said a few moments later. "They want to speak to you."

"This is Jenkins, Mister Sewell," the receiver crackled. "I just picked up a message from Honolulu that I think you should see."

"Was it addressed to the Asiatic Fleet?" asked Jack.

"No, Sir. It's an 'in-the-clear' broadcast. It says, 'AIR RAID ON PEARL HARBOR. THIS IS NOT A DRILL.'"

The impact of the words hit Jack like a blow between the eyes. "Write it out and bring it up, Sparks," he snapped as he picked up the circuit to the Captain's cabin. "You'd better come up to the bridge, Skipper," he said when Hoskins came on the line. "We just picked up a message that looks pretty bad."

"I'll be there in a minute," said Hoskins.

Jack went to the voice tubes and raised the engine room, ordering the duty chief fireman to get up steam in all the boilers. If an attack were imminent, *Rust's* survival might well turn on her ability to maneuver. Tom Hoskins came barreling into the wheelhouse moments later, asking for coffee as he hurried over to Jack. The New Englander handed him the clipboard with the message.

"Good God,"

Hoskins swore. "Do you know what this means?"

"I think so, sir. I've ordered steam up on all the boilers. We should be able to get underway shortly."

"Good thinking. Has anything come through from Asiatic Fleet command?"

"No, sir. Everything's quiet as a mouse except for this."

"Send this by light to the Marsman Building, 'HAVE MONITORED DISTURBING MESSAGE FROM PEARL. DO YOU HAVE ANY INSTRUCTIONS?'"

A few minutes later, a flashing lamp on the port signal bridge was rattling out the Morse message to the shore. A single word response blinked back, "WAIT." Fifteen minutes later, the signal lamp at fleet headquarters began to wink again. "PREPARE TO GET UNDERWAY. EXPECT ORDERS BY RADIO MOMENTARILY."

"We're one up on them already," said Hoskins. He looked at his watch and saw that it was 0300. "Let's let the crew sleep a little longer. God only knows when they'll get any more rest. If an attack comes, it won't be until dawn. Go down to the radio shack and stand by for that message. I have the con."

When Jack entered the radio room, Jenkins was bent over his pad transcribing the dots and dashes that were already buzzing in his earphones. When he finished, he whistled softly and tore the phones from his hear as he turned to get up. He jumped in surprise when he saw Jack.

"Goddamn, Mister Sewell, you like to scared the shit out of me. Read this. It's real dynamite."

The tersely worded message was typical of its author:
FROM COMMANDER ASIATIC FLEET...BREAK...JAPAN
HAS COMMENCED HOSTILITIES...GOVERN
YOURSELVES ACCORDINGLY.

When the sun crept up over the city, *Rust* was still moored to the buoy, but her crew was prepared to cast off at a moment's notice. From the crow's nest and bridge and another dozen high points on the superstructure, binoculars were scanning the sky, looking for the first sign of enemy activity. The gun crews all stood by their weapons. The barrels of the antiaircraft guns--the bow three-incher, the new 1.1-inch pom-poms and the .50-caliber machine guns-- pointed skyward.

All over the Philippines that morning, hundreds of eyes searched the dawn skies for the planes of their new, treacherous enemy. At Clark and Nichols Fields, aircraft were sent aloft to prevent being caught on the ground in a duplication of the sneak attack on Pearl Harbor. Strangely, the expected aerial assaults failed to materialize. Since no American reconnaissance flights reached Formosa that morning, the American high command received no inkling that the Japanese bases were blanketed in heavy fog and cloud cover. The enemy bombers were helpless until the weather cleared.

The anxieties of the first hours began to wear off at the American bases when no Japanese planes appeared. By mid-morning, the defenders started to relax. Low on gasoline from circling above their airfields, the Army Air Corps' big B-17 bombers and P-40 fighters came back to their roosts. At Clark Field, the Flying Fortresses were scattered around the edges of the airfield. With the surrounding ground too swampy to support their weight, it was impossible to disperse them properly. While ground crews refilled the fuel tanks, the pilots and aircrews grabbed a late breakfast.

Freed from their bases by improving weather, the Japanese finally struck at this worst of all possible moments. *Zero* fighters and Mitsubishi bombers swept down upon the American aerodromes, sowing bombs and cannon shells among the closely parked planes below. Within the space of an hour, two-thirds of the air force it had taken so many months to assemble was reduced to blazing wrecks. The fate of the Philippines was sealed in these first air strikes. Without control of the air, all the valiant efforts that followed were predestined to failure.

Near sundown, *Rust* returned to the mooring buoy from which she had sailed that morning. The constant hull vibrations from her engines suddenly ceased, and the noises made by the "sea and anchor" detail seemed unusually loud and threatening. Up on the fire control platform, Jack Sewell raised his glasses and swept them along the skyline of Manila. Huge fires were still burning at Nichols Field, which had been struck repeatedly during the day.

Several hundred yards north of *Rust*, the light cruiser, *Boise*, steamed slowly away toward Corregidor. Farther out, *Langley* was also underway, and the fleet's last two oilers were following close behind. Admiral Hart was clearing the port of his big ships, sending them south to join a task force he was forming under Admiral Glassford's command in southern Philippine waters.

"Bet those guys on *Boise* wished they'd stayed at Pearl," Chief Muldune intoned wearily. "They shoulda known that Admiral Hart would 'Shanghai' 'em if things turned sour out here."

"I wouldn't take any bets on how they feel," Jack responded. "They might be 'deep-sixed' by now if they'd been there when the Japs struck. Let's just be glad she came out with that convoy." He switched his gaze back to the new *St. Louis* class cruiser. She mounted fifteen six-inch guns which could be used against either surface or air targets. Better yet, her mastheads were festooned with rotating frames that looked like bedsprings--the antenna for the new radar devices. "With her around, the Japs won't be able to pull any surprise attacks on this fleet."

After the harbor was fully shrouded in darkness, Tom Hoskins secured the ship from General Quarters and sent the crew to dinner. The officers dragged hollowed-eyed into the tiny wardroom and sat down to salmon croquettes and French fries. The conversation revolved around the question of how soon they would be sent south to join Glassford.

"Admiral Hart will be getting all these merchantmen out right away," predicted Jerry Busch. "Ten to one we'll go along as an escort."

As if to prove Busch a seer, a light signal from the Marsman Building announced a conference of all masters in port on the following morning. Tom Hoskins was called ashore to attend, as were the other destroyer skippers.

"You were right, Jerry," Called Hoskins as he vaulted up the accommodation ladder upon his return. "Hart's clearing the port."

"What about us?" asked the exec.

"We stay put. The brass thinks the Japs will try a landing within a week. They're keeping the subs and a few of us 'cans' around to try and break it up."

(Two)
MK-KNIL Flying School
Andir, Java
Netherlands East Indies
8 December 1941

"The colonel will see you now, Captain," the prim young secretary said in crisp, sterile tones. She wore the uniform of the volunteer services.

"Thank you, Miss," said Garrit Laterveer with an equal lack of emotion. He was dressed in the workday uniform of MLKNIL officers: short-sleeved khaki shirt with black tie, green breeches and polished cavalry boots. Rising to his feet, he marched smartly through the open door and stopped before a massive mahogany desk. He saluted as he reported to Colonel Havenga, commander of the flying school.

"Stand easy, Garrit," said the paunchy, balding man behind the desk. Nearly sixty, Havenga had not lost the ramrod posture developed during his early years as a cavalryman. "I expect you know why I've sent for you."

"An operational command, Colonel?"

"Exactly. You are to assume command of Number 4 *Afdelingen* (squadron) of *Vliegergroep* (air group) V immediately. The unit is to be deployed in support of our British allies as soon as possible.

We need a man of your experience in charge."

"Where will we be going, sir?"

"Malaya. The Governor General has offered the full resources of our air forces and navy to help the British boot the Japs out. Damn bloody mistake, if you ask me. We'll be needing all our men and machines to save our own islands soon enough. But it's done, so we've got to make the best of it."

"When do we leave?"

"Tomorrow morning. All the Glenn Martins will also be going. Your initial destination will be Seletar Aerodrome outside Singapore. I shouldn't be surprised if they send you on to one of their upcountry airfields."

"What about Captain Leeuwenberg?" Garrit continued. Leeuwenberg had just organized 4-VLG V in mid-November. Former instructors from the Flying School manned the squadron. "Will he be staying on?"

"No. He's been posted to command a squadron of *Demons* at Soerabaja. He left an hour ago. You've worked with the RAF before, so you should get on quite well with them. You'll be given written orders, but I want you to clearly understand one thing. Don't let them throw your force away for no good reason. The British have been known to do some pretty stupid things in this war. They have a proclivity for heroic stands in the face of hopeless odds. If you refuse to undertake a mission that violates this directive, we'll back you to the hilt."

"I fully understand, sir. I'll keep it in mind."

"Now listen up and listen carefully," said Garrit to the knot of men clustered around him on the cool deck of the barrel arched hangar. Their faces were all familiar to him from their days in his training unit. "You all know that we'll be leaving for Malaya in the morning. I want some things clearly understood from the beginning. I've been in combat, and I know what I'm talking about. You've heard me say some of this before during your training, but now it's a matter of life and death.

"There's no room left in aerial combat for individual heroics. Teamwork is all-important. I've taught you the 'four-fingers' tactics. Stick with them, and you'll have a chance to survive.

"Don't overestimate the capabilities of our aircraft, and don't underestimate the enemy. The *Buffalo*'s a tough airplane, but it's no *Spitfire*. I've taught you its weaknesses and I've stressed its strong points. The main thing is to fight from a position that allows exploitation of those strengths.

"I know the British pretty well. I expect you'll hear lots of talk about the natural inferiority of the Japanese pilots and their equipment. Don't believe a word of it! Our intelligence is that the Jap pilots are a tough, smart enemy. Most of them have many months of combat flying under their belts. Their aircraft are extremely maneuverable. Their new *Zero* fighter is especially fast and nimble. Never, I repeat, never try to dogfight with these planes. They can fly circles around a *Buffalo*. We'll employ the diving attack tactics I emphasized during your training.

"Keep in mind from the beginning that our likely mission will be to protect the Allied ground and naval forces from air attack. Clashes with enemy fighters will be avoided if possible to preserve our strength.

"I must say that I'm confident that we can meet the enemy on even terms if we make him fight by our rules. The *Buffalo*'s a sturdy bird, and its armament can shred the light Jap planes if our gunnery is up to snuff. Questions?"

"How soon will our ground crews follow us to Malaya?" asked Lieutenant Moulders, the squadron second-in-command. "The orders haven't come through on them yet."

"Within two days, I understand," Garrit replied. "Lockheed transports have already been detailed for the lift."

"How long will we stay in Malaya, Captain?" inquired a young pilot whom Garrit recognized as Sergeant Symons. The slender, dark-haired youth had been one of his most responsive students.

"Several weeks, at least. Wrap up all your loose ends, if you can. It'll likely be a long time before we see this place again."

Garrit scanned the circle of eager faces. It was plain that they were straining at the leash to get into battle. He had felt that way once, eons ago. They would get over it soon enough. It struck him that their uniforms seemed almost ludicrous now that war was upon them. The riding breeches and cavalry boots would be a hindrance in combat; the neckties, an unnecessary and uncomfortable nicety. He decided on the spot that they would take only their green cotton flightsuits to Singapore. In the meantime, they could adopt a more practical outfit.

"No more questions?" Garrit's gaze met every pair of eyes in turn. "Then, gentlemen, I propose that we adjust out dress for real fighting." His fingers came up and unknotted his tie, then unbuttoned his collar. Walking to the nearest waste can, he ceremoniously deposited the necktie in the container. One after another, the pilots of 4-VLG V followed suit, grinning like bad little boys as they did so.

(Three)
Skies Above Sumatra
Netherlands East Indies
10 December 1941

Garrit rotated his head swiftly, surveying the airplanes flying around him. There were twelve Brewster 339D's, three flights of four, arrayed in the loose formation copied from the *Luftwaffe* by the RAF when their own pre-war "vics" failed disastrously during the early fighting. Powered by 1200-horsepower Cyclone air-cooled radial engines, the chunky *Buffalos* were reasonably fast, able to achieve 311 mph at 18,000 feet. Their armament of two .50-caliber Colt-Brownings in the wings and two .303-caliber Brownings in the fuselage firing through the propeller was as good as any Allied fighter in the Far East. Cockpit visibility was excellent, and the planes possessed a good diving speed. But they had one glaring deficiency for combat operations: a fighter plane must be able to maneuver like a nimble sports car. The Brewster 339D flew like an aerial truck.

Down below, the endless jungles of Sumatra stretched out to the horizon. A little while back, they had passed over the vast oil complex at Palembang with its Standard-Vacuum (Stanvac) and BPM refineries.

Their destination was the fortress of Singapore. The British had spent a fortune fortifying the place and building the naval base there. Now the Japanese were knocking on its back door. The ships of the big convoy that caused so much consternation at the Manila conference had dropped their hooks at a dozen points along Thailand's Kra Isthmus and put their troops ashore. General "Tiger" Yamashita sent his men storming across the border into Malaya at once. It was already known in Java intelligence circles that the advance British airfields had been overrun and their fuel dumps captured intact. Tokyo Rose, the Japanese propagandist, sarcastically thanked the Englishmen for their gift of "Churchill petrol."

Up ahead, the dark mass of Singapore came into view. Garrit was on the radio-telephone now, conversing with the Fighter Control Operations Room. After asking for a report on the Dutchmen's fuel situation, the ground controller vectored him toward Selatar Aerodrome. The huge city sprawled out beneath the *Buffalos* like a three-dimensional map. On Jahore, the naval base with its mammoth floating drydock seemed obscenely empty. Nothing bigger than a small gunboat was in evidence. Garrit was disappointed. After all the fanfare on the arrival of *Prince of Wales* and *Repulse*, he had hoped for at least a glimpse of them. He had seen the battleship once, back in May just after her return from the fight off Iceland when *Bismark* sank *Hood*.

Selatar was a well-developed airfield with paved runways. As his squadron circled to land, Garrit was puzzled to find no planes on at base. Not a single fighter could be seen. He surmised that they must all be dispersed at outlying fields. As was his long-standing custom, he stayed aloft until the last of his subordinates had landed, then brought his own *Buffalo* down to a perfect, three-point landing. Following the direction of a British aircraftsman, he taxied to the edge of the tarmac where a car was waiting. As he climbed out of his cockpit, a tall RAF lieutenant with sandy hair met him at the wing of his fighter.

"Captain Laterveer?" said the youth, saluting.

"That's correct."

"Woods is the name, sir. I'm honored to meet you. We've heard about your record in Europe." As he spoke, the lieutenant's eyes moved to the fifteen swastikas painted below Garrit's cockpit canopy. "Wing Commander Corby's most anxious to meet you at once, sir. Your pilots will be ferried to the squadron ready room we've assigned to you. Our ground crews will service your *Buffalos*. Is there anything special you need?"

"Not for the aircraft. They were combat checked before we left Java. The guns are loaded. Fill them with petrol, and we'll be ready to go back up."

"Very good, sir. We'll attend to it. If you'll get in the car, we'll be off to see the wing commander."

Corby was waiting for Garrit in the air operations room. He was in his mid-thirties, dark-haired and deeply tanned. His trim, fit body looked comfortable in in khaki shorts and shirt. "Ah, Laterveer, welcome to Singapore," Corby said warmly. "We're happy to have you operating with the RAF again."

"Thank you, sir," Garrit responded, suddenly aware that he was more at home with British fliers than with his own people. "I have the impression that you have something urgent laid on for us."

"You're very perceptive. As a matter of fact, things are in a muddle. All our fighters are up at the front. Admiral Phillips took his fleet up the east coast of Malaya yesterday to look for the Jap invasion convoys. He's been maintaining radio silence, so we're not sure where he's been. It really didn't matter until now, for we had no planes to spare to cover his ships anyway.

"Just as you were landing, we received a signal from *Repulse* that they're under attack by enemy aircraft. We don't have an exact position, but we have a good bearing on the transmission. How soon could you go out to give them cover?"

"As soon as we're refueled, sir. Shall I take the whole squadron?"

"Leave one flight here in reserve. We never know when the Nips are going to pop in for an air raid."

Garrit glanced at his watch as the wheels of his *Buffalo* folded into the chunky fuselage. It was 1215 hours on the 10th of December. A chill went up his spine. He had a premonition that this was not going to be a routine mission. Would it be his last?

Fighter operations control took charge and vectored the Dutchmen eastward across the Malay Peninsula. The terrain below was strikingly similar to that of the Dutch East Indies. Garrit took his formation up to ten thousand feet, giving orders to his pilots on what to look for as they climbed. Cruising at over two hundred and fifty miles an hour, they should reach the ships in about thirty minutes.

The iridescent green of the land below gave way to the brilliant blue of the South China Sea. Above, the sun was a blinding ball of yellow in an almost cloudless sky.

"Red Leader from Red Leader Four," Sergeant Symon's voice crackled in Garrit's earphones. "I think I've sighted a ship. Dead ahead, just on the horizon."

Squinting, Garrit could just make out the dim silhouette. He unhooked a hand-held mike from the instrument panel and brought it to his mouth. "Red Force from Red Leader," he said. "This is it. Look alive! If there're any Japs around, we have to spot them first."

With the distance to the ship shrinking at over four miles a minute, Garrit could soon make out the vessel clearly. It was a modern British destroyer. Then he sighted two others in quick succession. The three sleek greyhounds were almost dead in the water. But where were the capital ships?

"My God, Red Leader, look at that oil slick," Moulders said over the radio.

Garrit had already spotted the huge sheet of oil that covered the water around the destroyers. Now he picked out the Carley floats scattered about the surface. The awful significance of what he was witnessing hit him like a sledgehammer.

"Red Leader Two, keep your flight at this altitude for cover," Garrit ordered. "I'm going down for a look."

Nosing the *Buffalo* over, he led his four planes down to less that a thousand feet. From that height, he could see hundreds of heads bobbing among the waves between the destroyers. Unaccountably, many of the swimmers waved cheerfully as the *Buffalos* flew past. An icy claw tore at Garrit's vitals. There was no sign of either battleship. The oil slick and hundreds of men in the water could mean but one thing--they had both been sunk by Japanese aircraft. Never before had a capital ship been destroyed by aircraft while underway. Two days earlier, at Pearl Harbor, the American battlewagons had been immobile and relatively helpless. This was far more profound. At noon on this December day, the era of battleship supremacy ended.

The underpinnings of Allied strategy for the Far East had been shattered in less than two days. The cadres of MacArthur's fabulous air armada were now smoking wrecks on the ruined airfields of the Philippines. The last shipments of war supplies so vital to his ground forces had been diverted to Australia by a War Department fearful of the blockade that the Japanese Navy had already proclaimed. Now the loss of the British battleships destroyed any hope of forming a powerful naval force to contest the waters around the crucial Malay Barrier. The full onslaught of the powerful Japanese fleet would have to be borne by the cruisers, destroyers and submarines. With sufficient air support, they were a potentially viable force. Without it, they would be helpless against the enemy Juggernaut.

Garrit continued to circle the area, trying vainly to contact the destroyers below. In the haste to get the fighters away from Selatar, the British had neglected to give them the frequencies to converse with the ships.

No Japanese planes came out to mar the rescue operations. Garrit radioed a situation report back to Singapore, then stood by with his fighters for as long as their fuel supplies allowed. It was plain that the destroyermen down below were doing a first class job. When petrol reserves fell near the danger point, he formed up his *Buffalos* and headed back to Selatar. As they neared the aerodrome, the four destroyers of Commander Crouch's DesDiv 57 rounded the tip of the Malay Peninsula and dashed toward the scene of the disaster to help with the recovery operations. They had arrived at Singapore too late to help the valiant Admiral Phillips with his last battle.

"You're not going to believe this, Captain," Sergeant Symons said to Garrit as they walked back to the squadron ready room.

"What's that?"

"When we made our first low-level pass, I opened my canopy and lifted my earphones to see what I could hear. The British seamen in the water were singing."

"It's obvious that you don't know the Brits yet, my friend," Garrit replied, reflecting how very like their allies such conduct under adversity really was.

CHAPTER 13

(One)
Aboard USS *Rust*
Manila Bay
10 December 1941

The ear-splitting clang of the General Alarm jarred Jack from sleep. He felt the ship move as his feet hit the deck. Looking instantly at his watch, he saw that it was 1210. Only three days old, the war already seemed to have lasted forever. This was the first time he had enjoyed four hours of sleep at one time since hostilities started. Gambling that the Japanese bombers would maintain their routine of the past two days and not arrive before noon, the Exec had sent Jack and all his gunners to bed after *Rust* returned at dawn from another night patrol outside the minefields.

Strapping on his tin hat, Jack made straight for his battle station atop the bridge. He was struck by the purposeful manner with which the rest of the crew was reacting. There was no panic, no unnecessary talking. They were moving fast, but under control. He wondered if the old-time Navy professionals on the other ships were coping with the stresses of war as coolly as were these Reservists.

Rust was headed away from Cavite at about two knots when Jack reached Central Fire Control. She had been anchored off the Navy Yard while Tom Hoskins attended a conference at the headquarters of the Inshore Patrol, to which *Rust* was now assigned. The piers and wharves of the yard were crowded with vessels under repair, providing an inviting target to aircraft. Hoskins had taken his gig ashore rather than hazard his ship in the confined waters near the port facilities.

"All stations, report," Jack said to Seaman Jarvis, his telephone talker, just as Chief Muldune heaved his heavy bulk up the ladder.

"All guns manned and ready," Jarvis announced but moments

later.

"Very well," Jack responded, picking up his own sound-powered phone to the bridge. He reported his guns at the ready to the Exec. "Any report on what to look for?" he asked Busch.

"Large formation of enemy bombers approaching from the north."

"We'll be ready," said Jack just as the eerie wail of the air raid sirens in Manila drifted across the waters of the bay.

Just after 1230, the first sighting came in.

"Crow's Nest reports enemy aircraft bearing ninety degrees," Jack's talker said in clipped tones, anxiety evident in his voice.

"Very well." Jack wiped the sweat from his eyes and swung his glasses to the skies west of Manila. He caught the sharp glint of sunlight off silvery, unpainted wings. Focusing quickly, he made out a "vic" of the swift, radial-engined fighters already known to all hands as the *Zero*. Several more formations were stacked up behind the first "vic."

"Looks like they're headed for Nichols Field," Jack remarked. Almost as he spoke the words, he caught sight of more fighters diving into the enemy formations. They were P-40's! For once, the Air Corps was getting the jump on the enemy! The precise formations broke, and dogfights between the P-40's and *Zeros* swirled about the sunlit skies above Manila for several minutes. Crippled machines trailing long tails of flame and smoke began to plummet earthward. Here and there, white parachutes blossomed as the luckier pilots escaped the blazing deathtraps. Then, quite suddenly, the vicious air battle was over. The planes which formed up to circle about in search of further prey all bore the orange meatball of Japan on their wings. Incredibly, the skies over Manila had been swept clean of American aircraft. No defenders remained to oppose enemy bombers.

"Lookout reports bomber formation bearing seventy degrees, high," Jarvis intoned. His voice was firmer now, more under control.

Jack picked up the bombers with his glasses. They were the new, fat-bellied Mitsubishis of the Japanese Navy. The planes were in a triple "vic" formation, twenty-seven aircraft in all. They were moving fast, well over two hundred miles an hour. The formation wheeled into a precise turn towards Nichols Field and began dropping its deadly cargo of bombs a few minutes later. Black and brown clouds appeared like ugly flowers beyond the skyline of Manila. A deep-throated rumbling like distant thunder followed several seconds later. Their task of destruction completed, the Mitsubishis turned and sped away to the north. The *Zeros* continued to dive and strafe the Air Corps base.

"Here they come again, sir," said Jarvis, pointing west to a second bomber formation, a twin to the one that had just ravaged Nichols Field. This one seemed headed straight for *Rust*, and the planes were coming on fast.

"Get on the range finder, Chief," Jack ordered Muldune, "and we'll get a lock on their altitude." As Muldune swung the range finder around and focused its split telescope to get the diagonal distance to the oncoming raiders, Jack leveled his sextant on the horizon to read the angle of the planes above the horizontal. "Ready, mark," he shouted.

"Eighteen thousand, two hundred yards," Muldune barked.

Reading the angle on the sextant, Jack twirled a circular slide rule to get the proper scales aligned. "Damn!" he swore. "They're at twenty thousand feet."

"Too high for anything we got aboard," Muldune echoed.

And too high for the AA guns at Cavite, Jack thought. The heaviest antiaircraft guns at the Yard were nine old three-inch twenty-threes. He relayed the information on the enemy planes to the bridge and recommended that they not waste ammunition in futile firing.

"Okay, Jack," Busch's voice crackled back. "Keep on the line. I'll zig-zag around the bay to throw off their aim. The minute they drop anything at us, let me know and I'll start corkscrewing."

The bombers were definitely after shipping, and with more than forty merchant vessels in the harbor, presenting plenty of targets. The big formation split up into three, nine-plane groups and began stalking their prey. With no American fighters aloft to contest the skies, the Japanese could be quite leisurely about it. If they didn't like the set-up on a run, they circled around and repeated it. Almost all the other Navy ships were shooting at the enemy, crisscrossing the sky with colorful tracers. Just south of *Rust*, *John D. Ford* and *Pope* banged away with their three-inchers, but their bursts fell far short. Of all the ships left, only the China gunboats with their modern three-inch fifties could reach the height of the raiders.

Jerry Busch kept *Rust* maneuvering at high speed to discourage the Japanese from coming after her. For over an hour, his strategy worked. With wide-hulled merchantmen swinging indolently on their anchors like decoys at a duck shoot, the destroyer was not a promising target. One of the cargo ships took a hit, and black smoke belched up from her bulging sides.

Muldune grabbed Jack's arm and pointed toward a "vic" of "vics" that was just turning toward *Rust*.

"They're after us now, X.O.," Jack relayed to Busch.

"Keep me posted," came the reply. The ship heeled over hard to port. Through the crystal, tropical water, Jack glimpsed a submarine lying on the bottom for safety. High above, the Mitsubishis made a dry run without dropping any bombs.

"The bastards are trying to get our number, Lieutenant," Muldune shouted.

The enemy planes turned away, circled and came back for another run. Busch turned hard to starboard and laid on more speed. Again, the Japanese held their bombs. A wily veteran, their commander made his third pass from dead astern, high up. This time, Jack observed tiny black specks detach from the bombers. Warned by Jack's quick report, the Exec turned hard to starboard again and went full back on both engines. The screws churned the sea under the pointed stern into a boiling froth as they fought to stem the ship's progress. Jack's eyes were glued in fascination to the falling bombs. For an eternity, they seemed to be coming straight at him. Then the ship surged backwards away from the path of the deadly missiles. The entire barrage fell several hundred yards ahead of the bow. The topside crew broke into a ragged cheer.

Their bombs finally expended, the Mitsubishis turned lazily toward the west and winged away out to sea. Beyond them, over Corregidor, another group of planes was just coming into view. Jack caught the newcomers in his binoculars, recognizing these twin-tailed killers as older model Navy Mitsubishis. The Japanese again split up into smaller units as they approached the city. Over Sangley Point, ugly black puffs like dirty cotton balls appeared below the bombers as Cavite's antiaircraft guns opened up. Serenely unconcerned, the planes came on across the base and wheeled northward. Jack and Muldune repeated the exercise of calculating the altitude of the oncoming enemy. Like the earlier raid, the bombers were up over twenty thousand feet.

"They're goin' for the Navy Yard, Mister Sewell," Muldune shouted, and Jack saw that he was right. The formation was turning back toward Cavite. The first stick of bombs plowed up Bacoor Bay, doing damage only to the fish there. But then Manchera Wharf was suddenly enveloped in an enormous ball of flame and smoke.

"Goddammit, Lieutenant!" Muldune swore. "They hit *Otus* and *Sealion* dead on."

"Maybe just near misses," Jack responded. But even as he mouthed the words, a blazing torch shot skyward above *Sealions*'s narrow, submersible hull. Farther up the wharf, the minesweeper, *Bittern*, was also blazing.

"Look at those Jap bastards," one of the lookouts screamed. "You'd think they was on maneuvers."

Another nine-plane group, leisurely crossing Cavite in perfect formation, released its bombs. Jack raised his binoculars just in time to get a closeup view of the results. The area around Central Wharf was neatly plastered. A direct hit atop the *Peary's* bridge caused the destroyer to heel over sharply. The wooden shop buildings beyond went up like incendiaries. Moments later, the *Commandancia* and Inshore Patrol Headquarters collapsed under a storm of high explosive.

"God in heaven," Muldune muttered. "The Skipper was in there."

Jack surveyed the flaming wreckage, wondering if Hoskins could possibly have survived.

Time and again, the enemy formations crossed and recrossed Cavite, choosing their targets carefully. The power station was blasted into ruins. The floating drydock staggered beneath multiple hits. The lumber yard became a raging inferno. Torpedo warheads in the shop alongside Manchera Wharf began exploding, adding to the carnage. A dense smoke cloud boiled far up into the heavens.

The flotilla of moored minesweepers reacted like ants in a stirred nest. *Otus*, miraculously untouched by the bombs which had fallen close around her, was backing away from the wharf under her own power. *Pigeon* and *Quail* were also moving out, fleeing before heat and flames engulfed them. *Quail* was towing *Tanager*. Jack wondered how Dick Hawes was conning *Pigeon*, for he knew that the minesweeper's rudder had been removed for repairs. As he watched, his fears seemed confirmed, for *Pigeon* began moving back up the slip. Then he realized what an incredibly brave thing Hawes was doing. *Pigeon* was going back to help the stricken *Bittern*. As if inspired by her example, *Whippoorwill,* which had stood off Cavite during the attack, nosed toward Central Wharf, where *Peary* lay helpless.

"Fighter formation off the starboard bow," Jarvis's words jarred Jack's attention from the horror ashore. He picked up the enemy quickly, another nine-plane group. The *Zeros* were diving toward the waterfront as if intent on strafing.

"Three-incher," Jack barked. "Fire at will on fighter formation." The words were hardly out of Jarvis's lips when the sharp crack of the little gun just forward of the bridge rent the air. Jack ordered the pom-poms and the .50-calibers to stand by.

The Japanese split into three separate "vics" and dived straight for the minesweepers. Every gun ashore still capable of being fired was blazing away at them, but the enemy pilots seemed unconcerned. One of the "vics" pulled out of its strafing pass and turned almost straight for *Rust*. The ship heeled over to port as Jerry Busch turned her to present her stern to the enemy, unmasking the bulk of his antiaircraft battery.

"All pom-poms and machine guns open fire," Jack ordered.

A storm of tracers leaped up from the ship to converge on the lead plane in the "vic." The machine guns sent up continuous streams of fire; the tracer rounds from the one-point-ones seemed to drift lazily skyward. Startled, the Japanese broke their neat "vic" to flee in different directions. The lead plane started to turn away, but then Jennings's pom-pom caught him broadside. The explosive shells slammed into the fuselage from engine to tail, hammering it into a mass of twisted wreckage. Cheers and screams of joy reverberated about *Rust*'s upper works as the disintegrating *Zero* cartwheeled into the bay. After three days of helplessly enduring bombing attacks, the gunners had finally drawn their first blood of the war.

The public address system squawked out orders sending fire-fighting teams to their stations as *Rust* turned back toward Cavite. *Pigeon* had left the smoking *Bittern* in the stream and was heading back to help the submarine, *Seadragon,* which was moored just outboard of the blazing *Seadlion*. *Whippoorwill* backed away from Central Wharf, slowly dragging the powerless *Peary* after her. As they cleared the basin, Jerry Busch put *Rust* close alongside *Peary* to allow his firefighting parties to hose down the last fires aboard their sister destroyer. Jack guessed that the carnage on *Peary*'s bridge must have been ghastly. The bomb had struck the Crow's Nest, severing the mast and sending cascades of shrapnel across the fire control platform and through the roof of the wheelhouse, striking down the brains of the ship. Busch put two fire-fighting crews aboard *Peary* to help quell below-decks blazes, then stood clear.

The last of the enemy planes were speeding away to the north, their bomb bays and cannons empty. Ashore, the vital support facilities had been destroyed beyond any hope of repair. There could be no question now of the fleet returning to Manila.

An hour after the last raider departed, a battered whaleboat came chasing after *Rust*. Busch slowed the ship, and the boat pulled up to the accommodation ladder. Moments later, a hatless, soot-stained Tom Hoskins came vaulting up to the deck.

"Thank God you're alive, Skipper," said Jack as the Captain reached the bridge. "We thought you were a goner when Inshore Patrol headquarters was hit."

"Damn near was," Hoskins replied.

"What's it like ashore?" Busch inquired.

"As close to hell as I ever want to be. The Yard's gone for good. We can thank those old Spaniards for one thing, though. If they hadn't buried the magazines so deep, the fleet's ammo would've gone up in one big bang."

After darkness fell that fateful night, most of Admiral Hart's remaining ships slipped out through the minefields and headed south. With control of the skies now clearly lost to the enemy, surface ships could not hope to survive in these waters. Only the submarines of the Asiatic Fleet, supported by *Canopus* and the rescue vessel, *Pigeon*, were left to seriously contest the seas around the Philippines. The Inshore Patrol, now assigned the mission of protecting MacArthur's seaward flanks, was reinforced by minesweepers *Quail*, *Tanager*, and *Finch* and by three old China gunboats judged unfit for the long voyage to the Dutch East Indies. The six motor torpedo boats of PT Squadron Three and the destroyers, *Peary*, *Pillsbury*, and *Rust* filled out the command.

Captain Hoeffel would need them and more. While Japanese planes were bombing Manila that afternoon, an amphibious force seized the airfields at Aparri and Vigan near the north tip of Luzon. With enemy soldiers firmly ashore and their airmen already operating from the captured fields, Manila would soon know the full blast of total war.

Judging correctly that the initial Japanese landings were feints to draw his reserves northward, Lieutenant General MacArthur refused to take the bait. But with Clark Field now useless, his reconnaissance planes could no longer reach Formosa, where Lieutenant General Masaharu Homma's 14th Army was sweating through a combat loadout in invasion shipping. Three separate convoys containing eighty-five transports finally sailed with a close naval escort that outnumbered the Asiatic Fleet. Just over the horizon lurked two Japanese fleets made up of battleships, heavy cruisers and numerous destroyers. Washington's assessment had been right. Any attempt by Hart's surface forces to attack the convoys would have been suicidal.

During the early hours of December 22nd, the Japanese invasion force skillfully outmaneuvered Hart's submarines and reached the shoal waters inside Lingayen Gulf without losses. By 0500, the first troops began pouring in across the snow-white beaches. Within a few hours, more than a division and over a hundred tanks were ashore. Brushing aside light opposition from untrained Filipinos of the 11th Division, by sunset the Japanese seized a beachhead over five miles deep. In scenes reminiscent of the fighting in Poland, the elite U.S. 26th Cavalry battled valiantly but without hope against Japanese armor. By dark on December 23rd, the issue was decided. The raw recruits of the 11th and 17th Divisions had been savaged by Homma's battlewise veterans.

Realizing that he had a rout to contain, Lieutenant General Jonathan Wainwright, commander of the North Luzon Force, asked headquarters for the crack Philippine Division to help form a defense line on the Agno river, a mere ninety miles from Manila. It was painfully clear that the Japanese could not be contained on the beaches. Reluctantly, MacArthur ordered the gradual withdrawal of all ground forces to the Bataan Peninsula. Supported by the fortress of Corregidor, he would attempt to hold the entrance to Manila Bay until reinforcements arrived from America.

(Two)
Balikpapan, Borneo
Netherlands East Indies
14 December 1941

Frank Rhea circled his *Seagull* above Balikpapan Bay, looking for a place to put down. The mine-protected anchorage was literally packed with ships, and more were on the way in. Far out past the lightship, the cruisers *Houston* and *Boise* were barely visible against the horizon. Sub tenders *Holland* and *Otis* were approaching the minefield. *Marblehead* was already anchored in the roadstead, along with more than a dozen other vessels that included everything from fleet oilers and destroyers to seaplane tenders and ocean tugs. *Trinity* and *Pecos* were alongside the BPM piers, taking on fuel. The merchant liner, *President Madison*, was swinging on her hook out in the stream, as were three Dutch tankers and two British freighters.

Marblehead and DesDiv 58 had sortied from Tarakan on the previous morning to rendezvous with Admiral Glassford's Task Force 5, a mixed collection of warships and auxiliaries headed south for Java. *Houston* and *Boise* had been screening the force to the north. Since the enemy landings at Legaspi in South Luzon on December 12, even the southern reaches of the Sulu Sea were within range of his land-based aircraft. Still trying to digest the full impact of the sinking of *Prince of Wales* and *Repulse*, Glassford's staff was understandably concerned about the threat of air attack.

They were also concerned about Japanese submarines. *Langley* had already reported being attacked by torpedoes. A Dutch Dornier out of Tarakan had also confirmed that the motley collection of vessels was being shadowed by at least one unidentified "pig boat." The cruisers' *Seagulls* were required to keep up a constant antisubmarine patrol during daylight hours. Eddie Blessman and Frank were taking turns at the monotonous duty.

"Hey, *Kimo Sabay*," Tonto said over the intercom, "you gonna buzz the Doc's house before we land?"

"Not this time, *amigo*," Frank shot back. "We're running on fumes. "I'll call her when they let us go ashore."

Sweating profusely in the humid heat, Frank stood in the tin office at the head of the BPM fuel pier, waiting impatiently for the Dutch operator to connect him with the hospital. The place reeked of oil, and the sour odor of the nearby refinery added to the assault on his olfactory senses. He had already gotten through to the Van Wely residence, only to be told that Cinta was on duty. "Doctor van Wely, please," he said when the hospital operator came on the line.

The woman told him to wait. He heard another ringing on the line, then the click of a receiver being picked up.

"*Spreekkamer van de Dokter van Wely*," said a pleasant feminine voice.

"Is that you, Cinta?" Frank shot back, excitement welling up inside him

"No, this is Nurse van Zweden," came the reply in perfect English. "Who is calling, please?"

"It's Frank Rhea, Catherine. Can I speak to Cinta?"

"She's down the hall with a patient. I can get her. Are you here in Balikpapan?"

"At the waterfront. Please hurry. I have to go back aboard ship in a few minutes."

"Frank?" The very sound of Cinta's voice made him feel good inside.

"Yeah, it's me. Bad pennies keep turning up."

"I watched your ships come in this morning, and I hoped you might be with them. Can you come to dinner?"

"I'm afraid not. They only let me ashore because the ship's refueling. We're going right back out."

"Papa will be disappointed. He took quite a liking to you."

"I wish the same were true of his daughter. Look, Cinta, I don't have much time. When I saw you last week, you promised to go south if the war got out of hand. It's time you bailed out. The Japs have already grabbed part of the Philippines, and they'll be here before you know it. Get out now, while there's still time."

"I'll go as soon as Papa thinks I should. The Japs haven't declared war on us yet, you know. Not that it matters. Our Queen declared war on them right after Pearl Harbor."

"The oil here and at Tarakan is their main objective."

"Yes, that's what Papa says, too. Don't worry about me, Frank. I'll be well away before the Sons of Nippon arrive."

A knock came at the shed window, and Frank saw a CPO gesturing for him to come out.

"I have to go, now, Cinta," he said hurriedly. "I'll look for you in Java, if we make it that far. Always remember that I'll love you forever."

"Take care of yourself, Frank. Try to forget about me."

"Never!" he replied.

The banging came at the window again. The chief was more insistent with his gestures. The fuel hoses had all been disconnected now, and *Marblehead* was taking in her lines.

"This is it, sweetheart," he said quickly. "See you in Java."

"Goodbye, Frank. God be with you."

Marblehead sortied two hours before dawn, threading her way out through the minefields behind two escorting destroyers. Frank and Tonto sat in their *Seagull*, warming the engine for a pre-dawn launch. Commander Goggins's briefing had been short and succinct. The task force would head south at first light, with *Marblehead* screening ahead. He ordered Frank to fly an antisubmarine patrol a hundred miles down Makassar Strait, assuring that no enemy surprises awaited the force. Any submarines sighted could be assumed to be hostile. The admiral's staff had confirmed that no friendly subs were in the strait.

An antiaircraft alarm shattered the early hours of morning. An unidentified aircraft popped up onto *Boise's* air search radar screen for a few minutes, circling the harbor before flying off to the southeast. Neither the Dutch Air Force nor Navy knew where the plane came from. It could hardly have been Japanese, unless they had an aircraft carrier lurking somewhere to the east.

As soon as *Marblehead* cleared the minefield, Captain Robby worked her up to over twenty knots. With the wind whistling about his open cockpit, Frank decided conditions were ready for a launch. Pulling down his goggles, he warned Tonto and gave the signal to the catapult officer. Moments later, the cat shot the *Seagull* into the air.

Rising slowly to an altitude of five thousand feet, Frank throttled back his engine to just under 100 knots and dipped his wingtip to turn south. Endurance was of the essence now, not speed. Conservation of fuel would maximize his time aloft. Settling onto his outward leg heading, he began to search the sea for any signs of activity.   Down below, the phosphorescent wakes of the three warships shimmered beneath the bright tropical stars. Far off to the east, the first streaks of light appeared on the horizon.

Frank and Tonto kept up a banter over the intercom, coordinating the surface areas which each was searching. Even without moonlight, their binoculars picked up the whitecaps far below.   For the first half-hour, the seas were completely empty. Then Tonto let out a soft whistle.

"What's up, *amigo*?" Frank queried.

"I've got what looks like aircraft exhaust at two o'clock, low. What do you think?"

Frank raised his glasses and peered in the direction Tonto had specified. He picked up a moving faint red glow at once.   "My God, you're right. He's going about ten knots slower than we are. I'm throttling back."

"Think it's that bogey that buzzed the fleet this morning?"

"Could be."

"Want to report the sighting?"

"Let's maintain radio silence and see what happens."

Warrant Flying Officer Nobuo Nishina adjusted the throttle of his Yokosuka E14Y1 *Geta* to slow its 360-horsepower radial engine and then shifted his compass heading to the new course recommended by his navigator. If Petty Officer Fujita's calculations were correct, they would arrive at the rendezvous point with their mother ship precisely at dawn. The huge submarine, an I-Class B-2 Type vessel, would surface at first light to pluck her reconnaissance seaplane from the water. As soon as the hatches were sealed again, she would drop back beneath the waves, safe from the prying eyes of American aircraft.

Nishina knew that his report would galvanize the I-boat's crew to heroic action. He and Fujita had made a detailed survey of the American convoy through excellent night optics, information that would allow their captain to set a devastating ambush. The mother ship was among the most modern of Japan's submarines, carrying twenty of the new Type 95 torpedoes. Powered by oxygen, these 24-inch monsters travelled at 49 knots for the incredible distance of 11 miles, over twice the range of Allied torpedoes. Like its surface ship twin, the Type 93, the submarine torpedo packed an explosive charge of over 1,000 pounds, enough to break the back of even a cruiser. Better yet, they left no telltale wake of bubbles to give away the I-boat's position. Before this day was finished, Nishina expected Makassar Strait to be strewn with the wrecks of American ships.

"Final checkpoint," came Fujita's voice over the intercom.

"Acknowledge," Nishina responded and then began to descend towards the surface of the sea.

Dawn was coming on fast, streaking the eastern horizon like a Japanese battle flag. Down below, the moderate seas were still ink black. Frank pondered the situation, wondering if it were time to report the sighting.

"He's goin' down," Tonto said with excitement.

Frank leaned far over the control panel to get a better view of their prey. Sure enough, the glow was dropping toward the strait below. Just as the rim of the sun peeked over the horizon, the exhaust glow faded into the darkness on the sea.

"He must have landed on the water," said Frank as he circled back to the east to keep from overrunning the target. "Can you work out a pattern to hold us near him."

"Gimme a few seconds."

Frank orbited for several minutes to the east of where the plane had vanished while daylight spilled over the horizon behind him. Then Tonto solved the mystery with a new sighting.

"Holy shit," the Seminole suddenly exclaimed.

"What is it?" Frank asked quickly.

"The biggest Goddamed sub I've ever seen--even bigger than the *Narwhal*. Ninety degrees to port--just surfacing."

Frank swung his glasses left and picked out the large patch of boiling water at once. Tonto had not exaggerated. The submersible looked larger than any American submarine. A long cylinder filled the deck in front of its huge conning tower. What looked like a catapult extended almost to the bow. Ant-like figures swarmed out of open hatches, unlimbering a boom crane from the top of the cylinder.

"I'll be damned!" Tonto swore. "It's a goddamned aircraft carrier."

"I read something about them a few years ago. As soon as they take that guy aboard, they'll know everything about the task force. I'm going down before they see me." Dropping the *Seagull*'s nose, Frank leveled out at five hundred feet.

"What are we gonna do?"

"Sink the son-of-a-bitch. Send this to *Marblehead* by code: HAVE SIGHTED I-CLASS SUB RECOVERING SOC. WILL ATTACK UNODIR (unless otherwise directed)."

Frank took a quick mental inventory of his assets. The two 100-pound bombs slung beneath the *Seagull*'s wings were his main punch. One .30-caliber Browning machine gun was synchronized to fire through the propeller, while Tonto had a similar gun on a flexible mount. Considering that the sub doubtless carried antiaircraft weapons, the odds would be about even. His best hope was surprise.

"Just got a come backer from the ship," Tonto piped up. "ATTACK. HELP ON THE WAY. What's the drill, Lone Ranger?"

"We'll only get one crack at them. I'm going to attack at two hundred feet, coming straight out of the sun. If we're lucky, we'll put both bombs in her hull amidships. A couple of near misses might even split her pressure hull. Be ready to hose down her decks with your gun as we pass overhead."

"I'm with you. Give 'em hell, *Kimo Sabay*."

Frank worked the *Seagull* south until she was due east of the submarine. Raising his glasses, he saw that the crew was still involved with the aircraft recovery. Apparently, no lookout had spotted the American plane yet.

"Here we go, *amigo*. Hold onto your hat." Opening the throttles wide open, Frank dropped down to two hundred feet and headed straight for the I-boat. Skimming low over the waves with the sun directly behind it, the *Seagull* made a tiny blur of a target. The submarine grew larger by the minute as the plane picked up speed, finally hovering at just 150 knots.

Up ahead, the topside crew of the I-boat suddenly began milling about in a frenzy, redoubling their efforts to get their seaplane back aboard. Men were pointing toward the *Seagull*, while others unlimbered weapons on the big conning tower. Then orange tracer leaped out to meet the Americans as someone began firing a pair of heavy machine guns. Massive projectiles, at least .50-caliber, were whipping around the *Seagull*'s braced wings. Frank grimly hunkered down behind the instrument panel and flew on.

At a thousand yards, he lowered the plane's nose and pressed the firing button on his joystick, sending a stream of red tracer to lace the air around the conning tower. Everything was happening too fast! Heavy slugs were tearing holes in the wing above his head, shredding the canvas skin. He was almost on top of the I-boat now, skimming in at just above masthead-height. Grasping the bomb release firmly, he held his breath and pulled sharply.

A monstrous hand seemed to slap the *Seagull* from behind, sending it staggering skyward. When Frank finally regained control, he realized that Tonto was whooping at the top of his lungs.

"We got the bastard, Lone Ranger! At least one bomb hit, dead amidships!"

As Frank banked the plane to make a another pass, a huge secondary explosion rocked the I-boat, sending a plume of red flame shooting out of the hangar and up into the sky.

"There went his AVGAS," Frank opined. "Those poor-sons-of-bitches don't have a prayer, now."

A second attack was clearly unnecessary. A film of burning gasoline enveloped the sub and spread out on the waters around her, immolating those survivors still afloat. Caught in the flaming inferno, the little seaplane first caught fire, then disintegrated as her own fuel tank went up. With two gaping holes in her pressure hull, the big I-boat began slipping stern first beneath the waves.

"Here comes the cavalry--too late, as usual," Tonto commented.

A three-engined Dornier flying boat winged in from the south, arriving just in time to watch the I-boat's final plunge.

Frank picked up his intercom mike. "Send this to *Marblehead* in plain language: SCRATCH ONE I-BOAT AND ONE SOC."

(Three)
Aboard USS *Rust*
Manila Waterfront
24 December 1941

Jack was at his battle station when *Rust* nosed into a wharf near fleet headquarters at just before noon. Strung out and exhausted, he had felt irrational resentment when the signal arrived for the ship to steam across from Corregidor earlier that morning. No one had any idea what was behind Admiral Hart's peremptory order.

Fed by a dozen or more fires, a thin veil of smoke hung over the once-beautiful city. The early Japanese raiders had come and gone, but they would return quicker than in the first weeks of the war. Captured airfields in northern Luzon had drastically reduced their turnaround time..

A signal lamp began to wink from the third floor of the Marsman Building as Tom Hoskins nudged *Rust* against the camels just ahead of the little schooner, *Lanikai*. Filipino dockhands waited to take in her lines.

"Captain wants you on the bridge, Lieutenant," said Jarvis.

"Take over here, Chief," Jack said to Muldune. Handing his headset to the big CPO, he went down the ladder to the wheelhouse.

"Take a working party of twelve men from the deck force and get over to headquarters," Hoskins ordered. "Report to Commander Slocum. He has some classified files to be brought aboard. We're also to get some passengers for the run back to Corregidor, but they're not your worry. A truck will be here in a few minutes to pick you up."

"Manila's being evacuated?" asked Jack.

"Your guess is as good as mine on that. Get on with it."

"Aye, aye, Skipper," said Jack and then left the bridge at once. By the time he reached the weather deck, he'd decided which men to take with him.

"Wait here," Jack ordered Conroy Beavert, a tough little chief bosun who had been a railroad maintenance gang foreman in civilian life. "I'll take Jones with me and send him back for the rest of you when I find out what's wanted. Keep a close eye on that truck. Looks like anything could happen around here today."

Manila's main arteries were choked with Army trucks flowing northward toward the redoubt of Bataan. Civilian cars jammed the sidestreets in scenes that reminded Jack of the panics in Europe during the previous year. He sensed that order was on the verge of breaking down. It was easy to guess now why they were here.

Barreling through the door to the Marsman Building, Jack almost collided head on with a big, suntanned jaygee. He

recognized Kemp Tolley, the Skipper of the schooner, *Lanikai.*
"What's goin' on, Kemp?" he asked.

"You wouldn't believe the screwup," Tolley replied.
"MacArthur's about to declare Manila an open city. They've been
cooking on it over at Army headquarters for a couple of days, but
they didn't tell anybody in the Navy 'til this morning. Admiral
Hart's hopping mad, but it won't do any good. We've got spare
parts and torpedoes dispersed all over the city for protection against
bombing. Now we'll have to abandon them."

"What are you up to?"

"Heading south as soon as I take some of the staff to Corregidor.
Admiral Rockwell's already moved into Queen Tunnel, you know."

"Good luck, then," said Jack, shaking Tolley's hand. "I'd better
not keep Commander Slocum waiting any longer."

The fleet headquarters was a maelstrom of activity. Sailors
attached to the staff were purposefully scurrying about the offices,
some carting off extraneous files to be destroyed, others moving
signal equipment down from the roof. Jack sought out Commander
Slocum.

"Glad to see you finally made it," said Slocum in greeting.
"Jack, isn't it?"

"Yes, sir. Is it true that we're clearing out of Manila?"

"Afraid so. The Japs landed in force at Lamon Bay last night.
That's on the east coast, only sixty miles from here. They've got the
Army in a pincers now. MacArthur's pulling back to concentrate on
Bataan while he still has time. What I want you to do is move the
classified operations files to your ship. How many men did you
bring?"

"Twelve, plus a chief. They're with the truck out front. Show
me the load, and we'll get started."

Jack sent Seaman Jones off for the rest of the shore party.
Slocum had more than a dozen heavy filing cabinets with build-in
combination locks. Chief Beavert scrounged some hand trucks to
speed up the work. Within twenty minutes, the last of the safes was
carted away. Jack went searching for Slocum, finding him in the
hall talking to Commander "Rosie" Mason, the Fleet Intelligence
Officer.

"Can you handle seven more safes without making a second trip,
Jack?" asked Slocum.

"Yes, sir. We could take them and still have room for the men."

Mason was about to show Jack the cabinets when Admiral Hart came walking down the hall. Jack was surprised to see the taut, wiry little admiral wearing "River Rat" Whites rather than his usual stiff-collared blouse. He looked tired and strained, but his manner was confident.

"Have a look at this, Rosie," said Hart, shoving a dispatch at Mason. They talked in hushed tones about it for several minutes. "Those are my feelings exactly," the admiral finally said aloud. "We'll hold back only sufficient PBY's to take us out." He turned to go, but Jack caught his attention. "I don't believe we've met before, Lieutenant."

"Jack Sewell, Admiral. I'm gunnery officer on *Jonathan B. Rust*."

"Ah, yes. You're the one who talked Captain Collins out of *Houston*'s pom-poms. He told me about it."

"That's right, sir. We shot down a *Zero* with one of them."

"A fine piece of initiative. I must say that you Reservists have surprised me. You're doing first class work. One of the troubles with our profession is that only war itself proves whether we've been doing the right things to prepare for it. Keep up the good work."

"Aye, aye, sir," Jack answered, his chest swelling with pride.

"I need a word with you also, Harry," Hart said to Slocum, and the two of them went off down the hall together.

Rosie Mason personally supervised the transfer of his files to the five-tonner. He detailed a chief signalman named Tanner to accompany them to Corregidor. Chief Beavert took the wheel, and Jack and Tanner piled into the cab with him as they set out for the wharf. The short drive to the waterfront took only a quarter of an hour. When they neared the pierhead, Jack saw that a big Army truck blocked the entrance to the transit shed. A squad of soldiers was busily tearing down a sandbag emplacement around a 37-millimeter antiaircraft gun.

"Hey, Sarge," Chief Beavert yelled at a nearby NCO. "Can you move that rig? We've got urgent cargo for that destroyer out yonder."

"Hold your horses, sailor," the sergeant yelled back. "We're gonna pull this piece out of here in a minute or two."

"Hurry it up, then. We ain't got all day."

"Neither have we, Mac." The sergeant growled an order to one of his men, who jumped into the big truck and ground the gears. The vehicle lurched backwards, careening over the last of the sandbags to collide with the gun beyond. When it came to rest, the truck was still blocking the entrance to the pier. Exasperated, Jack bailed out of the cab and went over to see what was happening.

"What's the trouble, Sergeant?" Jack said impatiently.

"None of your goddamned business, swabbie," said the NCO as he started to turn. Then his eyes caught the twin bars on Jack's collar. "Oh, beggin' your pardon, Lieutenant," the man mumbled quickly. "No disrespect intended, sir. This dumbass just lost us a good sky gun. I'm Thomas, sir, 200th Coast Artillery."

"That's New Mexico National Guard, isn't it?"

"Yes, sir."

"We're Reservists too. Just about our whole crew is. Let's see your gun." Jack scrambled over the sandbags to have a look. The truck had crushed the left front wheel of the gun carriage, rendering it incapable of being towed.

"Get me a thermite grenade," Thomas said to one of his men.

"What are you going to do?" asked Jack.

"Blow up the barrel so that Japs can't use it, sir."

Jack thought for a moment, doing rapid calculations in his head, then said, "Don't destroy it. Drag it down the pier to our ship. Maybe we can get it to Corregidor."

"That's okay by me. I was gonna write it off as a battle casualty anyway."

Once alongside *Rust*, Jack had Thomas uncouple the 37-millimeter piece as close as he could get to the Wherry boat davits. The National Guardsmen, obviously relieved to be unburdened, sped away. Jack boarded the ship to report to the Captain. After getting directions on where to stow the filing cabinets, he outlined to Hoskins his ideas for the gun.

"Okay, Jack, we'll give it a whirl," said Hoskins. "Ten to one they take it away from us when we hit Corregidor, though."

When *Rust*'s lines were taken in an hour later, the Army flak piece was securely lashed to her boat davits. A dozen officers of the fleet staff came aboard a few minutes before for the run to "The Rock." Back at Central Fire Control, Jack raised his glasses and looked upriver as Hoskins conned the ship past the mouth of the Pasig River. The once-bustling wharves along the riverbank were deserted now. Farther up, the wide bridges were jammed with green Army trucks and garishly painted, commandeered buses loaded with troops. One thought must be dominating the minds of the men in the vehicles. They had to reach Bataan before the Japanese caught up with them.

CHAPTER 14

(One)
Aboard USS *Marblehead*
Soerabaja, Java
Netherlands East Indies
24 December 1941

While *Rust*'s crew was unloading her cargo of secret papers into lighterage off Corregidor, *Marblehead* and her escorts were 1800 miles to the south, approaching Holland Pier at Soerabaja in a rainstorm. The weather put a damper on the spirits of the crew. Expecting to be greeted by exotic sights at the landfall, their visibility was reduced to practically zero by the torrential downpour.

The voyage from Balikpapan had been harrowing to the point of exhaustion. After the exhilaration of their I-boat sinking, Frank and Tonto spent endless hours aloft in their *Seagull* flying patrols over the American ships as they threaded their way into Makassar Strait and steamed on toward safety. The procession covered hundreds of square miles of sea, any of which might hide more lurking Japanese submarines. Frank found it incredible that the enemy was letting dozens of valuable merchant ships escape without further efforts to sink them. Their loss and that of the auxiliaries would have crippled all Allied efforts to continue the struggle for Southeast Asia.

Viewed from above, the waters of Makassar Strait were so clear that Frank was certain he could have spotted any submerged submarine that ventured within a hundred feet of the surface. But despite day after day of searching, no additional enemy undersea craft were sighted. The scenery below gave no hint of the fast-approaching war. The lush vegetation of the tiny islands off Celebes shimmered like emeralds against the deep blue of the equatorial sea, where the *prahuas* of fishermen skimmed gracefully over the wavetops.

But now the long voyage was almost over. The last hour had been tense as the formation followed a Dutch patrol boat up the buoyed channel through the extensive minefield in the strait between Madura Island and the Java coast. Several near collisions with sailing *prahuas* occurred after they entered the harbor.

A welcoming party of Dutch Navy officials came aboard once *Marblehead's* gangplank settled in place. Word went around that a bigger reception had been planned, but the storm disrupted the preparations. Two officers from Admiral Glassford's staff were with the Dutchmen, and they stayed on after their hosts paid their respects and departed. A few minutes later, the bugle sounded "officer's call" throughout the ship.

Captain Robby rose to address his wardroom. "Gentlemen," he began in soft but confident tones, "I'm pleased to announce that Admiral Glassford has no immediate orders for our employment. We'll begin 'port and starboard' shore leave at 1600."

A murmur of approval went up from his audience.

"But first, I have an important announcement to make. Before leaving Manila, Admiral Hart approved decoration awards for two of our *Marblehead* shipmates. Lieutenant Rhea and Warrant Officer Coacoochie have each been awarded the Distinguished Flying Cross for sinking the enemy submarine in Makassar Strait. Admiral Glassford will award their medals at Quarters tomorrow morning. Congratulations, Frank and Tonto."

"Hear, hear!" the assembled wardroom cheered.

"Now, on with liberty matters. The admiral has moved his staff ashore to free *Houston* for operational duties. The staff offices are at 15 Reiniersz Boulevard. A BOQ is being set up at 118 Darmo Boulevard. The Exec has a list of the local points of interest to pass out. The Dutch have a chain of canteens around the city that serve free beer and sandwiches to servicemen. The *Oranjii* Hotel is supposed to be the classiest place in the city. They have a good restaurant and facilities for dancing. Impress upon your men the necessity of conducting themselves with proper decorum. We are all ambassadors here. The Dutch are our allies now, and it's important that we get on together well if we're going to beat the Japs. A word to the wise should be sufficient.

"By the way, we understand that Admiral Glassford's Supply Officer has cornered the local market on turkeys. We'll have a traditional Christmas dinner after all." The Captain went on to complete his instructions on policies to be followed during the in-port period. After a short time for answering questions, he dismissed them.

The "V" Division officers surrounded Frank and Tonto, pumping their hands and slapping their shoulders. All of the other ship's officers, including Sergeant York, queued up to offer congratulations.

"Those Dutch sure were stand-offish," Eddie Blessman commented to Frank as they finally left the wardroom.

"Condescending would be my word for it," Frank replied. "They were almost too polite."

"Don't ya'll know what's eatin' them?" asked Tonto.

"Enlighten us," said Blessman.

"Those guys think we're yellow. To them, it looks like we ran away from the Philippines without a fight and left our army in the lurch."

"They'll change their tune the first time they go through an air attack," said Frank. "Christ, after what happened to *Repulse* and *Prince of Wales*, you'd think they'd realize how helpless surface ships are without air cover."

"We've got a Navy full of admirals who didn't understand that before Pearl Harbor," Blessman reflected.

"I need to talk to you gents about something else," Tonto interjected. "Wilson's in a bad way. I was just down to sickbay a while ago to see him. He's got some kind of malaria that our docs don't know how to treat. I hear by the grapevine that old 'Shaky Jake' is over at the civilian hospital here. If anybody in the Navy would know what to do, he's the man."

"Who's 'Shaky Jake'?" asked Frank.

"One of the fleet MO's," said Blessman, "a lieutenant commander named Wassell. Spent nearly his whole life in China."

"I thought maybe we could get Doc Ryan to transfer Wilson ashore," Tonto continued.

"Let's go see him," said Frank. "Wilson's too good a man to lose."

"Best damned aircraft mechanic on the ship," Tonto added.

"I was going to suggest the same thing myself," Lieutenant Tom Ryan, *Marblehead's* junior doctor said to Frank. The thin medical officer with the habitual smile was well liked by the crew. "Doctor Wassell knows more about these Asiatic diseases than anyone I've ever met. I'll draw up the transfer papers right away."

"Thanks, Doc," said Tonto. "How long before we'll be able to move him?"

"Within the hour. I'm sure the Exec will approve."

"I'd like to take him over myself. We go back a long way together."

"I'll go with you," Frank offered.

Two hours later, Frank and Tonto were standing in a spotlessly scrubbed hall outside a ward in Central Burger Hospital. A Dutch ambulance had been provided for the transfer, but they had gotten soaking wet coming down the gangway and crossing the pier. Frank flexed his feet inside his wet shoes, feeling the swish of water between his toes. The antiseptic smell of the thick-walled stone building made his nose itch.

"Here he comes," said Tonto, who had been peering inside the ward.

A slim, plain-faced man of medium height came out the door. Even if his white smock and stethoscope had not identified him as a doctor, his professional demeanor would have.

"How is he, Doc?" asked Tonto.

"Your Wilson's a very sick man, Mister Coacooche," replied the doctor in a soft, southern accent. "Do you know if he's been taking his malaria pills."

"He confessed that he hadn't when he first got sick. The bitter quinine turned his stomach."

"He's paying for it now. I think he has tertian malaria."

"What are his chances, Doctor?" Frank put in.

"This is Frank Rhea, our number two pilot," said Tonto in a belated introduction.

"Corydon Wassell," the doctor replied. As he shook Frank's hand, the pilot felt the perpetual trembling that had earned Wassell the nickname, "Shaky Jake," throughout the fleet. While a missionary, he had survived innumerable bouts with Asian diseases. "The prognosis on Wilson isn't too optimistic. We may lose him.

It's according to how much of a fight his body can put up."

"Can we see him," asked Tonto.

"I'd rather you didn't. He's resting now. You can look in on him tomorrow." Excusing himself to complete his rounds, Wassell retreated into the ward.

"I guess we might as well go back to the ship," said Frank.

"Damn that stupid kid," Tonto swore as they started back toward the lobby. "All he had to do was take those goddamned pills." There were tears in the Seminole's eyes.

"He's young and strong," Frank responded. "Maybe he'll beat it."

Their leather heels echoed off the polished terrazzo floor, and they continued to converse in the low tones which everyone uses in a hospital as they approached an intersection of two corridors. Turning the corner without looking, Frank collided full force with a woman, almost knocking her off her feet. She let out a string of unintelligible Dutch expletives as she straightened, then stopped in mid-sentence.

"Good Lord, Frank," said Cinta van Wely in English. "You look like a drowned rat. What are you doing here?" She seemed genuinely pleased to see him.

"Just turned one of my men over to Doctor Wassell," he responded after recovering after his initial shock. "Are you working here now?"

"Yes. Papa ran me out of Borneo last week."

"That was sensible. He's still in Balikpapan?"

"At the moment. He's flying down for Christmas tonight. Is your ship in port?"

"We came in this afternoon. We're supposed to be here for several days."

"Would you have Christmas dinner with us?"

"Shouldn't you check with your father first?" Frank said calmly, hiding inner excitement.

"No. I'm mistress of our home, and he'll abide by my decisions. Can you get leave?"

"I have the midwatch tonight, but I'm scheduled for liberty tomorrow."

"I want you to come too, Tonto," she said to the warrant officer. "I don't know," he said with hesitation.

"None of that," she chided. "Unless you're standing duty, you're ordered to come for the sake of your health."

"Since you put it that way," Tonto chuckled, "I accept."

"I'll send a car for you at eleven thirty," Cinta went on. "Where are you tied up?"

"Holland Pier," said Frank.

"I'm late to the ward," she said, hastily checking her watch. "I have to run. I'll see you tomorrow morning." She started to go, then turned back to Frank. Reaching up suddenly, she hugged her cheek close to his for a moment. Then she was gone down the hall in a swirl of smock and skirt.

It stopped raining before Frank's watch that evening. The skies were clearing, and stars lit up the heavens when he stepped out of the superstructure. As his eyes adjusted to the darkness, he saw that the decks were covered with men on mattresses. Fleeing the stifling heat of the mess decks, a large number of the crew had dragged their bedding into the open.

Climbing the conning tower to the bridge, Frank stepped over the doorway combing and saluted the OOD. After the ritual of relief between oncoming and off going watches, he went out onto the bridge wing and raised his glasses to scan the harbor. A good bit of the fleet was here on this anniversary of the birth of the man called, "The Prince of Peace." He made out all the seaplane tenders, including *Langley*. *Boise* was moored just across Holland Pier. There was *Holland* with a brood of submarines alongside. Six destroyers were clustered around *Black Hawk*. The old gunboats that fled Manila after the holocaust of December 10th had all made it to this refuge, as had the yacht, *Isabell*, and the minesweepers, *Lark* and *Whippoorwill*.

The early part of Frank's watch was peaceful. He spent a long time considering what to do about a Christmas present for Cinta. His reverie was shattered when the duty signalman brought up a message that had just come in, an announcement from Hawaii that Commander Scott Cunningham's garrison at Wake Island surrendered the day before. First Guam, now Wake. Two key stepping-stones on the direct air route to the Philippines were now in Japanese hands. Any aircraft reinforcements would now either have to come up from Australia or fly halfway around the world through

Africa and India.

Frank finished getting ready to go ashore just before half past ten on Christmas morning. As he tied his white shoes and stood up in the humid heat of his cabin, he was thankful that the Captain had specified "River Rat" Whites as the officers' liberty uniform. Since Java lay in the Southern Hemisphere, mid-December was high summer here. Even this early in the day, the heat was oppressive. The open-collared shirts were infinitely more practical that choker-necked dress whites he had worn to morning Quarters for the decoration ceremony.

Admiral Glassford had been upbeat and cheerful. The slender, hawk-faced flag officer was known for his diplomacy when he headed the Yangtze gunboat force in China. He was almost totally bald and had an easy, disarming smile. Some said he was the most eloquent officer in the Navy. He was certainly eloquent at the short meeting with the decorated officers following the ceremony.

"Admiral Hart was adamant that you two be decorated at once," Glassford informed them. "It seems that Doug MacArthur has been handing out DFC's right and left at Clark Field, mostly for unconfirmed sinkings. Your kill in Makassar Strait was confirmed by the Dutch with a message of congratulations to the Fleet Commander. It's the best piece news we've had in this war."

Collecting his hat, Frank set out to get the Gunnery Officer's permission to leave the ship. Cooking odors permeated the corridors. The cooks in the galley were outdoing themselves to lay on the traditional Christmas feast. Otherwise, there was little holiday spirit to be seen. The men were worn out from constant watches. They badly needed liberty ashore to blow off steam.

Frank found Nick Van Bergen at one of the library tables in the wardroom, reading an old magazine. "I request permission to leave the ship, Commander," he said to his department head.

Van Bergen looked up, took a deep puff on his ubiquitous pipe, and blew out the smoke. "Not staying for Christmas dinner, Frank?" the big man boomed. "Oh, yes, you're eating with the oil man from Borneo, aren't you. What's his name?"

"Mister Nicolaas van Wely."

"I hear that it's his daughter you're really interested in." Van Bergen's eyes held a mischievous twinkle.

"Cinta and I were at UCLA together several years ago. I want to leave early so that I can pick up a present for her ashore."

"Go on, and enjoy yourself. Liberty expires at 2130. By the way, I understand that the Chinese goldsmiths here are famous for their work. You might give them a look for that present."

"Thank you, Commander. I'll do that."

Tonto was waiting at the gangplank. "'Bout time you showed up," he said reprovingly. "I was gonna go without you."

"Wouldn't have done any good," Frank retorted. "Van Wely's car isn't here yet, anyway." The words were hardly out of Frank's mouth when a white Lincoln Zephyr came nosing through the busy traffic beyond the wharf and approached *Marblehead.*

"Looks like we're goin' in style, *Kimo Sabay,*" said Tonto.

"Let's go," said Frank. Approaching the quarterdeck, he saluted the Officer of the Deck. "I have permission to go ashore, sir," he said.

"Very well," the ensign responded.

Taking two steps down the gangplank, Frank turned to the stern and saluted the American flag on the fantail gaff, then went rapidly down the incline to the shore.

The chauffeur, an islander resplendent in tailored uniform and tightly fitted turban, bowed to Frank. "Lieutenant Rhea?" the man said in English.

"That's right," Frank replied.

"I am Yuni. I am to take you to the home of my *tuan besar.*"

After boarding the luxurious vehicle, Frank explained to Yuni that he wished to visit a goldsmith along the way. The driver recommended a dealer and set a course for that section of the city.

In the immediate vicinity of the port, Soerabaja seemed to be more a European city than one of the Orient. The warehouses and waterfront facilities were totally modern. The business district was equally metropolitan, with broad, smoothly paved streets. The pastel buildings along the sidewalks were solid and well built, as one might expect of the Dutch. Soerabaja was the cleanest city Frank had seen since leaving San Francisco. Even on this Christmas Day, numerous motorcars of various vintages filled the streets.

As they neared the Asian section of the city, the character of the surroundings changed. The streets were still wide and smooth, but they teemed with a profusion of vehicles. Hundreds of *betjaks*, a sort of combination rickshaw and bicycle, buzzed about, propelled by the powerful legs of their drivers. Big gray oxen with rubber shoes tied onto their feet pulled oxcarts with six-foot wheels. Pedestrians in bright sarongs crowded the sidewalks. To the predominantly Moslem population, the Christian holiday was just another day of business. As the Lincoln passed a market that might have been lifted from any city in the Orient, the air was filled with the chirping of scores of birds in cages suspended from overhead poles.

At last, they reached the street of the goldsmiths. Yuni gave Frank some advice on how to deal with the proprietor of the shop at which they paused. A few minutes later, the aviator came back to the car grinning happily, having purchased a beautifully engraved bangle bracelet for a third of what the Chinese merchant originally asked.

After another half-hour's drive through the diverse city, they arrived at what would have been termed a "country club colony" in America. Sprawling stucco mansions with red tile roofs were set back from the street behind wide lawns teeming with blossoming trees. The whole area had an air of unbridled opulence. Yuni turned the Zephyr into a long, circular driveway that led to a villa atop a low hill. No more pretentious than its neighbors, the house seemed to bear the stamp of the tough oil man Frank had met in Balikpapan. Yuni parked the car before a recessed front entrance, then came around and opened the back door.

"This way, *tuan*," he said to Frank, leading the officers toward the door. Opening it without knocking, he ushered them into a high-ceilinged foyer. "Wait, please," Yuni requested before padding off on sandled feet.

A few moments later, Nicolaas van Wely came barreling into the room. Looking cool and comfortable in a white linen suit and open-collared shirt, he was carrying a glass of champagne.

"Welcome to my home," the big Dutchman said, pumping Frank's hand. "I'm glad you were able to come. I was sorry that we didn't get a chance to get to know each other in Borneo."

"It's a pleasure, *Mijnheer*," Frank responded.

"Enough of that. You must call me Nicolaas, and I shall call you Frank. And this must be Warrant Officer Coacooche." Nicolaas shook the Indian's hand.

"Tonto to my friends, sir."

"Then Tonto it is. Come into the drawing room. Cinta will be out presently. She's supervising the dinner preparations at the moment."

The leather heels of the officers' shoes clicked on the cool floor tiles as they went through an arched doorway into a wide room. Several fans spun slowly beneath the high ceiling. French doors opened onto a terrace beyond. Tonia Ivanovna rose from a fashionable rattan chair as they entered the chamber. For a moment, Frank was spellbound by her presence. In the months since their brief meeting in Manila, he had forgotten what a beautiful woman she was. The tight sheath of her yellow silk *cheongsam* accentuated her splendid figure, and, as she came to meet them, he saw that its skirt was slit up to the thigh, offering a glimpse of exquisitely tapered leg.

"Countess Ivanovna, I'm sure you remember Lieutenant Frank Rhea," Nicolaas said in introduction. "And this is Warrant Officer Tonto Coacooche."

"It's a pleasure to see you again, Lieutenant," Tonia said in thickly accented English, "and I'm pleased to meet you, Mister Coacooche."

"The pleasure is all mine," Frank responded, gallantly kissing the hand she proffered in continental fashion.

"Pleased to meet you, ma'am," said Tonto.

"What would you like to drink?" Nicolaas inquired.

"It's a little early for hard liquor," said Frank, "but if that's champagne you're drinking, I'll have one of those."

"I hear you have the best beer in the world on this island," said Tonto.

"Very true," Nicolaas agreed. He turned and spoke quickly in Javanese to a servant who had been standing by. In a few minutes, the man returned with Frank's glass of champagne and a frosty bottle of Heineken beer for Tonto.

Cinta came bustling into the room just then, smoothing the skirt of her blue taffeta cocktail dress. "Why didn't you tell me they were here?" she chided Nicolaas.

"You had your responsibilities in the kitchen. Besides, you learned quickly enough."

Cinta came straight to Frank and kissed his cheek. "I'm so glad you could come," she said, then turned and took Tonto's hand. "And you, too, Tonto. Are you keeping him out of trouble?"

"As best I can."

"Are those new ribbons you're both wearing? What outrageous things have you been doing since we saw you last?"

"I believe that's the Distinguished Flying Cross," Nicolaas exclaimed. "I should have noticed earlier. You must tell us about them. But first, let's sit down."

They settled into a circle of comfortable wicker chairs about a low brass table. As succinctly as possible without sounding boastful, Frank told them about the attack on the I-boat. His audience hung on every word, eager to ask questions when he had finished.

"Were you in terrible danger?" Cinta asked breathlessly.

"Apparently not too much," Tonto said with a laugh. "Anyway, we survived."

"You are very brave men," Nicolaas said with sincerity. "We must drink a toast to you." He clapped his hands, and Yuni immediately appeared and recharged the champagne glasses. "To Frank and Tonto," he said as he rose to his feet. "May their luck be ever so good."

"Hear, hear," said both women before they drained their glasses.

Somewhat embarrassed, Frank thanked them courteously.

"Do you know how long you'll be in port?" asked Cinta.

"It's a military secret," Frank responded. "It can't be for long, though. With no more ships than we have out here, there'll be plenty for us to do."

"I understand from some friends in our government that we've been promised all the help your Navy can send," said Nicolaas.

"We'll just have to wait and see on that," said Frank. "Nobody seems to know just how badly we were hurt at Pearl Harbor."

"Let's not talk about war," Cinta interjected. "Papa, did I ever tell you that Frank passed up a chance to go to the Berlin Olympics when he entered the Navy?"

"No. I didn't know that."

"It wasn't certain that I would have made the team," Frank corrected Cinta. "I didn't go to the tryouts. I was more interested in flying."

"I can understand that," Nicolaas nodded in agreement. "I can still remember when I soloed for the first time."

"I don't usually handle the controls, but I know just what you mean," Tonto reflected.

They continued to chat on various subjects for over an hour, pausing occasionally to refill their glasses of champagne and beer. No matter how hard they tried, the war crept back into their conversation. Discovering that Tonto had been stationed in San Francisco for several years, Tonia began plying him with questions about the great bayside city.

"You sound like you're planning to move to America," Nicolaas commented. "I thought you had your mind set on Sydney."

"I do, my sweet," Tonia cooed, "but it pays to develop alternate plans."

"Do you live here in Soerabaja now, Countess?" asked Frank.

"No. I flew over when I learned that Nicolaas would be in Java today. I have real estate holdings in Zwarte Gouden that I manage. I used to own properties in Balikpapan, but I've liquidated them."

"Zwarte Gouden is something of a boom town, like the gold rush towns in California," Cinta commented.

"Except that the gold is black instead of yellow," said Nicolaas. "That's what the name means—'Black Gold.' The oil strikes there are the richest in all Java. My company has built a new refinery and port facilities to process the product."

Somewhere deeper in the house, a telephone bell began to jangle. A moment later, Yuni came in to inform Nicolaas that he had a call from Houston, Texas.

"Excuse me for a few minutes, please," Nicolaas said to his guests. "That will be Alette and my grandchildren. Cinta and I must exchange our Christmas greetings with them. Would you entertain the gentlemen, Countess?"

The Van Welys left the room, Nicolaas obviously relishing the prospect of talking with his grandchildren.

"I didn't realize that the phone link was still open," Frank commented.

"Oh, yes," Tonia replied as she freshened Frank's champagne. "We can talk to just about anywhere in the world. If you want to call home, I'm sure that Nicolaas could arrange it."

"Nobody to call," said Frank. "My folks were killed in an auto accident when I was a kid. I don't have any other relatives. What about you, Tonto?"

"I come from so far back in the swamp they don't have telephones."

"May I ask you a personal question, Frank?" said Tonia, suddenly serious.

"Should I make myself scarce?" asked Tonto.

"Not if you're as good a friend to Frank as I've been told," the Countess countered.

"Fire away," said Frank.

"I saw how you looked at Cinta. You're in love with her, aren't you?"

"You really don't beat around the bush, do you? Yes. I've loved her since we were students together in Los Angeles."

"But she's given you no encouragement? Am I correct?"

"She doesn't seem to have any room in her life for anything but her work."

"I have some advice to offer, if you'll take it. Don't be discouraged. Cinta is just establishing her identity as a doctor. Once she feels comfortable in her profession, her womanly emotions will reemerge."

"That's the most welcome advice I've had in a long time," Frank said sincerely.

"Here they come," said Tonia as the sound of footsteps on the tiles came up the hall.

Nicolaas beamed as he entered the room. "My grandchildren think I'm the original 'Saint Nick,'" the oilman said with a belly laugh.

Tonia filled the room with musical laughter. "You'll never qualify as a saint of any kind," she said to Nicolaas.

"Dinner's about ready," said Cinta. "Ada has outdone herself this year."

Nicolaas led the way into a large dining room, which was richly furnished in Chinese rosewood. A crystal chandelier hung above a long table that could have seated twenty, but there were only five chairs clustered about one end. Nicolaas indicated the seating, with himself at the head, flanked by the two women. Frank sat beside Cinta and Tonto beside Tonia.

"We should give thanks for what we have," said Nicolaas, still glowing from his talk with Alette's children. He prayed in characteristically straightforward manner, praising his creator for the gifts of the earth and asking for strength to resist the heathen invader. When he finished, the servants began to bring in the food.

Knowledgeable now about Dutch eating habits, Frank had worn his loosest set of whites and skipped breakfast. He was not disappointed. The feast over which Cinta presided was a mixture of the best that the Dutch, British and East Indian cultures had to offer. They started with turtle soup and went through courses of shrimp cakes and sate' before tackling the main dish of roast goose with bread and apple stuffing. There was, of course, rice and all sorts of spicy vegetable side dishes. By the time dessert was served--half a dozen kinds of strudels and cakes and sweetmeats--Frank was full to the bursting point.

"No more," Frank said as a servant offered chocolate cake. "If I eat another bite, I'll pop the buttons off my uniform." He lifted his cup to sip the strong, rich coffee of Java.

"We could teach you to eat like a Dutchman if we had the time," Nicolaas chuckled.

"You won't need any more time with me," said Tonto, plucking a slice of strudel from a tray. "My people have a custom of feasting in times of plenty."

Tonia, who had long since stopped eating herself, laughed at the Seminole. She liked uncomplicated men. The warrant officer had the same lusty appetites she so admired in Nicolaas.

"I believe it's customary in your country, as in America, to give gifts at Christmas," said Frank, feeling that the moment was right to present Cinta with his earlier purchase.

"Quite correct," said Nicolaas. "You borrowed Saint Nick from us. We call him *Sinterklaas*. We like to keep what we will give a secret, so our custom is called 'giving surprises.' We usually exchange 'surprises' on Saint Nicolaas's Eve."

"In Russia, before the communists swept it all away, the children believed that Babuuschka brought their Christmas gifts," Tonia said wistfully. "I remember carolers going about the streets dressed as bears and stable animals. It was all very wonderful."

"I have a small 'surprise' for Cinta," said Frank, taking the box from his pocket. "I didn't have time to have it properly wrapped."

"Oh, Frank, you shouldn't have," Cinta exclaimed as she opened the lid. "Why, it's positively beautiful." She took out the bracelet and slipped it onto her wrist to show it to Tonia and her father. Then she turned and kissed Frank on the cheek. "We have 'surprises' for you and Tonto, also," she continued.

"It would be unthinkable to have a guest on this day without giving one," said Nicolaas. He turned and spoke to a servant. The man returned shortly with two small, wrapped packages on a tray. "I think you'll find these useful in your work," the Dutchman said as he handed the gifts to the Americans.

Frank broke the tiny ribbon and removed the paper, revealing a leather covered box with a spring-loaded lid. He popped it open and almost gasped in surprise. Inside was a large Rolex watch. "Wrist chronometer" might have been a better description of the elaborate timepiece. Its luminous dial was marked with both twelve and twenty-four hour notations, and it had a built-in stopwatch as well.

"I've never seen anything like it," Frank finally said. "It's the best Christmas present I ever had. There's no way I could ever adequately thank you for it."

"For once, even I'm speechless," Tonto said as he examined an identical watch in his box. "I didn't come here expectin' anybody to give me anything."

"It's our pleasure," said Nicolaas, obviously gratified at the reaction to the gifts. "Perhaps we should retire to the library for brandy and cigars while the ladies freshen themselves."

"That's one of your European customs I've always admired," said Tonto.

Nicolaas led the officers down a cool hall to a large room lined with bookcases. Once they were inside, he closed the sliding doors and walked to where a Zenith Transoceanic radio rested on a table.

"I really wanted to catch the early morning news broadcast from San Francisco," the Dutchman admitted, "but I didn't want to upset Cinta." He turned on the set, fiddled with the dials and soon brought in Glenn Miller Band music clearly. Then he offered a box of Cuban cigars to the Americans. After they lit up, he poured them brandy from a crystal decanter. "That's KGEI," he explained. "I've found their broadcasts more accurate than anything we can get out here."

After a few minutes, the record was finished, and the speaker began to spout the musical dots and dashes with which American stations preceded their newscasts.

"On this first Christmas of the war," the commentator began, "it's comforting for the people of San Francisco to see the sidewalks filled with servicemen in uniform."

"I'll bet," said Tonto with disgust. "When are they gonna send some of them out here to help us?"

"The War Department confirmed today that the first American soldiers have arrived in Northern Ireland to set up a training base there."

"Northern Ireland!" Frank said with exasperation. "The Japs are kicking the crap out of us in the Philippines and they're sending troops to Northern Ireland? What the hell are those idiots in Washington doing?"

"Giving first priority to defeating Hitler," said Nicolaas with fire in his eyes. "Our people in Washington have been warning us that this would happen. Roosevelt never meant to send us all the help he promised."

"The War Department also confirmed today that a second Japanese landing has been made south of Manila. General MacArthur's Fil-American Army is withdrawing in orderly fashion to cover the capital."

The library doors slid open, and the countess peered inside. "Ah, there you are, Darling," she said to Nicolaas as she fitted a cigarette into a long, ivory holder. "We knew you'd be listening to the news. We've come to hear it also."

"You just can't stay away from the war, can you, Papa?" Cinta chided as she followed Tonia into the library.

"The British War Office announced last night that the garrison of Hong Kong surrendered earlier today. There have been many rumors of Japanese atrocities. Neutral observers reported that berserk Japanese troops massacred the patients in British field hospitals and repeatedly raped the attendant nurses."

"The dirty rats!" Tonto swore.

"It shouldn't come as a surprise," said Tonia. "They've been acting like that in China for five years. In the Japanese lower classes, women have no rights. They exist only to serve men."

"How could civilized human beings behave in such a manner?" said Cinta, paled by the news of the massacre.

"They're not civilized," said Nicolaas, "at least not as we define the word. Less than a hundred years ago, they were still living in the Middle Ages. As far as their attitudes toward human rights are concerned, they've progressed to about where Europe was in the seventeenth century. They act about the same as the Spanish soldiers did in Holland back then."

"You hit the nail right on the head," exclaimed Tonto. "I never heard it expressed that way, but you're dead right. The Japs act just like the Spaniards who conquered Florida."

"Which makes it all the more imperative that we get you out to safety if it looks like we can't hold out here," Nicolaas said to his daughter.

"If that happens, at least it's some time off," Cinta replied hopefully. "They'll have to defeat the British in Malaya and the Americans up north first."

"Don't count on it," Frank responded. "The way the Japs are moving now, they might not take that long to get here."

They listened on to the American station. Time passed with surprising swiftness. When his new watch showed 8:30 p.m., Frank reluctantly announced that he and Tonto were due back at the ship.

"Must you go so soon?" asked Cinta with a touch of melancholy.

"Liberty expires in an hour," Frank replied. "We mustn't set a bad example for the men."

"I'll have the car brought around," said Nicolaas then clapped his hands. Yuni appeared as if by magic to receive his instructions. "My house is always open to you when you're in port here," the big Dutchman continued as another servant brought the officers their hats. "Come back at every opportunity."

They said their goodbyes at the car. Then the Americans got in and Yuni drove away.

Hand in hand, Nicolaas and Tonia wandered back toward the library. Cinta went to the kitchen, where Ada was supervising the cleanup from dinner.

"Ah, I saw your young American, *kesateria*," the old woman clucked to Cinta. "He had a Positive Peak (erection) when he was near you."

For a moment, the Dutchwoman's brain sought the meaning of the island word, but then it came back. The *kesateria* were a class of Javanese royal warriors before the Dutch conquest.

"A woman should be proud to couple with such a man," the *baboe* went on. "He is much like the *tuan besar*. Will you take him as a lover?"

"Of course not," Cinta snapped back. "Neither him or any other man. I've told you that a hundred times since I came home."

"A young woman should not be without a man," Ada continued, shaking her head. "Sooner or later, the wisdom of my words will become clear to you."

Cinta wished that she were as sure of her feelings as she made out to Ada. The logical, scientific part of her mind kept reaffirming that it made no sense to become romantically involved with anyone at this point in her life, much less someone like Frank who might be killed in combat at any time. Yet the physical attraction she felt for him was a palpable thing. His mere presence could envelope her in a flush of affectionate warmth, leaving her positively lightheaded. Was it really love that she felt for him, or were her long-suppressed biological urges reacting to subconscious memories of their past ecstasies? She pondered those questions long into the night, but found no answers.

CHAPTER 15

(One)
Aboard USS *Rust*
Manila Bay
25 December 1941

There were no turkey dinners for the sailors on the ships in Manila Bay. *Rust* spent Christmas afternoon alongside *Canopus*, anchored close beneath Marivelles cliffs at the tip of Bataan. The sub tender was the only shop facility available to the warships in Philippine waters, and Tom Hoskins was determined to make the most of the brief period she could spare for his ship. Most of the time was taken up installing Jack's purloined Army 37-millimeter gun.

Sparks flew all over the after part of the ship as Chief Collins's working parties improvised a new gun tub near the fantail where the other destroyers had their three-inchers. *Canopus*'s crew swung one of her big derrick cranes out over the destroyer to deftly pluck the Army gun from one of the boat davits and lower it into position. *Rust*'s shipfitters welded the gun to the deck and then surrounded it with open grating provided by the tender. When the metal cooled, *Rust* possessed the heaviest antiaircraft battery of any ship left in the harbor.

While Chief Collins was busy with the gun, Chief Muldune went ashore searching for ammunition. For the past week, both the Army and the Navy had frantically moved stores of every description from the city and dumped them near Bataan's quarantine pier. Supplies were there for the taking, without worry about requisition forms. Muldune came in with three boatloads of 1.1-inch and 37-millimeter shells just as Hoskins was about to slip away.

For some unaccountable reason, no enemy aircraft struck at the armada of small craft plying back and forth between the wharves of Manila and the evacuation sites on Bataan and Corregidor. No strikes disturbed the serpentine jam of vehicles on the roads leading to Bataan. About noon, a large formation of Japanese bombers

unloaded their ordnance on the deserted Walled City and then flew
off again to the north.

Early on the morning of December 26th, Tom Hoskins was
summoned to the new Navy headquarters in Corregidor's Queen
Tunnel. When he returned, he called a quick meeting of his officers.

"Admiral Hart left for Java this morning aboard *Shark*," Hoskins
announced. "Admiral Rockwell has taken command of what's left
here. DesDiv 'P' will continue our present duties until further
notice."

From mid-morning, that day was hell for the ships of the
destroyer division. Twenty-seven bombers came after them, and the
enemy airmen made savage, continuous air attacks until dusk finally
brought relief. The ships corkscrewed about the bay for hours,
straining their overworked engines and aged hulls. They put up the
best antiaircraft barrage they could when the planes came within
range, but only *Rust* could throw up anything bigger than .50-
caliber. By the time Hoskins dropped anchor off Marivelles in the
gathering darkness, his crew was completely played out. A hasty
conference between the destroyer skippers heated the TBS (Talk
Between Ships) airwaves soon after sunset. When it was over,
Hoskins called Jerry Busch and Jack to the bridge.

"We're going to ask the admiral to send us south," he told them.
"Grab all the ammo and stores you can from the beach, but finish
within three hours. We'll sail tonight if Rockwell gives us the green
light."

The smell of oil hung heavily over *Rust* as she lay alongside
Canopus, sucking vital, black lifeblood into her tanks. The tender
would never sail again, so her need for fuel was subordinate to that
of the destroyers. *Rust's* bunkers were only half-filled when the
Captain's gig returned. A few minutes later, Hoskins convened a
council of his department heads in the wardroom. Hollow eyes and
sagging cheeks showed that they were all close to exhaustion, but
their attention was riveted on the Captain.

"It was the damnedest thing I ever saw," Hoskins commented.
"Harold Pound, John Bermington and I all told the admiral that our
crews were burned out and we felt that our usefulness to him was
now negligible. Then he agreed and ordered us to join Task Force
Five in Java. We'll shove off as soon as our 'midnight requisitions'

teams are back aboard. Now, where's that chart I asked for?"

"Right here, Skipper." Jerry Busch unrolled a large map of the Philippines. Mindoro, Panay and Negros lay between the big Islands of Luzon in the north and Mindanao in the south. The long finger of Palawan ran along the western side of the Sulu Sea, suggesting an ancient land bridge to Borneo.

"The Japs took Davao on the twentieth," Hoskins continued, planting a finger on the port city in southern Mindanao. "They have shore-based planes there already. And they took Jolo yesterday." He indicated a little island in the middle of the Sulu Archipelago. "To make matters worse, Jap carrier planes have been sighted to the west."

"Japs every which way we turn," said Jack. "We're completely ringed in."

"The most direct course to join Admiral Glassford in Soerabaja would be to run down the east coast of Borneo through Makassar Strait," Hoskins went on. "The Brits still hold North Borneo and have aircraft there. I'm inclined to hug the coast of Palawan down to Borneo then slip through Tawi-Tawi Passage to the Celebes Sea. We can refuel at Tarakan and then run all the way to Java without stopping."

"You're right, Skipper," Busch agreed. "Let's head for Sandakan." He tapped the capital of British North Borneo on the chart.

Muldune's shore parties proved unusually effective that evening. His own boat made half a dozen passages between the ship and the shore, conveying thousands of rounds of .50-caliber, 1.1-inch and 37-mm ammunition. The other boats brought extra food, engineering gear and medical supplies. Chief Collins showed up with a boatload of olive drab paint in five-gallon cans.

"What the hell's that for, Chief?" asked Hank Logan as the first pails were hauled aboard.

"Camouflage, Lieutenant," the little CPO barked back. "We'll be hidin' close inshore during daylight. If we splash this around, old 'Rustbucket' won't look like a ship to a Jap pilot."

At 2230, *Rust* hauled her anchor and crept out through the swept channel to the open sea. Her crew was at General Quarters, every man at his battle station. A blinker light flashed in the darkness as the old Yangtze River gunboat on station outside the minefield issued a challange. One of the lamps on *Rust*'s signal bridge gave the correct response.

"GOOD LUCK," blinked the gunboat's light.

The ship took the moderate ocean swells like the old thoroughbred that she was. Adrenaline flowed through the veins of the exhausted crew, snapping them to alertness. Somewhere out there in the darkness were the blockading Japanese ships and airplanes. Nerves were perched on a razor's edge as scores of eyes scanned the dark seas for the first sign of the enemy, but none appeared.

"I want twenty-five knots," Hoskins said to the Exec. "It'll burn up fuel at a sinful rate, but so be it. Let's get the hell out of here."

Hoskins took his ship into Valencia Bay on the east coast of Palawan at 0830 the following morning. He knew exactly where he wanted to go. There was a steep, jungle-covered cliff along part of the bay with deep water beside it. He anchored there within an hour and set the crew to disguising the ship. Some work parties went ashore to secure mooring lines and cut branches to camouflage the decks. Others sloshed Chief Collin's Army paint over the hull and upper works to break the vessel's clean, grey lines. By 1030, with *Rust* randomly streaked with green and swathed in palm fronds, the Captain was satisfied that they had done their best. Except for vital watches on the boilers and the antiaircraft guns, he sent the crew to bed.

Less than two hours after the ship bedded down, a formation of twin-tailed Mitsubishi bombers flew directly over *Rust*'s position. Hoskins was out of the chartroom in a flash, his binoculars glued to his eyes. There was no sign that the enemy aviators had seen them, so he decided against waking the crew. His men desperately needed rest. Telling the OOD to call him at 1600, he went to his own cabin and fell, fully clothed, into his bunk.

The only aerial attackers to bother *Rust* that day were the huge mosquitoes that swarmed out from the steaming jungle shore. Sleeping men lay drenched in sweat as the thermometer rose steadily until the temperature stood at 110 degrees on the palm-shrouded decks. In the firerooms, it reached 120 degrees. The men on watch nodded with fatigue, dreaming of the time when they, too, might surrender to slumber.

The cooks were roused first to prepare a hot meal. Hoskins wanted his men at the top of their form when the southward run continued. After supper, he said a few words on the public address system, explaining where they were going and closing with a gentle exhortation for every man to do his duty. As the sun settled behind the island, *Rust* shed her mantle of vegetation and slipped her moorings to the shore. With all hands standing easy at their battle stations, Hoskins conned the ship out through the bay and turned south. Within half an hour, he had worked her up to twenty-five knots again.

The next ten hours were nerve-wracking but uneventful. The Sulu Sea was calm that night; the sky, moonless. But the bright tropical stars gave enough light to silhouette the ship to any lurking submarines. Hoskins eschewed zig-zagging to conserve fuel, depending on speed alone to counter any undersea threat. Their run of luck ended with the dawn, just as the cooks were distributing coffee and sandwiches to the crew at their battle stations.

"Horsecock and cheese," Chief Muldune snorted in disgust after biting into a fat sandwich. "That's a hell of a breakfast."

"A lot better than nothing," Jack responded. He braced his feet against the roll and pitch of the ship as he sipped his coffee. Since the fire control platform was the highest point on the ship except for the crow's nest, all movements of the hull were greatly magnified.

"Wish we had a rum ration like the Limeys," mused Muldune. "A shot of booze would sure taste good about now."

"Crow's nest reports aircraft contact, dead astern," barked Jarvis, Jack's telephone talker. "Altitude about five thousand feet."

Jack swung up his glasses and searched the sky beyond the ship's boiling wake. He picked out the tiny speck at once. It was too far away to identify the type. "Give that lookout a 'well done,'" he said quickly and then issued a string of orders to put all antiaircraft guns at full readiness. Reporting to the Captain by battle phone, he checked signals for the inevitable air attack. They had evolved an efficient drill under the incessant aerial harassment in Manila Bay. Jack would inform Hoskins when enemy planes released their bombs so that evasive action could be taken while the missiles were falling. So far, it had worked perfectly.

As the trailing plane rapidly overhauled *Rust*, Jack recognized it as a four-engined Kawanishi H6K flying boat. Climbing steadily as it approached the destroyer, the aircraft circled just outside the range of her guns.

"The bastard's sizing us up," spat Muldune. "Wonder if he's got the guts to tackle us?"

As if in answer to the chief's question, the Kawanishi dropped astern and took up station above *Rust*'s broad wake.

"He's radioing for help," said Jack. "In a minute, every Jap within five hundred miles will know our position."

For almost an hour, the Kawanishi hung like a trailing kite behind the little ship, weaving from side to side to keep from overrunning her. Hoskins did the only thing he could: increase speed to thirty knots to get *Rust* closer to Allied territory before the Japanese struck.

Just after 0730, one of the bridge lookouts spotted two more planes winging up from the southeast. Chief Muldune eyed the newcomers for several minutes through his binoculars. "Lieutenant," he finally said, "them's PBY's. I'd stake my life on it."

"You're right, Chief." Jack recognized the *Catalina* silhouette, with twin engines jutting from a high parasol wing. He called the Captain and reported his conclusions. One of the lamps on the signal bridge began to rattle out a message toward the amphibians, but instead of responding, they turned away and flew off to the south.

Almost at once, the crow's nest reported additional aircraft approaching from the north. Jack identified three more Kawanishis as they moved up to join forces with the plane that had been shadowing *Rust*. They circled together outside gun range for a quarter of an hour.

"They look like a flock of buzzards followin' a starving cow," Muldune observed.

Just then, one of the bombers poured on power and came after the destroyer, flying at about seven thousand feet. Jack ordered the gun crews to hold their fire until the plane was well within range. *Rust* could not afford to waste ammunition. Hoskins was holding the ship steady on course, waiting for Jack's signal. When the ugly flying boat was just over a mile astern, big balls of tracer began to float up from the 37-millimeter. Moments later, both the 1.1-inchers chimed in. Coming in from dead astern, the enemy was exposing himself to everything *Rust* could throw up, but he did not flinch from his attack. Following the plane closely with his binoculars, Jack instantly spotted two black specks detaching from the wings to hurl earthward.

"Bombs away!" he shouted into his battle phone then braced himself hard against the railing. The ship heeled over hard to port as Hoskins threw her into a tight turn. Jack followed the bombs with his glasses. For what seemed hours, they appeared to be falling directly at the ship. Then they seemed to veer away to plunge into the sea exactly where *Rust* would have been had she not circled back. Two dirty geysers of water shot skyward, and concussion waves buffeted the fire control platform.

"Here comes another son-of-a-bitch!" Muldune yelled above the rattle and thumping of the antiaircraft guns. A second Kawanishi was boring in, braving the fire of *Rust's* sky guns to get at her. The gunners continued to pump shells into the air, but with little effect. Jack began to worry about the ammunition supply. He screamed a warning when the pilot released his bombs, and Hoskins deftly dodged them again.

The Japanese fliers showed little imagination. After the third plane repeated the now familiar attack pattern, the first one started the cycle over again. The original shadow plane held back, flying now directly in the sun.

"How many bombs do those bastards carry?" Muldune wondered aloud after the flying boats completed their fourth cycle of bomb runs. Before Jack could reply, Jarvis grabbed his arm.

"Bridge reports three more Japs, two points off the starboard bow," shrieked the talker.

Jack swung his glasses to meet the new threat, and his heart skipped a beat. The aircraft were Nakajima single-engined torpedo bombers--carrier planes that carried deadly warfish beneath their bellies. They flew a hundred miles an hour faster than the lumbering Kawanishis.

The carrier pilots split their formation to come at *Rust* from all over the compass, two from the port side and the other from starboard. Hoskins zig-zagged furiously to throw off their aim, but the Japanese hung on like terriers. With the 1.1-inchers and machine guns lashing streams of tracers about their wings, the Nakajimas dropped down to skim just above the wavetops. Jack's stomach knotted as he watched both planes on the port side smoothly slip their monstrously large torpedoes into the water.

"Hang on!" Muldune bellowed as the fire control platform careened drunkenly. Hoskins had reversed the starboard engine, spinning the ship like a top. Then sparks were erupting all over her upper works as the Nakajimas' machine guns winked wickedly. Jarvis screamed, and his chest seemed to explode. Bullet splashes tore at Jack's cheeks, but he hardly noticed. His eyes were riveted on the twin wakes that appeared certain to tear out *Rust*'s vitals. Then the bubbling monsters streaked past close aboard, plowing harmlessly away into the open sea.

Rust felt almost dead in the water, and Jack realized that both engines were backing under full power. Searching the sea to starboard, he saw at once what was happening. The third Nakajima had dropped its fish while Hoskins was avoiding the others, and it was coming on with sickening speed. Until the last second, it seemed sure to take off the destroyer's bow, but her churning screws saved her. The frothing wake darted by a mere six feet from her stem. The men on *Rust*'s upper works caught their breath again.

"Here comes our shadow," yelled Muldune, who had taken up Jarvis's headset. A brace of seamen were hustling the talker to sickbay.

Jack saw that the Kawanishi was coming on fast. "Get that lousy son-of-a-bitch," he shrieked at the gun captain on the 37-millimeter. "He's down to where even a machine gun can reach him."

The Army gun opened fire at the limit of its range. Jack cursed, expecting the enemy to turn away, but the pilot pressed home his attack. Anticipating the moment of bomb release, Jack was sucking in his breath to report when the sky gun began to score. Pieces of metal flew off the Kawanishi's left wing between the engines, then orange flame leaped out to leave a trail of oily smoke. The propellers slowed, and the crippled wing dipped crazily. Tracers from the port 1.1-incher started slamming into the plane's fuselage. The Japanese pilot was very good. Instead of crashing, he brought the flying boat down to a rough water landing about two miles off *Rust*'s port beam.

"Number Four Gun," Jack barked into his battle phone, "fire at will."

Flame leaped from the four-incher on the after deckhouse. After three weeks of helplessly enduring air attacks, this was the naval rifle crew's first chance to shoot back. They went at it with vengeful glee. Their first shot was high, but the next three ripped into the crippled Kawanishi, reducing it to smoking rubble. The fuel tanks went up with the last hit, casting a mantle of flaming gasoline over the wreckage.

After seeing the fate of their comrade, the remaining Kawanishis circled once and flew off to the east. The Nakajimas had long since vanished over the horizon. Startled by the sudden silence, Jack pushed back his tin hat and looked around him. Spent cartridges from the .30-caliber Lewis guns littered the platform. He had not even noticed them firing. A pool of blood marked the spot where Jarvis had fallen.

"All guns, report casualties," he ordered, wiping what he thought was sweat from his cheek. His hand came away bright with blood.

"Already done, Lieutenant," said Muldune. "Nothin' but a couple of scratches. I'd better take a look at your face." The chief broke out a first aid kit and cleaned the shallow wounds on Jack's cheeks, then dabbed them with iodine. It stung like fire, bringing tears to his eyes.

"I'm okay," Jack muttered grimly. "Keep a sharp lookout. Those yellow bastards are bound to come back."

"Maybe not," Muldune said hopefully. "By now, we ought to just about be within range of the Limey's airfields on Borneo."

(Two)
Sandakan Harbor
British North Borneo
28 December 1941

Near dusk, *Rust* crept smoothly in across the placid waters of Sandakan Harbor. She had not come through unscathed. After losing two crew members killed in attacks by Japanese aircraft, she suffered another tragedy. A flight of RAAF Lockheed *Hudsons*, mistaking the destroyer for an enemy cruiser, bombed and strafed her when she entered British waters. Hoskins endured one bomb run while frantically trying to identify himself to the fliers, then turned loose Jack's antiaircraft gunners. More proficient after their morning's practice, they blasted one of the *Hudsons* out of the sky. After Hoskins got through tongue-lashing them, the Aussie airmen were not sure that they were glad to be rescued from their raft.

Scores of outrigger canoes, all filled with screaming, laughing natives in sarongs, swarmed out to surround *Rust*. Looking down at their happy brown faces, Jack found it hard to believe that these were the progeny of the once-feared Malay pirates. An official-looking launch came nosing through the smaller boats. A tall Britisher in a khaki safari suit stood in its bow. A naval officer in whites was at his side. Hoskins stopped the engines and ordered a Jacob's ladder thrown over the side, and the two white men scaled it nimbly. From his perch on the fire control platform, Jack could see that the naval officer was an American, a full commander. Hoskins met him at the rail and saluted, then took the visitors below. A few minutes later, word was passed for all officers to assemble in the wardroom.

"Gentlemen," Hoskins said after his officers had settled themselves around the table, "this is Mister Albert Finney, the Sandakan Harbormaster." He indicated the paunchy, slightly balding man in the bush jacket. "And this is Commander Murphy, our naval observer here."

"It's good to stand on an American man-o'-war again," said Murphy. "Congratulations on your escape from the Japanese."

"Mister Finney has agreed to fill our tanks from the government stocks here," Hoskins continued. "We'll be able to get fresh fruit and vegetables from the natives. I intend to stay here for twenty-four hours to rest the crew and repair damage. There aren't any recreational facilities, so all hands will remain on board."

"The entire European population here is less than a hundred," Murphy explained.

"We'll need to be able to get underway on short notice anyway," Hoskins went on. "We'll go directly to the pier to top off our tanks, then knock off except for in-port watches. After a good night's sleep, the men should be ready to get old 'Rustbucket' shipshape tomorrow. We'll shove off at dusk. I want to run Sibuto Passage after dark. A Jap 'pig-boat' has been reported in the vicinity. Questions?"

"Will we be stopping at Tarakan, Skipper?" asked Hank Logan.

"No. With full tanks, we can run all the way to Balikpapan.

We'll have more than one reason to stop there. I've agreed to take two passengers that far--the wife and niece of the Deputy Governor here."

"Women aboard a warship?" Logan said skeptically. "Isn't that bad luck?"

"You won't think so when you see Pamela Mallory," Commander Murphy spoke up. "She's the best-looking woman in North Borneo."

Near sundown the following day, Jack was just completing an inspection of *Rust's* weaponry. Every gun on the ship was now thoroughly cleansed of dirt and carbon and freshly lubricated. Spent shells from yesterday's battles had been cleared away, and new ammunition filled the ready issue magazines. Muldune pushed the men hard, but the lives of everyone aboard depended on the guns functioning properly.

After satisfying himself that all the weapons were ready for action, Jack went up to the fire control platform to check out the instruments there. It afforded a fine view of the port. Sandakan was mostly a thatched-roof native town, with only a sprinkling of solidly built colonial buildings to mark its British Empire status. The white beach was studded with big, outrigger-equipped sailing *praus.* Except for the launch that Finney and Murphy had used, there wasn't a white man's boat to be seen. Close behind the town loomed the dark Borneo jungle.

Jack was just checking the main range finder when a late-model Ford sedan turned onto the pier, driving right up to *Rust's* gangplank. Its uniformed driver jumped out and rushed around to open the rear door. A thick set middle-aged man in a white suit emerged first, followed by a large woman dressed in shapeless khaki coveralls. Last out was a young blond woman in a similar garment, and as she stood upright and raised her smoothly tanned face to look at the ship, Jack saw that Commander Murphy had not lied. She had that fresh, uniquely British beauty that harkened back to the days of the Viking conquests. Her face would have drawn notice in Monte Carlo or New York, and her coveralls could not fully conceal her splendid figure.

"Mother of God," Muldune muttered at Jack's elbow. "Will you look at that? Better break out the leg-irons from the brig,

Lieutenant. We'll have to chain up half the crew to keep them away from that one."

"The officers, too, Chief," Jack said with a laugh.

Supper was served to all hands about a half-hour after the arrival of the passengers. For the first time since the war began, the officers dined together. A party of British civilians and Commander Murphy assured a crowded table. Murphy introduced the white-suited man as Deputy Governor Landsbury. He seemed a harmless gaffer but befuddled by the calamities now befalling the empire. His wife was built like a tank. Rawboned and heavily fleshed, Madeline Landsbury would have made two of her husband. She had a personality to match her figure: hard-nosed and utterly disdainful of anything not British. She wore her brown hair in a bun at the back of her neck, and the small brown eyes set close together in her plain, red face had an icy glint. The younger woman was quite another matter. She had a pixie-like quality about her, accentuated by her closely bobbed golden hair. Immediately the center of attention among this pack of young warriors, she was enjoying every minute of it. Her musical laughter punctuated the conversation. The excellent meal of pork chops, the first fresh meat *Rust's* men had seen in weeks, went largely unnoticed.

"My wife and Pamela have already had quite an adventure," Landsbury observed as he finished his pork. "They've been knocking about the jungle for the better part of a fortnight."

"Uncle wanted Auntie and me to get to safety as soon as the Nips attacked," Pamela picked up the thread of the story in a soft, musical voice, "so he sent us south to Sarawak by road. We were about there when we learned that the Japs had already invaded the place."

"I knew from the beginning that it was wrong to go there," Mrs. Landsbury said haughtily.

"Now, now, my dear," said her husband. "You know that I couldn't bear the thought of you falling into the hands of those bloody barbarians."

"Anyway," Pamela went on, her intensely blue eyes sparkling, "we had to turn around and rush back with the Nips at our heels. To make matters worse, we just missed the last evacuation ship, the old *Baynain*. If you hadn't come to take us to safety, I don't know what would have become of us."

"We'd have taken you south in the launch," Commander Murphy put in, "but not nearly so safely as *Rust* can."

The conversation continued for over half an hour. Jack got to chat with Pamela for a few minutes. She expressed interest in his father's fishing fleet, explaining that her family had owned such vessels before the war. They were now serving the Royal Navy as antisubmarine ships.

"Guests and gentlemen," Tom Hoskins finally said, "I hate to break this up, but we must sail within the hour." He issued instructions for getting underway. The ship's officers filed out to go to their duties, and Landsbury said goodbye to his womenfolk. He seemed to take it much harder than his seemingly indestructible wife. There were tears in his eyes as he drove away.

Once *Rust* cleared the harbor and turned east, Jack left his post atop the bridge and went back to the wardroom for a cup of coffee. The ship was running on normal watches. He would be OOD for the First Watch--eight to midnight--and there was not time for a nap first. He took a mug of black, oily liquid from the duty steward and walked out to the rail to drink it. His eyes strained to make out the dim outline of the Borneo coast in the gathering darkness.

"Leftenant Sewell, isn't it?" Pamela Mallory's voice at his elbow startled Jack, and he spilled coffee on the deck.

"Yes, Miss Mallory. Excuse my clumsiness. I didn't hear you come out."

"I was sneaking away from old dragon Auntie." She laughed softly. "She's dreadfully seasick. Your doctor gave her something for it, and I think she's asleep now."

"How are you feeling?"

"Oh, marvelous. I love the sea and sailing. More than that, I'm delighted to finally be away from Uncle's dreadful little fiefdom. You have no idea how stifling such a place can be. There were only seventy white people in the whole town, and we had to keep up appearances to show the fifteen thousand natives how superior our culture is."

"If you hated it so much, why did you stay?"

"Oh, I was in exile. Mama decided she couldn't handle me, so she shipped me out to Aunt Madeline. Actually, I was having an affair with someone beneath my station, which was inexcusable in

Mama's view."

"You don't seem reluctant to talk about it," said Jack, not a little surprised by the turn of the conversation.

"Why should I be? I think the old double standard for men and women is a lot of malarkey. Why shouldn't women have the same freedoms as a man? Anyway, people of Mama's generation had affairs aplenty. They just didn't have the honesty to admit it."

"What about your aunt?"

"The 'Iron Maiden?'" Pamela laughed again. "I'll bet she hasn't slept with poor old Uncle a dozen times since they were married. She's been watching me like a hawk for over two years."

"Where will you go now?"

"Australia, for a start. I'll try to get home from there. What about you, Yank? Have you got a girl somewhere?"

"No such luck. Just my father's business."

"Those women in Glochester must be nitwitted," said Pamela, edging closer.

Jack checked his watch, finding that it was almost 1945. "I'm afraid I have to go," he said with reluctance. He was strongly attracted to this frank young woman. "I have the next watch."

"Yes, I remember. I saw your watch bill. I believe that Leftenant Logan, your cabin mate, will be relieving you."

"That's right," said Jack, surprise evident in his face.

"Papa was in the Navy in the last war. I know all about those sorts of things."

Just after midnight, Jack groped his way through the darkened ship toward his cabin. He was bone weary and drenched with perspiration. It had gotten hotter and muggier on the bridge as the night wore on, which was not surprising since they were approaching the equator. Only a dim, red battle lamp glowed in the wardroom as he entered officers' country. The two ensigns displaced from their quarters by the women were asleep on the transoms. The duty steward nodded at the table. Jack tiptoed quietly through the passageway and entered his pitch-black cabin. Going straight to the far corner, he located the pail of fresh water Hank had brought up earlier. Stripping off his sweat soaked uniform, he removed the collar devices before rinsing the garments in the bucket. After putting them on a hangar to dry, he wet a washcloth and sponged off his body. Only then did he realize that there was someone in the cabin with him.

"Who's there?" he asked quietly.

"Not to worry, pet." He recognized Pamela's musical voice. "It's only weak little me."

She was on him in a flash, her hands grasping his neck to pull his face down to meet sweet, hungry lips. He slipped his arms around her, discovering that she did not have a stitch on her body. Passion boiled up within him like an erupting geyser, and he pressed her back onto the bunk.

"Ah, Jack, swive me!" she purred into his ear. "I've waited two years for this, and I won't wait any longer."

Daylight found *Rust* plowing southward through the Celebes Sea at a steady speed of twenty knots. She had slipped through Sibutu Passage while Pamela shared Jack's bunk. Around mid-morning, the oil port of Tarakan slipped by off the starboard beam. Although they were now well into Dutch waters, Hoskins kept a double crew of lookouts scanning the horizon in all directions. Three times during the day, suspected periscope sightings sent the crew to General Quarters. Jack spent the better part of the day at his battle station. Not once during daylight hours did he set eyes on Pamela.

As dusk approached, the ship was nearing the point where Borneo and Celebes funnel the waters of the Celebes Sea into the long, narrow neck of Makassar Strait. She was right off Mangkalihat Point when the duty soundman reported a positive submarine contact off the port beam. As the general alarm rang through the vessel, Hoskins made an instant decision. A submarine in these waters could just as likely be friendly as Japanese. He turned away from the contact and ordered up flank speed. But even as the contact faded astern, he kept the crew at battle stations. If the "pig-boat" were Japanese, there might well be others of its kind nearby.

Dawn brought an aircraft sighting. It was a flying boat similar to a PBY, but it had three engines rather than two. The bow lookout was the first to identify the black and orange triangle markings of the Dutch Naval Air Force. Feeling safe for the first time in weeks, Hoskins secured the ship from General Quarters.

Jack headed for the wardroom for a late breakfast. Jerry Busch was there already, talking avidly with Pamela. He invited Jack to join them. Ford, the steward, brought them plates piled high with scrambled eggs.

"I've missed your company at meals, Leftenant," Pamela said to Jack.

"Duty called," he said with a shrug.

"I'd hoped to get to know you better," she went on, winking ever so slightly. Her eyes held an impish gleam.

"That would have been nice."

"There'll be no time now. Mister Busch was just telling me that we'll make Balikpapan before evening. Auntie won't stay aboard a moment longer than necessary."

"How is she?" Jack's poker face hid his great disappointment.

"Ghastly. She's still sick as a dog. Hasn't moved from her bed except to go to the lavatory. Will your ship stay long in Balikpapan?"

"We may lay up for a day or two to make repairs," Busch answered.

"Perhaps we'll get a chance to meet ashore," Pamela said to Jack. "We'll be staying with a friend of Uncle's, a chap named Van Wely."

Daylight was fading as *Rust* came up on Balikpapan lightship. A little Dutch minesweeper led her in through the minefields to the protected harbor, where pier space beside a refueling ship was made available. Hoskins put the destroyer alongside the wharf as darkness settled in. The gangplank was hardly in place when a white Cadillac came rumbling up to fetch the women to Nicolaas van Wely's mansion. Mrs. Landsbury insisted upon an instant departure after a perfunctory "thank you" to the Captain. She hustled Pamela off the ship before Jack had a chance to say goodbye.

Within the hour, Hoskins secured the boilers and turned half the crew loose on liberty. Jack went straight to a phone booth to call the Van Wely residence, but his request to speak to Pamela brought disappointment. The Dutchman had just taken the women to the aerodrome to fly them to Java. Dispirited and in no mood to celebrate, Jack went back to the ship. Besides Pamela, what he wanted most in the world was about twelve hours of sleep.

CHAPTER 16

(One)
Skies Above Central Borneo
Netherlands East Indies
15 January 1942

Garrit Laterveer kept adjusting the throttle of his battered *Buffalo* until he was satisfied that he had the best possible balance between fuel consumption and speed, then settled back into his seat and scanned the dark skies beyond his windscreen. About a thousand yards in front of his fighter and five hundred feet below, his keen eyes picked out the pale blue exhaust flames of four Glenn Martin bombers--the final survivors of a full squadron that his friend, Cornelis Van Den Brock, had brought to Borneo the previous week. Garrit was escorting the bombers with a flight of six *Buffalos* from his squadron.

The Dutch aircraft were far out over Makassar Strait, winging their way north for a dawn strike against the Japanese task force which had seized Tarakan Island three days before. Twice in the past two days, the Dutch fliers had surprised the enemy and inflicted casualties on the ships standing off the oil-rich island. Now they were challenging fate again, trying for a final, telling blow before the Japanese established their fighter forces on Tarakan aerodrome and drove the Allied air units from the skies of North Borneo.

The first two weeks of 1942 had brought continuing disaster to the Allied cause. When Roosevelt and Churchill met with their staffs over Christmas in Washington, they failed to comprehend the magnitude of the impending debacle in the Far East. Reaffirming their "Defeat Hitler First" policy, they ruled that only those forces that could be spared from the war against Rommel would be made available to their Asian commanders. They did establish the important principle of unity of Allied command, appointing General Sir Archibald Wavell, hero of the early campaigns in Africa, as supreme commander of the Southwest Pacific Area. Headquartered at Lembang, Java, his command would be known as ABDA--for American, British, Dutch, Australian. His air commander would be British; his ground forces commander, Dutch. Admiral Tommy Hart was named naval commander.

While the Allies planned and organized, the aggressive Japanese acted. They overran all of Luzon except for Bataan and Corregidor, where MacArthur's forces continued stubborn resistance. Lieutenant General Tomoyuki "Tiger" Yamashita's 25th Army steadily pushed General Arthur Percival's British and Commonwealth forces back down the Malay Peninsula until only Jahore, the southernmost province, remained in British hands. And now, finally declaring war on the Netherlands, the Japanese had seized Tarakan.

Flaming death stalked Allied airmen throughout the skies of Southeast Asia. The Brewster *Buffalos* being flown by both Dutch and British Commonwealth pilots were pitifully inadequate to deal with the nimble Nakajima Ki-43 *Hayabusas* of the Japanese Army. Almost a third of Garrit's squadron was blasted from the air over Malaya, and his unit was luckier than most. Employing the "attack diving--never dogfight" tactics being used by Chennault's Flying Tigers in Burma, Garrit's young proteges gave a good account of themselves, becoming experienced combat veterans while posting a kill ratio of 3:1 in their favor. His personal kill total rose to twenty-three. Their British comrades had fared far worse. Flying a version of the *Buffalo* with only 1100 horsepower, the inexperienced Brits had been decimated. Garrit felt relief when ordered to withdraw and transfer to Borneo. The rampant defeatism in Malaya had begun to affect even the Dutchmen.

All the Dutch *Buffalos* had been modified in Singapore. Armored glass salvaged from wrecked RAF Brewsters now filled their cockpit windows. RAF reflector gunsights replaced the cruder versions of the Dutch birds. Garrit's plane also had an internal wireless antenna instead of the drag-inducing external pole and wire. By reducing armament and petrol carried, his plane was some 30 mph faster than when he left Java. But on this mission, he needed all the firepower and range he could get. On the earlier Tarakan raids the Dutch had encountered the storied Mitsubishi *Zeros* of the IJN, a much more formidable opponent bearing 20-mm cannon.

Although fatigue gnawed at his consciousness, Garrit felt more vibrant and alive than at any time since leaving England. What turned his life around was unrelated to the cataclysmic events occurring about him. Precipitously and without reservation, he fell in love. More astonishing to his war-weary mind, his love was returned with equal intensity.

Garret met Catherine van Zweden on his first day at Samarinda II, the secret, magnificently camouflaged airfield on the Mahakan River in Central Borneo. Initially attracted by her uncanny resemblance to his martyred fiancee, Juliana Kortie, he quickly fell for her genuine goodness and sense of duty.

Catherine was viewed as an angel of mercy by the aircrews of the American 19th Bombardment Group. Driven off their bases in Luzon and Mindanao, these B-17 units had retreated all the way to Australia before moving their operations to Malang, Java. Now, they were flying shuttle-bombing missions against the Philippines, using Samarinda as a refueling stop. Whenever the planes returned from their combat missions, Catherine was always there beside the ambulance, her white uniform shining in the sunlight like a homing beacon. The Yank fliers claimed that several wounded crewmen managed to cling to life by dreaming of her tender care at the end of their agonizing flights.

Since every eligible male at the air base was courting Catherine, Garrit was surprised at first that she was willing to spend so much time with him. Finally blurting out his love to her, he was astounded when she admitted that she loved him as well but had been unable to verbalize her feelings. Within a few days, they were engaged. They planned to wed as soon as they could return to her home in Zwarte Goud, Java. Only one factor marred his complete happiness: Unlike Juliana, Catherine adamantly refused to go to bed with him until the church blessed their union.

The brightness of shared love burned the cancer of pessimism from Garret's mind, allowing him to tackle his work with renewed vigor. His flying skills became sharply honed again, and his former aggressiveness returned. Even in his stolid, obsolescent *Buffalo*, he was again a killer to be reckoned with.

Far to the east, the first hint of light appeared on the horizon.

Below, the waters of Makassar Strait were black as ink. The Dutch fliers passed unknowingly over the big Kawanishi flying boat riding smoothly down on the surface of the calm sea. Not monitoring the wireless frequencies used by the enemy, the Dutch pilots failed to intercept the signal that went winging in rapid dots and dashes from the picket plane. Still hoping for surprise, they approached Tarakan just after sunrise. A towering pillar of smoke from the burning oil installations marked the target clearly.

The fighter pilots coaxed the *Buffalos* up to almost 27,000 feet. As they came up on Tarakan, six sets of eyes were busily searching the skies for signs of the enemy. Far below, the Glenn Martins began their bomb runs. Van Den Brock planned to swing in over the northern tip of the heart-shaped island, skirt the smoke column and sweep down the anchorage from north to south.

Garrit sighted the *Zeros* first, and a sinking feeling hit him in the gut as he did. The nine enemy planes wheeled around the smoke column from the south at about fifteen thousand feet. They had obviously spotted the Glenn Martins and were racing to intercept. Hastily barking orders over the wireless, Garrit rolled his *Buffalo* over onto its back and went almost straight down. Only the quickest reaction could save Van Den Brock's planes from certain slaughter. Even as the *Buffalos* plummeted earthward, three of the *Zeros* broke away from the pack and came racing up to meet them.

"Cheeky bastards, aren't they?" Lieutenant Shultz commented over the radio.

The *Zero* had an exceptional rate of climb. As the opposing flights of fighters converged at mind-boggling speed, Garrit called out assignments of specific targets to each of his pilots and told them to hold formation. Tracers leaped out at him from the wings of the leading *Zero*. The Japanese pilot was ranging with his machine guns, waiting until he was on target before unleashing his 20-millimeter Oerlikons. He never got the chance. Garrit's own guns were rattling now, the heavy recoil of the wing .50-calibers shaking the aircraft. Orange tracers converged on the propeller hub of the *Zero*, then lifted slightly. Flames exploded from the engine and swept back along the fuselage. The *Zero* fell away to the right as Garrit's plane streaked past.

"Shultz just bought it," Lieutenant Moulders, Garrit's second-in-command, screamed over the circuit.

Without breaking his dive, Garrit glanced back over his shoulder. A *Buffalo* was falling toward the sea, trailing a long tail of fire. Garrit's target suddenly exploded, scattering flaming debris about half a mile of sky. The two remaining *Zeros* were turning to follow the *Buffalos* down, but they would never catch the heavy Brewsters.

"Close up on Moulders," Garrit ordered Sergeant Simmons.

Screaming earthward, Garrit could see that the other *Zeros* were already shredding Van Den Brock's formation. He headed straight for the melee, knowing all along that he would arrive too late. Two of the bombers were on their way down, belching oily smoke. The others were maneuvering frantically, trying to shake two "vics" of *Zeros*. Garrit sent Moulders and Symons after one "vic" while he took on the other. One pass was all that he would have, so it had to be good. He opened up at maximum range, wildly spraying the air about the enemy planes with tracers. The *Zeros* broke away immediately and looped up to get on his tail, but he never gave them the chance. He glanced a Glenn Martin flying into the smoke cloud as he continued his own dive almost all the way to the sea, opening the distance from his pursuers until he was too far ahead for the *Zeros* to overtake the *Buffalo*. With the throttle all the way through the emergency gates, he ran for home. A quick call over the radio brought only a response from Moulders.

"Symons went in, Captain," reported the lieutenant. "I'm about a kilometer to your left and a hundred meters lower. We head south, I assume?"

"Roger," Garrit responded. "Did any of the bombers get away?"

"One, I think. Yours. The Nips put ours down before we could help him."

Garrit overtook the single surviving Glenn Martin about fifty miles from Samarinda. It was badly shot up but still flying at maximum speed. He saw from its markings that it was Van Den Brock's plane.

About mid-morning, Garrit eased the formation of survivors down toward the Borneo jungle. They were scarcely a thousand feet above the Mahakan River before his sharp eyes picked out Samarinda II field. At first, it appeared to be merely an open space in the rain forest. Only when he came down to five hundred feet could he make out the two parallel sod runways. The camouflage was fantastic, the best he had ever seen. The field was covered with hundreds of wooden sawhorses. Not even a tiny observation plane could have found a path between them. Any aircraft landing uninvited would have been smashed to pieces.

Landing flares suddenly shot up from the control tower, and swarms of indigenous Dyaks broke from cover and began clearing the runway along the axis of the wind. It took only a matter of minutes. Garrit gave a hand-signal for Van Den Brock to take his bomber in first.

With Lieutenant Moulders glued to his wing, Garrit continued to circle the field until the bomber was safely down before landing his *Buffalo*.

Well-drilled ground crewmen directed Garrit to the aircraft dispersal area back under the tall trees. He taxied to the front of a solidly built revetment protected by dirt filled oil drums, swung around facing away from it and cut his engine. Two-dozen Dyaks, barefoot and dressed in their traditional sarongs, came out of nowhere and pushed the plane back into the protected shelter. Feeling unutterably weary, Garrit climbed out of his cockpit and jumped down from the wing onto the grass.

(Two)
BPM Refinery Complex
Balikpapan, Borneo
Netherlands East Indies
15 January 1942

Nicolaas van Wely was halfway up the newest thermal tower in the Sepoeloeh Cracking Plant, directing the placement of demolition charges, when the messenger came to tell him that the Controleur was urgently trying to reach him. Turning the work over to an assistant, Nicolaas went to the safety phone on one of the landings and had the refinery operator patch him through to the Controleur's Residence. Woltz came on the line at once.

"You'd better get over here quickly, Nicolaas," said the Controleur firmly. "There's been a serious development which can't be discussed by phone. It's extremely pressing."

"I'll be there in twenty minutes," the oilman responded,

checking his watch.

"Good. That's about when Rotteveel will be arriving."

Nicolaas went back to where the charges were being set and gave instructions to keep the work moving for the rest of the day. Then he clambered down the steep ladders to the ground with the agility of a man half his age.

Explosion after explosion rumbled in the distance. As soon as Tarakan fell, orders came from Batavia to begin demolition of the Balikpapan oil wells. Teams of specially trained oilmen with military training swarmed into the fields at once to begin with the lowest producing wells. They pulled casings, cut the pipe into short lengths, and jammed them back into the shafts along with pumps and any other metal they could get their hands on. Then they sealed the wells with blasts of TNT. At the pace the work was progressing, Nicolaas hoped to complete the destruction before the Japanese forces reached Balikpapan. Other teams were wiring the giant refineries for demolition. When the orders arrived, a fortune in oil works would be blasted to oblivion.

A company truck took him to the refinery administration building. He made a quick pass by his office to leave word on where he would be, and then went to a private lavatory to wash the oil and grime that streaked his face and arms. Taking off his sweat-soaked shirt, he sponged his torso and slipped into a clean bush jacket. Dictating a memo of instructions for completing demolitions to his secretary, he walked rapidly to his car, finishing just as he slid behind the wheel of his Alfa Romeo. Ten minutes later, he was entering the high-ceilinged office of the Controleur.

"Ah, Nicolaas, you're just in time," said Woltz. "Colonel Rotteveel was just recounting an extraordinary development. Could you start over again, Colonel?"

"Certainly," the thick-bodied officer answered. "About an hour ago, one of the Navy's Dorniers was patrolling off Cape Mangkalihat when they spotted a motor launch headed south. They circled to investigate and saw a white man signaling to them. When they landed in the water, the man jumped overboard and swam to the plane. It was Colonel Anton Colijn."

Nicolaas was thunderstruck. He had been certain in his own mind that Colijn was dead by now. They'd been friendly rivals for years, their careers at BPM closely paralleling each other. They held identical positions for the past two years, with Anton directing company affairs at Tarakan while Nicolaas held the same post at Balikpapan. A former Army officer, Colijn was recalled to active duty some months before. It was on his orders that the oil works at Tarakan had been put to the torch when the Japanese fleet was sighted.

"How the hell did he get away from the Japs?" Nicolaas inquired.

"He didn't, at least not until our flying boat arrived on the scene," Rotteveel went on. "There were two Jap officers with him. He was being sent to us with an ultimatum. That's all I know so far. The Dornier's about to land now."

Fifteen minutes later, a Navy car pulled into the driveway of the Controleur's Residence, and shortly afterward, Colijn entered the room. He looked even thinner than Nicolaas remembered, but he was solid, wiry muscle. An ill-fitting aviator's flight suit did little to help his appearance. Colijn's thin hair was askew, face, haggard with strain; his eyes, twin pools of anguish.

"Good God, Doctor Colijn," said Woltz, "tell us what happened."

Colijn made no reply but turned instead to his fellow oilman. "You must blow up your plant and wells at once, Nicolaas," he said in a calm, measured voice. "Destroy everything just as we did at Tarakan. The Japs will be here in a matter of days."

"How did you come to be in the launch, Colonel?" asked Rotteveel.

"It's a long story," Colijn replied. "I'd like to sit down."

"Of course," Woltz agreed. "Would you like a drink or something to eat?"

"Coffee. I haven't slept in three days. I must stay awake. I'm here because the Japs sent me to tell you not to damage the oil works."

"But you just told Nicolaas to do the opposite," Rotteveel exclaimed.

"What do you expect of me?" Colijn shot back. "The Japs must get nothing! Nothing, no matter what reprisals they take!"

"What do they threaten?" asked a suddenly sobered Woltz.

"General Toyama does not threaten," Colijn went on, all emotion drained from his voice. "He merely informs one of the facts."

"The Butcher of Nanking," Nicolaas muttered aloud. Reporters on the scene when Nanking, China, fell in 1937 swore that Toyama was responsible for the slaughter of over ten thousand helpless prisoners and civilians by rampaging Japanese soldiers.

"He hasn't changed his methods," Colijn continued. "We surrendered about mid-morning on the twelfth. When one of my batteries didn't get the surrender order, they fired on the ships. The Japs massacred them all. They treated the white women roughly and locked them up in the gaol. My wife, Zus, is among them."

"Good Lord," Woltz interrupted. "Do they have your daughters, too?"

"No. My girls are safe in Java. Toyama had me brought aboard his flagship and informed me that I was to be sent here ahead of his fleet to warn you not to destroy anything. Unless everything is left intact, he'll kill the Tarakan women and take similar measures here."

"He's bluffing," Rotteveel interjected. "No civilized man could order such atrocities."

"You underestimate both Toyama and Japanese brutality in general," Nicolaas put in. "He'll do exactly as he threatens."

"What are we to do?" asked the Controleur, dismayed. "We can't evacuate everyone."

"Just what Anton advised when he arrived," said Nicolaas calmly. "Blow everything up."

"I'd better inform the Governor General of these developments and seek further guidance," Woltz said shakily. He rang for his secretary to place the call to Batavia. It took but a few minutes to go through. Twenty minutes later, Woltz replaced the receiver on its hook.

"Well?" inquired Rotteveel.

"The orders remain as before. Complete demolitions on the outlying fields at once. The minute we get word that the Japs are moving south again, the refinery and everything else of potential use to the enemy is to be destroyed."

"There could be no other order," said Colijn. "Now, I want to go up to Samarinda. If I can fly with the bombers on their next raid on Tarakan, I can point out Toyama's flagship. If we kill him first, maybe the women won't be shot after all."

Rotteveel offered to have Colijn flown to Samarinda that

afternoon, and the two military men went off to get Colijn some fresh clothing.

"Well, Nicolaas, you have your marching orders now," Woltz said solemnly. "How soon can you begin?"

"We'll be blowing wells within the hour," the oilman replied. "By the day after tomorrow, everything will be wrecked but the refinery, the storage tanks and the docks. I'd like to place a call to Oosten, if I might, to tell him what I'm doing."

"Of course. Use my desk." Even in defeat and destruction, the oil rajah's power was as great as the politician's.

When Nicolaas finished his talk with Oosten, he asked Woltz's secretary to get Karl Mueller, his deputy at the refinery, on the line. "Execute Phase One immediately," he ordered.

By the time Nicolaas got into his Alfa Romeo a few minutes later, the distant rumble of explosions could be heard. Off to the north, oily black smoke boiled up into the sky from where TNT charges were sealing off the precious oil wells.

(Three)
Samarinda II Aerodrome
Netherlands East Indies
15 January 1942

The remnants of the air complement at Samarinda were at supper when the Lockheed bearing Colijn arrived at the field. The colonel came unannounced, so no one met the plane, but only a few minutes elapsed before he entered the mess in search of Major De Nooy, the base commander. A startled lieutenant called the group to attention. Colijn immediately put them at ease and sat down at the table with De Nooy and Van Den Brock. Garrit and Catherine were at the next table, so they overheard what Colijn was demanding.

"I'm afraid you've come for nothing, Colonel," Van Den Brock was saying. "After today's raid, I haven't a single Glenn Martin fit to fly from here to Tarakan. If we're lucky, we might be able to put up perhaps three in a week by cannibalizing the others."

"Does that mean that no one will be attacking the Japs at Tarakan?" Colijn demanded.

"The American Flying Fortresses will continue their strikes from Java," De Nooy replied.

"From where do they fly?"

"Malang."

"Then, I must go there. Can you arrange it?"

"I'll begin at once," said De Nooy and excused himself.

"It's been a long time, Garrit," said Colijn, turning to the fighter pilot. They had last seen each other when the ace surveyed the air defenses of the Indies the previous summer. "How many kills do you have against the Japs, now?"

"Eight."

"That makes a total of twenty-four, I believe."

"That's correct."

"One more and you're five times an ace. Now, tell me, who's this charming young lady?"

Garrit introduced Catherine to the Colonel.

"I've known this young man since he was a toddler," Colijn commented to Catherine. "All in all, he hasn't turned out so badly."

They chatted amicably for a few minutes before Catherine had to return to duty.

"I take it you care a great deal for her?" said the Colonel after the nurse left the mess.

"I'm going to marry her," Garrit confessed.

"Then get her out of here before the Japs arrive. They're holding the nurses at Tarakan hostage. They're threatening to kill them."

"I'll make her leave if I have to tie her up to do it."

The next few days at Samarinda II were filled with frantic efforts to get the damaged planes repaired sufficiently to fly again. The five remaining *Buffalos* were soon all airworthy, so Garrit sent his men to help Van Den Brock. The work under camouflage nets continued day and night. The mechanics literally tore the shot-up Glenn Martins to pieces, sorted out the good components from the bad, and put the good ones together into what amounted to different machines. There were enough parts for two complete bombers.

On January 17th, more bad news came in by radio. The Fortress group from Malang, which was continuing its attacks on the enemy force at Tarakan, spotted *Zeros* on the airfield there. From Tarakan, the range of the enemy fighters would allow them to operate as far south as Balikpapan. The days of the Dutch fliers in this part of

Borneo were clearly numbered. De Nooy began to execute the first stages of his contingency plans. Evacuation of the wounded and all skilled technicians was soon underway.

"We can't just let them sail unmolested into Balikpapan Harbour," Van Den Brock insisted at dinner that night. He was sitting with De Nooy and Garrit. Catherine was at the hospital, readying the worst of the wounded for air evacuation.

"We'll have to do the best we can," said De Nooy, an advocate for the art of the possible.

"The Japs will come with at least twenty transports," Garrit put in. "At best, we might be able to get two or three."

"Our Navy is sure to throw in their submarines," De Nooy went on. "Add to that the *Flying Fortresses* and, hopefully, some action by our naval surface forces. There has to be an outside chance that we might stop the Japs from moving down Makassar Strait."

"You're as hopelessly optimistic as Catherine," Garrit said with exasperation. "You know as well as I do that as long as the Japs control the air, we've got no chance at all of stopping them. We need three or four squadrons of first class fighters, right here and now. We both know that the only worthwhile machines in the whole theater are the *Hurricanes* in Malaya. Our British friends aren't sending any up here. Protecting Singapore's all they're interested in."

"In your shoes, you'd do the same," Van Den Brock observed.

"I never said I wouldn't. The point is that we shouldn't fruitlessly throw away any machines and men that we'll need later to defend Java itself."

"Such decisions are for the high command to make," De Nooy continued. "We must be prepared to strike the hardest blow possible against the Japs when they come south."

"We'll probably get off no more than one mission," said Garrit. "If the *Zeros* are out, they'll have located this field by then. I want to send all my people save for the barest minimum back to Andir at once."

"I should do the same," said Van Den Brock. "Those highly-trained people are irreplaceable now. Only those required to mount our final mission should remain here."

"Your assessment is quite correct," De Nooy agreed. "We'll ferry them south as soon as they can be fitted into the transport schedule."

"The nurses should go out early," Garrit observed. "We know what those Jap bastards did to the nurses in Hong Kong."

"I quite completely agree," De Nooy replied. "But getting them to leave might not be all that easy. They're civilians, after all, and not subject to my orders."

"You and Doctor Baltussen must insist," Garrit exclaimed. "If necessary, they should be forcibly put on a plane."

"Easy Garrit," said the major. "We all know how you feel about Catherine. We'll get them out, never fear."

"All right. I'll trust you to do it. Now, if we're going to fly this suicide mission, I have some other ideas. The Yank Navy *Buffalos* in the States carried bombs under their wings. We can rig at least two of ours the same way with racks left from the wrecked bombers. That should at least double our chances of hitting an enemy ship."

"See to it," De Nooy ordered.

De Nooy's promises were well and good, but Catherine kept stalling about being evacuated. As long as any of the wounded remained, she refused to leave. There were two severely burned airmen whom Baltussen was afraid to move, fearing that even a flight to Banjermasin might kill them. Although the other two nurses went out on the earlier flights, Catherine was still at Samarinda on January 21st when word came through from headquarters that a reconnaissance plane has sighted a Japanese convoy sailing south from Tarakan. Garrit confronted her right after breakfast.

"You must leave now," he said with finality. "The Japs will be here in a day or two. You have to take the next plane out."

"Oh, Garrit," she sighed, "I don't want to go unless you can come, too."

"Don't be foolish," he snapped back. "We're going out as soon as we dare to strike that Japanese convoy. We'll be hitting them for as long as we can. When it's sure that Balikpapan will fall, I'm certain that Van Oyen will recall all the fighters to Java. In the meantime, I have a job to do here. Worrying about you just makes it that much harder."

"I never meant for it to be," she said, tears welling up in her eyes. "I wouldn't consciously do anything to distract you. Of course, I'll take the next transport."

No transports made it to Samarinda II either that day or the next. A wide storm front moved down from the Celebes Sea, blanketing central Borneo and Makassar Strait with low-hanging clouds. All contact with the enemy naval force was lost. Dutch Navy Dorniers and American PBYs probed through the mists from above, trying to locate the enemy ships, but their efforts were fruitless. With visibility so severely limited, the few available Lockheeds could not be risked for evacuation missions. At Samarinda II, those two days were a nightmare of anxiety. Not knowing where the Japanese were or where they might be heading was the worst part. The pilots spent most of their time clustered in the operations building, listening to the scraps of information that came over the wireless. Heavy rain pelted the buildings and turned the sod airfield into a quagmire.

The early morning hours of January 23rd were much like those of the previous days. About mid-morning, however, the rain stopped, and the ceiling lifted to about five hundred feet. The ground crews were soon swarming over the revetments, removing tarps from the aircraft engines and checking for rain damage. Dyaks rolled the bombs from the magazines to the planes. Just before noon, De Nooy summoned Garrit and Van Den Brock to his office.

"Our worst fears have been realized," the major began. "The Navy has just spotted the Japs--fourteen transports and the same number of escorts. They've already passed the mouth of the Mahakan. They're between here and Balikpapan."

"Good God!" exclaimed Van Den Brock. "They'll be there by tonight. We must attack now."

"Those are the orders," De Nooy continued. "There's one piece of fortunate news. The Navy reports no fighter cover over the Jap fleet. Apparently this storm front is keeping their *Zeros* at Tarakan grounded."

"It's a free shot," said Garrit. "We'd better make the most of it."

"How soon can you get your planes up?" asked the major.

"Fifteen minutes," said Van Den Brock. Garrit nodded agreement.

"God bless you both," said De Nooy. "Get as many of them as you can."

The mission briefing was short and to the point. Van Den Brock's promised schedule was bettered. The first Glenn Martins were off in just over ten minutes. Garrit and Moulders were flying with the bombers. The extra burden of bombs beneath the wings made Garrit's *Buffalo* even more sluggish than usual. He glanced over his shoulder to catch a parting glimpse of Samarinda, wondering if he would ever see it again. Icy fingers of worry knotted his gut as he thought of Catherine still being there. He hadn't even had the chance to say goodbye. For a moment, his mind seemed to be outside his body, an observer to events rather than a participant. He shook his head to snap out of the mood. The last time he'd felt like that, a German sent him into the drink off Britain.

Van Den Brock turned the tiny formation toward the south when they reached the seacoast. Dirty smoke hung in a haze beneath the overcast, further reducing visibility. Down on the horizon, Garrit made out the thin black columns connecting the sea with the clouds above. The Japanese force was closing in on Balikpapan. At the speed reported by the Navy recce planes, the enemy would be offshore in the early hours of the night.

Making well over ten times the speed of the convoy, the aircraft overtook the ships rapidly. Van Den Brock's voice crackled in Garrit's earphones, assigning targets to the bomb-carrying planes. The enemy transports were steaming southward in two columns of seven ships each. A ring of big destroyers surrounded the thin-skinned troop carriers, and a pair of cruisers could be seen in the vanguard. The lookouts were apparently keeping a sharp watch, for the flash and smoke of antiaircraft guns commenced from the warships as the Glenn Martins and *Buffalos* came up from astern.

On Van Den Brock's command, the planes peeled off to attack the ships from a number of directions. Puffs of dirty smoke were blossoming all over the sky as the Japanese gunners tried desperately to get the correct range. Several times, Garrit's plane lurched this way or that as flak burst nearby, but his speed was throwing off the enemy's calculations. He was all concentration now. Unaware that he was sweating profusely, his only thought was to maneuver his plane for the bomb run on his target, the lead transport of the port column. He hoped it was Toyama's flagship. If only Colijn could have been with him today. Heavy machine guns and light flak were winking wickedly at him from the warships and transports. Balls of tracer whipped by the *Buffalo* from every direction as he skirted the ring of destroyers and turned toward his target. It lay there ahead, twisting away as the lone Dutch plane bore down on it.

Garrit had barely three hundred feet of ceiling with which to work. A moderate sea was running in the strait, and his wings seemed to be almost skimming the tops of the whitecaps. A wall of tracers leaped out at him from the high-sided transport as he closed in on it relentlessly. The *Buffalo* shuddered momentarily as heavy machine gun slugs whipped about the wings.

A stream of oil suddenly shot back from the radial engine and splattered against the windscreen. For a terrifying moment, Garrit was totally blind. Acting instinctively, he pulled the bomb release and yanked back on the stick. The *Buffalo* lurched upward as the unnatural load of the two fifty-kilogram bombs fell away. The masthead of the transport flashed by close against the sidepane of the cockpit, and then a terrific explosion buffeted the plane from the rear, sending it careening forward. The two bombs, released from almost wavetop level, had skipped off the sea like flat stones off a millpond, smashing into the side of the transport at the waterline.

Garrit was up into the low-hanging clouds now, fighting with all his skill to maintain control of his airplane. Red lights were on all over the control panel, and the engine was running erratically. He had to get the plane down fast if he was to avoid a crash. Knowing that he would never make it back to Samarinda, his only hope was to reach one of the airfields near Balikpapan. His bomb run had already pointed him in the right direction. The wiper blades cleaned away part of the oil on the windscreen, but he still could not see through it. He was flying totally on instruments. Keeping the nose of the *Buffalo* up, he clawed desperately for every foot of altitude he could gain before the engine inevitably quit running. If he could keep it aloft for twenty minutes, he thought that he might just make Maggor Landing Field.

An icy calm settled over Garrit's mind. He had done this all before in a different plane in another war. He knew that every split-second decision now could mean the difference between life and death, but that did not shake him. He was up over a thousand feet now. The engine was running extremely rough, but he thought that he might keep it alive just long enough.

The *Buffalo* broke out on top of the clouds into brilliant sunlight. The glare off the white undercast was blinding. The clouds stretched away in every direction, but up ahead, an ugly plume of dense smoke pierced the white surface and boiled upwards toward the heavens. Garrit knew what it was at once, for it was a twin of the smoke pillar over Tarakan. Beneath the undercast, tank farms and refineries must be blazing fiercely. He flew on toward the smoke, nursing his crippled bird to the safety that waited nearby.

He raised Maggor on the wireless and asked for clearance to land. The reply came back negative. The field had already been cratered to prevent a surprise landing by Japanese aircraft. Only the KNILM runways at Sepingyang were still open. He spiraled down through the clouds several miles from the smoke column, hoping against hope that the engine would not quit until he was safely down.

The *Buffalo* broke out beneath the overcast at six hundred feet. Off to the left, flames leaped up almost that high from the ruined BPM refinery. Smoke hung beneath the cloudbank like a black pall of death. Garrit slid back the cockpit canopy and stuck out his head. The slipstream tore at the flesh of his face, but his goggles protected his eyes. He made out Sepingyang in the distance and headed for it, intent upon a straight-in approach.

The engine began to rattle violently, shaking the whole plane like a rat in a terrier's mouth. He considered lowering the landing gear, then rejected the idea. That extra bit of drag might be more than the engine could bear. He was talking to the tower with detachment now, telling them his plans, asking for a crash truck. He could see the threshold markings on the macadam runway.

The engine suddenly quit. It was ghostly quiet in the cockpit, with only the sound of the wind shrieking past the canopy to break the silence. The grass alongside the runway came rushing up to meet the *Buffalo*, but he held the plane level and bellied her in perfectly onto the wet turf. She went skidding on with the dizzying speed of a bobsled for over a thousand feet before lurching to a halt in the thick mud. Garrit unstrapped himself before the plane stopped rocking and was out of the cockpit within seconds. He jumped off the wing and sprinted some fifty yards before diving into the grass. He lay there panting, waiting for the plane to explode, but it did not go up. A crash fire truck arrived and began to hose down the wreck.

"Are you all right, Captain?" asked a medical orderly who had appeared above Garrit.

The pilot sat up. "I'm still in one piece." He got to his feet and began brushing the mud from his battle dress. "I need to get to your ops center right away. I have to get back to my squadron at Samarinda."

"That'll be a tall order, sir. The only plane left on the field is the BPM Lockheed, and she'll be taking off for Java within the hour."

Nicolaas walked out the front door and turned to look one last time at his mansion among the flaming hibiscus. He had lived some happy moments within its walls, but none more pleasant than the five months that Cinta had been here. The Japanese would be ashore by morning. If left standing, the house would make a comfortable headquarters for some enemy official. Nicolaas had no intention of letting that happen.

The demolition men were backing out the front door now, pouring streams of gasoline from cans as they came. They stopped on the porch, capped the cans, and put them into a truck.

"Do you want me to fire it, sir?" Karl Mueller asked at Nicolaas's elbow.

"No, I'll do it myself." Taking a lighted flare from Mueller, Nicolaas drew back his arm and tossed the blazing stick into the front door. Fire erupted through every opening in the walls and licked rapidly up toward the roofline. "Let's get out of here," Nicolaas muttered as he climbed into his Cadillac. The driver spun the wheels on the gravel driveway, shooting rocks into the wilting hibiscus as he sped away.

"Where now?" asked Mueller.

"The Controleur's Residence. I must see Woltz before we go."

A blazing inferno raged for miles along the waterfront where one of the world's largest refineries had stood. Heat lightning shot between smoke plumes rising from blazing wharves soaked with gasoline and fires fed by kerosene and motor oil. Nicolaas had ordered the towering stills fired dry and run until they collapsed from the heat. The power plant and other refinery installations had been blown up with explosives. Only the tank farm remained to be destroyed, and he was delaying that final sabotage until Mueller's demolition crew was ready to flee the city. For those who would be unable to fly out at once, an evacuation camp was waiting far back in the jungle on a small river capable of accommodating BPM's twin-engined Grumman flying boats. With any luck at all, the entire European staff of the oil works would escape to Java.

There was a roaring bonfire on the clipped lawn of the Controleur's Residence. At least a score of native servants were shuttling between the house and the blaze, carrying cartons of papers. Nicolaas left Mueller with the car while he went into the house. He found Woltz in his office. The big man was in his shirtsleeves, and his necktie was askew. He was in the process of emptying a file cabinet onto the floor.

"So, you're still here," said the Controleur. "I thought you might have gone already."

"Not without saying goodbye, old friend. I had to ask you again to come with me."

"Out of the question. I have my responsibilities to those who must remain here. Half of them still don't believe that the Japs will intern us. They think we'll be able to live in our homes as our relatives do under German rule."

"They're badly deluded."

"Quite, but then, someone must look out for them. Will you have a final drink with me?"

"Of course."

"I have a surfeit of good Bols gin. It would be a pity to waste it on the Japanese." Woltz poured the clear, sparkling liquor into two whisky glasses. "To the Queen," he toasted, "and to a speedy liberation of all her dominions."

"The Queen," Nicolaas echoed before tossing down the gin.

"How many people are you flying out?"

"Twenty-two." Nicolaas ticked off the list, mostly technical men of the BPM complex and highly trained air force personnel for Rotteveel. He was also taking two nurses from the hospital.

As if summoned by the mention of his name, the swarthy colonel came elbowing his way in through the confusion.

"Ah, Colonel," said Woltz, "you're just in time to wish Nicolaas farewell. He's about to leave for Bandjermasin."

"Glad I caught you here," the colonel said to Nicolaas. "I've got a change in your flight plan. Garrit Laterveer crash-landed at Sepingyang about an hour ago. Fortunately, he wasn't injured. I want you to take him to Samarinda."

"That's in the opposite direction from Java," Nicolaas protested.

"Van Oyen just ordered all the fighters back to Java. You can top off your tanks at Samarinda and then have an escort of *Buffalos* all the way to Soerabaja. There's also a nurse and a spare fighter pilot still up there that we need to get out."

"In that case, I'll be glad to send the Lockheed. But someone from here will have to stay behind. She'll never make it off the runway at Samarinda with two more passengers and a full fuel load."

"I'm glad I don't have to make that choice," Woltz commented.

"It's not hard at all," said Nicolaas. "Larry Nobis can handle the piloting without help. I'll stay and fly out from the jungle in one of the company Grummans."

"Is that wise?" asked Rotteveel. "You're the one person we can't afford to have the Japs capture."

"I have no intention of getting captured. The Grummans will be at the evacuation camp before the Japs can take control here."

"Is there anything new on the enemy's position?" Woltz inquired.

"They'll be offshore not long after dark," Rotteveel answered. "I expect them to land on the beaches east of Klandasan, outside the mine field area. I'll resist the landings for as long as possible, then fall back into the jungle."

"I'd better get moving," said Nicolaas, putting down his glass. "I pray God we meet again in better times."

"We shall, my friend," said Woltz, taking the oilman's hand.

Nicolaas sensed that the Resident had little faith in his own words. Their splendid world of oil and guilders and living like white kings among the Asians was coming to an end. They both doubted that it would rise again like a phoenix from the ashes.

The flight from Sepingyang to Samarinda proved uneventful. Every seat in *Belle of Borneo* was filled, and several men were crouched in the narrow aisle. All of the passengers had looked hollow-eyed and frightened before takeoff, for they realized that they were escaping capture by a matter of mere hours. Garrit sat in the cockpit with Tommy Nobis, pointing out landmarks and explaining how to recognize the camouflaged airfield.

De Nooy was expecting them, and the Dyaks had the runways clear when they arrived. Tommy Nobis taxied over to the small tower, where Garrit disembarked while the pilot saw to topping off the fuel tanks. Garrit was talking to De Nooy when Nobis finally entered the base commander's office. Catherine was hugging Garrit tightly.

"Your fighters are ready to leave," De Nooy was saying. "You're to take off at once. Catherine and your spare pilot will go on the Lockheed if there's room."

"We've already made room," Nobis assured him. "Van Wely stayed behind in Balikpapan so that we could take them."

"Aren't you coming with us, Major?" Garrit asked De Nooy.

"No. I have unfinished business here. Then I'll fade into the jungle with my Dyaks."

"What about Van Den Brock?" Garrit continued.

"I forgot that you didn't know. He was lost on the second raid this morning, as was his other ship. Your *Buffalos* are the only flyable aircraft left on the field."

No time was lost in finalizing flight details. They would first go inland then turn south toward Bandjermasin. Pausing at the Borneo capital to refuel, they would go on at once to Java, landing at the KNILM field just south of Soerabaja. Garrit's orders were to remain overnight there, then take his *Buffalos* to the outlying field at Zwarte Gouden.

Nobis took off first then circled low over the jungle while the fighters lifted off. Garrit's planes assembled in a loose "four-fingers" formation. He led them back in a final pass over the base that had been their home for almost a month.

Garrit checked his watch. Two hours of flying time would see them in Bandjermasin. Another three after that would put them safely in Java. But for how long could even that stronghold remain safe with the Japanese coming on so fast? Unless the high command took notice of the steady advance south down Makassar Strait, the enemy would be at the back door before forces could be shifted from their focus on Malaya to face him.

There was no way for Garrit to know, but one man in Lembang had recognized the threat and was reacting to counter it with all the forces at his command. Earlier that day, Admiral Tommy Hart had ordered Glassford's task force to sortie and head for Balikpapan.

(Four)
BPM Refinery Complex
Balikpapan, Borneo
Netherlands East Indies
23 January 1942

"Is everything ready?" asked Nicolaas, wiping sweat and soot from his eyes. The heat on the hill above the upper tank farm was terrific. Down below in the ruined Pandansari Refinery, flames were leaping almost two hundred feet into the air.

"The detonators are all set and wired," answered Mueller. "We placed fifteen sticks of dynamite on each tank. The circuits are sequenced to start at the bottom and work up the hill."

"Let's get on with it, then."

"Fire in the hole!" Mueller called out the blaster's universal warning then pushed down on the detonator plunger.

Nothing happened. Cursing in a solid stream of Dutch, Mueller cocked the plunger and tried again without results.

"How long since we set the charges?" asked a puzzled Nicolaas.

"Three, some four days ago."

"It's the humidity. TNT deteriorates in this climate. We'll have to open the valves and set the oil afire."

"We can't open the valves," Mueller said, dejected. "The keys were in the tank farm office. We blew that up two hours ago."

Nicolaas's mind was ticking like a Swiss clock, replaying the old British report on the methods employed by their Colonel Norton-Griffiths to destroy the Rumanian oil works during the last war. "We'll think of something. How much dynamite do you have left?"

"About seventy-five sticks."

"Enough for five tanks. All right, here's what we'll do."

Keeping only a dozen of his best men to help, Mueller sent the rest of the demolitions crew down to the seawall by the wireless station, where a fleet of native *proas* waited to evacuate them. Nicolaas set the new charges himself, placing them on the highest tanks in the farm. With any luck, their oil would ignite and set off the fuel in the myriad tanks below.

The horrible heat and exhaustion were taking their toll. Nicolaas had planned to be ready to blast within half an hour. It took twice that long. When the final connections had been made, he sent the rest of the men except Mueller off to the *proas*.

"Are you a praying man, Karl?" Nicolaas asked as he made the final connections to the detonator.

"On occasion, *Tuan Besar*."

"You'd better make this one of those." Mentally saying his own a prayer, Nicolaas activated the firing circuit.

Five balls of fire shot up in succession, followed by the rumble of explosions. A sea of flaming gasoline roared down through the storage farm, igniting tank after tank until the whole world seemed to be ablaze. Typhoon-force winds streamed towards the center of the fire, tearing sheets of tin from small buildings, stripping trees of their vegetation.

"Let's get out of here while we can," Nicolaas yelled to be heard above the howling wind.

It was a quarter-mile from the tank farm to the wireless station, but the oilmen had to run three times that distance to avoid the flames. A cheer went up from the men already in the boats when the two bosses staggered down the quay. As soon as they were aboard, the men eagerly pushed off and fired outboard motors. Nicolaas felt suddenly chilled by the cool breeze blowing in from the sea.

With the daylight fast fading, the little armada of *proas* entered the wide mouth of the Riko River and proceeded upstream. Nicolaas and Mueller sat near the bow of the lead boat, navigating with a small hand-drawn map. The sky behind glowed red from the massive fires. Ahead, bright tropical stars appeared, casting enough light to make out the shadowy banks.

"Is this it?" Mueller asked about 10:00 p.m. as they approached the gap where a large tributary met the river.

"It must be," said Nicolaas. Instructing the helmsman to turn up the smaller stream, he shouted directions to the boat just behind. By voice and electric flashlight, word was passed back down the string of *proas*.

Once in the tributary, the dense jungle on either bank cut off even the slightest hint of wind. The helmsmen slowed down and barely crept ahead. After half an hour of creeping forward, Nicolaas spotted a dim light up ahead. It grew brighter and brighter until he made it out as a Coleman lantern hung on the end of a short pier. Other lights glowed from the windows of an entire village of tin-roofed bungalows on the shore behind it.

The camp supervisor, an Englishman named Barnes, met them at the pier. He was an old hand in the jungle, lean and with skin like tanned leather. Several Dyaks were with him.

"Any news on the flying boats?" Nicolaas asked after they had exchanged greetings.

"Not a word," growled the Englishman. "What's worse, the bloody transmitter's 'gone west.' We can receive, but we can't talk back. I haven't been able to raise Soerabaja since yesterday afternoon."

"They'll come in the morning," Nicolaas assured him. "I sent Oosten a personal note with Larry Nobis."

The camp was well stocked with good food and good beer. After wolfing down a meal of hot stew and bread, the exhausted oilmen bedded down for the night.

The planes did not come in the morning. The Hallicrafters transceiver in the camp headquarters sputtered only static on the frequency designated for rescue communications. Both Nicolaas and Mueller fiddled with the set, finally changing all of the vacuum tubes in an effort to get the transmitter working, but to no avail. Paul Snoek, the refinery chief electrician, offered to have a go at it. After removing the cabinet, he concluded that the fault lay in a burned out capacitor. With no spares available, there was no chance of successful repairs.

After waiting all day without relief, Nicolaas decided to take a small party back down the river to look for a transmitter. Leaving Mueller in charge at the camp, he took only enough men to handle a *proa* and set out near dusk. Darkness caught them at the juncture with the Rika. With a dense overcast shutting out the light of the moon and stars, they were forced to lay up until morning. None of the Europeans slept that night because of the swarms of mosquitoes that attacked throughout the hours of darkness. Puffing furiously on their pipes, the Dutchmen managed to veil their boat in a cloud of tobacco smoke to hold the voracious insects at bay. The lone Dyak aboard slept like a baby. Finally too tired to care anymore, Nicolaas dozed off near dawn.

The sound of aircraft engines tore him from sleep. He realized at once that the plane or planes were coming upriver from the direction of Balikpapan. But was they friendly or Japanese?

As the noise grew louder, Nicolaas heaved a sigh of relief as he recognized the familiar roar of Pratt and Whitney radial engines. Barking a string of orders, he untied the line that had held the boat fast to a tree on the shore and pushed off. By the time the plane appeared, they were in the middle of the river, waving wildly to attract the attention of the pilot.

The twin-engined flying boat, a Grumman G21A *Goose*, circled the canoe twice before lining up to land. The pilot throttled back on the engines and taxied to within a few meters of the boat before killing the engines. As the refugees paddled the *proa* alongside, the hatch to the cabin opened. Nicolaas recognized Reinhold Mussert, a BMP pilot from Soerabaja, standing in the entrance.

"My God, *Tuan Besar*, you look like you have a case of the pox," Mussert's bass voice boomed as the canoe came alongside. He was a lean, dark-haired man in his thirties.

"I was the main course at a mosquito feast last night," Nicolaas growled back, in no mood for levity. "Have you come for my people? There were supposed to be two planes."

"We've been socked in at Soerabaja by the weather--the same storm the Japs used to shield their attack. No one was sure you were still here. We've been trying to contact you for almost twenty-four hours."

"We didn't hear a thing. Must be atmospherics. We couldn't answer, anyway. Our transmitter's down."

"I've got to go upriver to pick up a fighter pilot who crash-landed at our exploratory rig. He's supposed to be in bad shape, so time is of the essence. I'll come back by here and take the five of you on the return light."

"Four," Nicolaas said firmly. "I'm staying until we can get the whole crew out."

Mussert was as good as his word. An hour after taking off, the *Goose* returned and put down on the water. Nicolaas sent his four white companions off with another scribbled note to Oosten, explaining the radio situation and requesting that the whole BPM flying boat fleet be dispatched to collect the remaining oilmen. There was method in his madness. He believed that, as long as he was in Borneo, Oosten would not dare withhold the planes.

It took Nicolaas and the Dyak a good hour to reach the evacuation camp. Barnes and Snoek met him at the dock, and he put them in the picture while wolfing a plate of eggs washed down by warm beer.

"So, what do we do now?" asked Barnes.

"Wait by the radio," Nicolaas mumbled around a mouthful of eggs. "I'm going to sleep."

Late in the afternoon, word came from Soerabaja to go back to Balikpapan Bay. The Japanese were not yet ashore, and it was still possible to make night landings on the Bay. Because of high overcast, the pilots were leery of landing on the Rika or the tributary.

Once again, the oilmen piled into the *proas* with the skilled Dyak watermen. Once they reached the Rika, they had both the outboard motors and the current to speed them seaward. As the boats neared the bay, the massive fires still blazing at the refinery lighted their way. At just after 11:00 p.m., Nicolaas passed the word to cut the engines and wait. The roar of the mighty fires made conversation impossible, and the awful heat reached them even across the broad bay. The Dutch and Englishmen fired their pipes again to discourage ravenous insects. The Dyaks slumped at their places and slept.

At just after midnight, Nicolaas picked out the clamor of aircraft engines above the roar of the fires. Then he spotted two sets of landing lights. Unbelievably, the BPM pilots were coming in lighted up so that the refugees could spot them. Nicolaas grabbed an electric lantern and flashed out the agreed upon signal. Ten minutes later, he was climbing into one of the Grummans. Larry Nobis was there to greet him.

"Welcome aboard, Boss," called Larry Nobis from the cockpit door. "Glad to see you made it."

"And why wouldn't I?" Nicolaas shot back good-naturedly. "Did you get everybody to Java in the Lockheed?"

"We made it okay. Laterveer's fiancee is with your daughter."

"Who's flying the other *Goose*?"

"Mussert. He's got to be exhausted by now. Why don't you fly her back?"

"I'm not going with this group. I'll stay until the last shuttle."

"I think you'd better read this." Nobis handed the Dutchman a heavy bond envelope.

Nicolaas tore open the letter and read it by flashlight, then cursed bitterly under his breath.

"From Oosten?" asked Nobis.

"The Governor General. I am ordered to Lembang at once to meet Conrad Helfrich."

"Admiral Helfrich?"

"Yes. It seems they think my services indispensable. God dammit! I can't just fly off and leave my people here."

"Looks like you don't have much choice, Boss."

"That doesn't mean I have to like it. How many people do you plan to take?"

"We've stripped everything out that we can. We'll take twelve per plane. That's a heavy overload, but these birds are tough."

"Make it fifteen. We've got plenty of searoom to play with here."

It took but a few minutes to load the planes. Nicolaas left Barnes in charge of those who would remain, promising to send the planes back as soon as they could be refueled. As the boats pulled away, Nobis and Mussert fired their engines and began their long run down the bay. With their heavy loads, it took the *Geese* almost three miles to become "unstuck" from the water and slowly rise into the air.

The Grummans put down their wheels and landed at Soerabaja just before dawn. Nicolaas deplaned to devastating news. The Japanese were beginning to land at Balikpapan, and the air base commander had forbidden the BPM planes to return. Barnes and seventy-four companions were stranded on the east bay. Their only choices were surrender or trying to get out through the jungle to Bandjermasin in the south.

CHAPTER 17

(One)
Aboard USS *Marblehead*
Soembawa Island
Netherlands East Indies
23 January 1942

Frank Rhea stood leaning against the main deck railing, watching *Marblehead's* deck gang disconnect the hose that had bound her to *Boise* for the past several hours. The reek of oil permeated the air of Wawarada Bay, where the cruisers lay close together. *Marblehead's* tanks were now topped off with precious fuel from the newer vessel. Boats shuttled back and forth between *Houston* and Admiral Glassford's flagship, bearing cargoes of new 5-inch antiaircraft shells. *Houston* had been plagued by dud flak ammunition since the start of the war. *Boise* would be leaving the battle area as soon as she could get underway. The most modern ship in the Asiatic Fleet--the only one with radar--had ripped open her bottom on an uncharted reef as she steamed through Sapi Strait. Even now, Captain Robby was heading a formal board of inquiry to determine how the casualty occurred. "Iron Mike" Moran's reputation was on the line. Running a ship aground was always potentially fatal to a skipper's career. To do so on the way to a battle was doubly damning.

Everyone on *Marblehead* realized at once that they would have to pick up the fallen baton. Frank felt they were more than ready, even eager to at last come to grips with the enemy. This mission should have been *Marblehead's* by right to begin with. She had been selected to lead the strike on the Japanese force moving on Balikpapan when it was first sighted the week before. Captain Robby had called the department heads to his cabin for a quiet but inspiring briefing on the attack and the logical reasons why they had been given the mission. He was right in saying that the porcupine-like placement of the ship's main battery allowed her to engage more targets at once, a definite advantage in the nighttime melee that was envisioned. It was also true that the old "Ghost of the China Coast" was slightly faster than any of the enemy's cruisers or destroyers, a definite asset when a quick get-away was in order. Left unsaid was the obvious fact that as the oldest and poorest armed of Glassford's three cruisers, she was also the most expendable for what was virtually a suicide mission. The enemy force was known to have at least three cruisers and a dozen modern destroyers.

Captain Robby's tiny task force was halfway across the Java Sea when orders came to return to Koepang Bay on Timor. The enemy force had moved to an unknown destination, aborting the mission. Disappointment was rife among the men of *Marblehead*. When the Japanese finally came on for the oil ports, the Marby was sidelined by a turbine casualty. Admiral Glassford took a scratch division of destroyers led by Commander Talbot of DesDiv 59 and headed for the enemy in *Boise*. Two unexpected events changed the situation completely. *Marblehead*'s black gang, accustomed to years of self-sufficiency in China, managed to repair the damaged turbine. Then *Boise* ripped out her bottom. Glassford turned loose his destroyers to speed on toward the enemy and ordered the cruisers to rendezvous at Wawarada Bay.

A knot of *Marblehead*'s officers who had taken part in the board of inquiry began returning over the gangplank between the two ships. Eddie Blessman came up the deck towards Frank.

"What's the verdict?" Frank inquired.

"Collision with an uncharted rock," said Blessman. "A clear case of incomplete charts. No blame to be placed on 'Iron Mike.'"

"That's good news, at least," Frank continued. "Our own charts of these waters aren't worth a damn, and who can read those tracings?"

The ABDA forces were reduced to reliance on pencil tracings of Dutch charts, with all the markings in the language of the Hollanders.

"Anyway," Blessman went on, "We've all got to double up. Admiral Glassford and his staff will be coming aboard any minute. The mission's on for sure. We've got to high-tail it north and try to catch the 'cans' before they get to Balikpapan."

Frank was back at the catapult checking the condition of his plane when Admiral Glassford and his staff boarded *Marblehead*. The slender, hawk-faced flag officer had been known for his diplomacy when he headed the Yangtze gunboat force in China. He was almost totally bald and had an easy, disarming smile. At the commanders conference before they sailed from Koepang Bay, he had been full of vigor and fight—"piss and vinegar" in Navy parlance--and had offered Commander Talbot detailed suggestions for a night torpedo attack based on his own experiences in the previous war. Now, unhorsed from his modern flagship, he was moving into Captain Robby's cabin, ready to hazard himself and his staff while seeing the dangerous undertaking through to its climax.

Heavy seas buffeted *Marblehead* as she steamed out of the bay and headed northward. At least the cruiser could plow through the big Indian Ocean waves. Tiny *Bulmer* bobbed about like a cork in a whirlpool, confirming the cruisermen's prejudice against service in small ships. The run of over a hundred miles to Sapi Strait must have been interminable to the men aboard the destroyer.

As *Marblehead* negotiated Sapi Strait, every man aboard was holding his breath, hoping against hope that they would not share the fate of *Boise*. Then they were through the Malay Barrier, steaming across the glassy surface of the Java Sea. As *Bulmer* came through in their wake, a signal lamp began to rattle on *Marblehead's* bridge, ordering on more speed. The heavy going had slowed their progress so much that it was doubtful that they could catch the destroyers in time. And now a further spur had been added. From his headquarters in Lembang, Admiral Hart had sent a one-word direct order to Talbot: ATTACK!

(Two)
Aboard USS *Rust*
Makassar Strait
23 January 1942

Jack Sewell looked up from his desk as Chief Muldune, clad in dripping oilskins, came into the Gunnery Department office. The chief braced himself in the doorway against the violent rolling and pitching of the little ship. She had been acting like this ever since they rounded Cape Laikang on the south tip of Celebes and headed up Makassar Strait into the teeth of the gale.

"I think you'd better come up and take a look, Mister Sewell," the big CPO growled. "We're taking green water all the way over Number One Gun. Chances are, she ain't gonna shoot at all tonight."

"Okay, Chief," said Jack, closing the gunnery book he'd been studying. "I need some fresh air, anyway."

The force of the wind tore at Jack's oilskins as they came out on deck and made for the ladder at the back of the bridge. He followed Muldune up its slippery rungs to the wildly gyrating fire control platform. Slate grey skies hung low overhead. The usually brilliant blue sea was almost black now and running high before the gale. *Rust* seemed to climb up the side of one monstrous wave and slide down into the following trough to have the next one break heavily over the forecastle. Muldune had been right. If Number One Gun lost its muzzle plug, it would be worthless in the upcoming fight.

Thankful that his youth spent on his father's fishing boats had made him immune to seasickness, Jack turned to the lookout lashed to the forward railing, tapping the man on the shoulder. "See anything?" he asked the seaman.

"Nothing, Lieutenant," the man yelled back.

"One thing's certain," Jack said loudly to Muldune. "No Jap recon plane is going to spot us under this cover."

Up ahead, the other vessels of Talbot's scratch force were pitching about in the towering seas, trying to keep in line ahead as they raced northward at twenty-seven knots. *Ford* was leading, with *Pope*, *Parrot*, and *Jones* in her wake. *Rust* was "tail-end-Charlie." Jack checked his watch. They had at least another twelve hours of steaming to reach Balkipapan. He marveled that the old relics would hold together under such pounding. Silently, he thanked the shipfitters of that past generation who had taken such pride in their work.

Jack braced himself against the mast and surveyed the ship's armament from his lofty perch. Number One Gun was the only weapon in danger of being disabled by the heavy seas. The other three, on raised platforms or atop deckhouses, were snugged down and safe. Elroy Brown's torpedo tubes were trained inboard and secured. Later, when they neared the target area, the overweight ensign and his men would be the most important members of the crew. The deadly fish in those twelve tubes were *Rust's* heavyweight punch.

Jack turned to Muldune and motioned for him to go back down. He followed the chief onto the main deck, where they sought shelter under the bridge wing.

"Have all the men who aren't on watch turn in, Chief," Jack ordered. "We're going to need them alert tonight."

"That's a good move, Lieutenant," said Muldune, "but I don't know whether anybody will be able to sleep. They're keyed up like crazy."

"Natural enough. Give it a try, anyway. I'm going to get some shuteye myself."

The door to the radio shack flew open, and a messenger stepped out onto the deck. "You'll never believe this, Mister Sewell," the man blurted out excitedly.

"What's that, 'Sparks'?"

"An Air Corps bomber just reported five Jap cruisers steaming north dead on our position."

Muldune let out a big belly laugh. "Let's hope that the Japs are as bad at ship identification as our flyboys," he muttered.

Jack came awake instantly as the steward, Ford, shook him gently. "Captain's ordered all officers to the wardroom, sir," Ford said softly. "In five minutes."

"Thanks, Ford," said Jack, rolling over from his wedged position against the bulkhead to swing his feet to the deck. He looked at the luminous dial of his watch and saw that it was ten twenty-five--2225 in Navy time. He knew before he stood up that the seas had abated considerably, for *Rust*'s movements were much more moderate than when he'd fallen asleep. Most of the other officers were already in the wardroom when he arrived. Their faces looked strained and ghostly in the red light of the battle lamps.

"Keep your seats, gentlemen," said Tom Hoskins as he slipped quietly in through the door. "We have only a few minutes." He moved to the center of the room.

"I want to fill you all in while there's still time. Fleet Intelligence places the enemy transport force anchored off Balikpapan. They have two light cruisers and about a dozen 'cans,' but those are all farther in, apparently shelling shore targets. The refineries ashore are said to be burning fiercely, which should silhouette our targets. Commander Talbot passed us these orders by TBS a while back." Hoskins took out a message pad and read:

"INITIAL WEAPONS WILL BE TORPS. TRANSPORTS CHIEF OBJECTIVE. CRUISERS AS REQUIRED TO ACCOMPLISH MISSION. LAUNCH TORPS AT CLOSE RANGE IF UNSIGHTED BY ENEMY. ATTACK INDEPENDENTLY WHEN TARGETS ARE LOCATED. WHEN ALL TORPS FIRED, CLOSE WITH ALL GUNS. USE INITIATIVE AND DETERMINATION.

"We'll go in at flank speed and raise all the havoc we can. If we're lucky, the Japs won't realize what's happening. Surprise will be our greatest asset. This is the first surface action our Navy's fought since the Spanish-American War. I'm sure that every man aboard will do his duty. Questions?"

The officers looked at the Captain and at each other. No one spoke up.

"Very well, then. We'll sound General Quarters as soon as I reach the bridge. Good luck and good hunting."

Sweating profusely inside his heavy lifejacket, Jack stood quietly at his battle station as *Rust* sped northward through the inky night. He took off his tin hat and mopped his forehead. The sea had calmed so much that the bridge was hardly swaying. He mentally ticked off situations that might occur in the coming battle, deciding how to react to each eventuality. This combat would be totally different from anything taught at gunnery school. There would be no time for deliberate target plots, no illumination with searchlights or star shells. It would be old-fashioned hit-and-run reminiscent of Drake and Hawkins. Split-second decisions would be called for, and he would have to make most of them.

"Mister Sewell," his talker suddenly broke the silence, "Crow's Nest reports blinking red light, bearing fifteen degrees relative."

The tension that had been building all night shot even higher. Muldune swung the big rangefinder towards the reported target and spun the dials.

"What is it, Chief?" asked Jack, trying to sound calm.

"Just a second, sir. There. Got it. It's a burning ship. Seems to be drifting."

Jack reported the target identification to Hoskins on the bridge.

"Must be one the Dutch bombers hit," the Captain speculated. "Good work. Keep it up."

Another tense two hours passed without a sighting. The crew checked and rechecked their weapons. Ammunition was broken out and the ready service racks filled. Before-battle nervousness reigned throughout the force. Then, dead ahead on the horizon, a dim orange glow appeared, growing bigger by the minute.

"God Almighty, what a fire that must be," Muldune exclaimed. "We're at least thirty miles away, and it's already lighting up the sky."

By 0230, they were running through a low-lying haze of oily smoke from the blazing refineries. Through breaks in the smoke, Jack caught sight of the anchored transports up ahead standing out starkly against the towering fires ashore. It looked like some ancient vision of hell. Jack began quietly giving orders to Ensign Brown to ready the torpedo battery.

A searchlight suddenly sprang out into the night to starboard. Jack got his glasses on it at once, and his stomach knotted as he recognized a *Hibuki* class destroyer. He quickly scanned the seas in its wake, picking out two more enemy "cans," then another. He started to call the gun crews, but it was already too late. The Japanese ships crossed rapidly in front of *Ford*, miraculously firing not a single shot. There could be but one explanation. If the Japanese saw them at all, they must have assumed that the four-pipers were some of their own ships. The American column swung a few points to starboard to widen the gap, then came back to port on a beeline for the anchored transports. Close-in sightings began to flood into fire control.

"The show's all yours now, Jack," Hoskins suddenly barked on the battle phones. "Have at them."

"Action port! Action port," Jack ordered Ensign Brown. His heart was racing, and he suddenly felt invincible. "Transport close aboard. Fire a spread of three." In his mind's eye, he could see the tubes swinging out to follow Brown's director. With a muffled explosion, the first torpedo left its tube, its propellers whining shrilly until it slid beneath the water. Two more fish quickly followed. Jack could hear his talker calmly counting off the seconds while he searched quickly for another target in the nightmare setting. He could see now that the Japanese were anchored in two columns.

Talbot had them running parallel to the outer column, shooting torpedoes as they passed.

"We missed, Lieutenant," the talker announced, his voice laced with disappointment.

"Dammit to hell!" Muldune swore. "How could we miss? That Jap was like the broad side of a barn."

Jack's stomach churned. The fleet's submariners had been saying for weeks that there was something fundamentally wrong with the Mark 14 torpedo. Could they be right?

Up ahead, *Ford* started a tight turn to starboard, looping back for another run on the enemy ships. They were passing the shoreward end of the Japanese column.

"We must have missed, Chief," said Jack, incredulous. Just then, a fresh explosion ashore silhouetted a new target, a ship of the inner column.

"Action port," Jack shouted to Brown, giving him the target bearing. Just before *Rust* followed the other "four-pipers" into the turn, Brown let loose three more fish. The port tubes were now empty. Half their load had been shot.

The talker counted impassively again as the ship heeled over sharply and followed Talbot's maneuver. She was halfway around when a sudden blinding flash lit the smoky surface of the sea. A deafening explosion rent the night air, and then the concussion wave buffeted the bodies of the fire control party. They hardly noticed, for they were jumping about in excitement, clapping each other on the shoulders.

"First blood," Muldune was screaming. "We drew first blood."

The ship steadied up on a straight course again, and all on the platform went back to searching for targets.

"Here comes the one we missed earlier, Brownie," Jack said to the torpedo officer. "Better drop to two-fish spreads. Fire when ready."

Searchlights shot skyward, and antiaircraft guns cut loose here and there about the Japanese force. It was clear that surprise was still in effect. The enemy was totally confused.

"Mark," the talker shouted just as a succession of explosions rumbled across the bay. The target ship had been literally blown to bits after hits from at least four torpedoes.

"The whole squadron must have shot at that bastard," screamed

Muldune, "but we got a piece of him, by God."

"Warships, dead astern!" came an electrifying report from the Crow's Nest.

Jack ran back to the rear rail and searched with his glasses. A chilling sight greeted his eyes. Two Japanese light cruisers, flanked and trailed by big, modern destroyers, charged out past the burning hulk of *Rust*'s last target. Jack barked frantic orders to both his guns and torpedo crews, but to his amazement the ships kept right on going out into Makassar Strait. Brown sent two torpedoes chasing after the lead cruiser, but they both missed. Later, the rumbling of distant depth charges clarified the situation. The enemy commander apparently thought he was under attack from submarines.

Talbot turned his ships again to starboard, running between the transports in the outer line. Jack searched vainly for fresh targets. He picked out two, only to see them torpedoed by the destroyers ahead before Brown could bring his tubes to bear. *Rust* dodged past the sinking wrecks. In the garish light, he could see men swarming down the sides of the largest vessel like monstrous water bugs. The sea was thick with the heads of swimmers. Then the "four-pipers" were past, turning north again for another run against the undamaged transports. They had hardly steadied up on course when Talbot turned them to port again. Jack glimpsed what looked like a Japanese destroyer off the starboard bow and ordered Brown to loose two fish at it.

"We just got the order to commence gunfire," Hoskins's voice came over the battle phones to Jack. Before he could issue the order, their last target blew sky high, the torpedo blasts augmented by exploding magazines.

"Guns One, Two, Three, and Four," Jack had to scream now to be heard above the battle noise, "commence firing at targets of opportunity. Local control. Gun captains, select targets."

The next few minutes were a destroyerman's dream. Talbot's ships ran amok among the helpless transports, shooting out searchlights with their .50-caliber machine guns, firing over open sights with their four-inchers as targets loomed up at point-blank ranges. The enemy was just now realizing that they were under a surface attack. Jack watched in glee as shells from his guns raked a fat transport, catapulting deck plates and other wreckage high into the sky. The enemy ship staggered as three shells in succession slammed into her waterline and then began to settle.

All the ships but *Ford* had turned away now, dashing back toward the freedom of the open sea. Behind them, another transport went up as the flagship's last torpedo struck home. Then, quite suddenly, there was nothing left at which to shoot. *Rust* was clear of the anchorage and dashing southward toward escape. The blowers aft were whining loudly as she slashed through the sea. Astern, the other ships of the division followed in her wake. Amazingly, as far as Jack could tell, the force had come away unscathed. He checked his watch and found that it was past 0400. They had been among the enemy ships for over an hour, though it seemed but a few minutes.

"Well done, Jack!" said Tom Hoskins over the battle circuit. "Your crews did splendid work."

"Thanks, Captain. I'll pass it along. Mind if I ask a question, sir?"

"Shoot."

"I've never seen us cut a wake like now. Just how fast are we going?"

"Over thirty-two knots. Bet the old girl hasn't done that since her builder's trials."

(Three)
Aboard USS *Marblehead*
Makassar Strait
24 January 1942

Frank Rhea sat in the cockpit of his *Seagull* on *Marblehead*'s port catapult, warming his engine in preparation for takeoff. The exhaust pipes glowed cherry-red in the predawn darkness. Off to the east, the sky above the mountains of Celebes showed signs of the coming day. Another quarter of an hour would bring them light enough for a worthwhile launch.

Frank's mind jumped from subject to subject with no logical pattern. He should have been totally concentrating on the plane, but he could not. He kept picturing the battle that should still be going on in the waters off Cinta's former home. Japanese warships would surely be pursuing the survivors of Talbot's force. If the enemy had a carrier in the area, the mission he and Tonto were about to fly might seal their fate. They would not last thirty seconds against the fast Japanese fighters.

Dawn came on rapidly, soon revealing the familiar features of *Marblehead*'s outdated superstructure. The long swells through which the ship ran hardly caused her to roll at all. Conditions would soon be favorable for a launch.

"Get ready, Tonto," Frank said over the intercom. "We'll be off in a minute or two." He looked down at Lieutenant Bishop, the acting catapult officer, and gave the "thumbs-up" signal. The catapult began to swing outboard. Revving the engine until it fairly screamed in protest, Frank gave Bishop the ready signal. The carriage shot forward with sickening speed, and the *Seagull* took wing. Frank put her nose up and climbed northward as fast as full power would allow. He leveled off at eight thousand feet and set a course straight for Balikpapan. Both cockpit occupants strained their eyes at the dim horizon ahead. For several minutes, they saw nothing but empty sea.

"Hey, Lone Ranger, I've got something in my glasses, two points to port off the nose."

Frank squinted hard, but could make out nothing with his naked eyes.

"It's ship's wakes!" said the Seminole with excitement. "I count five. Can't tell if they're ours or Japs."

"Only one way to find out," said Frank. "Let's have a look." He nosed the *Seagull* into a shallow dive to gain speed. Five minutes later, from four thousand feet, the unmistakable shapes of American "four-pipers" were clearly visible.

"Shall I radio the news?" asked Tonto.

"No. Don't break radio silence. Use your signal lamp when we're close enough for them to read it on *Marblehead*."

Frank circled north of the flagship while Tonto read the flashed reply to their report.

"What do they say?" Frank asked impatiently.

"Patrol twenty-five miles north to search for pursuit, then return."

"Let's hope there aren't any *Zeros* out there, *Amigo*. Here we go."

Frank flew directly over Talbot's retreating ships as he headed back up the Borneo coast. They were in precise formation, with flags whipping proudly in the wind. Their sterns were down almost below sea level as their screws churned at flank speed. He could not see a mark on any of them. Sailors waved enthusiastically from the decks as the *Seagull* flew past. They were a cocky bunch down there, indicating that they must have knocked the Japs about smartly.

The patrol revealed nothing but empty sea and sky. Before he turned back, Frank could make out the towering plume of smoke above Balikpapan. Heaving a sigh of relief, he reversed course and fled southward to join Glassford's retreating force.

Marblehead was at the end of the column when the *Seagull* overtook her. Signals flashed back and forth between the ship and Tonto's cockpit. Then *Marblehead* turned to port, smoothing the sea in her lee. Frank dropped the seaplane neatly onto the calmed waters and taxied quickly to the side of the ship, positioning the main float above the "sled." A few minutes later, a jubilant Eddie Blessman met him on the deck.

"Talbot's report just came in on the TBS," Eddie shouted. "They sank seven Jap ships and damaged God knows how many more. The only damage they took was a single hit on *Ford*."

"God takes care of fools and little children," Tonto muttered, "and we sure ain't kids. As many ships as the Japs had up there, they should've all been blowed out of the water."

(Four)
Nittabaru Aerodrome
Kyushu Island, Japan
24 January 1942

Chusu (lieutenant colonel) Katsura Okuma stood staring out his office window at the cold rain falling on the empty airfield. Impatience gnawed at the core of his consciousness. While he was stranded here in the winter chill of the home islands, his contemporaries were covering themselves with glory in the tropical lands to the south and west. Guam, Wake, Hong Kong and most of the Philippines were already in Japanese hands. General "Tiger" Yamashita's army was already more than halfway down the Malay Peninsula, continually savaging a British force of far superior strength. British Borneo had tumbled into the bag of conquests with hardly a fight, and now the northern Dutch oil port of Tarakan had also fallen. If he did not get into the fighting soon, the war might be over before he got a chance.

Upon his return to Nittabaru, Okuma had buried himself in the establishment and training of his regiment. The equipment he had ordered began arriving almost at once.   The base commander at Nattabaru detailed one of his ordnance shops to work full-time for Okuma, converting the rifles and machine guns into takedown models. The gunsmiths virtually rebuilt the Type 100 submachine guns, removing the heavy bayonet lug bars, morticing in pistol grips beneath the receivers and substituting hinged tubular stays for the clumsy wooden buttstocks.   The station parachute shop manufactured quick-opening chest packs for carrying the torn-down small arms into battle.   The aircraft maintenance department fabricated drop containers for the heavy weapons and ammunition.

Since he had ten volunteers for every spot in the unit, Okuma got superb human material. Almost all China veterans, they had been toughened by the brutal training and close combat which was the hallmark of the Japanese Army. He dressed them in loose-fitting green coveralls made of a tough silk and cotton blend and rimless, padded steel helmets adapted from German models captured in China. Then he plunged into his most immediate task--to get them all qualified as parachutists.

He based the regiment's training program on the Spandau curriculum.   The regimen was grueling, designed to assure remarkable physical conditioning, tactical expertise and political fitness. Within a month, every officer and man had completed the number of jumps required to qualify to wear the parachutist's wings--the Golden Kite of Tenno--on his right breast. Next came unit tactical exercises requiring jumps, first by platoon, then by company, then involving the entire regiment. Every exigency Okuma had witnessed while observing the *Luftwaffe* was simulated, along with his well thought-out countermeasures. With time extremely short, he drove both himself and his men mercilessly, but the results were worth it.   Yesterday, he filed the formal report informing the High Command that the 6th Independent Parachute Regiment was fully ready for combat. He was convinced that there was not a better comparably sized unit in the Japanese Army.

A knock at his door snapped Okuma's mind back to the present. "Come in," he said curtly.

"Good evening, Colonel," said Captain Akiyoshi Sakai, Okuma's best company commander, saluting smartly. Sakai was much smaller than Okuma but equally well muscled. He was an expert at martial arts. "A news bulletin just came in from the Supreme Command. I thought you'd be interested in it."

"Thank you, Akiyoshi." Okuma took the paper and read it quickly. The bulletin announced that Lieutenant General Toyama's expeditionary force had taken Balikpapan on Borneo's east coast. All the Borneo oil fields and production facilities were now under Japanese control. A combination of exhilaration and frustration boiled up within Okuma. The primary purpose for going to war had already been accomplished, but he had had no direct part in it! Worse yet, the infernal Dutchwoman might escape his clutches since his unit would almost certainly now be saved for Java.

"Do you think we'll get to fight before the war's over, Colonel?" Sakai echoed Okuma's inner thoughts.

"I believe that our chance will come somewhere in the Dutch East Indies. I just pray that the weak Westerners don't capitulate before the Supreme Command sends us South."

After dismissing Captain Sakai, Okuma took out his file on Cinta van Wely and went over it again. Perhaps even now she was in an internment camp in Balikpapan, waiting for him to come and extract his *tenchu*. The thought salved his disappointment that he had not been able to capture her personally. But duty had to come first. Once he had proven his concepts in the crucible of combat, there would be time enough to make the Dutchwoman suffer. Taking one long last look at the half-nude photograph, he closed the file and went off to dinner.

CHAPTER 18

(One)
Royal Netherlands Navy Headquarters
Lembang, Java
Netherlands East Indies
25 January 1942

Nicolaas van Wely found it pleasantly cool inside the massive underground bunker. Vice Admiral Conrad Emil L. Helfrich, commander of all Dutch naval forces in Java waters, got up from behind his large mahogany desk and came to meet the oilman. The admiral was a bulldog of a man: his face was almost square with sagging jowls and a double chin. His hair was grey and he had brown eyes.

"Nicolaas, old friend," said Helfrich, taking his hand, "thank God you made it safely out of Borneo."

"I almost didn't. The Japs were already ashore when I flew out on the last flying boat from Balikpapan. I had to leave some very good men back in the jungle. If the Japs find out they helped blow the refinery, we'll never see them alive again."

"It's a pity, but sometimes such things happen in war. You did an absolutely splendid job on the oil works. Sit down." Helfrich indicated an upholstered chair near the end of his large conference table. "Would you like a brandy?"

"Yes, please. I haven't had a decent drink in days."

The stocky admiral filled two snifters from a decanter on a side table, passing one to Nicolaas as he took the chair at the head of the table.

"Confusion to the enemy," Helfrich toasted, and Nicolaas echoed the words before they sipped the strong Napoleon.

"I understand you got your daughter out of Balikpapan earlier," said the admiral.

"Yes. Back in December. She's staying in Soerabaja now,

working at Central Beger Hospital."

"Ah, yes. She's a doctor, I recall. You must be very proud of her."

"You're right, but I'm also very anxious for her safety at the moment. I want her to leave Java if there's any chance we can't hold out here. Her sister's in Austin, Texas--in the States. What is the real truth about the war, Conrad? Do we have a chance to stop the Japs?"

"We damn well could if our allies were prepared to really fight for Java. You've seen the reports of what the American Navy did at Balikpapan the night you left?"

"Were they true, Conrad, or did the propaganda people embellish them?"

"You're damned right, they were true," Helfrich reacted testily. "One of my submarines was right on the spot and filed a full report. The problem is that the British and Americans just aren't pulling together with us. The idea of a unified command was good enough in theory, but it hasn't worked out. General Wavell is supposed to be in overall command, but like good Englishmen, he and his staff are preoccupied with Malaya. The Japs are beating the pants off the British Army up there, and he can't seem to stop it. Our naval commander, the American Admiral Hart, keeps talking about fighting the enemy with our surface forces, but he doesn't want to go anywhere without air cover. Since the Jap air force sank the British battleships, everybody is overly afraid of them. Air Chief Marshall Peirse has put Malaya first on his priority list and won't divert a thing for fleet support. So Hart keeps his ships out of range from the Japanese air bases and scatters his submarines all over the map. Until Balikpapan, nobody was sinking Jap ships except our own submarines."

"The press credits you with one for each day of the war," Nicolaas observed, trying to smooth his friend's ruffled feathers. The American reporters called the admiral "Ship-a-Day."

"An accurate statement, I assure you. If all the British and American cruisers in the theater were joined with ours into a single squadron and put under someone who was willing to fight, we could save Java. Hart agrees that we should have such a force but insists that it could operate only under strong air reinforcements. He bombards Washington constantly with requests for more planes. I think we'll have that cruiser force soon."

"You're convinced we can hold out, then?"

"We'll either hold Java or die in the attempt," said a grim Helfrich. "If we do lose, we'll exact a terrible price from Japan."

"I'm afraid that my daughter's life can't be a part of that price. I plan to fly her to Australia as soon as possible."

"You would desert the ship at this dark hour, my friend?" Helfrich seemed incredulous.

"I'll return if there's work for me here," Nicolaas shot back, stung by the criticism. "It's not fair to pull her down with me, though. She has her whole life ahead of her."

"The fact is," said the admiral, "there is work for you immediately. I'm afraid I can't let you leave just yet. I've already spoken to the directors of your company." Helfrich got up and stood by a large wall map of the Indies. "We've always had a wealth of oil, so much that we've been complacent in assuming its constant availability. We've depended on distribution by tankers from Borneo and Sumatra to satisfy our fleet needs. There's really no distribution system in Java for oil reserves. Now, we find ourselves facing an oil shortage. Tarakan and Balikpapan are gone." The admiral jabbed savagely at the map with his right forefinger. "Palembang, in Sumatra, is within range of the new Jap airfields in Malaya. They could destroy the refineries today if they so chose. That leaves us only one sure source of oil in the Java Sea, your new refinery at Zwarte Gouden. With its location between Batavia and Soerabaja, it's ideally suited to service both ports. The *Parfum* River can take ocean-going tankers right up to the refinery docks. The importance of this facility to our war efforts could not be overstated. It must be under the control of a production genius, but one who would not hesitate to destroy the whole complex if necessary to keep it out of the enemy's hands. There is only one man in Java to whom I could entrust such a task."

Nicolaas had guessed what was coming for several minutes. On the one hand, he was mildly flattered. On the other, a sense of desperation to see Cinta safely out of Java began to gnaw at him.

"Nicolaas, my old friend, you are the only man for the job."

"You underestimate Pieter Wildeboer, who's currently in charge at Zwarte Gouden," Nicolaas protested. "He's an excellent production man."

"He'd be all right if that were all there was to it. But he lacks your ruthlessness. He loves his machinery too deeply. He would never be able to blow it up without hesitation as you did at Balikpapan. Our homeland needs you, Nicolaas. You must do it."

"I have to get my daughter to Australia."

"Then send her now. I'll take care of whatever approvals are needed. You fly her out in your own plane if you wish, but your pilot must take her, not you. We need you in Zwarte Gouden tomorrow."

"She may not go without me. She's very strong-willed when she wants to be."

"I'll promise you this, old friend. If she refuses to go alone, I'll see that all necessary clearances are granted for both of you to leave when I give the word. I'll also see to it that the air force people don't confiscate your plane. If the situation turns against us, I'll send you word to destroy the oil works at once. After that, you'll be free to leave."

"I suppose I can't ask for more," Nicolaas said with resignation. "I only hope I can convince Cinta to leave now."

"You'll find our military people at Zwarte Gouden to be first class. The Army commander is Colonel Dijker, one of the regular officers sent out last year by the Queen."

"Yes, I know Jan Dijker."

"There's a fighter field nearby, but it has no regularly assigned units. It's really a dispersal field for the squadrons defending Soerabaja. I'm about to send a division of my new torpedo boats to protect tankers in the river estuary." The admiral set his now empty glass down on a tray. It was obvious that he had other matters that needed attending to. "You'll want to check with your company directors. The clearances I promised will be ready this afternoon." He took Nicolaas's hand again. "Good luck, my old friend. I hope I never have to give you that order to blow up Zwarte Gouden."

"Thank you, Conrad. I sincerely hope not, too."

The admiral was back on the phone before Nicolaas could get out of the room.

(Two)
Soerabaja, Java
Netherlands East Indies
25 January 1942

Jack Sewell settled into a comfortable armchair in the lobby of the Simpang Club and unfastened the high collar of his dress whites. He sipped a martini on-the-rocks as the body heat trapped inside the heavily starched blouse escaped around his neck. The sounds of the booming party in the ballroom restaurant rang in his ears. It was good to be away for a few minutes, to have time to relax and collect his thoughts.

All Soerabaja was one huge celebration on this late January evening. The Dutch had opened their arms and their homes to the returning Americans in a spontaneous outpouring of joy. It began when Glassford's task force approached Soerabaja lightship. A fleet of tugs and other small craft came out to escort them into the harbor amidst a cacophony of screaming whistles. The admiral took *Marblehead* into the naval base for repairs to her cranky shaft, but the destroyers went to Holland Pier, where a cheering crowd awaited them. Dutch ambulances were standing by at dockside to take off *Ford*'s wounded. The Americans had not, after all, come away from Balikpapan unscathed. The flagship had taken a single shell on her after deckhouse. Her damage control was so efficient that no one on the other ships realized the extent of her hurt. Tragically, another casualty occurred after they were well clear of the battle zone. Commander Talbot, who led the attack with such dash and courage, had suffered a heart attack the following day. Four sturdy bluejackets gently carried his stretcher to the waiting ambulance, which whisked him away to the hospital.

Once the ambulances were gone, parties of high-ranking military and civilian officials swarmed over the destroyers, smothering the American officers and enlisted men with congratulations. The Dutch, who had seemed so distant when the Asiatic Fleet first arrived, were now downright effusive. After all the ceremonial folderol was over, the senior officers were invited to victory parties in the homes of Dutch officials. Similar events were arranged for the enlisted men. All Soerabaja was on a bash. Jack reflected that the Dutch were due some good news, and the action off Balikpapan had filled the bill nicely. They had supported the British in Malaya from the first day of the war. Unselfishly pouring in their own slender air and naval resources, they had watched them melt away as the British defenses crumbled. Now it was clear that the Brits would lose all but Fortress Singapore itself. But if air reinforcements continued to flow into Java and the allied navies emulated Talbot's performance in Makassar Strait, the Malay Barrier might yet be held.

Jack was attending a party being given by Admiral Glassford himself. Glassford had received news when he reached his headquarters that Admiral Hart was to surrender operational control of all American ships in the Southwest Pacific to him the following day. While Hart concentrated on running the overall Allied naval effort, Glassford would command the U.S. forces. His third star was in the offing. A memorable celebration was called for, and the admiral was throwing it.

"There he is," came Ensign Brown's voice from the direction of the ballroom.

"Aren't you enjoying the party, boss?" asked Hank Logan.

"Just needed some fresh air," Jack said as the lanky jaygee and chubby ensign approached his chair.

"Button your collar and come with us," said Logan. "There's an old friend of yours inside who's dying to see you again."

The dimness of the lights inside the ballroom blinded Jack momentarily. Then his eyes came into focus, and he saw Pamela Mallory. She was even more beautiful than he remembered. He had last seen her dressed in shapeless coveralls, her hair a tangled mess piled atop her head. Now she was a sleek tigress, her magnificent body scarcely concealed by a gown of some shimmering, silvery material. The smooth skin of her bared shoulders and back was tanned to a golden hue, contrasting smartly with the pale platinum of her hair. Recognition flared in her light blue eyes as they met Jack's. She glided toward him in a blur of motion. He was so enthralled with her appearance that he did not notice the big Dutch Navy lieutenant at her side until they were almost on him.

"Jack, Jack, my luv," Pamela exclaimed, hugging him tightly. "I was hoping you would be here. Meet Jonkheer Hilling," she introduced her escort. "This is one of the gallant yanks who plucked me out of Sandakan when all seemed lost," she said to Hilling.

"I'm pleased to meet one of the heroes," said the Dutchman in thickly-accented English.

"Would you excuse us for a few minutes, Jonkheer?" Pamela said sweetly. "Jack and I have a lot of catching up to do."

"Of course, darling. I'll see you later."

"There're too many people in here," Pamela cooed, sipping gin and tonic. "I could use a breather."

"There's a game room off the lobby," said Jack. "It was deserted a few minutes ago."

"Sounds like just the privacy we need." Pamela's face broke into a wide grin.

They edged their way towards the doors. Jack saw Hank Logan coming their way and signaled him away with a nod of his head.

"Do you have an American cigarette?" asked Pamela as they slipped into the gameroom. There were lights over the billiard tables, but the edges of the room were in shadow.

Jack took out a Pall Mall, lit it and handed it to her. She took a long drag, inhaled deeply and blew out the smoke slowly. "Heavenly," she commented. "Only Americans know how to make good tobacco."

"I'm surprised to find you still in Java," said Jack as he lighted a cigarette of his own. "I would have thought you'd be in Australia by now."

"Auntie had a slight stroke the day we got here, and she's not able to travel yet."

"I hope she'll get well soon, but I'm glad that's what kept you here. I was afraid for a while that it might be your young Dutchman."

"Jonkheer? Dear God, no. He's a nice boy and eager to please me, but he's nothing more than a passing fancy. Now you, dear Jack, could be quite another matter. It's a pity that you have to stay out here and fight this stupid war."

"That almost sounds like a proposition." Jack's heartbeat quickened.

"It could be, luv," Pamela purred. "Last time we met, you were quicker off the mark."

Jack stubbed out his cigarette in an ashtray and reached for her. She came readily into his arms, her lips already parted to greet his crushing kiss. She ground herself against the length of his body, arousing him instantly to flaring passion. He slid a hand down her bare back and beneath her dress to the swell of her buttocks, gasping in surprise when he found that she was wearing nothing underneath. He pushed her back toward one of the billiard tables.

"Not here, Jack," Pamela whispered as she twisted away from his kiss. "You'll have to wait until the proper time."

"When, then? And where?"

"I'll give you the address," she promised as she rearranged her gown. "Leave the party about a half-hour after Jonkheer and me. I'll be waiting for you. Now, wipe my lip rouge off your face. If we don't go back soon, someone will come looking for us. Besides, I want you to meet Cinta van Wely, Auntie's doctor. She has a delightful pilot from your Navy with her."

Frank and Cinta stayed at the Simpang Club far into the night, enjoying the chance to dance together again to good American swing. They seemed to float across the polished hardwood, oblivious to the crowd around them.

To Frank, Cinta was a dazzling vision of beauty, elegant in the white gown she had loaned Catherine back in Balikpapan. Sapphires, which perfectly matched her eyes, sparkled in her earrings and necklace.

Just before 1:00 a.m., the band began to play "Goodnight Sweetheart," signaling an end to the party. Reaching the end of the tune, the musicians began packing away their instruments.

Frank took Cinta back to their table to finish their drinks.

"I've always felt that my inability to win you over was the greatest failure of my life," he said as he held her chair.

"Then, overall, you've been a great success. I'd have made a miserable wife."

"You'll never convince me of that. I remember too well the joys we shared."

"I was far too young and completely shattered by that first affair. What we shared wasn't any basis for a lasting marriage."

"It could have been if we'd given it a chance."

"It's too late, now, at any rate." Cinta's tone made clear that she wanted to drop this line of conversation.

"How are you and Doctor Wassell getting on?"

"Very well. He's a fine physician, and we share our knowledge.

He's a specialist on Asiatic diseases, and I've been able to fill him in on the new burn treatment theories from the States. I wish I could convince more of my colleagues that the conventional techniques for treating massive burns are outdated. The researchers in America have come up with a whole new set of concepts. We would have saved more lives if the war had held off a couple of years."

"I guess wars don't wait for convenient times to happen. What will you do now, go back to Texas?"

"If I had my way, we'd be there already. Papa did a splendid job of destroying everything at Balikpapan. He barely got away with his life. I think he's done his part. Unfortunately, the government doesn't. Admiral Helfrich has talked him into taking over at Zwarte Gouden."

"Will you be going back alone, then?"

"Never!" Anger laced Cinta's voice, and her eyes flashed. "If I did, he'd never leave, no matter how bad things got out here. He'll go in the end if he has me to worry about."

"That's a risky proposition, Cinta. Our victory night before last was a fluke. We won't catch the Japs napping again."

"I'll be all right, you'll see. Papa will get us out when the time comes. By the way, he has some excellent Napoleon that we won't be able to take with us. Would you care for a nightcap at my place before we call it a night?"

"It would be a sin to let good brandy go to waste."

The drive back to the villa was made more or less in silence, with each of them lost in their personal thoughts. Frank parked Nicolaas's MG sports car in front of the big entryway, and they went into the living room. Yuni fetched the brandy and poured it for them, then melted into the shadows.

"To what might have been," said Frank, raising his glass.

"To that, and to your safe return from the wars," Cinta responded.

They clicked their glasses and sipped the brandy.

"I suppose you'll be leaving again soon," she remarked.

"Probably tomorrow."

"Papa and I may be gone by the time you return."

"As you said back at the club, our time had about run out." Frank finished the brandy and set down his glass. He checked his watch and saw that it was past 0200. "If I'm going to fly tomorrow, I'll have to get some sleep. A goodbye kiss before I go?"

She stood up and put down her drink. Despite the strain of fatigue, she had never looked more beautiful to Frank. She came willingly into his arms, and he bent his face to hers. Then, as their lips met, all the careful control he had exercised throughout the evening dissolved, and the deep longing that had eaten at his soul for weeks came surging through his body. He crushed her to him, but when his hands tried to explore her body, her lips went limp. She pushed herself away.

"Cinta, please," he pleaded. "It may be our last chance."

"Our chance died eight years ago," she said with finality.

A wave of dejection broke over Frank. "Good luck with getting Nicolaas to leave for Australia," he said flatly. His shoulders sagged. "Better call Yuni to take me back to town."

Cinta closed the big front door as the car drove out into the street. Going back into the living room, she picked up her half-empty glass of brandy and sat down in one of the easy chairs. As she lifted the glass to her lips, she heard the tinkle of bracelets and the padding of bare feet across the floor tiles. Ada seemed to drift out of the darkened hall. Cinta looked up to find the old woman glaring at her.

"*Ayeeyah,*" Ada howled mournfully. "I have mothered a heartless devil. You shame me because I have failed so miserably to make a true woman out of you."

"Please, Little Mother," Cinta responded, holding up her hand, "let's not go into all that again tonight. I've told you a hundred times that I have to be a physician first and a woman second. I have to go to bed, now."

"Hhrumph," the *baboe* snorted. "You're no woman at all. You're a machine housed in a woman's body. The gods shaped you for love, but they left out your heart."

"Oh, Ada..."

"You're a self-centered witch. *Tuan* Frank worships you, though I can't imagine why. If you ever let anything into your mind besides medicine, you'll realize that you love him, too. I know that this is so. I can still read you better than you know yourself."

"Am I really that bad, Little Mother?" Cinta asked in a small voice, the tones coming from far back in her throat.

"Worse! *Tuan* Frank will go out tomorrow to fight the Japanese. He needed your love tonight. It was your duty as a woman to give him comfort and yourself the satisfaction of giving it. What are you saving yourself for? Have you already lost your ability to love?"

"No, Little Mother," Cinta replied, tears sparkling in her eyes. "I've only kept it on a tight rein. It's not dead."

"Then call it back, before it's too late."

"It's already too late with Frank. If he sails tomorrow, I may never see him again."

"Then I hope you can live with yourself," Ada snorted. *"Tuan* Frank has forgiven you already, but the gods may not."

Stung to the core by the penetrating truth of her *baboe*'s tongue-lashing, Cinta buried her face in her hands and began to weep quietly.

Her mind a maelstrom of confusion, Cinta lay awake for hours after the rest of the house was asleep. All the carefully constructed ramparts of cold reason she had built around her emotions over the years crumbled into the breach battered open by Ada's verbal onslaught. They came spilling out in a flood of long-suppressed feelings. The full realization that she had loved Frank through all the years they had been apart brought with it a tidal wave of desire. Her skin scorched to feel again the touch of his hands. She felt a great emptiness that only he could fill, a terrible yearning to be complete that only he could satisfy. But she had waited too long. Frank might be gone forever. Burying her face in her pillow, she cried herself to sleep.

Cinta woke just as the first rays of dawn crept in through the French doors that opened onto the terrace. She got up and peeled off her sweat-soaked nightgown before draping a silk sarong around her hips. Going out onto the terrace, she watched the orange orb of the sun creep up over the mountains to the east. A cool sea breeze pleasantly caressed the bare skin of her torso and streamed her unpinned hair away from her damp body. Her mind was now clear of confusion and filled with resolve. If ever she were blessed with another opportunity to be with Frank, she would never again withhold her love from him.

CHAPTER 19

(One)
Blimbing Aerodrome
Eastern Java
Netherlands East Indies
3 February 1942

G arrit Laterveer slowly circled the new fighter field at
Blimbing, admiring the effective camouflage job that the
Army engineers had done on it. Only at low altitude could
he discern the cleverly painted workshops. It took the eye of an
expert to make out the aircraft tracks on the thick sod field. After
two passes, he finally spotted the revetments under the trees.

Since early that morning, Major Charlie Sprague's 17th Pursuit
Squadron of the U.S. Army Air Forces had occupied the base. As
General Van Oyen's personal representative, Garrit had greeted this
first American fighter unit to reach Java when they arrived at
Tandjung Perak two days earlier. His own unit was now operating
from the auxiliary field near Zwarte Gouden. Together with 17th
Pursuit, they made up the better part of Soerabaja's air defenses.
According to Sprague, the 20th Pursuit Squadron would also come
up from Australia within a week. In less than a fortnight, American
fighter strength in East Java should reach more than fifty aircraft.

Garrit put his *Buffalo* down smoothly and taxied to the
revetment area. A fat sergeant with a stubby cigar in his mouth
directed him into one of the shelters. A new Nash motorcar drove
up, and Major Sprague vaulted from the front seat.

"Welcome to Blimbing, Garrit," said the bronzed, lean American
commander as Garrit saluted. Sprague walked over to stare at the
Dutchman's aircraft. The eight Japanese flags painted beneath the
sixteen swastikas were an awesome array. "I can't believe you're
still alive after flying that relic against the Japs," the major went on.
"If our replacement aircraft ever get here, I'll try to get you a P-40."

"I'd like a whole squadron of them," Garrit said earnestly.

"My pilots are assembled in the ops building, ready for your briefing."

"Good. Let's not keep them waiting."

"At ease, gentlemen," Sprague ordered his pilots, who had snapped to attention as the two squadron commanders entered the briefing room. They settled back into student desk chairs as he moved to a low dais across the front wall. "You'll all remember Captain Laterveer from Soerabaja. He's here to give us an update on the situation as the Dutch air staff sees it. I've also asked him to give us whatever advice he might have to offer on beating the Japs in the air. As I'm sure you're aware, he was a triple-ace in Europe before coming out here, and he has eight Japs to his credit already. Pay close attention to him. The floor's yours, Garrit."

"Thank you, Major," said Garret as he stepped up onto the platform and walked to a big map of the Indies which was pasted onto the front wall. Pausing for a moment, he let his eyes survey his American audience. Most were fresh-faced young men, but there was a sprinkling of wily veterans among them, men no older than the others but whose faces were gaunt and drawn. These were men who had survived the aerial slaughter in the Philippines to fight again. He hoped that they had learned the right lessons from their earlier defeats.

"Feel free to smoke, if you wish," Garrit began then paused until the flash of lighters ceased. "We'll have a look at the overall situation first. The Nips are following a definite pattern in their attacks. They send their amphibious forces out to the edge of the area where they have control of the air and seize an aerodrome from us. Then they rush in their air units to extend their zone of control."

He picked up a pointer and indicated a spot at the top of the map. "In the Makassar Strait area, they took your Philippine island of Jolo first, then Tarakan, then Balikpapan. The next logical target in this area will be Bandjermasin.

"On the east coast of Celebes, they moved down from Davao to seize Menado. Then, on the same day your Navy chaps knocked them about at Balikpapan, they grabbed Kendari. This was a very serious loss for us, as one of the best airfields in the Indies is located nearby. From there, we believe that the Nips will be able to begin striking at Soerabaja with their long-range bombers. Just yesterday, they invaded Ambiona on the east side of the Molucca Sea. Our naval aircraft based there got away just before the landings. Once Laha Aerodrome is in their hands, Timor will also be in range of their bombers."

"My God," muttered one of the Americans, "they're gonna cut us off from Australia."

"That's obviously their strategy. Fortunately, air reinforcements are coming from the opposite direction as well. Fifty *Hurricanes* were flown off H.M.S. *Indomitable* to Singapore last week. Within ten days we expect as many more to begin operating from our airfields near Palembang, Sumatra. A hundred *Hurricanes* should radically change the situation on our western flank. If enough of you Yanks can arrive in time, we'll hold the Nips at this end also.

"But I digress. As I was about to say, we can look for bombing attacks to begin from Kendari at any time. Unfortunately, we don't have any radar to give us an early alert. We do have a net of early warning stations on the smaller islands in the Java Sea. In clear weather, we should get sufficient advance notice to allow us to intercept before they reach Soerabaja. We've attempted to duplicate the RAF's ground control system, but I'm afraid we're in our infancy in that regard. Without radar, we can't give positive vectoring information.

"Now, as to tactics, I'm sure I don't have to tell you veterans from the Philippines not to dogfight with a *Zero*. The Jap will turn inside you every time. He can also outclimb you. His twenty-millimeter Oerlikons can cut you to pieces in a few seconds. Don't play the Nip's game. Make him play by your rules. The one thing that most American planes can do better than the *Zero* is dive. The first rule must therefore be to gain dominant altitude before engaging. Attack Japanese fighters only from above, and then only with enough space underneath for you to use your superior diving speed to escape pursuit. A word about attacking bombers. We learned in the battle of Britain that the surest way to kill a bomber is to get the pilot. A diving attack from ahead is the best way for that. It's the most vulnerable approach for the bomber as far as its defensive armament is concerned.

"I've rambled on for quite a bit. I'm sure you have questions. I'll take them now."

Half a dozen arms shot up. Garrit pointed to one of the younger, fresher-looking officers.

"Second Lieutenant Thompson, Captain. Is it true that the *Zeros* are so flimsy that one good burst will put them down?"

"The *Zero* is lightly built by Western standards, but the same could be said of the Focke-Wulf 190. The trick is to hit them with that one burst. I've flown *Spitfires*, and I've flown against the *Zero*. The Jap plane is by far the more maneuverable of the two."

The question and answer session went on for over half an hour. The younger American pilots clearly had a problem accepting that the Japanese aircraft were superior to their own. The Philippine veterans were not cursed with this prejudice. All in all, when Garrit left to fly back to his base that afternoon, he felt that he had accomplished his mission.

(Two)
Zwarte Gouden
Central Java
Netherlands East Indies
3 February 1942

Garrit broke out of the clouds surrounding the mountains that made up the spine of Java and winged out across the fringes of the Zwarte Gouden plain. Up ahead lay the city, bisected by the lazy *Parfum* River. The center of the metropolis was built around a long, open square with a massive courthouse at the north end and a park in the middle. The palm-fringed streets around the square were lined with solidly built government and private office buildings. The European shopping district contained several department stores. Four luxury hotels could house the executives and governmental officials who regularly visited the boomtown. A casual observer might have thought himself in Southern Europe until he crossed the river into the native quarter.

North of the city, the BPM refinery spread for hundreds of yards along the riverbank, its towering stills sending plumes of steam boiling up into the sky. Three tankers at a time could take on product at the long wharves that lined the riverbank. A railroad yard suitably sized for a fairly large city provided the landward link of the transportation system. To the east, the large square of the Army

Barracks was sandwiched between the suburbs and the mammoth East Oil Field, a jungle of steel derricks and oscillating pumps.

Garrit dipped the right wingtip of his *Buffalo* and turned due north to line up with the Zwarte Gouden aerodrome. The field was to the west of the city, close against the jungle and mangrove swamp that ran all the way to the north coast. Because of the importance of the oil center, the commercial airfield had tarmac runways, taxiways, and parking aprons. The control tower and terminal were as elaborate as anything in Europe. Strung along the edge of the jungle, oil drum and soil revetments covered by camouflage netting housed Garrit's fighters. All maintenance had to be performed in the open.

Garrit swept over a dome shaped hill that dominated the coastal plain. From the air, he would never have guessed that elaborate artillery bunkers were buried beneath the trees. After checking in with the control tower, he lined up on the main runway and dropped rapidly toward the earth. With flaps down and power curtailed, he soared in over the end of the threshold and made a perfect three-point landing. He slowed the plane to a stop and turned to taxi to his assigned protected area. Just before turning off the taxiway, he passed Nicolaas van Wely's *Belle of Borneo* parked in an oil drum revetment beneath a wide camouflage net.

Garrit parked his Chevrolet sedan in front of the Zwarte Gouden hospital and checked his watch. Catherine would be off duty momentarily. Today was an important day for both of them. They were going to the local Dutch Reformed Church to arrange with the pastor for their wedding. With Garrit now stationed at the nearby airfield and Catherine's family already in the city, it was possible to proceed without delay. Garrit met them on the day of his arrival. The father was a stoop-shouldered, clerkish man whose work in the bureaucracy had made him a little too respectful of authority. It had been embarrassing that the old fellow seemed awed that so rich and famous a hero would want to wed his daughter. Catherine's mother was another matter altogether. She was a whip-thin little woman with auburn hair just beginning to gray, a cheerful soul blessed with a stubborn determination. Garrit liked her instantly, and they got on comfortably from the first. The two younger sisters, Anna and Cora, were giggly teenagers who were even more impressed than their father with Garrit's reputation and position. The only hindrance to their early wedding plans was the absence of the two brothers, Johannes and Frans. Both were on active duty with the Dutch Navy. Everyone hoped that they could get leave to attend the ceremony, but were ready to proceed without them if necessary.

Garrit's own parents had been somewhat stunned when he told them by phone of his intentions. They agreed to abide by his decision, however, even seeming eager to get on with it before the conversation ended. It made him wonder if they were not just hopeful that he would sire them a grandson before his number came up in the deadly game of Russian Roulette he was playing in the sky. He was dead certain of one thing. He needed Catherine desperately. The terrible stresses of two straight months of combat flying were beginning to tell on him far worse than anything he had experienced in Europe. While airborne, everything seemed normal. But as soon as he hit the ground, the headaches began to build. He felt constantly as if a vise were squeezing in on his temples. He became irritable for no particular reason. He got inexplicable sore throats. His heartbeat fluctuated radically. He mentioned none of this to the flight surgeon for fear of being grounded. He was certain that what he needed was the soothing effect of the total love that Catherine promised. And if he did leave a new life growing within her body when his luck ran out, that would be but an added bonus.

Catherine came bounding down the hospital steps in her snow white uniform, a bright smile creasing her face. "Hello, Darling," she chirped happily, kissing his cheek as she got into the car. "Still sure you want to go through with this?"

"As sure as anything I've ever done," he replied with gravity then broke into a laugh. Starting the engine, he pulled out and headed for the town square, which the church bordered. "As far as I'm concerned, we could skip the big ceremony and get it over with today."

"We couldn't disappoint Mama and the girls. They're so looking forward to a big production."

Quite suddenly, the air raid sirens began to wail throughout the city. From the time of day, Garrit recognized immediately that this was not a drill. Either the warning service was spooked by war nerves, or the Japanese airmen had at last come to Java.

"Damn," Garrit swore, braking hard at a public phone. He

dashed to the booth, gave his name to the operator and got through at once to the duty officer of his squadron. Moments later, he was leaping back into the car. "Sorry, Darling," he said calmly. "Duty calls. The Nips are coming for Soerabaja. Maybe you should go on to the pastor and give him my regrets."

"No," she replied, her voice firm. "Let me go with you. I can get back to town later."

"No time to argue." He spun the Chevrolet into a tight U-turn amidst the honking of horns from other vehicles, heading for the big bridge across the river.

Garrit's ground crew had his *Buffalo* warmed up when he stopped the car at the revetment. "See you later, Darling," he said as he kissed Catherine quickly.

"Good hunting," she replied, hiding her turmoil with a cheerful smile.

He vaulted from the car and sprinted to where his crew chief was holding his parachute harness and flying helmet. "See that Miss Van Zweden gets home safely, Sergeant," he ordered as he struggled into the harness.

"Consider it done, Captain. Good luck, sir."

"We'll need it. How long ago did the alert flight get up?"

"Fifteen minutes, sir. They were off the ground within five minutes of the alarm being sounded."

"Good. I see five more machines ready to go. What about the others?"

"Equipment failures, Captain. Nine are all we can put up."

"They'll have to do, then." Garrit ran to his *Buffalo* and climbed into the cockpit. A quick check of the gauges showed everything normal. He keyed his radio set and got reports from the other four pilots. A few hasty instructions and they were ready to move. Garrit gunned the engine, released the brakes and taxied out to the end of the tarmac runway. Moments later, the five fighters roared down the strip abreast, taking off together.

No longer smiling, Catherine stood watching the planes fade into the horizon, silently praying that Garrit would come back to her.

(Three)
Bunda Roads
Off Madura Island, Java
Netherlands East Indies
3 February 1942

Frank Rhea finished checking his *Seagull* for battle readiness then climbed down onto *Marblehead*'s port catapult. Tonto was waiting for him on the deck.

"What do you think of this new setup, Lone Ranger?" the warrant officer asked.

Frank swept his gaze about the placid waters of the anchorage, which was hard against the southern shore of Madura Island. There were more Allied warships gathered here on this early afternoon of February third than had been assembled at one time since the war began. Besides *Marblehead* and *Houston* and their bevy of old "four-pipers," the Dutch light cruisers *De Ruyter* and *Tromp* were swinging on their anchors. The modern destroyers, *Van Ghent*, *Piet Hein* and *Banckert* completed the Dutch squadron. Here at last was the cruiser striking force for which Admiral Hart had been plugging since his first days at ABDAFLOAT. The real question was whether it had been formed quickly enough to affect the outcome of the campaign.

"I don't know yet," Frank finally said. "The Dutch ships look modern enough, but they don't have as much firepower as our old 'Ghost.' Seven six-inchers on *De Ruyter* and six on *Tromp* don't add that much to the battle line."

"They got more than the old cruisers the Japs are using as flagships of their desrons," Tonto observed. "They got lots of ack-ack, too." Both Dutch cruisers fairly bristled with 40-millimeter Bofors guns.

"Communications will be our biggest headache. They use a different flag system from ours, and we don't even have a common radio code. Commander Van Bergan said we're to get an English-speaking liaison officer later today. I guess we'll have to pass orders around by plain language on TBS until the communications types get this thing sorted out."

"What a screwed-up mess," Tonto said with disgust. "At least the TBS range is short enough that the Japs can't hear it unless they can see us. I don't like them putting that Dutch admiral in charge. What's his name again?"

"Doorman. Karel Doorman. Supposed to be some kind of a hotshot. He's an aviator-- commanded the Naval Air Service before he got his stars."

"Thank God for that. Still, I'd feel a lot better with an American flag officer in charge. We're furnishing most of the muscle for this lashup."

"It is their country. We and the British have hogged all the other major commands. I guess someone figured they rated a crack at running part of the show."

"Or Admiral Hart wanted to cut Glassford out of the action."

"You've been hearing that scuttlebutt, too?"

"Who didn't, the way Glassford's staff talked on the way back from Balikpapan?"

"Better forget it. We've got enough trouble on our hands without fighting among ourselves. At least Admiral Purnell's to be Doorman's chief of staff. He'll keep things on track."

"Wonder what's cooking over on *De Ruyter*?" The captains of all the allied ships had been at a conference on the flagship since Purnell flew in from Soerabaja in mid-morning.

"Something hot for the Japs," Frank mused.

"More likely, for us."

The clang of the General Alarm rattled them from their relaxation. The bugle began screaming the Air Defense call over the public address system.

"What the hell?" Tonto swore.

"Get someone on those cranes," Frank shouted above the noise. "We've got to put the planes in the water so that we can take off. If they hit them on the cats, they'll go up like bombs."

"Aye, aye," Tonto answered as he sprinted toward the crane housing. Frank ran back to the catapult and climbed onto his *Seagull*. The big aircraft crane was already swinging its hook his way as he dug the lifting slings from their hatch atop the high wing.

"I'll take over, Lone Ranger," said Tonto as he climbed up beside Frank after undogging the catapult clamps. "Get onto your pre-flight check."

As Frank slid into his seat, he saw that Eddie Blessman was scrambling into the other *Seagull*. With any luck, they would get them both off the ship. Frank's plane lurched drunkenly as the excited crane operator lifted it off the catapult. Then he calmed down and swung the aircraft smoothly clear of the deck, setting it into the water with hardly a ripple. Tonto unslung the hook in record time and snapped shut the wingtop hatch. Frank hit the electric starter as the Seminole dropped into the rear cockpit.

Weighed down by a full fuel load and two 100-pound bombs, the *Seagull* taxied sluggishly. To make matters worse, there was not even a breath of wind to help them get airborne. Frank gunned the engine hard, turning it up to maximum revolutions. The floatplane plowed on through the waves, unable to build enough aerodynamic lift to raise the main float clear of the water.

Off to the right, Frank spotted Eddie Blessman in a similar predicament. Beyond Eddie's plane, two *Seagulls* from *Houston* were also vainly attempting to take off.

Nearing the shoreline, Frank slacked off on the throttle and swung the nose of his plane to seaward just in time to see the two *Houston* aircraft streaking across the anchorage so closely in tandem that they seemed hooked together. Quite suddenly, the rear biplane rose up on the step of its float, then broke free and began to soar skyward. The other throttled back and taxied toward Eddie Blessman. Frank grasped at once what the *Houston* pilots were doing. The prop wash of the leading plane provided just enough extra lift to the wings of the trailing ship to allow it to lift out of the water. It was a brilliant piece of improvisation by the "Flying Wombats." The *Houston Seagull* was soon in front of Eddie Blessman's plane, duplicating the trick to perfection. Eddie's bird rose majestically and lumbered off to the south.

As the innovative pilot approached and waved instructions, Frank saw that he was "Little Jack" LaMade. They began their tandem run across the water. Frank's *Seagull* was still sluggish, but he could clearly feel the extra lift on the wings. With agonizing slowness, the plane rose higher and higher on the step of its float. Then he was airborne, clawing for altitude to get clear of the anchorage before the enemy airmen struck.

Somehow, LaMade got his own plane into the air without help and came up behind Frank as he joined in formation with the other floatplanes. Eddie Blessman led them on toward Bali, away from the approaching enemy aircraft.

"How many Japs are there?" Frank asked over the intercom.

"About fifty," Tonto responded. "They're not headed our way. They're going in the direction of Soerabaja."

"I hope those Air Corps guys who came in last week are ready." But even more, Frank prayed that the Japanese would not target Central Berger Hospital for destruction.

Despite the early sighting by Doorman's warships off Madura, the enemy bombers were almost to Soerabaja before the defending fighter units received orders to intercept. The Japanese had been over the city for over twenty minutes when Garrit's squadron reached the scene. Smoke billowed skyward from the warehouses at the naval base. Other fierce fires were raging at the Perak Naval Air Station. The commercial docks were in shambles, and several ships were settling to the harbor bottom.

Coming in at fifteen thousand feet, Garrit searched the bowl of the sky for the raiders, picking out a few dim specks retreating toward the north. He took his planes in a wide sweep over the wounded city, looking in vain for targets.

His fighter pilot's sixth sense told him that something was wrong. Then, straight up in the sun above, he caught the glint of diving wings.

"Break right!" he screamed into his wireless mike. "Dive! Dive! Bandits in the sun!" He snapped the *Buffalo* over onto its back and sent it screeching toward the earth below. As the ground swept up at him with mind-boggling speed, tracers began to zip past his cockpit. Then came the sickening crunch of cannon shells slamming into his engine. Oily smoke erupted from the cowling and swept back past the cockpit. Flames began to lick at his feet. With that icy calmness that had saved his life twice before, Garrit pulled the nose of the stricken fighter up and rolled it onto its back. Sliding his goggles down over his eyes, he released the canopy latch and shoved it backwards. With fire whipping about his face, he unsnapped his seatbelt and kicked hard against the floorboards, propelling his body clear of the crippled warbird. Cool air tore at the scorched skin of his cheeks, jarring his brain with pain. He grasped the D-ring of the ripcord and tugged it hard.

The snap of the opening parachute jarred every bone in his body. Drifting earthward, he beat at the smoldering cuffs of his trousers until he was sure that the fire was out and then began orienting himself. He was over the southern part of the city near the Dermo Barracks. The wind was pushing him eastward toward Ngagel. Tugging at the shrouds, he guided the parachute in the direction of an open field near one of the factories there. The descent seemed to accelerate as he neared the ground. It came rushing up to meet him at the last few seconds. He landed with flexed knees, rolled over in the grass and came up in full control of the collapsing canopy.

A squad of Javanese militia ran up to ring him in as he wrestled with the billowing silk. They gestured threateningly at him with Marlin M42 submachine guns until he tore off his helmet to reveal his blond hair. Then they helped him collapse his parachute.

"Sorry, Captain," said the fresh-faced young Dutchman in command of the group. "We thought you might be a Nip."

"No such luck," Garrit responded. "Any parachute you see is probably ours."

"We'd better get you to the hospital, sir," the sub-lieutenant said with some concern. "Those are nasty burns on your face."

"Sounds like a good idea." The fierce burning sensation in his cheeks galvanized his attention. "Let's go."

Garrit took no more than a dozen steps toward the militiamen's lorry before his legs suddenly turned to jelly. *Shock*! His brain screamed as his knees buckled and he stumbled forward. It took three of the little Javanese to carry him the rest of the way to the truck.

"You were very lucky, Garrit," said Cinta van Wely as she finished bandaging his face with Vaseline gauze. "If you hadn't been wearing your goggles, you would have been blinded."

"Luck had little to do with it," he observed wryly. "That's how they trained us to do it."

"At least your handsome face isn't damaged permanently. What you have is a second-degree burn. Most of it isn't much worse than you'd get by a bit too much time in the sun. You'll still be able to set Catherine's heart aflutter. Papa told me about you two."

"That's good news," Garrit replied thickly. The painkiller in his face made his speech sluggish. "We're supposed to get married next week."

"Why that's marvelous! Where will the wedding be? I'd like to come."

"Zwarte Gouden. We'd love to have you. Since your father's in charge of the oil works there, perhaps it would be possible."

"Just get me the exact time and date," she said as she cut the scorched part of his right trouser leg away. "Oh, dear, this is worse than I expected." The charred skin of his ankle was peeled back almost to the bone. "This is going to ground you for two or three weeks."

"I can't afford that, Cinta," he shot back, suddenly belligerent. "Patch me and let me fly."

"That's not rational, Garrit," she replied coolly. "You can do permanent damage to the tendons--end up a cripple for life. A few days of the proper care will work wonders. Your second-in-command will just have to fill in."

"We'll see about that," he responded, his sudden flare of temper subsiding.

As two Javanese orderlies wheeled Garrit out of the treatment room, a chubby-faced Air Corps lieutenant rushed up.

"Captain Laterveer?" the young man inquired anxiously.

"That's right."

"Thank God you're alive. We heard you'd been shot down. I'm Jan Mantel, air liaison officer on General Ilgen's staff. Is there anything I can do for you?"

"Yes, there is," Garrit replied, heaving himself up on his elbows. "Get me back to Zwarte Gouden, by plane if you can. I've got to see what's left of my squadron."

The Lockheed *Electra* banked gently as it lined up to put down at Zwarte Gouden aerodrome. The Army medical orderly who had accompanied Garrit from Soerabaja checked to see that the sleeping Captain was securely strapped to his litter, then settled into a seat and buckled the safety belt. The pilot was very good, making a smooth-as-glass landing. Garrit did not stir from his drug-induced sleep as the plane taxied to the parking apron, or when the men from his squadron came aboard to take him to the nearby ambulance. It was over three hours later, in a room at the Zwarte Gouden hospital, when his eyes finally fluttered open. A tired-faced, frumpy nurse with frowzy blond hair was sitting beside the bed, watching over him.

"Where am I?" he asked sleepily.

"You're back in Zwarte Gouden, Captain," the nurse replied in a motherly voice. "You just rest yourself. You'll be right as rain in a few days."

"I'd like to see Nurse Van Zweden. Is she on duty?"

"Oh, no. She'll be gone for several days, sir. She's in Soerabaja with her family."

"Soerabaja?" Garrit was confused. "Why would she go there now?"

"Of course, you wouldn't know. Both her brothers were killed in the bombing yesterday. They've gone to bring the bodies back for burying."

CHAPTER 20

(One)
Aboard USS *Marblehead*
Flores Sea
4 February 1942

Frank Rhea had the midwatch on the morning of February 4th. He paced *Marblehead's* bridge confidently, speaking quietly to the watch standers, occasionally stopping to check the plot of the ship's position. She was steaming eastward down Madura Strait in company with *De Ruyter, Tromp*, and *Houston*. The three Dutch destroyers were somewhere astern, while the American "four-pipers" covered the flanks. The Combined Striking Force left Bunda Roads at midnight, bound for an attack on an enemy invasion force near Makassar Town. The plan called for sailing round the eastern tip of Madura before heading north across the Flores Sea.

A scene from the previous afternoon kept running through Frank's mind, and he savored it with relish. It happened soon after the *Seagulls* were hoisted back aboard the cruisers. A PBY slipped in from Soerabaja to take Admiral Purnell back to headquarters. Just as the ungainly flying boat was lining up to land, a stray *Zero* swept down out of the sun and jumped its tail. For once, a Jap pilot had been too cocky. One of the waist gunners put a half-belt of .50-caliber slugs into the enemy fighter, sending it crashing in flames. Spontaneous cheers rang out across the roadstead from the assembled ships. It was a good omen for the fledgling Allied fleet.

At 0400, Frank turned the watch over to Lieutenant "Blades" Gillette and gratefully sought out his bunk. It had been a long exhausting day. He was given no second sight, no premonition that he was crawling between those sheets for the last time. The first brilliant rays of sunlight reflected off broken cloud cover as he fell into an exhausted sleep.

Four hours later, Frank passed on Eddie Blessman's order dismissing the men of "V" Division from Quarters then turned to the division officer. "I need another cup of java, Eddie," he said sleepily. "Care to join me?"

"Not right now. Tonto's found something wrong with my *Seagull's* engine. I'm going to check it out. Go on yourself, though. You look like death warmed over."

Stretching his aching muscles, Frank walked up the deck toward the wardroom. Off to starboard, he recognized the slightly different silhouette of the *Jonathan B. Rust* and wondered what Jack Sewell was up to this morning. Beyond the destroyers, the tall volcanic mountains of Bali hung between the clouds and the horizon. A soft breeze blew in from the west, providing a following sea. He leaned for a moment against the railing, hoping that at last the Allies would be able to strike a telling blow against the enemy. If only they had a little air cover, this fleet should have the firepower to turn the trick. On that optimistic note, he went into the wardroom for a late breakfast and coffee.

Frank was on the bridge being briefed for a reconnaissance flight when the signalman reported that a plain language message was being flashed from *De Ruyter*. Sublieutenant Luxemburg, the liaison officer who had come aboard the previous evening, stepped out onto the bridge wing and raised his glasses.

"Thirty-seven enemy bombers headed for Soerabaja," the Dutchman translated. "Sighted at 0810 in Southern Celebes."

Commander Goggins turned from Frank to the Captain. "They could be on us at any time, Skipper."

"Set Condition Three," Captain Robby ordered. "We'll have to go to General Quarters fast if they find us."

"*Houston's* signaling, Captain," the JOOD reported. "Strange aircraft sighted bearing 023 true."

"Crow's Nest lookout reporting, Captain," one of the talkers spoke up. "Planes approaching from the east."

"Sound General Quarters," snapped Captain Robby. "Order 'Air Defense.'"

The strident clatter of the General Alarm reverberated through the ship. The Bosun of the Watch keyed the speaker system and began calmly reciting the appropriate instructions. Then the bugler blew "Air Defense."

"We should launch the *Seagulls* to lessen the fire hazard, sir," the Exec suggested.

"Make it so." Robinson agreed.

"Get the planes up," Goggins told Frank. "Keep well clear until the action's over."

"Aye, aye, Commander," Frank acknowledged the order.

"And dump the AVGAS from the main deck fuel tanks," Goggins shot at him as he made for the bridge exit.

There was a clammor of noise throughout the ship as the men ran to their battle stations, clanging shut watertight doors and hatches behind them. But there was no confusion, no unnecessary verbiage being bandied about. Countless hours of silent drills were paying off.

Frank met Eddie Blessman at the catapults and relayed Goggins's orders.

"My engine's conked out," Blessman informed him. "We'll go ahead and launch you now. If it comes to it, we'll jettison my bird. Get Tonto and prepare to launch."

AVGAS was already streaming over the side as the starboard catapult swung outboard. Frank had his engine going full bore. Tonto came running up the deck, buckling on his parachute harness as he moved. He scurried up onto the catapult and vaulted into the rear cockpit. Nearby, gunners were unlimbering the antiaircraft battery.

"Ready back here, Lone Ranger," came Tonto's words over the intercom. "Very well. Here we go." Frank revved the engine and gave Eddie the "ready to launch" signal. With a hissing of air across the wings, the *Seagull* shot forward with blinding speed, clearing the catapult and climbing slowly away from the cruiser. Frank put her into a tight spiral climb, hoping to gain enough altitude to act as an early warning station for the ship. He barely had her up to five hundred feet when *Houston's* battery of five-inch antiaircraft guns cut loose. Concussion from the shock waves buffeted the floatplane's wings. A moment later, one of the heavy cruiser's catapults fired, flinging its aircraft into the sea.

"Goddamn!" Tonto swore. "They had a dead cat shot."

Frank glanced quickly at the wreck in the water. The canvas skin had been blown apart on the after part of the fuselage. "It's empty," he finally said. "They threw it overboard to get its gasoline off their decks. How many Japs do you count?"

"Thirty-six so far.   Looks like three squadrons--Type 96 Mitsubishis."

Down below, the Allied fleet was scattering. The farther apart the ships could get, the less chance that a single bombing run could damage more than one vessel. Each ship would have to fight its own battle with the enemy planes.

As Frank continued to climb, the Japanese formation split into three groups, each of which made for one of the Allied cruisers. They flew arrogantly over the heavy ships at 17,000 feet, oblivious to the bursting antiaircraft shells below them. The captains of the warships were doing corkscrew maneuvers to throw off the enemy's aim, leaving boiling wakes in the blue sea.

The Japanese squadrons shifted targets and came down to 14,000 feet, again making dry bombing runs over the warships.

"What are the bastards doing?" Tonto asked in exasperation.

"Testing the range of our ack-ack and seeing what our skippers do when attacked. Pretty soon, they'll drop their bombs."

A third formation was approaching *Marblehead*. From eight thousand feet up, the cruiser looked to Frank like a toy boat in a monstrous bathtub.

"They're bombing," Tonto shouted.

Ugly black eggs seemed to spring from the bomb bays of the Mitsubishis and rocket downward towards *Marblehead*. The cruiser suddenly turned to the right, away from the point at which the bombs had been aimed. Frank banked the *Seagull* so that he could see and held his breath. Great geysers of water erupted in the sea just off *Marblehead*'s port bow, drenching the foreparts of the ship as they crashed back into the sea. At that very moment, one of the Mitsubishis disintegrated in a ball of flame. A second bomber began to smoke and fell away from the formation.

"They got one of the son-of-a-bitches," Tonto exclaimed. "He's going down."

Frank watched the Japanese plane fall, thrilled to see one of the enemy finally hit. Then his practiced eye recognized what the pilot was doing. If he kept control of the burning bomber, he was going to crash directly into *Marblehead*.

Streams of orange tracer leaped up from the .50-caliber machine guns on the cruiser's mainmast as the Mitsubishi plunged straight for her bridge. Then the guns farther aft joined in. For a long awful interval, it looked as if the bomber was unaffected. Then its windscreen shattered into hundreds of glittering fragments, and the plane nosed straight over as the dead pilot slumped against the control column. It struck the sea with a scorching explosion of gasoline.

Frank was now up to ten thousand feet. He maneuvered toward the southeast to get away from the cone of steel being thrown up by the blazing antiaircraft guns on the ships.

"Here comes another squadron of Japs," Tonto reported. "They're single-engined jobs. I think they're Jap Navy Nakajimas."

"Report them to *Marblehead.*"

"I did already."

The Japanese carrier planes stalked the cruiser with stealth and skill. Again, dry runs were made to test the Americans' reactions. Then, guessing the direction Captain Robby would turn, the enemy squadron commander ordered "bombs away." Eight missiles plunged toward the sea, their speed increasing by the moment under the forces of gravity. *Marblehead* steamed a straight course until the moment of bomb release. Now she was turning to her left, her screws churning up a curved, frothy wake. Frank banked his plane again so that Tonto could watch with his binoculars.

"Goddammit! Oh, Goddammit!" the Seminole cursed. "That little yellow bastard guessed right. They're going to hit."

An instant later, *Marblehead* disappeared beneath a storm of water and blossoming balls of fire and smoke.

"Mother of God!" Chief Muldune muttered to Jack Sewell. "*Marblehead*'s a goner."

"Did I just see daylight under her keel?" asked Jack, incredulous. "Or am I imagining things?"

"Your eyes are okay, Lieutenant. I saw it, too."

Jack pushed his tin hat back from his forehead and raised his binoculars. The cruiser, which was about a thousand yards off *Rust's* port beam, slowed perceptibly. She was down by the bow, and fires raged in her amidships and near her stern. She began to turn away from the destroyer then continued around in a full circle.

Ships from all over the formation began speeding to *Marblehead*'s aid. *Tromp* was coming up fast. *Houston* was also on the way, her longer-range five-inchers blazing away at the Nakajimas. Their fire was still futile for the moment, their shells falling far short of the target.

"This is the Captain, Jack," came Tom Hoskins's voice in the battle phone. "Can our antiaircraft guns reach those Japs?"

"Not from here, Skipper. From closer in, maybe."

"Then stand by to open fire," said Hoskins. "We're going in until you can shoot. Those boys over on *Marblehead* need us."

Rust heeled over sharply as she turned toward the fiercely burning cruiser. Ugly, oily smoke shot up several hundred feet above the stricken ship. Another enemy squadron lined up for a run at her. They were down to about eight thousand feet and streaking in from the northwest. As soon as they were close to the reach of *Rust*'s guns, Jack ordered the gun crews to commence firing.

The little three-inch twenty-five on the forecastle barked defiantly but with little hope of hitting the enemy. Its shell exploded far below the oncoming planes. Then the pom-poms opened up, sending lazy tracers drifting up toward the Japanese. Seemingly unconcerned, the Mitsubishis came on toward their drop point.

Two thousand feet above and in front of the raiders, Frank Rhea looked down on his ship with a growing sense of despair. Even at this altitude, the fierce flames behind her bridge and on her fantail were visible through the billowing smoke. She was steaming in a circle, her steering gear apparently jammed by bomb hits.

"Holy shit!" Tonto swore over the intercom. "They really plastered the old 'Ghost.'"

"She's out of control. If they hit her again, she'll go under."

"Ain't there something we can do? I feel like shit just sitting around up here while our buddies are taking it on the chin down there."

"I know the feeling." Inside, Frank was seething. If the Allied high command had given the ships any air cover at all, this wouldn't be happening. The Japanese bombers were operating without any fighter escort.

"More bogies," Tonto announced. "Eight, at nine o'clock, about eight thousand feet."

Frank twisted around in his cockpit and squinted toward the

northwest. Sure enough, the bombers were coming back in for the kill. The germ of a thought took root in his mind and began to blossom. Pulling back on the steering column to put the *Seagull* into a tight, spiral climb, he explained to Tonto what he planned to do. When he finished, the Indian broke into a laugh.

"You're crazy as hell, Lone Ranger, but I'm with you. I'll do anything to stop the Japs from hitting the Marby again."

Frank closed the cockpit canopy and continued to climb. The Wasp engine strained hard on full power, its propeller clawing at the thin air to gain altitude. Frank glanced at the oncoming Japanese formation. They were coming straight in, flying in three tight "vics." There was no doubt in his mind that the squadron commander was in the lead ship of the first "vic." That was his target. He would get but one chance.

The Mitsubishi bombers had a good hundred miles an hour on the little *Seagull*. The only way he could attack at all was by getting above and in front of them, then scream down in one, head-on diving pass. If he misjudged, he would either miss altogether or collide with one of them. His eyes scanned the horizon in a full circle, again finding no sign of escorting fighters.

The bombers came on. As Tonto had surmised, they were the newer Mitsubishis, with fat, cylindrical fuselages. Sunlight glinted off the extensive glazing in their noses.

Aim for the cockpit, Frank's brain played back what Garrit Laterveer had told him. *Straight in through the canopy is the weakest point on a bomber. Kill the pilots and the machine dies with them.*

The moment to act was approaching. Frank cleared his .30-caliber machine gun and checked the sights. Yelling to Tonto to get ready, he nosed the *Seagull* over and dived straight for the formation leader. The airplanes were closing with fantastic speed. Below the bombers, black puffs of smoke began to erupt. *Marblehead* was putting up everything she had, but her guns could not reach the raiders. The Japanese were about to release their bombs.

On *Rust*'s fire control platform, Jack Sewell caught sight of the tiny seaplane diving into the raiders.

"That guy's either crazy or too brave for his own good," Chief Muldune shouted.

"That's Lieutenant Rhea, from *Marblehead*," Jack responded, admiring Frank's audacity.

The same question was flashing through the minds of dozens of officers throughout the tiny fleet. On *Houston*, Captain Rooks thought for a moment that it might be one of his planes. On *De Ruyter*, Admiral Doorman was standing on the bridge wing, his glasses glued to the high drama above.

A stream of red tracers leaped out from the single machine gun in the *Seagull's* nose and probed for the enemy bomber. The bullets began to strike the fuselage near the gun turret. Correcting the angle of attack swiftly, Frank hosed the tracer up to the cockpit and held them there. Balls of colored fire began floating toward his face from all over the enemy formation. The Japanese had spotted him now, and every gun in the force that could be brought to bear was firing at the seaplane. Tracers began whipping by close aboard.

The floatplane was a marvelously stable gun platform, and the Japanese pilot refused to waiver at all. For what seemed an eternity--it was actually closer to five seconds--Frank held the river of tracers dead on the cockpit. The windscreen of the bomber suddenly disintegrated, spraying fragments of Plexiglas back into the slipstream. The Mitsubishi loomed ominously close. He had to break away, or they would collide!

Frank dropped the *Seagull's* nose and broke left. They flashed by the enemy formation just ahead of the commander's wingman, clearing his starboard propeller by a scant thirty feet. As they fell away rapidly, Tonto cut loose with his flexible gun and stitched a neat row of holes down the fuselage of the lead bomber. Then they were out of range, and he released the trigger.

Suddenly, the floatplane was buffeted by a terrific shock wave. Black balls of smoke were blossoming all about them. In diving past the enemy, they had fallen into the ack-ack barrage of the ships they were trying to save. Frank pulled back on the stick and climbed frantically.

"We got 'em, Lone Ranger! We got 'em!" Tonto was screaming on the intercom. Frank twisted his head, searching for the target plane.

Far above, the leading Japanese bomber was pulling straight up, as if the pilot were trying to loop the big bird. Its nose rose until the fuselage was almost vertical, but then the plane fell away in a twisting dive and plummeted toward the sea.

On *De Ruyter's* bridge, Karel Doorman turned to his American liaison officer. "Get the name of that pilot," he ordered. "Bravery like that should not go unrewarded."

To the Japanese, the loss of their leader seemed not to matter at all. The next "vic" moved up, its point plane taking the lead. But as they wheeled in for a bombing run, a few shells began to burst right in among the aircraft. Captain Rooks had moved *Houston* close to the wounded *Marblehead* to cover her with his five-inch guns. Using the new ammunition from *Boise*, the *Houston* gunners were beginning to score hits. Stung by this interference, the new Japanese commander shifted targets and went after the heavier cruiser.

Frank was still straining for altitude, trying to get above the enemy again, when Tonto let out a war whoop. The plane they had hit earlier had just disappeared in a cloud of smoke and spray as it struck the sea.

Houston steamed majestically past *Rust* at less than a thousand yards, her upper works ablaze with the muzzle flashes of her ack-ack guns. Her bow wash sent the little destroyer bouncing on her beams' ends. Jack grabbed for the railing and held on tightly. The starboard pom-pom went silent as the violent roll put the ship's bridge between its muzzle and the enemy. *Rust* was just righting herself when a barrage of bombs plowed up the sea around *Houston*. For a moment, it seemed that none had struck home, but then a violent secondary explosion erupted in her after turret, venting flames and smoke through the hatches. Seemingly unaffected, the heavy cruiser steamed on to place *Marblehead* under the protective umbrella of her sky guns.

Another wave of fifteen Mitsubishis bored in. *Houston's* five-inchers opened up again, this time with stunning results. Ugly balls of black smoke erupted all over the enemy formation, tearing away wings, shattering engines, lacerating the thin aluminum fuselages with a torrent of shrapnel. Half a dozen fiery wrecks spiraled earthward, and still the ack-ack shells took their toll. The Japanese airmen were brave to the point of foolhardiness, continuing to press home their attack.   Three more flaming planes fell away, then another and another. Only three of the bombers made it to the drop point, and one of them took a hit as they released their bombs.

The damaged bomber drifted slowly away from its companions and went into a shallow dive. Flames and smoke streaming from its starboard engine, it set a course directly for *Marblehead*.   Within a few seconds, it was evident to everyone watching that the pilot was trying for a suicide dive into the crippled cruiser.

"Get the bastard, Chief!" Jack screamed at Muldune. "If he hits *Marblehead*, she'll go down like a rock."

Muldune passed the order on to the midships pom-poms. Every antiaircraft gun in the force that could be brought to bear was already firing, sending a storm of tracers up at the Mitsubishi. The pilot ignored the barrage, boring in on the damaged warship. Hoskins turned *Rust* to unmask the pom-poms, and both opened fire together. Their lazy tracers drifted up toward the diving plane and almost immediately began to score along its port wing root. As if in slow motion, the wing folded upwards and tore away, sending the rest of the plane into a spinning spiral. It hit the water with a billowing explosion of gasoline about two hundred yards from *Marblehead*.

"Good shooting, Jack," Hoskins barked over the battle phones.

The old light cruiser was down by the bow and listing badly to starboard. She was still steaming in circles, but the effects of her damage control crews could be seen already. The volume of smoke coming from both the big fires was perceptibly smaller. A signal lamp began to blink from her bridge in the direction of *De Ruyter*, reporting that the fires were under control.

"Those poor son-of-a-bitches," a fire controlman said to one of the lookouts. "They're going to fry or drown before the day's out. The Japs must have blown her bottom out, the way she's settling."

"Those are old Asiatic Fleet salts, son," Muldune shot back. "They ain't about to give up on her. If anybody in the U.S. Navy can save that ship, Captain Robinson will do it."

"I hope you're right, Chief," said Jack, fearing that the younger man's assessment was nearer the truth.

The Combined Striking Force milled around in the Flores Sea for another hour while the crews of *Marblehead* and *Houston* fought the fires to a standstill and plugged up the inrushing waters as best they could. More bombers came, but these concentrated on the Dutch cruisers, trying to put them out of action also. Finally, just before noon, the last of the raiders faded into the northern horizon. A few minutes later, *Marblehead* stopped circling and began to zig-zag southward. Miraculously, her jammed rudder had been worked back amidships. Captain Robinson reported to *De Ruyter* that he could steer with his engines. Orders came out from the flagship for *Marblehead* and *Houston* to retire to Tjilatjap, the new fleet base on Java's south coast. *Rust* was detailed as one of her escorts. The rest of the ships would stay with her until time for her to run for a strait in the Malay Barrier. The Dutch ships would then continue to Batavia.

Frank had been cruising high above *Marblehead* all this time, watching with grave concern. Now that the ship was headed to safety, steaming an erratic course and trailing an oil slick, he began to worry about his own fuel supply. It was getting dangerously low. Tom Payne, who had been up in one of *Houston's Seagulls* during the engagement, flew briefly in formation with him, then dropped away to land and be picked up by his mother ship. Finally Frank had Tonto report his fuel situation to *Marblehead* and ask for instructions.

"We won't be needing you for some time, Frank," Captain Robby's voice came through his headphones. It sounded burdened with sadness. "Fly to Soerabaja and report to headquarters there. Good luck."

"Good luck to you, too, Captain," Frank replied, somehow guessing that he had received his final orders from his beloved commander. At Tonto's last sighting, the Allied ships were retreating westward as fast as the cripples could limp along.

(Two)
Soerabaja, Java
Netherlands East Indies
4 February 1942

Major Sprague and Captain Leeuwenberg, commander of the other Dutch squadron at Soerabaja, were already in the briefing room when Garrit hobbled in on crutches. The commanders of the other two fighter squadrons guarding Soerabaja both sprang to their feet.

"Good God, Garrit, you should still be in the hospital," Sprague exclaimed.

"It's not as bad as it looks," Garrit replied. "The brace is to keep my ankle from moving until the burn heals. The bones are all right. Besides, the Nips aren't giving us any time for convalescent leave."

"That's the God's truth," Leeuwenberg agreed. "My squadron's down to half strength and shrinking. I lost most of them the day you were shot down."

"The Curtiss *Demon* fighters didn't work out well in combat, then?"

"They're another disaster--maneuverable enough but underpowered and pitifully undergunned. The Japs cut us to pieces."

"When will your second American squadron arrive?" Garrit asked Sprague.

"The first batch came in on the fifth. Trouble is, there were only three of them. Twentieth Pursuit left Darwin with fourteen P-40's. They lost one to engine trouble on Timor. The rest ran into a bevy of *Zeros* at Den Passar. Only three were still fit to fly when the fight was over. We took them into my outfit as replacements."

"That means that instead of the fifty *Tomahawks* you expected to have by now, you have only..."

"Fifteen," Sprague filled in the blank.

"Attention, gentlemen," came a voice from the doorway. As he rose, Garrit recognized Van Oyen's chunky aide.

Lieutenant General Ludolph H.van Oyen, commander of the NEI air forces, walked briskly into the room, his cavalry boots clattering on the concrete floor. He put them at ease immediately and told them to sit down. After inquiring about Garrit's injuries and greeting the American commander warmly, he got to the purpose of the meeting.

"Gentlemen, I called you here to impress upon you the gravity of our situation. As you know, our British allies pulled the last of their forces back into Singapore Island on the first of the month. All aerodromes on the island have been evacuated to our fields at Palembang, Sumatra. The RAF has a number of *Hurricanes* there, and some *Blenheim* squadrons. Air Marshall Peirse is insistent that all our resources in West Java be concentrated to defend Singapore.

You are going to have to make do here with what you have until more American forces arrive.

"The Third Pursuit Squadron is due to leave Australia within a week. Admiral Hart has ordered the old carrier, *Langley,* to Fremantle to bring up another two squadrons. Another thirty *Tomahawks* are coming on the ship, *Seawitch.* If we can hold the Japs at Singapore long enough, the Yanks should be able to shore up our defenses here in East Java. We have to husband our resources until then. Our priorities must be in order. The Navy's yelling bloody murder for fighter cover over their ships, but we just can't afford it. Above all else, we must protect our slender force of bombers, for these are the only weapons capable of keeping the enemy at bay. The Flying Fortresses at Malang are absolutely essential to a successful defense. We must keep our military installations and our war materiel factories intact, but even these are secondary to maintaining the integrity of our air attack units. When reinforcements arrive, we'll be able to consider aiding the Navy. Now, let's discuss how we shall implement this policy."

"How long will it take *Langley* and *Seawitch* to get here?" asked Sprague.

"Three weeks," Van Oyen replied. "Their cargoes should be operational by the end of February."

"We just might make it," Sprague continued. "The Limeys should hold Fortress Singapore for a lot longer than that."

"We must hope so," the general went on, "but it appears that Singapore Island isn't really a fortress at all. There are no defenses on the side facing Malaya. The British never envisioned an attack from that direction."

Van Oyen asked Garrit to stay after the others were dismissed. He offered the captain an American cigarette, and they both lit up. "It's all coming to pass, Garrit, just as you predicted when you first came out from England," the general said with a heavy sigh. "You were dead right about the Nips' equipment and the quality of their pilots. They've even massacred the new RAF *Hurricane* squadrons."

"I'd much rather have been a false prophet. I wish I'd had a chance to talk with the incoming RAF boys. I'm sure they tried to fight the *Zeros* like they did the Eyeties in North Africa."

"I fear you're right. If we hold out long enough, there'll be more

Hurricanes to replace your *Buffalos*. I'm sure your men will put them to good use. In the meantime, pray for time. If we can hold on long enough, the Yanks will be forced to provide the aid they've promised."

"We're going to have to buy that time, General."

"It's all on the shoulders of young men like you. Go and get it for us, Garrit. Otherwise, the last piece of free Dutch soil on earth will be lost."

Garrit brooded about the deteriorating situation during the flight back to Zwarte Gouden. The effects of his wounds, piled atop the strains of the past weeks had beaten down his natural optimism. The funeral for Catherine's brothers on the previous day had plunged him further into depression. Catherine's mother had come close to a complete nervous breakdown. Her father had withdrawn into himself. Catherine had been cast in the role of the rock supporting the rest of the family. For the moment, Garrit felt terribly left out of her life. The bright promise her love had offered just a few days ago seemed now unattainable. Instead, he would have to buckle down and do his job, even if he were ground to pieces in the process.

"Frank. Frank Rhea!" A familiar voice from the direction of the bar greeted Frank as he came into the lobby of the *Oranjie* Hotel. It was Steve Hurley, his old friend from Ford Island, waving from the entrance to the bistro. Frank went at once to join him.

"Steve, you old son-of-a-bitch," said Frank as he pumped his friend's hand. "What the hell are you doing out here?"

"Flying a PBY for PatWing Ten. I came out from Hawaii with VP-22. But you're the one with some explaining to do. I thought you were on *Marblehead*."

"I was. The Japs chewed her up pretty badly in the Flores Sea this morning. I was aloft when it happened, and they couldn't take me back aboard. The skipper sent me here to join PatWing Ten."

They retired to a table in the bar, and Frank gave Steve an account of the Flores Sea battle while they guzzled frosty bottles of excellent Dutch beer. Henley had an appreciation for what the men on the ships had endured, since he had been on duty during the Pearl Harbor attack.

"What are you supposed to do now?" Henley finally asked.

"I'm not sure yet. Commander Peterson told me to take a couple of days off to unwind. I'm looking for a place to stay."

"My roommate just 'bought the farm' yesterday--shot down flying a recon job up in 'Cold Turkey Alley.' Why don't you move in with me?"

"Sounds great. And you're about my size. Maybe I could borrow some khakis. All my gear's still on the ship."

The second-floor suite that Henley occupied proved to be spacious and airy, containing a small sitting room, a big bedroom and a dipper bath. There were no solid doors in the *Oranjii*. Louvered half-doors allowed the free flow of air from the narrow porch that overlooked the opulent restaurant in the courtyard below. The windows also had louvered shutters, but no screens. An enormous mosquito canopy hung above the large double bed.

"Pick your side, old buddy," said Henley. "I don't care where I sleep."

"Neither do I. How about those khakis? These I'm wearing are getting pretty rank."

"Yeah, I noticed that. Third drawer down in the bureau. I'm going back to the bar while you clean up."

"Does the phone work? I'd like to call Cinta."

"She's here in Soerabaja?"

"Working at Central Berger Hospital."

"Same old Frank. Yeah, it works fine. Just tell the hotel operator the number you want."

To Frank's disappointment, Cinta had night duty at the hospital. But when he reached her there, she seemed delighted that he was safe and in Soerabaja. She invited him to dinner at her villa the following evening, insisting that Ada could prepare them a meal far superior to anything offered in the city's restaurants. Frank accepted at once. Her friendly attitude buoyed up his mood. He decided to eat supper at the hotel and go to bed early.

A strong contingent of PatWing 10 fliers was already living it up in the bar when Frank returned. He recognized the strains of a ditty that had been popular in Cavite's Nutshell Cafe only a few short weeks before.

The girls, they wear no teddies in Manila.
The girls, they wear no teddies in Manila.
The girls, they wear no teddies,

They're a bunch of ever-readies.
Oh, the girls, they wear no teddies in Manila.

Steve Henley, now well into his cups, waved Frank over to the table he was sharing with two other lieutenants, whom he introduced as Hank Palmer and Steve Camp. There were already a dozen or more empty beer bottles littering the tabletop.

"Old Frank here flies one of those little old *Seagulls* off a cruiser," Henley said in introduction.

"Better than a PBY when the brass thinks they're a fucking Flying Fortress," Camp responded in slurred syllables. His tone was bitter, "Do you know what they've had us doing for the first six weeks of this goddamned war, Frank?"

"I don't follow you."

"They've been trying to use PatWing Ten for strike missions," Palmer chimed in. "Do you know how a PBY flies with a full load of fuel and bombs? The brass had us flying into those hornets' nests at Davao and Jolo to bomb Jap ships. They were nothing but suicide missions!"

"We're not trained for that kind of work," Camp resumed the refrain. "We're supposed to be the 'eyes and ears of the fleet,' for Christ's sake, not its main punch. The PBY can't even do two hundred all loaded up like that. The *Zeros* are slaughtering us."

"I figure that over half the casualties we've taken so far were thrown away for nothing," Palmer added.

"What a screwed up mess," said Frank as he took a liter bottle of beer from a passing barmaid. "They're not still doing that, are they?"

"Naw, they've quit now that half our buddies have bought it," Camp went on. "We're finally doing what we've been trained for, now that there's not anywhere near enough of us left to cover the beat. It's murder up there in Makassar Strait. We call it 'Cold Turkey Alley' because any PBY caught by all those *Zeros* is a cold turkey."

Two hours later, filled with good Dutch beer and spicy Javanese food, Frank crawled into the big bed in Henley's room. The warm glow of alcohol had melted the edges of fatigue and strain. He had the pleasant sensation of floating free in space for a few minutes before slipping into a deep, exhausted sleep.

CHAPTER 21

(One)
Soerabaja
Netherlands East Indies
6 February 1942

Excitement quickened Cinta's pulse as she sped homeward in her sports car through late afternoon traffic. In less than three hours, she would see Frank again! She had continually dreamed of this reunion since the night when Ada brought her to her senses. The two of them plotted every aspect of the coming evening with conspiratorial thoroughness--the menu, what she would wear, when the servants would conveniently vanish to allow a romantic climax.

The last two days had been hectic. Just as she came off duty on the night that Frank returned, she received word of the deaths of Catherine's brothers. Reluctantly postponing her planned assignation, she spent all that day and evening helping Catherine and her family with arrangements to transport the bodies to Zwarte Gouden. After Nicolaas flew her back to Soerabaya in *Belle of Borneo*, she grabbed a few hours of sleep. Then she returned to the hospital for rounds with her patients and to make arrangements to be off for the next two days. She made one final stop before leaving, a call on her friend Cora Baltussen in gynecology to be fitted with a new cervical cap. For one central theme permeated all her plans for the upcoming evening: before it was over, she and Frank would make love.

Ada met Cinta at the front door of the villa. "It took longer than usual at the market, but I got all the food we wanted," the *baboe* crowed. "Come, I'll show you." She led the way to the kitchen and took the meat tray from the refrigerator. It held four tenderloin steaks, each about two inches thick.

"Beautiful," Cinta commented.

Ada then dipped a pierced ladle into a steaming pot on the stove, fishing out a seven-inch prawn. It could have passed for a small lobster.

"You're a miracle worker, *Ibu*."

"We'll see about that. Go take your bath. I'll be along to instruct you later."

Cinta stood in the shower for a long time, letting the hot needles of water soothe away the stresses of the day. After toweling herself and brushing out her hair, she put on a sarong. She was at the closet laying out the clothes she planned to wear that evening when Ada padded noiselessly into the room.

"We must do what we can now to make you ready for love," the *baboe* announced. "I wish you'd paid more attention when you were a girl."

"I'm afraid I wasn't that good a pupil. Alette was your prize *kama* disciple."

"And she's a much happier woman than you. If I'm to help you at all, you must stop evading my questions about your affairs. Tell me truthfully, how many lovers have you had?"

(Two)
Aboard U.S.S. *Rust*
Tjilatjap Harbor
South Java Coast
6 February 1942

Wild cheering rang out across the narrow waters of Tjilatjap Harbor from the decks of the moored *Houston*. A shiver of awe and pride ran up Jack Sewell's spine as he stood on *Rust's* bridge watching *Marblehead's* battered hull being towed into the roadstead ahead. The determination and seamanship displayed by the old cruiser's crew was downright incredible. By all reasonable standards, she should have been resting now on the bottom of the Flores Sea. But Captain Robinson and his men had wrought a miracle.

The turbulent events of the hours since the Flores Sea battle flashed quickly through Jack's mind. There had first been the midnight run through Lombok Strait. *Marblehead's* navigational equipment was out of action, so a destroyer was posted on either side to guide her through. Twice during the passage, rainsqualls blinded them all for several minutes. The entire squadron came close to grounding on the reefs more than once. Then daylight bared them once more to the eyes of the enemy. A Kawanishi duly appeared to circle above the small force before flying off to the north. Later that morning, forty bombers swarmed all over the ships. A single bomb, even a near miss, would have sent *Marblehead* to the bottom. But then another miracle occurred. The enemy pilots apparently mistook *Paul Jones* for the damaged cruiser and concentrated their attacks on her. The maneuverable little "four-piper" corkscrewed about the blue waters of the Indian Ocean like a whirling dervish. When the Japanese finally gave up and flew away, Lieutenant Commander Hourihan of *Paul Jones* cockily reported by TBS to Captain Robinson, "PLANES GONE. NO HITS. ALL ERRORS."

Marblehead moored upstream from *Houston*, and a gangplank was quickly put ashore. By the time *Rust* berthed farther up the harbor, Jack could see wounded men being carried ashore to a waiting Dutch hospital train. He counted over forty stretchers before being relieved of the watch. He was anxious to get ashore and search for more ammunition for his antiaircraft guns. *Rust* was almost out of shells for her pom-poms.

(Three)
Soerabaja
Netherlands East Indies
6 February 1942

Yuni came in Nicolaas's Lincoln to fetch Frank to Cinta's home for dinner. He felt strange riding like a big executive in the back while the chauffeur drove.

Cinta had never looked more beautiful to Frank than she did waiting there for him in the living room. Dressed in the elegant green gown he remembered from Balikpapan, she wore a pearl-encrusted tiara in her pinned-up hair, while other pearls gleamed at her ears and throat.

"Oh, Frank, it's so good to see you safe and sound," she exclaimed, rushing to meet him. She hugged his neck and primly kissed him on the cheek. The fragrance of her perfume inflamed his senses.

"For a greeting like that, I'd come back every day."

"How long will you be in Soerabaja?" she asked as they sat down together on the rattan couch.

"No one seems to know. *Marblehead* got mauled by Jap planes. If the skipper saves her at all, she'll never fight again in this campaign. I'm sort of in limbo."

"I'm sorry to hear about your ship, but I'm glad that you'll be out of the fighting for awhile. Is Tonto all right?"

"He was flying with me when the ship was hit. He's out at the naval air station helping the mechanics from PatWing Ten. Morokrembangan took a real pasting in the air raid this morning."

"Well, at least we'll have some time together. We must make the most of it. How would a martini sound?"

"Great."

Yuni appeared with two drinks on a tray.

"To the happiness of the hour," Cinta toasted brightly.

"I'll drink to that."

"Ada's prepared a marvelous feast for us," Cinta bubbled happily as she sipped her drink. "She took quite a liking to you when you were here at Christmas, so she's outdone herself."

"I'd like to know how her mistress feels about me." Frank was puzzled by Cinta's effusive attitude. "The last time I was here, I wasn't sure you ever wanted to see me again."

"Every woman has the prerogative of changing her mind. The truth is, Ada gave me quite a tongue-lashing over my behavior that night. She opened my eyes to what a bitch I've been these past few months. I've been so wrapped up in my work that I ignored what I was doing to those who love me, especially to you."

"Aren't you being a little hard on yourself?"

"No. Not hard enough." She put down her drink and looked straight into his eyes. "I even hid my true feelings from myself. I never really stopped loving you, Frank. I just walled it in so that I could get on with my studies. That's why I never fell for anyone else."

"I can't believe my ears," he said in astonishment. "Don't pinch me. I don't want to wake up from this dream."

"It's no dream, Darling. If that long-standing proposal of yours is still open, I'll gladly become your wife."

"You just made me the happiest man in the world." Frank caught her in his arms and kissed her fiercely until they were both gasping for breath.

"Not here, my love," Cinta chided, pulling away when he let his hand drift up the inside of her leg. "Think of the servants. You'll have to wait for the proper setting."

Yuni came in to announce that dinner was being served. They ate by candlelight at a small table that the butler had placed in the dining room where they could watch the flaming sunset through the French doors. Ada served the shrimp and its side dishes first, then the filet mignon.

"I feel like a goat being fattened for sacrifice," Frank joked near the end of the meal.

"Nonsense," Cinta laughed. She sampled the chilly burgundy that Yuni had just poured. "You're just being fortified for things to come."

"Does that mean what I think it does?"

"Wait and see," she replied with a girlish giggle.

"Let me give you a tour of the house," she suggested when they had finished their dessert of *dame blanche*. She got up and led Frank out through the French doors that opened onto a terrace. The sun had gone now, and the twilight was fading fast. The first stars were twinkling, and a brilliant moon hung just above the peaks to the east.

"This one is mine," she said like a tour guide, ushering him through another set of glassed doors into a bedchamber. It was large and comfortable, with a sitting area and a breakfast table. The covers were turned down on the large, mosquito-canopied bed that dominated the room.

"Alone, at last," said Frank as he drew her into his arms again. Their mouths came together in unbridled passion, their lips constantly moving, their tongues probing and twining.

Cinta finally broke free to catch her breath. "I think you'd better have your brandy on the terrace while I powder my nose," she said coyly, leaning back from the waist.

"If you must," he said ruefully.

Cinta had Yuni bring the Napoleon before excusing herself, then hurried to her bathroom.

Rejoining Frank, she walked to the edge of the terrace and gazed at the rising moon, then turned and leaned back against the railing. A breeze sprang up off the Java Sea, swirling her skirt about her legs. "Why can't it always be like this, Frank?" she asked suddenly. "Why did this damned war have to come and spoil everything?"

Instead of answering, he took her in his arms and kissed her again.

She sensed the gnawing hunger of his passion, matched now by her own. "I want you, Frank," she panted in his ear. "Take me to bed while we still have time."

Ada stepped back from the darkened window where she had been watching and smiled triumphantly. Her mistress had at last come to her senses! Gliding silently out onto the terrace, she retrieved Cinta's dress and paused for a moment to listen to the little animal cries of delight coming out through the doors from her mistress's bedroom. It was plain that the gown would not be needed again tonight. She padded off to hang it up, musing about Cinta's good luck in finding so considerate and skilled a lover.

Cinta came awake in the hour before dawn. For a long time, she lay quietly, savoring the warm glow that still enveloped her body. A smile curled her lips as she relived the soaring, shuddering ecstasies that had blotted out all consciousness. Sometime in the years they had been apart, Frank had learned to do wonderful, wicked things with his fingers and mouth.

She slipped from the bed and sat on the edge of the chair where his uniform lay crumpled. Very quietly, she stripped off her garter belt and stockings. A faint ray of the dying moon crept in through the open door and fell across the bed. Frank lay flat on his back, lost in deep slumber. He seemed at peace with himself and the world. She felt a flush of accomplishment such as she had known before when she snatched a patient back from the brink of death. Quietly, she got up and tiptoed to the lavatory.

They spent the next day in Cinta's bedroom, adding new ecstasies from Ada's *Serat Centani* to those they had enjoyed when they were lovers before. By late afternoon, their desires utterly sated, they were both ravenously hungry. Ada served them supper at Cinta's breakfast table--another feast of langoustes, Chinese pea pods, water chestnuts and rice. They dressed for the occasion, Frank in one of Nicholas's sarongs, Cinta in her *kain* and frangipani blossom. They were just finishing when Ada came in with the message that Cinta was urgently wanted on the phone.

"It was Doctor Wassell calling from Petrinella Hospital in Jogjakarta," Cinta said as she resumed her seat at the table. "He's there to see about the wounded from *Marblehead* and *Houston*. He wants me to come down and help with the critical burn cases."

"Are you going?"

"I'm sorry, Darling. I simply have to. I called my boss to get permission then phoned Papa. He's sending *Belle of Borneo* to fly me over. Larry Nobis will have her at Soerabaja airport in about an hour."

"I'd like to come along and see my shipmates. I'll check with the PatWing Ten duty officer to make sure it's okay."

(Three)
Petrinella Hospital
Jogjakarta, Java
Netherlands East Indies
7 February 1942

"You can see Commander Goggins now," a prim Dutch nurse said to Frank in English.

"Thank you, Nurse," he responded, rising from a chair in the hospital hallway. He pushed open the door to the officers ward and peered inside. The sight of the figure on the bed stopped him cold in his tracks. "Sergeant York" was literally swathed in bandages. Flexible hoses ran from hanging bottles of fluids to needles buried in his bandaged arms. Incongruously, a lighted cigar protruded between the wrappings on his face. A large radio played soft music on a nearby table.

Frank tiptoed over to the bed. A strong smell of disinfectant and Vaseline competed with that of the cigar. "Commander?" he said softly.

The face turned towards him, and recognition flared in the eyes that peered out between the bandages. "Frank Rhea," the Exec said in drug-slurred tones. "Good to see you. They keep you busy at headquarters?"

"Yes, sir. Don't know yet whether they're going to stick me on *Houston* or give me to PatWing Ten. Looks like Eddie will have to do without me in 'V' Division."

"I'm sorry, you couldn't know. Eddie was killed during the attack."

The news of his friend's death hit Frank like a hammer blow. "How did it happen?" he managed to croak.

"He was in the wardroom at the temporary aid station. A bomb passed through and blew up in the compartment below. The concussion killed him. Didn't have a mark on his body. That's where I got all this--flash burns from the bomb blast. I should have known better than to wear shorts. Some of the boys caught it worse. The ones who were asleep when we sounded G.Q. went to battle stations in their skivvies."

Goggins went on to describe what he knew of the grim and determined fight *Marblehead's* crew had put up to save her, pausing every few minutes to gather his strength.

"There were too many heroes to do justice to them all. Nick Van Bergan took charge of damage control when I couldn't continue. Marty Druary bossed the fire-fighting effort. Remember Bull Aschenbrenner?"

"The Second Class Shipfitter who used to give the shore patrol a hard time?"

"That's him. They say he practically put out the fire below the wardroom by himself. Martinek, the turret captain for the after barbettes, got the fire on the fantail under control. Frank Blasdel took a party into the rudder room after the fires were out. They worked in a living hell down there to bleed off the hydraulic pressure and wrench the rudder yoke over to put it amidships. The medicos were all supermen. Doc Wildebush and Doc Ryan worked miracles to keep men alive. So did Chief Ace Evans. None of us would be here today except for them."

"Sounds like a miracle that you saved the old 'Ghost' at all."

"You could look on it that way, but don't discount training and leadership, and I'm not just talking about officers. The professional Navy men showed the stuff they're made of. And, come to think of it, I doubt the Captain ever considered abandoning ship."

"It's time for you to let the Commander get some rest," Cinta said from the doorway.

"Our beautiful angel of mercy can get cantankerous at times," Goggins commented. "Cory Wassell says that she's worked a few miracles of her own tonight. But I'll take her for my doctor any day."

"Simply the application of modern medical science," Cinta protested. "You really must rest, Commander. And for God's sake, put out that horrible cigar."

"They're about the only pleasure I'm going to have for a long time, Doctor. Let me at least enjoy them."

"For five minutes more," she said with mock severity. "Then, as you say in the Navy, 'the smoking lamp is out.' I'll send a nurse to see to it."

"Is he going to be okay?" asked Frank after they had left the sickroom.

"If he gets the proper care. He's got stamina and spirit. I wish I could say the same for all of them. The Chinese mess boys all seem to have given up hope, though some aren't as bad off as the commander. Some of the first aid performed during the battle was well meaning but quite harmful. Someone plastered diesel oil over burns in quite a few cases. It gave temporary relief and stopped some fluid loss but made tissue damage worse."

Frank saw that Cinta was nearing exhaustion. "You should find a place to lie down for awhile," he suggested. "You've been on your feet for over sixteen hours."

"After last night and this morning," she said with a mischievous smile, "I've been too tender to sit down."

As they walked down the corridor, Doctor Wassell's spare frame materialized from one of the wards. "Doctor Van Wely," he called quickly. Cinta stopped and turned towards his voice. The ex-missionary came swiftly to her side and took her hands. "I wanted to thank you for coming. We'd have lost those two without you."

"I was glad to do it. I just pray to God that we can save them all now."

CHAPTER 22

(One)
Headquarters U.S. Naval Forces Southwest Pacific
15 Reiniersz Boulevard
Soerabaja, Java
Netherlands East Indies
17 February 1942

"Where the hell's that Jap convoy, John?" Real Admiral William Purnell asked Lieutenant Commander Peterson. Impatience laced the flag officer's voice. Known affectionately as "Speck" because of his face full of freckles, the senior American naval officer in Soerabaja was usually noted for his coolheadedness. Constant strain was taking its toll on his nerves.

At the back of the crowded, hot conference room, Frank Rhea stood among the junior staff officers and fidgeted from one foot to the other as the PatWing 10 commander walked to Purnell's wall chart.

"They're hidden somewhere under that storm that's blanketing the whole Flores Sea area, Admiral," said Peterson, sweeping his hand over the chart. Dressed in wash khakis, Peterson was slender, dark-haired, and bore a close resemblance to the film actor, Dana Andrews. "We know they left Makassar Town during the night, but we haven't been able to find them today. They're using the weather to mask their movements, just as they did before grabbing Balikpapan."

"We've got to find out where they're headed," Purnell said emphatically. "Are they coming for Java already? Or are they after Kangear or one of the Lesser Sundas?"

"We just don't know yet," Peterson responded, adjusting his rimless glasses.

"What do you think, Rosie?" Purnell asked Commander Mason,

the Intelligence Officer.

"Bali. You can lay money on it. The pattern of their pre-invasion air attacks is unmistakable."

"Doorman won't let us move until we have hard intelligence," the admiral continued. "By then, it may be too late. If the Japs come on as fast as they did in Malaya and Sumatra, they'll have the place before we can react."

"Then we should sortie now," said Commander Slocum, the Operations Officer. "If we laid a trap in Lombok Strait tonight, we'd probably be able to take them by surprise. We might even force them to turn back."

"If they get Den Passer airfield, we're finished here in Soerabaja," Peterson commented.

"And at Tjilatjap, too," said Captain Wilkes, the submarine commander. "They'll be bombing us around the clock, just like they're doing at Singapore."

"What's *Langley*'s status?" asked Purnell.

"Still loading P-40's in Fremantle," said Slocum. "It'll be another ten days before she makes port in Tjilatjap."

"I'll talk to Doorman, but I doubt he'll let us sail until he knows for sure where the Japs are headed. Find them for me, John."

"Aye, aye, Admiral."

"Let me know if the Air Corps has any news as soon as you find out," Commander Peterson said to Frank as they left the morning conference. "Don't wait for the motor pool. Take the Nash and get cracking."

The streets of Soerabaja were cluttered with debris from the bombing, but so many residents had fled to the countryside that the traffic was light. Operating from fields around Kendari, on Celebes, the Japanese Navy's Eleventh Air Fleet came punctually at 0930 to pound the port then returned for a second raid at 1100. Anything that moved on the ground during the attacks was a potential target. Frank was headed for the bar at the *Oranjie* Hotel, the impromptu office of the new Allied air liaison group of which he was the Navy member.

Unmitigated disaster had dogged the Allied cause in the ten days since the Flores Sea battle. On the night of February 8th, General Yamashita's forces stormed the Straits of Jahore to begin the invasion of Singapore Island. Meanwhile, the outlying bastions of the Netherlands East Indies tumbled like ripe fruit into the hands of the enemy. Makassar Town fell on February 9th and Bandjermasin, the capital of Dutch Borneo, on the 10th. The entire north shore of the Java Sea was now under Japanese control.

Another huge convoy was already sailing south from Camranh Bay. After a stormy confrontation with Admiral Hart at Tjilatjap, Admiral Doorman took his strike force--now reinforced with the British heavy Cruiser, *Exeter*, and the Aussie light cruiser, *Perth*--north through Sunda Strait to intercept the enemy force. The surface forces never made contact, and the air support from the British squadrons based on Sumatra that Doorman had been promised never materialized. On the night of the 14th, Japanese paratroopers seized several of the fields and some of the oil works at Palembang. On the 15th, as Doorman's ships probed toward the enemy convoy, swarms of Japanese airplanes attacked, harrying the Allied vessels for hours until they broke and fled for Batavia. Slipping in behind Doorman's retreating force, the Japanese first seized Banka Island with its airfield, then Palembang itself. The skies over West Java would soon belong to the enemy. This was a first-class disaster, but it went almost unnoticed. Incredibly, after only a week of combat on the island itself, Fortress Singapore surrendered on February 15th.

Command changes at ABDA headquarters had shaken up the naval forces. On February 11th, Tommy Hart was startled by immediate recall to Washington "for reasons of health." On the 14th, he turned over command of ABDAFLOAT to Admiral Helfrich and departed, making Glassford the senior American flag officer in Java. Leaving Purnell in Soerabaja, Glassford moved at once to Bandoeng Priok to be near Helfrich. Captain Wagner's Commander Aircraft Asiatic Fleet headquarters was already colocated with the ABDA staff.

Java was ringed in from both north and west. Now this new threat from Makassar threatened to cut communications with Australia as well. The only good piece of military news Frank had heard in days was word that the half patched-up *Marblehead* had managed to sail for the safety of British Ceylon.

Although Frank's working hours were filled with frustration and gloom, his personal life was pure paradise. He spent every off-duty night with Cinta, and they were trying to cram a lifetime of loving into the short interlude allowed them by fate. His one regret was that both their lives were too hectic to allow getting married at once.

Frank found Major Harry Asher of the U.S. Army Air Corps sipping from a bottle of Heineken beer while doing paperwork at a corner table in the *Oranjie* Hotel bar. The blond, wiry bomber pilot was head of the liaison group, which he had personally proposed after the B-17's from Malang were almost sent to bomb the American destroyers returning from Balkipapan.

"Have you Navy guys found that Jap convoy yet?" Asher asked as Frank sat down and ordered a beer.

"Our PBY's can't penetrate the storm front."

"What about your subs?"

"Nothing from them, either. The sea's been too rough to stay at periscope depth."

"Well, our recon planes haven't seen anything. Our spare parts problems are so bad that we're having trouble putting anything up."

"Any chance of some air cover for our ships if we find the convoy?"

"You've got to be kidding," Asher exclaimed. "We're down to a couple of scratch fighter squadrons. You and I both know that this place will fold up any time the Japs want to come and take it. Maybe, if we got a whole bunch of new airplanes and pilots…"

"Any hope of that?"

"Not much. The *Langley* convoy's the only relief in sight. She and *Seawitch* are bringing up five squadrons, but they may already be too late."

"What's the Air Corps going to do?"

"Obey orders and fight for as long as we can. You can bet that we'll get our trained people out, though. We don't have enough of them to throw away in gallant last stands. The smart commanders are making contingency plans to evacuate. What about you Navy guys?"

"We've already sent our support ships to Broome, on Australia's west coast. The warships will stay and fight it out to the last. If the Japs close Bali and Lombok Straits, they'll have bottled up everything north of the Malay Barrier."

"Let's pray that *Langley* and *Seawitch* get here before the Japs do. If we get those five squadrons of fighters activated, I've got a hunch that air cover for your ships will go to the top of the priority list."

All through the day, the PBY's of Commander Peterson's shrinking force tried in vain to penetrate the clouds to locate the enemy convoy. Frank had duty at headquarters that night and continued to follow the search. The commander of the small Dutch contingent on Bali was the first to report the position of the Japanese fleet. He awoke on the morning of February 18th to find Badoeng Strait, just off the town of Den Passer, choked with enemy warships and transports.

Before the Allies could react, another disaster struck. Just after dawn on February 19, Vice Admiral Chuichi Nagumo's First Air Fleet--the force that had savaged Pearl Harbor--devastated the Australian port of Darwin. USS *Peary* and two American transports were sent to the bottom. A pair of Australian ammunition ships exploded. The town was flattened, and every American fighter in Northwest Australia shot down. Commander Peterson lost his entire recon force in the Eastern Sundas. Three anchored PBY's were sunk and another shot down at sea.

(Two)
Aboard USS *Rust*
Madura Strait
19 February 1942

Jonathan B. Rust steamed eastward from Soerabaja on the night of February 19th in company with *Stewart, Parrott, Edwards* and *Pillsbury*. The destroyers of DESDIV 58 were escorting *Tromp*. It had taken the Allies almost thirty-six hours to mount a counterstrike to the invasion of Bali. Besides the units from Soerabaja, Doorman was bringing *De Ruyter* and *Java* from Tjilatjap, along with destroyers *Piet Hein, Ford* and *Pope*.

Jack Sewell did not like the battle plan and told his captain so in no uncertain terms. "We should hit with torpedoes first with all the 'cans,' like we did at Balkipapan," he had argued. "The cruisers shouldn't open fire until the fish are in among the Japs. As it stands, we're throwing away surprise at the outset."

Doorman's plan called for three successive sweeps through Badoeng Strait. He would personally lead the first attack with his ships from South Java. The cruiser-destroyer force from Soerabaja was to follow some minutes later. Finally, as a follow-up, a group of Dutch Higgins torpedo boats that had slipped through Bali Strait would move in to pick off any enemy ships missed by the earlier sweeps.

Jack manned his post at Central Fire Control and tried to keep his mind on the upcoming battle. That was not easy, for he had spent another tempestuous night ashore with Pamela before they sailed. Her sexual repertoire was almost beyond belief; her appetites, insatiable. He would remember that encounter for a long time to come.

The column of warships rounded the eastern tip of Java and turned into the boiling froth of Bali Strait. Progress slowed perceptibly as the destroyers bucked the swift currents where the Indian Ocean spilled through the narrows into the Java Sea.

Jack lifted his glasses and scanned the seascape ahead. The cold light of tropical stars clearly outlined the shores on either side of the strait. Worse yet, the silhouettes of the Allied ships were quite visible. The enemy off Bali could be expected to hug the shoreline for cover, while the attackers would be easy targets for sharp-eyed lookouts several miles away. Not that it would matter. The first wave, which should be striking already, was being led by *De Ruyter* and *Java*. The cruisers planned to illuminate targets with their searchlights and open fire as soon as the enemy was spotted. There was no finesse at all in the attack plan, no application of cunning. It was all to be brute force.

Commander De Master of *Tromp* had decreed a more conventional plan for the second wave. The destroyers, led by Commander Binford's flagship, *Stewart*, would steam through the anchorage making torpedo attacks while the cruiser stood off and provided cover. Had they been attacking before Doorman's task force, this would have made imminently good sense. With the enemy fully alerted by the first strike, no element of surprise would remain.

"Who's on the searchlights, Chief?" Jack asked Muldune.

"Toliver, sir. He's a good petty officer."

Jack remembered well the secondclass boatswain from Memphis. He was solid and dependable, as he would need to be in this night action. *Rust* had not attacked by searchlight before. There was a well-structured battle drill for it, but drills and procedures often broke down under the first stress of battle use.

"Check the phone circuits again," Jack ordered his talker. Quick communications with the guns and torpedo crews would be essential in the coming action.

As *Rust* swung down the Bali coast in *Stewart*'s phosphorescent wake, a rumble of gunfire came rolling across the water to meet them. Searchlight beams were dimly visible swinging about in the darkness, the blue hue of Dutch lights contrasting with the blinding white of the American. The glow of shipboard fires flared up.

"Alert all weapons crews," Jack ordered. "We're about to be in the middle of that."

Up ahead, the gun flashes abruptly ceased, and the searchlights faded. As the *Tromp* group approached the Badoeng Strait anchorage, the battle had completely quieted. Signal lamps could be seen blinking back and forth between ships that Jack presumed to be Japanese. The breeze tore at his hair as *Rust* plunged forward at twenty-five knots. A low-lying mist hung near the shoreline, half concealing the dim shapes of the enemy vessels.

"Bridge reports Commodore orders TORPS attack on enemy ships to port," said Jack's talker. "Fire on his signal."

"Very well. Get me Ensign Brown." Jack took the handset from the talker. "Action Port, Mister Brown. Looks like a destroyer, close in to Nusa Besar. Get on target and fire a spread of three on my order."

"Aye, aye, sir," came Brown's terse reply.

Ahead, *Stewart* swung hard to starboard, presenting her beam to the target. As *Rust* turned in her wake, the forward portside tubes rotated outward, following the enemy ship.

"Bridge orders, 'open fire,'" barked the talker.

"Fire," Jack repeated to Brown.

From down on the weather deck, three muffled explosions occurred in rapid succession, followed by the *swoosh, swoosh, swoosh* of the deadly fish springing out of their tubes. The talker calmly counted off the seconds. The Allied column turned to port, dashing up Badoeng Strait.

"They missed, Mister Sewell," the talker informed Jack.

"Damnation!" swore Muldune. "There must have been fifteen fish shot at the bastards. How could they all miss?"

No hits had been scored, but the Japanese had obviously seen the torpedo wakes. Two ships that looked to be light cruisers came charging toward the little destroyer force. A searchlight stabbed out from *Stewart* and latched onto the leading enemy ship. Twin turrets were clearly visible on its forecastle. The "four-piper's" four-inch guns opened up all together, blasting away at the illuminated cruiser.

"Guns One, Two, and Four, open fire on *Stewart's* target," Jack ordered.

The sharp report of *Rust's* four-inch fifties tore at Jack's eardrums as three of his guns fired simultaneously. More searchlights flared up on two enemy ships, catching *Rust* in their blinding beams. Muzzle flashes spouted from the newcomer's guns. Seconds later, shells began raining down all around the "four-piper," rending the air with their tumultuous roar. Geysers of water sprang up on both sides of the ship as the thunder of exploding shells buffeted her sides. *The Jap gunners are too damned good*, Jack thought. *A bracket on their first salvo*!

Rust heeled over to starboard, shuddering as if struck a giant hammer blow then righted herself. Jack hung onto the railing for dear life as she rolled sharply among the shell splashes. Then she was through, her guns still blazing away at the enemy ships, which were now falling astern to port.

Tromp's blue searchlight sprang out and caught one of the Japanese ships as the destroyers fled to the northeast. The Dutch six-inchers opened up. Just seconds later, a starshell burst above the Allied cruiser, showing her outlines as if it were mid-day. Shells started raining all around her. In the fading light of the starshell, Jack saw that the other three destroyers were still following *Rust*, but *Pillsbury* was out of column to port.

"Lookout reports enemy ships off the starboard bow," announced the talker.

"Guns One and Three, prepare to fire on enemy off starboard," Jack barked as he brought his glasses up, catching what looked to be a column of Japanese destroyers. "Searchlight, illuminate target bearing forty-five degrees, relative."

The big arc lamp on the after tower sprang to life, shooting its powerful beam towards the oncoming enemy. The range was going to be point blank.

"Guns One and Three, open fire," Jack shouted. "Gun Four,

open fire as you bear."

Recoil and blast forces buffeted *Rust*'s bridge structure once more, but now the shells could be seen striking home. Explosions blossomed all over the enemy destroyer. She seemed to stagger under the barrage, and fires erupted in half a dozen places. The men around Jack were screaming in excitement at seeing their projectiles tearing holes in the enemy. Then *Pillsbury* came charging up on the enemy's other quarter to pour more fire into her. In the few minutes that their guns could be trained on the crippled ship, the two "four-pipers" blasted her into a wreck.

As Gun Number Four fell silent, Jack swept his glasses about, looking for further targets.

"I was watching *Tromp* just before we started that last fight," said Muldune. "She took a couple of good shots on the chin, maybe eight-inch hits."

"Did we take a hit back there?"

"I thought we did for a minute, but there wasn't any explosion."

"We must be doing close to maximum revolutions." Jack could feel the ship vibrating heavily beneath his feet. They were out into Lombok Strait now, dashing north toward the Flores Sea.

Jack reported the condition of the armament to the bridge.

"Good show, Jack," said Tom Hoskins on the phone. "I think we sank that bastard."

"What hit us?" inquired Jack.

"As best we can make out, an eight-inch armor-piercing shell. It passed right through the ship without exploding. We'll have to eat standing up tomorrow. It made a wreck of the wardroom."

"Mother of God," muttered Muldune when Jack relayed the story of the dud shell. "If it'd gone off, we'd all be roasting in hell already. But we hit the Japs a good lick tonight, Lieutenant."

"That's true," Jack agreed. "The trouble is, the Japs still have Bali."

(Three)
Oranjie **Hotel**
Soerabaja, Java
Netherlands East Indies
20 February 1942

Frank found Harry Asher staring into space when he brought his afternoon report to the liaison officer. "Why so morose?" he asked, sitting down at Asher's table. The bar was almost empty, and they were the only Americans in the room.

"Bud Sprague bought it this morning," said Asher heavily.

"The C.O. of Seventeenth Pursuit?"

"Yeah. An old buddy of mine from way back. He was trying to dive bomb ships off Bali with his P-40. He found out the hard way that the Japs already have *Zeros* on Den Passer."

"That's what our recon boys say, too. No chance that he crash landed?"

"Not much. He went into a bomb run and didn't come up. Would you believe it? He was just promoted to lieutenant colonel this morning. He didn't even have time to get his silver oak leaves. And if losing Bud wasn't enough, Seventeenth also had three other planes missing. They're down to a skeleton force."

"What about the Dutch squadrons?"

"Worse off than us. That bevy of *Zeros* that came in with the bombers yesterday savaged them badly. They downright slaughtered the old Curtiss *Hawks*. Garrit Laterveer's squadron at Zwarte Gouden is the only one that's close to half-strength."

"Did the bombing at Bali do any good?"

"The *Forts* and *Liberators* knocked down a hangar or two and set fire to some fuel. But those *Zeros* are still using the field. When they get bombers in there, they'll be able to hit Malang and Tjilatjap at will."

"The jig's up, then." Asher's depression had infected Frank.

"You said it."

"Come in, Frank," said Lieutenant Commander Peterson, looking up. "Sit down." Peterson's office fleet headquarters was not much more than a cubbyhole, with room for his desk, a filing cabinet, and two chairs for visitors.

"You wanted to see me, Commander?"

"Yes. I wanted to tell you that we'll be buttoning up here soon. The daily Jap air raids are making the place untenable as anything but an advance base. Even Wilkes is taking the last of his 'pig boats' to Tjilatjap. That being the case, your liaison job won't be necessary much longer. I've exchanged messages with Captain Rooks of *Houston*. He wants you and Tonto assigned to him when he returns from Australia."

"I've been expecting that, Commander. That's where we could do the most good."

"I'm glad you feel that way. You can stay on with us until we evacuate. By then, *Houston* should be back. We've really appreciated your help with the liaison job, and Tonto's been worth his weight in gold helping repair our PBY's."

"Would it be presumptuous to ask what's happening with the command setup, sir? There've been lots of rumors."

"No reason why you shouldn't know, if you'll keep it under your hat. The ABDA command is going to fold up next week, turning over to the Dutch CINC's. We'll stay on under Admiral Helfrich for as long as we're ordered to."

"That means they don't believe we can hold out here?"

"Not necessarily. The *Langley* convoy is still coming. With all those fighters, we'll give the Japs some hell."

"Still, if you had family here, you'd try to get them out?"

"Damn right! Women and kids have no place in a war zone."

"The Dutch weren't given any choice."

"It can't happen too quick for me," said Tonto when Frank telephoned to tell him of their new assignment. "When's *Houston* due back?"

"Can't say over the phone. Not soon."

"Damn. We'll have Japs breathing down our necks in a few days. I'm ready to be a 'Flying Wombat' tomorrow."

"Keep the plane in good shape. I'll come and look it over in the morning."

Later that day, word came in from Bandoeng that assured that Frank and Tonto would remain in Soerabaja indefinitely. Admiral Helfrich, expecting attempts to invade Java momentarily, had regrouped his slender forces into two strike forces. Despite the constant threat of air attack, both had to be based north of the Malay Barrier to have any hope of success. In addition, the only source of fuel now available to supplement the dwindling stocks of bunker oil was the refinery at Zwarte Gouden. The Eastern Striking Force would be based on Soerabaja and the Western at Tandjong Priok, near Batavia. The Dutch and American forces were allotted to Soerabaja under Admiral Doorman. The Western Striking Force was composed of British and Commonwealth forces under Commodore J.A. Collins of the Royal Australian Navy. *Houston* would be coming to Soerabaja as soon as she returned from escorting the fleet Auxiliaries to Broome, Australia.

(Four)
Skies Above Balikpapan, Borneo
Netherlands East Indies
20 February 1942

Chusa (Lieutenant Colonel) Katsura Okuma scowled as he looked down at Balikpapan through the observer's window in the nose of the big Kawanishi flying boat that was circling the long bay. He had no idea that the destruction was so great. The oil fields around the city looked like a forest after a tornado, with some crippled derricks lying flat on their sides and others still standing at odd angles. The great refinery was but a maze of twisted steel; the storage tanks looked like massive wilted flowers. And everything was scorched black by the raging fires that had consumed all assets of any value in producing oil. The Dutch had lost this prize but denied its immediate use to Japan.

If only my regiment had been here, Okuma thought. *We could have prevented this!*

Okuma had been elated when the order finally came to move the 6th Independent Parachute Regiment by air to Borneo. Two hastily assembled squadrons of Nakajima-built DC-2's and Kawasaki K-46's (Lockheed Super *Electras*) were assigned to the mission, but they were insufficient to lift his entire command. The Navy provided a half-dozen Kawanishis to make up the difference. Their destination was Balikpapan, where Lieutenant General Senjuro Toyama, the conqueror of Nanking, China, was staging his forces for the invasion of Central Java. Okuma looked forward to landing for more reasons than the professional challenge. Gazing down at his semi-nude photograph of Cinta van Wely, he felt confident that she would soon be within his power, to deal with as he pleased. As soon as the business of war allowed the time, he would go and find her in the Dutch internment camp. After he was finished with his personal vengeance, he would have to finally decide whether to follow Shirai's advice or send her to one of Miyaga's "comfort stations" on some island at the front.

The Navy pilot knew his business. He put the big flying boat down gently into Balikpapan Bay and taxied to the former Dutch seaplane base. A boat from the expeditionary force commander's flagship was waiting for Okuma. Within twenty minutes, he was standing at attention in front of General Toyama's desk.

Lieutenant General Senjuro Toyama was an ex-cavalryman with a reputation for dash and fierceness in battle. Medium-sized for a Japanese, he was somewhat overweight but tough. He shaved his head Prussian style and wore pince-nez glasses.

"Let me make myself perfectly clear from the beginning," Toyama growled at Okuma, keeping him at attention. "I'm not convinced that you and your *rakkasan-butai* can be of any use to me. I don't believe in elite units. They just skim the cream off line formations. Airborne operations work only when complete surprise is achieved, and after the near debacle at the refineries at Palembang in Sumatra, I'm not sure that's even remotely possible."

Okuma inwardly flinched. On February 14th, Colonel Kume's 1st Parachute Brigade had dropped as planned on the Palembang airfield and the Sungeigelong and Uyodiraff Refineries. Their mission was to seize the oil works and hold them until the seaborne invasion forces could relieve them. But a sortie by the Allied fleet had delayed the Japanese invasion convoys, allowing the Dutch Army to concentrate on eliminating the paratroopers. Kume had taken heavy casualties before landing craft finally arrived with reinforcements.

"However, it is imperative that we take the oil production facilities at Zwarte Gouden, Java, intact," Toyama went on. "The Dutch must not be allowed to repeat what they did here. I'd use Satan himself if he could help achieve my objectives. Your task is to conceive a workable plan to seize the Zwarte Gouden refinery in a *coup de main* and hold it until my amphibious forces fight their way up the *Parfum* River. My staff does not believe that it's possible. You have twenty-four hours to prove them wrong."

Toyama's chief of staff, an ascetic colonel named Honda, provided Okuma with an office aboard the flagship and all the available intelligence data. The paratrooper poured over the maps of the Zwarte Gouden area with his senior company commander, Captain Sakai, who had come with him on the Kawanishi. They next carefully analyzed the excellent aerial photographs provided by the Navy. Toyama had given them a day to come up with a plan. It took them only four hours. Okuma had no doubts that it would succeed. Its thesis was simple and direct. He would turn the Dutchmen's careful anti-air assault preparations against them.

Toyama listened impassively as Okuma briefed his plan the following morning. Like every other airborne operation of the war, this one would begin with a parachute drop on the nearest airfield. The common pattern called for the quick landing of additional troops in transports to expand the airhead. The Dutch commander would doubtless rush his mobile forces to the field. Then Okuma would spring his trap, capturing the refinery before the Dutchmen could recover.

Toyama sat quietly for a few minutes after Okuma stopped talking; his face, expressionless; his eyes, almost closed. Okuma guessed that he was visualizing the assault.

"It might work," Toyama finally said. "Make all the necessary preparations. We must be ready to sail within two weeks."

"It will be done," Okuma replied, his chest swelling with pride.

"I have another detail for you to attend to. I assume that you've heard by now that I had all the Hollanders here executed in reprisal for the destruction of economic resources."

Okuma was stunned. He had been too busy with his plan to inquire about the Van Welys. Now the general was telling him that the object of his hatred was already dead, cut down in a mindless act of general reprisal. "No, sir," he managed to reply. "No one informed me."

"I ordered every *gaijin* from Controlleur Woltz down to the youngest child slaughtered. Some were beheaded; the rest were shot."

Okuma understood the general's motives and would normally have approved. But his disappointment that he would not get his hands on Cinta van Wely was a sharp pain in his gut.

The general continued, "The major culprit, the General Manager of the Dutch oil firm, escaped. Our intelligence reports indicate that he's now in Zwarte Gouden, along with his daughter. Here are some pictures of them."

Okuma's disappointment changed to elation as he glanced at the snapshots. He recognized the big bear of a Dutchman at once, but it was the sight of the woman beside him that sent his hopes soaring. Cinta van Wely was waiting in Zwarte Gouden, available for him to seize and exact his sweet revenge. This had to be an omen of the highest import. The gods were promising him victory!

"The man is Nicolaas van Wely," Toyama continued. "I want both him and his daughter alive. An example must be made of them so that the other *Oranda-jin* (Dutch) and the natives of Java will understand that we are to be obeyed without question."

"Van Wely must surely die," Okuma agreed, "but it seems a waste to merely kill women who could provide well-earned sport for our officers and troops. I have a suggestion on how the daughter and other white women deserving punishment could render useful service to the New Order. I've already discussed it with Major Miyagi of the General Staff..."

"That's an inventive scheme, Colonel," Toyama said after hearing Okuma's proposal. "It's too bad no one recommended that to me before I had the *gaijin* women here executed. It would have been interesting to compare their 'pillowing' skills with those of our *joro*s."

"What about the Dutchwomen in Tarakan?" Colonel Honda eagerly offered. "I could send a Kawanishi to fetch some of them. It would be fitting since Colonel Colijn did betray us."

Toyama thought quietly for several moments. "It would certainly be entertaining. But they're far too old. *Ianfu* should begin young, when they're easier to train. As far as Zwarte Gouden is concerned, prepare the necessary orders to impress those Dutchwoman whom Colonel Okuma suggested as soon as we take over."

"As you command, my General," Honda said with enthusiasm.

"One thing further, Colonel Okuma. If you succeed with your

mission, you and your men can have your pick of the new *gaijin Ianfu.*"

CHAPTER 23

(One)
BPM Refinery
Zwarte Gouden, Java
Netherlands East Indies
23 February 1942

Nicolaas van Wely stood on the highest platform of Catalytic Cracking Tower Number One and cast his eyes lovingly over the jungle of piping and machinery below him. Catalytic cracking was the latest in oil technology, capable of vastly increasing the volume of 100-octane aviation gasoline that could be extracted from crude. Since his days as a young engineering student in Holland, Nicolaas had been fascinated by the mechanics and chemistry of petroleum products manufacturing. One of his early heroes was William Burton of Standard Oil of Indiana, the father of both thermal cracking and catalytic cracking. Nicolaas had spent his entire adult life climbing to the pinnacle of success in the oil business, enjoying his work as some men can only enjoy women. It had taken the collective brains and brawn of thousands of men to put together this intricately designed plant and set its processes in motion. He was called in several times to personally resolve knotty problems back in the days when he was BPM's chief trouble-shooter. His inquisitive mind always produced practical solutions. It was a labor of love. Now he was preparing to ruthlessly destroy this great industrial treasure rather than yield it to the Japanese. The Zwarte Gouden cat crackers were the only such units left in the Far East, so it was doubly vital that they not fall intact to the enemy. His crews were almost finished wiring in the demolition circuits. Explosives were in position. By noon the following day, only the detonators would be required to progressively demolish the entire complex from the safety of a bunker outside the gates.

The hollow ring of footsteps on the stairway gratings announced that someone else was coming up to the platform. A moment later, Pieter Wildeboer came puffing into view.

"I thought I'd find you here," said the general manager between gasps for breath. He was much heavier than Nicolaas and had a bald head, but his skin was just as dark from the sun. He pulled a handkerchief from his sweat-soaked bush jacket and mopped his forehead. "How's it coming?"

"All the preliminary work will be done tomorrow. I could blow it by tomorrow night if necessary."

"I hope to God it doesn't come to that. Oosten was right to send you here. I could never have blown it all up."

"You underestimate yourself. Men do the things that they have to do. You'd have pulled the detonator switch as readily as I will."

"I'm glad I don't have to learn if you're right.'

"Any news from Batavia?"

"Not from Oosten. I talked to De Pril an hour ago. He confirmed that we're the only plant still delivering fuel to the armed forces."

"We won't be able to keep that up long," said Nicolaas, pointing to the long wharf along the river where two Dutch Navy tankers were loading fuel for Doorman's force at Soerabaja. "The Japs won't bomb our refinery, but their planes will sink all the tankers. Have you finished packing to leave?"

"Not really. Christine just can't believe that we'll have to run away."

"She'd better, and damned quickly." A vision of Pieter's lovely wife flashed before Nicolaas's eyes. She was a devoted mother and charming hostess, but she tended to ignore unpleasantness, hoping that it would just go away. "We can't let anyone with your knowledge fall into the Japs' hands. They'd be torturing you and her to make you help them put this place back together. There'll be seats for your family on *Belle of Borneo*, and I'm damned well going to see you in them."

"We will be, even if I have to carry my wife aboard. Now, to something more pleasant. Christine has suggested a small dinner party tonight. We'd be pleased if you'd come."

"I'd love to. Might as well enjoy our way of life while we can."

"At seven, then."

(Two)
Commanding Officer's Quarters
Zwarte Gouden Army Barracks
Netherlands East Indies
23 February 1942

Jan Ditker wiped down the final part of his Browning High Power automatic and started putting the pieces back together. Finishing in a few seconds, he pulled the slide back and let it slam forward with a satisfying *click*, then let down the hammer and inserted a full magazine. After slipping the loaded weapon back into his holster, he checked the time and saw that he still had another hour before going to Pieter Wildeboer's party.

Stripped to his shorts, he was comfortable in his large bedroom despite the heat outside. The thick brick walls of his quarters held out much of the heat, and the electric fan dangling from the high ceiling fan stirred the air pleasantly, causing the mosquito net canopy over his double bed to sway back and forth. He considered what to do next for a few seconds then decided to mentally review his defense plan again.

With the way the war was developing, he might be dead or a prisoner within a week. Jan had few illusions about the ability of his command to hold the region against a determined Japanese assault. If Garrit Laterveer's fighters had been at his disposal, it might have been possible, for his force was the most heavily armed unit in Java.

Immediately upon taking command the previous summer, Jan realized that his only hope of a success lay in building a mobile defense. The one Dutch and two colonial battalions available to him could not hope to hold such a vast expanse of real estate from static defenses. The excellent interior communications provided by the road network that the oil company had built offered a potential solution. His superiors in Soerabaja and Bandung had given him all the material help that was available. His Dutch battalion, commanded by Major Frans de Visser, was now the equivalent of a German *panzer* unit. Built around a squadron of American Marmon-Herrington tanks, the mobile infantry was mounted in Krupp armored trucks. Four German 20mm antiaircraft guns provided mobile flak support.. The unit was equipped with new

American .30-caliber small arms: Johnson self-loading rifles and light machine guns; Browning belt-fed machine guns; Marlin M42 submachine guns. The artillery observers were mounted in British Alvis-Straussler armored cars. He had enough Chevrolet trucks to transport one of his colonial battalions. These units were still armed with Dutch 6.5 mm rifles and Madsen light machine guns, but they would be able to give a good account of themselves. The constant drills which he had conducted since September had put the whole force on a war footing.

The thick swamps between the plain and the coast severely limited an attacker's options. From the first, Jan's premise had been that the Japanese would attack up the river from the sea with an amphibious force. With extensive help from Pieter Wildeboer's BPM workforce, his troops had constructed log bunkers to house small cannon at the big bend of the river north of the city. They had also constructed a series of bunkers on the dome shaped hill at the south edge of the plain. From there his battery of twelve Bofors 105 mm guns could dominate the entire Zwarte Gouden plain. Buried telephone lines ran from the bunkers to his underground command post at the Zwarte Gouden Barracks. His capable second-in-command, Major Cornelis Huygen, was on duty there even now, ready to call the reaction force to action on a moment's notice.

Based on his experiences in Europe, Jan had also prepared for another contingency that none of his subordinates thought to be possible—a Japanese airborne attack on the aerodrome. An Australian antiaircraft unit with 40 mm Bofors guns defended the field. If the Japanese struck there, they would have to hold out until his tanks crossed the river and came to their rescue.

Checking his watch again, he saw that it was time to get ready. He went into his bathroom to take a dipper bath.

(Three)
BPM Residence
Zwarte Gouden, Java
Netherlands East Indies
23 February 1942

Nicolaas got out of his sedan in front of the Pieter Wildeboer's mansion and stood for a minute admiring the place. It was a small palace, befitting the community station of the local oil rajah. The stuccoed exterior reflected the latest trends of modern architecture. It contained dining spaces and ballrooms suitable for entertaining the local society with proper pomp and elegance, with all the necessary kitchens and wine cellars. BPM was never parsimonious where the prestige of the firm was concerned.

A uniformed houseboy led Nicolaas from the entryway to a small sitting room where the guests were gathering. As he came through the door, he recognized Garrit Laterveer chatting with their hostess. Pieter's wife was a classic Dutch beauty: blond with finely chiseled features and her sparkling blue eyes. The curves of her shapely body were well set off by a floor-length blue silk gown.

"Good evening, Nicolaas," said Christine Wildeboer, offering her hand for his kiss. "I'm so happy you could come."

"I'd never pass up a chance for your company, my dear," he replied gallantly. He took a gin and tonic from a servant. "Where's Pieter?"

"Showing Garrit's fiance the house. She's an utter darling. You must meet her."

"I know Catherine well. She worked with Cinta in Balikpapan."

"It's such a shame that her brothers were killed. She had to postpone the wedding."

"I hadn't heard."

Christine and Garrit related the story of how Catherine's family had been shattered by the deaths of the two young men.

"It was a terrible loss," Nicolaas finally said to Garrit, "but you should go ahead and get married anyway."

"It may be too late for that now. We'll be attacked here any day now."

"My *Lodestar's* fueled and ready to take off. I'll take Catherine to Australia with me when the time comes."

"I wish you two wouldn't talk like that," said Christine, distress evident in her voice. She was spared pursuing the point by the arrival of Pieter and Catherine. Upon sighting Nicolaas, Catherine fairly flew across the room.

"Nicolaas," she exclaimed. "You're looking wonderful. How's Cinta?"

"Working too hard," he replied, kissing her cheek. Standing back to survey the young nurse, he saw that her black cocktail dress could not detract from her fresh beauty. "You're looking well."

"As are you. What happened to Cinta's American lieutenant?"

"He' in Soerabaja, and she's seeing him regularly. I think it may be serious."

"I think that fate has taken a hand," said Catherine. "It was inevitable that Cinta would fall in love with him."

"Here's our brave protector," said Pieter as Colonel Jan Dijker entered the room. There were greetings all around for the Colonel, whose deeply tanned skin bespoke many hours in the scorching tropical sun.

"Are we safe for the night, Colonel?" asked Pieter.

"For a few days more, at least," Jan advised, taking a drink from the waiter.

"I heard one piece of good news from Oosten this afternoon," Pieter continued. "Nicolaas, you'll be glad to hear that over forty of the men you had to leave in Borneo got to Java today. Mueller and Barnes are among them."

"I thought the Japs had all of Borneo," Catherine exclaimed.

"Only the coastal cities," Pieter replied. "Our men trekked through the jungle to Samarinda II airdrome. Oosten sent company planes to get them."

Nicolaas and Pieter discussed the rescued BPM men for several minutes.

"Can't we forget this awful war and remember happier times," Christine proclaimed. "Tomorrow will take care of itself."

Christine worked very hard to lend an air of gaiety to the evening. When they retired to a small dining room for dinner, her ample staff of servants served a *rijsttafel* that rivaled that of the *Hotel des Indies*. The wine was French and very old. But no matter how hard they tried, the conversation always came back to the war.

Nicolaas felt a great sense of melancholy as the chauffeur drove him back to the Wilhelmina Hotel. His heart told him that the wonderful life the Dutch had enjoyed in these islands for four hundred years was nearing extinction. He could build a new life in America, but it would never be as good.

He found the lights already on when he let himself into his suite. The radio in the bedroom was playing classical music, and he recognized the voice humming along with the melody. "Tonia?" he called out.

She appeared in the doorway, seductively dressed in a *robe-de-chambre* of black silk. Rushing into his arms, she gave him a passionate kiss but then pulled away. "Before we go too far," her tone was very businesslike, "you had a call a few minutes ago. There's a number for you to call in Lembang. It's supposed to be very urgent."

Nicolaas took the paper she offered, recognizing Admiral Helfrich's private number. "I'd better do it now," he said, taking off his coat and pulling his necktie down. He walked to the phone and recited the digits to the operator. As he waited, Tonia slipped her robe off her shoulders and dropped it onto a chair.

"Nicolaas?" came the familiar voice over the phone.

"Yes, Conrad, it's me. What can I do for you?"

"Stay put and wait. I called to tell you that I'm keeping my part of our bargain. All the clearances have been granted for you and your daughter to leave. You can transfer your accounts out of the country tomorrow. As soon as you've thrown the switch to blow up the refinery, you can push off. But don't throw it yet. You're the only place left where I can get oil for my ships and AVGAS for van Oyen's fighters. I'll give you the word when I must, but not before."

"I won't have another Palembang here," said Nicolaas. The refinery at Pledju had fallen almost intact into Japanese hands less than a week before when the local military commander refused permission for BPM executives to begin demolitions.

"There won't be. You'll be warned. I'll speak to you myself when the time comes."

"I can't ask for better than that."

"Take care, old friend." Helfrich rang off.

"And you also." Nicolaas put down the phone. Tonia, who'd waited patiently until now, took his hand and led him into the bedroom.

(Four)
Holland Pier
Soerabaja, Java
Netherlands East Indies
24 February 1942

Frank was standing on the pier when *Houston* docked in Soerabaja. He was anxious to get aboard the cruiser and back into the close company of a ship's wardroom. For the past few days, he and Tonto had been more or less footloose. Most of the staff had been sent off either to Australia or Tjilatjap. Admiral Purnell was preparing to fly to Exemouth Gulf on Australia's west coast to set up shop there. Captain Wilkes was in Tjilatjap making sure that the auxiliaries necessary to support his submarines were sent off promptly to join Purnell.

Frank's last glance at Rosie Mason's intelligence reports had been alarming. A convoy of fifty-four transports, guarded by carriers, cruisers and destroyers, had sailed from Camrahn Bay on the 18th. The next day, General MacArthur signaled that a slightly smaller fleet had sortied from Jolo. And from Balikpapan, General Toyama's armada moved out on the 20th on a course for central Java. As these octopus-like tentacles approached the shores of Java, a completely different force, spearheaded by paratroopers, seized the island of Timor, directly between Java and Australia. The trap was beginning to snap shut.

Houston was an impressive sight as the tugs pushed her in to the wharf. She was sleek of line, and the powerful eight-inch rifles jutting from her triple turrets had an awesome effect. Alongside the Dutch light cruisers, she looked like a giant among pygmies. But only two-thirds of her main armament could fire. She was powerless to respond to an attack from astern. Her heavy amidships battery of five-inch antiaircraft guns would be a most welcome addition to the strike force. None of the Dutch vessels had guns which could reach nearly so high.

The gangplank was hardly in place before Frank dashed up it to report aboard. Fifteen minutes later, he was in the "V" Division offices talking to Lieutenant Tom Payne.

"Glad to have you aboard," Payne welcomed him. "Drag up a chair. Want some coffee?"

"Sounds great. It's good to be back aboard a warship."

"We all felt bad about Eddie. Walt and I were pallbearers at his funeral."

"It was a shock." Frank took a mug of coffee from Payne's yeoman. "At least he died instantly."

"A better way to go than some of our boys. The whole crew of "Z" Turret burned to death."

"When do you want me to bring my *Seagull* aboard?" Frank changed the subject.

"Better wait until we get word on our orders. We can't leave our planes on the catapults because they mask the five-inchers. We had to jettison one during the Flores Sea fight after she was damaged by the muzzle blasts. Little Jack flew off to Australia just before an air attack last week to prevent the same thing happening again. If we're going out tonight, you'll want to leave your bird where she is. We won't want the extra fire hazard on deck."

"Tonto's got her hidden over in the swamp. Where do I bunk in?"

"You can have Little Jack's rack. There'll be room with the other warrant officers for Tonto. Let's get you around to meet the brass."

Within the next hour, Frank paid office calls on Commander Maher, the Gun Boss, the Exec and Captain Rooks. All made him feel instantly welcome. Both Maher and Rooks mentioned his attack on the Japanese planes that were bombing *Marblehead*.

"We can always use men of your caliber," Rooks assured him. "The next couple of weeks are going to be brutal."

At that moment, the General Alarm went off, and the bugle began to blare, "Air Defense."

"Care to join me on the bridge?" asked Rooks while strapping on his tin hat.

"Yes, sir," Frank responded, not sure that he really meant it.

The Japanese formation came in at ten thousand feet. There were two nine-plane groups of the fat-bellied new Mitsubishis. With the arrogance born of weeks of air superiority, the enemy pilots separated into "vics" of three planes and began to stalk the Allied shipping in the harbor. Captain Rooks held fire until most of the enemy was well within range.

"They must not have recognized us," Rooks commented to Frank as they stood together on the exposed starboard bridge wing. "Here comes a nasty surprise for them." He turned to his talker. "Open fire."

The concussion of *Houston's* powerful sky guns sucked away Frank's breath and almost shattered his eardrums. Moments later, eight ugly black puffs sprouted in the midst of the enemy formation, sending the bombers scattering wildly. One seemed to visibly stagger, then turned and fled out to sea.

"Damn, what a sight!" Rooks shouted above the gunfire. "Those new shells *Boise* left us work like a charm. Half the ones we had before were duds."

Shaken by the fierceness of *Houston*'s barrage, the enemy commander took his bombers up above their range before returning to the attack. Most of the bombs fell harmlessly into the sea. But near the end of the strike, the merchantman, *Kota Radja*, was hit and caught fire. Seemingly satisfied with inflicting this damage, the Japanese wheeled toward the north and faded into the skies over Madura.

"Better leave your plane at the air station until tomorrow," the Captain said to Frank. "Our antiaircraft crews won't be getting much rest here."

The Flying Wombats readily took Frank into their closely-knit group. He ate with them in the wardroom that evening and sat up with them far into the night exchanging sea stories.

When he finally turned in, the slap of the waves against *Houston*'s hull quickly sang him to sleep.

The General Alarm and the ubiquitous notes of "Air Defense" shattered Frank's reverie. He rolled out of his bunk and fumbled in the darkness of the unfamiliar cabin for his clothes and shoes. Stumbling into the passageway, he ran pell mell into John Stivers.

"I don't have a battle station yet," Frank mumbled. "Where's the best place to go?"

"Hell, we might as well go up and watch the gunners work," Stivers shot back. "If these Japs aren't any better than the ones yesterday, they're not going to hit anything."

Strapping on a tin hat, Frank made his way up to the weather deck, staying out of the way of the scurrying crew. During the night, *Houston* had shifted to nest outboard of *De Ruyter*, doubtless to give the flagship the added protection of her five-inchers. The noise of the antiaircraft barrage being put up by the Allied ships was deafening. The thump of *Houston's* 1.1-inchers overlaid the steady crack of the five-inchers and the rattle of *De Ruyter's* 40-millimeter Bofors guns. The dawn sky was filled with tracers and bursting shells.

Nine enemy bombers came on, very high up. Their commander was apparently a prudent man. He cruised back and forth across the harbor, dropping bombs from above the range of the guns below. The Mitsubishis flew away after half an hour, having inflicted some damage to the port but none to the warships.

Tom Payne called the Flying Wombats together after he returned from an early afternoon meeting with the Gun Boss. "Here's the scoop," he began. "There's a big Jap convoy--about fifty ships-- coming down Makassar Strait. John Robinson of PatWing Ten sighted it this morning, just before they shot him down. A few hours ago, the Japs invaded Bawean."

"God, that's only a hundred and fifty miles from here," said Walt Winslow.

"That's right," Payne continued. "The Strike Force will sail at dusk and sweep towards Bawean in case the Japs come on tonight. Frank, you'd better go ashore and wait there with your plane. We'll radio the Dutch seadrome if we want you to fly out in the morning to join us."

'Is there any need for me to stick around the base tonight, or can I stay with the PatWing Ten boys at the *Oranjie*?"

"Go on to the hotel. Hell, go see your girl. There's no chance we'll need you before morning."

Frank was lucky enough to catch a Dutch bus to Morokrembangan. He found Tonto and explained the situation to him.

"I'll watch the bird, Lone Ranger. If I was you, I'd be seeing the Doc tonight."

"Exactly what I had in mind. See you in the morning."

"Frank, you're still here!" Cinta's voice over the phone seemed delighted when he reached her at the hospital. "I was afraid you'd been sent off without us saying a proper goodbye."

"I thought you might have gone by now."

"Papa called this afternoon. He wants me to drive to Zwarte Gouden the day after tomorrow. Things must look black."

"They do. I'll tell you tonight. How's the Simpang Club sound?"

"Expensive."

"Might as well spend it while we can."

"Are you at the hotel?"

"Yes."

"I'll pick you up in an hour. You can wait while I change and then take my car."

"How bad is it?" Cinta asked as they drove through the nearly deserted streets of the city.

Frank told her about the convoy and the invasion of Bawean.

"Papa should be leaving now," Cinta said angrily. "Why won't they just let him blow up that infernal refinery so that we can go?"

"It's the only place left that we can get fuel for our ships," Frank said soothingly. "We can't give it up as long as there's any hope that we can turn back the Japs."

"I suppose you're right, but I'm getting frightened. The Nips are too close for comfort."

They sat at their table at the Simpang Club long after dinner, surrounded by revelers but seemingly alone. They talked for hours about the good times they had shared together, which were perhaps now ending forever.

"I think we should go home now," Cinta finally said. "We're wasting time that we could put to better use."

CHAPTER 24

(One)
Aboard USS *Rust*
Holland Pier
Soerabaja, Java
Netherlands East Indies
26 February 1942

"Where's the Skipper off to?" Chief Muldune asked Jack as they supervised the restocking of *Rust's* pom-pom ready magazines. Once again, *Houston* had come to their rescue when the cupboard was bare.

"Doorman's having a big confab at ABDAFLOAT Soerabaja."

"We gonna make another night patrol north of Madura?" *Rust* had come out of repairs just in time for the previous night's sweep.

"That's what I'd guess. It makes sense. The first Jap convoy was about out of Makassar Strait at the last sighting."

"I hope to hell they get the signals worked out. Last night was a regular three-ring circus. If we didn't have the TBS to talk to *Houston*, we'd still be lost out there."

The intercom blared for all hands topside to render honors to starboard. Jack and the chief stepped to the railing and came to attention.

"Son-of-a-bitch!" said Muldune. "There's some reinforcements that'll really count."

Steaming slowly in from the *Westervaarwater* were two cruisers flying the White Ensign of the Royal Navy. The lead ship was the larger, a heavy cruiser of about nine thousand tons. Jack recognized HMS *Exeter* at once. She was famous throughout the world for her duel two years before with the German pocket battleship, *Graf Spee*. As important as her heavy guns to the strike force was the prominent radar antenna on her mast. The Australian light cruiser *Perth* followed in her wake, with three modern destroyers bringing up the rear.

"We may stop those Jap bastards yet," Muldune exclaimed with enthusiasm. "That gives us two heavy cruisers and three lights. If we find that Jap convoy, there could be a massacre."

"If we can get some air cover," Jack observed wryly.

Tom Payne called a conference of the Flying Wombats in *Houston's* hangar at six that evening. "The Captain just got back," he informed them. "We sortie at 1830 for another night sweep. The Jap convoy may be close to Bawean now. I've been ordered to unship my SOC and hide it with Frank's. We'll both sit this one out and be ready to fly out and join the fleet tomorrow."

Frank helped the mechanics roll the aircraft trolley bearing Tom's *Seagull* onto the deck so that the crane could put it in the water. He was going to show Tom where to hide the plane, so he climbed into the rear cockpit. After unhooking the crane, Payne started the engine and slowly taxied across the harbor to the naval air station.

Out in the roadstead, the Allied fleet began to form up for the sortie. All along the headlands, people were gathering to watch the ships depart. Many were relatives of the Dutch Navy personnel, but there were also droves of other wellwishers. For the Dutch, Java was their last free bastion. If Doorman did not stop the Japanese, everything they had left would be forfeited.

De Ruyter spoiled what might have been a stirring sailing by colliding with a tug boat and sinking her. The ships finally sorted themselves out and threaded their way out through the western approach into the Java Sea.

"If it's okay with you, I'm going over to Cinta's now," Frank said to Tom after the last vessel had disappeared. He had earlier cleared his plans for the evening with Tom.

"I have the number. I'll call you if I need you. Otherwise, be back here at 0700."

"Want to go into town?" Frank asked Tonto.

"I'll stick it out here," the Indian replied. "Me and some of the boys from PatWing Ten are putting together a PBY from pieces of the wrecked ones. We should just about finish her up tonight."

(Two)
Andir, Java
Netherlands East Indies
26 February 1942

While Frank and Cinta were spending that last night together, Garrit Laterveer was driving out to the hidden revetments at Andir aerodrome. Van Oyen had called him back to headquarters the previous evening.

"Bring your three best pilots with you," the general had ordered. "I have some replacement aircraft for you."

A Lockheed *Electra* from Batavia picked up Garrit's party an hour later and flew them to Andir. Moulders went off with the others to arrange billets for the night while Garrit reported to Van Oyen's posh office.

"Our British friends have left us in the lurch," the old cavalryman commented after asking the young ace to be seated in a stuffed leather armchair. "I'm sure you know that the ABDA Command was dissolved yesterday. Everything that's left had been turned over to us."

"Yes, sir," Garrit replied. "The word came down the chain."

"The RAF units have packed up and gone. The Yanks are still trying to help, but they've withdrawn their heavy bombers to India. Only the fighter units are staying. *Langley* and *Seawitch* should reach Tjilatjap tomorrow. Pilots and ground crew are already there. We've built a new landing field for them to fly the *Tomahawks* out. Within a day or two, Soerabaja command should be back up to strength. If Karel Doorman can delay the invasion convoys north of Bawean, we should be able to stabilize the air situation."

"Am I going to Tjilatjap for aircraft?"

"Oh, good Lord, no. I've something much better than *Tomahawks* for you. The RAF squadron that pulled out this morning left us four brand new *Hurricanes*."

The general talked on for some time before dismissing Garrit. He was clearly embittered by the RAF's hasty withdrawal. After throwing everything that the Dutch had into the early defense of Malaya, it offended his sense of propriety that the British were so ready to scurry out of Java without a similar unselfish gesture. Garrit had finally gone off to his billet, tired but excited about the prospect of finally flying a decent combat aircraft again.

Lieutenant Moulders was waiting for Garrit with Sergeants Marinus and Schulte in the first revetment. They were standing around one of the big, hump-backed Hawker fighters, eyeing it with wonder. They snapped to attention as Garrit limped up in the golden glow of sunrise. He put them at ease and patted the wing of the airplane.

"A *Hurricane* Two-C," he commented with authority. "A *Spitfire's* a spirited mare. These chaps are more like a knight's charger. They're solidly built--lots of steel tube framing--and can take plenty of punishment. We'll need that virtue, for they're a bit slower than those damned *Zeros*. *Hurricanes* are probably the most stable gun platform you'll ever fly, and they have plenty of firepower."

"They only mount rifle-caliber machine guns, Captain," Moulders protested.

"Yes, but a dozen of them. We won the Battle of Britain with eight-gun fighters mounting these same .303 Brownings. If we can catch a *Zero* with one burst from this battery, it'll tear the Jap to pieces.

"The finest aircraft engine in the world's in here," he went on, patting the cowling. "That's a fourteen-hundred horsepower Rolls Royce Merlin. It will give you close to three hundred and fifty knots at twenty thousand feet."

"What can the pylons carry, sir?" asked Schulte, fingering one of the weapons attachments just outside the landing gear.

"Bombs of up to five hundred pounds. This model was designed as a fighter-bomber. Come on up, and I'll explain the cockpit."

Garrit spent the next half-hour going over the controls and giving tips on how to fly the British airplane. There would be no time for familiarization missions. They would take off and fly directly back to their base to resume combat. After what he considered sufficient ground indoctrination, he sent the others scattering to their machines, donned his helmet and parachute and struggled into the cockpit. After the *Buffalo* he had been flying, the *Hurricane* seemed oversized. After going through the preflight checklist, he signalled the attendant ground crew that he was ready and hit the starter.

The familiar roar of the Merlin engine washed over him like the presence of an old, very dear friend. He sat for a long while letting it warm up, enjoying the prospect of the flight ahead. When he called the control tower for takeoff clearance, the flight controller also informed him that the early warning net had sighted no enemy aircraft that morning. Giving a rapid set of commands to his pilots, he swung the *Hurricane* out of the revetment and onto the field.

The *Hurricane* roared skyward like no aircraft Garrit had flown since leaving England. The unparalleled performance of the Merlin sent a thrill up his spine. After flying planes with bulky radial engines all these months, it came as a pleasant shock to enjoy the sleek power of the Rolls Royce V-12. His pilots were startled at their new aircraft's operating characteristics. They began to chatter gleefully over the R/T until he was forced to quiet them.

"Calm down and remember basics," he told them sternly. "The *Zero* can still turn inside you. We stick to the tactics we've used since the first."

Less than an hour after leaving Andir, Garrit's formation approached Zwarte Gouden. When he called for landing instructions, he was redirected to the secret American fighter base at Blimbing. The last Allied fighter strength was being concentrated to allow striking a telling blow against the oncoming Japanese.

(Three)
Morokrembangan Naval Air Station
Soerabaja, Java
Netherlands East Indies
27 February 1942

Frank stopped Cinta's Alfa Romeo at the operations building. "This is it, sweetheart," he said with resignation. He turned and kissed her tenderly. She held his face between her hands, reluctant to let him go. "You'll be leaving now?" he continued.

"Yuni will be packed when I get back to the villa. We'll be in Zwarte Gouden by noon."

"Don't let Nicolaas tarry. Jap tanks may be crawling all over this island in a day or two."

"We may fly out this afternoon."

"I hope you do. Look, I'll be wherever *Houston* ends up. I'll write you at your sister's address in Texas. We'll set the wedding as soon as we can get together."

"Take care of yourself, Darling," Cinta whispered in his ear, her voice close to breaking. She kissed him again, this time with passion. He got out then, and she slid over to the driver's seat. He stood in the doorway until the sportscar disappeared down the road then went inside to look for Tom Payne.

Near noon, Frank and Tom were sitting in the radio room at the tower, anxiously awaiting word from their ship. All morning, they had been expecting a call to fly north and join the strike force, but none had come. Finally, a signal was monitored that the ships were just outside the harbor, returning for fuel and rest.

"Looks like we might as well break for chow," said Payne, getting up from his chair. "It'll be a good two hours before the ships tie up."

"Good idea," Frank agreed. "I had an early breakfast."

As they were about to leave, the radio operator, who spoke fluent English, put his hand up to stop them. "I'm getting a queer signal from a ship that may be a Yank," he informed them.

"What are they sending?" asked Payne.

"A four-letter pattern, repeated over and over. 'NERK'."

"It's our signal for air attack," said Frank. "Is it one of the ships outside the harbor?"

"No," the Dutchman said with certainty. "It's coming from a ship south of Tjilatjap."

"Oh, my God!" Tom exclaimed, exchanging knowing glances with Frank.

"*Langley?*" asked Frank.

"It has to be."

"Not the ship with the fighter reinforcements?" asked the radio operator.

"That's the one." Payne responded.

The operator put his hand to his headset for a moment then shook his head. "She's gone off the air."

"That just about cooks our goose," said Frank with despair, sitting down heavily.

"Wait. He's back, broadcasting in plain language Morse." The Dutchman began to write furiously, and the two pilots leaned over his shoulders to read the word.

For over an hour, they suffered with the unknown radioman,

who was trumpeting *Langley*'s agony to the world. Caught without air cover by Japanese bombers from Den Passer, she was helpless beneath their attack. Bombs burst among the precious fighters parked on the flight deck, starting raging gasoline fires. Then other missiles shattered her hull.

"JAP PLANES TOO HIGH FOR OUR GUNS. WE HAVE A DECIDED LIST. POWER OFF IN THE SHIP. AC TO BATTERIES..." the message continued. "THE JAPS ARE JAMMING US AS MUCH AS POSSIBLE. WE ARE SECURING SOON. THE SHIP IS LISTING. SHOT TO HELL. LANGLEY SIGNING OFF."

"Damn!" swore Frank, pounding a wall bitterly. "You'd have thought this was one time the Air Corps could have given us some cover. There's so hope now of regaining air supremacy."

"There's still *Seawitch*," said Tom.

"It'll take several days to put her crated P-40's together," Frank said with a shake of his head. "Jap tanks will be in Tjilatjap before then."

"Do you have any idea where she was?" Tom asked the Dutchman.

"I was just checking with my contact in Batavia. He took my bearing and plotted it against his. Wait... here it is now."

"Well?" asked the impatient Payne.

"*Langley* was just fifty miles south of Tjilatjap--less than three hours from docking."

(Four)
Aboard USS *Rust*
Soerabaja Harbor
1430, 27 February 1942

Jack Sewell was asleep on his feet. The early afternoon sun beat down unmercifully on the tin hat that he had tilted to shade his eyes, sending cascades of sweat streaming down his collar, but he was unaware of the discomfort. His body wedged tightly against the gun controller, he had been oblivious to everything since relaxing when *Rust* threaded her way in through the northern entrance to Soerabaja's *Westervaarwater*. It had been over fifty hours since he last slept. A day of beating off air attacks had been sandwiched between two successive nights of patrolling the seas to intercept the enemy invasion convoys. He was fast approaching the limits of his stamina, as were all the other men on the ship. Only the lookouts were still alert. Even Chief Muldune was dozing lightly as he leaned against the rail.

Jack's talker jerked upright and held his headset to his right ear. "Fire Control, aye, aye." he responded to the order, then shook Jack's shoulder gently. "Bridge orders, 'Secure from General Quarters,' Lieutenant."

Jack blinked his eyes, and then comprehension registered. "Very well," he said hoarsely. "Pass it on to the weapons crews."

"Will we be getting a chance for some shut-eye now, Mister Sewell?" Muldune inquired.

"I hope so. What I need now is some chow, and I'll bet most of the men feel the same." Jack took off his tin hat and mopped his brow, then started down the ladder at the back of the bridge. Glancing at his watch, he saw that it was just past 1430.

Down on the signal bridge, one of the signalmen put a long telescope to his eye and peered at *DeRuyter,* which was steaming several hundred yards ahead. An Aldis lamp was blinking furiously from the flagship's bridge, and the Dutchman appeared to be turning about in mid-channel.

"Jesus-H-Christ!" the petty officer with the telescope swore then began copying the message on a pad. Moments later, a messenger almost collided with Jack behind the bridge.

"What's going on?" asked Jack, now wide awake.

The messenger held the pad for him to read it. Admiral Doorman had signaled: "FOLLOW ME. THE ENEMY IS NINETY MILES AWAY."

The Combined Strike Force emerged from the entrance to the *Westervaarwater* in almost total confusion. Signal flags whipped in the breeze, and shuttered lamps blinked wildly as Doorman tried to sort out the mess and get the vessels into some sort of battle formation. With no common code or even a common flag system, he was reduced to plain-language radio broadcasts to pass his orders for the coming battle. For the Americans, messages were sent in Dutch to a liaison officer aboard *Houston*, who translated them into English. The cruiser's TBS relayed the orders to the old "four-pipers." A similar situation existed with the British vessels, but the Royal Navy lacked the convenience of TBS. To prevent breaking long-range radio silence, *Exeter*'s skipper was reduced to using signal lamps and flags.

Despite the communications foul-ups, by 1500 the force had settled into the formation Doorman had ordered. The big British destroyers, *Jupiter, Electra,* and *Encounter*, were in the van, spread out in line abreast. The cruisers followed in single file, with *DeRuyter* in the lead. *Exeter* came next, with *Houston* close behind. *Perth* and *Java* completed the battle line. The Dutch destroyers, *Witte deWith* and *Kortnaer*, guarded the port flank of the cruiser column, while Binford's "four-pipers" steamed in column behind the heavy ships. *Rust* was at the tail end of the line. The force was on a heading of 315 degrees, steaming at twenty-five knots.

"What's happening, Skipper?" Jack asked over the battle phones.

"The Jap convoy's been definitely sighted off Bawean," Hoskins replied. "About forty-five transports with cruiser and destroyer escort. We're headed to attack them. Primary targets will be transports."

"What's the battle plan?"

"There isn't one. No time to make it up. We're to close with the enemy and sink him."

"Who the hell does Doorman think he is, Nelson? The Japs won't be shooting smoothbore cannon. Those orders are suicidal."

"Those are the orders," Hoskins said dryly. "Hang loose and play it by ear."

Jack rang off and passed the word to his weapons crews so that they would know what to expect. Just as he was finishing, bombs began to fall around *De Ruyter*, and the ships broke formation and scattered.

"Masthead reports SOC over the cruisers," said Jack's talker in matter-of-fact tones.

Jack raised his glasses and spotted the floatplane cruising nonchalantly above *De Ruyter*. *Houston* let loose a barrage with her five-inchers, and the enemy plane retreated to the north. Lights blinked from the flagship, and the force resumed its former formation. A high overcast began to mar what had been a day of unlimited visibility.

"The Captain's calling," said the talker. Jack lifted his battle phone.

"*Electra* just made a sighting report," said Hoskins. "One cruiser and an unknown number of destroyers bearing 330 degrees, speed eighteen knots, course 220 degrees. This is it, Jack. Make every shot count."

Jack glanced at his watch and saw that it was 1615. Astern, the Java coast was still in view. They were barely twenty-five miles from Soerabaja.

"Another sighting, Jack," the Captain reported a few minutes later. "*Houston* just reported a Jap force almost due north--a bevy of cruisers and destroyers, headed west."

"Get on the gun director, Chief, bearing dead ahead," Jack snapped to Muldune then turned to his talker. "Ask Crow's Nest what he sees up ahead."

"Mother of God," Muldune muttered as he spun the focus wheels on the big range finder.

"What do you see?" Jack demanded, raising his own glasses.

"Jap heavy cruisers, at least two. *Nati* class, I think. Four...no, five turrets. Twins. Might be the *Mogami*. Range 28,000 yards."

"Let me have a look," said Jack, nudging the chief aside. He pressed his eyes to the eyepiece guard to seal out extraneous light. He had trouble adapting his eyes for a moment, and *De Ruyter's* mast kept bobbing up to blot out the horizon. Then he saw the lead enemy ship clearly. Its five turrets were trained on the Allied force, the twin guns in each raised to maximum elevation. At that moment, bright flashes erupted from the gun muzzles, followed instantly by sprouting plumes of smoke.

"Dammit to hell!" Jack exclaimed. "They're about to 'cross our T.'" He suddenly found himself staring at empty sea as *Rust* heeled over sharply in a turn to port.

Realizing that the enemy would indeed soon steam across his bows, Doorman was turning left to avoid that worst of all tactical situations. Had he continued his previous course, the Japanese would have been able to bring all their guns to bear, while the Allied ships would have been limited to the use of their forward weapons. Jack realized that Commander Binford was also shifting the position of the "four-pipers," sliding over to the disengaged side of the cruisers to trail the Dutch "cans." The men on *Rust's* upper works had an excellent view of the developing situation.

The column was still turning when *Houston* and *Exeter* opened fire with their eight-inchers. A resounding crash rolled across the water as smoke shrouded the Allied heavies. Geysers of water sprouted from the sea around them a few seconds later. The enemy gunners were good, Jack reflected. Too damned good. *Houston's* guns spoke again, beating *Exeter* by several seconds. Then a storm of Japanese shells came plunging down around *De Ruyter*, *Houston*, and *Exeter*.

"They got a bracket on their second salvo!" Muldune exclaimed. "Those little yellow bastards know how to shoot!"

"They've got help," Jack yelled, pointing up to two enemy floatplanes cruising serenely overhead. "Where the hell is our air force? We're in sight of the coast, and they still won't come out and help."

"Crow's Nest reports hit on enemy cruiser," said the talker.

Jack got his glasses focused. Bright orange flames and smoke was boiling up on one enemy cruiser's fantail. "*Houston* got an SOC on the catapult," he said excitedly. "That's a gasoline fire."

A light cruiser followed by a squadron of big destroyers came charging across his field of vision, passing between the damaged heavy cruiser and the Allied ships. The enemy's guns were blazing as they came on, apparently aiming at Doorman's leading ships. Water spouts in brilliant reds, yellows, and greens shot up all around the British destroyers. These hardy veterans of the North Atlantic dodged and twisted among the splashes, emerging, miraculously, untouched.

Once more in danger of having his "T" crossed, Doorman ordered another twenty-degree turn to port. As the column swung around, the Dutch and American destroyers moved farther up on the port flank of their heavy ships. *Houston* and *Exeter* continued rapid fire with their 8-inch main batteries.

"When are we going to fight, Mister Sewell?" asked an exasperated Fire Controlman.

"When we're ordered to," Jack shot back. "Don't worry. We'll get our licks in."

"What are you bitching about?" yelled Muldune. "This is better than a front row seat at turkey shoot."

The fleets were steaming on parallel courses now, throwing

shells at each other as fast as they could reload.   Jack timed *Houston*'s broadsides, discovering that she was firing an incredible six salvos a minute. Captain Rooks's gunners must be working like supermen to compensate for the loss of their after turret. The accuracy of the Japanese gunners continued to be phenomenal. Shells were raining down heavily upon the Allied force now, and every second or third salvo was a straddle.

"Can't we do something about those SOC's, sir?" Muldune pleaded. "They're calling those shots right down on the cruisers."

"Can the 37-millimeter reach them?"

"Maybe not, but we could make them damned nervous."

Back aft the ex-Army gun began to thump away, sending lazy tracers up toward the enemy floatplanes. They broke away and went into tight spiral turns to climb well out of range.

"Crow's Nest reports aircraft off the port beam," said the talker. "Looks like friendlies."

Jack swung around and searched the sky toward Java. He picked out the incoming planes quickly. They were high and headed straight for the sea battle. He recognized three A-24's--the Army version of the Navy's *Dauntless* dive bomber. The escorts were P-40's. He counted ten.

"Hot damn!" Muldune swore. "We're finally going to get some air cover. They'll knock those SOC's down in a minute."

Jack put his glasses back on the lead enemy destroyers. As he caught them in his vision, they swung left in a maneuver usually associated with a torpedo attack. His suspicions were confirmed moments later when he saw flashes of fire from their waists. "I think the Japs just launched a TORPS attack," he reported to Hoskins.

A few minutes later, orders came from the flagship for a hard turn to starboard. Doorman was closing the enemy so that his light cruisers could join in the fray. The Japanese destroyers were dashing back toward their heavy ships now, trailing a thick smokescreen as they went. The Allied turn was hardly completed when reports of torpedo tracks began to flood into *Rust's* nerve centers. Captain Hoskins steered nimbly between half a dozen wakes in the next few minutes. Explosions rocked the ship as the deadly fish exploded harmlessly at the ends of their runs.

"Submarines?" Hoskins asked Jack.

"I don't think so. I believe it was those Jap 'cans.'"

"Couldn't be. They were over twenty thousand yards away."

The Allied ships swung back to the left, paralleling the enemy fleet once again. *De Ruyter, Perth,* and *Java* began blazing away with their 6-inch guns at the Japanese battle line, which was pulling slightly ahead. Doorman's force had hardly steadied on their new course when tight shell patterns started falling all around them.

"Where the hell did our planes go?" Jack shrieked, spotting the enemy floatplanes still cruising overhead.

"I was too busy to look," Muldune responded.

"They're there, off to the north," one of the lookouts reported, pointing to a cluster of specks on the horizon. Incredibly, the American pilots had flown right over the sea battle without intervening in any way.

"Those fuckin' bastards!" Muldune cursed bitterly. "They're going for the transports and leaving us to fry in our own juice. One damned fighter plane for three minutes was all we needed to get rid of those damned Jap spotter planes!"

Muldune had no further chance for reflection on what might have happened. Without warning, the Allied formation began to come apart at the seams, the ships milling around in complete disarray.

A monstrous smoke cloud suddenly blossomed in *Exeter's* waist. The British cruiser lurched drunkenly and slued out of line to the left. Froth boiled beneath *Houston's* fantail as Captain Rooks turned sharply to avoid colliding with his stricken ally. The following ships, *Perth* and *Java,* also swung to port, assuming the flagship had ordered a general turn. Unaware of the turmoil behind him, Doorman kept *De Ruyter* steaming towards the enemy, still preceded by the British destroyers. The Dutch and American destroyers dodged wildly about to keep from running into the turning cruisers. *Perth's* captain, seeing *Exeter* slowed to a crawl with fire and smoke pouring out of her hull, broke formation and steamed between the damaged ship and the enemy to lay a smoke screen.

Finally realizing what was happening, Doorman turned the flagship and the lead destroyers back to join the rest of the force. Just then, whole schools of torpedoes began to streak through the Allied fleet. Again, the captains turned into the barrage to "comb" the torpedo wakes. Luck ran out on *Kortenaer*. A towering geyser of white water shot up a hundred feet as a warfish struck her amidships. The destroyer turned turtle, broke in half and sank instantly.

Sensing victory within his grasp, the Japanese commander was looping back to charge in for the kill. *De Ruyter* came churning eastward past the milling cruisers, her signal lamps frantically ordering that the battle line reform. *Houston, Perth* and *Java* turned to follow the flagship. *Witte de With* and the American "four-pipers" fell in line astern of *Java*. While the rest of the Allied force was reforming, the three British destroyers dashed south to place themselves between *Exeter* and the Japanese. Executing a full 180-degree turn, they started laying a thick smoke screen to mask the crippled cruiser from the enemy's gunners. Then they darted through the smoke into the very teeth of the oncoming Japanese force. From the bitter end of the Allied line, which was steaming away from the action, Jack could see little but an occasional shell flash from the melee in the smoke.

De Ruyter went into a tight turn to starboard, bringing the battle group back towards the limping *Exeter*. Smoke hung in patches all over the scene. Twilight was fast approaching, lending an eerie cast to the seascape. *Witte deWith*, damaged moments before when her depth charges were accidentally released to explode close against her hull, fell out of line and made off to cover *Exeter*. *Encounter* came racing back with a great "bone in her teeth" to rejoin the Allied force. *Electra* had vanished somewhere out in the smoke.

Still turning counterclockwise, the Combined Strike Force broke out of the smoke screen. Jack's Crow's Nest lookout quickly spotted the enemy heavy cruisers steaming westward at about twenty thousand yards. Fire sprouted from their upper works at once. *Houston's* eight-inchers spoke in reply, firing very slowly now. The signal lamp on *De Ruyter's* bridge began to flash again.

"This is it, Jack," came Hoskins's voice over the battle phones. "Commodore's just relayed orders by TBS. We're to make a TORPS attack on the Jap heavies. We'll be firing both batteries. Stand by."

"Stand by for TORPS attack," Jack passed on to Ensign Brown. "Train all tubes outboard. All gun crews, stand by."

As the Allied cruisers completed their circle and turned away to the east, Commander Binford peeled his wheezing old "four-pipers" off to starboard and raced to the north, directly toward the Japanese fleet.

"Mother of God," Muldune was actually praying now, "pray for us sinners now and in the hour of our death."

"What's the range, Chief?" Jack interrupted. The American destroyers were plunging forward at twenty-five knots.

"Fifteen thousand and closing," Muldune shouted to be heard above the shriek of the wind over the open platform.

"Stand by, Jack," the Captain ordered. "We're to attack at maximum torpedo range."

Up ahead, the targets were clearly visible in the fast-fading light. Muldune identified them as two heavy cruisers and a destroyer.

"Steady TORPS on target," Jack ordered the torpedo officer.

"TORPS, aye, aye," came the swift response.

"Fire TORPS,'" barked Hoskins on the battle circuit.

"Fire when ready," Jack passed on to Brown. Muffled explosions were audible amidships within seconds, followed by a quick verbal report.

"Six TORPS salvo fired."

Almost at once, Binford swung his squadron to starboard, ordering a smoke screen as they turned. Steadying on an eastward course, he then ordered all portside tubes fired. Their torpedoes expended, the "four-pipers" blazed away with their deck guns while they could bear, scoring several hits on the Japanese destroyers.

Loosed at their extreme range of ten thousand yards, the warfish had little chance of actually hitting the enemy cruisers. But as the "four-pipers" strained to overtake Doorman's column, Jack saw that the attack had the desired effect. The Japanese heavies turned away to the northwest, steaming rapidly away from the Allied battle group. Free for the moment from the threat of being finished off, *Exeter* was limping in the direction of Soerabaja as fast as her damaged engines could take her.

The Dutch admiral turned his force back to the north, heading once again towards Bawean, where the invasion convoy was believed to be lurking. The next hour was one of great confusion for the American destroyers. Communications almost completely broke down. *Houston*'s TBS ceased to function, and only the most essential signals could be passed by blinker lamp. No one knew

Doorman's intentions for certain. They could only hang on at the end of the battle line and improvise as the situation developed.

Just after 1930, green parachute flares blossomed over the battle group, lighting the seascape like day. *Houston* let loose a single broadside to port, and star shells burst in the distance a few moments later, revealing the distant outlines of more Japanese cruisers. The heavy ships exchanged a few salvos in the dark, and then the night went black again. Doorman ordered a complete turnabout, steaming his force south to dodge away from the enemy heavy ships. Periodically, more flares floated down from the shadowing floatplanes.

At about 2100, the shoal waters of the Java coast were sighted ahead. *De Ruyter* turned right to parallel the shore. *Houston* followed with *Perth* and *Java*. But *Edwards*, the leading American destroyer, turned to port instead.

"What's up, Skipper?" Jack inquired over the battle phone.

"We're all sucking air from our tanks," Hoskins replied. "The Commodore's taking us into Soerabaja to refuel."

Jack raised his glasses and watched the strike force fade away in the starlight. Twenty minutes later, the crack of a heavy explosion rolled across the waters. Far away, Jack caught a momentary flash of fire, which quickly flickered out.

"Any word on what that was?" Jack asked the bridge.

"Sparks picked up a report," the Captain answered. "*Jupiter* was hit by a torpedo. She went down with all hands."

It was just past 2300 when Binford's little force steamed into Soerabaja Harbor from the Western Approach. Jack was slumping wearily against the range finder, thankful for the prospect of rest but apprehensive over the fate of their comrades still sailing the troubled waters to the north. *Edwards* suddenly started executing a 180-degree turn, the other ships ahead following suit. Then they all slowed to a crawl. Jack called the bridge, and Jerry Busch came on the line.

"We just got orders to sail to Batavia," said the Exec. "The Commodore's holding a conference on the TBS. Hold on."

Jack leaned against the railing and reflected on the order. It made little sense. There were no stocks of American ammunition in Batavia.

"They've decided to ignore the order," Busch informed him. "We're going to top off our tanks here and clear the docks by dawn if we can get some direction from Admiral Glassford's headquarters."

Once again, the destroyers reversed course. An hour later, their boilers running on the dregs of their tanks, they tied up at the Naval Base fuel piers. By then, the fate of Java had been sealed. At 2320, *De Ruyter* and *Java* received multiple torpedo hits and burst into flames. Immediate orders went out from the flagship for *Houston* and *Perth* to flee to Batavia at once. Karel Doorman went down with *De Ruyter* when she sank a few minutes later.

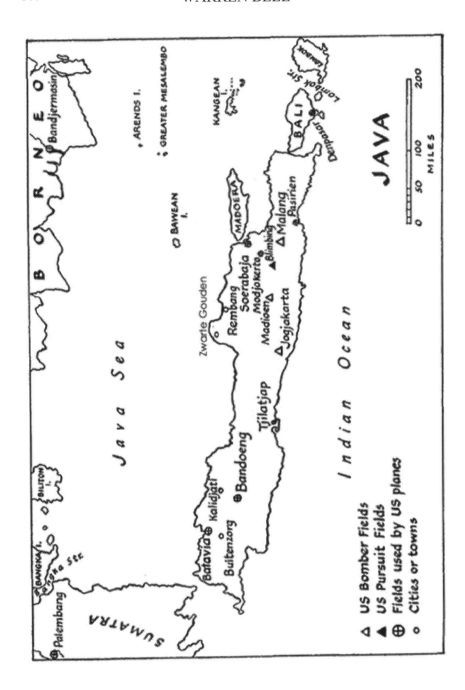

CHAPTER 25

(One)
Morokrembangan Naval Air Station
Soerabaja, Java
Netherlands East Indies
27 February 1942

Frank and Tom Payne spent the tense hours of the Java Sea battle in the air station operations building, momentarily expecting orders to fly out and join the Combined Strike Force. Inexplicably, the call never came. The few fragments of radio signals intercepted ashore were not sufficient to actually follow what was transpiring to the north. Doorman sent a signal to ABDAFLOAT at 1830 that stated, "ENEMY RETREATING WEST. WHERE IS CONVOY?" It was plain that he was still pursuing his original aim--to get in among the soft-skinned transports and destroy the invasion force. Much later, the shore stations heard the signal to the American destroyers to proceed to Batavia for fuel and torpedoes. Their final interception was the Dutch admiral's signal to *Houston* and *Perth* to make for Batavia rather than stand by the sinking *De Ruyter*. It was clear then that the battle had been lost.

"We'll be up to our asses in Japs by tomorrow night," Frank commented as he lighted his forty-fifth cigarette of the stress-filled day.

"No question about it," Tom responded. "We'd better be ready to fly to Batavia in the morning to catch the ship."

"I'm going to sleep at the hotel. Might as well get one last crack at a good bed."

"We'd better fill Tonto in before we go. He may want to come along."

The three officers drove to the *Oranjie* through blacked-out, deserted streets. What was left of PatWing 10 was in the process of clearing out, so they had no trouble getting rooms. A roaring party was still in progress at the bar, but they passed it up to get some sleep. Frank paused in the lobby to make two phone calls. No one answered at Cinta's villa, so he called the hospital, finally getting a nurse who spoke English.

"Oh, no," she answered Frank. "Doctor van Wely has left us. She hasn't been here since the day before yesterday."

Thanking the nurse, Frank hung up and headed for bed, confident that Cinta was by now on her way to Australia.

(Two)
Aboard USS *Rust*
Holland Pier
Soerabaya, Java
Netherlands East Indies
28 February 1942

"What the hell's goin' on, Lieutenant?" Chief Muldune asked in exasperation.

Jack Sewell sat hunched in a chair in his tiny office. Exhaustion had hollowed his cheeks and drawn deep lines in his face. A half-eaten plate of Vienna sausages and an empty coffee cup littered his desk, the remnants of a hastily eaten breakfast. "All I know is that we're waiting for orders," he said wearily.

"If we don't get outta this place soon, we're gonna get trapped like rats."

It was evident to even the lowliest seaman on the six "four-pipers"--*Pope* had been in port under repairs and had now joined Binford's force--that the Japanese would be ashore in Java within hours. Yet here they sat in Soerabaja Roads, their fuel tanks topped off and ready to sail, while staff officers in the far-off Lembang headquarters procrastinated.

"Commander Binford talked to Admiral Glassford on the Green Line to headquarters a little while ago," Jack continued. "We should be hearing something pretty quick."

"Which way do you think we'll go?"

"If they've got any sense at all up there, they'll send us east through Bali Strait. We can make it through the shallows there.

Thank God we're not as big as *Exeter*."

"Yeah. She'll have to go west to Batavia and Sunda Strait."

A seaman appeared in the doorway. "Lieutenant, there's a native civilian down on the pier with a message for you," the man reported.

"What now?" said Jack, heaving himself up from his chair. He reflected that he was an utter mess; his uniform, stained with sweat and soot from the guns; his face, unshaven. He ambled slowly off to the gangway. When he saw the Malay, he recognized him at once. He was Pamela Mallory's houseboy.

"Ah, Lieutenant *Tuan*," the man said, bowing. "Miss Mallory asked me to deliver this to you." He handed Jack an envelope.

Jack thanked the servant and offered him a twenty-guilder bill. Smiling, the man took it and dashed off. Jack tore open the letter and read it quickly.

Dearest Jack, Sorry I couldn't see you again. Have arranged with your darling PatWing 10 to fly to Australia with Auntie. We're for Perth, where I'll get Auntie back in hospital. Look for me there. I must tell you one thing in parting. You're the best lover I've ever had. Keep your pecker up.

Ever your,

Pamela

Glad that Pam had escaped, Jack felt a new optimism as he went back up to the ship. Perth, he mused, might prove an interesting liberty port after all.

(Three)
BPM Refinery
Zwarte Gouden, Java
Netherlands East Indies
28 February 1942

"You've got to let me blow it up now, Conrad," Nicolaas said heatedly into the telephone. "The Japs may get here today."

"I can't agree," came Admiral Helfrich's gruff voice in reply. "I still have ships to fight, and you're my only source of fuel. I'm reforming the Combined Strike Force at Tjilatjap. *Houston* and *Perth* will be there tomorrow, as will the American destroyers. I've appealed to Washington and London for reinforcements. *Seawitch* has made port. As soon as we put her *Kittyhawks* together again, Van Oyen will need your petrol to fly them."

"We'll never get another tanker out of here," Nicolaas protested. "Jap ships are cruising right offshore between here and Soerabaja."

"The rail links across the island are still open," Helfrich shot back. "Oosten is sending you every tank car in Java."

"It's too late, Conrad. If we don't start our demolitions, the Japs will get this plant just as they did the one at Palembang."

"I'm in a better position than you to know the overall situation," the admiral said soothingly. "I'll give you sufficient notice if and when it's warranted."

"I'll be expecting your call," said Nicolaas angrily before ringing off.

"Well?" said Pieter Wildeboer, from whose plush office the call had been made.

"They can't believe that we've already lost," Nicolaas replied, sighing heavily. "Conrad's still dreaming of breaking up the invasion convoys. If we wait for his orders, it will be too late to destroy the refinery and the oil fields."

"What are you going to do?"

"Set all my detonators and firing circuits today. If I'm not given permission by noon tomorrow, I'll take it on my own head and throw the switches. Plan to be at *Belle of Borneo* by mid-morning. I'll be flying off as soon as the charges explode."

An air raid siren sent them scrambling outside to a beehive shaped concrete shelter. As they reached it, Nicolaas suddenly paused at the entrance.

"What are we doing?" he asked sheepishly. "This is the last place on Java the Japs would want to bomb."

They walked out onto the lawn and stared skyward. Very high up, a nine-plane formation of twin-engined bombers was winging toward the south, escorted by an equal number of *Zero* fighters.

"They're headed for Tjilatjap," Pieter commented. Nicolaas agreed with the observation. Conrad Helfrich was the one who was not facing facts. With complete control of the skies over Java, the Japanese were already the victors.

(Four)
Morokrembangan Naval Air Station
Soerabaja, Java
Netherlands East Indies
28 February 1942

Frank, Tonto and Tom Payne horsed Payne's *Seagull* around on its dolly and pushed it over to the ramp that led down to the water.

"Sure you don't want to fly together?" Frank asked Tom, who was pulling on his flying helmet.

"We'll be better off alone," said Payne. "Less chance of being spotted by the Japs. You follow in about half an hour."

"Aye, aye," Frank responded. "Good luck." They shook hands, and then Tom climbed into his cockpit. Tonto let out a yell in Malay, and four native seamen came running to help push the dolly down the ramp. Once afloat, Tom cranked up his engine and taxied out into the harbor. Smoke from the early morning air raid hung low over the water, occasionally obscuring the *Seagull* from view. Then Payne gunned the floatplane across the harbor, lifting smoothly into the air. He circled low over the air station once and flew off to the west. *Houston* would be waiting in Batavia.

"Let's get cracking," Frank said to Tonto. "By the time we get ready, it'll be time to go."

Frank flew low above the canefields that stretched between Gunung Luwa, the holy mountain, and the blue Java Sea, hoping to escape the notice of any enemy planes that might be lurking overhead. He had plenty of fuel to make it to Batavia, so he was pushing the *Seagull* for all she was worth. An hour out of Soerabaja, the coastline swelled out to the north to form the large, forested plain of the Zwarte Gouden district. Frank followed the coast, not wanting to be exposed above the jungle. Up ahead, he could see the flashing water of the *Parfum* River.

"Trouble, Lone Ranger," Tonto said over the intercom. "There's a *Zero* coming in from nine o'clock, about five thousand feet up."

Frank craned his neck around to the left and caught the glint of the sun off the fighter's wings. "Maybe he won't see us," he hoped aloud.

Belying that expectation, the Japanese plane suddenly nosed over and came streaking down.

"Unlimber your gun and hang on," said Frank. Nosing the *Seagull* over, he did a "Split-S" and plummeted earthward, pulling out of the dive just above the treetops. Throttling back as far as possible without stalling, he slowed the biplane to just over seventy knots. Frank knew that his only chance was to limit the time that the enemy pilot could keep the floatplane in his sights and to maneuver violently during those moments. If he had calculated right, the *Zero* would never be able to slow down enough to properly line up its guns.

As tracers from rifle-caliber machine guns began to zip around the *Seagull*, Frank flipped the plane onto its side and turned tightly to the left. The *Zero* flashed by astern, then climbed to make another firing pass.

"You spoiled my aim," yelled Tonto.

"Want me to hold her steady for you?"

"And make me a sitting duck! No, thanks."

The *Zero* came screaming back to the attack. This time, the Japanese pilot anticipated Frank's turn. Bullets shredded the *Seagull's* wings and opened the fuel tanks. Miraculously, they did not catch fire.

"We've had it," Frank exclaimed. "I'm putting her down."

The *Zero* came back in for the kill, but strangely no fire came from its guns. The pilot flew alongside and watched Frank plop the floatplane down into the muddy river, then turned north and flew out to sea, cursing himself for the last strafing run he had made on the roadstead at Tjilatjap earlier. His guns had run out of ammunition just as he was about to flame the American floatplane.

Frank taxied up the river, looking for a sheltered place to moor. With fuel streaming from his damaged tanks, the plane could catch fire at any moment. Finally, off to the right, he saw a break in the shoreline where a tributary from the adjacent swamp met the river. The boughs of huge trees on either side formed a massive green archway. Turning the *Seagull*, he taxied her under the sheltering trees, proceeding about fifty yards up the leafy tunnel before cutting the engine. Tonto climbed out and grabbed an overhanging tree limb, then went hand over hand to the shore. Frank threw him a line, which he tied to a massive tree.

"Think we dare fold the wings?" asked Frank.

"Not now. Too many fumes around. One spark and she'll explode."

"Can you patch her up?" asked Frank as they surveyed the damage.

"Sure, given a few hours and the right tools and materials. Question is, where am I gonna get 'em."

"There's a big refinery about twenty miles upriver. They should have what you need."

"Guess I'd better break out the dinghy. It's gonna be a long paddle."

The little inflatable rubber boat was barely big enough to hold the two of them. They climbed into it gingerly and paddled out onto the big river. They had hardly started upstream when a sleek-hulled motor torpedo boat came cruising up behind them. The Dutch sailors hailed them and threw over a rope. Within five minutes, they were drinking coffee with the Captain, a bearded Dutch Navy lieutenant named DeGraff.

"We'll not only get you the materials and tools," DeGraff was saying. "I'll send along a pair of native shipfitters to help out. You can use our power launch."

"Sounds great," said Frank. "How long should it take to fix, Tonto?"

"We oughta be ready to go by noon tomorrow."

The MTB nosed into the wharf of the refinery and tied up. Frank was on deck, staring in wonder at the size of the place. He had seen refineries before, both in Southern California and in Borneo, but nothing like this. What might the enemy be willing to pay to get the plant in operating condition?

Two men in khaki pants and bush jackets were standing near the shoreward end of the wharf. Frank prayed to God that his eyes were playing tricks on him, for the bigger man looked like Nicolaas van Wely. That meant that Cinta had not yet escaped!

"Is that who I think it is?" asked a squinting Tonto.

"I'm afraid so. It's Cinta's father."

"You know the *Tuan Besar*?" asked DeGraff.

"I'm engaged to his daughter."

"That's fortunate. We'll have to get the equipment and supplies from him or Wildeboer, the gentleman he's with."

Nicolaas turned toward the trio of naval officers when their footsteps neared. "Good God, Frank," he exclaimed. "What are you and Tonto doing here in Zwarte Gouden?"

Frank described the encounter with the *Zero* and the subsequent crash landing in the river.

"And you survived?" said Wildeboer. "You must be a very lucky man."

"He is," Tonto agreed. "That's why I fly with him."

Nicolaas introduced the Americans to Wildeboer, who already knew DeGraff. Frank summarized the situation with their aircraft and asked for the loan of some tools. Tonto quickly sketched out his requirements.

"Of course, we'll help," Nicolaas agreed. "I'll take you to our central tool room."

"Is Cinta still here?" asked Frank as they walked across the compound.

"I'm afraid so," Nicolaas replied. "She's at the hotel. We're leaving tomorrow."

"You should get her out today. The Japs whipped our tails out there in the Java Sea yesterday. They'll be landing in a day or two."

"I know. Batavia's still trying to get oil from here across to Tjilatjap. Tomorrow noon's my limit though. I won't keep Cinta and Tonia in Java any longer."

The tool room foreman let Tonto go through his inventory to pick out what he needed. He crammed his selections into a metal toolbox and came out grinning. "Look what that guy gave me," he said to Frank, holding up a sealed can. "It's caulking compound for oil tanks, just what the doctor ordered."

As they started back for the pier, a dark green staff car pulled alongside them. It braked abruptly, and Colonel Dijker swung out of the rear door.

"News from Lembang?" Nicolaas inquired.

"Nothing," said Dijker. "I came to check on your demolition preparations."

"I'll be ready tonight."

Frank introduced Tonto to Dijker and explained their predicament.

"You seem to be well taken care of," Dijker remarked. "Can I can do anything for you?"

"Could you let us have a couple of rifles, Colonel?" asked Tonto. "We don't have any guns. I feel naked goin' back to that swamp without one."

"Every firearm I have has been issued to the reserve units and militia," Dijker replied. He started to turn away and then paused. "Wait, I do have something--a souvenir pistol from my days as a spy. I'll send it to DeGraff's launch as soon as I get back to the barracks. It should be there in an hour." After a short exchange with Nicolaas on demolition plans, Dijker got back into his car and drove away.

"Look, Lone Ranger," Tonto said as they neared the wharf. "You're not gonna be that much use to me until I finish patchin' up the plane. This may be your last chance to see the Doc for a long time. Why don't you stay in town tonight, and I'll come get you when I'm through."

"I should stick with you," Frank said halfheartedly.

"Tonto's right," Nicolaas interjected. "You'll need to sleep tonight if you're to fly tomorrow. I'll get you a room at the Wilhelmina. Cinta will be delighted to have you here."

"Okay," said Frank, torn by conflicting loyalties. "One thing's sure. Tonto can't leave without me."

"Don't count on that. I've handled the controls enough to fly if I had to."

Tonto went on to DeGraff's mooring float, where the small launches were kept. He had just finished loading his gear and several full drums of AVGAS when Dijker's driver returned and brought him a small leather suitcase. He recognized the 1932 model Mauser pistol at once when he opened the lid, for it was a popular weapon in China. Loading with detachable magazines rather than the strip-in method of earlier models, it had the additional advantage of fully automatic fire. This one had a feature Tonto had never seen before, a bulbous silencer surrounding the barrel. He wished he could test fire a few rounds to see how well it really worked, but he needed to get back to the plane before dark. Closing the case, he stowed it in the launch and called out in Malay to the two Javanese petty officers who DeGraff had detailed to help him. A few minutes later, they were on their way downriver.

"Is my daughter here?" Nicolaas asked Ada as he and Frank

entered the living room of his sumptuous hotel suite.

"No, *Tuan Besar*, she is visiting the hospital," the *baboe* replied.

"She just can't stay away," Nicolaas sighed. "How would you like a gin and tonic?"

"Sounds great," Frank replied, digging his cigarettes from the pocket of his sweaty shirt.

"I arranged for you to have the room next door."

"I appreciate that. Any idea where I could scrounge some clean clothes?"

"You look about the size of one of my assistants who lives downstairs. I'll send Yuni down to see what he can spare."

They sat sipping their drinks for half an hour, talking about the military situation. When Yuni returned with fresh khaki trousers, a bush jacket and underwear, Frank excused himself and went to his room to take a dipper bath. He was just coming out of the bathroom, toweling vigorously, when a knock came at his door.

"Frank?" He recognized Cinta's voice.

"It's unlocked," he replied, draping the towel about his hips.

She came across the room in a blur of motion, straight into his waiting arms. Their mouths locked as he crushed her to him, his hands moving over her body.

"Oh, Frank," she gasped, catching her breath. "I can't believe you're really here."

"Courtesy of a *Zero*," he answered and kissed her again. He slipped a hand inside her blouse, his passion rising.

"Not now, Darling," she protested, leaning back in his arms. "Papa is taking us to dinner upstairs. He's expecting us in a few minutes."

"I'd rather take you to bed," he laughed.

"My feelings exactly, but you know how fathers are about their little girls. I have to freshen up myself. Come over to Papa's suite when you've dressed."

The nightclub restaurant in the hotel penthouse was pure bedlam. The band blared American popular music, and the dance floor was packed with men in a variety of uniforms and women in evening dresses. Liquor flowed freely. Everyone seemed to be talking at the top of their lungs.

The headwaiter steered Nicolaas and his party through the crowd to a small, private dining room at the rear of the restaurant. After seating them at a round table, he left menus and closed the door as he went out.

"It was like this in Shanghai back in 'thirty-seven'," Tonia commented, "just before the Japs took over.""

"I've read the same about the cities in Europe," said Cinta. "People instinctively try to grab that last instant of happiness when the world is crashing down around their ears."

"It's natural," Nicolaas agreed. "We should do the same although, God willing, we won't be here to see the walls cave in."

Nicolaas invited them to indulge their appetites with whatever they wished. Frank and Cinta chose tenderloin steaks, the older couple more exotic island dishes. The Dutchman ordered the finest *pinot noir* in the wine cellar, a twenty-year-old French import, declaring that it was too good to leave to the Japanese. After dinner, they sat chatting over coffee for the better part of an hour. Nicolaas and Cinta did most of the talking, reminiscing about the various places they had lived in the Indies. Then their conversation turned to their expected refuge in Houston, Texas.

"I still think it's scandalous that the Americans won't let us bring our servants," Cinta said in exasperation.

"The Yanks, especially those on the West Coast, are touchy as hell about Asians right now," said Nicolaas. "I've heard that they're putting the Japanese there, even American citizens, in concentration camps."

"The *Nisei*?" asked Frank, astounded. "You can't be serious."

"I'm afraid I am. They had a near panic in California after the Pearl Harbor attack. Alette sent me some press clippings about it.

"It wouldn't matter about Yuni and Ada at any rate," Nicolaas went on. "They won't leave these islands. I've bought them a house in the native quarter. I gave Yuni the deed this afternoon."

"And what about you, Countess?" Frank inquired. "Will you be going on to America?"

"They're not anxious to welcome the old nobility now that they're allied with the Bolsheviks. I'll probably settle in Australia for the duration. Where will you go if your ship's left Batavia by the time you arrive?"

"Over to Tjilatjap. That's where she's bound to head. If she's left Java already, we'll ditch the *Seagull* and get a ship for Australia."

"We'd better make an early evening of it," said Nicolaas after checking his watch. "We all have to be up early. Tomorrow night, we should be dining in Perth."

"I think I'll stay here with Frank for a while," said Cinta, looking Nicolaas straight in the eye. "You and Tonia go ahead. I'll not disturb you when I come in."

Nicolaas and Tonia exchanged knowing glances. "Very well," said Nicolaas, pushing back his chair. "We'll have breakfast at seven, and I'll take Frank back to the refinery with me."

"Sounds fine to me," said Frank, rising as Nicolaas pulled back Tonia's chair.

"They'll not bother us tonight," said Cinta as Nicolaas and the countess elbowed their way through the crowd.

"Is she his mistress?"

"I thought you'd figured that out by now. They've been lovers for a couple of years."

"I suspected as much. Now, what about us? Do you want to stay and dance for a while?"

"Only long enough to get them settled. What I really want is to make love right now."

"Then, let's get out of here."

Frank's hand trembled with expectation as he slipped his key into his door lock. Cinta looked both ways down the hall then followed him into his room. She came at once into his arms, her fingers already working at the buttons of his shirt, as he kicked the door shut.

CHAPTER 26

(One)
Aboard USS *Rust*
Madura Strait
28 February 1942

Two hundred miles to the east of Zwarte Gouden, Jack Sewell tilted back his tin hat to wipe his forehead with his shirtsleeve. A stiff, warm breeze tore at his hair.

"Damn that moon," Chief Muldune swore from the shadowy darkness nearby. "Makes you feel naked as hell."

Jack shared the feeling. Just ahead, the glowing wake of *John D. Ford* seemed bright as a beacon on the silvery sea. Commander Binford's squadron was running eastward down Madura Strait toward Bali. Speed was paramount on this moonlit night. To have any hope of escape, the destroyers must be through the narrow passage between Bali and Java and well out into the Indian Ocean before dawn. Although no one aboard had slept for over thirty-six hours, all hands were alert at their battle stations, surviving on coffee and adrenaline. Sleep could come later when they reached safety. For now, every pair of eyes was needed to search for the enemy.

Until late afternoon, they had all expected to be sent west to Batavia, where *Houston* and *Perth* spent the day. Then Tom Hoskins called *Rust's* officers to meet in the wardroom.

"Here's the scoop," said the Captain. "Commander Binford just got off the phone with Admiral Glassford. We're ordered to Exmouth Gulf in Australia to rearm from the tenders there. We sail at 1700 so that we can transit Bali Strait after dark. If we make it into the Indian Ocean, we should be home free. By dawn, we'll be too far south for the bombers from Den Passer to find us. Questions?"

No one spoke up. They were all too numb from fatigue for their usual cheerful banter. One thought dominated their minds: they had been reprieved from almost certain destruction. If their luck held for one more night, they would have a chance to live.

Binford's skippers wasted no time. By 1700, the line of "four-pipers" was following the flagship, *Edwards*, out through the *Oostervaarwater* toward Madura Strait. In a spontaneous demonstration of admiration and comradeship, the crews of the American vessels lined their rails and cheered as they steamed past the anchored *Exeter*. They knew that she would be leaving shortly to head for Sunda Strait at the other end of Java. *Pope* and *Encounter* would go with her as escorts. Very few in Binford's force had much hope that the gallant, crippled cruiser would make it safely to Tjilatjap. The Java Sea was swarming with Japanese task forces.

"Poor old *Pope*," Muldune muttered as they left that slender ship astern. "We'll not be seein' her again."

It was already March first when the line of destroyers turned south to round the eastern tip of Java. Word was passed through *Rust*'s battle phones to keep a sharp watch. Bucking the stiff currents of Bali Strait, the ships slowed noticeably. The ghostly shores of the islands on either side towered above the boiling seas. The breeze from the shore was rank with rotting vegetation. They were almost out into the Indian Ocean when the first combat report came in.

"Crow's Nest reports unidentified ship, bearing 100 degrees relative," said Jack's talker.

Jack swung his glasses to the high Bali shore and strained his eyes. Then he picked out a ship's silhouette moving just inside the shadow of the land. It was a destroyer, a big one.

"Captain on the line for you, Mister Sewell," the talker reported.

"The Commodore's sighted two Jap destroyers to port," Hoskins informed Jack. "Our orders are to hold fire but be ready to cut loose. We're going to try to slip by undetected."

"Aye, aye," Jack responded, then issued a rapid set of orders to his gun crews. In his mind's eye, he could see the slender barrels of the four-inch fifties swinging round to point at the enemy warships. There would be no torpedo attack tonight. Brown's tubes were as empty as Mother Hubbard's cupboard.

A signal lamp began to blink from the bridge of the leading

Japanese ship, obviously a challenge.

"Stand by to fire," Jack ordered his gun captains. Flame suddenly spouted along the lines of the enemy warship. "Open fire!" Jack barked without waiting for further orders from the bridge. The sharp crack of the four-inchers overlaid the rumble of enemy gunfire.

Just as *Rust* got off her third salvo, the ship heeled over in a sharp turn to port, heading almost directly at the Japanese ships. Jack's momentary puzzlement vanished as he glimpsed the boiling shoal waters of a reef astride their former course. The next few minutes were all noise and confusion. Salvos from the Japanese ships bracketed the destroyers and exploded on the Java shoreline beyond, but none scored hits. Jack could have sworn that his guns hit the enemy several times, although he could not be certain. Twice more the American column turned quickly to avoid reefs. Then, inexplicably, the Japanese ships turned away and ceased firing.

Smoke began to pour from the funnels of the American destroyers, covering the moonlit surface of the sea with a thick haze.

"Commodore's ordered a smoke screen," Hoskins passed to Jack. "We're going to run for it now."

"Guns report," Jack directed, bracing himself against the rail as the engine room worked up to maximum revolutions on the screws.

"You're not gonna believe this, Lieutenant," said Muldune a few moments later.

"What's that, Chief?"

"Best I can figure, we were in action about fifteen minutes, and we only had three guns engaged. We fired off sixty rounds of four-inch."

"I hope they hit something."

"They did their job," Muldune said with certainty. "We got away."

Standing at the back of the fire control platform, Jack watched the shapes of Bali and Java retreat with the horizon. He checked his watch and saw that it was 0230. Moving at close to thirty knots, the squadron would be over a hundred miles to the south by sunrise. For the first time in days, he relaxed, sure in his mind that they were going to escape.

WARREN BELL

CHAPTER 27

(One)
Blimbing Aerodrome
Eastern Java
Netherlands East Indies
1 March 1942

Garrit Laterveer opened a fresh pack of Lucky Strikes, took out a cigarette and passed the rest around the circle of pilots who were gathered about him. Even in the hour before dawn, it was stifling in the small ready room with the blackout curtains closed. He scanned the tired, drawn faces as lighters flared one after another, thinking that he must look as haggard as they. His entire squadron, or what was left of it, was here at Blimbing with the battered American 17th Pursuit Squadron. The Yank unit had lost so many of its senior officers that a first lieutenant now commanded it.

"The day we've all dreaded has finally come," Garrit announced gravely. "The Japs began landing on the beaches at Rembang just after midnight. We'll be going out with the Americans at dawn to strafe the landing craft and the troops in the beachhead. We'll keep at it as long as any of our planes can fly and our ammunition supply lasts. There's not much to say beyond that."

"Is it true that another Jap convoy is off Zwarte Gouden, Captain?" asked Sergeant Schulte.

"It would appear so," Garrit responded. He knew that the sergeant's young wife was in the oil port. "One of our submarines sighted an invasion force just off the *Parfum* estuary during the night."

Schulte cursed and pounded his fists together.

"We have to do the best we can," Garrit continued. "We still have the capability to do substantial damage to the enemy."

"Don't worry about us, Captain," said Moulders. "We'll follow you into hell if necessary."

"That may be exactly where we're going."

The ragged formation of Allied fighters was flying very low as they approached the coast. Iridescent green rice paddies whipped by just below with dizzying swiftness. The nine *Kittyhawks* of 17th Pursuit were leading. Garrit's planes followed in two flights, the four *Hurricanes* first and then his last four *Buffalos*. Garrit had the Merlin engine of his *Hurricane* throttled well back to keep from overrunning the American planes ahead.

As so often happened in combat, Garrit's mind was completely cool and clear. He knew that the odds were against his returning from this mission, but that seemed almost irrelevant now. The enemy was at the gates of his home. He had to protect his hearth.

The coastline came rushing to meet them. Out on the flat, blue water, Garrit could see at least thirty transport ships anchored off the beaches. Hundreds of boats were plying between the ships and the shore like swarms of obscene water bugs. Without thinking, his hands flipped the switch to activate the firing circuits.

"This is it," Garrit said to his pilots over the radio-telephone. "Remember, the Yanks take the beaches. We go for the landing craft."

Even as he spoke, the *Kittyhawks* peeled off and dived for the ant-like lines of Japanese soldiers on the snowy sands below. Tracers came floating up to meet them. The enemy already had his antiaircraft guns ashore!

Garrit nosed over and went for a line of square-bowed barges chugging toward the beach. He could see the electric flashes of antiaircraft guns winking from the ships ahead, but he ignored them and the tracers that were lacing the air about his plane. His whole attention was riveted on the gunsight and the landing craft that was rapidly filling it. Very gently, he squeezed the firing button.

Tracers leaped from the six guns in each wing to converge on the water just ahead of the barge. Then they went plunging up the length of the craft, leaving a path of shattered bodies and splintered wood. As the following planes took out the next few barges in the string, Garrit was already searching out another group to attack. He saw at once that it would not be so easy again. The neat lines of landing craft had broken up, and the individual boats were milling about in confusion. He stood the *Hurricane* on its wingtip and went roaring off after one boat that appeared larger than the others. Overhauling it rapidly, he made out the lines of a light tank inside. The fighting vehicle's automatic cannon was firing back as he bore in from the side and depressed his trigger again. Hundreds of bullets from his guns literally sawed the bow off the boat. It was settling as he pulled up and zoomed skyward again.

The sudden hammer blows of direct hits behind his cockpit shook the *Hurricane* for a moment as he barrel-rolled to pursue another barge. An icy nausea momentarily gripped his vitals, but no explosion followed. He dived again for the sea, heading straight for a boat crammed with infantry. The entire surface of the boat came alive with flashes. In the split second of clear visibility he had before his tracers slashed up the length of the craft, he saw that the soldiers inside were kneeling in phalanx formation, firing their rifles at him in volleys. Then his twelve machine guns lashed the barge like a scythe, splitting it lengthwise and whipping the water beneath into a bloody froth. After that, he lost count of the number of boats he went after. He was dimly aware of reports coming in from his other pilots as they swept back and forth across the anchorage. Incredibly, no enemy fighters appeared to halt the slaughter, but the antiaircraft guns took their toll. Pillars of oily flames along the beach marked the funeral pyres of several of the attacking aircraft. Garrit's guns finally stopped firing, and he realized that he was out of ammunition. Calling to his mates to reform, he turned inland and began to climb out of range of the Japanese guns. As the reports came in, he was shocked to find that only two of his *Buffalos* were left, but all the sturdy *Hurricanes* had come through. Setting a course for Blimbing, he flew at the greatest speed that the *Buffalos* could muster.

As he taxied to the revetment area, Garrit saw that only six of the *Kittyhawks* had made it back. The Americans were all clustered near a pair of heavy trucks. The Dutchman cut his engine and climbed out of his cockpit. Sergeant Van de Vanter was waiting for him on the ground.

"Give them all a full load of petrol and ammunition," Garrit instructed the dependable crew chief. "We'll be going back as soon as you can turn them around."

"The Yanks aren't going out again, sir," the sergeant replied with bitterness in his voice.

"What's that?" Garrit was incredulous.

"The trucks have come to take the Yanks away."

Garrit strode rapidly over to the knot of American fliers. As he neared the trucks, he recognized Harry Asher at the center of the group. "What's the meaning of this?" Garrit demanded.

"Orders came through from our headquarters to evacuate all pilots to Australia," Asher replied. "We're about to take off for Jogjakarta. The operational fighters are yours if you want them."

"Rats from a sinking ship?" Garrit said with sarcasm.

"Face it, Garrit," Asher said forcefully. "Java's as good as gone. This is gonna be a long, hard war. We'll need all the trained pilots we can get our hands on. We can't afford to throw them away on lost causes."

"For you, that may be true," Garrit said sadly, "but this is our home. Forgive us if we can't help being bitter. We gave everything we had to help out in Malaya, and now we're being abandoned, first by the British and now by you."

"Look, why don't you come with us? Better to keep fighting from Australia than to die for nothing."

"My orders are to fight to the last plane, and that's what I'll do. You Americans will have to take the war to the enemy."

The American pilots and ground crews were hastily cramming the last of their gear into their duffel bags. Their cooks passed around a final serving of good Java coffee and handed out apples and sandwiches. Then they began piling into the trucks.

"God bless you, you dumb Dutchman," Asher blurted out as he pumped Garrit's hand. Then he got into his sedan and closed the door.

As their allies faded into the distance, Garrit turned to his little knot of fliers. "All right, boys, we go back as soon as we finish rearming. I need five volunteers to fly the *Kittyhawks*."

Over a dozen hands shot up. He was just beginning to make his choices when the air-raid siren went off. Over its raucous whining, he made out the sound of Japanese aircraft engines. The enemy had finally discovered Blimbing.

As the pilots scattered to the trenches, Garrit sprinted to his

Hurricane. The armorers were frantically closing the hatches on its wings as he arrived, panting for breath. The fuel truck was still alongside, the hose stuck in the aircraft's fill spout.

"Get that damned thing out of here," Garrit screamed at the truck driver.

"But we've only started refueling," the man protested.

"There's no time." Garrit vaulted into the cockpit. "Now, get going. If the Japs hit that truck in here, we'll lose all the *Hurri's*."

Sergeant Van de Vanter crawled up onto the wing as Garrit hit the engine starter. "The guns are all ready, Captain," he reported. "Full load."

"Good man. Now get to shelter."

Gunning his engine, Garrit swung the *Hurricane* out onto the runway and taxied toward the far end. High above, the first enemy planes began to peel off. He recognized the spatted undercarriage of the Aichi navy dive-bombers. They reminded him of the German *Stukas*. Finally reaching the end of the runway, he whipped the Hawker fighter into the wind. Shoving the throttle all the way to the firewall, he willed the plane to take off. The engine was tired and overworked, but it was a Rolls Royce Merlin. The *Hurricane* gathered speed rapidly. Bombs started bursting all around, but he ignored them, pulling back on the stick and praying. Then the nose of the fighter snapped up, and he was airborne. He was barely ten feet off the ground when he retracted the landing gear.

The bomb bursts were at last below and behind him. He glanced quickly about the sky, searching for the hated *Zeros*, but none were in sight. The enemy apparently thought that the Allied air forces were finished. A grim smile crooked Garrit's lips. Now the hunters would become the hunted. He picked out an Aichi as it pulled out of its dive, locked onto its tail and quickly overtook it. Waiting until its ugly shape filled his gunsight, he cut loose on it.

The twelve 7.7-millimeter wing guns sent a storm of tracer zipping toward the dive-bomber, and Garrit guided them straight across the right wingroot. With almost ten thousand bullets per minute sawing through the duraluminum, the wing buckled upwards and tore away. The Aichi went into a flat spin and slammed into a sugar cane field, disintegrating in a ball of orange flame. It was Garrit's twenty-sixth kill, but he no longer thought of such things. Another Aichi flashed into view, and he went after it. Closing easily on the dive-bomber, he sent his tracers converging on its cockpit. The windscreen exploded, and with its pilot dead at the controls, the Japanese plane nosed over and flew into the ground.

Garrit circled, craning his neck in every direction in search of the enemy. Then he saw the survivors, eight black specks beating a hasty retreat in the direction of the Java Sea. He flew back over Blimbing, where dark plumes of smoke rose above the field. Making a low-level pass to inspect the damage, he saw that the P-40's and the other *Hurricanes* were shattered, flaming wrecks. Just as bad, the runway was badly cratered. If he put the *Hurricane* down, he would never get her up again. Checking his fuel gauge and making mental calculations, he concluded that, with a little luck, he could barely make Zwarte Gouden before his tanks went dry. He should be able to refuel there for one final sortie against the Japanese.

He flew on a direct compass heading toward the oil port, staying very low and hoping that his camouflage paint would hide him from any enemy planes lurking aloft. When he saw more clouds of smoke boiling skyward on the northern horizon, he guessed that the authorities must have fired the Zwarte Gouden oil fields. The fuel gauge was getting alarmingly low, but he thought that he could just make it. Then, without warning, the Merlin went dead.

It was eerie in the cockpit with only the whistling of the wind around the canopy to break the silence. Garrit banked the aircraft, searching for the main east-west highway. Then he picked it out, a black ribbon of asphalt between the glowing green of the rice paddies. Banking the powerless plane gently, he headed for the road as he cranked down the landing gear by hand. Lining up carefully on a mile-long straightaway, he made a perfect dead-stick landing.

He had hardly braked to a halt when a truckload of Javanese soldiers came around the bend ahead. As they scrambled out of their vehicle and rushed wildly toward him, he climbed out on the wing to meet them. Their noncom ran up, saluted smartly and reported that they were on their way to Zwarte Gouden. This suited Garrit's purposes exactly. He had the soldiers push the *Hurricane* under a grove of coconut palms then got into the truck with them. With any luck, he would be back in a couple of hours with enough petrol to fly a mission. As the Chevrolet bounced along the road, he suddenly realized how tired he was. He began to nod and fell asleep a few minutes later.

Garrit's head bounced off the windshield as the truck lurched to a stop. Dazed, he lay in a heap beneath the dashboard, only vaguely aware of a few scattered gunshots. Then the door flew open and rough hands dragged him out onto the road. He struggled up onto all fours, trying to stand. His vision began to clear, and his eyes focused on a pair of highly-polished paratrooper boots. Raising his eyes, he stared down the barrel of a Japanese machine carbine. The realization that his war was over hit him like a sledgehammer. Letting go completely, he sank back into unconsciousness.

(Two)
Wilhelmina Hotel
Zwarte Gouden, Java
Netherlands East Indies
1 March 1942

The shrill wailing of air raid sirens rattled Frank from slumber. From a distance, he heard the *crumph* of bombs and the rattle of antiaircraft cannon. Cinta came awake instantly and rolled naked from the bed, frantically gathering up her clothes before dashing to the bathroom. Frank got up and began dressing.

As the young lovers went out into the hall a few minutes later, they met Nicolaas and Tonia. The Dutchman scowled briefly at his disheveled daughter. "I just talked to Dijker on the phone," he said as they hurried to the elevator. "Jap paratroopers have seized the airfield. He's mobilizing his forces for a counterattack."

"There must be something I can do to help," said Frank.

"I'm going to the colonel's headquarters now to get permission to start my demolitions. You can come with me."

"Cinta and I will go to the hospital," said Tonia. "White women and children are to gather there in case of an attack."

"We'll not be coming back here?" asked Cinta, surprised.

"It's according to how the military situation develops," Nicolaas replied.   "Then I'm going back for more practical clothes and my medical gear." Cinta turned and made off for Nicolaas's suite.

"Wait!" Frank called after her, concerned for her safety.

"Let her go," Nicolaas interjected. "She's right. It's unlikely they'll bomb this close to the refinery anyway."

"I'm going for my clothes, too," said Tonia before following Cinta up the hall.

The two women returned in a little over five minutes. Cinta had changed into a blouse and skirt, and Tonia was wearing slacks. They both brought small suitcases, and Cinta had her medical bag.

"I've called the Shanghai Hotel to send my car," said Tonia. "I'll take Cinta with me."

Tonia's sedan was waiting at the hotel entrance. Other guests were streaming out around them as they paused before parting.

"Take care of yourselves," Nicolaas said, embracing the women in turn. "We'll come for you as soon as we can. If *Belle of Borneo* will still fly when the airfield's been cleared, we're going to leave at once."

"Don't do anything foolishly brave, Frank," Cinta said as she threw her arms around his neck and kissed him.

"Don't worry," he replied. "I'll stick to what I've been trained for."

Nicolaas and Frank found Dijker in his underground command post near the barracks. He was talking on the radio-telephone when they arrived.

"Can I start blowing up the refinery?" Nicolaas demanded as Dijker switched off his set.

"Wait here. Lembang has promised us an answer within the hour."

"Is there something I can do to help?" asked Frank.

Dijker thought for a moment before replying. "Can you spot for artillery?"

"That's a cruiser pilot's *forte*."

"The artillery liaison officer for my reaction force was injured in a motorcar accident on the way here. Will you take his place?"

"I don't speak Dutch."

"All my officers speak English. Let me put you in the picture."

Dijker showed Frank the location of the airfield on a map, then pointed to the spot where his artillery bunker dominated the plain. "You'll be riding in an armored car," he concluded. "I'll have you driven out to the assembly area."

(Three)
Skies Above the Java Sea
1 March 1942

Katsura Okuma checked his watch for perhaps the twentieth time within the last half-hour. As always when he was waiting for battle, the minutes were creeping by at a snail's pace. He leaned forward and tapped the pilot of the Douglas DC-3 on the shoulder. The Army Air Force captain pushed up his right earphone so that he could hear.

"How long to the Java coast?" asked Okuma.

"Another twenty minutes, Colonel. Don't worry. We'll put you on target precisely as scheduled."

Okuma was not worried. His command was well drilled on the requirement for split-second timing during this operation. He looked out the window of the former Dutch airliner and checked the formation spread out behind it. Fifteen of the aircraft were Nakajima-built DC-2's. The other ten were Kawasaki K-46's. Until recently, all had been passenger liners with *Dai Nippon*. Like Okuma's command ship, all now wore KNILM livery, a ruse to confuse the enemy.

"Contact with Major Nishazawa, Colonel," the radio operator said. "Drop completed. Resistance slight. Securing airfield."

Okuma's face broke into a smile. "Acknowledge receipt," he ordered. "Tell him to proceed according to plan."

Up ahead, Toyama's convoy was closing with the coast. A squadron of cruisers stood by to shield the transports from enemy surface forces. A small carrier was protecting against the unlikely event of air attack. From this point on, clockwork execution was required. Within an hour, the transports would drop anchor off the Parfum River and the accompanying Military Landing Craft Carriers would disgorge schools of blunt-bowed boats to take the assault troops up the broad river to Zwarte Gouden.

"Java coast in sight, Colonel," the pilot yelled.

Okuma stepped forward between the cockpit seats and peered through the windshield. In the distance, he could see thick, green jungle behind a fringe of white beach. Far off on the horizon, blue-green mountains towered up toward the heavens. Except for a few, distant thunderheads, the brilliantly blue sky was clear. Wind was negligible.   Weather could not have been more perfect for a parachute drop. The transport planes flew directly over the fleet, so low that he could see soldiers waving to the aircraft from the decks of the ships.

"Time to hook up, sir," said the pilot.

Making one final check of the weapons in his chest pack, Okuma snapped it firmly shut, checked his harness, and then went back into the passenger compartment.   His felt a warm flush of satisfaction as he surveyed the troops in the drop line.   He had chosen Captain Sakai's company for the main objective because they had been more aggressive in training than the others.   They were the toughest of the tough, all old China veterans who had become inured to killing by conducting bayonet practice on live prisoners.   Okuma joked with his men as he made his way to the front of the line, where he snapped his static ripcord strap to the rail. His runner hooked up directly behind him.   Spontaneously, the soldiers began to sing, their words sending shivers of patriotism up Okuma's spine.

Umi yukaba, mizuku kabane,
Yama yukaba, kusamusu kabane,
Okimi no he ni koso shiname.
Kaerimi wa seji.
(Across the sea, corpses soaking in the water,
Across the mountains, corpses heaped upon the grass,
We shall die only for the Emperor.
We shall never look back.)

Okuma nodded to an aircrewman, and the man opened the door. Down below, the thick mangrove swamp swept by at dizzying speed. As the plane edged out over the river, the channel buoys were clearly visible.   Then a light came on over the door, and Okuma moved into the opening. The refinery was dead ahead. He took a deep breath and stepped out into space.

Okuma felt the brief exhilaration of free fall, and then the bone-jarring jerk of his parachute opening ended his reverie.   He was directly over the target area and floating toward the center of the cleared space. All about and above him, other parachutes were blossoming, white flowers against the blue background of the sky. The transports swept over in precise "V" formations, disgorging stick after stick of paratroopers.

The ground came rushing up to meet him. A parachute drop from two hundred meters left little time for reflection. He flexed his knees and made a textbook landing on the soft grass. Collapsing the parachute and shucking the harness were but a moment's work. He sprinted to the shelter of the berm, the predesignated command post assembly point. The field was covered with billowing silk now. Noncoms were gathering their squads and setting off to their objectives. Ripping open his pack, he took out his submachine gun and snapped a curved 30-round magazine into place. Leaving the stock folded, he slung the weapon across his chest.

As the last man hit the ground, two final "vics" swept past, dropping heavy weapons containers with cargo canopies. All but one, which opened late to splash in the river, landed in the drop zone.

The roar of the transports' engines faded, and the din of battle from the airfield could be heard. The discriminating ear could distinguish the dry rattle of small arms fire, the crump of mortars and the deep-throated roar of heavier artillery. The drone of small aircraft was barely discernible. Looking up, Okuma saw the sun glint off the silver wings of Navy *Zeros*.

Okuma's runner joined him, and then his two-man radio crew appeared, carrying their set and generator on a litter. They reported that the equipment was in good working order.

Captain Sakai dashed up. "All accounted for, Colonel," the company commander reported. "Only one injury, a broken leg. The units are proceeding to their targets."

"Very well. What was in the container that fell in the river?"

"Anti-tank satchel charges, two machine guns and a platoon mortar. We can do without them with no difficulty. Not much chance of having to fight tanks in here."

"Carry on," Okuma dismissed Sakai.

Okuma stayed put for over fifteen minutes, taking reports from runners and marking the battle progress on his map board. His men were sweeping unopposed through the maze of pipes, tanks, distillation units and condensers. Only a few BPM security guards were encountered, and the tough *paras* easily dealt with them. The airborne engineers quickly disarmed the demolition charges.

"Major Nishazawa reports being heavily counterattacked by tanks," the radio operator relayed to his commander.

"Order him to hold fast," Okuma replied. Tanks! It was a nasty surprise, but one for which his men were trained and equipped. Nishawaza's troops had anti-tank grenades and satchel charges to complement their twenty-millimeter Type 97's.

Sakai's runner appeared. "The Captain reports the refinery grounds are secured," the man blurted out breathlessly. "All demolition charges are deactivated."

"Good," said Okuma. He checked his Swiss wristwatch. His unit was ahead of schedule. The flying boats were due within a matter of minutes, so he told the radio operator to order the Kawanishis to put down. Then he packed up his staff and headed for the refinery operations building, which he had chosen as his headquarters.

Out over the river, the first Kawanishi came skimming in across the water. Once down, the pilot cut back on his throttles and taxied toward the docks. Okuma was in the doorway of the office building when he heard a locomotive-like roar pass overhead. He instinctively ducked, for he knew the sound well from China-- incoming artillery. The salvo plunged into the river beyond the Kawanishi, sending towering columns of water skyward. Okuma guessed that it was medium artillery, at least 105-millimeter.

The flying boat rocked violently in the waves, buffeted by torrents of water from the shell splashes. The pilot poured on power, valiantly dashing for the docks. From far off, Okuma heard the muted bellow of the guns. Seconds later, the rush of shells again rent the air. The second salvo fell directly on the Kawanishi, disintegrating the plane in a flash of exploding shells and gasoline. A mushroom of black smoke soared upward as pieces of debris rained down upon the river. Then the water quieted, and no trace of the aircraft or the platoon of soldiers it carried remained.

"Get the radio working," Okuma snapped at his operator. "Order the remaining flying boats to circle downriver and await orders."

Okuma was dumbfounded. How had the Hollanders reacted so swiftly and with such accuracy? They could not have been informed by anyone inside the refinery. One of the first actions his troops had taken was to cut the telephone trunk line to the city.

When the siren went off announcing the dawn attack on the airfield, Frans Memelink, the graveyard shift supervisor on Catalytic Cracking Unit Number One, remained at his post. His Javanese workers all high-tailed it for one of the beehive-shaped bomb shelters, but Frans figured that Cat One was the safest place he could be. The Japanese had not put a bomb inside the refinery yet, and they were not likely to start now. They wanted the place intact for their own use. Instead of hiding, Frans climbed to the highest platform on Cat One to get a better view of the action at the airfield. He had been a ringside spectator to Okuma's airdrop forty minutes later. As he watched the paratroopers fan out through the refinery, Frans's first reaction was to feel like a trapped rat. He flattened himself against the tower and remained motionless for several minutes. Down below, he could hear the soldiers jabbering in Japanese as they tore out the demolition charges Nicolaas van Wely had placed the day before. Then their footsteps retreated, and the tower was silent again. Frans edged over to a communications box and lifted the receiver of the fire phone, hearing a buzz in the instrument as the instrument in the firehouse rang. Then the night fire chief came on the line.

Frans talked fast, telling his friend about the Japanese and asking him to call Army headquarters. The fireman came back with the word that the outside telephone lines were dead. There was one last chance, however: the direct line to the city fire department, a separate circuit buried in armored conduit for protection. Within moments, Frans was talking to the city fire chief, trying to get him to comprehend what was happening. When Okuma's paratroopers broke in and slaughtered the refinery firehouse crew, they did not bother to destroy the switchboard, knowing that the cable to the outside world had been cut.

CHAPTER 28

(One)
Zwarte Gouden Aerodrome
Netherlands East Indies
1 March 1942

Frank was standing with his head outside the turret of his armored car when his radio operator tugged on his leg to signal that new orders were coming in. He ducked down into the vehicle to confer, saving his life. A Japanese sniper's bullet pinged off the hatch within inches of his scalp.

"That was a near thing," he said to his Dutch operator. "What's up?"

Dijker was about to regroup his forces to move back across the river, and all unit commanders were to report to a conference at the base of the airfield control tower.

Frank was filled with admiration for the Dutchman's tactical skill. The colonel had fought German *panzers* in Europe, and he had learned his lessons well. His attack on the airfield was right out of General Guderian's textbook. Deploying his motorized infantry to contain the enemy and relieve pressure on the Australian antiaircraft troops who had been putting up a last stand, he massed his company of Marmon-Harrington tanks and two companies of armored dragoons for a sweep straight up the field--a classic *Scherpunkt*. The fighting had been fierce, but the enemy was ill prepared to deal with massed armor. In less than two hours of battle, those Japanese forces that survived were driven back into the mangrove swamp to the north. With the combat too close to employ artillery, Frank had joined the general melee, firing the machine gun in his turret at anything that moved along the Japanese lines.

The Dutchmen's victory was total, but not without casualties. Every aircraft on the field was destroyed. Nicolaas's *Belle of*

Borneo was a sorry sight, her back broken by an explosion and her once-shiny skin blackened by fire. Nicolaas had waited too late to flee. Now he would have to find an alternate way to get out of Java.

Most of the unit commanders were already at the base of the tower when Frank arrived. They were clustered about a pair of captured artillery pieces, tiny things with barrels no more than two feet long.

"Don't let their appearance fool you," Dijker was telling his officers. "The 70-millimeter battalion gun is one of the best of its type in the world, and it's light enough to be broken down and man-packed."

Just then, the radio operator from Dijker's command car stuck out his head and called for the colonel. Dijker strode quickly to the vehicle and talked into his headset for a moment. "Lieutenant Rhea," he said loudly, "come over here at once." When Frank reached his side, he continued, "Do we have any four-engine flying boats operating with our forces?"

"No, sir. The only four-engine jobs out here are Jap Kawanishis."

"Thank you. That's all for now." As Frank turned to go, Dijker returned to his microphone. "Tell Major Hoek to open fire on the docks," he ordered then climbed into his command car. Several minutes later, he came back carrying his map board.

"Gentlemen," Dijker said to his assembled officers, "it seems that we're up against a clever enemy. While we've been clearing the airfield, another group of parachutists seized the refinery."

A murmur of surprise shot through the group.

"I've dispatched Major Snoek's 41st Java Battalion to surround the refinery grounds. We must move back and retake it before enemy forces off the coast come upriver. I've had no report from Lieutenant DeGraff's torpedo boats, so we don't know how much time we have." He went on to explain his plans for a forced march to the oil works to attack and drive out the invaders.

"One more thing, Lieutenant Rhea," Dijker said as the officers broke for their units. "We won't be able to use Major Hoek's guns so close to the city. Better bring along these Jap pieces. See Major MacIntosh, the Australian commander, about the loan of some gunners."

Back at the refinery, Okuma had established his command post on the flat roof of the administration building, from which he had a panoramic view of the perimeter. As soon as the radio came on-line again, Nishazawa reported that he had been driven off the airfield into the swamp. He had less than a hundred men left. Okuma told him to lie low until pressure slackened before infiltrating the airfield again. Then he sent his runner to find Captain Sakai.

Okuma spread out his map and looked at the area about three miles downstream. Just before the parachute drop, he had noticed a low bluff behind a long sandbar. There was clearly firm ground in the vicinity, and if there was some sort of path through the jungle, it might be an ideal place to bring down his Kawanishis. He badly needed the remainder of his command if he was to hold the refinery.

When Sakai arrived, Okuma pointed out the bluff and ordered him to send a squad-sized recon force to find a way to the site. They were to take a radio so that they could call down the flying boats then guide the reinforcements to the refinery. The captain darted off to pick his men.

A lookout spotted movement at the edge of the *kampong* to the south. Through his binoculars, Okuma made out enemy troops among the buildings. The distinctive Dutch steel helmets were easily recognized. He toyed with the idea of calling in an air strike but decided to wait. Until his reinforcements arrived, he preferred to postpone the fighting. Sakai's troops had taken up strong defensive positions among the refinery works, but they might be too few to hold off a determined attack. The ferocity of the Hollanders' reaction at the airfield had been unexpected. Better to put off any further shocks as long as possible.

About forty-five minutes after Sakai's patrol was dispatched, the sergeant in charge reported that they were on the bluffs. They had discovered a concealed road leading directly from the refinery and unmanned underground bunkers mounting antitank guns overlooking the river. The first flying boat was just landing.

Okuma gave orders to bring up the new forces to wait at the edge of the jungle until a coordinated attack could be mounted to pierce the Dutch troops now ringing the refinery. He was beginning to get worried, for there was increasing enemy activity around his perimeter. Calling up the commander of the Navy air units overhead, he asked for air strikes on anything moving on the roads to the south.

Just over forty minutes after leaving the airfield, Dijker was in the *kampong* south of the refinery, marshaling his forces for a counterattack. Nicolaas was at his elbow with the detailed drawings of the oil works he had used for his demolition plan, while Frank stood by with a knot of staff officers. Dijker now had two battalions of native infantry manning the north and east boundaries of the refinery. His mobile troops were massed in the village. His plan was simple: the tanks and dragoons would drive through the plant from north to south, closely supported by dismounted infantry and Frank's impromptu troop of infantry guns. They would stay in line abreast, pausing to destroy all Japanese strongpoints encountered. That way, he could be certain that no enemy troops remained behind his lines.

Just as the counterattack was forming up, enemy dive bombers struck. Nosing over at five thousand feet, the Aichis came screaming down in an attack reminiscent of the *Stuka* attacks in Europe. They met with a hot welcome. The six Bofors guns and four self-propelled twenty-millimeter flak pieces in Dijker's force threw up a cone of fire at the bombers. One of the Aichis burst into flames and came tumbling earthward. The others released their bombs early and beat a hasty retreat to the coast.

Up on the roof of the office building, Okuma cursed the pilots bitterly. They should have pressed their attack home! He had seen tanks in the *kampong,* and he knew now that he could not hold the refinery with the forces at hand. His reinforcements were still coming ashore on the sandbar, and it would be close to an hour before they would be of any help. He called Captain Sakai to the command post and quickly reshaped their defensive strategy. They must delay the enemy as long as possible while minimizing damage to the refinery installations. If they could hold the Dutchmen inside the oil plant, the amphibious forces coming upriver might arrive in time to prevent its destruction.

From the stirring along the enemy front, Okuma was sure that the attack would come soon. As he waited, another report came in from Major Nishazawa. He had collected almost a hundred survivors of the airfield attack force in the swamps. Okuma gave him new orders to make a forced march to the general vicinity of the Hollanders' artillery emplacements. Those guns had to be destroyed if Toyama's amphibious forces were to come directly to his assistance.

Okuma heard the *crump* of heavy mortars and instinctively ducked. Mortar bombs began falling all around him on the roof. One close blast lifted his body and slammed him against the parapet wall. As he dragged himself to his feet, he saw that his radio crew and their equipment were blown to bits. His runner was at his elbow, unwounded. The two of them dashed for the staircase and down into the building. They did not see the line of tanks burst out of the *kampong* to break down the perimeter fence with their tracks.

Sheltered with his team of Aussie gunners behind an armored car, Frank watched the attack go in from a field outside the village. The Marmon-Harringtons rumbled toward the refinery works with their turret machine guns blazing. The armored trucks with the dragoons closely followed the tanks, and he could see the shapes of Dutch infantrymen darting along behind the screen of armor. The Japanese soon opened up with everything they had. Twenty-millimeter tracers began zipping toward the tanks, only to ricochet harmlessly into the air. Then one of their gunners started aiming for the tracks. By the time the tanks reached the first maze of piping, two of them were immobilized. Frank banged on the armored car then moved forward with his guns. As the tank commanders began picking out the enemy strongpoints and machine gun nests from the muzzle blasts of the weapons, they swung their turrets around to bear and fired round after round of 37-millimeter high explosive. Catching up with the dragoons, Frank pointed out targets for his gunners. The Diggers laid their tiny pieces over open sights, firing flat-trajectory at the Japanese antitank guns. Fifteen minutes after battle was joined, they knocked out the last one.

Once the fighting moved into the maze of oil tanks, towers and pipes, the armored vehicles lost their ability to maneuver. The job of digging out the Japanese *paras* fell to the infantry. The flexible tactics employed by the enemy made the going extremely rough. They would hold a position until the last possible moment, pouring a hail of automatic weapons fire into the advancing Dutchmen, then abandon that point and sprint to another farther back within the plant. Without the steady flow of information coming in from Frans Memelink on Cat One, it might have taken Dijker all day to root them out. A constant stream of runners fed the locations of strong points to Frank, who then blasted them with his little cannon. After an hour and a half of combat, the remnants of the enemy force were cornered in a pocket near the northwest boundary of the refinery.

Nicolaas remained at Dijker's side during the whole of the fight to regain the refinery. They were driving through the recaptured portion of the plant on the way to where the last Japanese holdouts were pinned down when an urgent signal came in from DeGraff. Patrolling downstream with his motor torpedo boats, he had stumbled onto a convoy of about forty transports anchored off the mouth of the river. An armada of landing craft was already headed toward the shore. He was attacking with torpedoes.

"How long will it take to set new charges and wreck this place?" Dijker asked Nicolaas.

"Half a day, at least. We'll have to round up more explosives."

"We don't have that kind of time. Show my officers what to do, and we'll blast as much as we can with the tanks and Frank's infantry guns."

"What about the aviation gasoline? There's over two hundred thousand metric tons in the tanks by the wharves."

"We can't burn it with our troops in here. We'd all roast."

"We could crank up the pumps to the tanker loading pipes and dump it in the river."

"Do it now."

In the pocket at the northern end of the refinery, Okuma and Captain Sakai were planning a breakout. They believed that they could cut their way through the containing native troops along the riverbank, but their remaining mortar crew and three of their seven machine gun teams would have to fight a *gyokusai*--a sacrificial battle. The mortar would remain in place and blow a pathway through the enemy lines while the three machine guns pinned down the Dutchmen on the refinery side. The plan lacked finesse, but it was the best they could come up with under the circumstances. It at least offered some chance of saving about forty crack *paras* for the continuing battle. The slackening pressure from the South encouraged Okuma. The enemy tanks were pulling back to regroup.

"If we don't make it, our souls shall meet at the Yasukuni Shrine," Sakai said solemnly when the orders had been passed. The shrine was a temple for Japan's fallen heroes.

"Don't worry about the afterlife," Okuma snorted in return. "Cut your way out through the Dutchmen."

As the breakout party assembled, the sacrificial gun teams opened up with a withering fire along the south perimeter. As the mortar began pounding the edge of the jungle, Sakai's remaining *paras* rose up and dashed toward the trees, firing furiously as they ran. The colonial troops in front of them broke before the vigorous assault, melting back into the undergrowth. With Okuma and Sakai bringing up the rear, the paratroopers burst through this small opening in the Dutch cordon, dashing off to the north. It was all over in a matter of moments. Dutch officers rallied the scattered colonial troops and reclosed the pocket. The Japanese rearguard sold their lives dearly but were eventually wiped out to a man.

Nicolaas managed to assemble over a dozen of his Dutch supervisors. Under their direction, the turret guns of the tanks and Frank's gun troop began firing at the critical equipment of the refinery. The waterfront pumps were going full bore, sending a thick stream of AVGAS gushing into the river.

Dijker was regrouping his units to counter the amphibious force that was coming up the Parfum. He knew now that there was little chance of repulsing the Japanese. His main task was to hold them long enough for Nicolaas to cripple the refinery. He dispatched one of his native battalions to pursue the small party of paratroopers who had escaped and to occupy the prepared positions at the big bend of the river. The machine guns and antitank guns in the bunkers should wreak havoc with the wooden invasion barges. In the meantime, he was reforming his tanks and armored infantry to use as a reaction force when the amphibious threat materialized.

"Report from a lookout," Dijker's radio operator shouted. "Boats sighted on the river."

"Damn!" Dijker swore. "I didn't expect them this soon." He turned quickly to his runner. "Find the American Lieutenant. Tell him to get to the top of the catalytic tower. I want him to spot for out artillery."

Fifteen minutes later, Frank stood beside Frans Memelink high up on Cat One, his chest heaving from the exertion of the climb. Picking up the fire phone the Dutchman had used all morning, he checked out the circuits. Major Huygen at Dijker's fixed command post was at the other end of the line, waiting to relay orders to Hoek's guns.

Frank lifted his binoculars and looked downriver. The size of the approaching force was staggering. From the minesweeper at the point of the formation to the big bend in the river, the surface of the water was covered with square-bowed landing craft. He checked his map and did some quick calculations, finding that the lead boats were already within range of Hoek's 105-millimeter pieces. Reporting the coordinates of the minesweeper to Huygen, he stood by to spot the fall of shot.

From far up the valley, Frank heard the boom of Hoek's big cannon. The roar of shells in flight passed high overhead. Plunging into the river astern of the minesweeper, they sent tall columns of water hurling skyward. Frank stood galvanized by the scene in his binoculars. Great sheets of fire sprang out from the explosions, spreading with incredible speed until over two miles of the river was enveloped in flames. Ignited by the artillery shells, the skim of AVGAS on the water was now a blazing inferno, trapping hundreds of Japanese barges. The wooden boats began to blaze as their coxswains vainly tried to steer for the shore. Thousands of Japanese troops were dying in the inferno.

"Relay to the Colonel that he ought to come up and take a look," Frank told Major Huygen. "The AVGAS we dumped in the river is on fire."

Katsura Okuma viewed the northern fringe of the holocaust with rage in his heart. Almost an entire brigade of his countrymen was being incinerated alive out on the water. The Dutchmen must be made to pay dearly for this! Then he shook himself. He could not allow anger to cloud his reason. Even as the enemy was striking this telling blow against the invasion forces, the seeds of his ultimate defeat were being sewn. Major Nishazawa reported that he had located the position of the Hollanders' artillery. His hundred-man unit would be there in twenty minutes.

Okuma had already reversed Japanese fortunes north of the refinery. The survivors of Sakai's company linked up with the troops from the Kawanishis about a mile from the breakout point. Together, they ambushed and routed the pursuing colonial battalion, capturing eight big trucks in operating condition. Okuma came on to the bluffs, intent on contacting the amphibious force with the radio there. He arrived too late to save the assault brigade. But quickly establishing communications with the following wave downstream, he arranged for its troops to come ashore at the big sandbar. Using the hidden roads through the jungle, Okuma planned to lead them in a sweep to outflank the Dutch forces.

A knot of men stood on the platform of Cat One watching the fiery hell on the Parfum. Dijker was there with Nicolaas, Frank and a soldier they'd brought along to search the skies for aircraft.

"We'd better shut down the pumps," Nicolaas observed, "or else that fire will come right back up to the pipes."

"Good thinking," Dijker observed. To the colonel, the swift turn of events simply meant that he had more time to destroy the refinery. He had no hope of any part of Java holding out now. In the last half hour, he had learned that the Japanese had put a large force ashore at the western tip of Java. The fall of Batavia was imminent. In the east, another army had invaded the beaches at Kragan. He also received a piece of news he thought best to withhold from Frank for the present. The American was too valuable to chance upsetting him. Dijker left Frank up on the tower and went back to his task at hand--freeing his armor to reform his reaction force. He was beginning to worry about the battalion he had sent in pursuit of the Japanese survivors. He had received no report yet that the river bend defenses were manned.

At that moment, Okuma was in a bunker on the river bluffs conferring with Brigadier General Shinada, commander of the second wave of the invasion. The general's troops were already pouring ashore onto the sandbar to ford the narrow shallows and form up under the trees. Captain Sakai's patrols had just found a route through the jungle to the oilfields east of Zwarte Gouden. It offered the opportunity for a concealed movement to outflank the Dutch forces and pin them against the river. Okuma outlined the possibility to Shinada, who snapped it up immediately. Okuma volunteered to lead the thrust with the remnants of his *rakkasan-butai*, who were standing by in the Dutch trucks. They were taking the four 47-millimeter antitank guns they had found in the bunkers with them.

An hour later, Okuma's troops were sweeping unopposed through the western suburbs of Zwarte Gouden, closing in on the refinery. As yet, the Dutch had not discovered their presence. In a few minutes, the enemy units in the oil plant would be surrounded.

Okuma decided to go up onto the roof of one of the taller buildings to get a better look. His advance patrols had moved past the city hospital, an imposing, three-storied structure, a few minutes before. It would make a good observation post. Bringing along his radio crew and a squad of *rakkasan-butai,* he vaulted up the steps to the hospital entrance.

The lobby was an absolute bedlam. Japanese soldiers were running amok, smashing equipment, bayoneting and clubbing wounded Dutchmen and chasing female orderlies and nurses. Okuma was incensed. Didn't these idiots realize that the facility would shortly be needed for their own wounded? He grabbed a senior sergeant, dressed the man down severely and told him to restore order. Then he demanded to be taken to the officer responsible for this madness. Another noncom led Okuma's party to an office just off the main lobby.

The overweight lieutenant who was sitting on the edge of a desk did not even notice Okuma at first. His attention was riveted on the naked, blond-haired girl who was kneeling between his feet. Okuma saw that her pale blue eyes held an expression of abject terror, and no wonder. The private who was standing behind her had a knife at her throat.

"*Kiuotsuke!*" Okuma shrieked in cold fury. "Attention."

The two men snapped upright, the private nicking the girl's throat in his surprise. He released her hair, and she collapsed sobbing onto the floor. The lieutenant was thunderstruck.

"Incompetent swine!" Okuma raged and struck the officer hard across the face. "The enemy remains to be defeated, and you waste your time with this *gaijin* whelp while your men destroy equipment our medics will need. Get your ass out of here and get them under control before I have you shot on the spot for dereliction of duty. There is to be no more raping, and I hold you personally responsible for the safety of the medical equipment."

The lieutenant saluted and dashed off, buttoning his trousers. Okuma ordered one of his *rakkasan-butai* to bandage the girl's neck and give her back her clothes. Then he went looking for the staircase to the roof.

Cinta let out a sigh of relief as she finished closing a nasty abdominal wound in a Dutch corporal. Closing her eyes, she rewarded herself with a brief moment of relaxation. She had been in the operating room for over three hours, working on a steady stream of military and civilian casualties. Of the hospital staff, only two doctors reported for duty that morning. The three of them were barely able to treat the wounded at a rate faster than they were being brought in.

"Doctor!" Catherine screamed as she burst into the room, snapping Cinta awake. "Doctor, you have to stop them! The Japanese are murdering the patients!"

Cinta rushed out into the post-op ward behind Catherine, stripping off her bloodstained rubber gloves as she went. She recoiled in horror at what she found there. The place was a slaughterhouse. Packs of Japanese were moving from bed to bed, butchering the wounded soldiers with their long bayonets. Her first thought was to find someone with the power to stop the carnage. *An officer. I must find an officer.* Darting out into the hall, she ran full tilt into a squad of enemy soldiers.

The storm troopers ringed her in, cackling derisively as they drove her in circles with their bayonets. They had the eyes of predatory cats, cruel and menacing. Hysteria clawed at the core of her sanity, shredding the last vestiges of her composure. The soldiers backed her into a corner. Two of them slung their rifles and seized her by the arms, while another ripped off her cap and surgical mask. Their stench of sweat and fresh blood turned her stomach, sending vomit boiling up her throat. A corporal unsnapped the bayonet from the barrel of his rifle and stepped forward to grab a handful of her hair and pinion her head, his pockmarked face so close that she could smell rotting fish on his breath. Bringing his blade up against her throat, he pricked through her skin with its needle-sharp point. She stopped breathing, sure that the next moment would be her last. Then the corporal turned the long knife down and slid it under the yoke of her operating gown. The fabric parted easily to the razor edge of the knife as he slashed downward through the lower hem of the garment. A few more quick strokes of the blade, and rough hands were snatching away the last scraps of her underclothing.

"Don't! Oh, please, please, don't!" she begged instinctively, knowing all the while that her pleas were in vain.

The soldiers laughed uproariously at her babbling. Determined to fight them with all of her strength, she tried desperately to pull free as the men on either side pawed at her body.

"*Baku da yo!*" the noncom shrieked in rage. "Stupid idiot!" He jabbed his fist up under her rib cage, slamming the air from her lungs. Her whole torso exploded with searing agony as she desperately struggled to get back her breath. Drowning in a sea of pain, she slipped into unconsciousness.

When her mind drifted back to awareness, she found that they had put her on a gurney, her wrists and ankles bound to the side rails. She heard a shrill keening, and it was several moments before she realized that it sprang from her own lips. Then something snapped inside her head, and a trance-like calm settled over her. She seemed to be floating outside her body, observing what the men were doing rather than experiencing it. Their raucous laughter sounded far away; their movements appeared inordinately slow. She accepted as inevitable that they would violate her in turn, slacking their rage and battle euphoria with the pleasures of her body. Somehow, she must endure the abuse and survive.

The soldiers howled with glee and egged on their corporal as he mounted the cart and positioned himself above her.

"*Tomemas* (stop)!" A sharp voice of command snapped the soldiers to attention. Their faces reflected surprise, then outright fear. The corporal fell clumsily off the gurney before jumping to his feet, his trousers bunched about his ankles.

Four men clad in paratrooper battle dress moved into Cinta's field of vision. A tall, brawny officer with a submachine gun slung across his chest stalked over to the would-be rapists and began to berate them. Whatever he said was obviously scathing, for their faces flinched as if struck by physical blows. Then the officer stomped his foot and shouted, and they all saluted and ran off down the hall.

The officer said something to one of the *paras*, and the man picked up a sheet to cover Cinta's nakedness. Two others cut the lashings that held her down. Clutching the sheet to her quivering body, she sat up on the cart. She was dumbfounded to recognize Katsura Okuma's face beneath the German parachutists' helmet.

"I apologize for this outrage, Doctor van Wely," said Okuma. "Our troops are overwrought because of atrocities committed by your people against their comrades. I shall restore order, and there will be no further trouble. How many white women are in the building?"

"Over fifty," she barely croaked. Her body was now shaking violently, and she knew that she was on the threshold of shock. "I'm sorry, Mister Okuma, but I don't know your rank. How should I address you?"

"*Chusa*--lieutenant colonel. Is there a place where we can assemble all the women for safekeeping?"

"Perhaps in one of the empty wards upstairs."

"I'll leave two of my men to assure your safety. Gather the women at once and take them to that ward. I have a battle to fight. When it's over, I'll see that you're properly cared for."

Okuma jubilantly vaulted up the last of the stairs to the roof. He was confident that victory was but hours from his grasp, and now the Van Wely bitch was under his control! The incident in the hall had affected him much more than he had let show. Lust had coursed through his veins at the sight of the naked Dutchwoman. As soon as the battle was over, she would be his for the taking, the delights promised by her splendid body at his disposal for as long as they interested him. Had not General Toyama promised him his pick of the *gaijin* women? He knew now that Shirai had been right all along--she was much too valuable to be wasted on enlisted men. What a game of cat-and-mouse he would play with her before crushing her spirit, perhaps even seeing how far she would let him go of her own free will. He had had no chance to exercise his seductive skills since leaving Europe. But first, there were the Dutch forces to be dealt with.

From high atop Cat One, Frank saw that Dijker was holding another council of war. Their situation was deteriorating rapidly. He'd lost

contact with Major Hoek's artillery a half hour before, but at least
the line to Major Huygen at the command post was still open.

The knot of officers around Dijker broke up, the men moving in
haste back to their units. The tanks started concentrating near the
Krupp armored trucks, and the Aussie gunners hooked their Bofors
guns up to their tractors. It was obvious that the force would soon
move. Frank was about to ask Major Huygen what was happening
when the Dutch private who had been scanning the skies touched his
arm and pointed to the north. Frank took the glasses and peered
intently toward the horizon. The black specks against the pale blue
sky came into focus. Four "vics" of Aichi divebombers were
approaching with a dozen *Zero* escorts.

Frank dropped his gaze to the river bend almost as an
afterthought. Cold terror stopped his breath for a moment, for
framed in the binoculars was the forepart of a *Hubuki* class destroyer
coming on at high speed. Moments later, a second destroyer
appeared. He lifted the phone and told Huygen, who passed word
from Dijker to come down at once. The refinery was being
evacuated.

"How far along did we get?" the colonel was asking Nicolaas as
Frank approached.

"We hardly dented the main stills. I'd need heavy explosives to
take them out. I'd say that it'll take six or seven weeks to get the
plant back into production."

"Excuse me, Colonel," Frank interrupted. "Did you get my
message about the destroyers coming upriver?"

"Good Lord, no! I've been away from my radio."

Frank gave a quick summary of what he had seen.

"Let's set the river on fire again," Nicolaas proposed. "We
should burn that AVGAS anyway. Maybe we can damage the piers
as well."

"Do it quickly," said Dijker. "We've got to get moving. When
that's done, get the hell out of Java. And take your daughter with
you. I'm releasing you."

"It may be too late, but I'll sure have a go at it. May I take
Lieutenant Rhea along? The Americans will be needing all their
pilots.

"You might as well," Dijker allowed. "There's not much more
he can do here. I'd head for Tjilatjap. The Japs are already ashore

at Kragon. You can't reach Soerabaja." He turned to Frank. "There's something I should have told you earlier, Lieutenant. You probably owe your life to the *Zero* pilot who shot you down. The Japs sank *Houston* and *Perth* in Sunda Strait the night you got here. It was in our last message from Batavia."

CHAPTER 29

(One)
Zwarte Gouden Hospital
Central Java
1 March 1942

C inta was still half dazed and trembling in shock as the two paratroopers herded the white women of Zwarte Gouden into the upstairs ward. Tonia managed to get her into some clothes from her suitcase –a pair of tan slacks and a white *kabaja* blouse--and guide her up the stairs. The hundred or so women sorted themselves out and sat on the empty beds. Everyone was too afraid to speak except in whispers. A number were silently crying. The guards closed the doors behind them and took up station outside. The women could hear Japanese soldiers stomping around on the roof overhead.

"You need to get hold of yourself," Tonia said softly to Cinta, who was staring blankly ahead. "We'll have to keep our wits about us if we hope to survive."

"I'm trying," Cinta shot back panic lacing her voice. "They stripped me naked. They were going to rape me."

"But they weren't allowed to," Tonia said soothingly. "You're here, and you're alive. We have to decide what to do now."

"What can we do? We're prisoners."

"For the moment. We have to be alert to any chance to free ourselves."

Cinta squared her shoulders and closed her eyes. Her face took on an expression of extreme concentration. Her quivering subsided, and after a few minutes stopped altogether.

The sounds of footfalls on the roof moved in the direction of the stairwell and then faded. A few minutes later, orders barked in Japanese could be heard through the door, then more receding footsteps. An eerie quiet settled over the ward.

The women began to cluster in groups, speaking rapidly in muted tones. Catherine left her dazed mother and sisters to come over to Cinta and Tonia.   "I'm so sorry, Cinta," she said, eyes downcast. "If I hadn't fetched you, none of that would have happened to you."

"It wasn't your fault, Catherine," Cinta's voice was still shaky. "It was those Jap brutes."

"We're looking for a way to escape," Tonia spoke up. "Will you come with us?"

"I can't leave Mama and my sisters," Catherine responded. "I'm all they have left."

"Please stay with Cinta for awhile," said Tonia. "I need to check something out."

"Of course."

Tonia edged over to a French door that led out to a balcony. Cracking it open, she peered outside. Seeing no activity, she slipped through the door and flattened herself against the stucco building. She heard gunfire from the direction of the refinery and saw black smoke billowing far up into the sky. The stench of burning petroleum hung heavy in the air. At the moment, she observed no trace of the Japanese Army.

Moving very slowly, she inched along the wall until she came to a corner. Peeking around the wall, she saw another empty stretch of balcony. This was the back side of the hospital, out of sight from the entrance and the direction of the fighting. A fire escape leading down to a stone patio beckoned halfway down the wall. She had parked her sedan less than three blocks away.

Scurrying back to the detention ward, Tonia went straight to Cinta and Catherine, who were holding each other tightly and gently rocking back and forth. "We can get out of here if we go now," she said quickly. "There may not be another chance."

"But what if you run into more soldiers?" Catherine blurted. "You may be safer here."

"One is never safe in the grasp of the Japanese," Tonia responded. "I'd rather take my chances while I have them."

"Colonel Okuma promised to protect us," Cinta said tentatively, unsure of what to do.

"I trust him as much as I would a cobra. I dealt with the Japs in Shanghai. I know what I'm talking about."

"I can't think straight," Cinta replied. "I put myself in your hands." She turned to Catherine. "Please come with us. I can't stand the thought of them ravaging you."

"It's out of the question," Catherine said plaintively. "Mama won't survive without me."

"That's it, then." Tonia spoke with finality. "Let's get out of here."

Cinta marveled at Tonia's composure under such desperate circumstances. The Countess went ahead of her as they tip-toed around the balcony to the fire escape then slinked down the ladder to the stone patio. The gunfire from the direction of the refinery had intensified, and all the attention of the Japanese troops was apparently focused there. They reached Tonia's Cadillac without being discovered and quickly slipped inside. The closed interior was hot as a blast furnace, but that was but a minor distraction.

'Say a prayer, Cinta," said Tonia. "Starting the car may alert the Japs."

The big V-8 engine turned over instantly and began to purr like a contented cat. Tonia eased the car away from the curb and crept slowly down the street

(Two)
Zwarte Gouden Refinery
1 March 1942

Nicolaas spun the wheel on the big valve rapidly, sending a long stream of AVGAS far out into the river. "We'll let it run awhile before we set it afire," he said to Frank. "I want it to be all around those Jap ships by then." They were standing on the fuel pier. The destroyers were still a good way down river.

"That won't be very long. Let's get the boat fired up." Several small launches were still moored to the pier against a float. One was a speedy luxury boat with mahogany woodwork. Frank slung the Japanese submachine gun he'd taken off a paratrooper and hopped down into the fancy boat. Examining the controls, he decided he could run it. A push of the starter button brought a roar from its diesel engine. Nicolaas cast off the lines then climbed aboard. Frank eased the boat away from the float and crept around the end of the pier until they could see the approaching destroyers.

"I think they're close enough," offered Nicolaas.

"I agree. Let's give the Jap Navy a hot-foot."

Nicolaas took a road flare from the emergency box and ignited it. Drawing back his arm to the limit, he heaved the flare in a high curving arc to land in the pool of gasoline. With a loud *whoosh,* flames sprang out to race across the water and envelop the two Japanese ships. Sirens suddenly screamed on the river, and both ships careened away to escape the blaze.

Nicolaas patted Frank's shoulder. "Get us the hell out of here. Head upriver. We'll go around the Jap troops."

In the *kampong* outside the refinery, Okuma crouched behind one of the captured 47-millimeter antitank guns right up in the front line. He had instructed the gunners on all the other Dutch pieces to hold their fire until he signaled. He intended to wait until there was absolutely no chance of missing. The Hollanders out there had no idea what they were walking into. Besides the guns manned by Okuma's *rakkasan-butai*, Shinada's troops had brought up four 70-millimeter infantry cannon. Light and heavy mortars were standing by. Guessing that the Dutch commander would try for a massed breakout, Okuma had disposed his forces accordingly.

The first Marmon-Harrington nosed through the smokescreen the Dutch had laid earlier, and Okuma tapped his gunner on the shoulder. The antitank gun recoiled on its carriage as its tracer rocketed into the tank, which burst at once into flame and slewed to the right. Its crew tried to bail out through the turret, but machine guns cut them down. The same scene was being played out all along the line as the wedge of tanks cleared the smoke. The American armor could not withstand the 47-millimeter solid shot. Exactly as Okuma had planned, the Dutchmen were being slaughtered.

Colonel Dijker raised his head above the shell hole in which he'd been sheltering when the fire from the Japanese lines slackened, then ceased altogether. Even the two destroyers out in the river stopped shooting. A ghostly quiet settled over the battlefield. Then static sputtered from a loudspeaker.

"This is a message from the Japanese commander to Colonel Dijker," a voice said in perfect Dutch. "You have fought a good fight, but your situation is hopeless. Further killing is completely pointless. Surrender now, and save your men. You have five minutes to decide."

"Give me your undershirt, Corporal," Dijker said to the soldier sharing his hole.

"You're giving up?" the corporal said in disbelief.

"The Jap's right. There's no point in further bloodshed. We're trapped like rats."

The last signal Dijker had received before his command car was destroyed confirmed that the enemy now held the airfield and the big bridge across the river. The men in the refinery were the last organized resistance left on the Zwarte Gouden plain.

Reluctantly, the soldier peeled off first his shirt and then the white vest underneath.

Dijker took the undershirt and tied it to a stick, then began waving it in the air.

"I see your flag," came the voice of the speaker. "Stand up and walk in this direction."

Dijker got up and stood at attention. He passed the flag to the corporal, and they moved out together, walking in step. The Japanese soldiers suddenly started to sing, and Dijker recognized the stately strains of *Kimigayo*, the Japanese national anthem.

The emperor's reign will last
For a thousand and then eight thousand generations
Until pebbles become mighty rocks
Covered with moss"

(Three)
Zwarte Gouden City
1 March 1942

Frank nosed the launch into the bank just south of Zwarte Gouden. Nicolaas leapt ashore and tied a mooring line to a tree. Frank took stock of their equipment before leaving the boat. Nicolaas was presently unarmed, but Frank had both his Colt .45 automatic and the Japanese submachine gun. He also had a chest pack with six spare magazines. Nicolaas dug a long machete from a boat's toolbox, along with a sturdy fishing knifeand a portable irst-aid kit.

"You'd better take this," said Frank, unbuckling his pistol belt and handing it to the Dutchman. "We both need to be armed."

The older man adjusted the web belt to fit his girth then buckled it in place. "The women are probably still at the hospital," he mused. "It's about a kilo from here."

"Let's make tracks. We may not have much time."

A shift in the wind blew a thick haze of oil smoke over the city, bringing with it the foul odors of burning oil and scorched human flesh. The sounds of the refinery battle grew more intense. Tonia drove the Cadillac slowly through the smoke, keeping engine noise as low as possible to avoid detection. She had the windows rolled up, but acrid fumes still burned the women's eyes and irritated their sinuses.

"How much farther?" Cinta asked, squinting to see ahead.

"About ten blocks," the Russian said softly. "Pray for good luck."

"I think our luck just ran out." Cinta's voice cracked with emotion.

Up ahead, three Japanese soldiers suddenly loomed out of the smoke--short, bandy-legged men carrying incongruously long rifles with fixed sword bayonets. Their green uniforms were sweat-soaked and smeared with mud. The cloth campaign caps above their unshaven faces had attached neck cloths like those of the French Foreign Legion. A corporal holding a Dutch Luger pistol put out his hand for the car to stop while the other two leveled their rifles at the windshield. Reluctantly, Tonia pressed down on the brake pedal.

Some monstrous force suddenly slammed one of the riflemen forward into the auto's grill. At the same instant, the other began to jerk and dance about like a marionette before crumpling to the pavement. Astonished, the corporal was just turning toward a nearby alley when a hail of gunfire stitched across his chest and knocked him backward.

Cinta screamed without realizing it as she stared at the slaughter before her eyes. Then she saw two crouched figures slink out of the alley and stealthily approach the fallen soldiers. The newcomers were so covered with soot and oil that it took a moment to recognize them.

"My God," Tonia exclaimed. "It's Nicolaas and Frank."

Cinta was out of the car and running to Frank within seconds.

Then she was clinging desperately to him while savage sobbing racked her body. Nicolaas rose from relieving the dead corporal of his Luger and stood dumbfounded by his daughter's outburst.

"God in heaven," the Dutchman swore when Tonia told him what Cinta had endured. "I'll tear out their black Jap hearts with my bare hands."

"Later, my love," Tonia advised. "We need to flee at once or the Japs with catch us again. Get in the car." She again took the wheel, while Nicolaas rode shotgun. Frank and Cinta, who was regaining her composure, got in the back.

"Where are you going?" Nicolaas asked when Tonia started the car and turned left at the first intersection.

"To my hotel. We'll need food and more petrol. And you two could do with a bath. You smell like goats."

"No time for that, now. Let's just grab the supplies and go."

A half hour later, Nicolaas was speeding the Cadillac south at a steady speed. They had encountered no more Japanese troops in their foray to the Shanghai Hotel. The trunk now held spare cans of gasoline and boxes of British bully beef and dry biscuits. Large thermos bottles of fresh water rested on the floorboards. Cinta had rescued an extensive first aid kit, and Tonia recovered a small Mauser pistol and a fistful of cash from the hotel safe.

After the first few miles outside the city, the road ran through an open forest that screened their movements from Japanese planes. Then the trees suddenly ended, and verdant fields of rice spread out before them. Nicolaas braked to a stop under the last of the shade.

"This is no good," said Tonia, who was peering intently at a BPM road map. "The paved highway runs right along the coast for several miles. There's no cover at all."

"Does the map show native paths?" asked Frank, who had been napping in the back seat.

"Our maps record all passable tracks," said Nicolaas stiffly. He took the chart from Tonia and studied it for several moments. "There's a logging road along the foot of the mountain." He pointed at the wooded slopes of a tall volcanic peak that loomed to the east. "It should keep us covered until nightfall. After that, we can run across the open country to Semarang in the dark."

"Let's just drive all night," Frank proposed. "We can take turns at the wheel. The quicker we get to the south coast, the better our chances of getting out."

"I agree," Cinta chimed in. "I'm all right, now. I can take my turn at the wheel."

Tonia quickly concurred. Nicolaas turned off onto a dirt road and angled to the east. Soon, dense forest cover placed them in deep shade. There was no traffic to be seen. The Javanese, rather than fleeing before the invasion, appeared to be sitting out the conflict in their homes.

As darkness approached, Nicolaas stopped so that he and Frank could place tape from the first aid kit over the lens of the headlights, leaving but a thin slit of light to escape from each lamp. Thus prepared, they crept forward at as great a speed as their vision permitted.

(Four)
Zwarte Gouden Hospital
1 March 1942

With his blood running high, Okuma fairly swaggered into the entrance to the hospital. After Dijker's surrender, General Toyama had sent a personal message of congratulations upon being informed of the light colonel's bravery and initiative. IJA medical orderlies were dashing about the place, bringing in wounded troops and sorting them out for treatment. Okuma ignored them all and, with Lieutenant Nagara trailing close behind, made straight for the ward where the white women were being held. It was time to bring his plan for Cinta van Wely to fruition.

The two *rakkasan-butai* outside the closed doors snapped to attention and presented arms as he approached. The corporal-in-charge reported that the situation was secure.

"Open the doors," Okuma ordered.

As he stepped into the room, the women herded close together, and he heard them sigh in apprehension. His eyes ran swiftly over the crowd, searching for his target. Then the realization struck him that Cinta van Wely and the older woman who'd been with her were not there. Rage boiled up within his brain, and he turned in a fury to the corporal.

"*Baka* (idiot)!" he screamed at the man, then struck him hard across the face. "You've let two of the women escape."

The corporal made no protest, but drew himself up straight for the next blow. Okuma, however, turned back to the women.

"I know that Doctor van Wely and an older woman were here before," he addressed them in Dutch. "What happened to them? Tell me now, or you will all be punished."

The women shrank away from him and spoke quickly among themselves in Dutch. Then a striking blond woman in the uniform of a nurse edged forward.

"They left through the French doors over an hour ago,' the woman said in a trembling voice. "We don't know where they've gone."

Okuma began to get control of his temper. Despite being disheveled, this woman was quite beautiful, and the nurses' garb did not disguise her splendid body. He had bedded many women of her like in Germany. Lust now shoved fury to the back of his brain.

"What is your name?' he asked sternly.

"I'm Nurse Catherine von Zweden," she replied, her head slightly bowed.

"You knew Dr. van Wely?"

"I was her surgical nurse."

"Then you could discuss the techniques she uses to treat burns?" A diabolical scheme was beginning to form in his mind. If his men failed to find the runaway women, Catherine would make a very satisfactory replacement in his bed.

"Yes, Colonel. I've assisted her many times."

A sweating courier ran into the ward just then and handed a piece of paper to Lieutenant Nagara. The officer read it quickly and turned to Okuma. "You are to report to the temporary HQ in the Wilhelmena Hotel. The message says immediately."

"I'll want to talk with you later, after security is restored." Okuma said to Catherine, then turned and issued orders to Nagara to scour the city for the fugitive Dutch doctor. Then he stalked out to see what General Toyama wanted of him.

"You've done extremely well, Colonel Okuma," said General Toyama. He was seated behind a table in the hotel lobby, where his staff was busily setting up headquarters. "I have another task for you, now. Our casualties have been much more than expected. The loss of all those burned boats is especially holding up getting all the troops ashore. We must not let up on the Dutch. We need to press on to Semarang immediately, but our tanks are not yet ashore.

"I want you to form a battle group from the remnants of the formations that have been decimated. Take whatever captured equipment you need and move out down the Semarang road as soon as possible. Don't let the Dutchmen have time to mount a defense of that city.

"Your unit will be the size of a regiment. I'm brevetting you full colonel as of this moment. Do you have any questions?"

"No, my general." Okuma's morale shot skyward. "It shall be done at once."

Three hours after leaving Toyama, Okuma stood in the suicide seat of a captured White M3A1 4x4 armored truck and watched his impromptu regiment move out of Zwarte Gouden. First off was his reconnaissance team, three Bantam GP *Blitzbuggies*, American jeeps with pintle-mounted machine guns. Okuma's driver moved to take the head of the column. Next came his paratroopers mounted in White armored trucks and Dodge 2-ton trucks. The companies organized from the remnants of the assault regiments made up the bulk of the convoy. All the vehicles drove with their headlights on. There was no longer any danger of attack by Allied aircraft.

Okuma sat down and fingered his captured Thompson submachine gun. His paratroopers now carried all these weapons that the defeated Dutchmen had surrendered. Browning machine guns in both .30 caliber and .50 caliber were liberally sprinkled throughout his force. If fortune smiled on him, he planned to blast his way into Semarang before daylight. After taking that city, he planned to drive "hell for leather" toward Tjilatjap. He was not yet ready to give up on recapturing Cinta van Wely.

CHAPTER 30

(One)
Jogjakarta
South Central Java
2 March 1942

Sometime after midnight, Frank came instantly awake when the noise of the engine suddenly stopped. He could tell they were in a city from the characteristic aromas. "Where the hell are we?" he asked Tonia, who was at the wheel.

"In front of the Grand Hotel in Jogjakarta," she responded. "We're almost to the south coast."

Frank stretched and looked around the car. The first thing that struck him was that the streetlights were still on. And despite the hour, crowds of Dutch civilians were clustered about the street corners, their low murmuring sounding like a swarm of insects. The temperature was hovering around 70 degrees Fahrenheit, downright frigid to Frank after the heat of the north coast.

Tonia parked on the edge of a large, European style plaza. The surrounding streets were bordered by solid Dutch colonial stone buildings, some of two stories and a few of three. The architecture of the uniformly white structures was stolid nineteenth century. The Grand Hotel had wide verandahs around each of its three stories, the lower level supported by white Romanesque columns, the upper by wrought ironwork that reminded Frank of New Orleans French Quarter. A wide striped canvas canopy sheltered an outdoor café that was still serving customers.

"I think I might have a better chance of getting us a room," observed Nicolaas, who was vigorously rubbing the back of his neck to drive away sleep. "Why don't you stay with the ladies, Frank?"

"Okay, but maybe we can stretch our legs."

The two women beat Frank out of the car, eager to unkink their muscles.

Nicolaas hailed a doorman and spoke rapidly to him in Dutch. Then the two of them went inside.

"If Nicolaas thinks I'm going to wait out here when there are flush toilets this close, he's a crazy man," Tonia suddenly exclaimed before stalking quickly to the hotel entrance.

"I'll wait with you," Cinta whispered in Frank's ear. "I don't want to let you out of my sight."

"The feeling's mutual." He kissed her lightly on the lips.

"Doctor van Wely!" a familiar voice broke their reverie. "What in the world are you doing here?"

Frank spun to find Doctor Cory Wassell fast approaching them from across the square, his cigarette holder held jauntily between his teeth. He wore a khaki uniform and a darker tan sun helmet. As befitted a junior officer, Frank snapped to attention and saluted the lieutenant commander. Cinta opened her arms and warmly embraced the slight doctor.

"I could ask you the same question, Cory," she said as they parted.

"The reason I've always been here. I still have wounded men to care for."

"The guys from the "Marby" are still here?" Frank was appalled by the revelation.

"I still have nine patients. A couple from *Houston*, but most are from the "Marby.""

"What about 'Sergeant York'?"

"He's one of them. I got the walking wounded out through Tjilatjap, but the boarding officers wouldn't let us put the stretcher cases on a ship. There was nothing to do but come back to the hospital." Wassell took off his helmet and mopped his damp brow with a handkerchief. His thinning, light brown hair was plastered to his skull. "I thought I had a deal with the local Air Corps to fly us out last night, but that fell through yesterday when the Japs destroyed some of their planes. Now that the Japs have landed on Java, I've got to find a way to get my men to safety. None of them would survive a Jap POW camp."

"My father and I will do all we can to help," Cinta put in. "He still has some influence with our Navy."

"I'd appreciate any help I can get," Wassell said sincerely.

"Help with what?" asked Nicolaas, who was just walking up.

After introductions, Cinta explained Wassell's predicament to her father.

"If we can get them to Tjilatjap, I'm fairly sure I can find them a berth," Nicolaas finally pronounced. "Do you have any transport?"

"Just one Ford sedan," The doctor answered. "I can only take three in it."

"We could cram one in with us," Tonia offered, "but not with a stretcher."

"We need a lorry or an ambulance," Cinta chimed in.

"There are none to be had at the moment," Wassell sadly intoned.

"Keep looking," said Nicolaas. "We're all done in and have to get some rest. I managed to get the manager to let us have his personal rooms."

The large hotel lobby had a high, coffered ceiling. Electric fans languidly stirred the warm air. Weary travelers fleeing the Japanese, all trying to grab precious sleep, sprawled across the many chairs and settees that filled the space. The hotel manager, a stiff-necked, florid-faced man in a wrinkled white suit, led Nicolaas and his party to his personal suite. It reminded Frank of the *Oranji* Hotel in Soerabaya. The large sitting room held two rattan couches, and the bedroom had a big, canopied four-poster. Just as important, the suite had a personal bathroom.

The manager gave Nicolaas the room keys and told him that if they left their soiled clothes outside the door, his staff would clean them before morning.

"I claim the first dipper bath," Cinta exclaimed.

"And I'm next," said Tonia.

Nicolaas went over to a small bar and poured four snifters of brandy. "We can all use a touch of this."

"Confusion to the enemy," Frank toasted before taking a sip. He suddenly felt unspeakably weary. "I'm turning in. Wake me when it's my turn with the bath." Collapsing on one of the couches, he fell instantly asleep.

An insistent pounding on the doorjam rattled Frank from slumber. He felt like he had just lain back down after bathing and dressing in a set of the manager's underwear.

"Wake up, Frank," came Cory Wassell's voice through the louvered door. "I need you now."

"What's up?" Frank said as he swung open the door.

"A British convoy just pulled in," said Wassell. "We need to see if they'll take us with them."

"Okay. Is our clean laundry out there?"

"There's some clothes on a rolling rack."

"Push it through and I'll be ready in a minute."

Frank woke the others, and they went about gathering their few possessions. Frank slipped into his freshly washed pants, then paused to pin his "railroad tracks" to the collar points of the bush jacket before putting it on. Lastly, he buckled on his pistol belt.

"Let's get cracking," Wassell admonished as the aviator stepped out into the hall.

The hotel lobby was teeming with activity when the two naval officers came down the stairs. A group of Javanese cooks was circulating among the refugees, passing out bowls of rice and mugs of tea. Frank's attention was drawn at once to the front desk, where a tall officer dressed in the wide-legged shorts, bush jacket and sun helmet of the British Army was arguing with the harried hotel manager. The Americans made a beeline for this officer, who had an aloof air of authority. As they came close, Frank recognized the crown and single pip of a lieutenant colonel on the Brit's bush jacket shoulders. Following Wassell's lead, Frank saluted the newcomer and introduced himself.

"Humphries, H.R., 77th Heavy Antiaircraft Regiment," the tall man replied coolly. "Is there something I can do for you gentlemen?"

Frank found Humphries' aloofness offputting. But then he noticed the man's bloodshot eyes and sagging face. The Colonel was skating on the ragged edge of exhaustion.

"Are you evacuating to Tjilatjap?" asked Cory Wassell.

"Where else would we go?" Humphries stared into the distance. "What is it you need?"

Wassell quickly outlined the predicament of the wounded sailors. "Could you take us with you?"

"I suppose." Humphries stifled a yawn. "Your men would have to be able to ride in the trucks."

"That's no problem at all, if there's room for their stretchers," Wassell assured him

"All right, then. I plan to leave in two hours, as soon as my men are fed. Have them here by then, and we'll take you."

"No problem Colonel," Wassell pronounced. "We'll be ready."

"Are you sure we can make that deadline?" Frank asked as he and the doctor walked away.

"We'll have to," Wassell said grimly. "Can you get Cinta to help us? I really need to redress most of the burns before we shove off."

"I'm sure she'll be glad to. I'll bring the Countess's Cadillac to help move the men here."

Nicolaas and the women were just coming down the stairs. The oilman wore one of the manager's white suits. Its sleeves were too short and the pants sagged where Nicolaas had cinched the excess waistband with a belt. Both women were in the same outfits they'd worn the day before.

Cory Wassell quickly explained what he had arranged, and Cinta agreed at once to help with the wounded. Nicolaas offered to round up a member of the local BPM staff to guide the convoy.

"The Colonel will need someone who knows the back roads," Tonia offered. "We don't dare make the run on the open highway."

"I know just the man," Nicolaas responded. "Let me get on the phone."

The rising sun turned the white stucco of Petrinella Hospital pink as Frank drove up the curving driveway to the entrance to the building. A cool breeze from the south caused shade patterns to dance across the roofs of the one-story ward buildings. Cory Wassell's Air Corps sedan was already parked under the entrance portico. The imposing figure of Doctor Groot pushed through the doors and came to meet the Cadillac. His cheeks seemed redder than ever, but his steely blue eyes still blazed with fervor.

"Welcome back to my hospital, Doctor van Wely," said the big Dutchman. He gallantly kissed her proffered hand. "You're here to assist Doctor Wassell?"

"That's right," Cinta replied, then introduced Frank.

"I remember the Lieutenant from your earlier visit." Groot pumped Frank's hand.

"Could you let me have some medical equipment?" Cinta went on. "I lost my entire kit in Zwarte Gouden."

"Of course," said the Dutchman. "Come with me. I assume the Lieutenant wants to see the sailors."

"Yes, sir. Are they still in the same ward?"

"That's correct. Doctor Wassell is with them now."

Frank paused before entering the ward, peering over the louvered barroom half doors to survey the situation. The men who could move about were hastily packing their few possessions. Nurse Teramina, the little Javanese woman the men called, "Three Martini," was sitting beside recumbent Ben Hopkins, a "Marby" Signals striker, holding a cigarette holder to his mouth to take a puff. Many other sailors were smoking through identical Chinese holders.

"Hey, Mister Rhea," an ambulatory sailor called out when Frank stepped into the ward. He recognized the tall, sandy-haired man as Joe Leinweber, a cook's striker from the "Marby." "What the hell are you doin' here?"

"Trying to get out of Java, just like you," Frank said with a grin.

"I thought you went to the *Houston*, sir," said a man Frank didn't know. "I'm EM2c Bob Whaley. *Houston*'s my ship."

"You knew that *Houston*'s gone, sir?" said another man from that ship. "I'm Tom Berghetti, FC1c." Berghetti had an arm and one leg encased in plaster casts.

"I got the word yesterday," Frank replied. "Where's Doctor Wassell?"

"I think he's across the hall with Commander Goggins," Leinweber answered. "The Doc said we have one last chance to get to Tjilatjap. We're all for it."

"A British Army convoy," Frank confirmed. "You men finish getting ready. I'll be back in a minute."

Frank found Cory Wassell, Cinta, and Doctor Groot huddling outside Commander Goggins's doorway. Cinta now had a white lab coat over her clothes. A stethoscope was around her neck, and a Dutch Army medical satchel hung from her shoulder.

"We should redress all the burns if we have time," Wassell was saying.

"What medications do we have?" Cinta asked.

"We have a little Sulfanilamide and Vaseline ointment left," Wassell responded,

"That's by far the best treatment," Cinta opined. "Coagulants like tannic acid tend to dry out the surface and perhaps stimulate sepsis.

"The sulfa treatment has worked wonders since the Air Corps brought us a supply from the states," Wassell went on. "Problem is, we don't have half enough."

"Do you have any powdered Sulfanilamide?" Cinta asked Groot.

"A small supply from the Dutch Army," the big Dutchman admitted.

"I'm sure you have mineral oil?" Cinta continued.

"Of course."

"Then I know what to do," said Cinta, animated. "In Houston, we sometimes dipped the gauze in mineral oil and then sprinkled on the sulfa powder. It worked very well."

"Okay, that's what we'll do," Wassell agreed. "Why don't you take charge of preparing the oiled gauze?"

"I'll be glad to."

"I'll have Nurse DeKraufre assist," said Groot, indicating a tall nurse with black hair.

"Frank, I have a job for you, too," Cory Wassell went on. "As soon as we have a few patients ready, you can start moving them to the Grand Hotel. Joe Leinweber's in good enough shape to help with that."

"I'm on it," Frank replied. "Do I have time to look in on Commander Goggins?"

"We'll have a few patients ready in about twenty minutes," Wassell agreed.

Frank was surprised to find Goggins sitting up in bed. The XO's face, arms and calves were still encased in heavy bandages, but his voice was strong and his eyes sparkled with humor.

"I'll be damned," Bill Goggins swore when he caught sight of Frank. "You keep turning up like a bad penny. I thought you were lost with *Houston.*"

"They left me in Soerabaya when they went out to fight the Japs in daylight. I got shot down trying to join them in Batavia."

"Help me up," Goggins went on. "I've got to be able to walk to make it onto a ship. I've been practicing. Just catch me if I fall."

Goggins sucked in his breath with a hiss, and Frank could see intense pain in his eyes as the XO pushed himself to his feet. Nevertheless, the commander shuffled slowly across the floor to the door, then turned to limp back to the bed. He was breathing heavily by the time he sat down on the mattress.

"Where's Tonto?" the XO croaked between gasps of breath.

"He's either a POW or still loose somewhere on the north coast." Frank related the story of their encounter with the *Zero* and Tonto's mission to repair the SOC. "There were several thousand Japs on the river between us," he concluded. "We had no way to reach him."

"That's a damned shame. He's one hell of a good man."

"He is that."

Cory Wassell decided to evacuate the patients in reverse order based on the seriousness of their wounds. As the worst of the burn cases, Bill Goggins would be among the last to leave. Frank and Joe Leinweber helped the first group out to Wassell's and Tonia's sedans then drove them through the clogged streets to the hotel plaza.

The British convoy was already beginning to reform. Colonel Humphries's driver had moved his sedan to the front of the queue and was standing by outside. Humphries was having a discussion with a junior officer just outside the hotel entrance. He was just turning away when Frank walked up. "Ah, there you are, Rhea," the colonel barked out. "Have you brought me some passengers?"

"Just the first load, sir," Frank said after saluting. "Most of them can ride in a truck, although one with both a broken arm and a broken leg might find that hard."

"We'll sort this out." Humphries called to the junior officer he'd previously been chatting with, "Come back, Leftenant Mills. I have a task for you.

"Mills is my Embarkation officer," Humphries said to Frank. "He's been making space for your men. He'll take it from here. But, I say, why don't I take that fellow with all the casts in my sedan with me. I have the room."

"That would be great, Colonel."

Lieutenant Mills called up several Tommies to help transfer the patients from Tonia's car to the Army vehicles. Tom Borghetti was settled as comfortably as possible in the back seat of Humphries staff car. Leaving Joe Leinweber with the men in the truck, Frank drove back to the hospital to pick up a second load.

The doctors were just finishing up with re-bandaging the other patients when Frank walked into the ward. The aromas of mineral oil and sulfa powder hung in the air. Commander Goggins looked a bit like Lon Chaney's "The Mummy" with his face and limbs swathed in new gauze. The mood of the sailors was definitely upbeat.

"Don't worry," a sailor said to the Javanese nurse who was attending him. "We'll be back. The Doc is just taking us for a day at the beach."

"I'll take the worst cases in my car," Cory Wassell informed them. "Once I get them settled, I don't want to have to move them. Mister Rhea will take those who can ride in a truck."

"Before you leave," said Doctor Groot to Wassell, "I'd like a word in my office. Please come, too, Cinta, and bring along Lieutenant Rhea."

As the travelers filed into the Dutchman's office, Groot went to his cabinet and took out a bottle of Bols gin and poured four glasses.

"It has been an honor to treat your American sailors," Groot said with sincerity. "They have made great sacrifices for the sake of my homeland, and we will be forever grateful. Now, let us drink to our friendship and to the defeat of Japan."

"Here, here," Wassell and Frank said together. They all downed a stiff slug of gin. "You have given our men the finest medical care in the world," Cory continued. "We'll remember you for the rest of our lives."

"Farewell, then," said the big Dutchman. He shook both of the American's hands and briefly embraced Cinta. "God go with you."

The Javanese attendants settled Bill Anderson, Bob Whaley, and Bill McCurdy, who still had a catheter installed, in the seats of the Air Corps sedan. Pao San Ho, the horribly burned Chinese mess attendant, was placed in the middle and his legs draped over the front seat. Commander Goggins took the shotgun seat. Frank took Ben Hopkins and two others in the '38 Cadillac. Two stretchers were stored in the trunk, which had to be tied down because they stuck out several feet. Neither Frank nor Cory Wassell saw "Three Martini" slip into the trunk.

When the Americans arrived at the Grand Hotel, they found the British convoy nearly ready to start. Frank drove back along the line of lorries until he found the 3-tonner that was to carry the sailors. Leinweber already had the first load of patients waiting in the truck, He jumped down to help Frank transfer the sailors from Tonia's car, first taking the stretchers from the trunk and placing them on the pavement. Two Tommies left the truck cab to come and help with the transfer. Frank took a quick muster when all were aboard the truck. Besides Leinweber, coxswain Bob Krauss, Ben Hopkins, and a skinny seventeen-year-old named Melvin Francis. Bob Whaley joined them from Wassell's car a little later. Cinta checked the men to see that they were as comfortable as possible, then returned to the car.

"Let's drive just behind the truck with the patients," she told Frank. "That way, if there is a crisis, I can help at once."

"That makes sense," Frank agreed. "We'd better get your father and Tonia."

They found Nicolaas and Tonia talking with Wassell and Colonel Humphries back near the head of the convoy. With them was a wiry Dutchman with a tan to match Nicolaas's leathery skin. The newcomer was dressed in a khaki bush suit and was carrying a large road map. Nicolaas introduced him as Dirk Ryk, BPM's field superintendent for Central Java. Ryk would ride in Colonel Humphries's car, guiding the convoy to Tjilatjap over back roads to avoid air attack.

Cinta explained her plan to drive behind the lorry with the wounded sailors, which Wassell thought a good idea.

"I'm going to be 'tail-end Charlie' in this procession," Wassell pronounced. "That way, I can be sure that all my men are aboard."

Nicolaas took the wheel for the first leg of the journey. Tonia sat with him in the front, and Frank and Cinta in the rear. The British vehicles began to slowly pull away. Nicolaas waited until the lorry with the Americans drove past, then nosed in behind it. The sailors in the back waved at them. As the vehicles crept out of town, they slowly spread out into open convoy order. True to his word, Cory Wassell watched while the cars, lorries, and heavy AA guns with their big tractors passed by. Field kitchens, mobile repair shops and heavy trucks loaded with AA shells brought up the rear of the convoy. All in all, over two hundred vehicles passed by before Wassell pulled in at the tail end.

The perfect cone of Mount Merapi to the north spewed forth a cloud of steam as the convoy cleared the suburbs of Jogjakarta. They were passing now through miles of terraced rice paddies that stepped down the hills toward the Indian Ocean. All phases of rice production could be seen in the fields. Some flooded paddies held green shoots, others half-grown stalks. A number of the fields contained ripened grain on browning shafts. Java had no limited growing season. Because of its latitude and climate, rice could be cultivated year round. Oblivious to the approach of battle, hundreds of Javanese farmers, their faces shaded by umbrella-shaped bamboo hats, labored on the terraces. They apparently considered food production more important in the scheme of things than their Dutch masters' war. Opposing traffic towards Jogjakarta confirmed this attitude. Bearing the produce of the hinterland, two-wheeled oxcarts drawn by skinny white cattle lumbered by to the right of the convoy.

It was supposed to be the rainy season in Central Java, but the weather gods did not favor the convoy with cloud cover. Motorcycles buzzed up and down the column of vehicles, passing orders to spread out even more. All along the line, hundreds of eyes swept the sky, alert for prowling Japanese aircraft. Many of the vehicles had pintle-mounted Bren Machine guns, manned by skilled gunners. But .303 rifle-caliber rounds stood small chance against the 20mm cannon of strafing *Zeroes*. Everyone on the line of vehicles heaved a sigh of relief as Piet Ryk directed Colonel Humphries to turn off onto a dirt road that ran beneath a corridor of bordering tall trees.

In addition to sheltering them from the view of overhead airplanes, the shade granted relief from the scorching sun. The temperature in the city had been in the lower seventies. But as the convoy dropped gradually down towards the sea, the mercury and humidity crept up apace. The wounded Americans began to sunburn so friendly Tommies spread their overcoats to cover their exposed skin.

The Allied personnel paid a price for the shade in roughening road surface and speed. They fairly crept along over countless potholes and shallow mud holes. The vehicles rocked and jerked as they moved forward, giving the wounded sailors in the truck a very hard time. But relentlessly, the convoy moved forward. After awhile, the road swung back to the northeast, and the vehicles made a gradual climb back up into the piedmont. Then, taking a sharp left turn at a village called Purworejo, it ran parallel to the south coast through intermittent forest and farms. Making about twenty mph, the convoy moved inexorably forward. Noon came and went. Tonia broke out a bag of sandwiches she'd brought from the hotel. Nicolaas ate his at the wheel, for there was no midday break in the journey. Cold water from the thermoses slaked the travelers' thirst, and Nicolaas passed around a flask of Scotch as dessert. An hour later, Frank swapped places with Nicolaas, who went immediately to sleep.

About 5:00 p.m., a motorcycle rider came back to announce a pause for rest and, of course, a "brew-up" of tea. The selected spot was a long stretch of heavy shade bordered by wide rice fields, where Javanese farmers toiled beneath their wide-brimmed shade hats. As Frank closed up on the lorry ahead, he noticed that all along the line ahead, the road was swarming with Tommies released from the trucks. Some were "brewing up" on improvised camp stoves. Others were washing the sweat from their clothes in the nearby irrigation canals or bathing in the moving water. Considering their respective professions, Frank was not surprised that neither seemed phased by the sight of the cavorting naked men. In fact, Tonia observed wryly that the Tommies seemed better endowed than most Europeans. Cinta suggested that the subject would make an interesting medical study. Nicolaas seemed mildly amused by their banter. Frank stopped the car close behind the lorry carrying the Americans and turned off his motor.

Cinta got out at once and hurried to the lorry ahead. Leinweber reached down to help her up into the truck bed. "Hopkins is really hurting, Doc," said the cook's striker. "Could you give him something?"

"Let me look at him." She knelt beside Hopkins's stretcher and pulled back the British overcoat. The seaman first class was gritting his teeth and squirming on his cot. Cinta took out a syringe, filled it with morphine, and slipped it into Hopkins's arm. In a few moments, his face relaxed, and he slid back into slumber.

Cinta noticed a small movement in the pile of British overcoats that the men had discarded when they reached the shade. "All right, Nurse Teramina," she said sternly, continuing in Javanese, "You can come out, now. I've known you were on the truck since mid-morning. What do you think you're doing here?"

The diminutive nurse spoke rapidly in her own language for about a minute, obviously pleading with Cinta. While doing so, she protectively knelt over the recumbent Hopkins.

Cinta replied in the same language and turned to Frank, who was standing at the tailgate. "She believes that Hopkins will die without her special care," Cinta explained. "I would let her stay, but I don't know if Doctor Wassell will agree."

"Agree with what?" came a voice from the shoulder of the road. Wassell's car had crept unnoticed along the right side of the road until it was almost beside them. His ever-present cigarette glowed in its long holder.

"It seems we have extra medical help," Frank responded. "Nurse Teramina came on the truck."

Wassell was out of his car in an instant, headed straight for Leinweber with fire in his eyes. "God dammit to hell, Leinweber, I know this is your doing," Wassell raged. "What'll we do with her when we get to Tjilatjap?"

"Honest, Doc, I didn't ask her to come. She must have some plan of her own."

"I've been speaking with her," Cinta cut in. "She believed that Hopkins might die if she weren't here to help him."

That stopped Wassell cold. "How is Hopkins?" he asked quietly.

"Not good. I gave him a shot of morphine, so he's out of it for a while.

The two doctors discussed the condition of the other men in hushed tones.

"Don't let Colonel Humphries see 'Three Martini,'" Wassell finally said. "He'll blow a gasket for sure." Then he turned back to his sailors. "How are these Britishers treating ya'll?" he asked in his soft Arkansas accent.

"They're okay," Leinweber responded, and the others agreed.

"They gave us corned beef for lunch with candy for dessert," Bob Kraus spoke up." They're making tea for us now."

"That diet will kill you before we get to the coast," Wassell said jokingly.

"Can you do something about the square wheels on these trucks, Doc," asked Mel Francis, who had a patch on his left eye. His torso and arms were swathed in gauze.

"I'm afraid they're standard British Army issue." Wassell went on joking with the men until the lorry crew came back with mess kit cups of dark, steaming coffee. Frank and Cinta took theirs and strolled over to the tree line, a combination of towering palms and hardwood trees varying from about ten to fifty feet high. Javanese boys from the fields were shinnying up the palms to throw green coconuts down to the Tommies. The soldiers knocked holes in the shells to drink the milk from within.

"They'll be sorry for that," Cinta observed as she sipped her tea. "In a couple of hours they'll come down with diarrhea."

"We'd better tell the men," Frank responded.

"I'm sure that Doctor Wassell is doing that now."

"What are those trees with the droopy limbs and fuzzy leaves?" Frank inquired.

"The natives call them *Kalok*. I believe the English name is Capulin. They're all over Java. They'll grow in anything, even the poorest soil."

"We'd better get back," said Frank, observing that the British were packing up. He saw that Wassell was getting back in his car. He motioned them to come over.

"A motorcycle messenger just told me that Colonel Humphries sent his embarkation officer ahead to Tjilatjap. Seems he took Berghetti with him," the doctor informed them. "There's little daylight left. I've decided to go on ahead and drive straight through to Tjilatjap, too. That way I can get the lay of the land and try to find us a ship. I assume that Doc van Wely will look after these boys until you reach the port."

"Of course, Doctor. I think Nurse Teramina and I can handle the situation handily," Cinta responded.

"Let's get one thing perfectly clear," Commander Goggins growled from Wassell's shotgun seat. "Dr. van Wely can be responsible for the medical treatment of the men, but Lieutenant Rhea's in military command."

"Of course, Commander," Frank responded.

"I'm off, then. See ya'll in Tjilatjap." Wassell pulled away up the road.

Nicolaas was behind the wheel again when the lovers approached their car. Tonia sat beside him.

"I think I'll nap for awhile," Frank said as he and Cinta slid into the back seat. He sprawled across the bench and pillowed his head on Cinta's lap. Nicolaas let the lorry get fifty yards ahead before he eased out on his clutch. The Cadillac responded smoothly, speeding up to cruise at twenty mph. Cinta stroked Frank's temples until he fell asleep.

(Two)
Karagangar City
Central Java
2 March 1942

Frank became vaguely aware that the vehicle had stopped again and that the others were conversing in low tones. As he sat up and opened his eyes, he saw that a bright moon was shining, lighting the surroundings almost as bright as twilight. Closed up now, the convoy had paused in a small city that strung out on either side of the highway. Dutch colonial buildings with tile roofs were interspersed with tin roofed native structures. Nightfall had brought a decrease in temperature and humidity, but perhaps that might be due to climbing to a slightly higher altitude.

"Anybody know where we are?" Frank asked as he dug a cigarette from his shirt pocket.

"Some town on the road," Nicolaas responded. "I've lost track of exactly where we are."

"I wonder what Leinweber wants," Cinta said with a yawn.

The sailor had jumped down from the truck ahead and walked quickly to the sedan. "I think you'd better have another look at Hopkins, Doc," Leinweber said softly. "He's in an awful lot of pain again, and Three Martini's really concerned."

"Of course," Cinta answered, climbing out of the car. Frank slid out also and followed her up into the truck bed. Cinta conversed rapidly in Javanese with the nurse for a few moments, then turned on her flashlight and examined Hopkins. He was obviously in agony.

"What do you think?" Frank asked.

"He's in a bad way." Cinta's voice was laced with concern. "I don't dare give him more morphine yet. It might put him over the edge. Nurse Teramina is convinced that he'll die if he goes on like this. I tend to agree."

"You've got to get me off this truck, Doc," Hopkins suddenly croaked. "I just can't take this anymore."

"We'll have to see what we can do. Just hold on."

A British motorcycle runner drove up from the front of the column. Stopping beside Tonia's car, he pushed up his goggles and wiped sweat from his face. "Is there a Leftenant Rhea here?" the rider asked.

"That's me," said Frank, jumping down from the truck.

The rider saluted from his seat. "Colonel Humphries's respects, sir. He'd like to see you at once. You can ride behind me."

Wondering what was up now, Frank climbed on the back of the motorcycle, and the driver eased slowly up the right side of the road. Many of the Tommies were clustered around their trucks, smoking cigarettes. As the cycle approached the head of the column, Frank made out Colonel Humphries conversing with one of his officers. When he saw Frank, Humphries came over and returned Frank's salute.

"Hell of a mess," Humphries snorted. "One of my messengers wrecked his motorcycle and broke both his legs. My MO is with him at the local infirmary. The man can't travel, so I guess I'll have to leave him here."

"Is your MO staying with your injured man?"

"That won't be necessary. They have Dutch Army doctors here."

"Doctor van Wely thinks one of our other men can't live through the journey. Maybe we should leave him here also."

"You'll need to be quick about it. I'll have my runner show you the way."

The Tommies manning the wounded sailor's truck gently lifted Hopkins's stretcher and carried him to the Dutch Army clinic. Cinta spoke quickly with the doctors there, introducing Nurse Teramina who insisted on staying with her sailor, and explaining her plan for treatment. Frank was the last to leave.

"Hang in there, Hopkins," Frank said in parting. "It's been an honor to serve with you."

Lost in a haze of pain, Hopkins did not respond.

A deep sense of sadness flooded over Frank as the convoy pulled out of the city. Leaving a man to the mercies of the Japanese was just slightly better than having the trip claim his life. He kept envisioning the horror at the hospital in Zwarte Gouden that Tonia had described. The burdens of command weighed heavily on his soul.

Frank was back at the wheel of the Sixty-Special when the long column of vehicles started to close up again. This had occurred several times in the last few hours at the approaches to rivers and canals, where KNIL sappers were busy wiring bridges for demolition. Most of the trucks had to creep across each span one at a time since the engineers had already loosened the bolts securing the bridges to their abutments.

"That looks like a suspension bridge up ahead," Frank commented to no one in particular.

"Then we're at the Serajoe River," Nicolaas spoke up. "Only about twenty kilometers to go

"Another hour or so," Cinta joined in. "We'll get there a little after dawn."

A slow drizzle of rain began to fall as the Cadillac crept across the swaying suspension bridge. Between slapping windshield wipers, Frank could see Leinweber spreading British overcoats over the stretcher cases in the truck bed. The wool garments would hold in heat, but they were not waterproof. If the rain kept up, the sailors would be soaked before long. Wet bandages were hell on infections.

KNIL soldiers were all over the bridge structure, laying charges and stretching wire.

"We may be the last convoy across," Nicolaas observed. "Looks like the sappers are almost ready to blow her."

"Poor Hopkins," Cinta said softly. "I shudder for his future."

The rain began to pick up until it was falling steadily. The black asphalt of the highway ate up what little illumination the taped-up headlights threw out. The pavement also became slick, and more than one of the Tommies' trucks ended up in the side ditches. In contrast, the Cadillac kept a firm grip on the road. Frank peered intently through the windshield, trying to keep the truck ahead in sight. They were all the way down on the coastal plain now, and the temperature and humidity became oppressive. Sweat streamed into Frank's eyes and constantly had to be wiped on his shirtsleeve. His shirt was plastered to his back. He wondered whether he or the men in the truck were more soaked.

Despite the rain, the sky above the jagged mountains far to the east began to lighten. Dawn on March 3rd was fast approaching. The same question hung heavily in the minds of all of the Americans: would there be ships left in port to spirit them away before the Japanese caught up with them?

(Three)
Hotel Bellvue
Tjilatjap, Java
3 March 1942

Frank's first impression of the Hotel Bellvue was that it looked like the other hotels he'd seen in Java—columned balconies, impressive portico, and a plaza in front. He eased the Cadillac up the right hand lane, passing trucks and guns and jeeps until he reached Colonel Humphries' staff car. The big Colonel was leaning wearily against the fender of the car, talking to a cluster of his staff officers. One of them was a tall Dutch officer in a green uniform.

"Ah, there you are, old chap," Humphries said to Frank. "Lieutenant Voorhuys was just briefing us on the situation here. Your doctor friend is down at the harbor looking for a ship. The men he brought with him are in a room upstairs."

"Is Berghetti there, too?"

"No. He had a spot of good luck. My officer got here just before your ship, *Isabell*, sailed. Berghetti made it aboard.

"So he's out of it," Frank observed. U.S.S. *Isabel* was a 700-ton patrol yacht, formerly classified as a destroyer. Until the previous year, she had been the flagship of the Yangzi River Patrol. Steam powered with a top speed of 25 knots, she had a better chance than many of escaping the Japanese blockade.

"If you'd like, I could show you where your patients are," Voorhuys offered.

"I'd be grateful," Frank responded.

Going back to the car, Frank explained the situation.

"I need to check all the patients," Cinta said with determination.

"I'm getting out here."

Nicolaas explained that he and Tonia meant to visit the local BPM offices to seek help finding a berth. "Is there anything I can get you?" he asked the young lovers.

"Some clean clothes would be great," Cinta answered.

"Same here," said Frank.

The truck with the remaining patients had now pulled up behind the Cadillac. Cinta did a quick check of their situation then told Frank he could move them. A number of Tommies assisted in lifting the stretchers out of the truck bed and taking them inside the hotel.

The situation inside the hotel lobby was exactly like that in Jogjakarta. Refugees were swarming all over the place. Javanese cooks circulated among the crowd with bowls of rice and meat and sauces, serving an impromptu *rijsttafel*. When Frank discovered that the elevators were too small to take the stretcher cases, the determined Tommies carried them up the stairs to the level Voorhuys indicated. The Dutchman went straight to their destination and opened the door without knocking.

"So, you finally got here," Commander Bill Goggins said to Frank.

"Better late than never, Commander," Frank shot back, his eyes taking in the room. It was about twelve feet square and held two beds and an easy chair. Goggins was ensconced in the chair, looking relatively dry when compared to the newcomers. Bill McCurdy and Pan San Ho were lying on the beds. Wassell's other two passengers sprawled on the floor. "Where's Doc Wassell?" Frank asked.

"Down at the harbor trying to find us a ship," Goggins replied. "You'll have to put the rest of the men on the floor."

Following Cinta's direction, the British soldiers arranged the stretchers to allow passage among them, then saluted the officers and said their goodbyes. Cinta began examining the patients, beginning with the most serious. After a few moments, she turned to Frank. "Those wet bandages need changing," she said seriously, "and I'm not sure I have enough gauze left."

"Just do the best you can, Doc," Goggins spoke up. "We'll just have to make do."

Frank and Leinweber helped Cinta take off and replace the wet bandages. She had no sulfa left, but she did have one bottle of Vaseline. She used it sparingly. Several of the men were in intense pain, so she injected them with more morphine. They had attended to about half the men when the door swung open again, revealing a soaked, dripping Corydon Wassell. Inexplicably, the doctor was actually grinning beneath his wet sun helmet.

"You boys look like a bunch of drowned rats," Wassell said jokingly.

"What are you so cheerful about, Cory," asked Goggins.

"I got us a ship to take us out of here," Wassell replied. "We'll leave as soon as we finish fixing you boys up."

"Hooray for the Doc," Leinweber shouted, and the others joined in.

Wassell looked over the room then suddenly frowned. "Where the hell are Hopkins and Berghetti?" he said forcefully.

"Berghetti got out last night on the *Isabell*," Frank explained. "Hopkins got so bad off we had to leave him in a Dutch Army clinic."

"Who gave you the authority to leave a man behind?" Wassell shouted, obviously agitated.

"I did, Cory," Bill Goggins cut in. "I left Frank in command."

"Hopkins would not have made it here alive," Cinta said soothingly. "My medical judgment said to leave him where he could be cared for. Now, perhaps you and I should compare notes on the patients."

Wassell heaved a heavy sigh. "I wanted to get them all out," he said sadly. "But you're right. How are the men you brought in?"

The two doctors conferred briefly, then went about re-bandaging as many men as they had supplies for. Lieutenant Voorhuys disappeared for about half an hour before returning to announce that he'd found a bus to take them to the waterfront.

Just then, the air raid sirens began to wail.

"Do you want to go to the shelter?" asked Voorhuys.

"Hell, no," Wassell shot back. "When we leave here, we're going straight for the ship. Are you with me, boys?"

"Damned right, Doc," Leinweber answered at once. The others quickly concurred.

"Anyway," Wassell went on. "There can't be much of a raid in this weather, not with this heavy rain."

"The rain won't stop the bombs," Voorhuys observed.

"Maybe not, but they can't see where they're aiming. That's a regular toad-strangler out there. In Arkansas, a rain like this turns the roads to black gumbo."

Voorhuys looked puzzled at the term.

Just then, a messenger from the local BPM office came in bringing fresh clothes for Cinta and Frank. They took turns changing in the dipper bath, leaving their wet clothes behind.

"Look what the cats drug up and the dogs wouldn't eat," Cory Wassell said to Frank when he came out in his new dry khakis.

Behind Wassell, dripping wet and still wearing his dirty flight suit, stood Tonto. "Hey, Lone Ranger," Tonto grunted. "Got any more dry clothes around here?"

"How the hell did you get here?" Frank exclaimed, grabbing his observer in a bear hug.

"Flew myself in old 'Silver.' I got her patched up yesterday. I waited until the Japs quit using the river after dark and took off by moonlight. Had a hell of a time getting through those damned mountains."

"You didn't see any Japs at all?" asked Bill Goggins.

"Nope. The only people trying to shoot me down were those British Tommies around the port here. They put some holes in old 'Silver.'"

Upon seeing Tonto when she returned from changing, Cinta rushed over and hugged him. He had to repeat his story for her.

"There was a message from Papa with my things," Cinta told Frank later. "He's found passage for himself and Tonia on the Motor Ship, *Janssens*."

"That's the same ship we're on," Wassell spoke up. "We're all going together."

"I'd already told Papa that I was staying with you and your patients."

"The bus is here," Voorhuys announced. "We'd better get the men down."

With Wassell, Frank, Tonto, Voorhuys, and Leinweber the only men able to carry the stretchers, it took several relays to get all the wounded downstairs. The bus was an American Dodge. Except for its dull green paint job, it could have been a school bus. Those who were able sat in the seats. The stretcher cases went in the aisle. Before they left, Doctor Wassell went back in to thank Colonel Humphries one more time. The Colonel was so exhausted that he fell asleep while they were talking.

The drive through the empty streets of the city took only a few minutes. The Dutch Army driver drove right onto Fortseiger Pier before stopping. At the end of the wharf, men from Colonel Humphries's regiment were setting up a heavy anti-aircraft gun.

The roadstead at Tjilatjap was little more than a wide place in the estuary of the Segara Amnakan Strait. Port facilities were clustered around the right-angle bend where the Kali Donan River met the bay. The low-lying Kambangen Island formed the far side of the harbor. Two ships were barely visible through the steadily falling raindrops. Cutters carrying Dutch Navy personnel plied back and forth between the wharfs and the ships.

Frank found himself strangely emotional when he sighted the wreck of 'Silver' half-submerged near the end of the wharf. Tonto had not joked about the local flak units shooting the SOC full of holes. Looking at the derelict, Frank felt surprise that his friend had survived.

"This is it, Boys," Cory Wassell announced from the front of the bus. "I've hired a private launch to haul us out to the *Janssens*."

From her blunt bow to her rounded stern, *Janssens* was about two hundred and fifty feet long. She had superstructure with a single stack amidships. Open but awning-covered steel decks extended from her deckhouse to both stem and stern. She was about two thousand tons displacement, and through her hull, her big diesel engine could be heard idling. Dutch sailors in white uniforms swarmed about her decks. She would clearly be heavily laden on the voyage out.

Frank and Wassell carried the first stretcher from the bus to the launch, with Goggins limping alongside. Voorhuys and Tonto brought the second stretcher. When Frank came down the steps with the third litter, a pack of half a dozen Tommies were waiting to relieve him of the load. Having seen what was happening, the gunners had come at once to help. With so many helping hands, the transfer to the launch took but a few more minutes. As soon as the last were aboard, the Javanese crew cast off and headed out toward the ships. Cinta crouched beneath a small canopy in the stern. The others just hunkered down in the rain. Frank's new khakis were soon as soaked as the ones he'd taken off.

As the launch approached the little coastal passenger ship, Frank saw Nicolaas waiting for them at the rail. Dressed in oilskins, the big Dutchman looked formidable.

Most of the passengers were climbing a steep accommodation ladder, but that would never do for the Americans on stretchers. Cinta went up the ladder and spoke in Dutch to an officer on the deck. Moments later, nimble Javanese deckhands lowered slings over the side and gently lifted the litters in a level position, taking the sailors directly from the launch to the deck above. With Cinta giving directions, Dutch sailors came down the ladder and carried the other men piggyback up to the ship. Other Dutchmen took up a number of mattresses the bus driver had scrounged up for the sailors. Commander Goggins made it up under his own power. Before following with Frank, Doctor Wassell pressed a fistful of Dutch Guilders into the launch owner's hands and thanked him profusely.

Cinta commandeered deck space for the men near the stern. The area was open but covered by an awning. As long as the rain fell more or less straight down, they would remain dry. Those without stretchers lay down on the mattresses. Cinta and Wassell passed among them, making each as comfortable as possible under the circumstances.

"Those beds are made of kapok," Cinta told the men. "In a pinch, they'll double as life rafts." She then turned to Frank. "I'm going to look for Papa and Tonia.

Cinta went into the main smoking salon of the ship, which was well appointed with gaming tables and a long bar. Fairly large, it was almost packed at the moment with soldiers and sailors from all the Allied nations. Besides a preponderance of Dutch Navy, there were British, Dutch, and Australian soldiers and airmen, as well as many Dutch civilians. Although they were speaking in muted tones, the din was still unintelligible. She spotted Nicolaas near the bar, talking in Dutch with a tall, blond-haired man in a blue beret. When he caught sight of her, he pushed his way through the crowd to meet her.

"You're finally here," Nicolaas said with relief, then grabbed her in a bear hug. "I was getting worried about you."

"We were bringing the patients aboard," she replied. "They're all settled on deck, now."

"Come meet Captain Jan Praas," Nicolaas continued. "He's assigned us a stateroom with three bunks." He led her over to the Captain and introduced them. Praas seemed a very no-nonsense man.

"You're a medical doctor?" Praas asked Cinta.

"That's right, sir," she answered. "I'm a burn specialist."

"You may prove very valuable before this voyage is over," Praas went on. "I have no medical officer. We have no sick bay either."

"Commander Wassell is also a doctor," Cinta commented. "The two of us make a good team."

"Ah, yes. Doctor Wassell. I didn't want to let him bring his patients aboard. If we're sunk, they have no chance. But the man wouldn't take, 'no,' for an answer." Praas turned and looked over at a group of men in the corner, who were pouring over a book. "Excuse me," he said quickly. "I think I see something I need." He went over and spoke to the men, who reluctantly surrendered the book. He came back baring it proudly. "It's a detailed world atlas," Praas informed them. "This may be priceless. I have no charts of the Indian Ocean. I can make them with this." Excusing himself again, he hurried off to the bridge.

"Those men with the book are American war correspondents," Nicolaas told Cinta. They came in from Bandoeng this morning. Come, now let me show you our room."

There were no staterooms for Frank or the other American officers. Like the men, they had to sleep on the open decks. But they made no complaints. The prospect of escape before the Japanese arrived trumped all other considerations.

Loading the ship continued until about 5:00 p.m By then, the rain had slowed to a fine drizzle. The crew pulled up the accommodation ladder and made preparations to get underway. Anchors were soon weighed, and the big diesel engine below decks roared to life. *Janssens* crept out through the channel between the minefields for about half a mile, then stopped and dropped anchor again.

"What's that crazy Dutch Captain up to?" Leinweber said impatiently.

Frank pointed inland to boiling black clouds, which were fast approaching. "I think he's waiting for darkness and more rain, hoping the Japs won't see us coming out."

Sure enough, heavy rain began to pour down in a few minutes. Nightfall came close behind. The engine roared alive again and the anchor chain rattled up through the hawsepipe. The ship slowly gained way, moving deliberately out through the minefield until it cleared the tip of Kambangen Island, then swung westward. As the big Indian Ocean waves caught the ship, she rolled gently.

"I just thought of something," Cory Wassell said to Frank. "Back at the hotel, I promised myself a still drink when we finally cleared Java. I believe it's time I indulged in a wee dram."

"That sounds like a plan," Frank responded. "May I join you?"

"Sure. Let's go find one."

The two Naval Officers entered the crowded lounge and pushed their way toward the bar. A big, ruddy-faced man turned from his drink and came to meet them. To Frank, he bore a striking resemblance to Hermann Göring, the German *Luftwaffe* commander.

"I'm Bill Dunn of CBS Radio," the man said, extending his hand. "Where did you boys come from?"

Wassell explained their situation and introduced himself and Frank.

"Frank Rhea," Dunn repeated. "I've seen that name. You were 'mentioned in dispatches' the other day."

"What are you talking about?" asked a puzzled Frank.

"You are the pilot who took on a formation of Jap bombers in a Navy floatplane, aren't you?"

"I guess so, but how did you know?"

"Admiral Doorman mentioned you in his report on the Makassar Straight battle," Dunn went on. "Would you give me an exclusive interview?"

"Maybe later on. Right now, the Doc and I want a drink."

"They only have beer at the bar, but it is Heineken. If you need something stronger, I have a personal bottle of White Horse Scotch."

"That would be perfect," Wassell chimed in, patting his pockets as if searching for something.

"Did you lose something, Doc?" Frank inquired.

"My cigarette holder. I thought I had it in my shirt pocket. I guess I left it in my briefcase." A look of shock suddenly spread over Wassell's face. "Oh, my God," he exclaimed. "I left my briefcase in the launch."

"We'll find you another cigarette holder, Doc."

"It's not the holder, Frank." Anguish laced Wassell's voice. "I had all my receipts in that briefcase. I have over five hundred Guilders to account for when we get to Australia. The Navy's going to court martial me!"

"I really doubt that, Doctor," Dunn tried to reassure him. "But I think now's a good time for that drink." Dunn led them over to two other Americans in one corner and made introductions all around. Frank recognized one of them at once--Frank Cuhel, a former football star and Olympic medal winner whose career Frank had closely followed as a youth. Cuhel now represented the Mutual Broadcasting Company. The other journalist was George Weller of the *Chicago Daily News.* Dunn rounded up some glasses and poured the scotch. They all talked amiably for several minutes while consuming the whiskey, but then Cory Wassell made his excuses.

"I'd better be getting back to my boys," Cory said in parting. "Are you coming, Frank?"

"I think I'll look for Cinta and her father."

"I believe they've turned in for the night," Dunn advised.

"I guess I'll catch them at breakfast." As the warmth of the scotch spread throughout his body, Frank suddenly realized that he was exhausted. Going back out onto the deck, he found a dry place near the rear of the deckhouse and lay down on the steel plates. Sleep came almost at once.

CHAPTER 31

(One)
Aboard M.S. *Janssens*
South of Java
4 March 1942

"Wake up, sleeping beauty." Frank felt a toe nudging him in the ribs. As his brain emerged from the fog of sleep, he recognized Cinta's voice. "Did you spend the night there on the deck?"

"I was so tired I could have slept on a bed of nails." Frank stretched and sat up, feeling scuzzy. His teeth seemed to be wearing sweaters.

"You make me feel guilty for sleeping in a cabin." Cinta looked fresh and perky in clean slacks and a blouse. Her hair was combed, and she was wearing makeup. "And I think I cramped Papa's and Tonia's style."

"Speaking of which," he said as he rose to his feet, "when are we going to get some time alone?" He folded his arms around her and held her close. She melted into his body.

"I think I know how to be could manage that. Ship captains can perform marriages, can't they?" Her eyes held a sparkle, and she gave him a lop-sided smile.

"That's a brilliant idea!" Frank said with exuberance. He kissed her fiercely, but she pulled away after a moment.

"What did you drink last night?"

"A little White Horse Scotch."

"You need to work on your breath, and while you're at it, get rid of that three-day beard. It scratches like sandpaper."

"Anything for the bride-to-be," he said expansively.

"We have a small lavatory off our cabin. I'm sure Papa will let you use it. Meanwhile, I'm going to check on our patients"

Nicolaas not only shared his head with Frank. He also loaned him a toothbrush, Listerine, and a razor. Clean-shaven for the first time in days, Frank emerged from the cabin to the ringing of a bell. Javanese stewards began circulating among the passengers serving plates of breakfast. Frank went up to the after deck where the sailors were billeted. He found them wolfing down food. Cinta and Cory Wassell were consulting near the stern.

"Hey, Mister Rhea," Leinweber called through a half-chewed mouthful of bully beef. "Have you tried any of this slop?"

"Not yet," Frank responded as he inspected the sailor's plate. "The pancake's soggy and this jam must have been made a long time ago. The fresh bread's really good, though."

"It's a hell of a lot better than we'd get in a Jap POW camp."

"You can say that again," Bill Goggins chimed in."

Frank "BSed" with the sailors for a few more minutes, then snagged a plate of breakfast and a cup of milky coffee. Afterwards, he went to join Cinta and Cory.

"The Dutch make a good *café au lait*," Wassell commented.

"Our Java coffee's the best in the world," Cinta agreed.

"How are the men this morning?" asked Frank.

"Better than I expected," answered Wassell. "If this tub can get us to Perth, they're all going to be okay."

Frank glanced to starboard and saw that they were running east only about a mile off the Java coast. "Why are we still in sight of Java?" he asked with alarm. "I thought we'd be well out to sea by now."

"I asked Captain Praas that very thing a while ago," Bill Goggins spoke up as he joined the group. "He was advised to steam east before running for Australia. Dutch Intelligence thinks the Japs have a big task force astride the plumb line from Tjilatjap to Perth. We may be the only refugees still afloat."

"Hey, Doc," Francis called out. "Any chance we could have some more beer?"

"Yeah, that would sure be good," Leinweber put in.

"Sure, boys. We'll get you some."

"I'm coming along," Goggins commented. "I could use a cold one myself." Still swathed in bandages, he followed Wassell and Frank into the smoking lounge. The place was a bedlam of languages and accents: Dutch, American, British, Australian, even Javanese. All seemed to be debating their closeness to the shore.

Wassell found a table for Goggins while Frank waited at the bar for drinks. After getting a Heineken to his X.O., he went back with Cory and started shuttling beers to the men on deck, finding that Cinta had gone off to rejoin her father.

After all the men had their beer, Frank and Wassell returned to Goggins' table. They sat there for some time, enjoying the good Dutch beer and listening to the war correspondents who were at a nearby table arguing American politics. The naval officers were all lost in their own thoughts.

"What are you boys thinking about?" Wassell finally said.

"I'm having trouble concentrating on anything," the commander responded. "What about you?"

"I'm thinking about all the fried catfish and squirrel I'm going to eat when I get home."

"You really eat squirrels down in Arkansas?" Frank asked, surprised.

"You're damned right," Wassell shot back. "Cook it right, and it tastes just like fried chicken."

"They eat squirrels in Texas, too, Frank," said Cinta, who was just walking up. "My brother-in-law loves to hunt them."

Goggins frowned for a moment. "We're changing course," he remarked. "Finally going south, I guess."

Just then, an alarm sounded throughout the ship. "Aircraft approaching," the word was quickly passed.

"We need to get the men below decks," Goggins said quickly. "Or at least drag them under the deckhouse overhang."

"I'll get some help," said Cinta before running to find Dutch sailors to man the stretchers.

"I'm going up to see what's happening," Frank said to the others.

"Be careful," cautioned Goggins. "Don't hesitate to find cover."

When Frank climbed up atop the deckhouse, he found a young Dutch sailor manning a pintle-mounted Browning machine gun. The man pointed to the skies ahead.

Frank recognized nine IJN bombers in their standard "vic of vics" formation. The distinctive sound of their engines, the fearful

"Mitsubishi moan," was just becoming audible. The bombers didn't worry him too much. They would have bigger fish to fry around Tjilatjap. The planes flew on toward the west, confirming his judgment. But then a chilling thought popped into his mind. *They will have reported our position to their base.*

As Frank watched the bombers receding, another glint of sunlight caught his attention. Above the bomber formation, a string of smaller planes was peeling off to dive toward the sea. Curse words formed in his head. The newcomers were *Zeroes!*

The fighters leveled off at wave-top level about a mile to the north, then came screaming toward the *Janssens.* Flashes of fire erupted just above their engines and from their wings.

"They're strafing," Frank screamed to those around him, then dived for a companionway that led down to the lounge. As he skidded across the deck inside, machine gun bullets and cannon shells began to pound the ship. Looking across the room, he saw Bill Goggins beneath their table, still sipping from his glass of beer. Frank slithered across the floor to join him.

"Keep your head down," Goggins shouted above the thunder of 20mm cannon shells bursting against the steel hull of the ship.

Frank didn't need to be told twice. He clasped his hands behind his head and pressed his face tightly against the deck. He could have sworn he felt each explosion reverberate through the cool metal. He sensed the ship swing from side to side as Captain Praas tried to throw off the enemy's aim. The attack seemed to go on forever as the passengers cowered behind whatever cover they could find. Then all was suddenly quiet except for the murmur of *Janssens's* engine.

The passengers began to rise up and look around them. Surprisingly, few seemed to be injured at all.

"I'm going to see about Cinta," said Frank, springing up and racing to the lounge door. He found her with the American sailors sheltering beneath the overhang at the back of the deckhouse.

"We're all okay," she reassured him. "But some of our Dutch sailors are wounded. We need to set up a dressing station somewhere."

"The bar below the lounge," Cory Wassell shot back. "I saw the ship's first aid cabinet down there."

A few minutes later, an impromptu emergency room was

functioning in the bar. Aided by a Dutch pharmacist's mate, Cinta triaged the ten wounded sailors as they were brought in. Most were from the ship's gun crews. Doctor Wassell worked to patch up the worst of the injured, using the bar surface as an operating table. Cinta joined him as soon as the wounded had all arrived. They toiled for almost an hour, injecting morphine, cleaning and bandaging wounds, and splinting broken limbs. When the last patient was lifted from the bar, both doctors heaved a sigh of relief. Javanese crewmen brought them buckets of water to wash the blood from their hands, arms, and faces. Little could be done for their bloodstained clothing, although Cinta had the foresight to don a bar apron before starting.

Captain Praas pushed back his beret and thanked them profusely in Dutch. Cinta explained that he'd also said that they'd have to have their suits cleaned.

"I'm going to see about my boys," Wassell said. He followed Captain Praas up the companionway to the lounge. Cinta checked the men they'd patched up then slowly heaved her weary body up the stairs as well. She was surprised to find Praas nose to nose with a Dutch Navy captain, both red-faced and arguing at the top of their lungs.

"That Dutchman's been pitching a hissy-fit ever since we came up," Doc Wassell informed her. "I don't have the foggiest notion what about."

Cinta listened to the argument for a few minutes, then said, "He's demanding to be put ashore at once. The other passengers there are all supporting him."

Captain Praas suddenly stomped his feet and screamed, "Enough" in Dutch. "All who want to go ashore may do so. I'll put into the first port we find." He stalked away with a stormy face and went out onto the deck.

Cinta explained Praas's words to Wassell.

"I'll have to decide what to do with my boys," Cory replied. "I don't know if I should subject them to more air attacks."

"You can't be thinking of surrender," Cinta shot back. "I saw wounded men disemboweled in their beds in Zwarte Gouden. That's the best you can expect from the Japs."

"You may be right. Still, my official orders were to stay in Java with my patients." Skirting on the ragged edge of exhaustion,

Wassell was clearly agonizing over what to do.

The ship turned toward Java, soon entering a small bay with a tiny port town. The anchor rattled down, and the crew began unshipping the lifeboats. Panic was evident in the passengers who went quickly down ladders to the boats, led by the whimpering captain who'd thrown a tantrum at Praas. The boats shoved off for the shore, which Cinta learned was called Patjitan.

All the Americans able to stand, along with Cinta, Nicolaas, and Tonia gathered behind the bridge to discuss what to do.

"There's no question about my family and me," Nicolaas put in. "We're for Australia."

"That includes me," Tonia put in.

Just then, Captain Praas came out of the bridge carrying a clipboard and handed it to Nicolaas. The typed document clipped to its face was in Dutch.

Nicolaas took the clipboard and read the document quickly. "It's a contract," he said firmly. "It says that anyone who wishes to continue to Australia must agree to obey all orders Captain Praas issues without question. Anyone who won't sign must go ashore."

"Let's get on with it," said Tonia, handing Nicolaas her pen.

The oilman signed quickly then passed the contract to Cinta, who added her signature. Frank, Tonto, and Tonia followed suit. Bill Dunn hesitated but a moment before signing with a flourish. Weller, Cuhel, and Turner then added their signatures. Turner passed the clipboard to Cory Wassell.

Cory hesitated for a few moments, anguish evident in his face. Then he slowly shook his head. "My orders were to stay in Java with my patients, and that's what I'd better do. We'll have a better chance ashore."

"Now wait a minute, Doc," Bill Goggins said forcefully. I think we should let the men make their own decisions. Why don't we take a vote?"

"Remember what I told you about Zwarte Gouden," Cinta intervened. "How the Japs butchered the wounded."

Wassell bowed his head for a while, as if praying. "All right," he said with a positive nod. "We'll let the men decide."

"I'm signing before we go talk to them," said Frank.

"All right, boys, listen up," Wassell said with uncharacteristic volume. He was standing against the back of the deckhouse looking down at his men. Frank and Bill Goggins were beside him, leaning back against the bulkhead. "We have a hell of a decision to make. Lots of the passengers want to go ashore and take their chances with the Japs. Captain Praas says that anyone who wants to jump ship here may do so. Anyone who stays on board will have to sign this contract to obey all his orders. So there you have it: a Jap prison camp ashore or the chance of being bombed or torpedoed on the ship. I think you should make your own decision. Whatever you want to do, I'll stick with you all the way. I'm going to give you a few minutes to think about it."

Frank followed Cory down the deck to the smoking lounge. The room was packed with passengers, all arguing with each other in hushed tones. Tension permeated the atmosphere. These people were being forced to make what might prove to be a life-or-death decision in a limited amount of time. Families might be separated, perhaps for years. Despite the conduct of the terrified captain, the Dutch Navy people were under orders to go on to Australia. Their wives and children were under no such obligation. Was a life in a Jap internment camp preferable to the chance of death in an air or surface attack?

"I guess they've had enough time," Wassell finally said. "We'd better get back."

When they returned to the fantail, the patients were still bantering with each other.

"Well, what's it to be, boys? Heads we win, tails the Japs lose?"

"We don't know yet, Doc," Leinweber spoke up. "What do you think Commander Goggins?"

"I don't want to influence your decision. In the final analysis, it's the Doc's call."

"What would you do if you only had yourself to worry about, sir?" Kraus asked the doctor.

"That's a fair question. I guess I look at it this way. If the fish are biting where you're standing, why take a chance of moving upriver? If it were just me, I'd stick with the ship and trust in the Lord and Captain Praas."

"We're with you, Commander," Leinweber answered for the men. The decision made, they all broke into smiles, even Pao San Ho.

Wassell spoke to Pao in Chinese for a few moments, and the steward nodded his head. "He says okay. It's unanimous. You boys had better put your monikers on this sheet." He passed the contract and a pen among the men. Bill Goggins signed last.

Once those going ashore had all disembarked, Captain Praas took stock of the situation. Of his original crew, only one cook and his Dutch chief engineer remained. The Captain tasked the engineer to recruit a crew from among the Dutch Navy men. The officer soon had the matter in hand and was ordering teams to clean up the battle damage and find materials to repair the shrapnel-riddled lifeboats. The one good boat made more trips to the ramshackled pier, bringing back fresh food and water. Even with all the activity, time seemed to stand still, the sun barely crawling across the sky. Cory Wassell wrapped himself in a towel and did his best to wash the blood and filth from his uniform, taking a bit of ribbing from his patients in the process. After drying in the sun, both pants and shirt were about a size smaller, providing the sailors more ammunition for joking.

Captain Praas personally took on the task of reassigning space aboard the ship. He gave Doctor Wassell and Bill Goggins cabins on the first deck and offered to put the stretcher cases in cabins as well. The sailors declined, preferring to stay on the cooler deck near their lifeboat.

Frank and Cinta took this opportunity to broach the subject of a shipboard marriage, first to Nicolaas and then to Praas. The Captain agreed to marry them when there was time and promised them a private cabin. As father of the bride, Nicolaas took charge of making the arrangements. He insisted on two days to get everything ready.

"I won't have time before then, anyway," Praas responded.

As dusk settled over Patjitan Bay, *Janssens* weighed her anchor and crept slowly out into the Indian Ocean. A full moon rose from beyond Bali, sending a silver sheen across the water. The passengers gathered on deck, almost all wearing their life jackets. Every eye was focused on the horizon, searching for the glow of aircraft exhausts or the spume of submarine periscopes. Praying for clouds to shroud them in darkness, Captain Praas set a direct course for Fremantle, Australia. After the volunteer crew served an impromptu supper in the dining hall, Praas ordered an all-hands meeting in the smoking lounge at ten o'clock.

Cory Wassell was just joining Frank and the Van Welys at a table when the Captain stalked into the room. He went straight to the small bandstand and stepped onto the raised platform. The room quieted as he began to speak. His first words were in Dutch, and they were forceful to the point of shouting. Before Frank could ask Cinta for a translation, Praas switched to his heavily accented English.

"We are now sailing due south at nine knots," Praas began. "Barring unforeseen events, we should reach Fremantle in about ten days." He turned to face the Americans. "I am pleased that the American sailors stayed with us. They show great courage. But courage is not enough. We all have to work together as a team. We don't have enough people to run the ship. Everyone must work, no matter what rank or station. That includes women as well as men. You all agreed to follow my orders. I will set watches and duties for everyone aboard."

Praas looked around the lounge, frowning at the litter left by the departed passengers. "Some of you start by policing this room. Never in my career have I allowed such a pigsty to exist aboard my ships. Get to work at once." With that parting shot, Praas marched out of the salon and went back to his bridge.

"I guess we'd better get busy," Cory Wassell said to Frank. "Have you ever swabbed a deck?"

"Not since my ROTC training. I guess it's something you don't forget how to do."

Wassell's new cabin-mate, a burly Dutch clergyman, agreed to help. By the time they went off to their respective cabins, the lounge was as shipshape as a warship mess hall.

(Two)
Aboard M.S. *Janssens*
South of Java
6 March 1942

By the third day out of Java, life aboard *Janssens* had fallen into a fixed routine. True to his word, Captain Praas published watch lists that assigned duties to everyone. Once the Captain learned that

Frank was a qualified OOD Underway, he assigned him as a bridge watch officer. Many of the Dutch wives took charge of the kitchen and dining room, serving wholesome if boring meals of sausages, cabbage, and boiled potatoes. Cory Wassell and the American correspondents became the lounge cleaning crew. Nicolaas and Tonto volunteered as an engine room watch officer. Cinta and some Dutch Pharmacist Mates set up a daily sick call in the barroom. Scores of lookouts constantly scanned the seas around the ship, looking for both enemy ships and aircraft. A spirit of camaraderie began spreading among the castaways, dulling the constant fear of attack that gnawed at their minds.

Nicolaas and Praas scheduled Cinta's wedding for just before dinner that evening. The ship had neither the space nor the supplies for an elaborate celebration. Cinta and Frank settled for a simple ceremony on the open deck followed by a slightly enlarged dinner for the passengers. Frank suggested the afterdeck so that the American sailors could watch. Captain Praas arranged also for the newlyweds to occupy one of the larger cabins on the ship for the rest of the voyage.

Several Dutch Naval Officers pieced together a white uniform for Frank to wear. It met neither American nor Dutch regulations, but no one really cared. One of the senior Dutch Navy wives loaned Cinta a pale blue dress. She was happy enough as there were no white ones aboard that would fit her. Commander Goggins, still swathed in bandages, stood up for Frank. Tonia was Cinta's matron of honor.

As the wedding gathered under the afterdeck awning, cool breezes enveloped the ship. Winter already held sway in the Southern Hemisphere, bringing chillier temperatures with each day sailing toward the Pole. The ceremony was simple and straightforward. Captain Praas asked the requisite questions of the bride and groom, accepted their answers, and, citing his authority granted by Queen Wilhelmina, quickly pronounced them husband and wife. The American sailors cheered and whistled when Frank kissed Cinta, and Dutch observers politely clapped. Everyone then filed into the dining room for the normal meal, washed down by large mugs of Heineken beer. Private stocks of wine and liquor also appeared. Bill Dunn gave the head table a full bottle of White Horse Scotch.

"Happy, Cinta?" asked Frank as they settled in at the head table.

"Supremely, Darling," she cooed in response. "What about you?"

"I feel like the luckiest man alive."

"We'll certainly have an unusual wedding story to tell our children."

"I can't wait to get started on that."

Lubricated by consumption of beer and strong drink, a festive mood soon pervaded the ship that evening. The captain even suspended the ration on beer, and the passengers made the most of it. But still, beneath the celebration lurked the possibility of Japanese attack, spoiling the perfection of the moment.

Without orders, various people closed the blackout curtains on the portholes as the sun sank into the sea to the west. Others went out to relieve the lookouts in their search for hostile ships or aircraft. Completely full of good Dutch beer, other guests said goodnight and drifted off to the comfort of the open decks. With the room nearly empty, Cinta suggested to Frank that they retire to their cabin. He was in no mood to disagree.

Captain Praas escorted the newlyweds to the cabin and handed the key to Frank. "May you have a long and happy marriage," he said in his gruff version of English.

"Thank you, Captain," Cinta said softly. "Would you like to kiss the bride?"

"Of course."

Cinta rose on her toes and gave Praas a long kiss on the mouth, then pulled away.

"I'll be on my way. Try not to rock the ship too much."

Cinta covered her mouth to smother a peel of laughter as Praas walked away.

Frank fumbled with the key and finally got the door open. "Stay here a moment." Stepping inside, he made sure the curtains were over the porthole then snapped on the light. The space fairly radiated Dutch competence—well-scrubbed white walls and ceiling, a polished linoleum floor, and good quality linens. The two-person bunk was crisply made up, and a generous teak bureau stood against one wall. Stepping back outside, Frank kissed Cinta fiercely, then swept her into his arms and carried her across the threshold. He began working on the fastenings of her dress as soon as he put her down.

"Just hold up there a minute, Lone Ranger," she laughed as she pulled away. "This is a borrowed dress. I'm responsible for keeping it in one piece."

"Well hurry, then," Frank laughed back. "I've dreamed of this night for years." He began unbuttoning his borrowed shirt.

While Frank stripped off his uniform, Cinta stood by the bed and languidly undressed, folding each garment carefully and storing them in the bureau. When she was down to her bra and panties, she turned to face him before unhooking her snaps.

Frank sighed in delight as she unveiled her marvelous breasts. A moment later, her panties slipped down to her feet. She stepped out of them and flung them up with a flick of one foot, catching them in her hand. Frank drank in the sight of her beautiful body for several moments, afraid to break the spell. Then desire raged through his body, and he raced to wrap his arms around her and pull her tightly against him. They kissed and caressed each other for a few moments, then tumbled together onto the bed. When Frank slipped a hand between her thighs, she started to quiver and make little animal sounds. He thought she was responding to his expert lovemaking, but her body suddenly stiffened. Drawing back, he saw that her eyes were wide open and frozen, and her face held an expression of abject terror. "What's wrong, Darling?" he whispered, perplexed.

At the sound of his voice, Cinta's stiffness relaxed, but then she broke into tears, then racking sobs. "Oh, Frank, I'm sorry. Oh, so sorry," she managed to say after a few minutes. Tears still streamed down her face. "The moment you touched me down there, I was back on that gurney in Zwarte Gouden. Japs were groping me all over and pulling down their pants."

"Oh, baby," Frank said soothingly. "What can I do to help?"

"Just hold me, Darling. Hold me close." Crying softly and trembling once more, she molded herself into the safety of his arms. They lay quietly like that for over an hour, Cinta finally falling asleep. Frank reached over and turned out the light, feeling utterly helpless. After awhile, he too drifted into slumber.

The feel of a warm hand exploring his groin jarred Frank from sleep, and he made out Cinta propped on one elbow beside him. "I'm awake." He said hopefully.

"I'm so terribly sorry, Frank," Cinta almost whispered. "I thought I'd be all right, but I know enough psychiatry to understand now that I need therapy. I just can't stand to be touched like that, not even by you. It breaks my heart that I can't give you what you deserve. It's so goddamned unfair to you." She broke into tears again.

"Oh, Baby," Frank said, stroking her arm. His heart was bursting with compassion and heartbreak. "Don't worry about me. I love you enough to wait 'til you're healed."

"I can't let you wait that long, Darling. I have a duty as a wife to give you pleasure tonight. So now I'm going to do what I can. Just relax and enjoy it."

(Three)
Aboard M.S. *Janssens*
7 March 1942

A vague feeling that something was wrong began to tug at Frank's brain, dragging him up from the comforting limbo of slumber. As consciousness slowly seeped back, he realized that the ship was gently turning, the hull occasionally creaking. For some time, alarm failed to register. Then he realized that the centrifugal forces were constant, as if *Janssens* were steaming in a circle.

"Good morning, my husband," Cinta cooed softly in his ear. She was lying close against him with an arm and a leg thrown across his body. The sheets were damp with perspiration.

"Good morning, marvelous wife," he whispered back. He turned his head and kissed her gently on the lips.

"What's that groaning noise that woke me?"

"The ship's in a sharp turn to starboard, and she's not straightening out."

"Perhaps we'd better put on some clothes. I don't want to go 'skinny-dipping.'"

"I hate to. I'm enjoying the view."

Reluctantly, Frank rolled out of the bunk and began to dress in his khakis, never taking his eyes off Cinta. She got up as well and slipped quickly into her underwear, blouse and slacks. Taking turns in the small head, they were groomed and ready to go outside within a quarter hour.

As they came out on deck, Frank noticed that *Janssens* was indeed cruising in a wide circle, currently headed north. Those passengers who were up seemed all headed for the entrance to the smoking salon. Just then, Cory Wassell and Bill Goggins came forward to greet them

"What's happening, Doc?" Frank asked.

"Something's wrong with the steering gear," Wassell replied. "Captain Praas has called a meeting to discuss it."

"How are the patients this morning?" Cinta inquired.

"Hangin' in there. We'll check them together after the meeting."

The lounge felt strangely empty with so many of the original passengers absent. Most of the crowd was Dutch Navy people, with a sprinkling of Brits and Aussies. Captain Praas mounted the dais and spoke bluntly to his audience, telling them that a bearing had blown completely out on the steering mechanism. Until it was repaired, the ship was helpless. He asked for volunteers to make repairs, and a large number of engineering personnel came forward. Nicolaas also asked to help. The Chief Engineer soon had a skilled team assembled. They went straight down to the hold and went to work. After awhile, the engine went silent. *Janssens* sat motionless on a quiet sea. Without the constant breeze of motion, the ship grew hot as the sun advanced. *A painted ship upon a painted ocean,* Frank thought as he went to stand his bridge watch.

Banging, chopping, and sawing sounds resounded through the hull all day. By sunset, the crew in the hold completed a new wooden bearing supported by a maze of timber bracing. The captain restarted the engine and gently tried the rudder. A momentary shudder ran through the hull but then subsided. Praas swung the ship slowly back toward the south, then picked up speed. Everyone aboard heaved a sigh of relief that they were back on course for Fremantle.

CHAPTER 32

(One)
Tjilatjap Harbor
8 March 1942

Katsura Okuma stood on Fortseiger Pier and stared out across the smoke shrouded waters. Conflicting emotions raged in his mind--elation at the lightning conquest of Java tempered with bitter frustration at not recapturing Cinta van Wely. Months of carefully plotting his revenge were all but wasted. He had come so close, actually having her under his control for a few hours. Even in the frantic chase across the island, he had never been that far behind. He'd interrogated staff at the hotels in Jogjakarta and Tjilatjap, learning that the white witch had been in both places shortly before. He could only hope that Admiral Nagumo's forces in the Indian Ocean would put an end to her. He must move on now. The thought of the blond nurse in Zwarte Gouden brought a hint of a smile to his face. With her, there would be no revenge to worry about. He could concentrate fully on taking every pleasure offered by her splendid body. He wondered if she were still a virgin. A dispatch rider on a motorcycle roared onto the pier and came straight to Okuma. The message he carried sent a thrill of accomplishment through the colonel. General Toyama was ordering him to return at once to Zwarte Gouden to become military governor with the mission of restoring the oil works to operation.

(Two)
Aboard M.S. *Janssens*
12 March 1942

"I'll see you and raise you two," Frank Rhea said with a blank face. He was playing poker with Tonto, Bill Goggins, and the American

journalists at a table in the smoking lounge. A stern-eyed portrait of
Queen Wilhelmina looked down on them from behind the bar. Blue
cigarette smoke hung in a haze just above the players. Dr. Wassell
and Cinta were conducting sick call in their improvised infirmary
near the aft end of the compartment.

As Tonto considered his bet, the saloon doors burst open and
Frank Cuhel barreled between them. "We've got a sub on our tail,"
the Mutual reporter said breathlessly. "Too far away to tell if it's a
Jap or not."

"Oh shit!" Tonto muttered. "This old tub can't outrun a turtle."

"Let's go have a look," Goggins suggested, throwing down his
cards. Obvious pain reflected in his face as he heaved himself up
from his chair. The commander steadfastly refused help from others
in moving himself around.

The outside air temperature hovered in the sixties, bringing
goosebumps to Frank's bare arms. A clear sky exposed the ship to
any aircraft within miles. Captain Praas and several Dutch officers
stood at the fantail, viewing their pursuer through binoculars. The
space beneath the canopy soon filled as passengers learned about the
submarine and came to see for themselves. Enlisted Dutch sailors
uncovered a little 5cm gun and checked its instruments.

"That pop-gun won't do much good," Tonto commented to
Frank. "Jap pig-boats carry 140 millimeter deck guns."

"Let's pray it doesn't come to that," Frank responded. He tapped
a Dutch lieutenant on the shoulder and gestured to borrow his
glasses. Spinning the central wheel to focus on the target, he saw
that the submersible was only about two miles astern. Try as he
might, he could not distinguish whether it was enemy or friendly.
Tonto had no better luck when he took a turn with the binoculars.

"We're on the same course," Praas said in English to the
Americans, "but I'm not sure that ship is actually following us. If we
can stay ahead until nightfall, I think I can shake him."

"Exactly where are we," Bill Goggins asked.

"Just off the northwest coast of Australia," Praas replied. "I was
beginning to let myself hope."

Time crawled by as the crowd on the afterdeck continued to
stare behind the ship and speculate on the identity of the tailing
vessel. People on galley duty passed around a nondescript lunch at
the usual time. No one wanted to go inside with the submarine still

gaining on them. A sense of dread pervaded the gathering.

"Air contact!" the crow's nest lookout, an RAF sergeant, broke the spell of gloom.

"Where away?" Praas shouted back in English.

"Dead on the bow. About seven hundred meters up."

Praas and his party elbowed through the passengers and quickly climbed onto the deckhouse. Frank and Tonto followed close behind, squinting their eyes to try to make out the approaching plane.

"It's a PBY, Lone Ranger," Tonto exclaimed. "I'd bet my life on it."

About that time, a signal lamp began to blink from the aircraft. Tonto watched intently then turned to Captain Praas. "They're Australian," the warrant officer translated. "That's a challenge, demanding to know who we are. If you have a hand signal light, I can answer them."

Praas barked an order to a crewman, and the man dashed off to return with a portable Aldis lamp. "Tell him who we are and ask him to check out that submarine," the Captain ordered.

The shutters of the lamp rattled as Tonto sent out the reply. The plane looked much larger now, and the familiar shape of the *Catalina* was evident to all onlookers. Another signal blinked from the flying boat.

"I'll be damned," Tonto muttered. "They hadn't seen the pigboat yet. They're going to have a look."

The PBY lumbered by overhead and made straight for the submarine, then began to circle. Lights flashed back and forth between the warship and the plane for several minutes. Tonto tried to follow the signals, but the distance was too great. Finally the aircraft flew back to the *Janssens*. Its signal light began to blink again.

"The sub's Dutch!" Tonto shouted excitedly.

Captain Praas immediately repeated the good news in Dutch to the crowd down on the deck. A collective sigh of relief swept through the gathering. Tensions that had plagued the refugees since before leaving Java began to relax. Hopeful cheers soon followed.

Cinta met Frank as he climbed down to the deck. "Is it true, darling?" she asked, tightly grasping his arm. "Are we really safe now?"

"Safe enough," he answered. "At least the Aussies know where we are. And having a sub as an escort's a big comfort."

"Oh, thank God!"

"Thank God, indeed," Cory Wassell echoed.

(Three)
Aboard M.S. *Janssens*
13 March 1942

At 0830 on Friday morning, M.S. *Janssens* sat idling her engines off *Wadjenop* Lighthouse on Rottnest Island, waiting for an RAN pilot to come aboard. Ahead lay Gage Roads, a large roadstead protected from Indian Ocean rollers by Garden Island to the south, Rottnest Island, and the limestone reefs that stretched between. On the mainland shore, the wide mouth of the Swan River led to the wharves and warehouses of Fremantle's Inner Harbor. The sky was clear, a blue dome marred only by the RAAF *Hudson* bombers that had shadowed the ship for the past few hours. The calm waters of the anchorage were a deep shade of blue, while those near the shore modulated to a bright green hue before breaking onto wide, sugar-white beaches. Ships of many nations lay scattered about the sheltered waters, all refugees from the fierce fighting to the north. About a hundred yards off the bow, a large white launch flying Australian colors approached the battered Dutch ship.

Frank stood at the rail with Cinta, Nicolaas, and Tonia taking in the sights. Close by, Tonto was helping Commander Goggins adjust a pair of binoculars to scan Rottnest Island.

"Those are hellacious big guns up on that ridge," Goggins exclaimed. "Must be at least eight-inchers."

"I believe they're nine-point-twos," Nicolaas offered. "Just like those at Singapore."

"A lot of good those did," Tonto remarked. "I think the guns on the point are six-inchers."

"Let's hope they don't take us for Japs," Tonia muttered. "Those bombers overhead seem to think we might be. They've been there for hours."

"At least we don't have to worry about Jap subs," Frank responded.

A shiver shot through Cinta. Dressed in khaki slacks and a short-sleeved white blouse, she was hugging herself tightly. "God, I'm freezing out here," she said. "I can't wait to get some warm clothes." With the temperature hovering around seventy degrees F, many of the refugees from Java's tropical climate were suffering in their hot weather clothing. Used to equatorial temperatures, their bodies had yet to adapt to Western Australia's temperate climate.

"Take this," said Tonia, passing a cotton shawl to Cinta. "It should help some."

The RAN launch slowed and pulled up to a ladder the crew had put over the side. An Australian civilian wearing a sea captain's hat came quickly up the ladder. After shaking hands with Praas, he followed the captain up to the wheelhouse. A few minutes later, the engine growled as the gears engaged. The ship moved slowly forward, heading toward the bouys that marked the passage through the protecting minefield. At barely three knots, *Janssens* crept up the channel until the mines were astern, then moved on to drop anchor off Fremantle's North Mole. Minutes later, the low black submarine that had shadowed *Janssens* glided by on her way to the Inner Harbor. Her white-hatted captain saluted the survivors for several moments.

The passengers gathered their possessions on deck, expecting a reasonably fast debarkation. But the noon hour came and passed without any further contact with the shore. Another makeshift meal was served in the dining hall while they continued to wait. Finally, at about 1530, another launch set out from South Fremantle and headed toward *Janssens*. It brought a party of bureaucrats—officials from quarantine, customs and immigration. All had fistsful of forms that had to be filled out by all those aboard. While Cinta helped Dr. Wassell get his patients ready for transport ashore, Frank and Tonto assisted Commander Goggins fill out all the paperwork for the sailors. When they were all finished, Cory looked them over and then passed them to a man from immigration.

"How soon can I get these men ashore?" Wassell asked. "They all need to be in a hospital right now."

"All in due time, Doctor," the man replied. "These forms have to be read and evaluated first."

"Why can't I just take them now?"

"Procedure must be followed," the man said and walked away.

"This is ridiculous," Bill Goggins growled. "I'd like to kick that guy's ass up between his shoulder blades."

"Wouldn't do any good," Wassell replied. "Bureaucrats are bureaucrats the world over."

After collecting the paperwork, the port party departed, taking with them the few Australian citizens aboard. It soon became apparent that the refugees would have to spend another night on the ship. Disappointed, those with cabins took their possessions back to their berths, while the others searched for a comfortable place to spend the night. Those with galley duty began putting together a makeshift supper of boiled eggs, rice, and a thin gruel. Everyone aboard felt let down by the Aussie government.

"I sent several letters ashore with the Immigration man," Nicolaas told the others at their supper table. "I'm hoping that either the Dutch Consul or the Royal Dutch Shell boss will have the pull to get us ashore soon."

"It's a disgrace they won't let Dr. Wassell take his men to a hospital," Cinta put in.

"We might as well get a card game going," Bill Dunn spoke up. "I still have one bottle of White Horse left. Why don't we crack it open, now?"

"That's the best idea I've heard all day," Tonto agreed.

(Four)
Aboard M.S. *Janssens*
Fremantle Harbour, Western Australia
14 March 1942

Travelling at about three knots, *Janssens* plowed slowly up the Swan River into the wide basin of the inner harbor. Frank and Cinta stood in a group that included Nicolaas, Tonia, Tonto, and Bill Dunn near the prow. Ships crowded the docks along either shore, and Frank recognized a number of old Asiatic Fleet veterans among them. Off to the right, sub tender *Holland* was tied up beside a long warehouse. Five low-slung Fleet subs and S-boats were nested alongside. A number of Dutch submarines were moored close by. At the far end of the harbor, on the north side, he recognized the silhouette of U.S.S. *Blackhawk* with four four-piper destroyers nested near her. The destroyer-like seaplane tender, U.S.S. *Childs*, was tied up at the North Quay as well, suggesting that PatWing Ten might be nearby.

Captain Praas brought *Janssens* in gently against the fenders of Victoria Quay. The wharf was typical—a seawall of concrete sheet piling topped with a concrete beam. Asphalt pavement stretched right up to the wall, and railroad tracks paralleled the shore, supporting several large portal cranes. A cluster of vehicles, including three RAA ambulances waited on the hardstand. As stevedores snugged down the berthing hawsers, a tall portal crane swung a gangplank into place. An Australian Army major came bounding up the brow and onto the ship. He went straight to Cory Wassell and snapped a salute. "Major Smyth, One-tenth Australian Army Hospital," the sandy-haired Aussie said. "Are you Commander Wassell?"

"I am," replied Cory, returning the salute.

"I have orders to transport you and your patients to our Hollywood Hospital in Nedlands. We have ambulances waiting."

"That's the best news I've had in a long time, Major," Cory exclaimed. "We're ready to go right now."

"My orderlies will carry your litters. I understand some of the men can walk."

"That's right." Wassell turned and walked over to Cinta. "I guess I won't need you anymore, Doctor." He took her hand and then continued, "You'll have my gratitude forever. I don't know if we could have made it without you."

"I was proud to help," she replied softly. "It was an honor to be your assistant." She stood on her tiptoes and kissed his cheek.

"You take good care of this woman," Cory went on as he shook Frank's hand. "You'll not find another like her."

"I know that, sir." He saluted Wassell. "Fair winds and a following sea, Commander."

Soon after the American sailors were driven away, a tall Aussie in a pin-stripe suit came aboard and conferred briefly with Captain Praas. Praas then made a short announcement in Dutch. A smile curled Nicolaas's lips as Praas finished speaking.

"We are free to go ashore, now," the oilman announced in English. "Officials from our Consulate and Navy are here to take care of Dutch citizens."

"I have to check in with someone in my Navy," said Frank. "There's no telling how long I'll be tied up." "I'll stay with Papa and Tonia," Cinta advised. "I'm sure you can find us through the Consulate." "I guess that's the drill, then." Frank hugged Cinta tightly and then went down the gangplank. Tonto, who had helped transport Wassell's patients, was waiting for him on the wharf.

"I already checked with a guy from the Port Captain's office," said Tonto. "He said we should report to PatWing Ten. They're processing all us 'Airdales.'"

"Did he say where they're located?"

"Some place called 'Pelican Point.' If we stop at a bank and change our cash to local money, we can take a cab."

(Five)
PatWing Ten Headquarters
Swan River Yacht Club
Australia II Drive
Crawley Western Australia
14 March 1942

After Frank paid the elderly Aussie cab driver with his new local currency, he and Tonto turned to take in the spectacular view from the driveway. The Swan River Yacht Club was a sprawling, one-story building on a finger of land jutting out into the blue waters of Matilda Bay, a wide basin of the Swan River. Three PBYs lay beached on the broad band of white sand along the bay, and a group of sailors was putting up a makeshift nose hanger not far away. Both U.S. and Australian colors flew from flagpoles in front of the club.

"If you don't mind, I think I'll go check with those boys on the beach," Tonto said to Frank. "They're most likely my buddies from Java. They can fill me in on the setup here."

"Go ahead. I'll go meet with the brass."

"Attention on Deck," barked the petty officer manning the desk in the yacht club lobby as Frank entered. "Officer on the quarterdeck."

"As you were," Frank quickly responded. He took out his ID card and handed it to the PO. "I'm Lieutenant Rhea, lately of *Houston*. I just got in from Java, and I'm looking for a place to check in."

"You came to the right place, Lieutenant. Let me make a note in the log, and I'll get someone to escort you."

A few minutes later, a yeoman from the Personnel Department came to get Frank and take him to check in. "I'm Yeoman Jones, Lieutenant," the sandy-haired, freckled faced man introduced himself. "Do you have your records with you?"

"My original records burned up in *Marblehead*," Frank replied. "I had a replacement set made in Soerabaya, but those went down in *Houston*."

"Looks like we'll have to start from scratch," Jones said with a shake of his head. He led Frank down a broad hall to a room with a view of Matilda Bay. The space was crammed with desks and filing cabinets. "Have a seat in that chair, and we'll get on with it." Jones went to a filing cabinet and extracted a thick sheaf of forms. Putting the first in his typewriter, he began to ask Frank's particulars.

More than an hour elapsed before the administrative ordeal finally drew to a close. "I think that does it," Jones remarked. "You'll have to bring in your marriage certificate to finish up. You can take that pay record to the Paymaster and get some cash."

"Thanks loads, Jones," said Frank. "You might as well break out another set of forms, though. Warrant Officer Jim Bob Coacooche should be here in a few minutes. We got out of Java together."

"Hot-damn," Jones exclaimed, snapping his fingers. "Tonto's here? We all thought he bought it up in Java."

"He's down with the maintenance crews. Is there somewhere to eat around here?"

"Lunch is over, but I'll bet we can rustle up some ham sandwiches. I'll show you to the wardroom."

The officer's mess was in what looked like a club party room. White tablecloths covered a number of round tables, each sitting six in rattan chairs. Wide windows opened toward the beach. A familiar looking broad-shouldered officer with curly hair occupied one of the tables.

"Hey, Steve," Frank called out. "Can a guy get something to eat around here?"

"Good God, am I seeing a ghost?" Steve Henley exclaimed. He sprang up from his seat and rushed to shake Frank's hand.

"Not likely," Frank shot back. "Tonto and I came in on *Janssens* yesterday."

"I heard another survivor made it out, but I sure didn't expect you to be on it. I thought you were lost with *Houston.*"

"Never got to *Houston.* A Jap *Zero* shot me down over Java."

"I want to hear that story. You look starved. Here, have a seat, and I'll call the steward."

Frank ordered steak, fried eggs, and toast. While the staff prepared the food, he regaled Henley with the tale of his escape from Java.

"So you're one of us old married men at last," Henley commented as Frank dug into the best food he'd tasted since Java.

"I jumped while I had the chance."

"Where's Cinta?"

"With her father trying to get us a place to stay. One thing I have to do is try to round up some uniforms. The only clothes I have are those I'm wearing."

"You can get khakis on one of the tenders. Blues are impossible. None of the tailors in Perth have any Navy Blue cloth left. Even Admiral Glassford had to settle for RAF Blue."

"What about Aviation Greens?"

"There you're in luck. No shortage of green cloth. I'll give you my tailor's card. He should be able to knock you out a set in a day or two.

"Have you called on Commander Peterson yet?"

"Haven't had the chance."

"I'll go set you up an appointment while you finish eating."

"Get word to Tonto, too. We should go in together."

LCDR John V. Peterson, Commander, Patrol Wing Ten, rose from behind the former yacht club manager's desk and came to greet Frank and Tonto. Dressed in a crisp Aviation Green uniform, Peterson was slender, dark-haired, and bore a close resemblance to the film actor, Dana Andrews. He shook both their hands with evident pleasure.

"Welcome to the 'Swan River Flying Club,'" said Peterson. "I'm really pleased you guys made it out of Java."

"We're hoping you could use another SOC crew, Commander," Frank replied.

"We've got two SOCs and a *Kingfisher* in the Utility Squadron.

Another experienced crew would be a Godsend. And Joe Antonides has already hit me up to grab Tonto for his Maintenance Department. So, until I get orders otherwise, both of you belong to me."

"That's great, Commander," said Frank, and Tonto nodded agreement.

"I want to hear about your escape. Have a seat. How about some coffee?"

"Sure thing, Commander," Tonto spoke for both himself and Frank.

Peterson listened intently as the newcomers related their tale of survival, frequently interrupting with questions. After half an hour and several cups of coffee, about everything had been told.

"Sounds like Doctor Wassell is the big hero of that story," Peterson finally remarked.

"You bet, Commander," Tonto spoke up. "Without him, those boys would either be dead or rotting in a Jap POW camp."

"Let's get down to practical matters. I'll get the Supply Officer to round up some khakis for you. The local tailors make some pretty good Greens. Blues are out of the question at the moment."

"Steve Henley told us about the material shortage," Frank remarked.

"As to billeting, we have space in the nearby Nedlands Hotel for Tonto. What's the situation with your bride, Frank?"

"Don't know about that, Commander. She went with her father to the Dutch Consulate."

"We have a few private houses in Nedlands. We'll see what we can do for you."

"I'd really appreciate that, sir."

While Tonto went with a CPO from Supply to draw uniforms and equipment, Henley borrowed a motor pool jeep to take Frank to visit a tailor in Nedlands. After taking exhaustive measurements of Frank's physique, the elderly Aussie filled out orders for two sets of Aviation Greens and one set of Service Dress Whites. The deposit took almost all the Australian cash Frank had obtained at the Fremantle bank.

"I haven't been paid since the first of February," he told Henley. "I'm almost broke."

"Don't sweat it. I'll float you a loan until you make it to the Paymaster."

"I should try to get in touch with Cinta."

"You can do that from the 'Swan River Flying Club.'"

When the two officers drove into the PatWing 10 driveway, they saw that Tonto had arrived just before them. With his usual initiative, Tonto had obtained two sets of new wash khaki uniforms with belts and garrison caps, summer-weight flying suits, canvass aviator helmets, three sets of skivvies each, brown shoes, and two new canvas flight jackets. New canvas seabags held most of the clothing and gear.

"Looks like you hit the jackpot," Frank remarked.

"The Chief helped a lot. These guys are really glad to have us, *Kemo Sabe.*"

"Why don't you go check in at the hotel? I'm about to try to find Cinta."

"We gotta get paid tomorrow morning, Lone Ranger. I'm about dry."

"Same here. See if you can get us a jeep for about zero-eight-hundred."

"Consider it done."

It took Frank almost half an hour to get through to an English-speaking official at the Dutch Consulate. The man said that Nicolaas and the two women had been checked into the Wentworth Hotel in Perth and provided a telephone number. The operator at the Wentworth informed Frank that Mrs. Rhea had gone out but offered to connect him to Nicolaas's room.

"Frank, how are you doing," Nicolaas asked after they exchanged greetings.

Frank gave his father-in-law a rundown of his day, then asked, "What are Cinta and Tonia up to?"

"Shopping, of course. And Cinta had a medical appointment of some kind. By the way, we got you a very nice room here. And we're planning a celebratory dinner in the restaurant at eight tonight. I assume you can make it."

"I'll get someone to run me over. What's the address?"

"The Wentworth's at the corner of Murray and William Streets. It's a limestone three-story building. You can't miss it."

Steve Henley offered to drive Frank into Perth in one of the jeeps. They piled Frank's gear in the back seat and drove out Australia II Drive to Hackett Drive, an unpaved macadam road that ran along the shore. To the right, a brisk breeze kicked up little whitecaps in Matilda Bay. Signs proclaimed that the sparsely developed land to the left belonged to the University of Western Australia. Hackett Drive soon dead-ended into with the wider Highway 5, the main road from Fremantle, called Mounts Bay Road at this point. The ride was much smoother on asphalt pavement. The land rose ahead of them until the river was a good forty feet beneath them at the foot of a bluff. To the left lay undeveloped scrubland. A wooded hill about 300 feet high loomed above. Steve told Frank that the wild land was called King's Park. To Frank, it looked like the rolling hills of Southern California.

The river narrowed ahead where a finger of land from the east jutted out into the water. They were in the suburbs of Perth now, an area of residential homes. Tall eucalyptus trees flanked the road providing shade. Ahead was the skyline of Perth, sporting only a few buildings taller than three stories. Soon after entering the city, Steve took Riverside Drive, which forked off to the right. Then he made a sharp left turn onto Williams Street.

"Only about three more blocks," said Steve.

Perth looked like a town in the U.S. Midwest. Buildings with varying Victorian facades lined the streets. Here and there was a sprinkling of others that reminded Frank of the French Quarter in New Orleans with cast iron balconies, iron columns, and lacy iron railings. Traffic on the streets was light by U.S. standards. Driving on the left side of the road seemed quaint to Frank.

Crossing a broad thoroughfare named St. George's Terrace, Steve pointed to the right. "See that white tower at the end of the block? That's where Navy Headquarters is."

Frank glimpsed a tall office building set between a park and a row of brick structures with fancy turrets and domes.

"There's the Wentworth." Steve pointed to a three-story, light beige stone building on the northwest corner of the intersection ahead. It had an impressive façade, with arched windows on the third floor and a stone frieze with peaked pediments along the top of the corner walls. The hotel street entrance was at the beveled corner of the building. A canopied, open-air restaurant filled most of the

Murray Street sidewalk.

Steve parked on Williams Street near the door and helped Frank unload his gear. Under the disapproving gaze of the middle-aged hotel doorman, Steve shook Frank's hand before driving away.

"Could I be of assistance, sir?" the doorman asked in a pronounced accent. The man was gray-haired, red-faced and a good sixty pounds overweight.

"Thanks, but I can handle it myself." Frank shouldered the seabag and walked into the lobby. The décor was typically British Empire—lots of dark wood paneling and overstuffed chairs. He walked over to the check-in desk and dropped the bag to the carpet. A slight, stooped clerk with a balding head came to greet him.

"Good afternoon, Leftenant," the man said warmly. "Might you be Mister Rhea?"

"That's right. I believe my wife's already checked us in."

"Earlier this afternoon. And I believe she's returned from her outing. You're in Room 316. I gave her two sets of keys."

"That'll be fine. I'll go on up."

The elevator was old-fashioned with collapsing grid doors. A boy no more that fourteen dressed in a uniform operated the car. He took Frank up to the third floor, where Room 316 was near the front of the building. Frank knocked lightly on the door."

"Yes?" came Cinta's voice from within.

"It's Frank."

"Come on in."

Cinta was standing next to a large bed that was completely covered with new clothing. She wore a blue rayon robe over her underwear. Her hair was now cut in a stylish pixie and her face was made up. "You did make it in time for dinner," she chirped happily. "Papa wasn't sure you would be able to."

"I'm done for the day, but I'm almost broke." Dropping his bag, he moved quickly across the room and took her in his arms for a passionate kiss.

"Easy, Lone Ranger," she cautioned as they broke away. "I need to finish getting ready."

"Looks like you have plenty to choose from," said Frank, admiring her new wardrobe.

"Oh, I have something better than any of this. Go get yourself a bath, and I'll show you when you finish. Another shave wouldn't do any harm, either."

Frank saw now that the room was large and well appointed. Besides the over-sized bed, there were several stuffed chairs and a small breakfast table with dining chairs in one corner. A number of seascape paintings graced the walls. A sitting area with a small dining table filled an alcove in the outside wall. Glenn Miller dance music played softly from a large cabinet radio. He found the bathroom equally spacious, with a large cast-iron tub on lion's feet. He ran it full of deliciously hot water and soaked away the stresses and sweat of the day. When the water began to cool, he got out, put on his skivvies, and began to shave.

When he went back into the bedroom, Frank froze in place when he saw Cinta. She was wearing a cocktail dress of light blue silk chiffon. Pearls gleamed at her throat and ears. The fragrance of *Chanel No. 5* wafted from her throat and earlobes.

"My God, Cinta," he replied, the spell broken at last. "You look fabulous."

"Like it?" she asked, spinning on her toes to show off her dress. The top bared her shoulders except for spaghetti straps, and the skirt fell from the waistband to just above her knees in hundreds of tiny pleats.

"Where did you find such a thing in Perth?" Frank said. "These people have been on war restrictions for years."

"It's borrowed--belongs to the wife of the head of the Dutch legation here. The nylons are hers, too. She tried to insist that we stay at their home, but I didn't want to impose. Besides, after the last few days, I really cherish our privacy."

"I'm afraid I'll be underdressed. All I have is clean khakis."

"I bought you a ready-made suit. I had to guess at the sizes, but I think I got them right." Cinta went to a big wardrobe and took out a blue suit of light worsted wool. "I guessed your leg length at thirty-one inches."

"You're right. Let me try it on."

Although the waistband was slightly loose, the suit otherwise fit perfectly. There was also a freshly laundered white shirt and a red tie, which Cinta tied for him in a Windsor knot.

"Would you like a drink now?" she asked after he'd removed and hung up the suit coat.

"What do we have?"

"Gin, scotch, and bourbon."

"I developed a taste for scotch on the *Janssens*."

"I'll have one with you."

"Where all did you go today?" Frank asked after they sat down on the couch with their drinks.

"We went to the Consulate first." Cinta took a sip of her scotch-and-water. "The staff set us up with these rooms and helped us settle our immigration status. Then we came here to check in and have lunch. After I took a long bath, Tonia and I went shopping."

"You obviously found a lot you liked. Where did you find them?"

"Mostly near the hotel. We had the most fun in a shopping arcade called London Court. They have all kinds of neat shops there."

"Nicolaas said you had a medical appointment."

"That, too. I told you I needed therapy. The Consul set me up with a psychiatrist."

"Did it help?" Frank asked expectantly.

"I think so. He said that my feelings are typical of women who've been sexually assaulted. They usually fade away with time. I have another appointment tomorrow."

"Did he suggest anything I can do to help?"

"Mostly just have patience, Darling. And always believe I want to make you happy."

When Frank and Cinta arrived at the dining room that evening, they found Nicolaas in a somber mood. He'd just received word from the Consulate that most of his bosses and contempories at BPM were now dead. Divebombers from Admiral Nagumo's carriers had caught the Dutch liner, *Poelau Bras,* a day out of Java, sinking her with great loss of life. Wilhelm Oosten, Anton Colign, and Colijn's three daughters were among the missing. RADM van Staveren, Admiral Helfrich's chief of staff, also perished. But there was even more bad news. A report from the Dutch Army in Java stated that all the oilmen left in Zwarte Gouden had been executed by the Japanese for sabotaging the refinery. The captured white women endured gang rape by the enemy soldiers.

"Oh, my God," exclaimed Cinta, utterly horrified. "Poor Catherine and her sisters. We shouldn't have abandoned them."

"Don't take responsibility for their plight," Tonia counseled. Getting yourself put in a Japanese brothel would not have helped them at all."

The excellent meal of steaks and longousta did little to cheer their spirits. None of them slept well that night.

(Five)
Colonial Mutual Life Assurance (CML) Building
55 St. Georges Terrace
Perth, WA
15 March 1942

Walking down the broad seventh floor hall with Tonto, Frank felt that he could have been in any U.S. Navy office in the world. Typewriters clattered incessantly from every room they passed on their search for the Paymaster, and enlisted men in "crackerjack" blues darted in and out of the spaces. They were about to enter the Paymaster's office when the door flew open and a red-faced Cory Wassell stormed out. He was wearing fresh khakis and even a necktie.

"What's wrong, Doc?' Tonto spoke up.

Wassell blinked his eyes for a moment, and then his scowl relaxed as he recognized the aviators. "It's that damned Dutch money from Java!" he said forcefully. "I still have five hundred guilders, and no one will take it off my hands. They all say it's 'not their department.' Guess I'll just have to mail it to Washington."

"Have you gotten new orders yet," Frank continued?

"I'm sort of attached to the staff. They put me in charge of medical supplies around here."

"How are the boys doing?" asked Tonto.

"Oh, they're right as rain. Those Aussie sawbones out at Hollywood are good, and the hospital's well equipped. Some of the boys are going home on the *West Point*, the ship that brought in all those Australian soldiers. Bill Goggins is one of them. He needs a first-rate burn center, and they have one at Pearl Harbor."

"Say hello for us," Tonto requested.

"You bet. I'll quit my bellyaching and let ya'll get on with your business."

An hour later, with their wallets bulging with Australian currency, Frank and Tonto got onto the 'Down' elevator. They immediately recognized the slight, balding captain standing against the back wall.

"Good morning, Captain Wagner," Frank piped up. "It's good to see you again, sir."

Wagner, who'd been reading a document, looked up, and then his eyes sparkled with pleasure. "Well, I'll be damned. The Lone Ranger and Tonto. I heard you two made it out."

"By the skin of our teeth, Captain," Tonto commented.

"Is it true that you flew across Java all by yourself, Tonto?"

"I did, Captain. I been flyin' off and on for several years."

"You'll have to tell me that story sometime. I'm off to Fremantle for a meeting."

"Guess we might as well head back to the Swan River Flying Club," Frank said as they came out into the bright sunlight. "I'm sure Commander Peterson has something to keep us busy."

CHAPTER 33

(One)
Aboard U.S.S. *Childs*
North Quay
Fremantle WA
18 March 1942

"Okay, Lone Ranger, crank up the engine and see what she does," said Tonto from the weather deck of the *Childs*. Dressed in a flight suit, Frank was sitting in the cockpit of a repaired *Seagull* resting in a cradle on the open deck. A former destroyer, *Childs* had been converted to a seaplane tender by converting her forward fire room to aircrew quarters and clearing most of the structure behind her cookhouse for repair space. She had a boom capable of lifting small aircraft aboard. Although usually a tender for the PBY squadrons, *Childs* had been drafted to service the Utility Squadron when *Heron* was heavily damaged in the attack on Darwin back in February.

"Here we go," Frank shouted back and reached for the electric starter.

"Hold up, Lieutenant" screamed a messenger running across the deck. "I've got an op immediate signal for you."

"Now, what?" Tonto groused as the man climbed up and handed Frank a slip of paper.

"A command performance," Frank replied after scanning the dispatch. "I've got less that an hour to spiff up and get to Admiral Glassford's office."

"You're in serious trouble if brass that high is lookin' for you."

"Wonder what the hell this is about? Did we pull some major screw-up I can't remember?"

"Not that I can think of."

Forty-five minutes later, dressed in his new aviation greens, Frank entered the elevator in the lobby of the CML Building. Just as the doors were about to close, Cory Wassell rushed in to join him. The doctor, who was carrying a thick manila envelope, looked very worried.

"What floor, Commander?" Frank asked.

"The eighth, I guess," Wassell wheezed. "I've been summoned by Admiral Glassford."

"You, too? Do you have any idea what this is about?"

"They're going to court martial me," Wassell said bitterly. "That's what it has to be. I've got half that Dutch money here, but I lost the receipts for all that money I spent up in Java."

"After what you did to save those boys? I don't think so."

"I disobeyed written orders when I brought them out of Java. I was supposed to sit tight and take whatever came down the road."

"I guess we'll have to wait and see."

When the elevator doors opened on the eighth floor, Captain Wagner was outside impatiently waiting for them. "You're cutting it awfully close, Frank," Wagner commented.

"Sorry, Captain. I didn't get much notice. What's this about?"

"You'll find out in a minute." Wagner turned to Cory Wassell. "You look like a schoolboy summoned to the principal's office, Doctor. The Admiral's not that bad."

"He's going to court martial me, isn't he?"

"Hardly. Come on, and we'll go meet him."

Admiral Glassford's office occupied a corner room with tall windows that gave a panoramic view of the city. As Frank followed Captain Wagner through the door, he was surprised to find quite a gathering. A dozen or more staff officers, including Admiral Purnell, were present, as well as a number of civilians. Frank was startled to recognize Cinta and Nicolaas among them. A Dutch Navy captain stood next to Nicolaas.

"This is quite a hanging party," Wassell muttered under his breath.

Admiral Glassford, dressed in the RAAF blue uniform Frank had heard about, came forward to meet the newcomers. He shook Dr. Wassell's hand first and then Frank's as they exchanged formal greetings. The bald admiral was at his most charming today, with a warm smile on his face.

"I need you to take this money off my hands, Admiral," Wassell blurted out, trying to hand his envelope to Glassford. "There's five hundred guilders in there."

"That's not my department, Doctor. That has nothing to do with why you're here." The admiral turned to face the guests.

"May I have your attention, please," Glassford began. "We are gathered here to honor two of America's newest heroes. First, I have an announcement from the Navy Department. It gives me pleasure to tell you that Lieutenant Commander Corydon Wassell will be awarded the Navy Cross for his heroic actions in saving the wounded sailors under his command from capture by the Japanese. Congratulations, Doctor."

The assembled guests broke into sustained applause. When it subsided, Glassford continued.

"We'll have a formal awards ceremony for Doctor Wassell as soon as the paperwork arrives from Washington. I just didn't want to wait to give him the news."

Cory Wassell looked thunderstruck. "The Navy Cross?" he almost croaked. "I didn't do anything…"

"Now, now, Doctor, no more denials. All the people here know that you've earned this honor.

"Our other reason for gathering is that the Dutch Government has an award to present to Lieutenant Frank Rhea. I'll yield the floor to Doctor K.E. van der Mandele, Acting Consul-General of the Netherlands Government."

The Consul-General came forward to first congratulate Doctor Wassell, and then he turned to Frank. "The Queen of the Netherlands takes great pleasure in awarding the Airman's Cross to Lieutenant Frank Rhea, United States Naval Reserve, for valor as set forth in the following citation." He nodded to the Dutch Naval Captain, who was now holding a paper in his hand.

The captain spoke excellent English with perfect diction. The citation described how Frank, flying a reconnaissance floatplane, had attacked a formation of enemy bombers over Makassar Strait, shooting down one and scattering the formation. He was credited with saving *Marblehead* from complete destruction.

An aide stepped forward and handed the Consul-General a box containing a bronze metal cross suspended from a white ribbon with diagonal gold stripes. Van der Mandele pinned the medal on the left side of Frank's blouse then air-kissed him on both cheeks.

Not really knowing what to do, Frank saluted the Dutchman and thanked him.

Another round of applause swept through the room. Then everyone began congratulating Cory and Frank, starting with the admirals.

When Cinta reached Frank, she kissed his cheek and whispered in his ear. "I'm so proud of you, Darling! We'll have a private celebration tonight."

After all the guests left, Frank Wagner took Frank aside. "There're some other things I need to discuss with you, Frank. Let's go down to my office."

Wagner's space was much less impressive than the admiral's, although there was room for a leather couch and a small conference table. They sat down at the table while Wagner's yeoman brought coffee.

"I have some good news for you and some bad news for me," the captain began. "I tried like hell to hang onto you, but the Navy Department disagreed." He opened a manila folder and took out a naval message. "I guess they figured that anyone who would attack Jap bombers in a *Seagull* ought to be in fighters. I have orders here for you to detach and go to Corpus Christi, Texas, for retraining as a fighter pilot. You'll be booked on the *West Point*, the next ship out."

Conflicting emotions immediately tore at Frank's mind. "That's exactly what I'd hoped for, Captain, but what about my wife? Will she be able to come with me?"

"She's a Dutch national, I believe?"

"*Indish* Dutch. She was born in Java. But we're legally married."

"We'll have to coordinate with the Dutch Consulate. We may be able to work something out. I also need to tell you that you're out of uniform. Your name is on a promotion list that just came out. Get another half-stripe put on your sleeves and come back tomorrow morning for the swearing in. Congratulations, Lieutenant Commander."

(Two)
Wentworth Hotel
109 William Street
Perth, WA

Following a celebratory dinner at the Dutch Consul-General's residence, Frank and Cinta finally made it back to their hotel. The events of the day, liberally flowing cocktails at the party, and the effects of a heavy meal left them both a little tired.

"Want a nightcap, Darling?" Cinta asked after Frank turned on the lights.

"Might as well."

"You go ahead and get one. I'd like to get into something more comfortable and my bladder's about to pop." She went into the bathroom.

Frank pulled loose his tie and took off his uniform blouse, poured some Scotch into a glass, and sank wearily onto the couch. Sipping the fiery liquid, he let its heat spread from his throat through his body. His eyelids drooped and then fell shut. His mind drifted toward slumber.

"Don't tell me you've gone to sleep on me." Cinta's words snapped Frank awake.

"Guess I did," he said sheepishly as he stretched and yawned. Then his eyes snapped open, and the site of Cinta drove all thoughts of sleep from his mind.

She wore a batik sarong about her hips, a flower behind her left ear, and nothing else.

"This is what I usually wear around the house. Think I'll scandalize the proper ladies down in Kingsville?"

"You'll get us kicked off the base!" He sprang up and took her into his arms, their lips fusing in a passionate kiss.

"I've had enough therapy, Darling. It's time we properly consummated our marriage."

"You sure you're ready?

"No question about it."

Without another word, Frank picked her up and carried her to the bed.

Snuggled close against Frank's sleeping body, Cinta lay awake in the hour before dawn. Still basking in the warm glow that lingered in her belly, her face reflected inner peace and contentment. She knew now that she was still capable of sexual fulfillment, that she was going to make it all the way back to a normal life. In the past several hours, they had replicated their magic morning in Soerabaya. Frank's gentleness made each embrace an act of tender loving and giving. Their love life would certainly never be boring.

She finally slept, her head pillowed against Frank's shoulder. For the first time since Zwarte Gouden fell to the Japanese, her dreams were sweet.

Author's Note

Hold Back The Sun has a number of actual historical characters. I have portrayed each of them as accurately as exhaustive research allowed. Many of the naval officers attained high rank before the end of the war. Captain Arthur G. Robinson and Commander William Goggins of *Marblehead* both became rear admirals. Lieutenant Commander Corydon Wassell also rose to real admiral. Admiral Tommy Hart served in the Navy Department until being appointed U.S. Senator from Ohio to complete the term of a deceased incumbent.

The saga of Doctor Wassell and his wounded sailors became legend during World War II. I have attempted to tell it exactly as it actually occurred. The motion picture, *The Story of Doctor Wassell,* produced in 1944 by Cecil B. DeMille, was mostly factual but deviated from the real history when the screenwriters thought drama might better be served. A good bit of wartime propaganda was also included. Readers may be pleased to learn that Petty Officer Hopkins survived the war in a Japanese POW camp. He stayed in the Navy and became a Chief Petty Officerbefore retiring. It was from an article in his hometown newspaper that I learned the spelling of the actual name (Teramina) of the Javanese nurse the sailors called, "Three Martini." The fact that she was a real person and was confirmed by Dr. Wassell himself in a speech to the British Empire Club in Canada during the war.

In relating the fall of the Philippines, I have endeavored to clear up the confusion about how so many aircraft were caught on the ground during the initial Japanese attack. Expecting a dawn air raid, all planes were ordered aloft just before sunrise. No one knew that the enemy aircraft were grounded in Formosa by a heavy fog. The Americans eventually ran out of fuel and had to come down. Coincidentally, the Japanese arrived at that moment.

The Asiatic Fleet battled valiantly for months against impossible odds. Captain W.G. Winslow aptly titled his history of their exploits, *The Fleet the Gods Forgot.* The fact that they were defeated should not diminish the quality of their courage.

Warren Bell
Williamsburg, VA, July 2013

Also by **Warren Bell**

FALL EAGLE ONE

SEMIFINALIST IN KINDLE BOOK REVIEW'S BEST INDIE BOOKS OF 2012!

It's 1943, and Nazi Germany is reeling from nightly battering of her cities by the RAF. Catastrophe looms at Stalingrad. Siegfried von Rall, Hermann Göring's technical advisor, hatches strategic missions to buy time for his country to refine cutting-edge technology into "Victory" weapons.

Two targets galvanize Siegfried's attention: Soviet hydro plants in the Urals and killing FDR. He chooses aircraft and recruits a team of experts for the missions. *Reichsmarschall* Göring fast tracks detailed planning and training.

In Britain, codebreaker Evan Thompson reads Siegfried's radio messages but can't detect his objective. The chilling truth emerges only after an Amerika-Bomber bearing "smart bombs" leaves Norway for the U.S.

FALL EAGLE ONE has aerial combat, trans-Atlantic assassination flights, Eastern Front action, codebreaking at Bletchley Park, intrigue at the highest levels of the German High Command, and fast-paced wartime romance.

FALL EAGLE ONE is available from Amazon.com in both Kindle and paperback. The paperback is also available from other Internet bookstores.
https://sites.google.com/site/warrenbellauthor/home

Made in the USA
Charleston, SC
09 November 2013